BATMAN:

TALES

OF THE

DEMON

BATMAN CREATED BY BOB KANE

WARNER
BOOKS

DC COMICS INC.

JENETTE KAHN
President & Editor-in-Chief

DICK GIORDANO
V.P. – Editorial Director

PAUL LEVITZ/JULIUS SCHWARTZ
Editors Original Series

DENNIS O'NEIL
Editor Collected Edition

JIM CHADWICK
Director – Design Services

ROBBIN BROSTERMAN
Art Director

JOE ORLANDO
V.P. – Creative Director

PAUL LEVITZ
Executive V.P. & Publisher

BRUCE BRISTOW
V.P. – Sales & Marketing

PATRICK CALDON
V.P. & Controller

TERRI CUNNINGHAM
Director – Editorial Administration

CHANTAL d'AULNIS
V.P. – Business Affairs

LILLIAN LASERSON
V.P. – Legal Affairs

BOB ROZAKIS
Production Director

COVER BY BRIAN STELFREEZE
PUBLICATION DESIGN BY DALE CRAIN

ISBN 0-446-39364-9
PUBLISHED BY ARRANGEMENT WITH DC COMICS INC.,
1325 AVENUE OF THE AMERICAS, NEW YORK, NY 10019
WARNER BOOKS, INC., 666 FIFTH AVENUE, NEW YORK, NY 10103
A TIME WARNER COMPANY
PRINTED IN CANADA
FIRST WARNER PRINTING, JANUARY 1992

BATMAN: TALES OF THE DEMON

ALL STORIES WRITTEN BY DENNIS O'NEIL

INTRODUCTION
BY SAM HAMM

4

INTO THE DEN OF THE DEATH DEALERS!
ART BY BOB BROWN & DICK GIORDANO

9

DAUGHTER OF THE DEMON
ART BY NEAL ADAMS & DICK GIORDANO

24

SWAMP SINISTER
ART BY IRV NOVICK & DICK GIORDANO

46

VENGEANCE FOR A DEAD MAN
ART BY IRV NOVICK & DICK GIORDANO

61

BRUCE WAYNE — REST IN PEACE!
ART BY IRV NOVICK & DICK GIORDANO

78

THE LAZARUS PIT!
ART BY NEAL ADAMS & DICK GIORDANO

92

THE DEMON LIVES AGAIN!
ART BY NEAL ADAMS & DICK GIORDANO

116

I NOW PRONOUNCE YOU BATMAN AND WIFE!
ART BY MICHAEL GOLDEN & DICK GIORDANO

132

THE VENGEANCE VOW!
ART BY DON NEWTON & DAN ADKINS

152

WHERE STRIKE THE ASSASSINS
ART BY DON NEWTON & DAN ADKINS

172

REQUIEM FOR A MARTYR
ART BY DON NEWTON & DAN ADKINS

182

AFTERWORD
BY DENNIS O'NEIL

204

The other day I was sitting around thinking, as I sometimes do, about a certain pointy-eared super-hero, and I
got to wondering why certain characters haunt the public imagination for decade after decade while others
drop by the wayside. I came up with the following four-
part recipe for concocting mythic heroes — feel free to
use it if you'd like to make an enduring contribution to
pop culture:

1. The hero is, in some crucial way, *other* — stronger,
faster, smarter, more implacable than the average run of
humanity. He might be naturally gifted. He might be the
product of years of training. He might have been bitten
by a radioactive crab louse. Although he is superior to,
and alienated from, the normal folk who populate his
world, his exaggerated competence makes him a natural target for reader identification.

2. His personality, motivations, and *modus operandi*
must be strongly defined, but at the same time "loose"
enough to accommodate periodic revisions and
reinterpretations, so that succeeding generations of
readers will continue to find him fresh and exciting.

3. A lively origin story helps. Primal is best; it's
always nice if our hero is obsessive, and a vividly
rendered trauma scene, involving some sort of univer-
sally comprehensible anguish, goes a long way toward
making obsession palatable. (Alternatively, we may
choose to keep our hero's roots "shrouded in mystery.")

4. He must face and thwart a succession of powerful
antagonists — a few sizable enough who will recur on
a semi-regular basis until they come to be indelibly
linked, in the public mind, with our hero and his legend — *viz.* Holmes and Moriarty, James Bond and
Blofeld, etc. In some real sense, the hero's nature will
be defined through conflict with his archenemy/ies.

It's requirement #4 that interests us here. Batman has
been around for more than fifty years, and the great
Batman villains have proven almost as evergreen as
their caped adversary. Among the rogues in the pan-
theon, the Joker, the Penguin, and the Catwoman have
been around almost since Batman's inception. The
Riddler and Clayface (in his various manifestations) are
relatively recent additions to the roster, dating from
1948 and 1961, respectively. But since then, it seems,
precious few of Batman's enemies have managed to
attain classic status.

Now, all this may mean that the originators of Batman
got it right from the outset, and that a proper hero needs
only a handful of perfectly-chosen nemeses to thrive.
Or it may mean that few of Batman's subsequent inter-
preters knew how to create villains with the conceptual
resonance to make a permanent dent in the mythos.

In fact, it strikes me that, of all the Bat-villains flung
up against the wall in the last quarter-century, only one
has managed to stick — and I don't mean Poison Ivy. I
don't mean Blockbuster, or Solomon Grundy, or Man-
Bat, or Killer Croc.

Here, at the moment of maximum suspense, let us pause for a brief but edifying dose of historical perspective.

I first encountered Batman circa 1959, during what I call his pink-alien-and-time-travel phase. The stories would typically revolve around Our Hero's discovery of an Inca Batman. Or, to cite just one of the zoological monstrosities that seemed so common at the time, a Mer-Batman. The new adventures looked pretty pale in comparison to the stronger stuff from the forties and fifties which turned up occasionally in the annuals and "80-Page Giants," in which the villains were at least humanoid — psychopaths and walking deformities, like the Joker and Two-Face.

Although I couldn't quite formulate the difference at the time, these stories seemed to me to represent the "true" Batman. I later realized that by the late fifties, something had gone dreadfully awry; the character had completely lost his sense of menace — and with it, his individual flavor. He'd become virtually interchangeable with any other superdoer in the DC line. And at

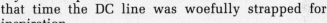

that time the DC line was woefully strapped for inspiration.

Then came the infamous television series.

THE BATMAN--!!

Nowadays it's fashionable to snipe at that icon of sixties camp as if its very existence somehow sullied the Batman we all know and love — betrayed his spirit. Personally, though, I've always felt that the television series horrified fans because it was an altogether too literal interpretation of the comic book. The feeble, slapdash plots, the outlandish contraptions, the hilariously stilted dialogue — all seemed perfectly natural in the garish four-color setting of a 1960's comic. But when you wrenched those familiar elements out of their undemanding context and ported them, intact, to the small screen ... dissonance ensued. The sight of live actors in gaudy costumes behaving exactly like their comic-book prototypes ruthlessly exposed the fundamental silliness of the source material.

It could have been worse; just imagine if Bat-Mite, or Ace the Bat-Hound, had made it onto the small screen.

Anyway, in the wake of the series, the more charitable observers pronounced Batman a charming manifestation of pop art, a sort of amusingly naive *objet trouve* discovered on the cultural slagheap. The rest of the world at large chuckled for a while, then lost interest. And serious comic-book fans sulked, feeling that Batman's reputation had been irreparably damaged.

I'm not trying to suggest that the character deserved the sort of treatment he received at the hands of the television producers. Jokes wear thin, and after all, Batman is still with us; no pop-culture character endures for fifty-plus years unless his legend embodies some nugget of emotional truth — unless he retains, in some small measure, the power to reverberate in the minds of his audience.

In other words, there have been *many* "Batmans." The

problem was not that the makers of the TV show had been untrue to Batman. They'd been true to the *wrong* Batman.

Cut to 1969, and the publication of a Batman story entitled "The Secret of the Waiting Graves." It was dark, mysterious, gothic. It was moodily, and beautifully, drawn. It was subtly unlike anything that had appeared in the Batman titles for years. Two young turks named Denny O'Neil and Neal Adams, fresh off an award-winning run on *GREEN LANTERN/GREEN ARROW,* had remembered — and been true to — an altogether different Batman.

"That story," said Denny, "was a conscious desire to break out of the *Batman* TV show; to throw in everything and announce to the world, 'Hey, we're not doing camp.' We wanted to reestablish Batman not only as the best detective in the world, and the best athlete, but also as a dark and frightening creature — if not supernatural, then close to it, by virtue of his prowess."

Within a few months, O'Neil and Adams had reinvented not only Batman, but his most famous foe as well — restoring the Joker to his original glory as psychopathic wild card, an interpretation that remains in favor to this day. But there was still more work to do.

Denny again: "There was no doubt that Batman needed a worthy opponent. We set out consciously and deliberately to create a villain in the grand manner, a villain who was so exotic and mysterious that neither we nor Batman were sure what to expect."

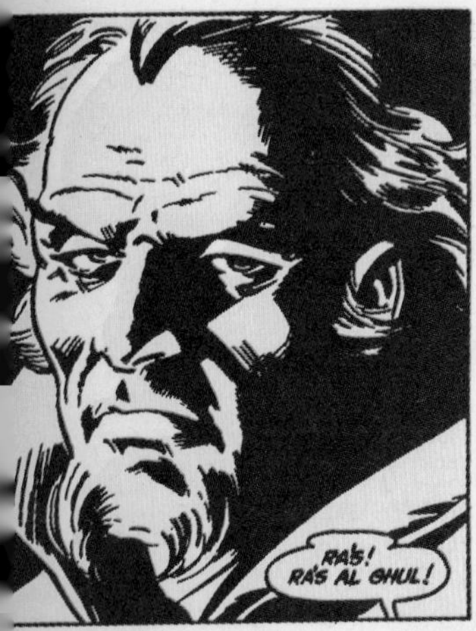
RA'S!
RA'S AL GHUL!

Hence, Rā's al Ghūl — "the demon's head."

Now, Denny O'Neil is a man well schooled in the ways of pulp literature (his twelve issues of *THE SHADOW* remain, to my mind, the perfect how-to manual for aspiring comics writers), and at first Rā's may seem an obvious avatar of Sax Rohmer's Dr. Fu Manchu. But it was O'Neil's inspiration to realize that the stock pulp figure of the nefarious Asian mastermind could be neatly retooled to embody the anxieties of the second half of the twentieth century — in particular the anxieties of an America that, poised between the twin upheavals of Vietnam and Watergate, was beginning to question its own long-cherished cultural verities — as well as the morality of its own actions at home and abroad.

Rā's would transcend racial stereotype. As Neal Adams described him, he was a figure of indeterminate ethnic origin, a citizen of many cultures: "I created a face not tied to any race at all. It had to have evidence of a great many things having happened, a face that showed the man had an awareness of his own difference at a very early age ... Rā's's face had to convey the feeling that he'd lived an extraordinary life long before his features were ever committed to paper."

Where the standard villains confined their activities to robbery, revenge and the like, Rā's's schemes were at once more ambitious and more nebulous. He hinted

darkly at a "new world order," and his encounters with Batman often seemed only marginally relevant to an infinitely larger master plan. The Darknight Detective often found himself a pawn in some dimly-perceived game of intrigue and conspiracy, played out across continents, the participants shadowy factions whose ultimate goals we would never discern. Even when Batman prevailed against Rā's, his victory was never complete; a quick dip in the Lazarus Pit, and evil would resurrect itself. The old, comforting order could never be fully restored...

It was a notion new to comics, that some types of corruption could not be neatly rooted out by the final frame of a 15$\frac{1}{2}$-page story. And Rā's's evil was of a particularly modern type — it sought to co-opt what it could not destroy. Through one subterfuge or another, Rā's would frequently enlist Batman as a reluctant ally. And of course, Batman was quite stricken to learn that Rā's regarded him not only as a deadly adversary, but also as a potential successor!

It's a splendid joke, actually. Note that Batman's "origin" — the murder of his parents, the moment that sparked his lifelong obsession with fighting crime — is reprised at the precise moment when he first meets the heinous master villain who hopes to become not only his mentor, but his *father-in-law.* The vehicle of temptation is Talia, Rā's's daughter, the one woman Batman is capable of loving — and the one woman he can never allow himself to have. Her shifting loyalties generate the constant moral convolutions at the heart of the tale — and infuse the "joke" with very real pain.

I'm tempted to say that his first meeting with Rā's was the point at which Batman's moral certainty began to dissolve — the point at which the "dark side" of the Dark Knight began to show through the cracks. Instead, I'll shut up and invite you to enjoy the extraordinary saga that begins in these pages and that will, with any luck, continue well into the future — through any number of reinventions and reinterpretations.

Let the duel begin.

Sam Hamm
Christmas, 1990

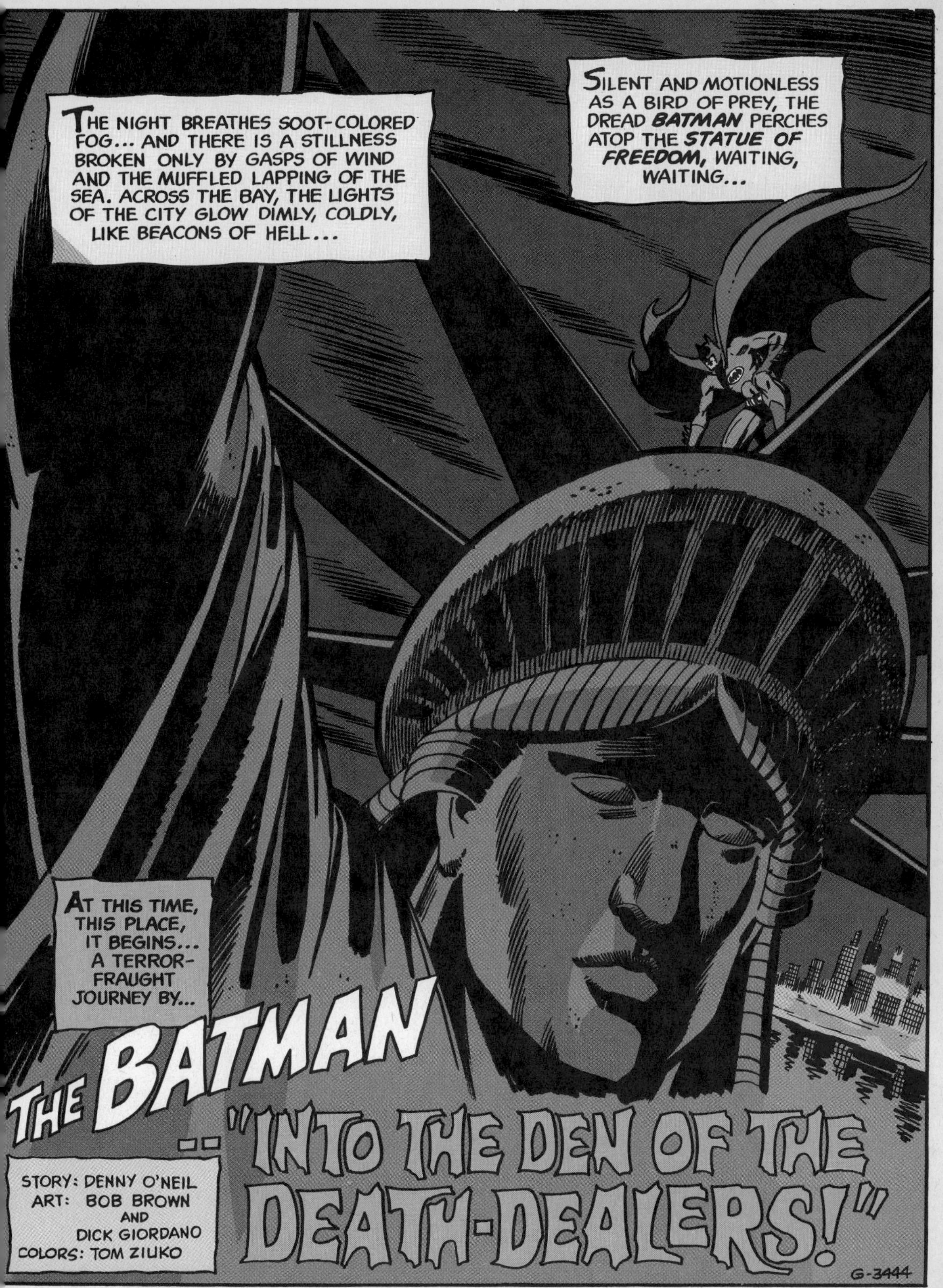
THE NIGHT BREATHES SOOT-COLORED FOG... AND THERE IS A STILLNESS BROKEN ONLY BY GASPS OF WIND AND THE MUFFLED LAPPING OF THE SEA. ACROSS THE BAY, THE LIGHTS OF THE CITY GLOW DIMLY, COLDLY, LIKE BEACONS OF HELL...
SILENT AND MOTIONLESS AS A BIRD OF PREY, THE DREAD BATMAN PERCHES ATOP THE STATUE OF FREEDOM, WAITING, WAITING...
AT THIS TIME, THIS PLACE, IT BEGINS... A TERROR-FRAUGHT JOURNEY BY...
THE BATMAN
.. "INTO THE DEN OF THE DEATH-DEALERS!"
STORY: DENNY O'NEIL
ART: BOB BROWN AND DICK GIORDANO
COLORS: TOM ZIUKO
G-3444

E SAGA OF RA'S AL GHUL 1 Published monthly and Copyright © 1987 DC Comics Inc., 666 Fifth Avenue, New York, N.Y. 10103. All Rights Reserved. The stories, racters and incidents mentioned in this magazine are entirely fictional. All characters featured in this issue and the distinctive likenesses thereof are trademarks of Comics Inc. Printed in Canada.
Comics Inc. A Warner Communications Company

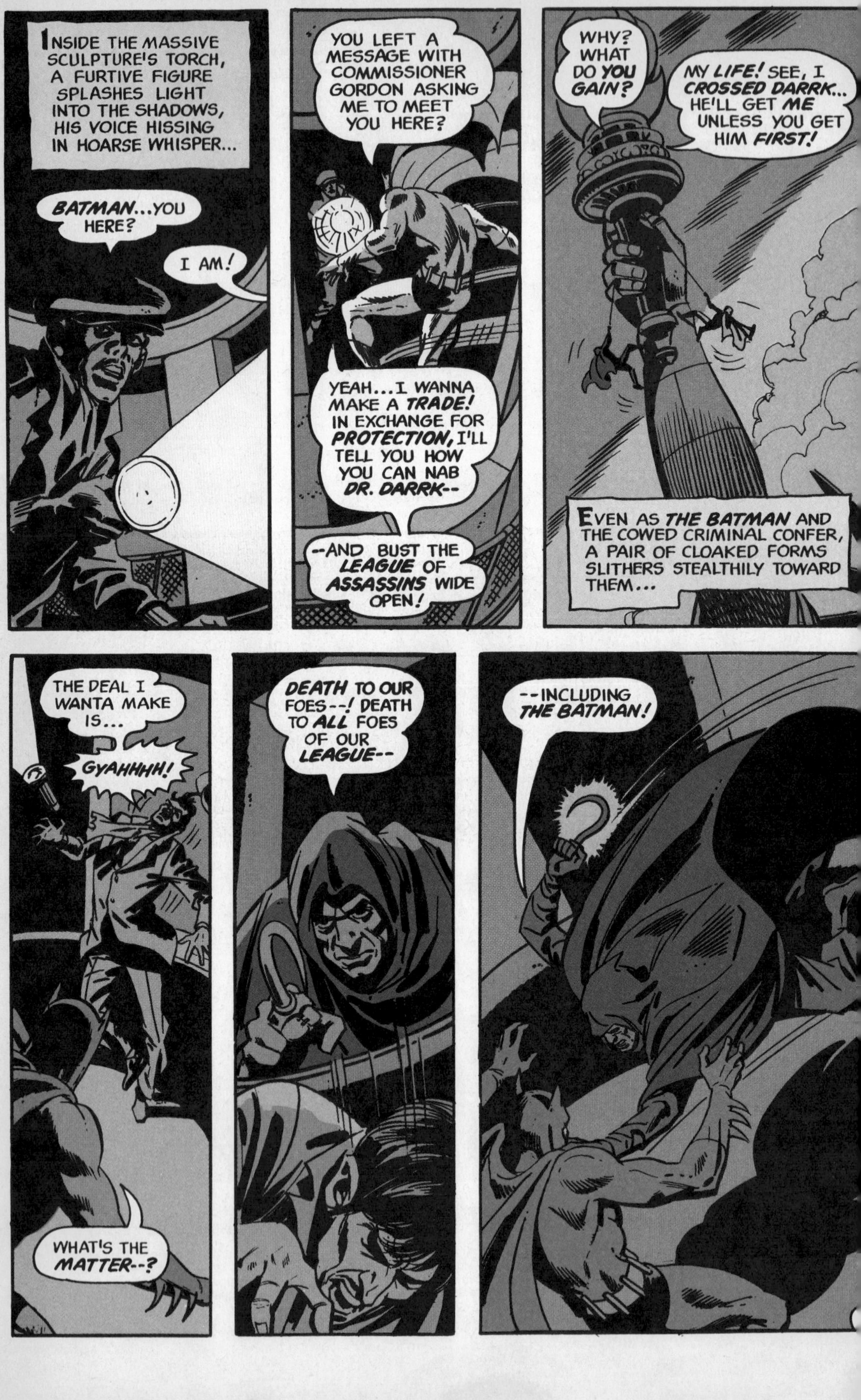
INSIDE THE MASSIVE SCULPTURE'S TORCH, A FURTIVE FIGURE SPLASHES LIGHT INTO THE SHADOWS, HIS VOICE HISSING IN HOARSE WHISPER...
BATMAN...YOU HERE?
I AM!
YOU LEFT A MESSAGE WITH COMMISSIONER GORDON ASKING ME TO MEET YOU HERE?
YEAH...I WANNA MAKE A TRADE! IN EXCHANGE FOR PROTECTION, I'LL TELL YOU HOW YOU CAN NAB DR. DARRK--
--AND BUST THE LEAGUE OF ASSASSINS WIDE OPEN!
WHY? WHAT DO YOU GAIN?
MY LIFE! SEE, I CROSSED DARRK... HE'LL GET ME UNLESS YOU GET HIM FIRST!
EVEN AS THE BATMAN AND THE COWED CRIMINAL CONFER, A PAIR OF CLOAKED FORMS SLITHERS STEALTHILY TOWARD THEM...
THE DEAL I WANTA MAKE IS...
GYAHHHH!
WHAT'S THE MATTER--?
DEATH TO OUR FOES--! DEATH TO ALL FOES OF OUR LEAGUE--
--INCLUDING THE BATMAN!

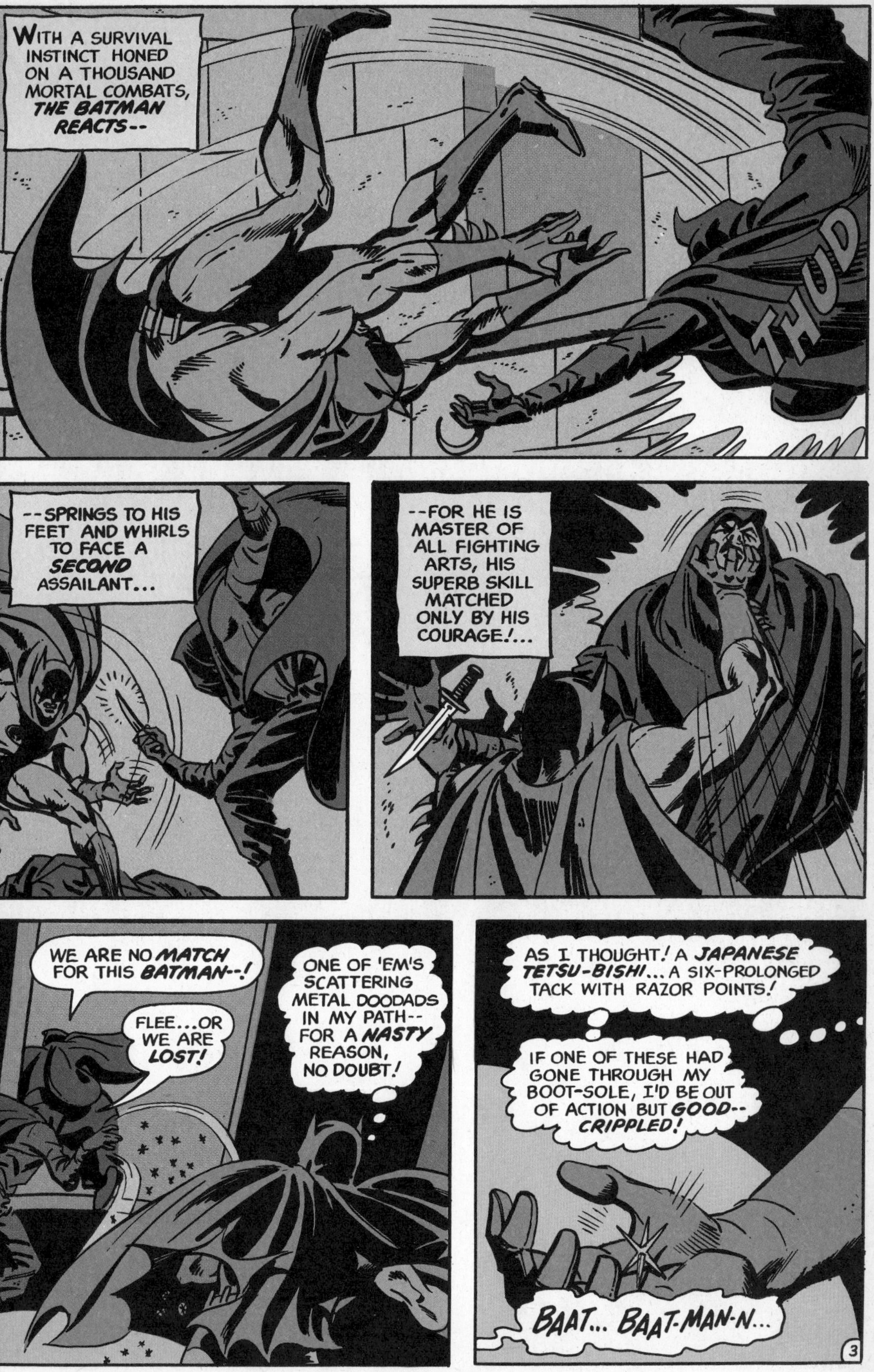
WITH A SURVIVAL INSTINCT HONED ON A THOUSAND MORTAL COMBATS, THE BATMAN REACTS--
THUD
--SPRINGS TO HIS FEET AND WHIRLS TO FACE A SECOND ASSAILANT...
--FOR HE IS MASTER OF ALL FIGHTING ARTS, HIS SUPERB SKILL MATCHED ONLY BY HIS COURAGE!...
WE ARE NO MATCH FOR THIS BATMAN--!
FLEE...OR WE ARE LOST!
ONE OF 'EM'S SCATTERING METAL DOODADS IN MY PATH--FOR A NASTY REASON, NO DOUBT!
AS I THOUGHT! A JAPANESE TETSU-BISHI... A SIX-PRONGED TACK WITH RAZOR POINTS!
IF ONE OF THESE HAD GONE THROUGH MY BOOT-SOLE, I'D BE OUT OF ACTION BUT GOOD--CRIPPLED!
BAAT... BAAT-MAN-N...
3

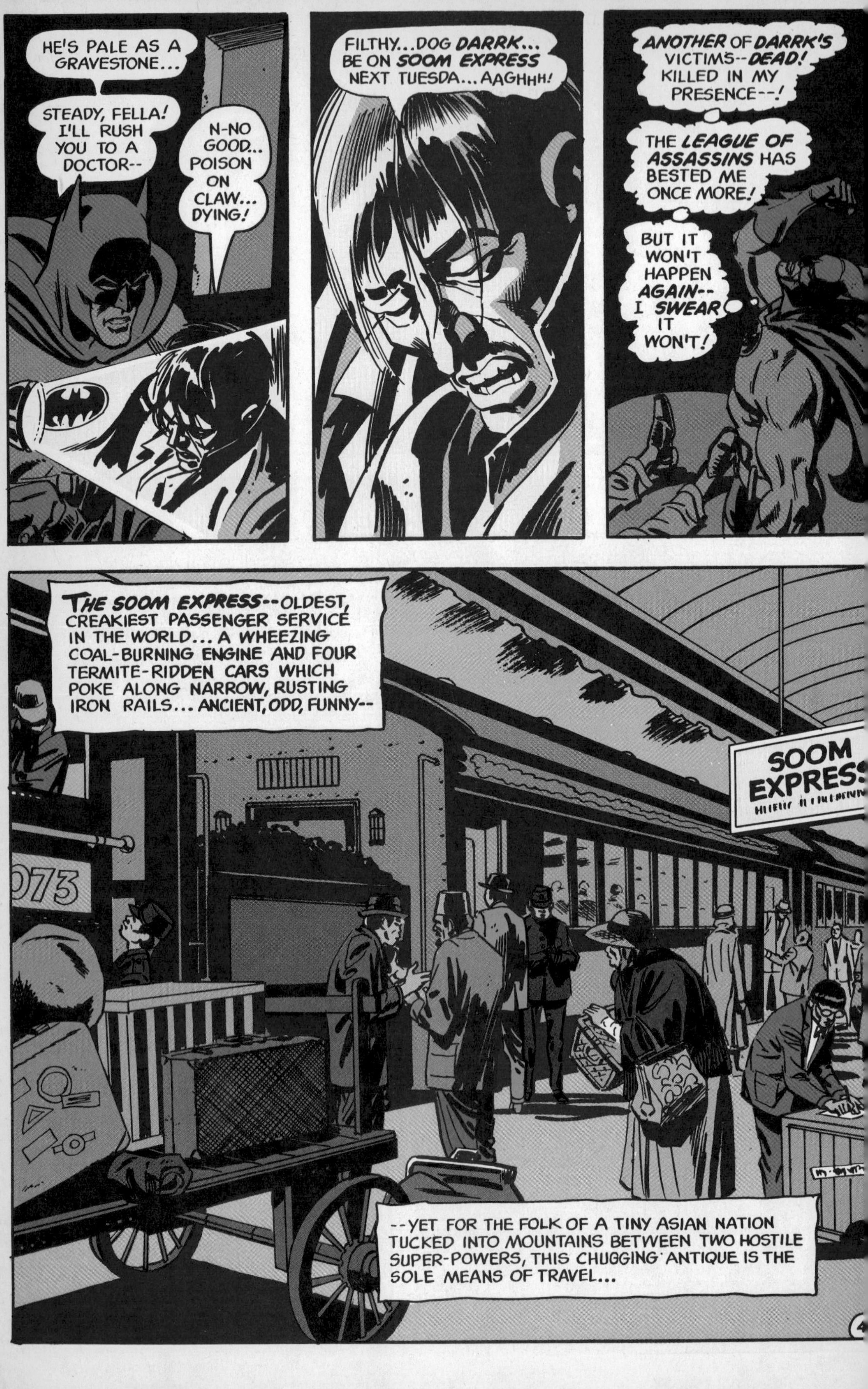
HE'S PALE AS A GRAVESTONE...
STEADY, FELLA! I'LL RUSH YOU TO A DOCTOR--
N-NO GOOD... POISON ON CLAW... DYING!
FILTHY...DOG DARRK... BE ON SOOM EXPRESS NEXT TUESDA...AAGHHH!
ANOTHER OF DARRK'S VICTIMS--DEAD! KILLED IN MY PRESENCE--!
THE LEAGUE OF ASSASSINS HAS BESTED ME ONCE MORE!
BUT IT WON'T HAPPEN AGAIN-- I SWEAR IT WON'T!
THE SOOM EXPRESS--OLDEST, CREAKIEST PASSENGER SERVICE IN THE WORLD... A WHEEZING COAL-BURNING ENGINE AND FOUR TERMITE-RIDDEN CARS WHICH POKE ALONG NARROW, RUSTING IRON RAILS... ANCIENT, ODD, FUNNY--
SOOM EXPRES
073
--YET FOR THE FOLK OF A TINY ASIAN NATION TUCKED INTO MOUNTAINS BETWEEN TWO HOSTILE SUPER-POWERS, THIS CHUGGING ANTIQUE IS THE SOLE MEANS OF TRAVEL...

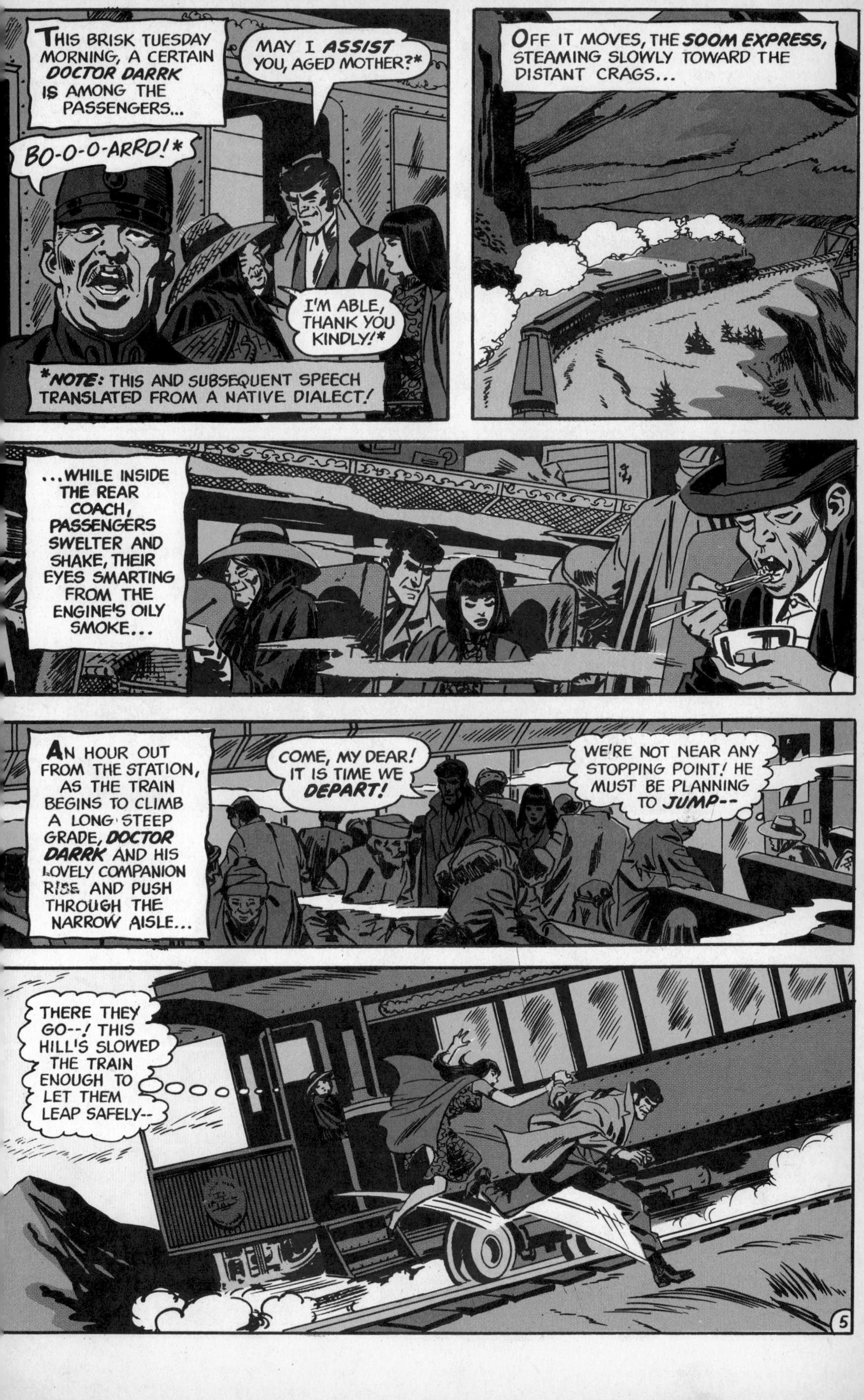
THIS BRISK TUESDAY MORNING, A CERTAIN DOCTOR DARRK IS AMONG THE PASSENGERS...
MAY I ASSIST YOU, AGED MOTHER?*
BO-O-O-ARRD!*
I'M ABLE, THANK YOU KINDLY!*
*NOTE: THIS AND SUBSEQUENT SPEECH TRANSLATED FROM A NATIVE DIALECT!
OFF IT MOVES, THE SOOM EXPRESS, STEAMING SLOWLY TOWARD THE DISTANT CRAGS...
...WHILE INSIDE THE REAR COACH, PASSENGERS SWELTER AND SHAKE, THEIR EYES SMARTING FROM THE ENGINE'S OILY SMOKE...
AN HOUR OUT FROM THE STATION, AS THE TRAIN BEGINS TO CLIMB A LONG STEEP GRADE, DOCTOR DARRK AND HIS LOVELY COMPANION RISE AND PUSH THROUGH THE NARROW AISLE...
COME, MY DEAR! IT IS TIME WE DEPART!
WE'RE NOT NEAR ANY STOPPING POINT! HE MUST BE PLANNING TO JUMP--
THERE THEY GO--! THIS HILL'S SLOWED THE TRAIN ENOUGH TO LET THEM LEAP SAFELY--
5

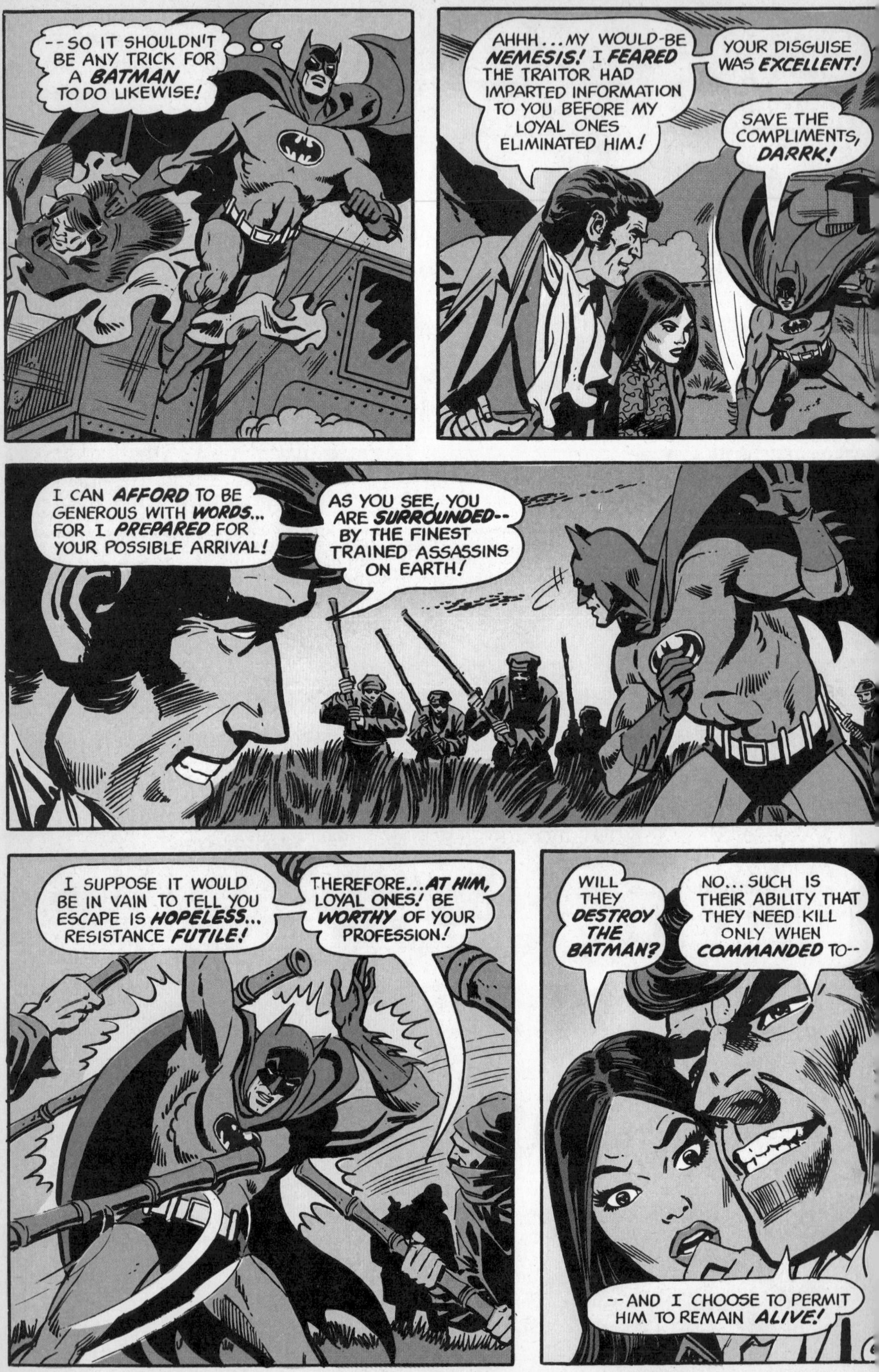
--SO IT SHOULDN'T BE ANY TRICK FOR A BATMAN TO DO LIKEWISE!
AHHH...MY WOULD-BE NEMESIS! I FEARED THE TRAITOR HAD IMPARTED INFORMATION TO YOU BEFORE MY LOYAL ONES ELIMINATED HIM!
YOUR DISGUISE WAS EXCELLENT!
SAVE THE COMPLIMENTS, DARRK!
I CAN AFFORD TO BE GENEROUS WITH WORDS... FOR I PREPARED FOR YOUR POSSIBLE ARRIVAL!
AS YOU SEE, YOU ARE SURROUNDED-- BY THE FINEST TRAINED ASSASSINS ON EARTH!
I SUPPOSE IT WOULD BE IN VAIN TO TELL YOU ESCAPE IS HOPELESS... RESISTANCE FUTILE!
THEREFORE...AT HIM, LOYAL ONES! BE WORTHY OF YOUR PROFESSION!
WILL THEY DESTROY THE BATMAN?
NO...SUCH IS THEIR ABILITY THAT THEY NEED KILL ONLY WHEN COMMANDED TO--
--AND I CHOOSE TO PERMIT HIM TO REMAIN ALIVE!

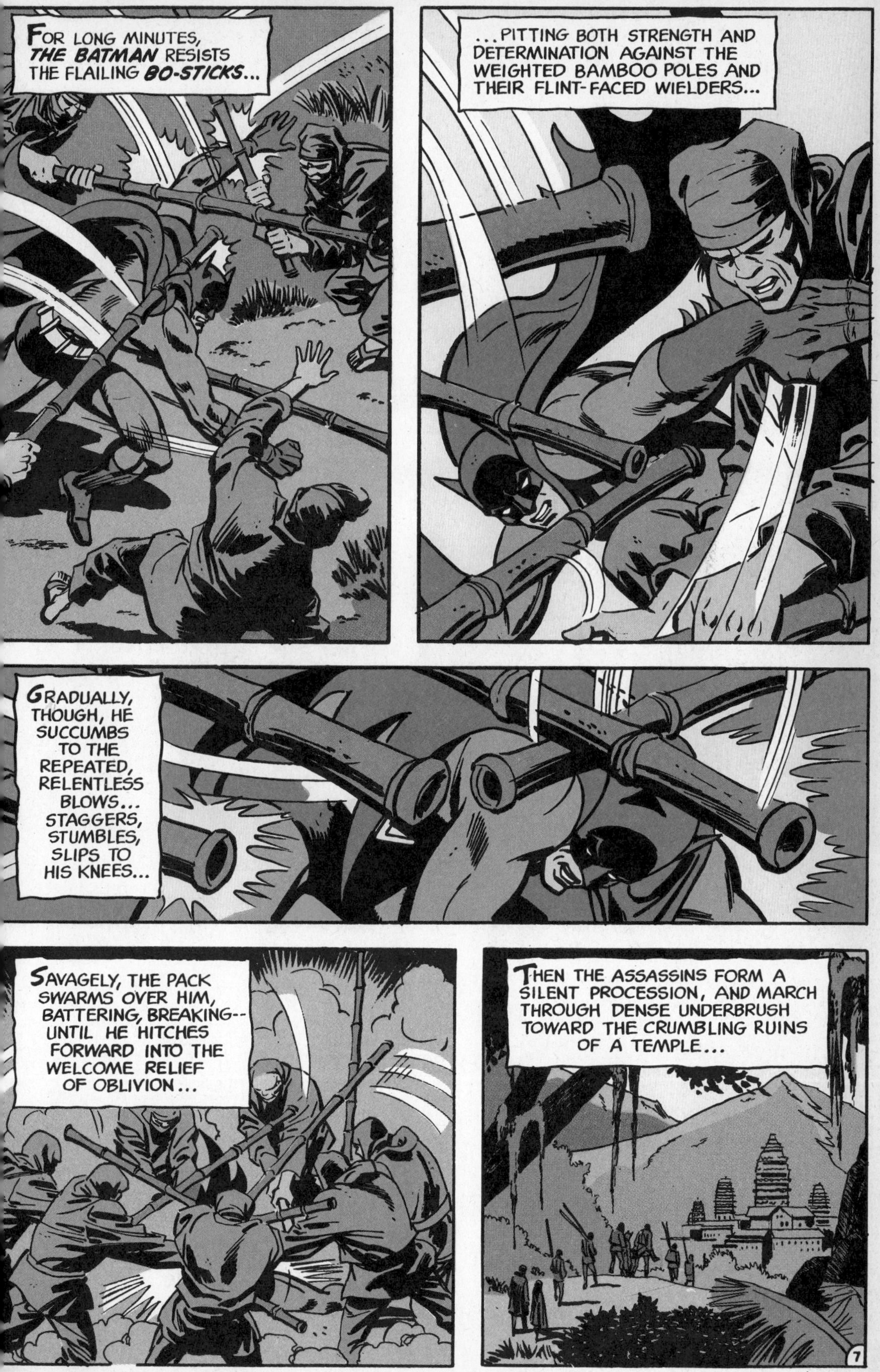
FOR LONG MINUTES, THE BATMAN RESISTS THE FLAILING BO-STICKS...
...PITTING BOTH STRENGTH AND DETERMINATION AGAINST THE WEIGHTED BAMBOO POLES AND THEIR FLINT-FACED WIELDERS...
GRADUALLY, THOUGH, HE SUCCUMBS TO THE REPEATED, RELENTLESS BLOWS... STAGGERS, STUMBLES, SLIPS TO HIS KNEES...
SAVAGELY, THE PACK SWARMS OVER HIM, BATTERING, BREAKING-- UNTIL HE HITCHES FORWARD INTO THE WELCOME RELIEF OF OBLIVION...
THEN THE ASSASSINS FORM A SILENT PROCESSION, AND MARCH THROUGH DENSE UNDERBRUSH TOWARD THE CRUMBLING RUINS OF A TEMPLE...
7

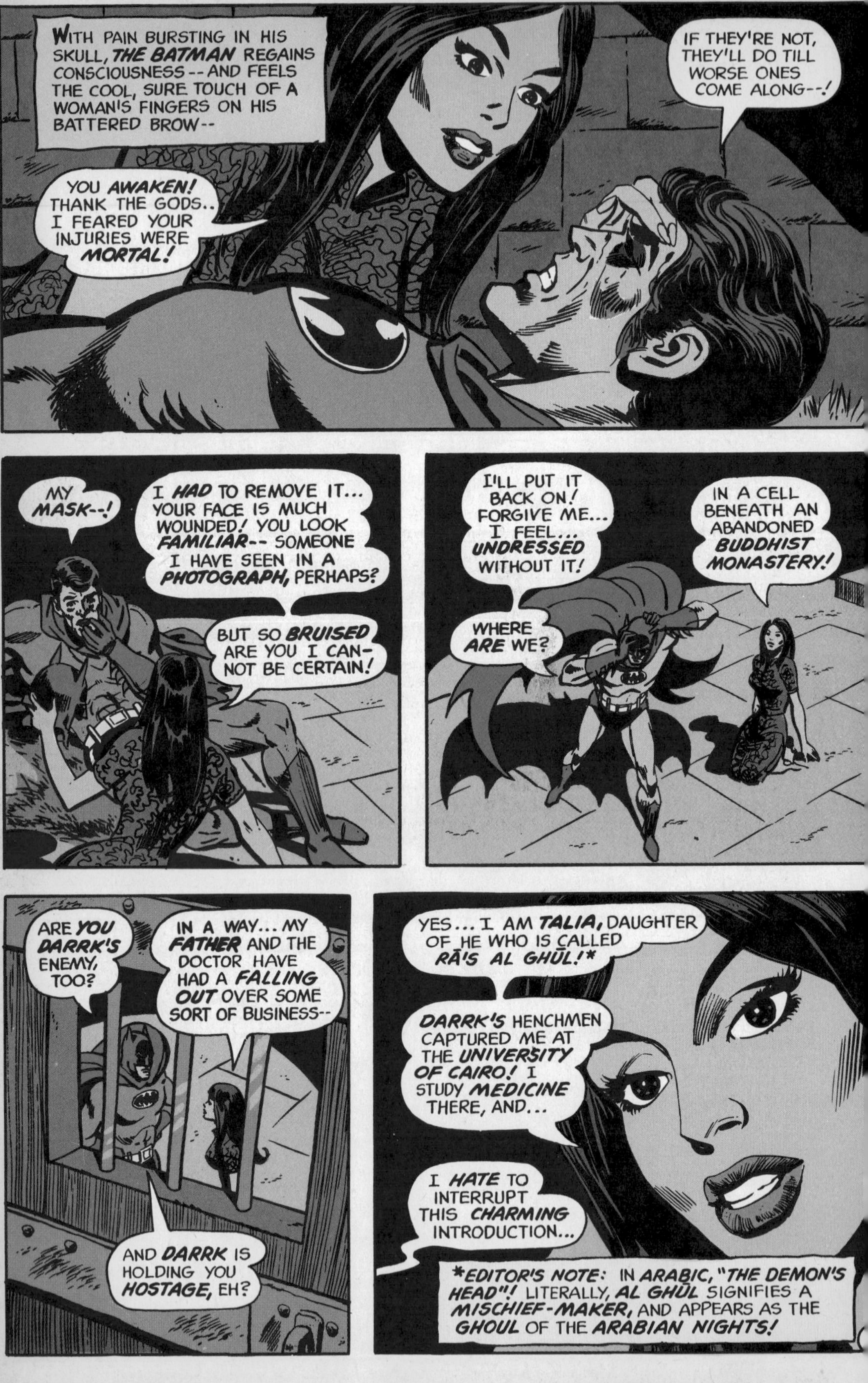
WITH PAIN BURSTING IN HIS SKULL, THE BATMAN REGAINS CONSCIOUSNESS -- AND FEELS THE COOL, SURE TOUCH OF A WOMAN'S FINGERS ON HIS BATTERED BROW--
YOU AWAKEN! THANK THE GODS.. I FEARED YOUR INJURIES WERE MORTAL!
IF THEY'RE NOT, THEY'LL DO TILL WORSE ONES COME ALONG--!
MY MASK--!
I HAD TO REMOVE IT... YOUR FACE IS MUCH WOUNDED! YOU LOOK FAMILIAR-- SOMEONE I HAVE SEEN IN A PHOTOGRAPH, PERHAPS?
BUT SO BRUISED ARE YOU I CAN-NOT BE CERTAIN!
I'LL PUT IT BACK ON! FORGIVE ME... I FEEL... UNDRESSED WITHOUT IT!
WHERE ARE WE?
IN A CELL BENEATH AN ABANDONED BUDDHIST MONASTERY!
ARE YOU DARRK'S ENEMY, TOO?
IN A WAY... MY FATHER AND THE DOCTOR HAVE HAD A FALLING OUT OVER SOME SORT OF BUSINESS--
AND DARRK IS HOLDING YOU HOSTAGE, EH?
YES... I AM TALIA, DAUGHTER OF HE WHO IS CALLED RĀ'S AL GHŪL!*
DARRK'S HENCHMEN CAPTURED ME AT THE UNIVERSITY OF CAIRO! I STUDY MEDICINE THERE, AND...
I HATE TO INTERRUPT THIS CHARMING INTRODUCTION...
*EDITOR'S NOTE: IN ARABIC, "THE DEMON'S HEAD"! LITERALLY, AL GHŪL SIGNIFIES A MISCHIEF-MAKER, AND APPEARS AS THE GHOUL OF THE ARABIAN NIGHTS!

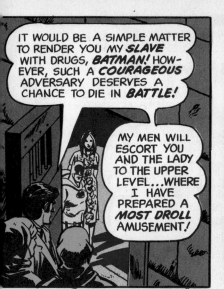

IT WOULD BE A SIMPLE MATTER TO RENDER YOU MY *SLAVE* WITH DRUGS, *BATMAN!* HOWEVER, SUCH A *COURAGEOUS* ADVERSARY DESERVES A CHANCE TO DIE IN *BATTLE!*

MY MEN WILL ESCORT YOU AND THE LADY TO THE UPPER LEVEL...WHERE I HAVE PREPARED A *MOST DROLL* AMUSEMENT!

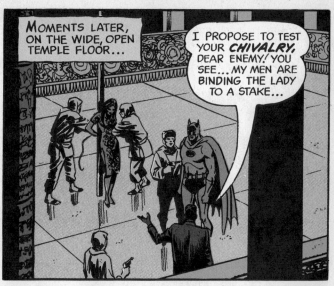

MOMENTS LATER, ON THE WIDE, OPEN TEMPLE FLOOR...

I PROPOSE TO TEST YOUR *CHIVALRY*, DEAR ENEMY! YOU SEE... MY MEN ARE BINDING THE LADY TO A STAKE...

...AND *BEHOLD!*-- AT THE FAR END OF THE AREA, A CAGED *BULL!* -- MOST *FIERCE*, I ASSURE YOU!

AT MY SIGNAL, THE ANIMAL WILL BE *RELEASED*, AND YOU WILL HAVE A *CHOICE*--

--EITHER RUN AND SAVE YOURSELF... OR STAY AND PROTECT MISS *TALIA!*

EITHER WAY, THE RESULTS SHOULD PROVE *HIGHLY* ENTERTAINING!

DARRK RAISES A HAND... THE CAGE DOOR FLIES OPEN... AND *THE BATMAN* IS FACED WITH TWO TONS OF BELLOWING, KILL-CRAZED *BEAST*--

MUSTN'T *PANIC!*

THAT CRITTER CAN BE *WHIPPED!*

IT'S BIG-- BUT ALSO *DUMB!*

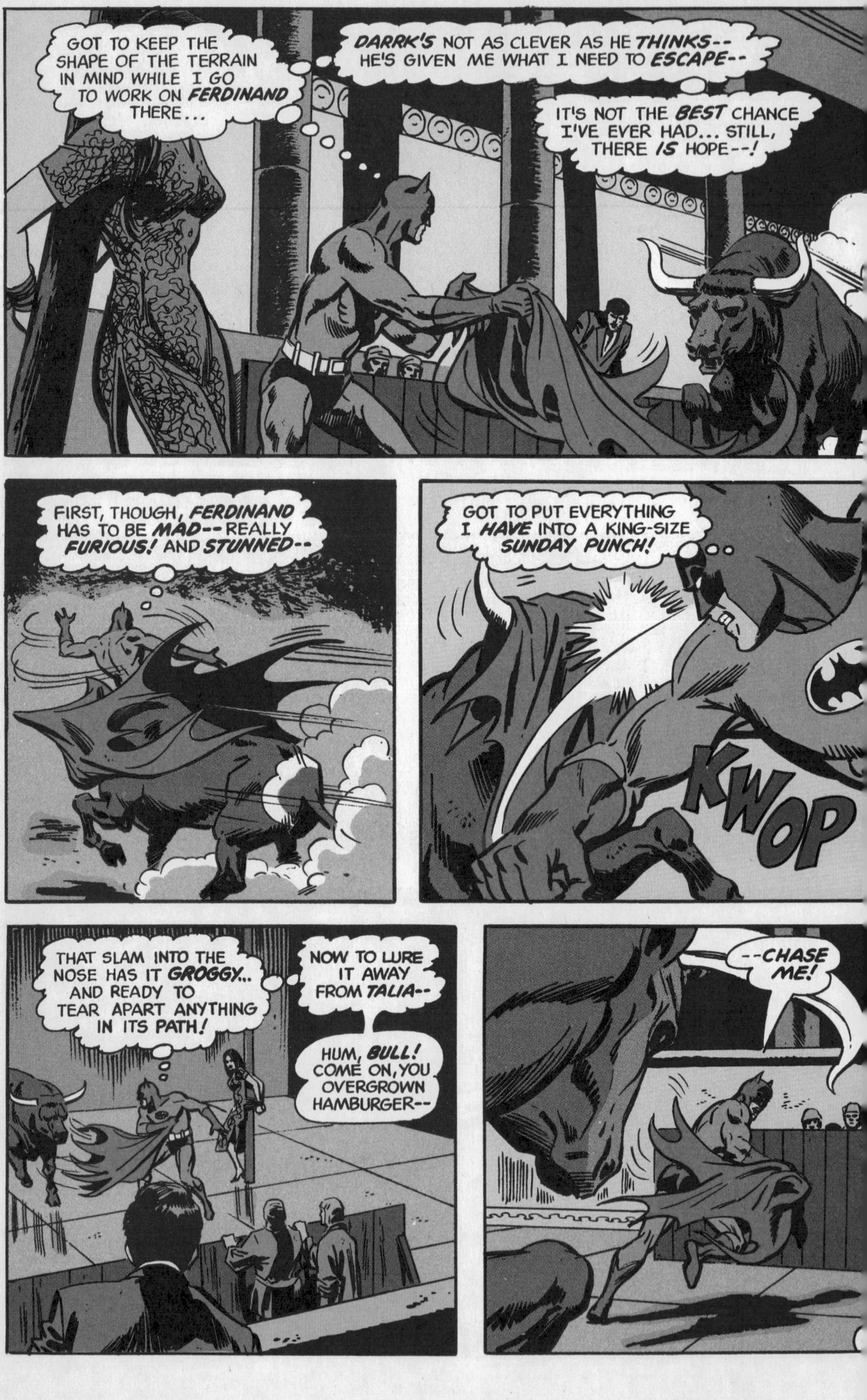
GOT TO KEEP THE SHAPE OF THE TERRAIN IN MIND WHILE I GO TO WORK ON FERDINAND THERE...
DARRK'S NOT AS CLEVER AS HE THINKS-- HE'S GIVEN ME WHAT I NEED TO ESCAPE--
IT'S NOT THE BEST CHANCE I'VE EVER HAD... STILL, THERE IS HOPE--!
FIRST, THOUGH, FERDINAND HAS TO BE MAD-- REALLY FURIOUS! AND STUNNED--
GOT TO PUT EVERYTHING I HAVE INTO A KING-SIZE SUNDAY PUNCH!
KWOP
THAT SLAM INTO THE NOSE HAS IT GROGGY... AND READY TO TEAR APART ANYTHING IN ITS PATH!
NOW TO LURE IT AWAY FROM TALIA--
HUM, BULL! COME ON, YOU OVERGROWN HAMBURGER--
--CHASE ME!

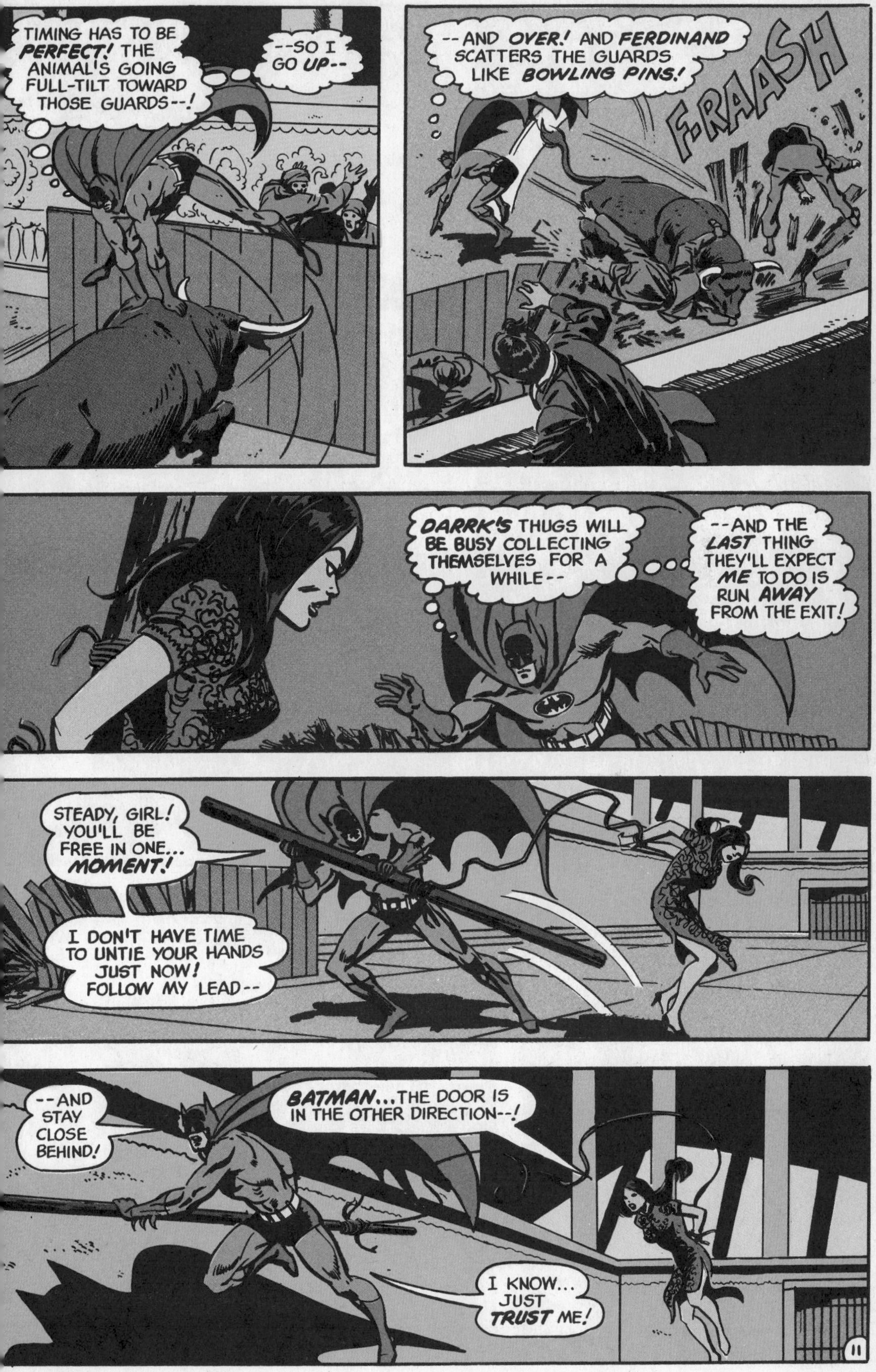
TIMING HAS TO BE PERFECT! THE ANIMAL'S GOING FULL-TILT TOWARD THOSE GUARDS--!
--SO I GO UP--
--AND OVER! AND FERDINAND SCATTERS THE GUARDS LIKE BOWLING PINS!
F-RAASH
DARRK'S THUGS WILL BE BUSY COLLECTING THEMSELVES FOR A WHILE--
--AND THE LAST THING THEY'LL EXPECT ME TO DO IS RUN AWAY FROM THE EXIT!
STEADY, GIRL! YOU'LL BE FREE IN ONE... MOMENT!
I DON'T HAVE TIME TO UNTIE YOUR HANDS JUST NOW! FOLLOW MY LEAD--
--AND STAY CLOSE BEHIND!
BATMAN...THE DOOR IS IN THE OTHER DIRECTION--!
I KNOW... JUST TRUST ME!
11

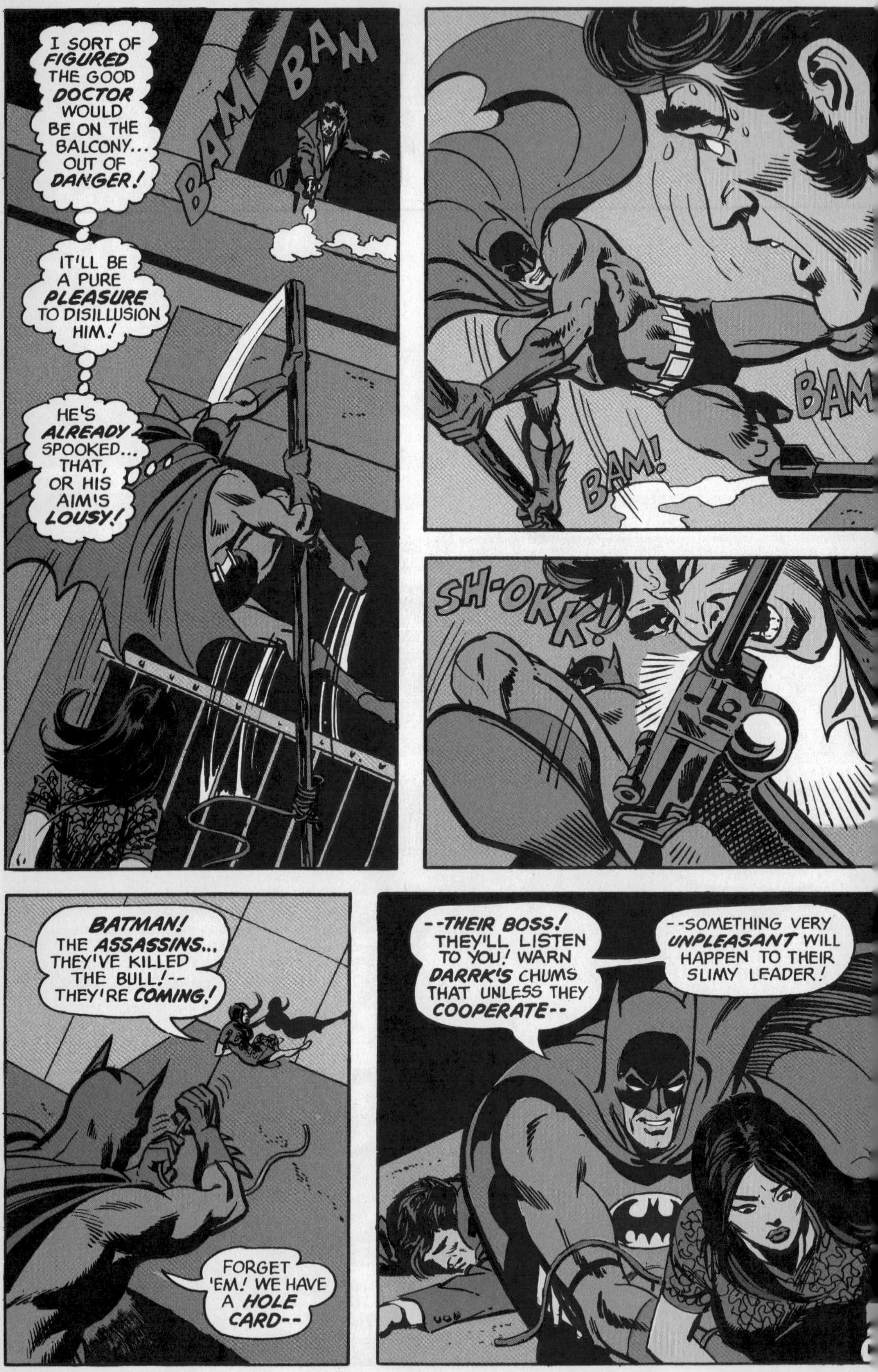
I SORT OF FIGURED THE GOOD DOCTOR WOULD BE ON THE BALCONY... OUT OF DANGER!
BAM BAM
BAM
IT'LL BE A PURE PLEASURE TO DISILLUSION HIM!
HE'S ALREADY SPOOKED... THAT, OR HIS AIM'S LOUSY!
BAM
BAM!
SH-OKK!
BATMAN! THE ASSASSINS... THEY'VE KILLED THE BULL!-- THEY'RE COMING!
FORGET 'EM! WE HAVE A HOLE CARD--
--THEIR BOSS! THEY'LL LISTEN TO YOU! WARN DARRK'S CHUMS THAT UNLESS THEY COOPERATE--
--SOMETHING VERY UNPLEASANT WILL HAPPEN TO THEIR SLIMY LEADER!

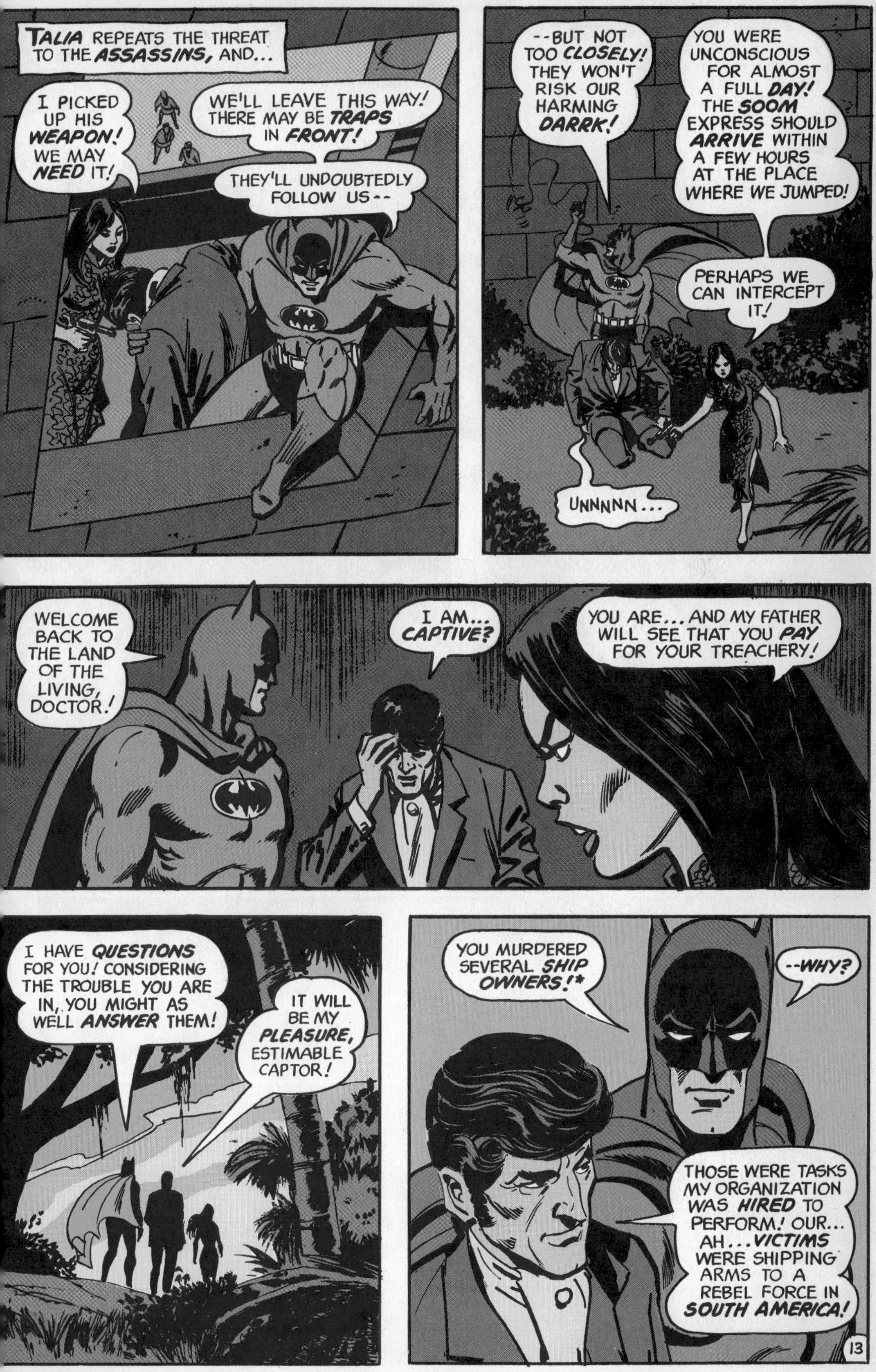
TALIA REPEATS THE THREAT TO THE ASSASSINS, AND...
I PICKED UP HIS WEAPON! WE MAY NEED IT!
WE'LL LEAVE THIS WAY! THERE MAY BE TRAPS IN FRONT!
THEY'LL UNDOUBTEDLY FOLLOW US--
--BUT NOT TOO CLOSELY! THEY WON'T RISK OUR HARMING DARRK!
YOU WERE UNCONSCIOUS FOR ALMOST A FULL DAY! THE SOOM EXPRESS SHOULD ARRIVE WITHIN A FEW HOURS AT THE PLACE WHERE WE JUMPED!
PERHAPS WE CAN INTERCEPT IT!
UNNNNN...
WELCOME BACK TO THE LAND OF THE LIVING, DOCTOR!
I AM... CAPTIVE?
YOU ARE... AND MY FATHER WILL SEE THAT YOU PAY FOR YOUR TREACHERY!
I HAVE QUESTIONS FOR YOU! CONSIDERING THE TROUBLE YOU ARE IN, YOU MIGHT AS WELL ANSWER THEM!
IT WILL BE MY PLEASURE, ESTIMABLE CAPTOR!
YOU MURDERED SEVERAL SHIP OWNERS!*
--WHY?
THOSE WERE TASKS MY ORGANIZATION WAS HIRED TO PERFORM! OUR... AH... VICTIMS WERE SHIPPING ARMS TO A REBEL FORCE IN SOUTH AMERICA!
13

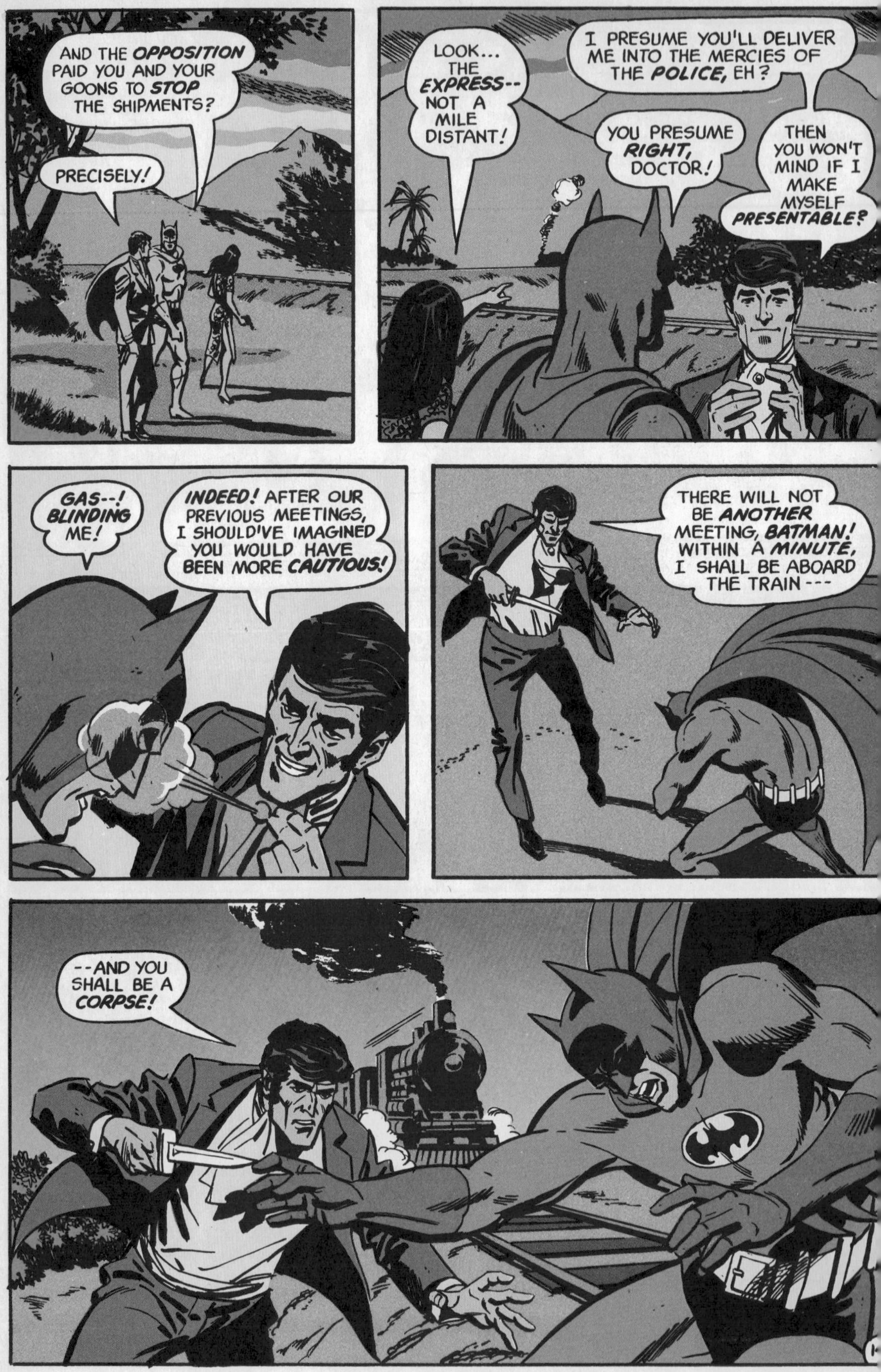
AND THE OPPOSITION PAID YOU AND YOUR GOONS TO STOP THE SHIPMENTS?
PRECISELY!
LOOK... THE EXPRESS-- NOT A MILE DISTANT!
I PRESUME YOU'LL DELIVER ME INTO THE MERCIES OF THE POLICE, EH?
YOU PRESUME RIGHT, DOCTOR!
THEN YOU WON'T MIND IF I MAKE MYSELF PRESENTABLE?
GAS--! BLINDING ME!
INDEED! AFTER OUR PREVIOUS MEETINGS, I SHOULD'VE IMAGINED YOU WOULD HAVE BEEN MORE CAUTIOUS!
THERE WILL NOT BE ANOTHER MEETING, BATMAN! WITHIN A MINUTE, I SHALL BE ABOARD THE TRAIN---
--AND YOU SHALL BE A CORPSE!

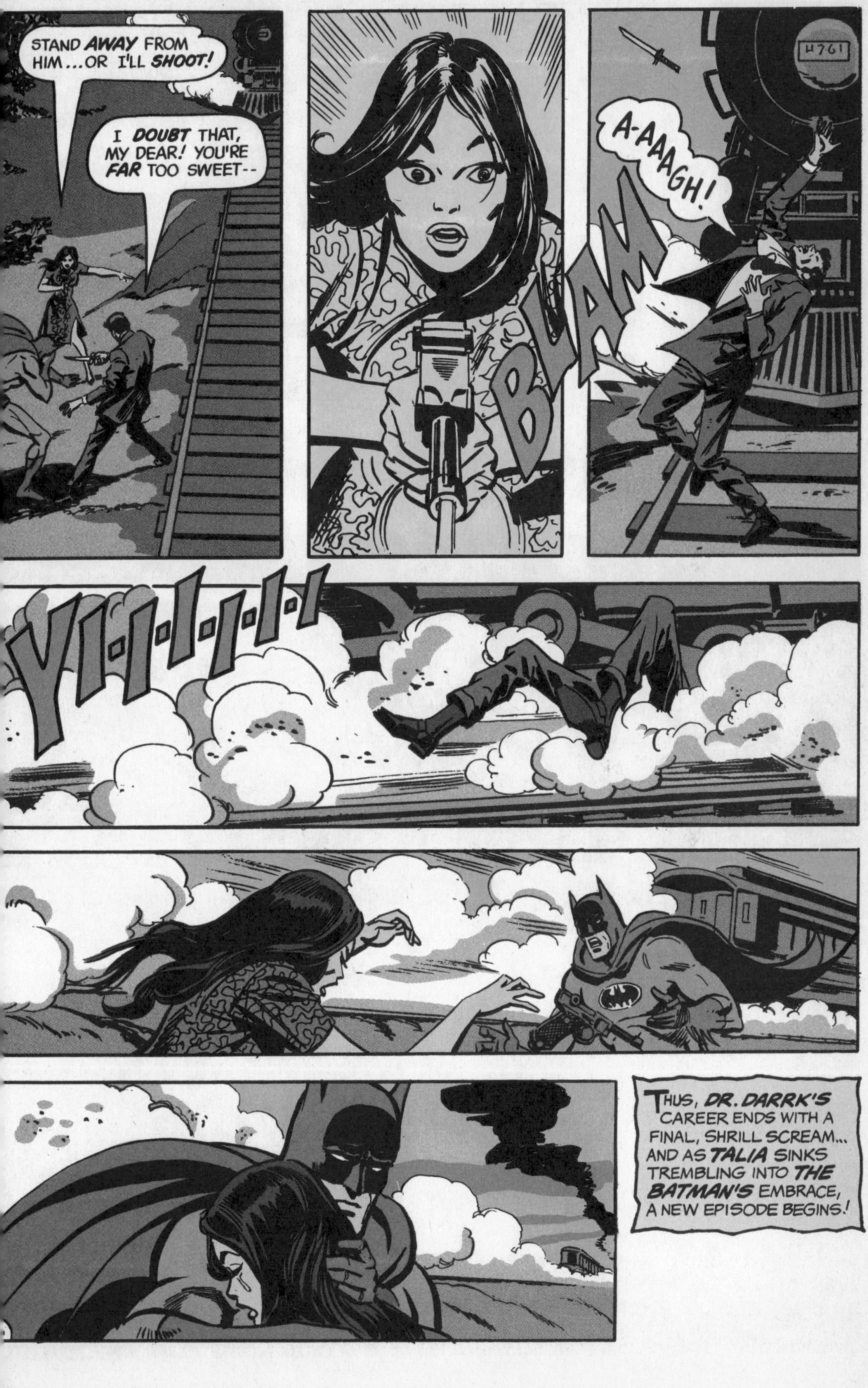
STAND AWAY FROM HIM...OR I'LL SHOOT!
I DOUBT THAT, MY DEAR! YOU'RE FAR TOO SWEET--
BLAM
A-AAAGH!
YI-I-I-I-I-I
THUS, DR. DARRK'S CAREER ENDS WITH A FINAL, SHRILL SCREAM... AND AS TALIA SINKS TREMBLING INTO THE BATMAN'S EMBRACE, A NEW EPISODE BEGINS!

NIGHT... A COLORFULLY CLAD FIGURE SLIDES SILENTLY THROUGH THE SHADOWS TOWARD A BOARDING HOUSE NEAR *HUDSON UNIVERSITY.* HE SHINNIES SWIFTLY UP A DRAINPIPE... THEN PAUSES AT AN OPEN WINDOW...

WHO IS THAT...? WHO'S *THERE?*

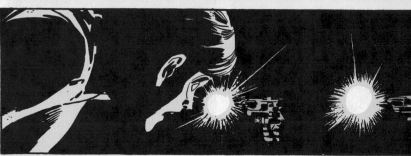

AARGH...!

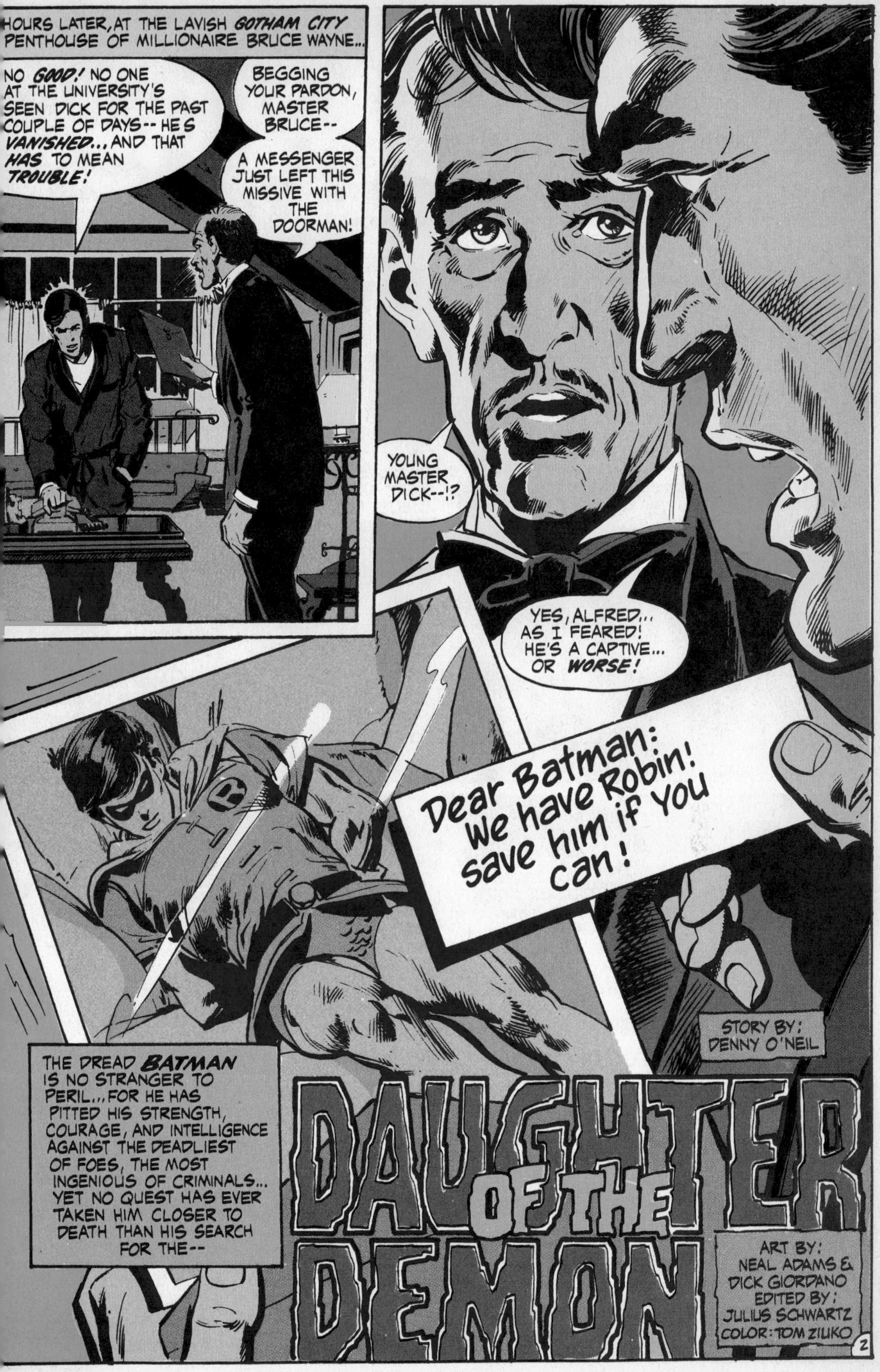
HOURS LATER, AT THE LAVISH GOTHAM CITY PENTHOUSE OF MILLIONAIRE BRUCE WAYNE...
NO GOOD! NO ONE AT THE UNIVERSITY'S SEEN DICK FOR THE PAST COUPLE OF DAYS-- HE'S VANISHED... AND THAT HAS TO MEAN TROUBLE!
BEGGING YOUR PARDON, MASTER BRUCE--
A MESSENGER JUST LEFT THIS MISSIVE WITH THE DOORMAN!
YOUNG MASTER DICK--!?
YES, ALFRED... AS I FEARED! HE'S A CAPTIVE... OR WORSE!
Dear Batman: We have Robin! save him if You can!
STORY BY: DENNY O'NEIL
THE DREAD BATMAN IS NO STRANGER TO PERIL... FOR HE HAS PITTED HIS STRENGTH, COURAGE, AND INTELLIGENCE AGAINST THE DEADLIEST OF FOES, THE MOST INGENIOUS OF CRIMINALS... YET NO QUEST HAS EVER TAKEN HIM CLOSER TO DEATH THAN HIS SEARCH FOR THE--
DAUGHTER OF THE DEMON
ART BY: NEAL ADAMS & DICK GIORDANO
EDITED BY: JULIUS SCHWARTZ
COLOR: TOM ZIUKO
2

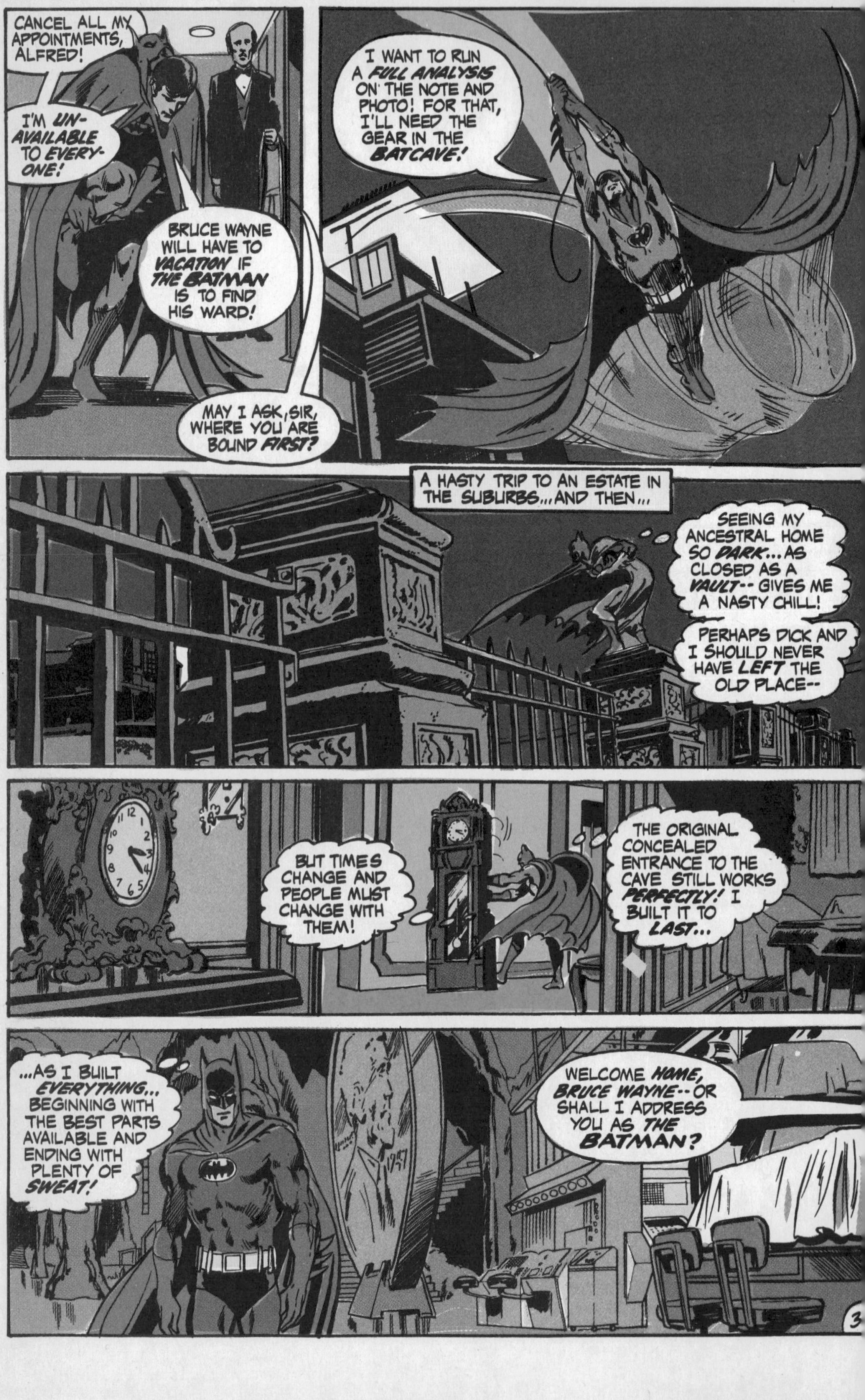
CANCEL ALL MY APPOINTMENTS, ALFRED!
I'M UN-AVAILABLE TO EVERY-ONE!
BRUCE WAYNE WILL HAVE TO VACATION IF THE BATMAN IS TO FIND HIS WARD!
MAY I ASK, SIR, WHERE YOU ARE BOUND FIRST?
I WANT TO RUN A FULL ANALYSIS ON THE NOTE AND PHOTO! FOR THAT, I'LL NEED THE GEAR IN THE BATCAVE!
A HASTY TRIP TO AN ESTATE IN THE SUBURBS...AND THEN...
SEEING MY ANCESTRAL HOME SO DARK...AS CLOSED AS A VAULT-- GIVES ME A NASTY CHILL!
PERHAPS DICK AND I SHOULD NEVER HAVE LEFT THE OLD PLACE--
BUT TIMES CHANGE AND PEOPLE MUST CHANGE WITH THEM!
THE ORIGINAL CONCEALED ENTRANCE TO THE CAVE STILL WORKS PERFECTLY! I BUILT IT TO LAST...
...AS I BUILT EVERYTHING... BEGINNING WITH THE BEST PARTS AVAILABLE AND ENDING WITH PLENTY OF SWEAT!
WELCOME HOME, BRUCE WAYNE--OR SHALL I ADDRESS YOU AS THE BATMAN?
3

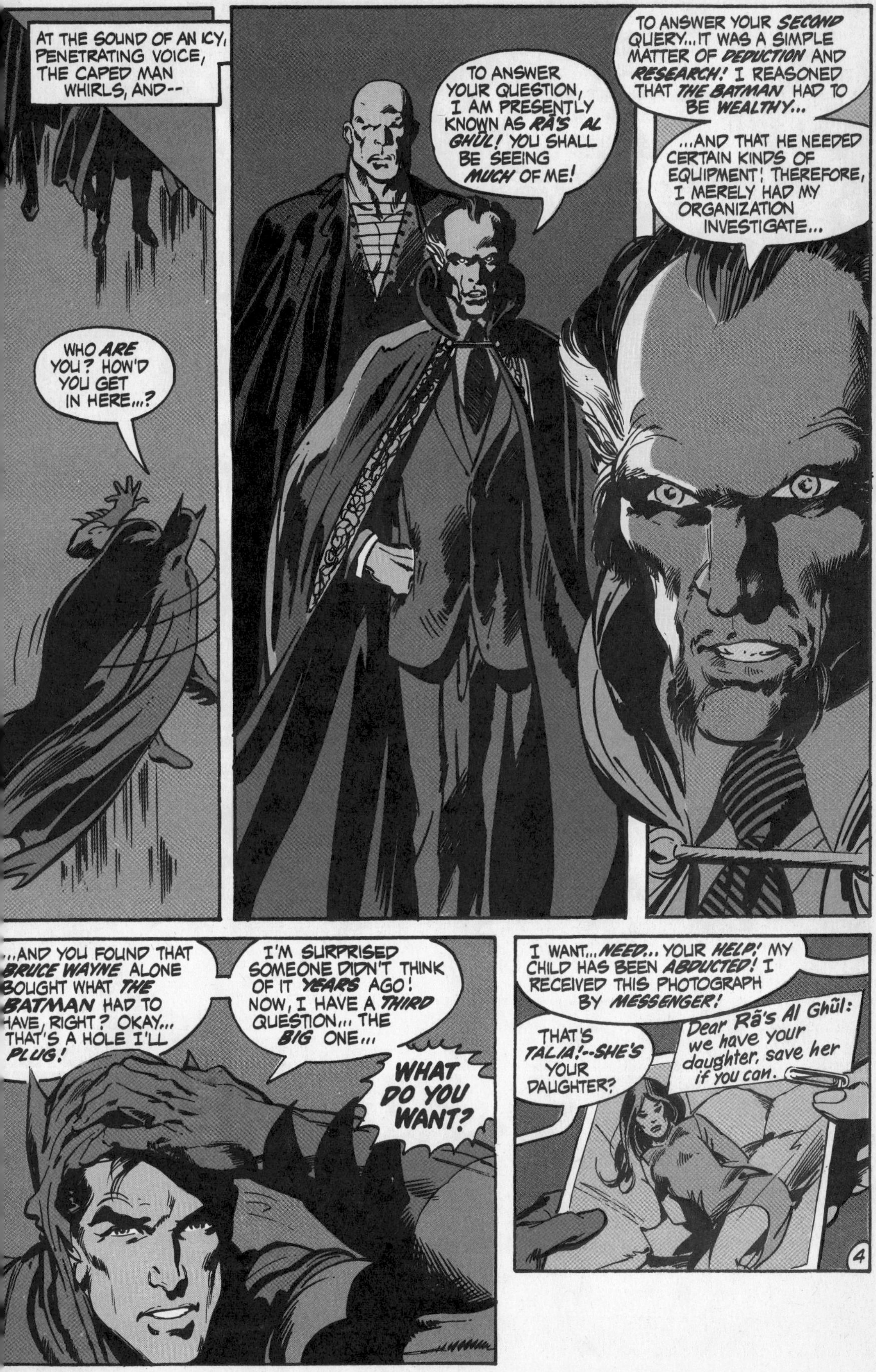
AT THE SOUND OF AN ICY, PENETRATING VOICE, THE CAPED MAN WHIRLS, AND--
WHO ARE YOU? HOW'D YOU GET IN HERE...?
TO ANSWER YOUR QUESTION, I AM PRESENTLY KNOWN AS RĀ'S AL GHŪL! YOU SHALL BE SEEING MUCH OF ME!
TO ANSWER YOUR SECOND QUERY...IT WAS A SIMPLE MATTER OF DEDUCTION AND RESEARCH! I REASONED THAT THE BATMAN HAD TO BE WEALTHY...
...AND THAT HE NEEDED CERTAIN KINDS OF EQUIPMENT; THEREFORE, I MERELY HAD MY ORGANIZATION INVESTIGATE...
...AND YOU FOUND THAT BRUCE WAYNE ALONE BOUGHT WHAT THE BATMAN HAD TO HAVE, RIGHT? OKAY... THAT'S A HOLE I'LL PLUG!
I'M SURPRISED SOMEONE DIDN'T THINK OF IT YEARS AGO! NOW, I HAVE A THIRD QUESTION... THE BIG ONE...
WHAT DO YOU WANT?
I WANT... NEED... YOUR HELP! MY CHILD HAS BEEN ABDUCTED! I RECEIVED THIS PHOTOGRAPH BY MESSENGER!
THAT'S TALIA!--SHE'S YOUR DAUGHTER?
Dear Rā's Al Ghūl: we have your daughter, save her if you can.
4

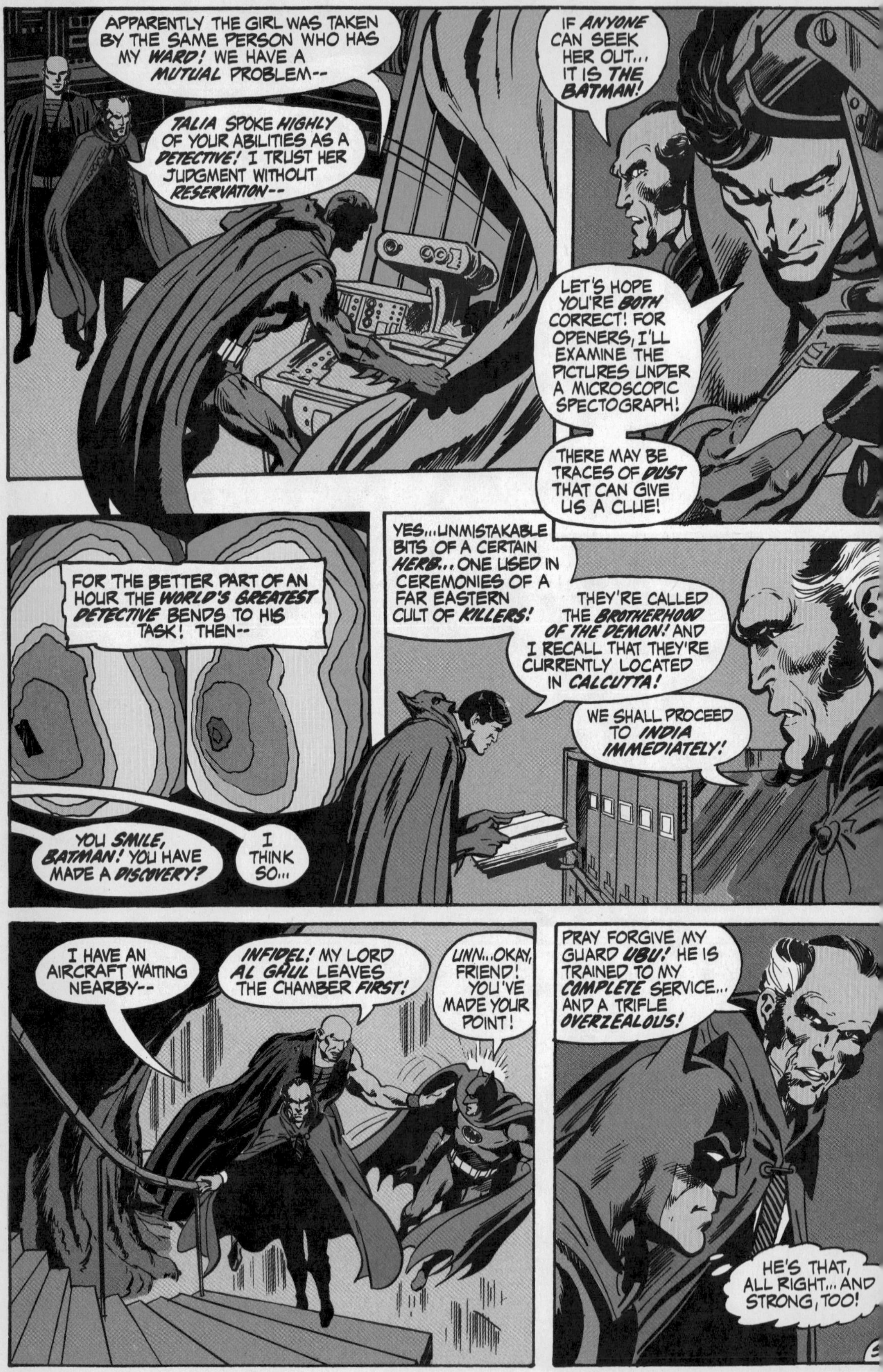
APPARENTLY THE GIRL WAS TAKEN BY THE SAME PERSON WHO HAS MY WARD! WE HAVE A MUTUAL PROBLEM--
TALIA SPOKE HIGHLY OF YOUR ABILITIES AS A DETECTIVE! I TRUST HER JUDGMENT WITHOUT RESERVATION--
IF ANYONE CAN SEEK HER OUT... IT IS THE BATMAN!
LET'S HOPE YOU'RE BOTH CORRECT! FOR OPENERS, I'LL EXAMINE THE PICTURES UNDER A MICROSCOPIC SPECTOGRAPH!
THERE MAY BE TRACES OF DUST THAT CAN GIVE US A CLUE!
FOR THE BETTER PART OF AN HOUR THE WORLD'S GREATEST DETECTIVE BENDS TO HIS TASK! THEN--
YOU SMILE, BATMAN! YOU HAVE MADE A DISCOVERY?
I THINK SO...
YES... UNMISTAKABLE BITS OF A CERTAIN HERB... ONE USED IN CEREMONIES OF A FAR EASTERN CULT OF KILLERS!
THEY'RE CALLED THE BROTHERHOOD OF THE DEMON! AND I RECALL THAT THEY'RE CURRENTLY LOCATED IN CALCUTTA!
WE SHALL PROCEED TO INDIA IMMEDIATELY!
I HAVE AN AIRCRAFT WAITING NEARBY--
INFIDEL! MY LORD AL GHUL LEAVES THE CHAMBER FIRST!
UNN... OKAY, FRIEND! YOU'VE MADE YOUR POINT!
PRAY FORGIVE MY GUARD UBU! HE IS TRAINED TO MY COMPLETE SERVICE... AND A TRIFLE OVERZEALOUS!
HE'S THAT, ALL RIGHT... AND STRONG, TOO!

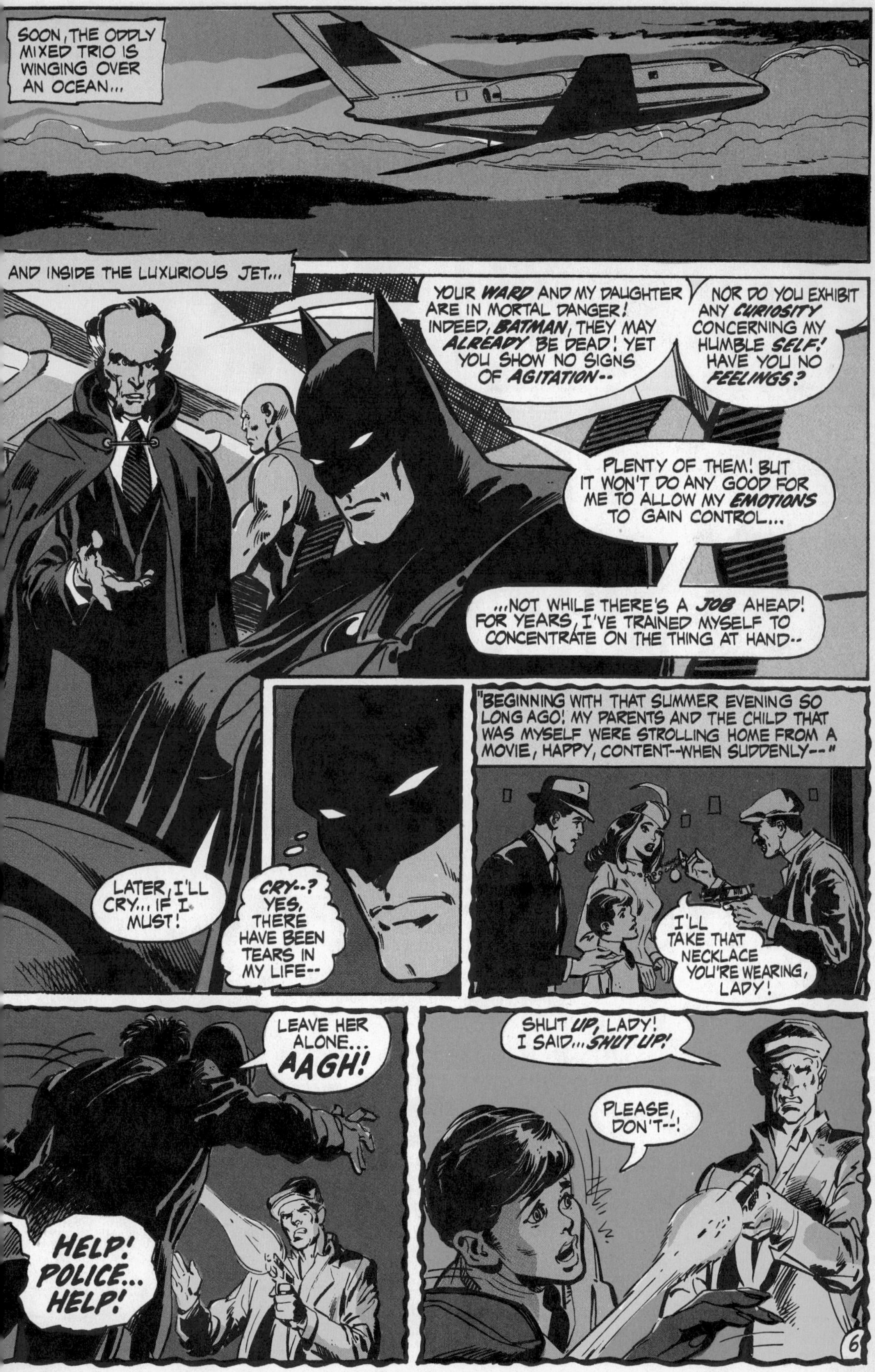
SOON, THE ODDLY MIXED TRIO IS WINGING OVER AN OCEAN...
AND INSIDE THE LUXURIOUS JET...
YOUR WARD AND MY DAUGHTER ARE IN MORTAL DANGER! INDEED, BATMAN, THEY MAY ALREADY BE DEAD! YET YOU SHOW NO SIGNS OF AGITATION--
NOR DO YOU EXHIBIT ANY CURIOSITY CONCERNING MY HUMBLE SELF! HAVE YOU NO FEELINGS?
PLENTY OF THEM! BUT IT WON'T DO ANY GOOD FOR ME TO ALLOW MY EMOTIONS TO GAIN CONTROL...
...NOT WHILE THERE'S A JOB AHEAD! FOR YEARS, I'VE TRAINED MYSELF TO CONCENTRATE ON THE THING AT HAND--
LATER, I'LL CRY... IF I MUST!
CRY--? YES, THERE HAVE BEEN TEARS IN MY LIFE--
"BEGINNING WITH THAT SUMMER EVENING SO LONG AGO! MY PARENTS AND THE CHILD THAT WAS MYSELF WERE STROLLING HOME FROM A MOVIE, HAPPY, CONTENT--WHEN SUDDENLY--"
I'LL TAKE THAT NECKLACE YOU'RE WEARING, LADY!
LEAVE HER ALONE... AAGH!
HELP! POLICE... HELP!
SHUT UP, LADY! I SAID... SHUT UP!
PLEASE, DON'T--!
6

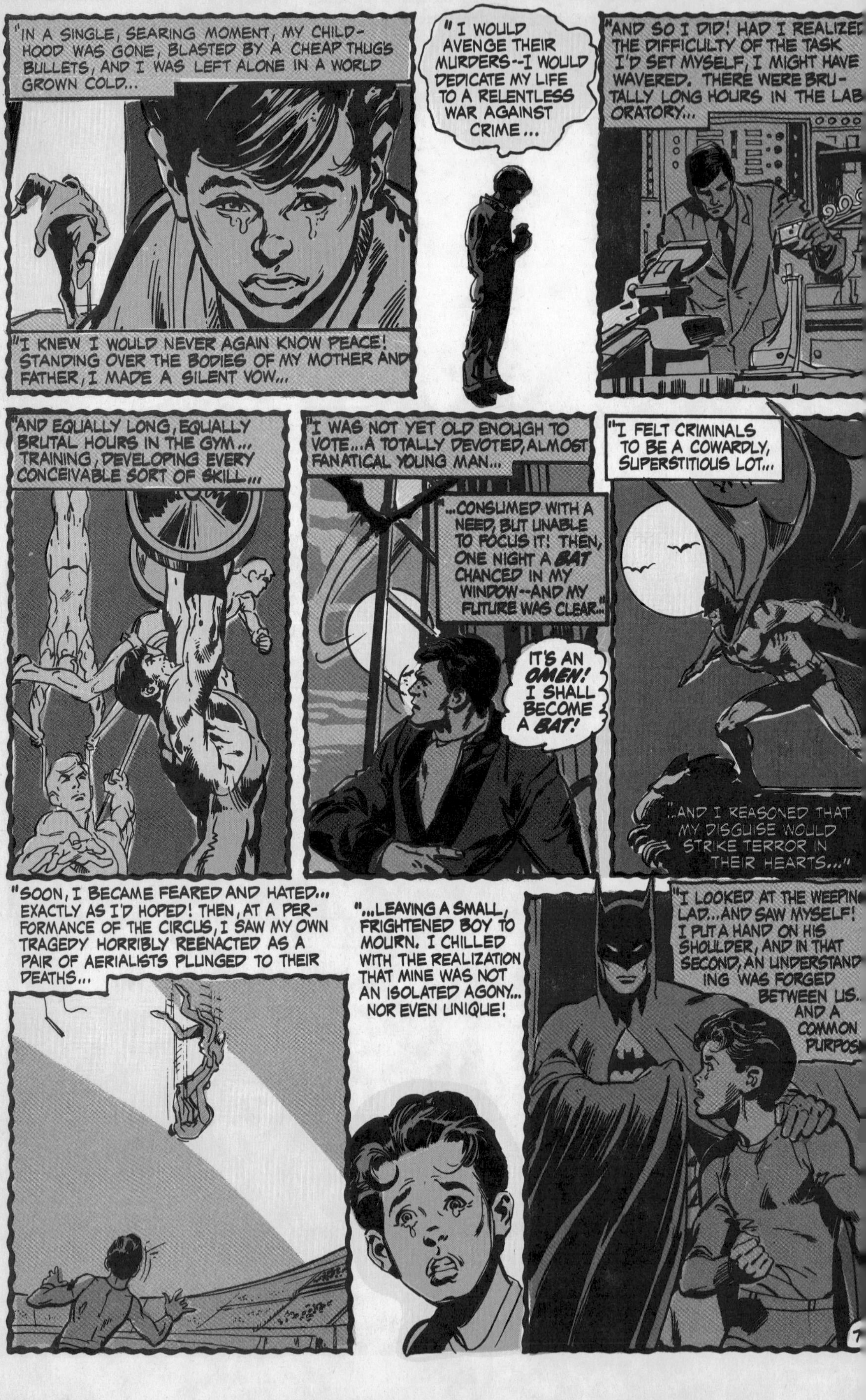
"IN A SINGLE, SEARING MOMENT, MY CHILDHOOD WAS GONE, BLASTED BY A CHEAP THUG'S BULLETS, AND I WAS LEFT ALONE IN A WORLD GROWN COLD...
"I KNEW I WOULD NEVER AGAIN KNOW PEACE! STANDING OVER THE BODIES OF MY MOTHER AND FATHER, I MADE A SILENT VOW...
"I WOULD AVENGE THEIR MURDERS--I WOULD DEDICATE MY LIFE TO A RELENTLESS WAR AGAINST CRIME...
"AND SO I DID! HAD I REALIZED THE DIFFICULTY OF THE TASK I'D SET MYSELF, I MIGHT HAVE WAVERED. THERE WERE BRUTALLY LONG HOURS IN THE LABORATORY...
"AND EQUALLY LONG, EQUALLY BRUTAL HOURS IN THE GYM... TRAINING, DEVELOPING EVERY CONCEIVABLE SORT OF SKILL...
"I WAS NOT YET OLD ENOUGH TO VOTE... A TOTALLY DEVOTED, ALMOST FANATICAL YOUNG MAN...
...CONSUMED WITH A NEED, BUT UNABLE TO FOCUS IT! THEN, ONE NIGHT A BAT CHANCED IN MY WINDOW--AND MY FUTURE WAS CLEAR."
IT'S AN OMEN! I SHALL BECOME A BAT!
"I FELT CRIMINALS TO BE A COWARDLY, SUPERSTITIOUS LOT...
...AND I REASONED THAT MY DISGUISE WOULD STRIKE TERROR IN THEIR HEARTS..."
"SOON, I BECAME FEARED AND HATED... EXACTLY AS I'D HOPED! THEN, AT A PERFORMANCE OF THE CIRCUS, I SAW MY OWN TRAGEDY HORRIBLY REENACTED AS A PAIR OF AERIALISTS PLUNGED TO THEIR DEATHS...
"...LEAVING A SMALL, FRIGHTENED BOY TO MOURN. I CHILLED WITH THE REALIZATION THAT MINE WAS NOT AN ISOLATED AGONY... NOR EVEN UNIQUE!
"I LOOKED AT THE WEEPING LAD... AND SAW MYSELF! I PUT A HAND ON HIS SHOULDER, AND IN THAT SECOND, AN UNDERSTANDING WAS FORGED BETWEEN US... AND A COMMON PURPOSE

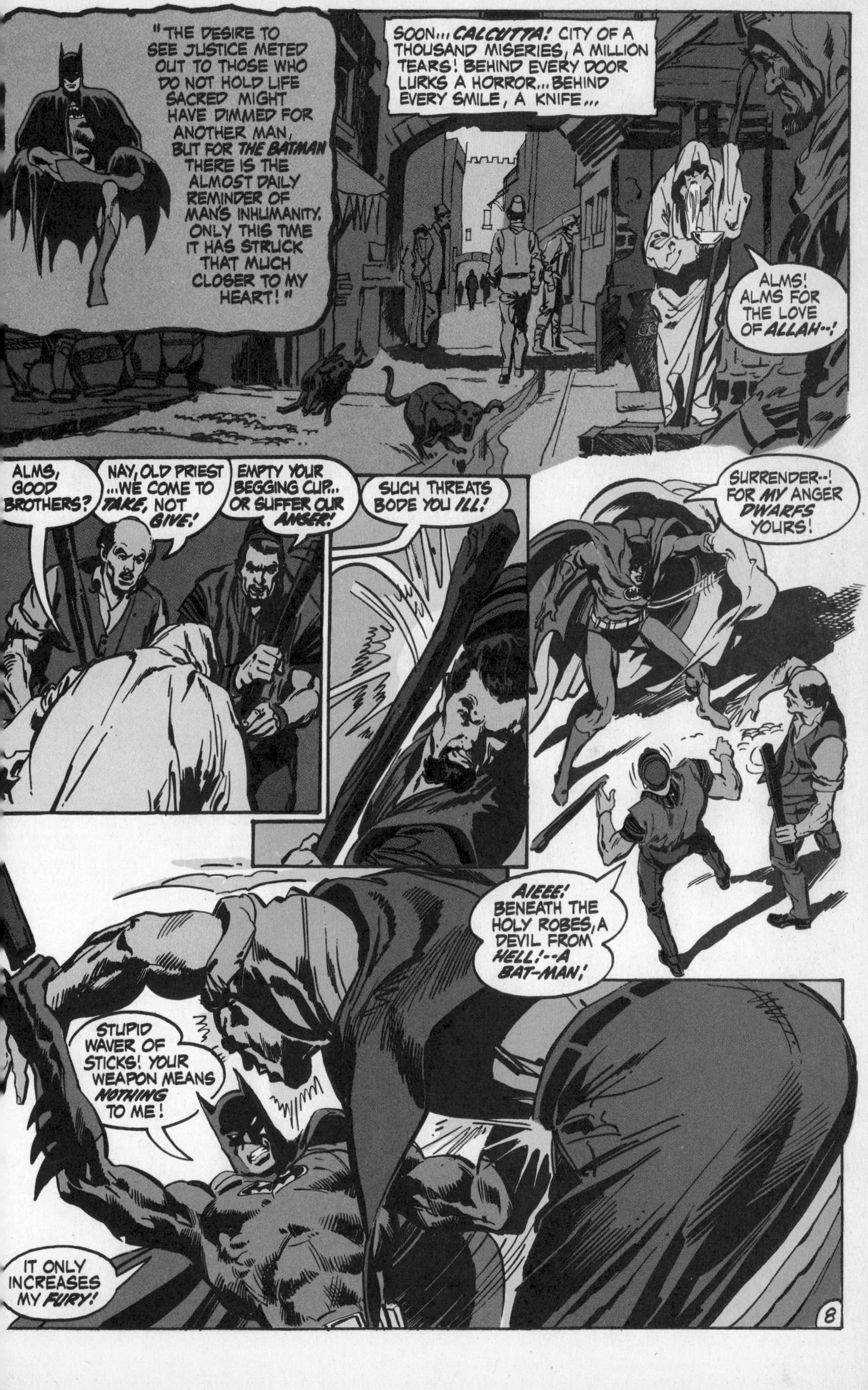
"THE DESIRE TO SEE JUSTICE METED OUT TO THOSE WHO DO NOT HOLD LIFE SACRED MIGHT HAVE DIMMED FOR ANOTHER MAN, BUT FOR THE BATMAN THERE IS THE ALMOST DAILY REMINDER OF MAN'S INHUMANITY. ONLY THIS TIME IT HAS STRUCK THAT MUCH CLOSER TO MY HEART!"
SOON... CALCUTTA! CITY OF A THOUSAND MISERIES, A MILLION TEARS! BEHIND EVERY DOOR LURKS A HORROR... BEHIND EVERY SMILE, A KNIFE...
ALMS! ALMS FOR THE LOVE OF ALLAH--!
ALMS, GOOD BROTHERS?
NAY, OLD PRIEST ...WE COME TO TAKE, NOT GIVE!
EMPTY YOUR BEGGING CUP... OR SUFFER OUR ANGER!
SUCH THREATS BODE YOU ILL!
SURRENDER--! FOR MY ANGER DWARFS YOURS!
AIEEE! BENEATH THE HOLY ROBES, A DEVIL FROM HELL!--A BAT-MAN!
STUPID WAVER OF STICKS! YOUR WEAPON MEANS NOTHING TO ME!
IT ONLY INCREASES MY FURY!
8

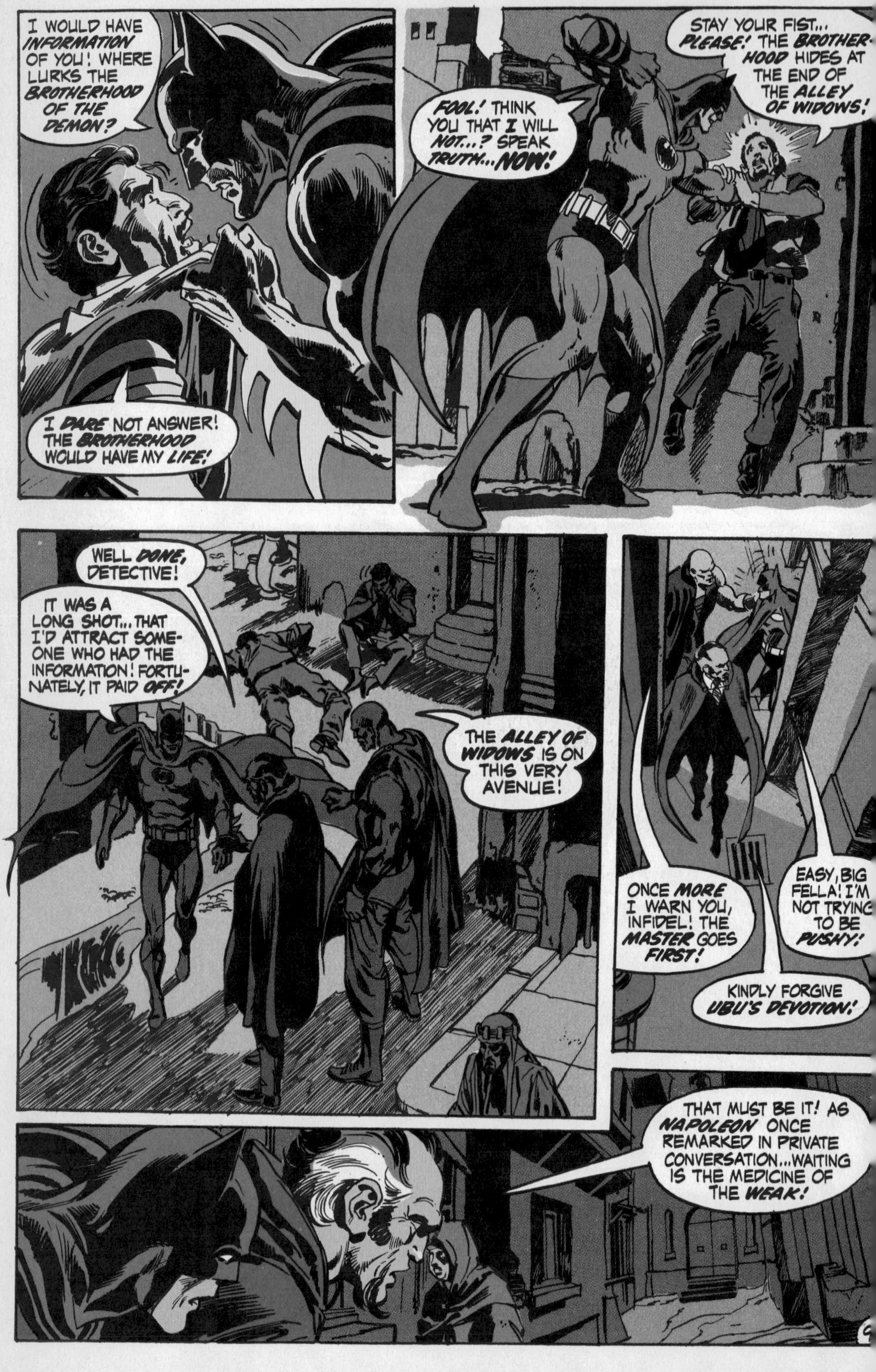
I WOULD HAVE INFORMATION OF YOU! WHERE LURKS THE BROTHERHOOD OF THE DEMON?
I DARE NOT ANSWER! THE BROTHERHOOD WOULD HAVE MY LIFE!
FOOL! THINK YOU THAT I WILL NOT...? SPEAK TRUTH...NOW!
STAY YOUR FIST... PLEASE! THE BROTHER-HOOD HIDES AT THE END OF THE ALLEY OF WIDOWS!
WELL DONE, DETECTIVE!
IT WAS A LONG SHOT...THAT I'D ATTRACT SOME-ONE WHO HAD THE INFORMATION! FORTU-NATELY, IT PAID OFF!
THE ALLEY OF WIDOWS IS ON THIS VERY AVENUE!
ONCE MORE I WARN YOU, INFIDEL! THE MASTER GOES FIRST!
EASY, BIG FELLA! I'M NOT TRYING TO BE PUSHY!
KINDLY FORGIVE UBU'S DEVOTION!
THAT MUST BE IT! AS NAPOLEON ONCE REMARKED IN PRIVATE CONVERSATION...WAITING IS THE MEDICINE OF THE WEAK!

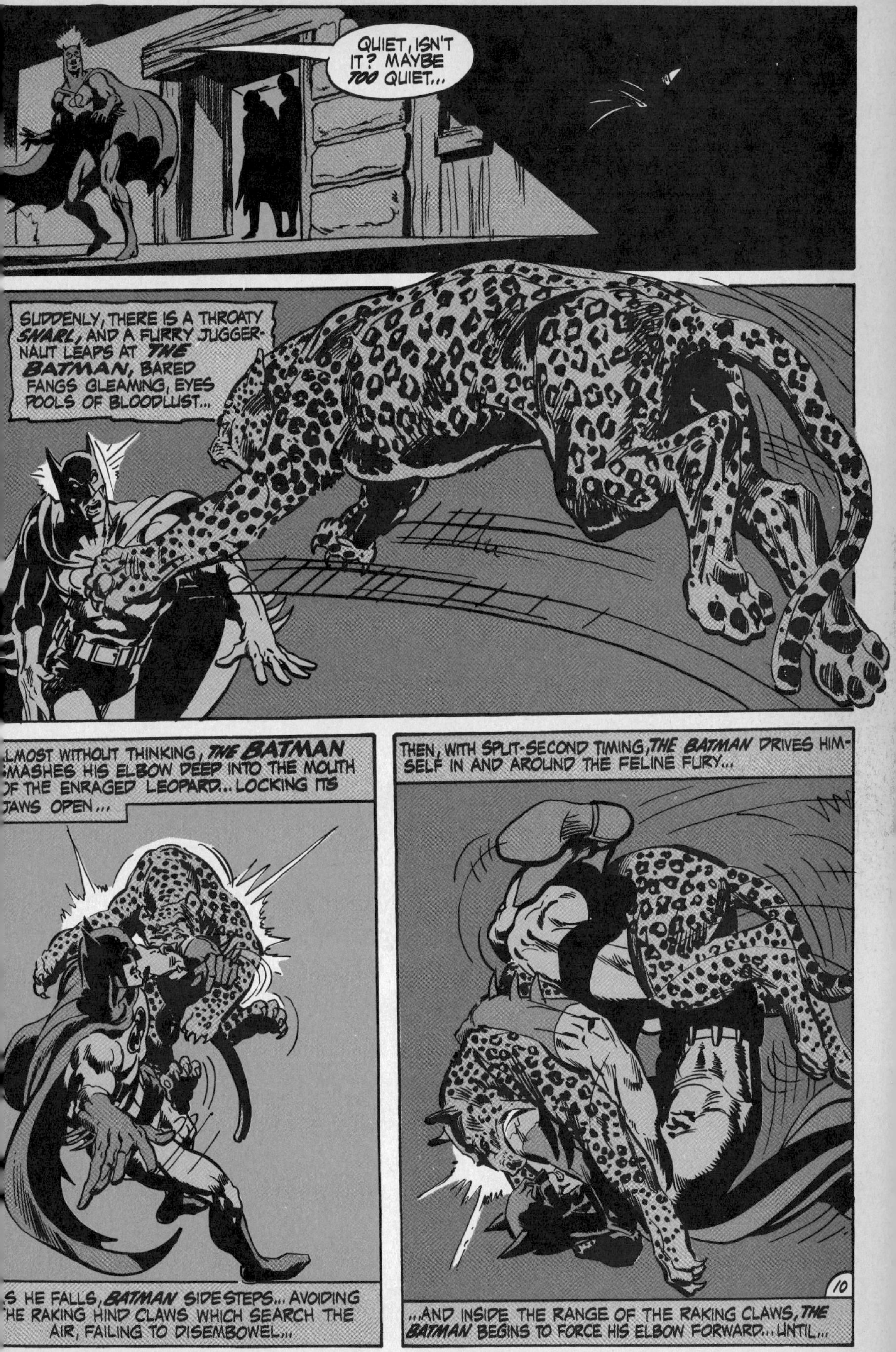
QUIET, ISN'T IT? MAYBE TOO QUIET...
SUDDENLY, THERE IS A THROATY SNARL, AND A FURRY JUGGERNAUT LEAPS AT THE BATMAN, BARED FANGS GLEAMING, EYES POOLS OF BLOODLUST...
LMOST WITHOUT THINKING, THE BATMAN MASHES HIS ELBOW DEEP INTO THE MOUTH OF THE ENRAGED LEOPARD... LOCKING ITS JAWS OPEN...
S HE FALLS, BATMAN SIDESTEPS... AVOIDING HE RAKING HIND CLAWS WHICH SEARCH THE AIR, FAILING TO DISEMBOWEL...
THEN, WITH SPLIT-SECOND TIMING, THE BATMAN DRIVES HIMSELF IN AND AROUND THE FELINE FURY...
10
...AND INSIDE THE RANGE OF THE RAKING CLAWS, THE BATMAN BEGINS TO FORCE HIS ELBOW FORWARD... UNTIL...

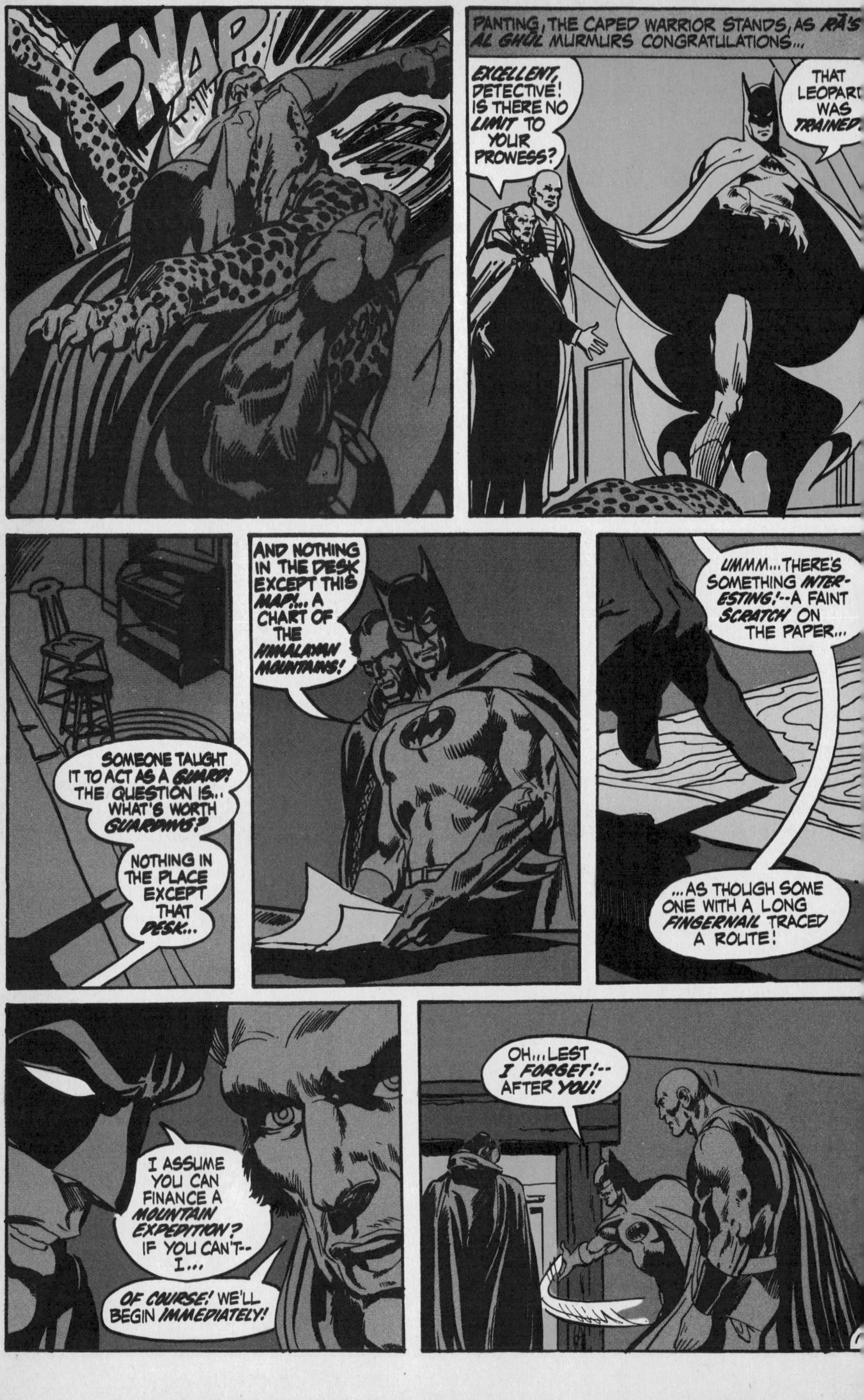
SNAP!
PANTING, THE CAPED WARRIOR STANDS, AS RĀ'S AL GHŪL MURMURS CONGRATULATIONS...
EXCELLENT, DETECTIVE! IS THERE NO LIMIT TO YOUR PROWESS?
THAT LEOPARD WAS TRAINED!
SOMEONE TAUGHT IT TO ACT AS A GUARD! THE QUESTION IS... WHAT'S WORTH GUARDING?
NOTHING IN THE PLACE EXCEPT THAT DESK...
AND NOTHING IN THE DESK EXCEPT THIS MAP!... A CHART OF THE HIMALAYAN MOUNTAINS!
UMMM... THERE'S SOMETHING INTER-ESTING!--A FAINT SCRATCH ON THE PAPER...
...AS THOUGH SOME ONE WITH A LONG FINGERNAIL TRACED A ROUTE!
I ASSUME YOU CAN FINANCE A MOUNTAIN EXPEDITION? IF YOU CAN'T-- I...
OF COURSE! WE'LL BEGIN IMMEDIATELY!
OH... LEST I FORGET!-- AFTER YOU!

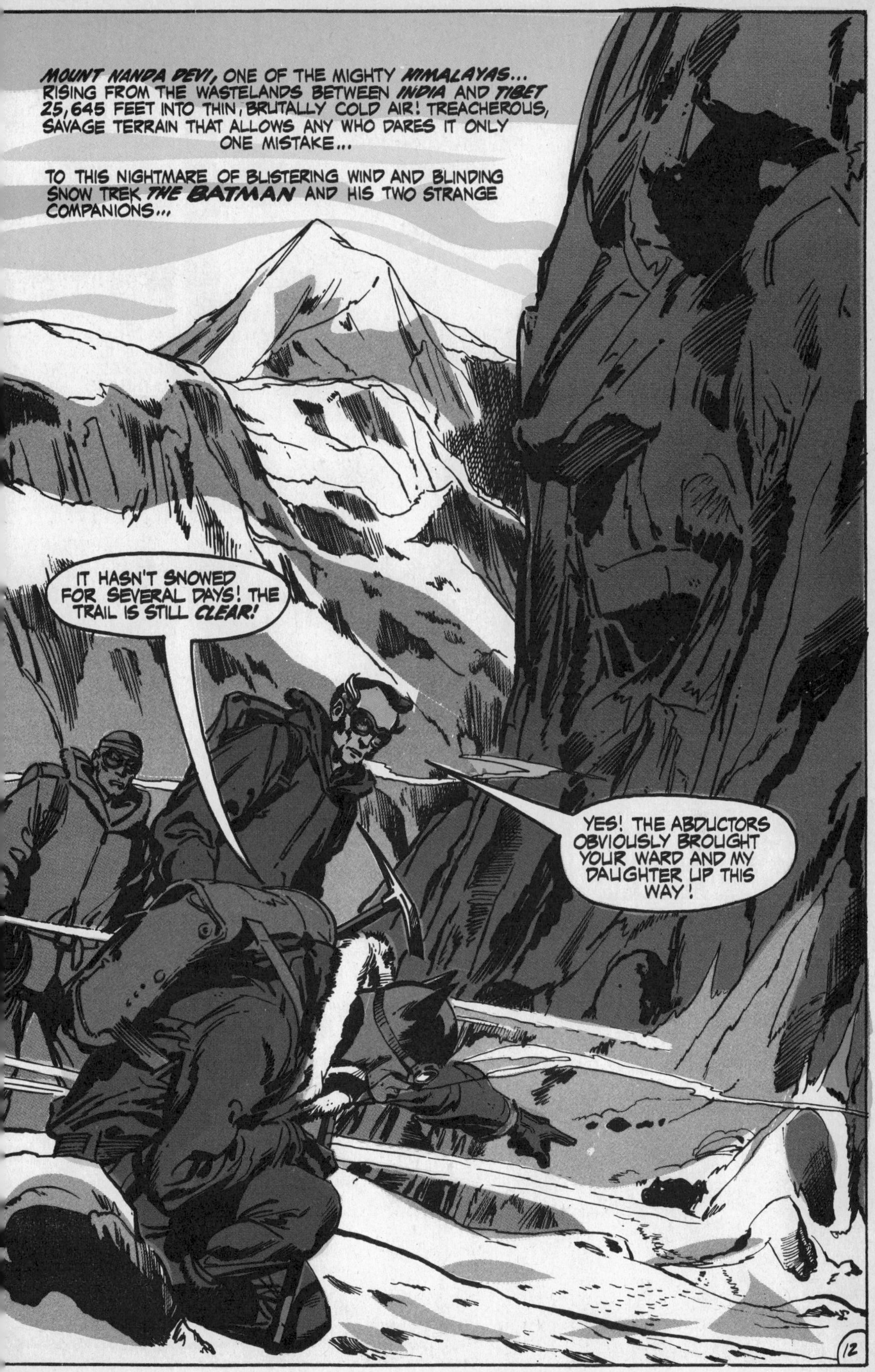
MOUNT NANDA DEVI, ONE OF THE MIGHTY HIMALAYAS... RISING FROM THE WASTELANDS BETWEEN INDIA AND TIBET 25,645 FEET INTO THIN, BRUTALLY COLD AIR! TREACHEROUS, SAVAGE TERRAIN THAT ALLOWS ANY WHO DARES IT ONLY ONE MISTAKE...
TO THIS NIGHTMARE OF BLISTERING WIND AND BLINDING SNOW TREK THE BATMAN AND HIS TWO STRANGE COMPANIONS...
IT HASN'T SNOWED FOR SEVERAL DAYS! THE TRAIL IS STILL CLEAR!
YES! THE ABDUCTORS OBVIOUSLY BROUGHT YOUR WARD AND MY DAUGHTER UP THIS WAY!
12

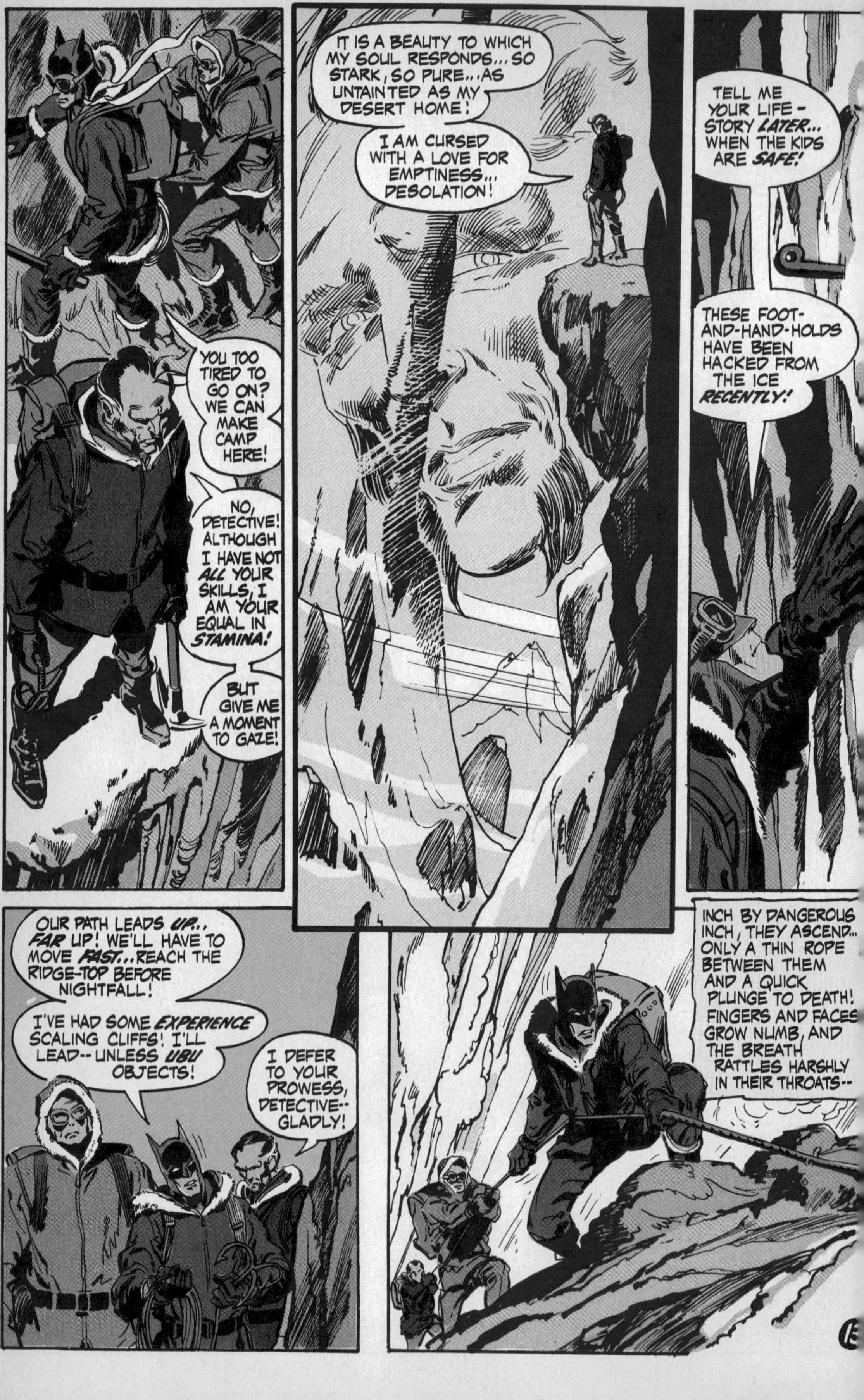
YOU TOO TIRED TO GO ON? WE CAN MAKE CAMP HERE!
NO, DETECTIVE! ALTHOUGH I HAVE NOT ALL YOUR SKILLS, I AM YOUR EQUAL IN STAMINA!
BUT GIVE ME A MOMENT TO GAZE!
IT IS A BEAUTY TO WHICH MY SOUL RESPONDS... SO STARK, SO PURE... AS UNTAINTED AS MY DESERT HOME!
I AM CURSED WITH A LOVE FOR EMPTINESS... DESOLATION!
TELL ME YOUR LIFE-STORY LATER... WHEN THE KIDS ARE SAFE!
THESE FOOT-AND-HAND-HOLDS HAVE BEEN HACKED FROM THE ICE RECENTLY!
OUR PATH LEADS UP... FAR UP! WE'LL HAVE TO MOVE FAST... REACH THE RIDGE-TOP BEFORE NIGHTFALL!
I'VE HAD SOME EXPERIENCE SCALING CLIFFS! I'LL LEAD-- UNLESS UBU OBJECTS!
I DEFER TO YOUR PROWESS, DETECTIVE-- GLADLY!
INCH BY DANGEROUS INCH, THEY ASCEND... ONLY A THIN ROPE BETWEEN THEM AND A QUICK PLUNGE TO DEATH! FINGERS AND FACES GROW NUMB, AND THE BREATH RATTLES HARSHLY IN THEIR THROATS--
13

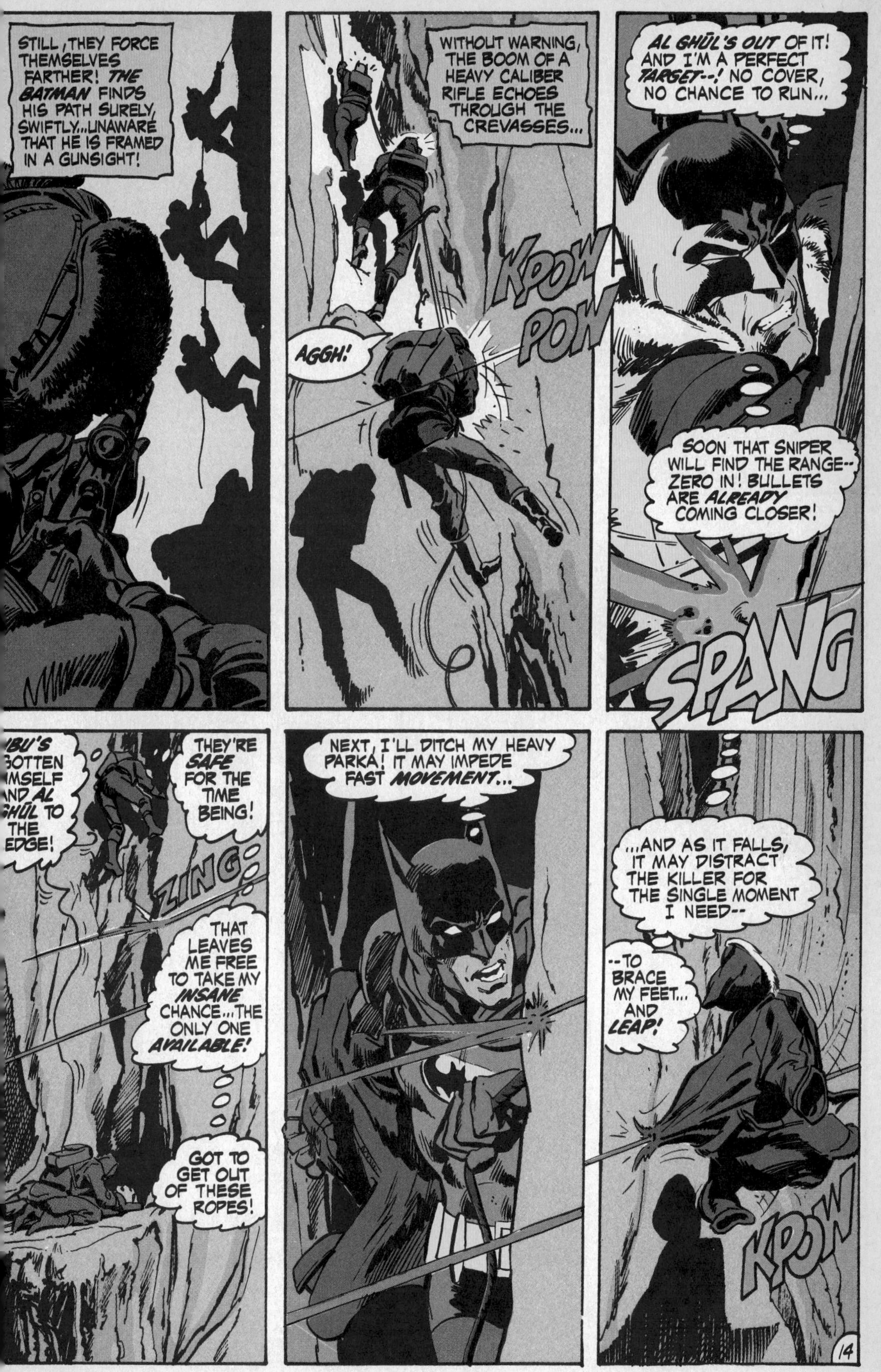
STILL, THEY FORCE THEMSELVES FARTHER! THE BATMAN FINDS HIS PATH SURELY, SWIFTLY...UNAWARE THAT HE IS FRAMED IN A GUNSIGHT!
WITHOUT WARNING, THE BOOM OF A HEAVY CALIBER RIFLE ECHOES THROUGH THE CREVASSES...
KPOW
POW
AGGH!
AL GHŪL'S OUT OF IT! AND I'M A PERFECT TARGET--! NO COVER, NO CHANCE TO RUN...
SOON THAT SNIPER WILL FIND THE RANGE--ZERO IN! BULLETS ARE ALREADY COMING CLOSER!
SPANG
UBU'S GOTTEN HIMSELF AND AL GHŪL TO THE EDGE!
THEY'RE SAFE FOR THE TIME BEING!
ZING
THAT LEAVES ME FREE TO TAKE MY INSANE CHANCE...THE ONLY ONE AVAILABLE!
GOT TO GET OUT OF THESE ROPES!
NEXT, I'LL DITCH MY HEAVY PARKA! IT MAY IMPEDE FAST MOVEMENT...
...AND AS IT FALLS, IT MAY DISTRACT THE KILLER FOR THE SINGLE MOMENT I NEED--
--TO BRACE MY FEET... AND LEAP!
KPOW
14

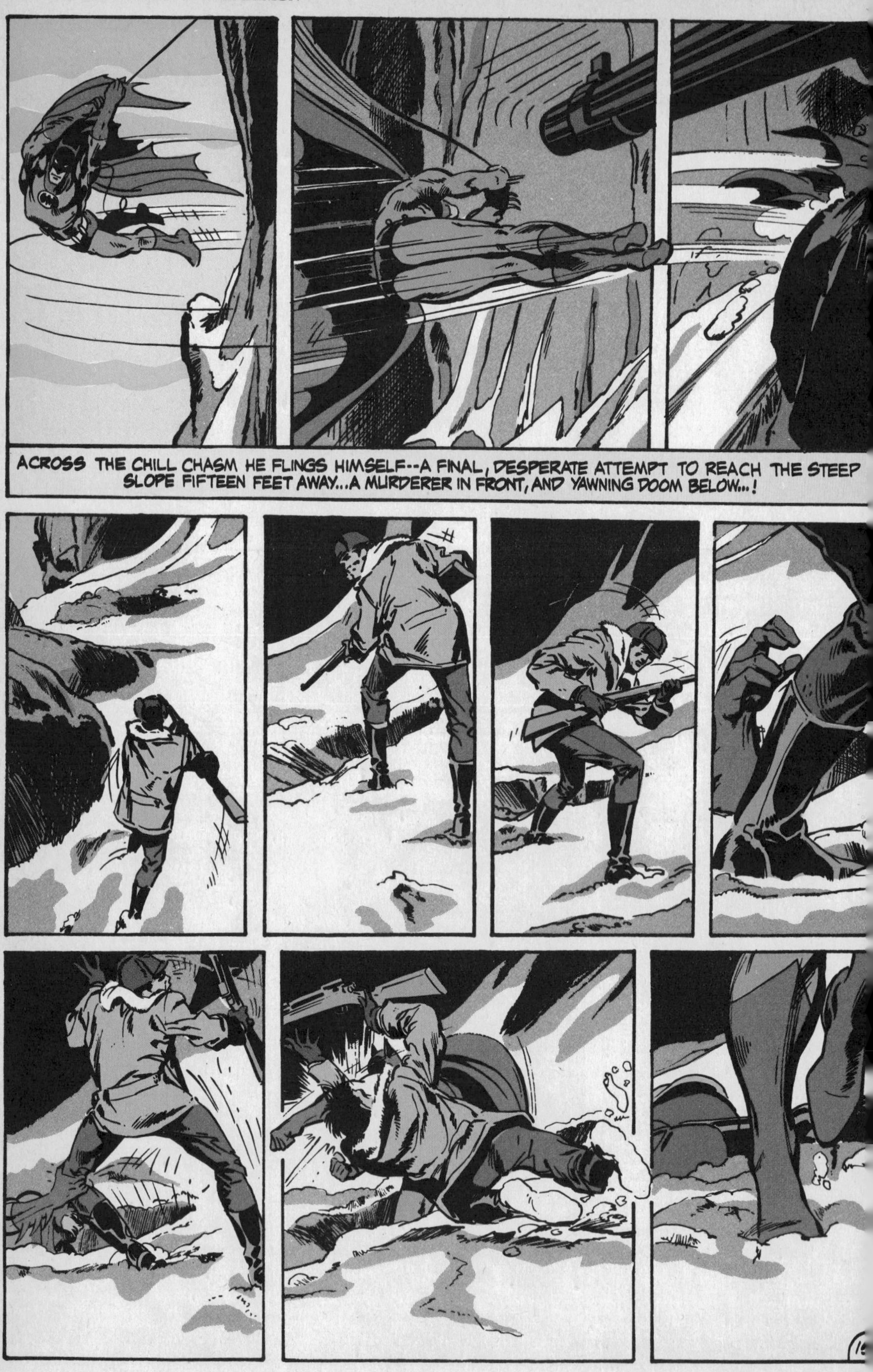
ACROSS THE CHILL CHASM HE FLINGS HIMSELF--A FINAL, DESPERATE ATTEMPT TO REACH THE STEEP SLOPE FIFTEEN FEET AWAY...A MURDERER IN FRONT, AND YAWNING DOOM BELOW...!

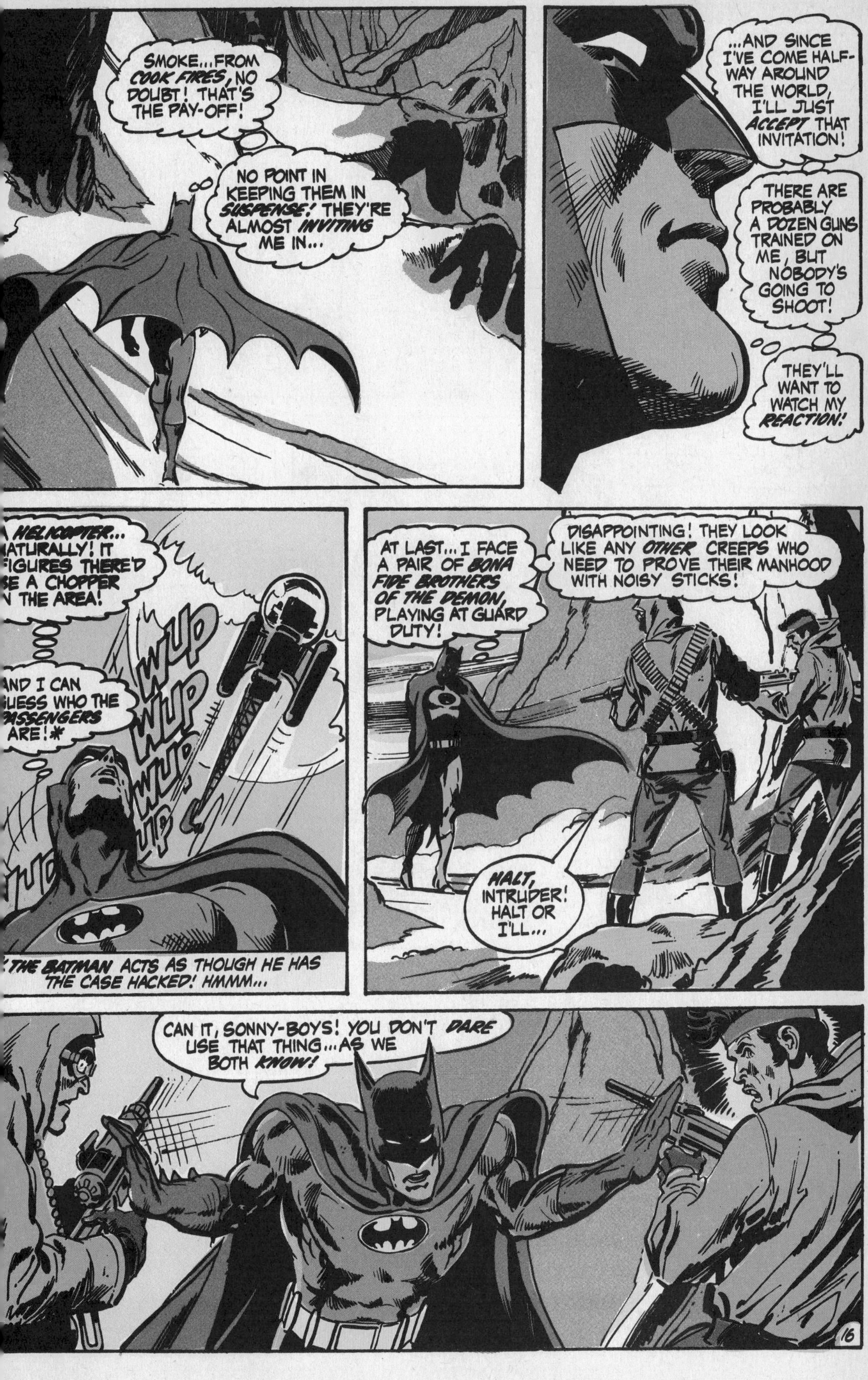
SMOKE...FROM COOK FIRES, NO DOUBT! THAT'S THE PAY-OFF!
NO POINT IN KEEPING THEM IN SUSPENSE! THEY'RE ALMOST INVITING ME IN...
...AND SINCE I'VE COME HALF-WAY AROUND THE WORLD, I'LL JUST ACCEPT THAT INVITATION!
THERE ARE PROBABLY A DOZEN GUNS TRAINED ON ME, BUT NOBODY'S GOING TO SHOOT!
THEY'LL WANT TO WATCH MY REACTION!
A HELICOPTER... NATURALLY! IT FIGURES THERE'D BE A CHOPPER IN THE AREA!
AND I CAN GUESS WHO THE PASSENGERS ARE!*
WUP WUP WUP WUP
THE BATMAN ACTS AS THOUGH HE HAS THE CASE HACKED! HMMM...
AT LAST...I FACE A PAIR OF BONA FIDE BROTHERS OF THE DEMON, PLAYING AT GUARD DUTY!
DISAPPOINTING! THEY LOOK LIKE ANY OTHER CREEPS WHO NEED TO PROVE THEIR MANHOOD WITH NOISY STICKS!
HALT, INTRUDER! HALT OR I'LL...
CAN IT, SONNY-BOYS! YOU DON'T DARE USE THAT THING...AS WE BOTH KNOW!
16

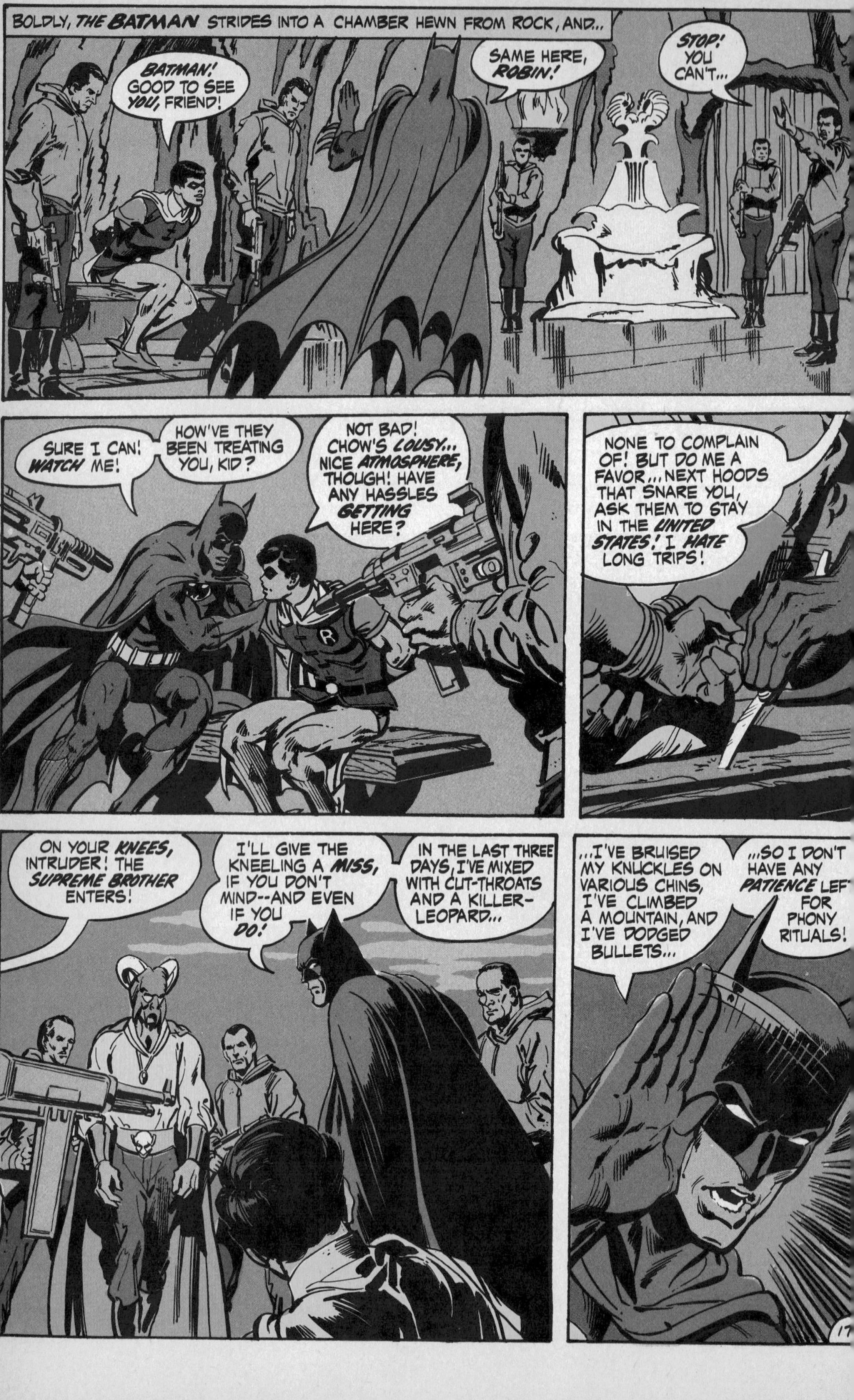
BOLDLY, THE BATMAN STRIDES INTO A CHAMBER HEWN FROM ROCK, AND...
BATMAN! GOOD TO SEE YOU, FRIEND!
SAME HERE, ROBIN!
STOP! YOU CAN'T...
SURE I CAN! WATCH ME!
HOW'VE THEY BEEN TREATING YOU, KID?
NOT BAD! CHOW'S LOUSY... NICE ATMOSPHERE, THOUGH! HAVE ANY HASSLES GETTING HERE?
NONE TO COMPLAIN OF! BUT DO ME A FAVOR... NEXT HOODS THAT SNARE YOU, ASK THEM TO STAY IN THE UNITED STATES! I HATE LONG TRIPS!
ON YOUR KNEES, INTRUDER! THE SUPREME BROTHER ENTERS!
I'LL GIVE THE KNEELING A MISS, IF YOU DON'T MIND--AND EVEN IF YOU DO!
IN THE LAST THREE DAYS, I'VE MIXED WITH CUT-THROATS AND A KILLER-LEOPARD...
...I'VE BRUISED MY KNUCKLES ON VARIOUS CHINS, I'VE CLIMBED A MOUNTAIN, AND I'VE DODGED BULLETS...
...SO I DON'T HAVE ANY PATIENCE LEF FOR PHONY RITUALS!
17

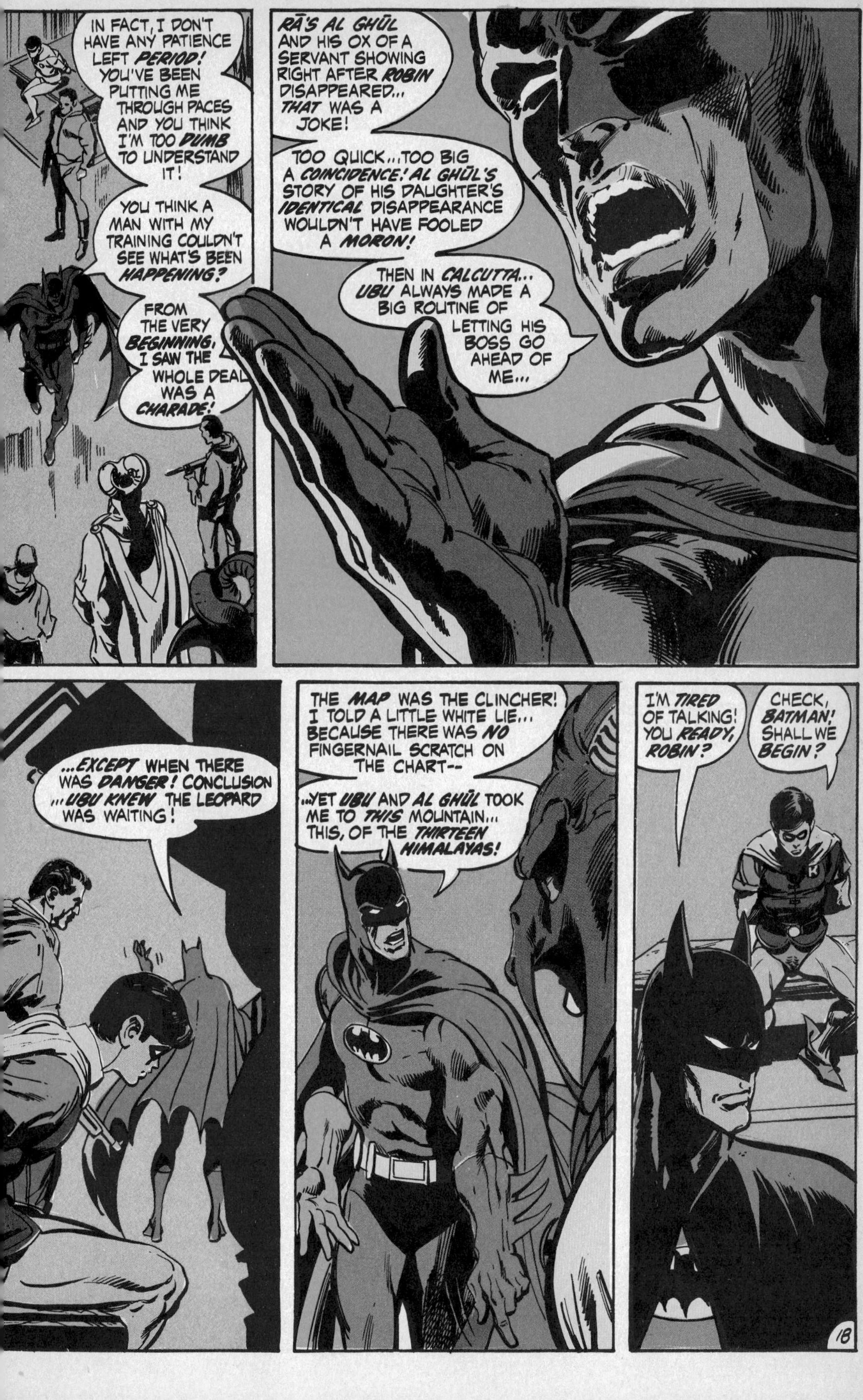
IN FACT, I DON'T HAVE ANY PATIENCE LEFT PERIOD! YOU'VE BEEN PUTTING ME THROUGH PACES AND YOU THINK I'M TOO DUMB TO UNDERSTAND IT!
YOU THINK A MAN WITH MY TRAINING COULDN'T SEE WHAT'S BEEN HAPPENING?
FROM THE VERY BEGINNING, I SAW THE WHOLE DEAL WAS A CHARADE!
RĀ'S AL GHŪL AND HIS OX OF A SERVANT SHOWING RIGHT AFTER ROBIN DISAPPEARED... THAT WAS A JOKE!
TOO QUICK...TOO BIG A COINCIDENCE! AL GHŪL'S STORY OF HIS DAUGHTER'S IDENTICAL DISAPPEARANCE WOULDN'T HAVE FOOLED A MORON!
THEN IN CALCUTTA... UBU ALWAYS MADE A BIG ROUTINE OF LETTING HIS BOSS GO AHEAD OF ME...
...EXCEPT WHEN THERE WAS DANGER! CONCLUSION ...UBU KNEW THE LEOPARD WAS WAITING!
THE MAP WAS THE CLINCHER! I TOLD A LITTLE WHITE LIE... BECAUSE THERE WAS NO FINGERNAIL SCRATCH ON THE CHART--
...YET UBU AND AL GHŪL TOOK ME TO THIS MOUNTAIN... THIS, OF THE THIRTEEN HIMALAYAS!
I'M TIRED OF TALKING! YOU READY, ROBIN?
CHECK, BATMAN! SHALL WE BEGIN?
18

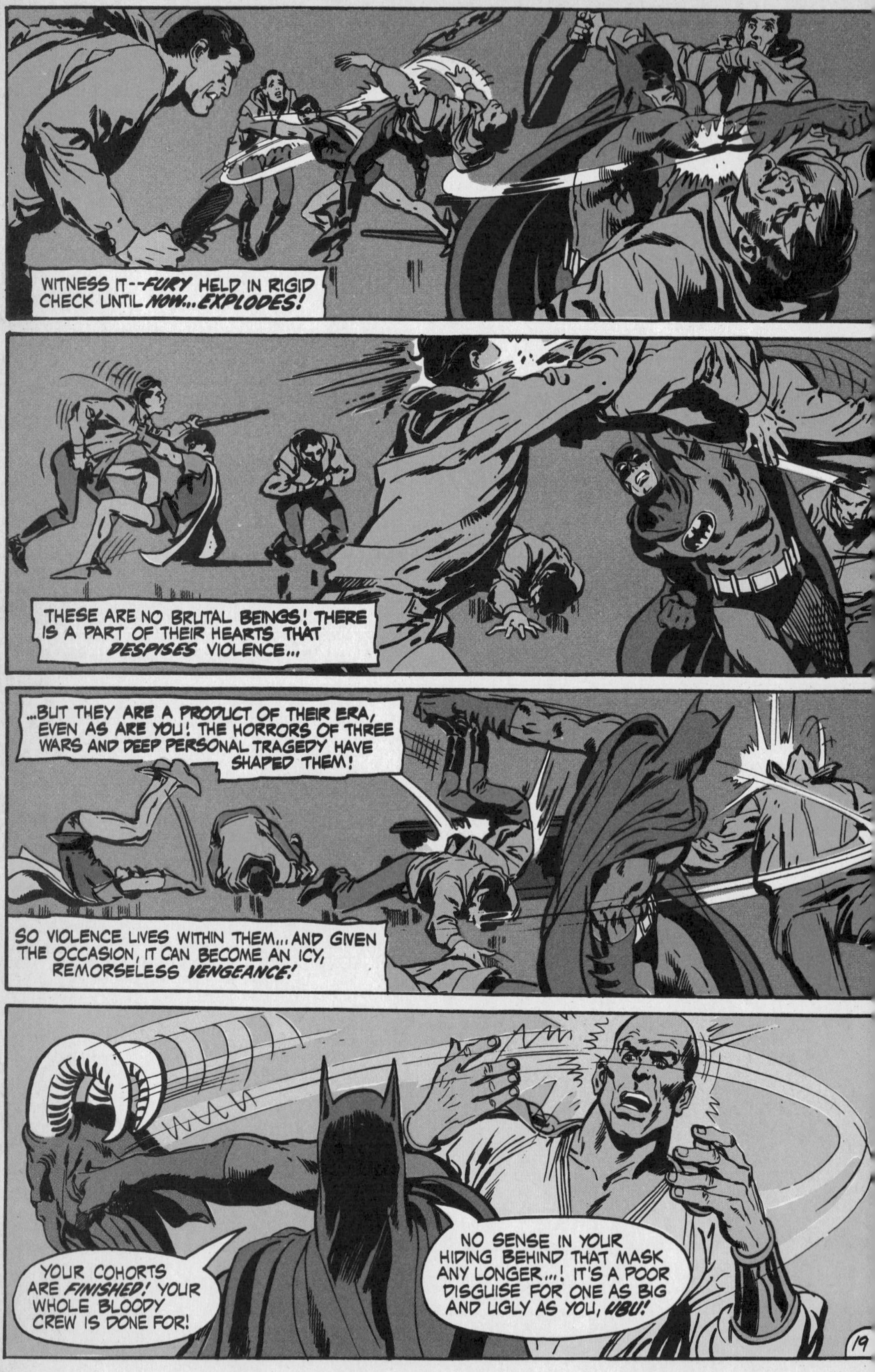
WITNESS IT--*FURY* HELD IN RIGID CHECK UNTIL *NOW*...*EXPLODES!*
THESE ARE NO BRUTAL BEINGS! THERE IS A PART OF THEIR HEARTS THAT *DESPISES* VIOLENCE...
...BUT THEY ARE A PRODUCT OF THEIR ERA, EVEN AS ARE YOU! THE HORRORS OF THREE WARS AND DEEP PERSONAL TRAGEDY HAVE SHAPED THEM!
SO VIOLENCE LIVES WITHIN THEM...AND GIVEN THE OCCASION, IT CAN BECOME AN ICY, REMORSELESS *VENGEANCE!*
YOUR COHORTS ARE *FINISHED!* YOUR WHOLE BLOODY CREW IS DONE FOR!
NO SENSE IN YOUR HIDING BEHIND THAT MASK ANY LONGER...! IT'S A POOR DISGUISE FOR ONE AS BIG AND UGLY AS YOU, *UBU!*
19

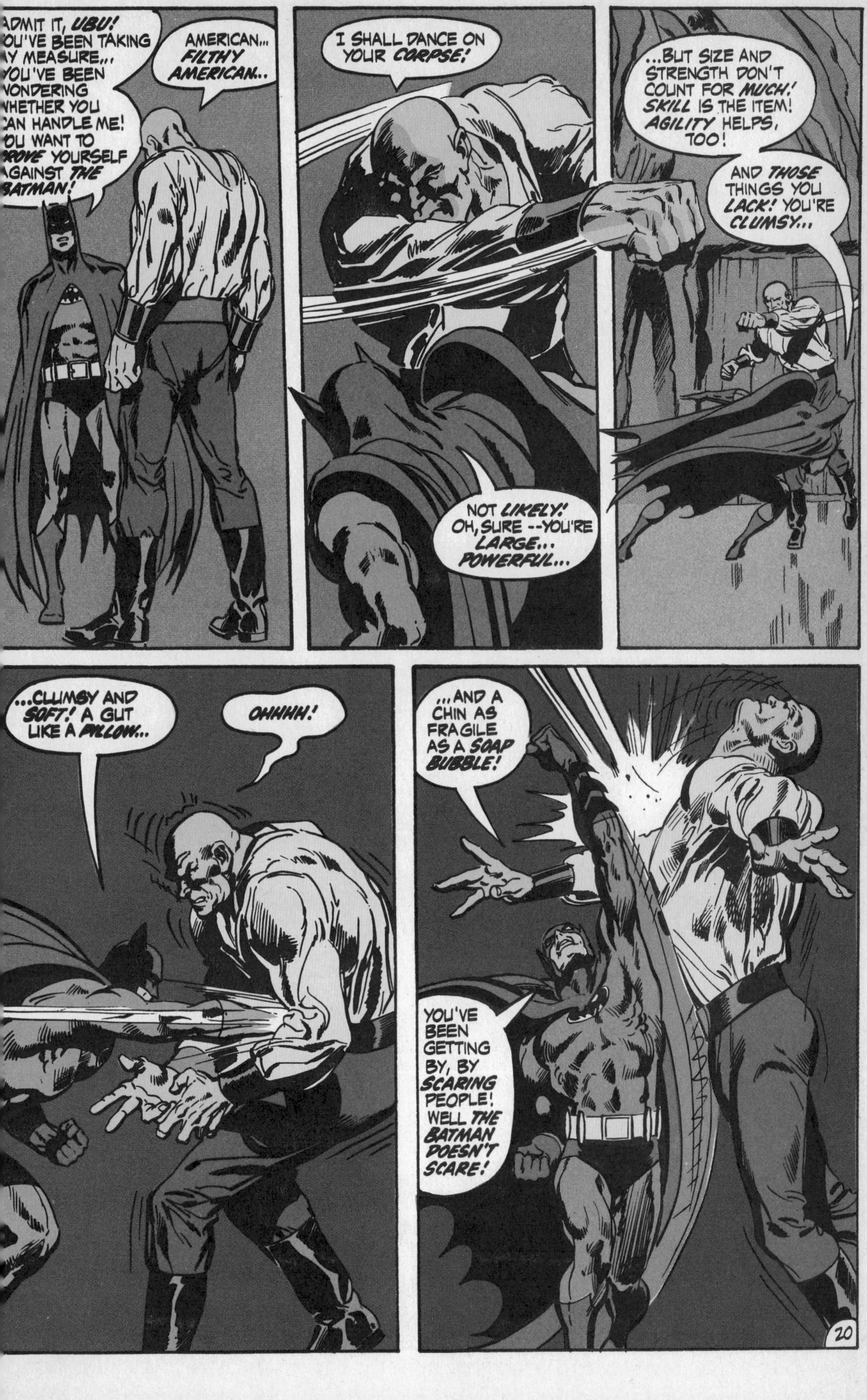
ADMIT IT, UBU! YOU'VE BEEN TAKING MY MEASURE... YOU'VE BEEN WONDERING WHETHER YOU CAN HANDLE ME! YOU WANT TO PROVE YOURSELF AGAINST THE BATMAN!
AMERICAN... FILTHY AMERICAN...
I SHALL DANCE ON YOUR CORPSE!
NOT LIKELY! OH, SURE --YOU'RE LARGE... POWERFUL...
...BUT SIZE AND STRENGTH DON'T COUNT FOR MUCH! SKILL IS THE ITEM! AGILITY HELPS, TOO!
AND THOSE THINGS YOU LACK! YOU'RE CLUMSY...
...CLUMSY AND SOFT! A GUT LIKE A PILLOW...
OHHHH!
...AND A CHIN AS FRAGILE AS A SOAP BUBBLE!
YOU'VE BEEN GETTING BY, BY SCARING PEOPLE! WELL THE BATMAN DOESN'T SCARE!
20

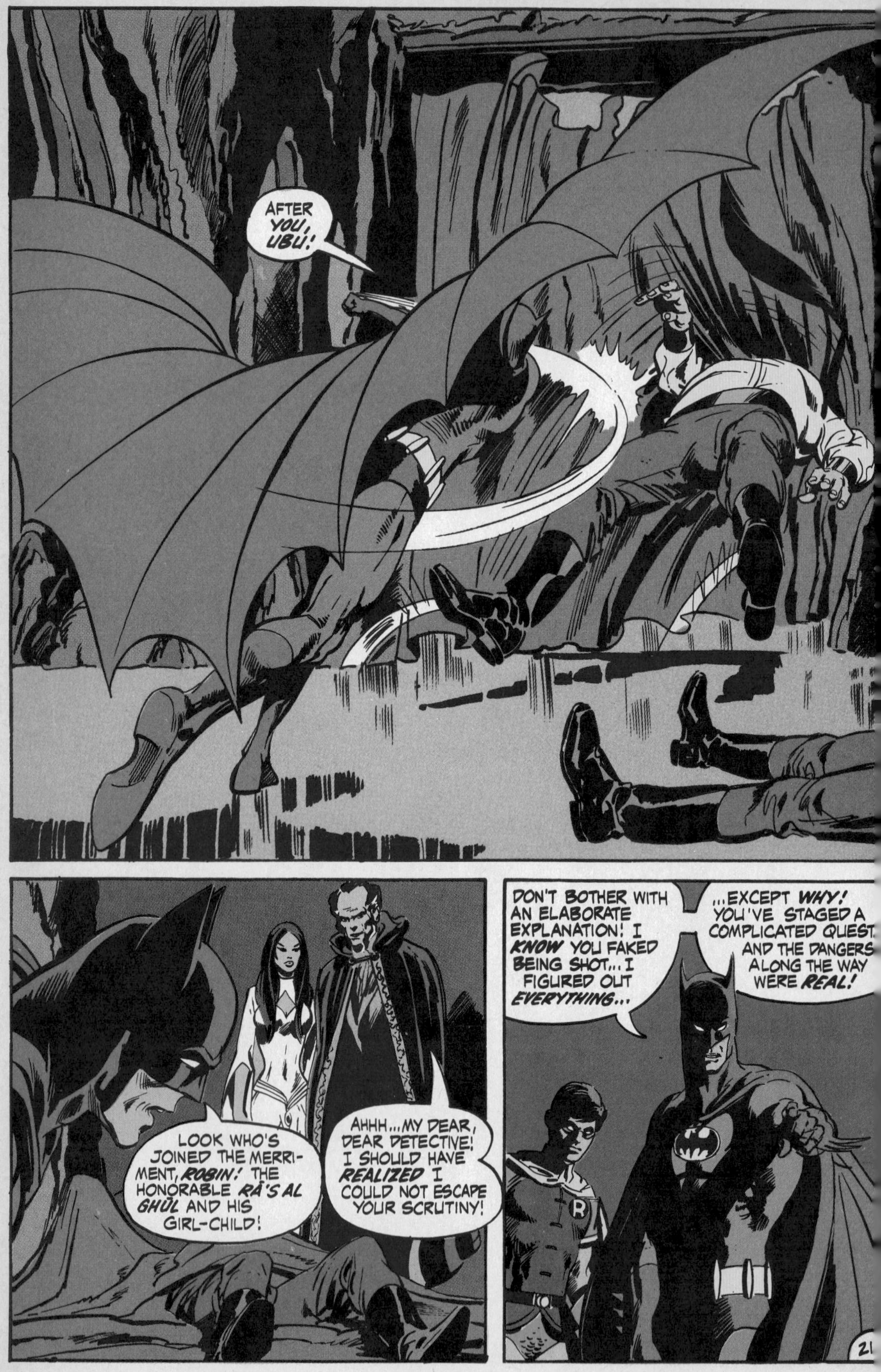
AFTER YOU, UBU!
LOOK WHO'S JOINED THE MERRIMENT, ROBIN! THE HONORABLE RĀ'S AL GHŪL AND HIS GIRL-CHILD!
AHHH... MY DEAR, DEAR DETECTIVE! I SHOULD HAVE REALIZED I COULD NOT ESCAPE YOUR SCRUTINY!
DON'T BOTHER WITH AN ELABORATE EXPLANATION! I KNOW YOU FAKED BEING SHOT... I FIGURED OUT EVERYTHING...
...EXCEPT WHY! YOU'VE STAGED A COMPLICATED QUEST AND THE DANGERS ALONG THE WAY WERE REAL!
21

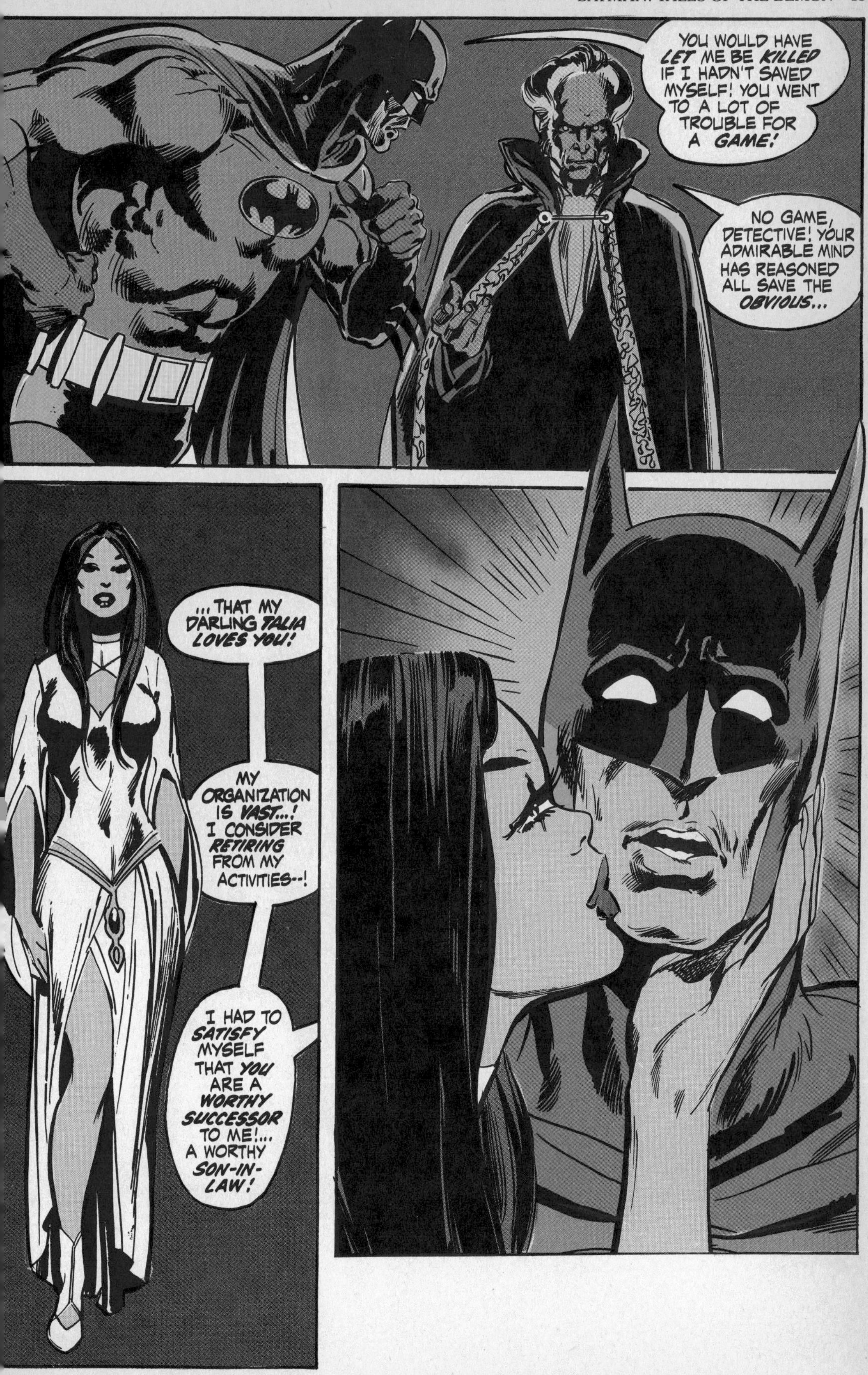
YOU WOULD HAVE LET ME BE KILLED IF I HADN'T SAVED MYSELF! YOU WENT TO A LOT OF TROUBLE FOR A GAME!
NO GAME, DETECTIVE! YOUR ADMIRABLE MIND HAS REASONED ALL SAVE THE OBVIOUS...
...THAT MY DARLING TALIA LOVES YOU!
MY ORGANIZATION IS VAST...! I CONSIDER RETIRING FROM MY ACTIVITIES--!
I HAD TO SATISFY MYSELF THAT YOU ARE A WORTHY SUCCESSOR TO ME!... A WORTHY SON-IN-LAW!

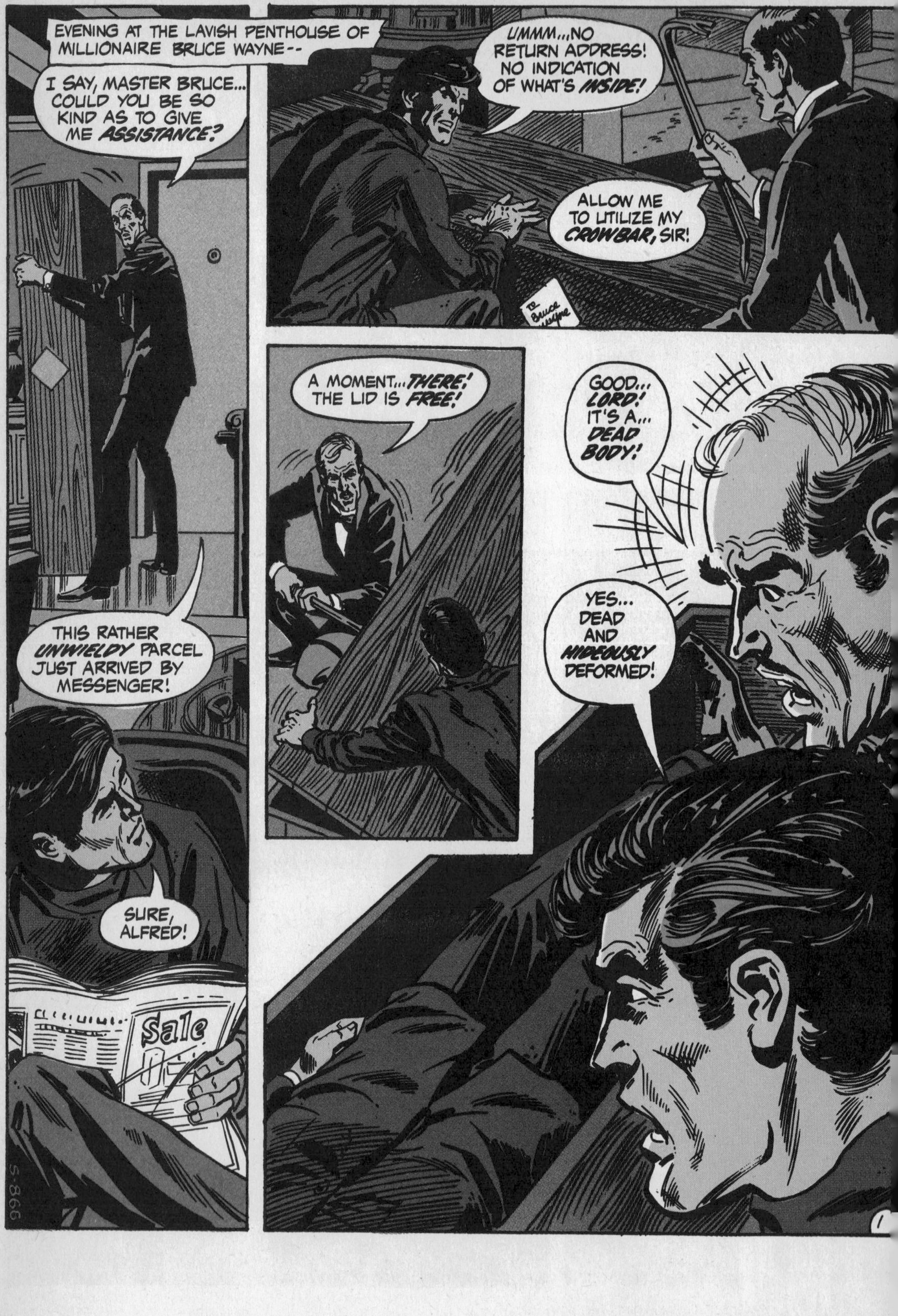
EVENING AT THE LAVISH PENTHOUSE OF MILLIONAIRE BRUCE WAYNE--
I SAY, MASTER BRUCE... COULD YOU BE SO KIND AS TO GIVE ME ASSISTANCE?
THIS RATHER UNWIELDY PARCEL JUST ARRIVED BY MESSENGER!
SURE, ALFRED!
Sale
UMMM...NO RETURN ADDRESS! NO INDICATION OF WHAT'S INSIDE!
ALLOW ME TO UTILIZE MY CROWBAR, SIR!
A MOMENT...THERE! THE LID IS FREE!
GOOD... LORD! IT'S A... DEAD BODY!
YES... DEAD AND HIDEOUSLY DEFORMED!

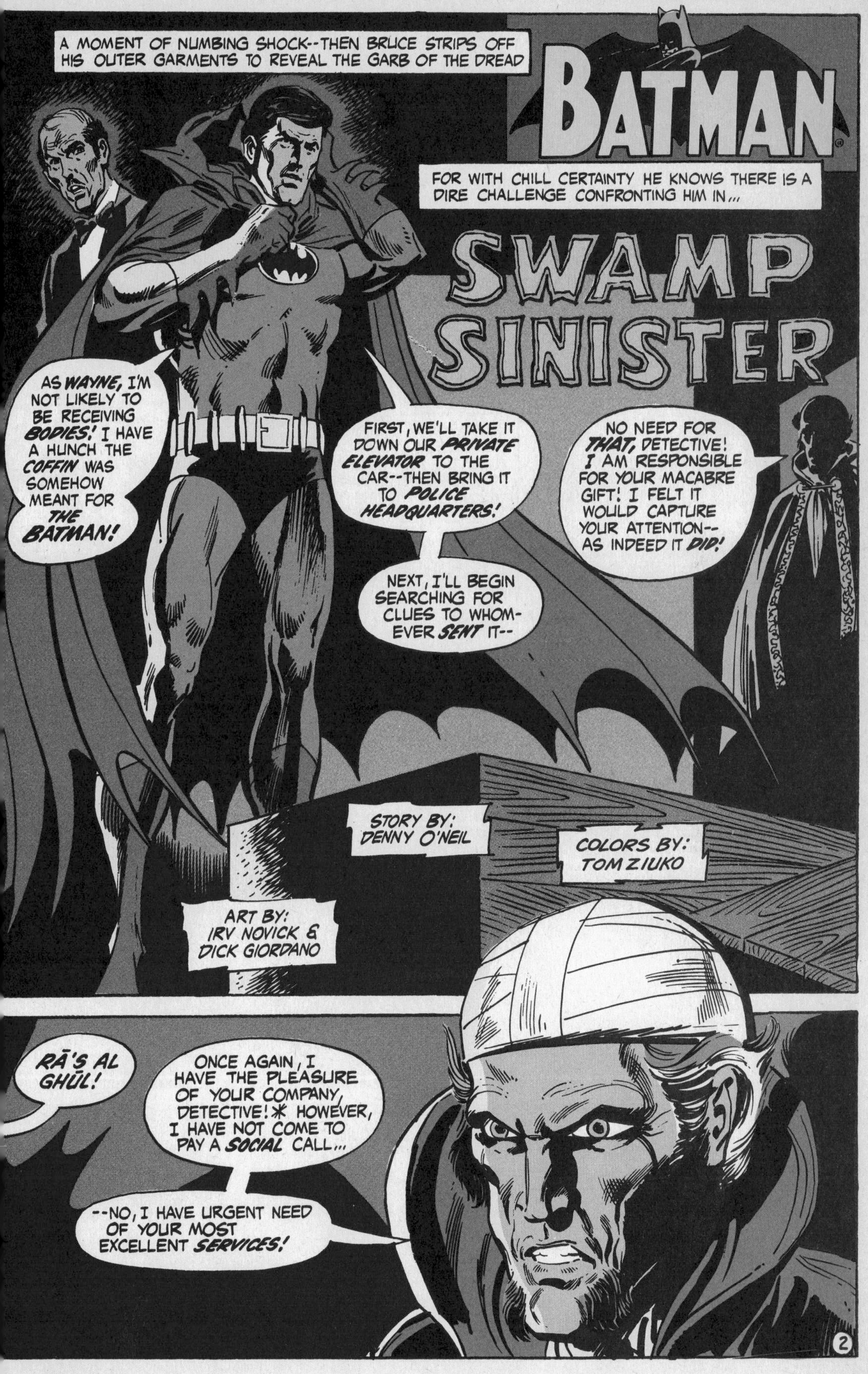
A MOMENT OF NUMBING SHOCK--THEN BRUCE STRIPS OFF HIS OUTER GARMENTS TO REVEAL THE GARB OF THE DREAD
BATMAN
FOR WITH CHILL CERTAINTY HE KNOWS THERE IS A DIRE CHALLENGE CONFRONTING HIM IN...
SWAMP SINISTER
AS WAYNE, I'M NOT LIKELY TO BE RECEIVING BODIES! I HAVE A HUNCH THE COFFIN WAS SOMEHOW MEANT FOR THE BATMAN!
FIRST, WE'LL TAKE IT DOWN OUR PRIVATE ELEVATOR TO THE CAR--THEN BRING IT TO POLICE HEADQUARTERS!
NEXT, I'LL BEGIN SEARCHING FOR CLUES TO WHOMEVER SENT IT--
NO NEED FOR THAT, DETECTIVE! I AM RESPONSIBLE FOR YOUR MACABRE GIFT! I FELT IT WOULD CAPTURE YOUR ATTENTION--AS INDEED IT DID!
STORY BY: DENNY O'NEIL
COLORS BY: TOM ZIUKO
ART BY: IRV NOVICK & DICK GIORDANO
RĀ'S AL GHŪL!
ONCE AGAIN, I HAVE THE PLEASURE OF YOUR COMPANY, DETECTIVE! * HOWEVER, I HAVE NOT COME TO PAY A SOCIAL CALL...
--NO, I HAVE URGENT NEED OF YOUR MOST EXCELLENT SERVICES!
2

LOOK UPON THE TWISTED DEATH-MASK OF THIS PERSON--UNTIL RECENTLY, ONE OF MY... AH... EMPLOYEES!

SHOULD YOU FAIL IN THE TASK I AM ABOUT TO SET YOU, THOUSANDS OF INNOCENT PEOPLE WILL PERISH SIMILARLY!

YOU'D BETTER TELL THE STORY FROM THE BEGINNING--!

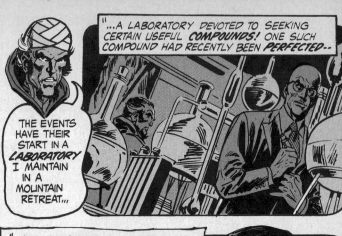

"...A LABORATORY DEVOTED TO SEEKING CERTAIN USEFUL COMPOUNDS! ONE SUCH COMPOUND HAD RECENTLY BEEN PERFECTED--

THE EVENTS HAVE THEIR START IN A LABORATORY I MAINTAIN IN A MOUNTAIN RETREAT....

"--AND I DISCOVERED THE TECHNICIAN RESPONSIBLE FOR PACKAGING IT IN THE ACT OF STEALING IT!...."

AH, MY DEAR STRISS! DOUBTLESS, YOU PLAN TO SELL THE CONTENTS OF THE VIAL BENEATH YOUR JACKET... TO THE HIGHEST BIDDER?

YOU'VE FOUND ME OUT, MASTER--!

BUT YOU SHALL NOT STOP ME!

STRIKE HIM, POLARD!

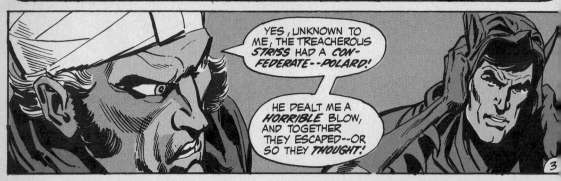

YES, UNKNOWN TO ME, THE TREACHEROUS STRISS HAD A CONFEDERATE--POLARD!

HE DEALT ME A HORRIBLE BLOW, AND TOGETHER THEY ESCAPED--OR SO THEY THOUGHT!

3

MOMENTS LATER, MY *DAUGHTER--TALIA--* DISCOVERED ME! THE BLOW TO THE SKULL HAD *STOPPED MY HEART--* SHE COULD DETECT NO SIGN OF LIFE WITHIN MY BEING...

"I HAD PREVIOUSLY SPOKEN TO HER OF SUSPECTING *STRISS* OF PLANNED DISLOYALTY! THE GIRL GUESSED WHAT HAD OCCURRED-- AND ORDERED MY BODYGUARDS TO SEEK OUT THE VILLAIN AND... WREAK *VENGEANCE!*...

"HOWEVER, MY PERSONAL PHYSICIANS WERE ABLE TO *REVIVE* ME, AS THEY HAVE SO OFTEN BEFORE! YES, IT WAS NOT THE *FIRST* TIME I HAD TASTED *DEATH...*"

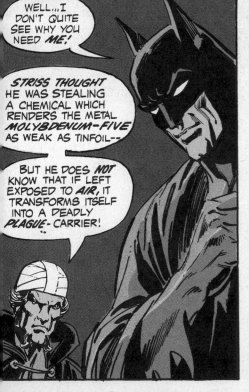

WELL... I DON'T QUITE SEE WHY YOU NEED *ME!*

STRISS THOUGHT HE WAS STEALING A CHEMICAL WHICH RENDERS THE METAL *MOLYBDENUM-FIVE* AS WEAK AS TINFOIL--

BUT HE DOES *NOT* KNOW THAT IF LEFT EXPOSED TO *AIR*, IT TRANSFORMS ITSELF INTO A DEADLY *PLAGUE*-CARRIER!

THERE IS YOUR EVIDENCE! THIS CREATURE WAS ONCE *POLARD-- STRISS'* ACCOMPLICE!

APPARENTLY WHEN HE ATTACKED ME, SOME OF THE CHEMICAL *SPLASHED* ON HIM!

YOU MEAN THAT THING'S INFECTED WITH *PLAGUE?!* WE BETTER GET *OUT*--

MY MEN FOUND HIM IN AN ALLEY!

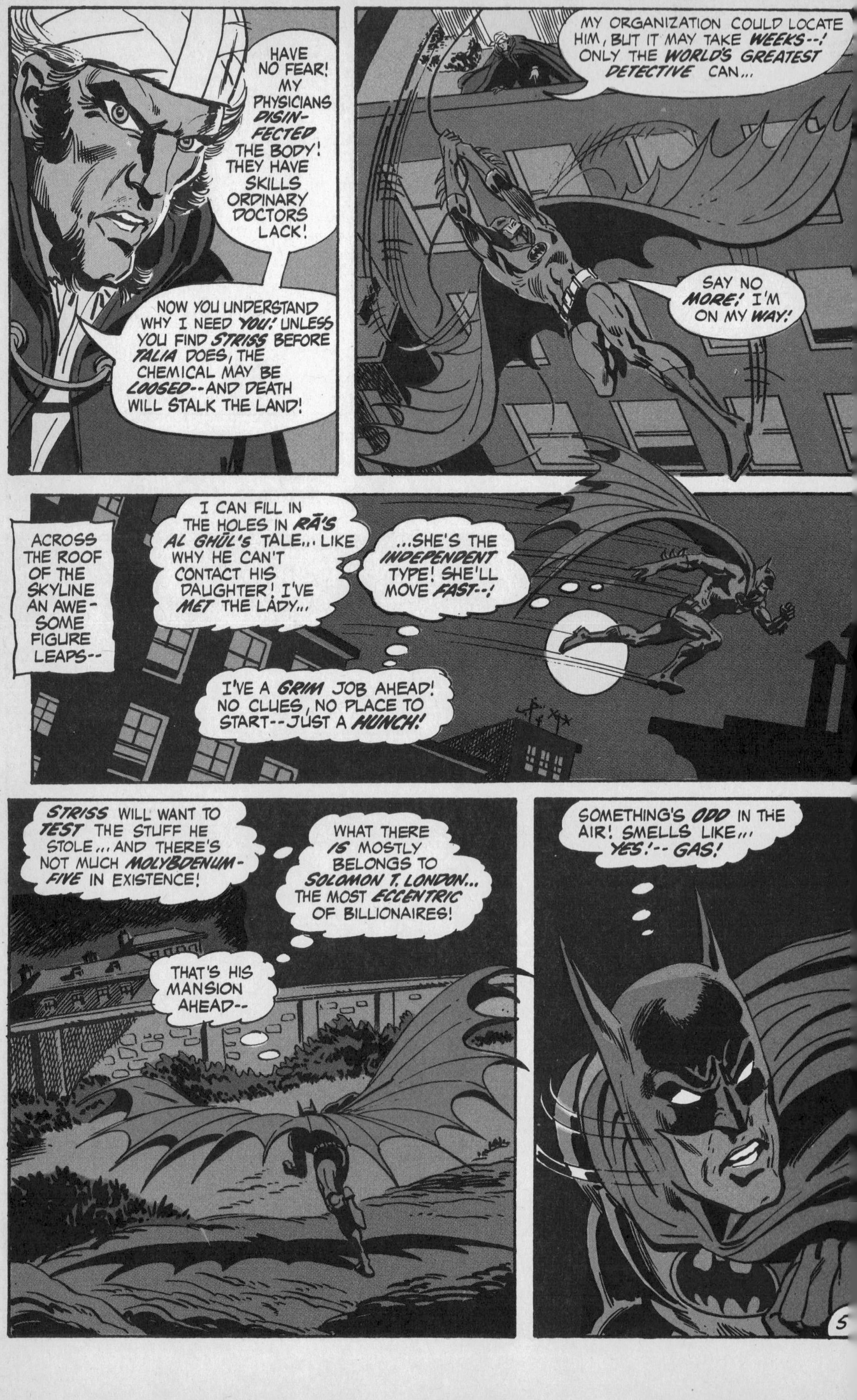
HAVE NO FEAR! MY PHYSICIANS DISIN-FECTED THE BODY! THEY HAVE SKILLS ORDINARY DOCTORS LACK!
NOW YOU UNDERSTAND WHY I NEED YOU! UNLESS YOU FIND STRISS BEFORE TALIA DOES, THE CHEMICAL MAY BE LOOSED--AND DEATH WILL STALK THE LAND!
MY ORGANIZATION COULD LOCATE HIM, BUT IT MAY TAKE WEEKS--! ONLY THE WORLD'S GREATEST DETECTIVE CAN...
SAY NO MORE! I'M ON MY WAY!
ACROSS THE ROOF OF THE SKYLINE AN AWE-SOME FIGURE LEAPS--
I CAN FILL IN THE HOLES IN RĀ'S AL GHŪL'S TALE... LIKE WHY HE CAN'T CONTACT HIS DAUGHTER! I'VE MET THE LADY...
...SHE'S THE INDEPENDENT TYPE! SHE'LL MOVE FAST--!
I'VE A GRIM JOB AHEAD! NO CLUES, NO PLACE TO START--JUST A HUNCH!
STRISS WILL WANT TO TEST THE STUFF HE STOLE... AND THERE'S NOT MUCH MOLYBDENUM-FIVE IN EXISTENCE!
WHAT THERE IS MOSTLY BELONGS TO SOLOMON T. LONDON... THE MOST ECCENTRIC OF BILLIONAIRES!
THAT'S HIS MANSION AHEAD--
SOMETHING'S ODD IN THE AIR! SMELLS LIKE... YES!--GAS!
5

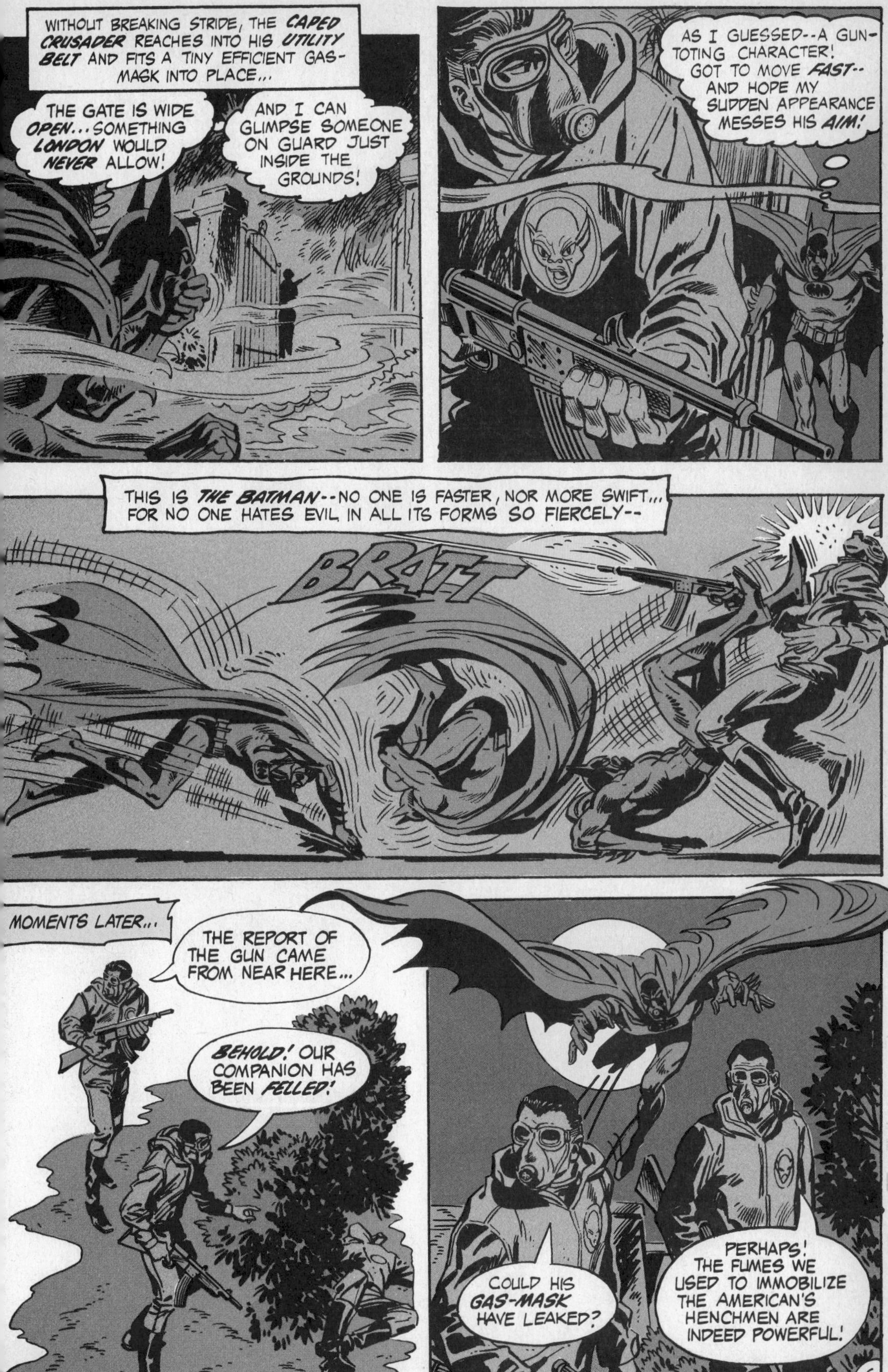
WITHOUT BREAKING STRIDE, THE CAPED CRUSADER REACHES INTO HIS UTILITY BELT AND FITS A TINY EFFICIENT GAS-MASK INTO PLACE...
THE GATE IS WIDE OPEN... SOMETHING LONDON WOULD NEVER ALLOW!
AND I CAN GLIMPSE SOMEONE ON GUARD JUST INSIDE THE GROUNDS!
AS I GUESSED--A GUN-TOTING CHARACTER! GOT TO MOVE FAST-- AND HOPE MY SUDDEN APPEARANCE MESSES HIS AIM!
THIS IS THE BATMAN--NO ONE IS FASTER, NOR MORE SWIFT... FOR NO ONE HATES EVIL IN ALL ITS FORMS SO FIERCELY--
BRATT
MOMENTS LATER...
THE REPORT OF THE GUN CAME FROM NEAR HERE...
BEHOLD! OUR COMPANION HAS BEEN FELLED!
COULD HIS GAS-MASK HAVE LEAKED?
PERHAPS! THE FUMES WE USED TO IMMOBILIZE THE AMERICAN'S HENCHMEN ARE INDEED POWERFUL!
6

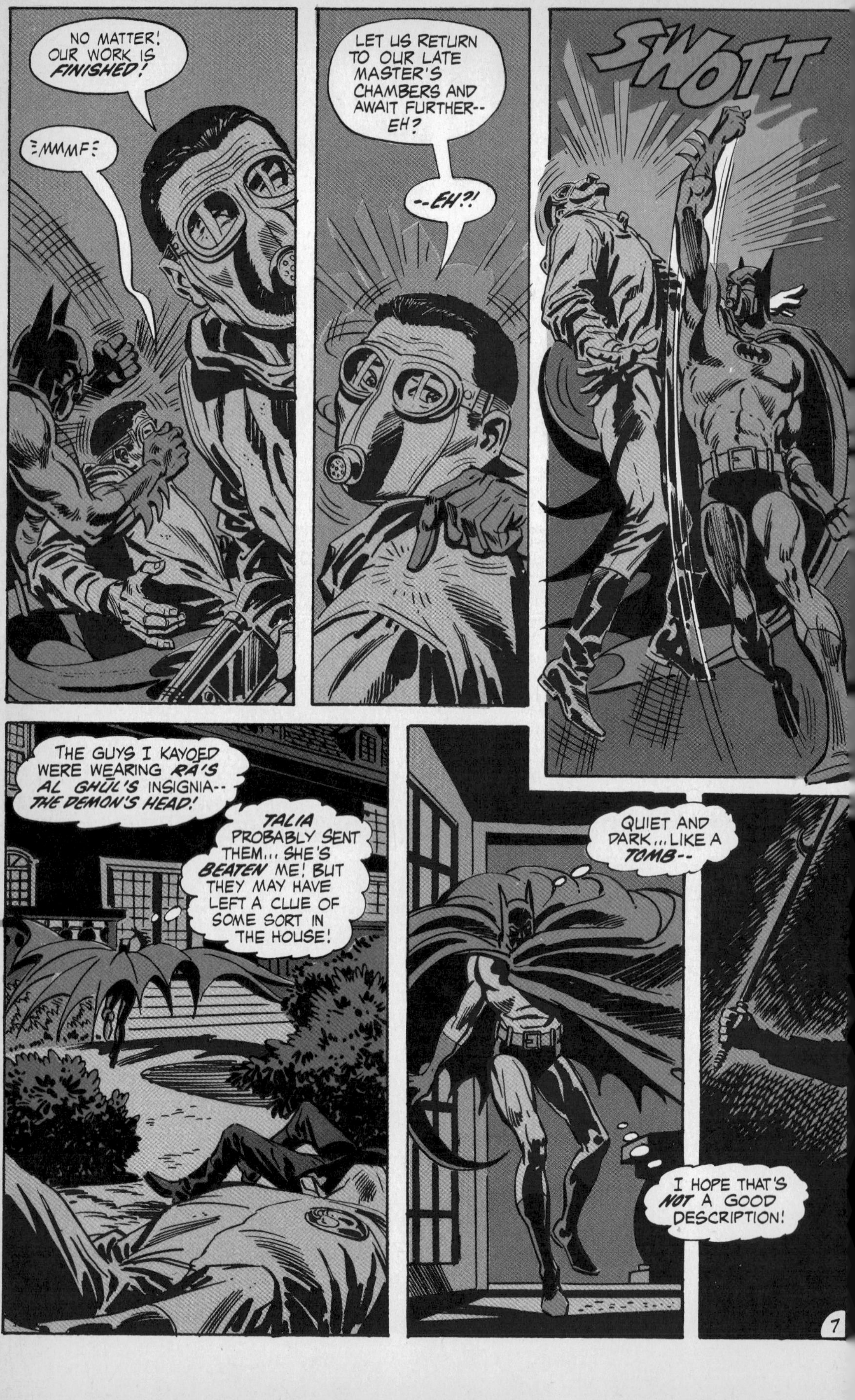
NO MATTER! OUR WORK IS FINISHED!
MMMF
LET US RETURN TO OUR LATE MASTER'S CHAMBERS AND AWAIT FURTHER--EH?
--EH?!
SWOTT
THE GUYS I KAYOED WERE WEARING RA'S AL GHUL'S INSIGNIA--THE DEMON'S HEAD!
TALIA PROBABLY SENT THEM... SHE'S BEATEN ME! BUT THEY MAY HAVE LEFT A CLUE OF SOME SORT IN THE HOUSE!
QUIET AND DARK...LIKE A TOMB--
I HOPE THAT'S NOT A GOOD DESCRIPTION!
7

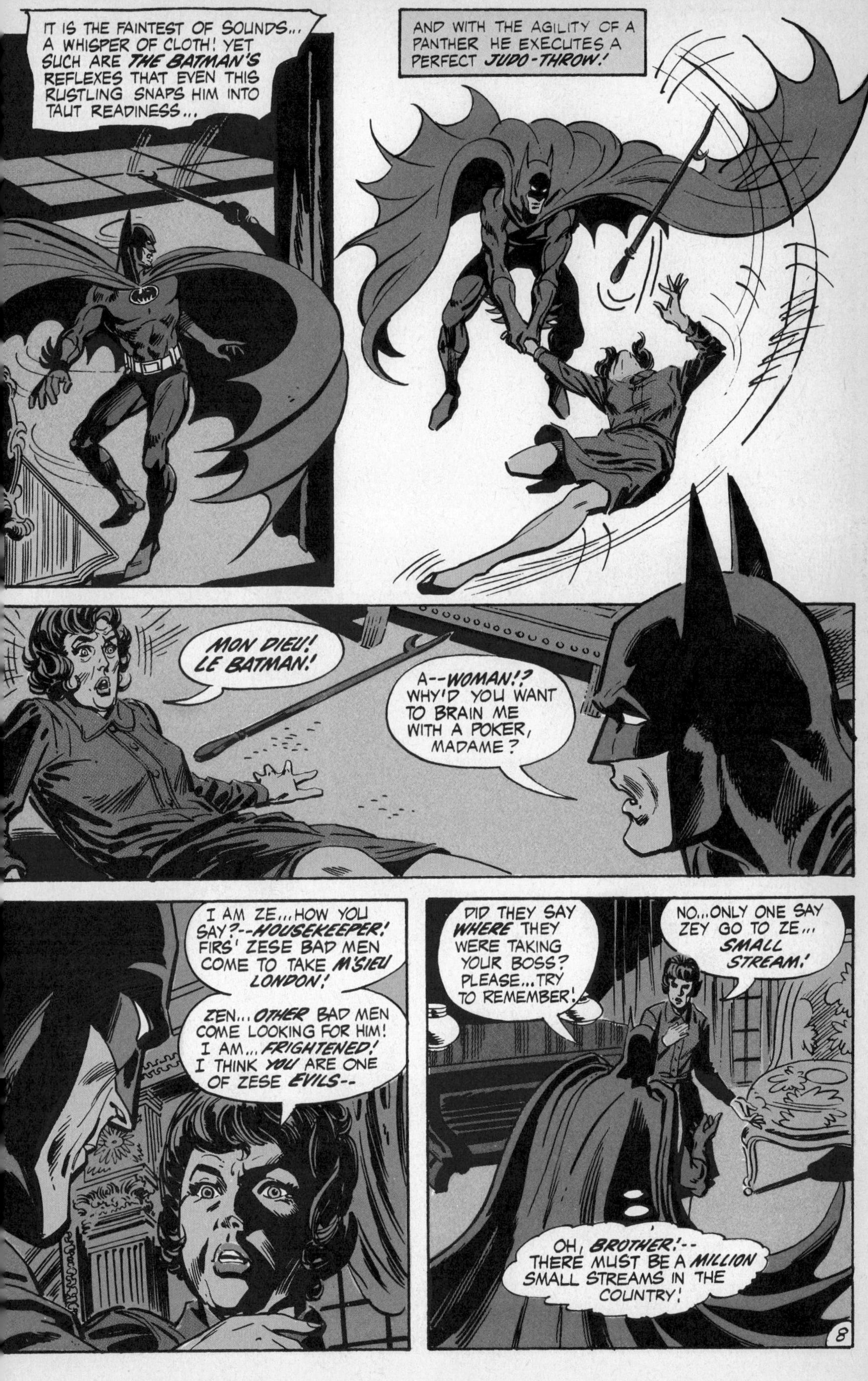
IT IS THE FAINTEST OF SOUNDS... A WHISPER OF CLOTH! YET SUCH ARE THE BATMAN'S REFLEXES THAT EVEN THIS RUSTLING SNAPS HIM INTO TAUT READINESS...
AND WITH THE AGILITY OF A PANTHER HE EXECUTES A PERFECT JUDO-THROW!
MON DIEU! LE BATMAN!
A--WOMAN!? WHY'D YOU WANT TO BRAIN ME WITH A POKER, MADAME?
I AM ZE... HOW YOU SAY?--HOUSEKEEPER! FIRS' ZESE BAD MEN COME TO TAKE M'SIEU LONDON!
ZEN... OTHER BAD MEN COME LOOKING FOR HIM! I AM... FRIGHTENED! I THINK YOU ARE ONE OF ZESE EVILS--
DID THEY SAY WHERE THEY WERE TAKING YOUR BOSS? PLEASE... TRY TO REMEMBER!
NO... ONLY ONE SAY ZEY GO TO ZE... SMALL STREAM!
OH, BROTHER!-- THERE MUST BE A MILLION SMALL STREAMS IN THE COUNTRY!
8

THE *FIRST* GROUP WAS IN THE SERVICE OF *STRISS!* PROBABLY HOODS HE BOUGHT WITH THE PROMISE OF BIG MONEY!

AND THE *SECOND* GROUP BELONGED TO *TALIA!* SHE WAS *ALSO* TOO LATE!

IF ONLY I UNDERSTOOD THAT REFERENCE TO A *SMALL STREAM!*

WAIT! MADAME, YOUR NATIVE LANGUAGE IS *FRENCH--?*

OUI... I MEAN-- *YES!*

THAT'S *ALL* I NEED TO KNOW!✱ SHOW ME A *TELE-PHONE* PLEASE!

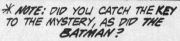

✱ *NOTE: DID YOU CATCH THE KEY TO THE MYSTERY, AS DID THE BATMAN?*

QUICKLY, THE *COWLED AVENGER* CALLS HIS BUTLER--ALFRED--AND SNAPS INSTRUCTIONS...

AND LESS THAN FORTY MINUTES LATER, THE LOYAL SERVANT MEETS HIS EMPLOYER AT *GOTHAM AIRPORT...*

I CALLED EVERY MARINA IN THE AREA YOU MENTIONED, SIR! A CHAP AT A TOWN NAMED *PORT-AU-LAC* SAW THE PARTY YOU WANT!

THANKS, ALFRED! SEE YOU SOON-- I *HOPE!*

THEN, IN *RÄ'S AL GHÜL'S* PRIVATE JET...

YOU HAVE DEDUCED *STRISS'* HIDING-PLACE, DETECTIVE?

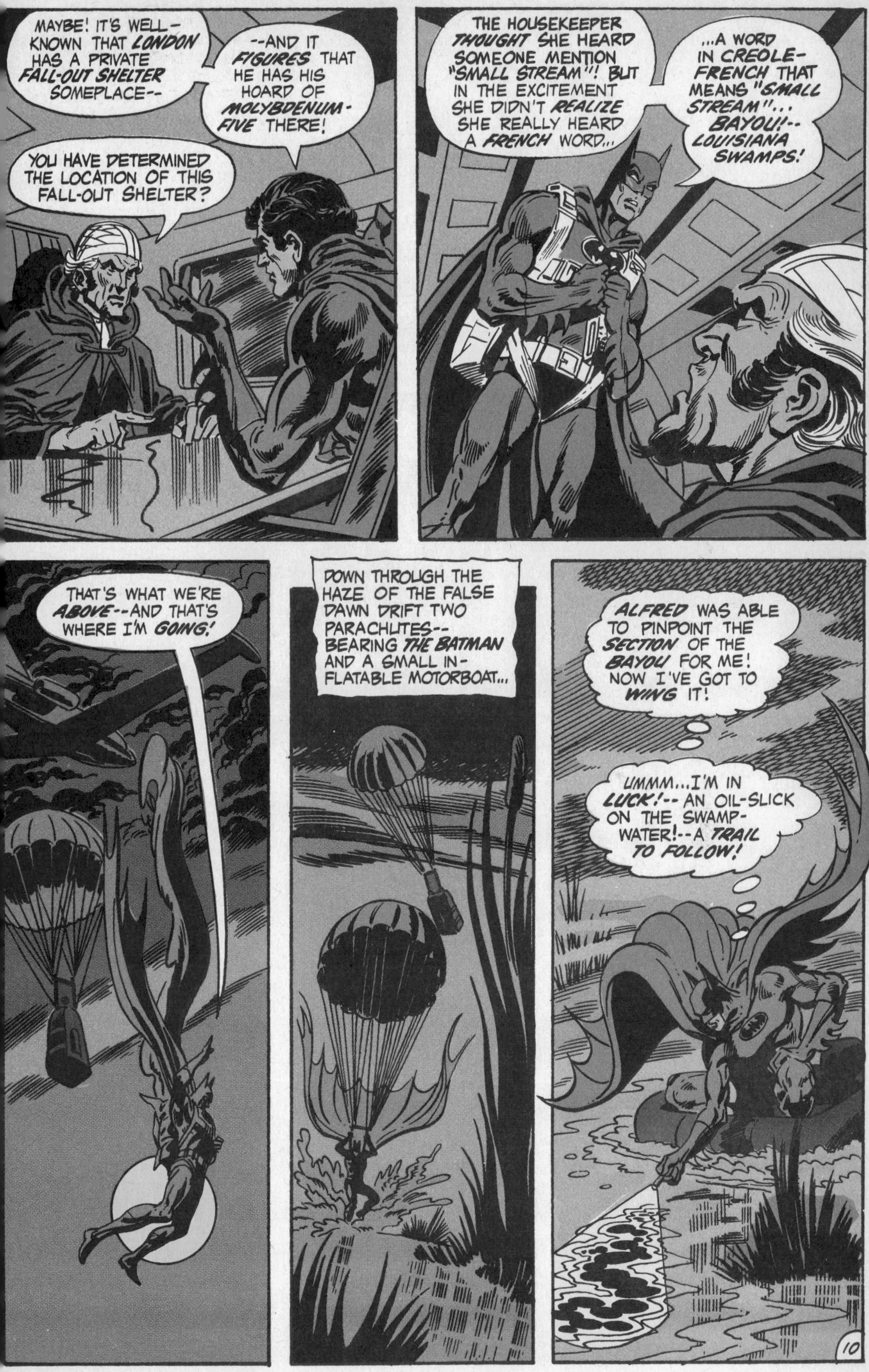
MAYBE! IT'S WELL-KNOWN THAT LONDON HAS A PRIVATE FALL-OUT SHELTER SOMEPLACE--
--AND IT FIGURES THAT HE HAS HIS HOARD OF MOLYBDENUM-FIVE THERE!
YOU HAVE DETERMINED THE LOCATION OF THIS FALL-OUT SHELTER?
THE HOUSEKEEPER THOUGHT SHE HEARD SOMEONE MENTION "SMALL STREAM"! BUT IN THE EXCITEMENT SHE DIDN'T REALIZE SHE REALLY HEARD A FRENCH WORD...
...A WORD IN CREOLE-FRENCH THAT MEANS "SMALL STREAM"... BAYOU!--LOUISIANA SWAMPS!
THAT'S WHAT WE'RE ABOVE--AND THAT'S WHERE I'M GOING!
DOWN THROUGH THE HAZE OF THE FALSE DAWN DRIFT TWO PARACHUTES--BEARING THE BATMAN AND A SMALL IN-FLATABLE MOTORBOAT...
ALFRED WAS ABLE TO PINPOINT THE SECTION OF THE BAYOU FOR ME! NOW I'VE GOT TO WING IT!
UMMM...I'M IN LUCK!--AN OIL-SLICK ON THE SWAMP-WATER!--A TRAIL TO FOLLOW!
10

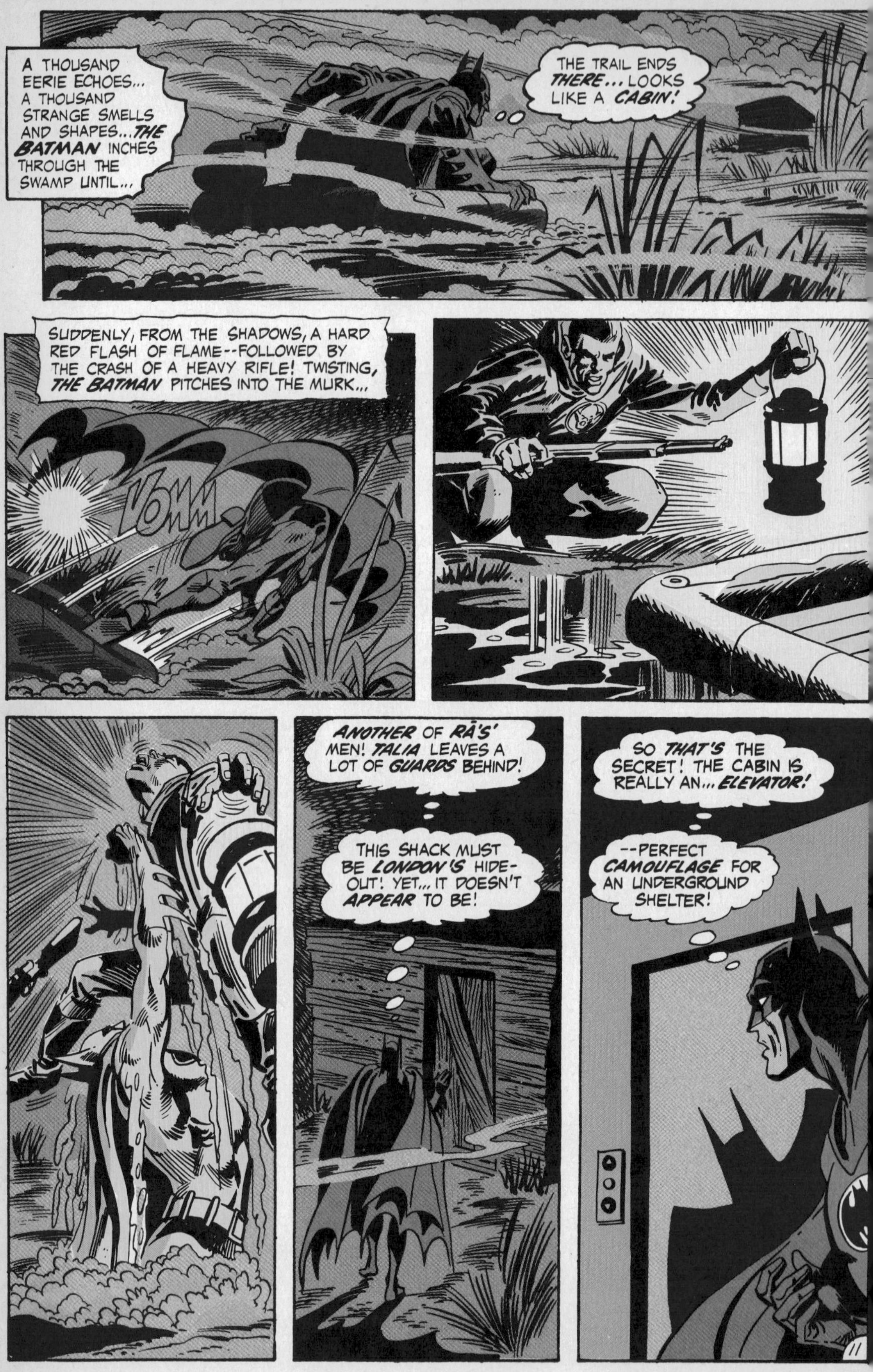
A THOUSAND EERIE ECHOES... A THOUSAND STRANGE SMELLS AND SHAPES...THE BATMAN INCHES THROUGH THE SWAMP UNTIL...
THE TRAIL ENDS THERE... LOOKS LIKE A CABIN!
SUDDENLY, FROM THE SHADOWS, A HARD RED FLASH OF FLAME--FOLLOWED BY THE CRASH OF A HEAVY RIFLE! TWISTING, THE BATMAN PITCHES INTO THE MURK...
VOMM
ANOTHER OF RĀ'S' MEN! TALIA LEAVES A LOT OF GUARDS BEHIND!
THIS SHACK MUST BE LONDON'S HIDE-OUT! YET... IT DOESN'T APPEAR TO BE!
SO THAT'S THE SECRET! THE CABIN IS REALLY AN... ELEVATOR!
--PERFECT CAMOUFLAGE FOR AN UNDERGROUND SHELTER!
11

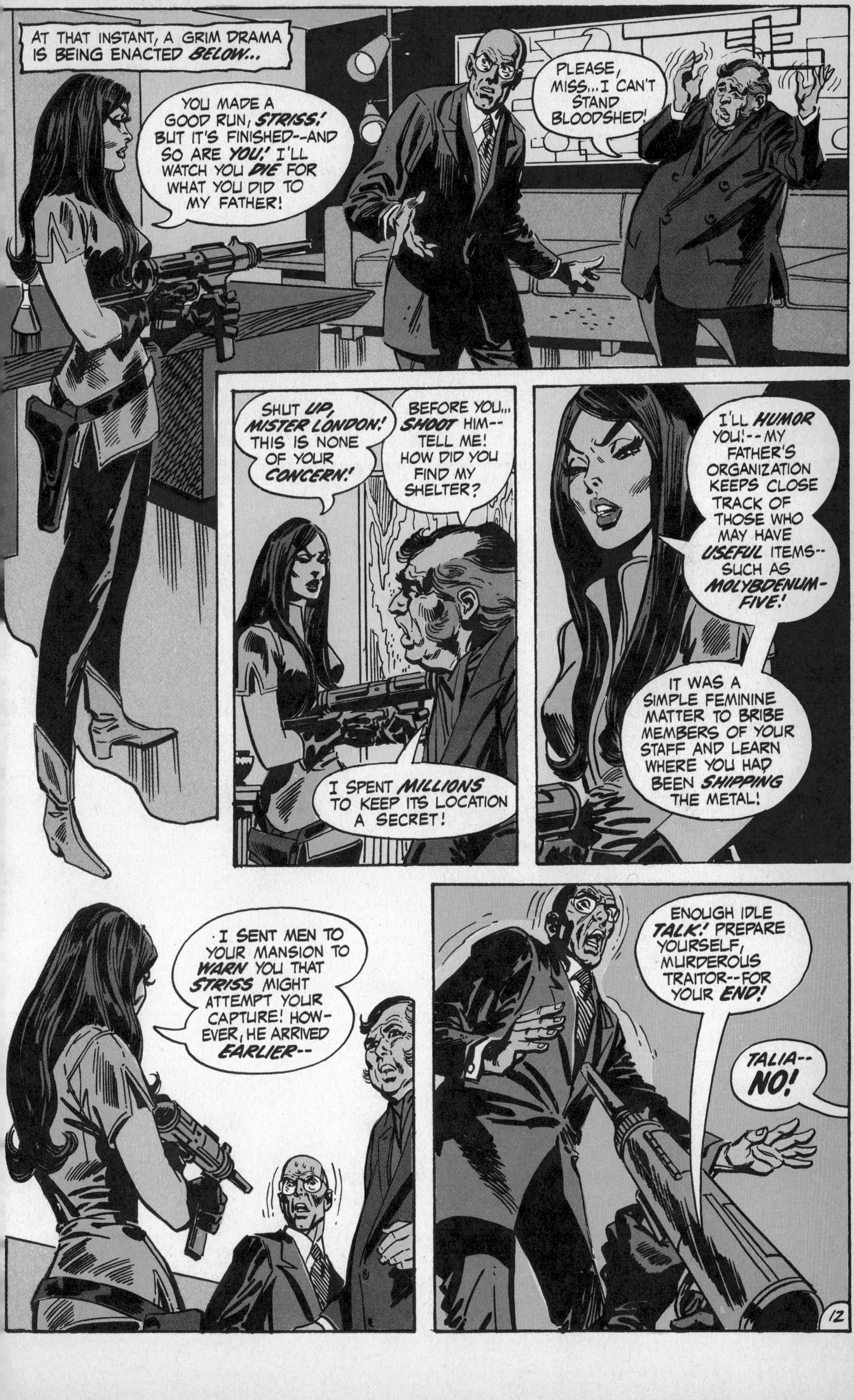
AT THAT INSTANT, A GRIM DRAMA IS BEING ENACTED BELOW...
YOU MADE A GOOD RUN, STRISS! BUT IT'S FINISHED--AND SO ARE YOU! I'LL WATCH YOU DIE FOR WHAT YOU DID TO MY FATHER!
PLEASE, MISS...I CAN'T STAND BLOODSHED!
SHUT UP, MISTER LONDON! THIS IS NONE OF YOUR CONCERN!
BEFORE YOU... SHOOT HIM--TELL ME! HOW DID YOU FIND MY SHELTER?
I SPENT MILLIONS TO KEEP ITS LOCATION A SECRET!
I'LL HUMOR YOU!--MY FATHER'S ORGANIZATION KEEPS CLOSE TRACK OF THOSE WHO MAY HAVE USEFUL ITEMS--SUCH AS MOLYBDENUM-FIVE!
IT WAS A SIMPLE FEMININE MATTER TO BRIBE MEMBERS OF YOUR STAFF AND LEARN WHERE YOU HAD BEEN SHIPPING THE METAL!
I SENT MEN TO YOUR MANSION TO WARN YOU THAT STRISS MIGHT ATTEMPT YOUR CAPTURE! HOW-EVER, HE ARRIVED EARLIER--
ENOUGH IDLE TALK! PREPARE YOURSELF, MURDEROUS TRAITOR--FOR YOUR END!
TALIA--NO!
12

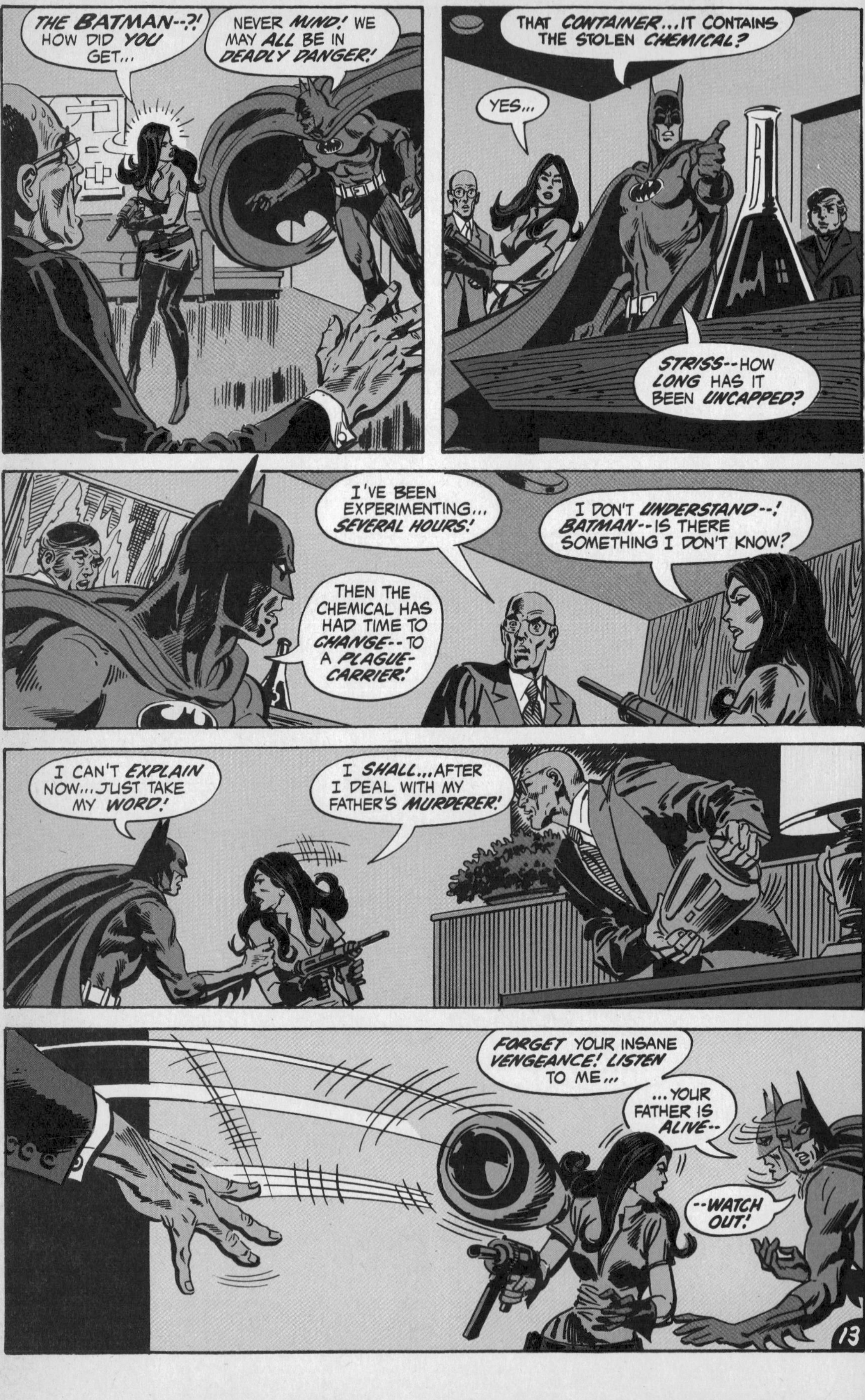
THE BATMAN--?! HOW DID YOU GET...
NEVER MIND! WE MAY ALL BE IN DEADLY DANGER!
THAT CONTAINER...IT CONTAINS THE STOLEN CHEMICAL?
YES...
STRISS--HOW LONG HAS IT BEEN UNCAPPED?
I'VE BEEN EXPERIMENTING... SEVERAL HOURS!
THEN THE CHEMICAL HAS HAD TIME TO CHANGE--TO A PLAGUE-CARRIER!
I DON'T UNDERSTAND--! BATMAN--IS THERE SOMETHING I DON'T KNOW?
I CAN'T EXPLAIN NOW...JUST TAKE MY WORD!
I SHALL...AFTER I DEAL WITH MY FATHER'S MURDERER!
FORGET YOUR INSANE VENGEANCE! LISTEN TO ME...
...YOUR FATHER IS ALIVE--
--WATCH OUT!
13

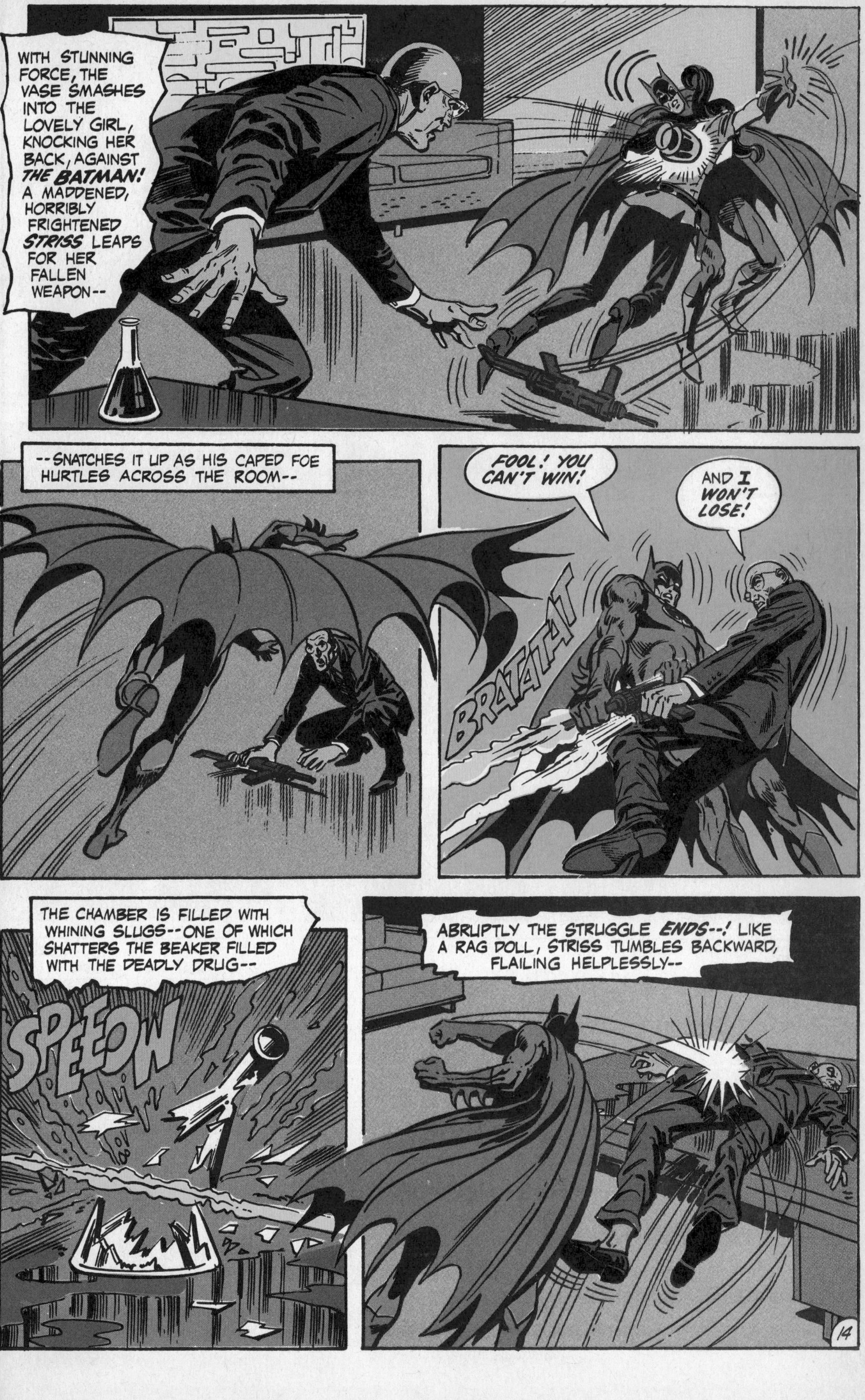
WITH STUNNING FORCE, THE VASE SMASHES INTO THE LOVELY GIRL, KNOCKING HER BACK, AGAINST THE BATMAN! A MADDENED, HORRIBLY FRIGHTENED STRISS LEAPS FOR HER FALLEN WEAPON--
--SNATCHES IT UP AS HIS CAPED FOE HURTLES ACROSS THE ROOM--
FOOL! YOU CAN'T WIN!
AND I WON'T LOSE!
BRATATAT
THE CHAMBER IS FILLED WITH WHINING SLUGS--ONE OF WHICH SHATTERS THE BEAKER FILLED WITH THE DEADLY DRUG--
SPEEOW
ABRUPTLY THE STRUGGLE ENDS--! LIKE A RAG DOLL, STRISS TUMBLES BACKWARD, FLAILING HELPLESSLY--
14

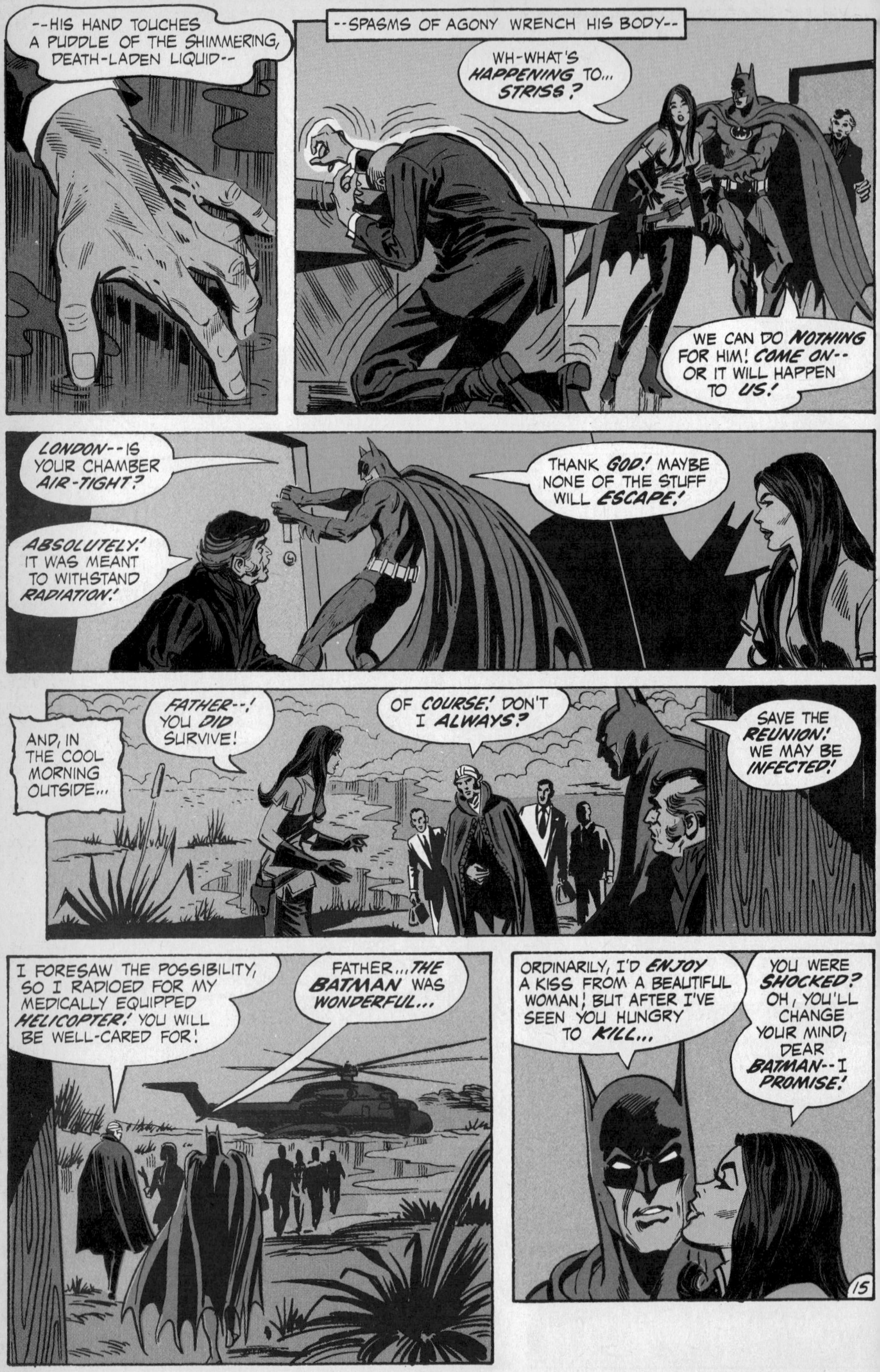
--HIS HAND TOUCHES A PUDDLE OF THE SHIMMERING, DEATH-LADEN LIQUID--
--SPASMS OF AGONY WRENCH HIS BODY--
WH-WHAT'S HAPPENING TO... STRISS?
WE CAN DO NOTHING FOR HIM! COME ON--OR IT WILL HAPPEN TO US!
LONDON--IS YOUR CHAMBER AIR-TIGHT?
ABSOLUTELY! IT WAS MEANT TO WITHSTAND RADIATION!
THANK GOD! MAYBE NONE OF THE STUFF WILL ESCAPE!
AND, IN THE COOL MORNING OUTSIDE...
FATHER--! YOU DID SURVIVE!
OF COURSE! DON'T I ALWAYS?
SAVE THE REUNION! WE MAY BE INFECTED!
I FORESAW THE POSSIBILITY, SO I RADIOED FOR MY MEDICALLY EQUIPPED HELICOPTER! YOU WILL BE WELL-CARED FOR!
FATHER... THE BATMAN WAS WONDERFUL...
ORDINARILY, I'D ENJOY A KISS FROM A BEAUTIFUL WOMAN, BUT AFTER I'VE SEEN YOU HUNGRY TO KILL...
YOU WERE SHOCKED? OH, YOU'LL CHANGE YOUR MIND, DEAR BATMAN--I PROMISE!
15

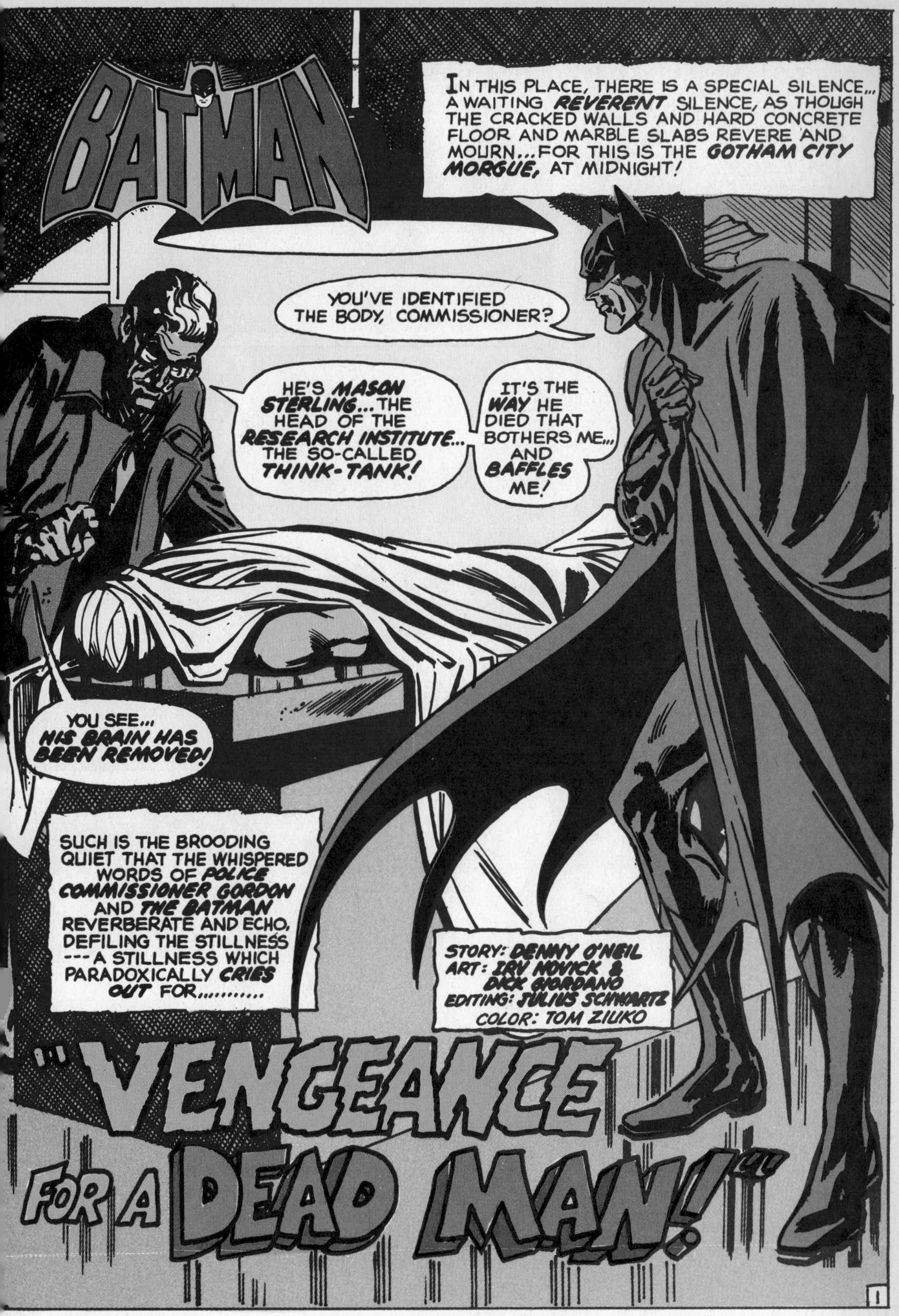
BATMAN
IN THIS PLACE, THERE IS A SPECIAL SILENCE... A WAITING REVERENT SILENCE, AS THOUGH THE CRACKED WALLS AND HARD CONCRETE FLOOR AND MARBLE SLABS REVERE AND MOURN... FOR THIS IS THE GOTHAM CITY MORGUE, AT MIDNIGHT!
YOU'VE IDENTIFIED THE BODY, COMMISSIONER?
HE'S MASON STERLING... THE HEAD OF THE RESEARCH INSTITUTE... THE SO-CALLED THINK-TANK!
IT'S THE WAY HE DIED THAT BOTHERS ME... AND BAFFLES ME!
YOU SEE... HIS BRAIN HAS BEEN REMOVED!
SUCH IS THE BROODING QUIET THAT THE WHISPERED WORDS OF POLICE COMMISSIONER GORDON AND THE BATMAN REVERBERATE AND ECHO, DEFILING THE STILLNESS ---A STILLNESS WHICH PARADOXICALLY CRIES OUT FOR..........
STORY: DENNY O'NEIL
ART: IRV NOVICK & DICK GIORDANO
EDITING: JULIUS SCHWARTZ
COLOR: TOM ZIUKO
"...VENGEANCE FOR A DEAD MAN!"
1

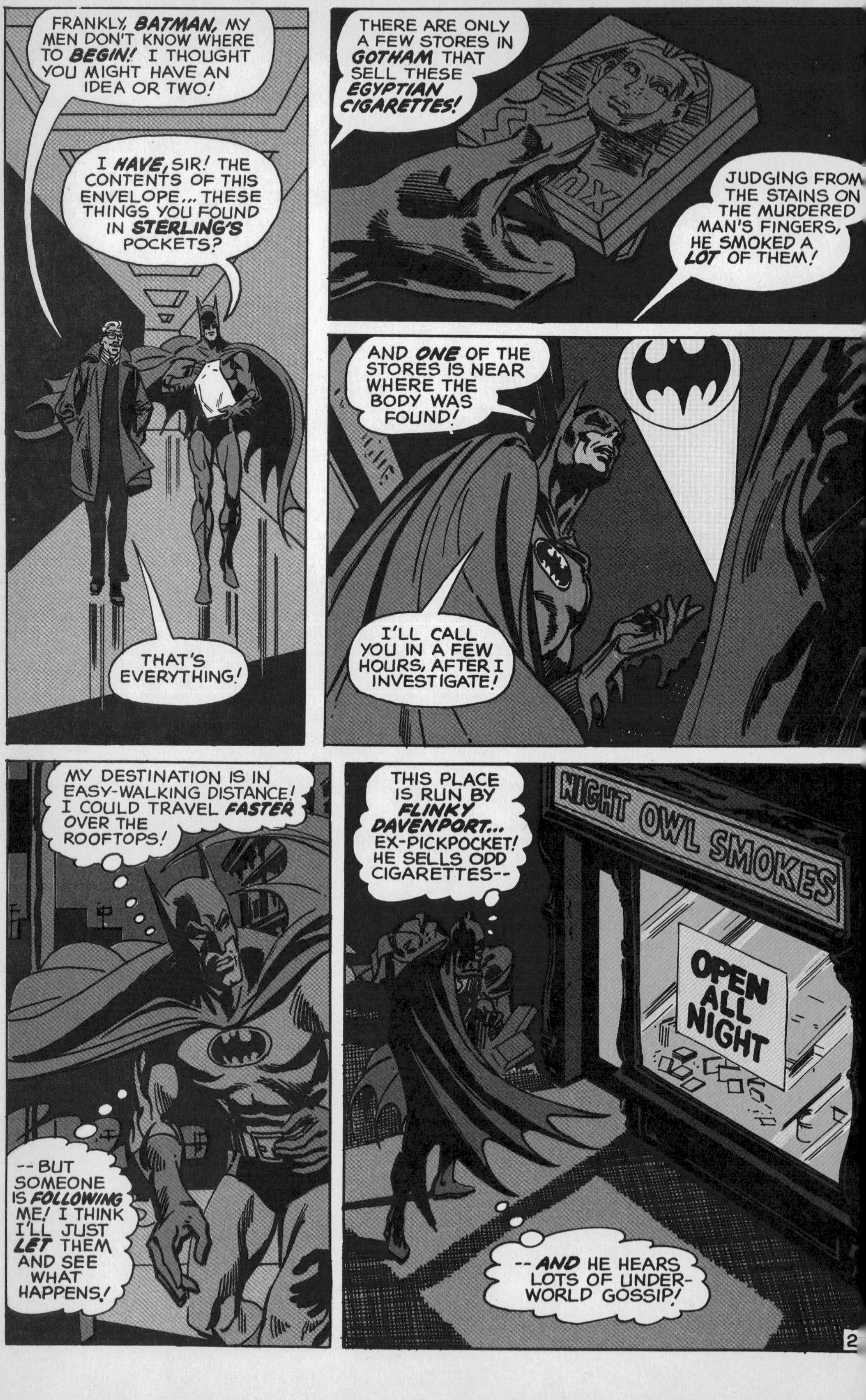
FRANKLY, BATMAN, MY MEN DON'T KNOW WHERE TO BEGIN! I THOUGHT YOU MIGHT HAVE AN IDEA OR TWO!
I HAVE, SIR! THE CONTENTS OF THIS ENVELOPE... THESE THINGS YOU FOUND IN STERLING'S POCKETS?
THAT'S EVERYTHING!
THERE ARE ONLY A FEW STORES IN GOTHAM THAT SELL THESE EGYPTIAN CIGARETTES!
JUDGING FROM THE STAINS ON THE MURDERED MAN'S FINGERS, HE SMOKED A LOT OF THEM!
AND ONE OF THE STORES IS NEAR WHERE THE BODY WAS FOUND!
I'LL CALL YOU IN A FEW HOURS, AFTER I INVESTIGATE!
MY DESTINATION IS IN EASY-WALKING DISTANCE! I COULD TRAVEL FASTER OVER THE ROOFTOPS!
-- BUT SOMEONE IS FOLLOWING ME! I THINK I'LL JUST LET THEM AND SEE WHAT HAPPENS!
THIS PLACE IS RUN BY FLINKY DAVENPORT... EX-PICKPOCKET! HE SELLS ODD CIGARETTES--
NIGHT OWL SMOKES
OPEN ALL NIGHT
-- AND HE HEARS LOTS OF UNDER-WORLD GOSSIP!
2

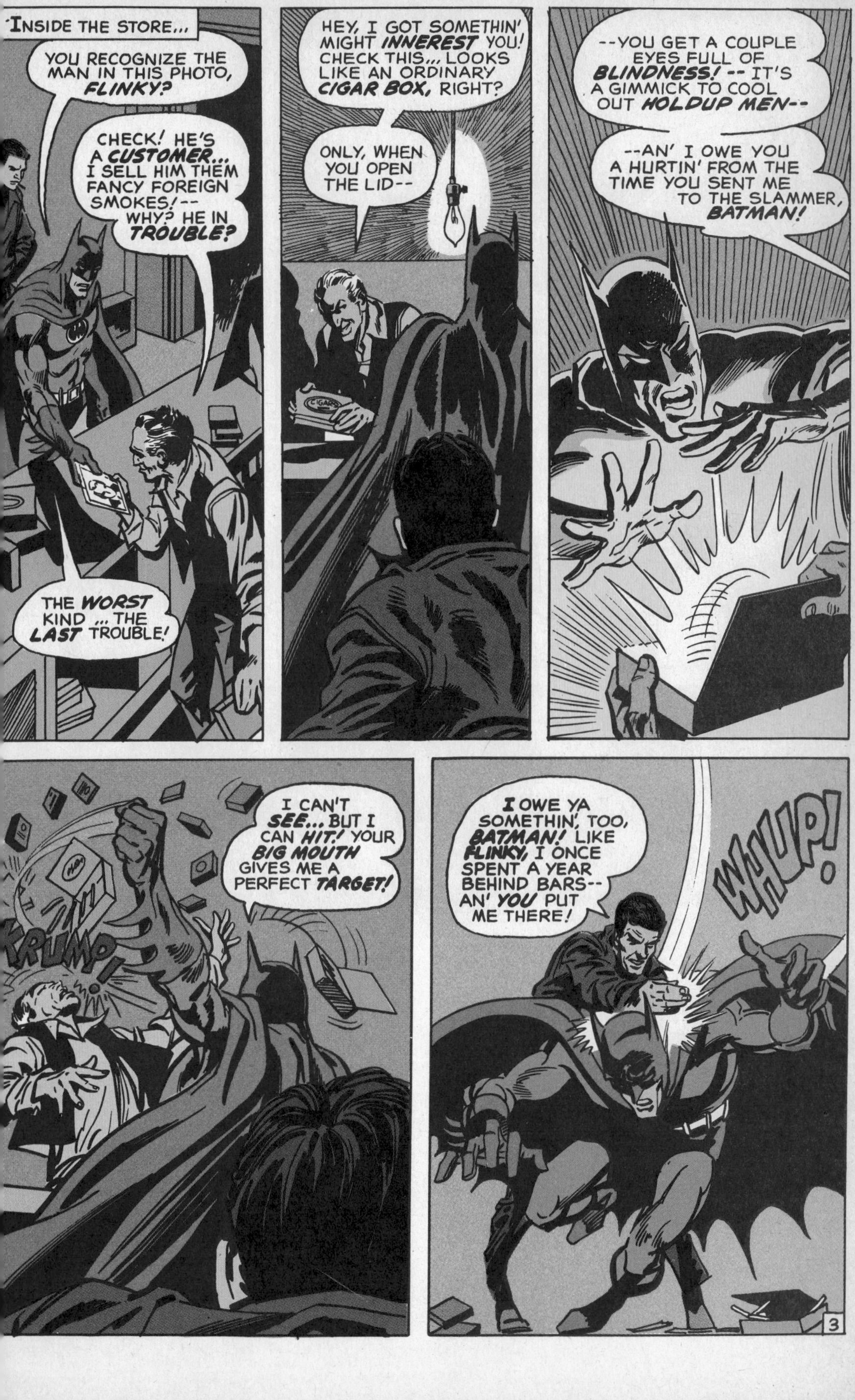
INSIDE THE STORE...
YOU RECOGNIZE THE MAN IN THIS PHOTO, FLINKY?
CHECK! HE'S A CUSTOMER... I SELL HIM THEM FANCY FOREIGN SMOKES!-- WHY? HE IN TROUBLE?
THE WORST KIND ... THE LAST TROUBLE!
HEY, I GOT SOMETHIN' MIGHT INNEREST YOU! CHECK THIS... LOOKS LIKE AN ORDINARY CIGAR BOX, RIGHT?
ONLY, WHEN YOU OPEN THE LID--
CIGARS
--YOU GET A COUPLE EYES FULL OF BLINDNESS! -- IT'S A GIMMICK TO COOL OUT HOLDUP MEN--
--AN' I OWE YOU A HURTIN' FROM THE TIME YOU SENT ME TO THE SLAMMER, BATMAN!
I CAN'T SEE... BUT I CAN HIT! YOUR BIG MOUTH GIVES ME A PERFECT TARGET!
KRUMP!
I OWE YA SOMETHIN', TOO, BATMAN! LIKE FLINKY, I ONCE SPENT A YEAR BEHIND BARS-- AN' YOU PUT ME THERE!
WHUP!
3

I BEEN *WAITIN'* FOR A CHANCE TO GET EVEN...

KLIK

...*PRAYIN'* FOR IT!

SUDDENLY THERE IS THE MUFFLED COUGH OF A SILENCED *PISTOL* -- AND THE GLITTERING BLADE SPINS FROM NUMBED FINGERS --

VOOP!

AND THE WOULD-BE ASSASSIN IS CATAPULTED THROUGH THE WINDOW BY THE BODY-BLOCKING OF THE ALMOST SIGHTLESS *BATMAN!*

KREESH

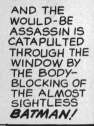

SOMEONE FIRED THAT SHOT... SOMEONE WHO'S *COMING!* --MUST CLEAR MY VISION...

IS IT A *FRIEND*... OR YET ANOTHER *ENEMY?*

4

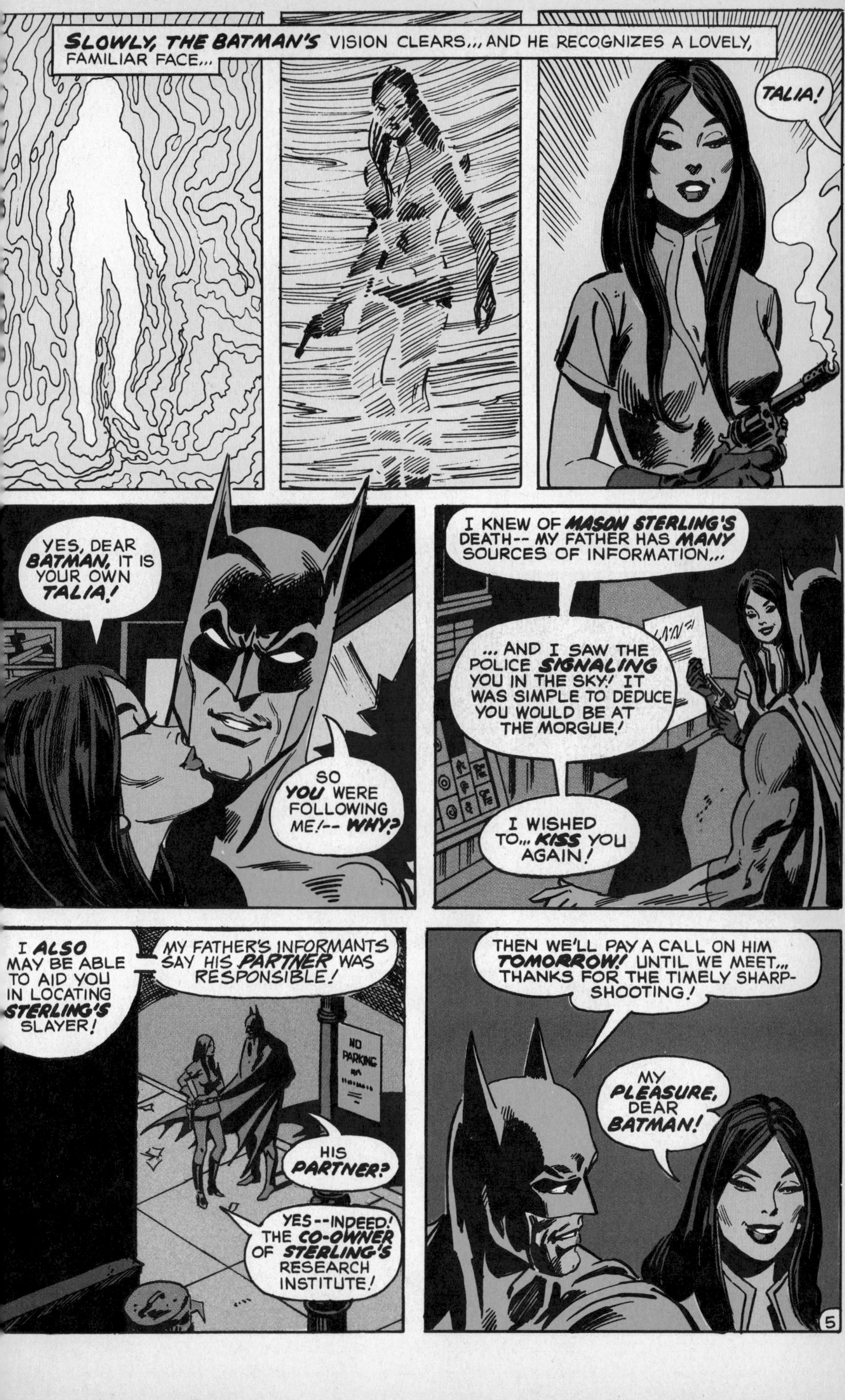
SLOWLY, THE BATMAN'S VISION CLEARS... AND HE RECOGNIZES A LOVELY, FAMILIAR FACE...
TALIA!
YES, DEAR BATMAN, IT IS YOUR OWN TALIA!
SO YOU WERE FOLLOWING ME!-- WHY?
I KNEW OF MASON STERLING'S DEATH-- MY FATHER HAS MANY SOURCES OF INFORMATION...
... AND I SAW THE POLICE SIGNALING YOU IN THE SKY! IT WAS SIMPLE TO DEDUCE YOU WOULD BE AT THE MORGUE!
I WISHED TO... KISS YOU AGAIN!
I ALSO MAY BE ABLE TO AID YOU IN LOCATING STERLING'S SLAYER!
MY FATHER'S INFORMANTS SAY HIS PARTNER WAS RESPONSIBLE!
NO PARKING
HIS PARTNER?
YES--INDEED! THE CO-OWNER OF STERLING'S RESEARCH INSTITUTE!
THEN WE'LL PAY A CALL ON HIM TOMORROW! UNTIL WE MEET... THANKS FOR THE TIMELY SHARP-SHOOTING!
MY PLEASURE, DEAR BATMAN!
5

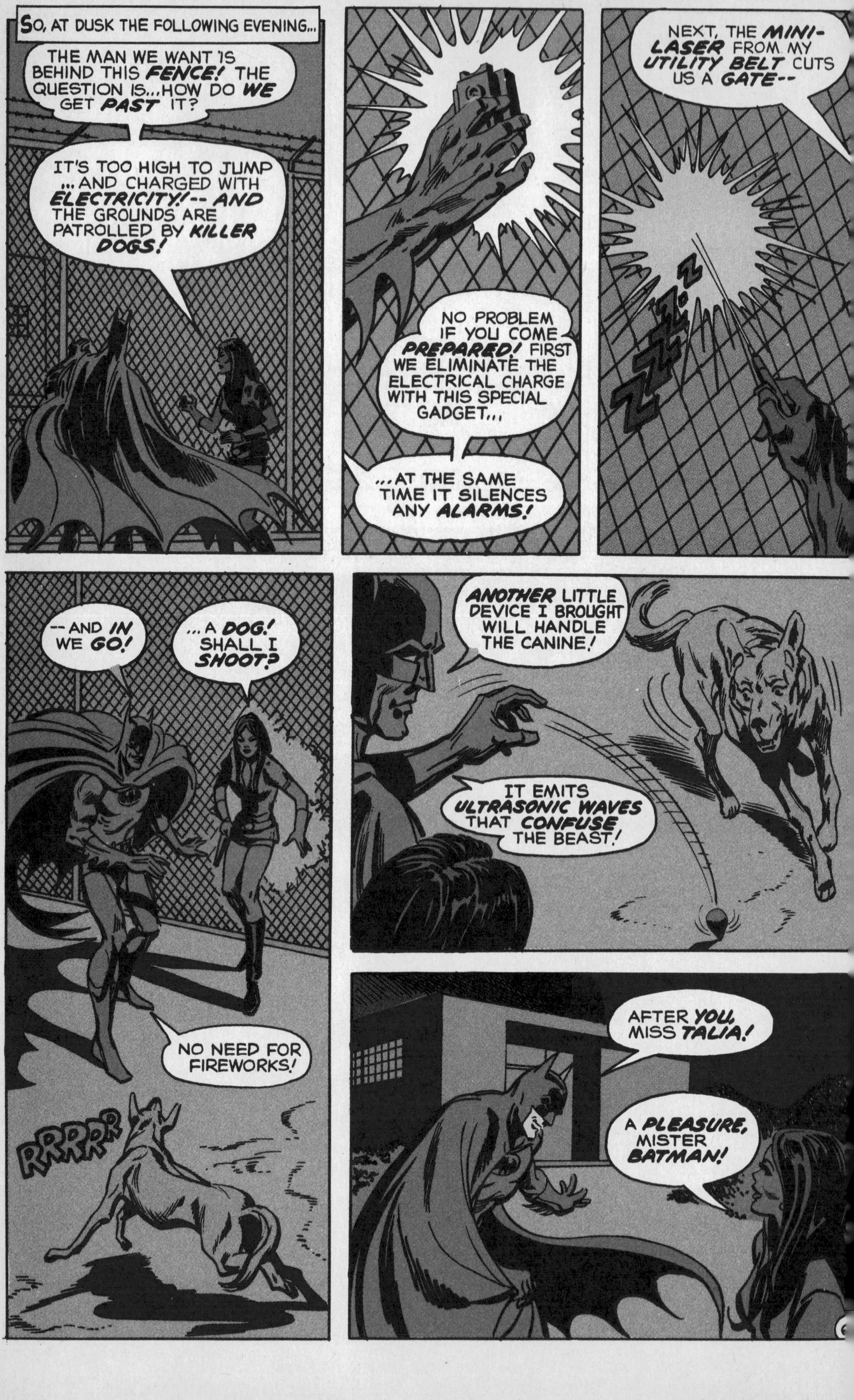
SO, AT DUSK THE FOLLOWING EVENING...
THE MAN WE WANT IS BEHIND THIS FENCE! THE QUESTION IS...HOW DO WE GET PAST IT?
IT'S TOO HIGH TO JUMP ...AND CHARGED WITH ELECTRICITY!-- AND THE GROUNDS ARE PATROLLED BY KILLER DOGS!
NO PROBLEM IF YOU COME PREPARED! FIRST WE ELIMINATE THE ELECTRICAL CHARGE WITH THIS SPECIAL GADGET...
...AT THE SAME TIME IT SILENCES ANY ALARMS!
NEXT, THE MINI-LASER FROM MY UTILITY BELT CUTS US A GATE--
ZZZ
-- AND IN WE GO!
...A DOG! SHALL I SHOOT?
NO NEED FOR FIREWORKS!
RRRRR
ANOTHER LITTLE DEVICE I BROUGHT WILL HANDLE THE CANINE!
IT EMITS ULTRASONIC WAVES THAT CONFUSE THE BEAST!
AFTER YOU, MISS TALIA!
A PLEASURE, MISTER BATMAN!

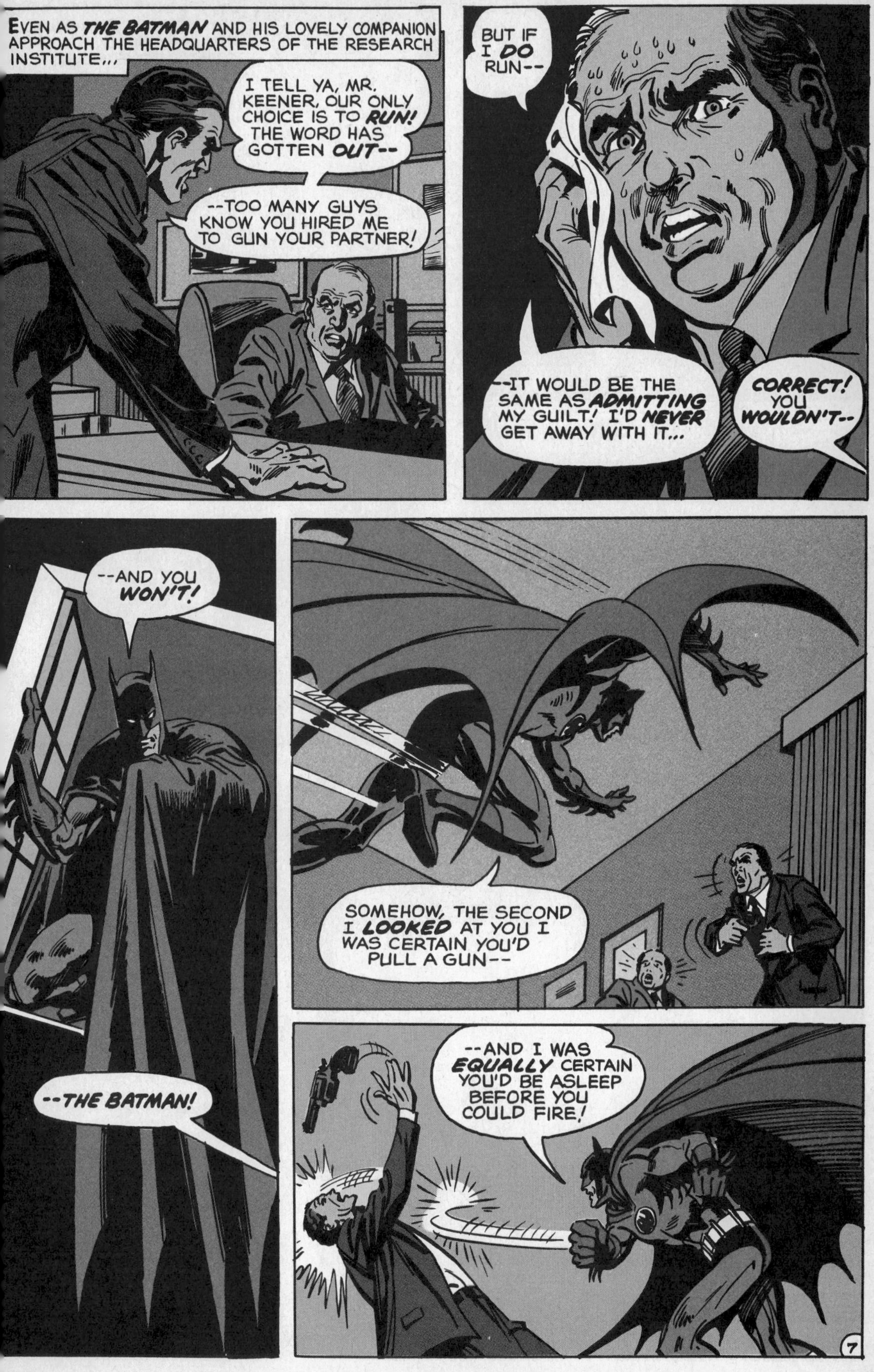
EVEN AS THE BATMAN AND HIS LOVELY COMPANION APPROACH THE HEADQUARTERS OF THE RESEARCH INSTITUTE...
I TELL YA, MR. KEENER, OUR ONLY CHOICE IS TO RUN! THE WORD HAS GOTTEN OUT--
--TOO MANY GUYS KNOW YOU HIRED ME TO GUN YOUR PARTNER!
BUT IF I DO RUN--
--IT WOULD BE THE SAME AS ADMITTING MY GUILT! I'D NEVER GET AWAY WITH IT...
CORRECT! YOU WOULDN'T--
--AND YOU WON'T!
--THE BATMAN!
SOMEHOW, THE SECOND I LOOKED AT YOU I WAS CERTAIN YOU'D PULL A GUN--
--AND I WAS EQUALLY CERTAIN YOU'D BE ASLEEP BEFORE YOU COULD FIRE!
7

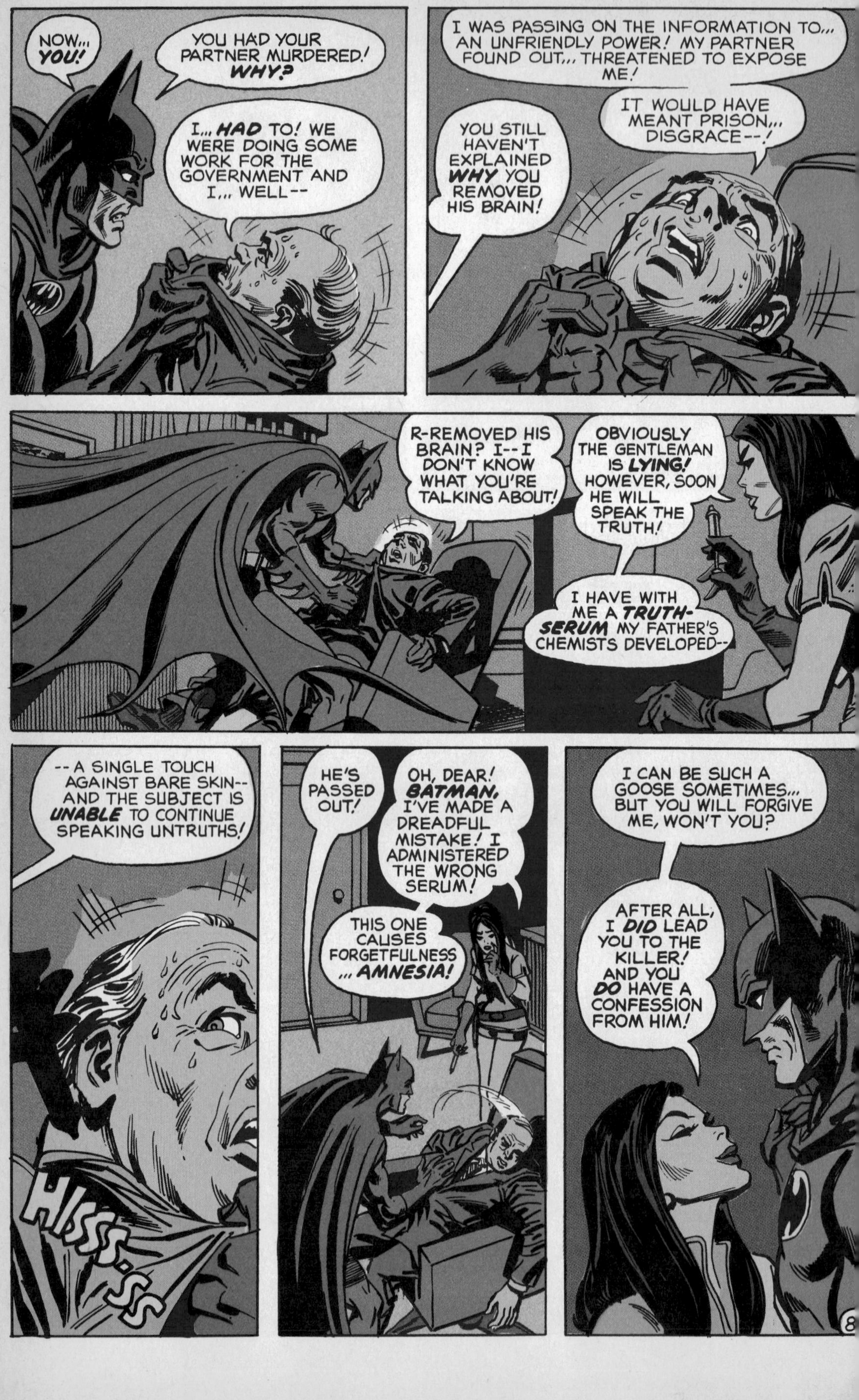
NOW... YOU!
YOU HAD YOUR PARTNER MURDERED! WHY?
I... HAD TO! WE WERE DOING SOME WORK FOR THE GOVERNMENT AND I... WELL--
I WAS PASSING ON THE INFORMATION TO... AN UNFRIENDLY POWER! MY PARTNER FOUND OUT... THREATENED TO EXPOSE ME!
IT WOULD HAVE MEANT PRISON... DISGRACE--!
YOU STILL HAVEN'T EXPLAINED WHY YOU REMOVED HIS BRAIN!
R-REMOVED HIS BRAIN? I--I DON'T KNOW WHAT YOU'RE TALKING ABOUT!
OBVIOUSLY THE GENTLEMAN IS LYING! HOWEVER, SOON HE WILL SPEAK THE TRUTH!
I HAVE WITH ME A TRUTH-SERUM MY FATHER'S CHEMISTS DEVELOPED--
--A SINGLE TOUCH AGAINST BARE SKIN--AND THE SUBJECT IS UNABLE TO CONTINUE SPEAKING UNTRUTHS!
HISSS-SS
HE'S PASSED OUT!
OH, DEAR! BATMAN, I'VE MADE A DREADFUL MISTAKE! I ADMINISTERED THE WRONG SERUM!
THIS ONE CAUSES FORGETFULNESS ...AMNESIA!
I CAN BE SUCH A GOOSE SOMETIMES... BUT YOU WILL FORGIVE ME, WON'T YOU?
AFTER ALL, I DID LEAD YOU TO THE KILLER! AND YOU DO HAVE A CONFESSION FROM HIM!

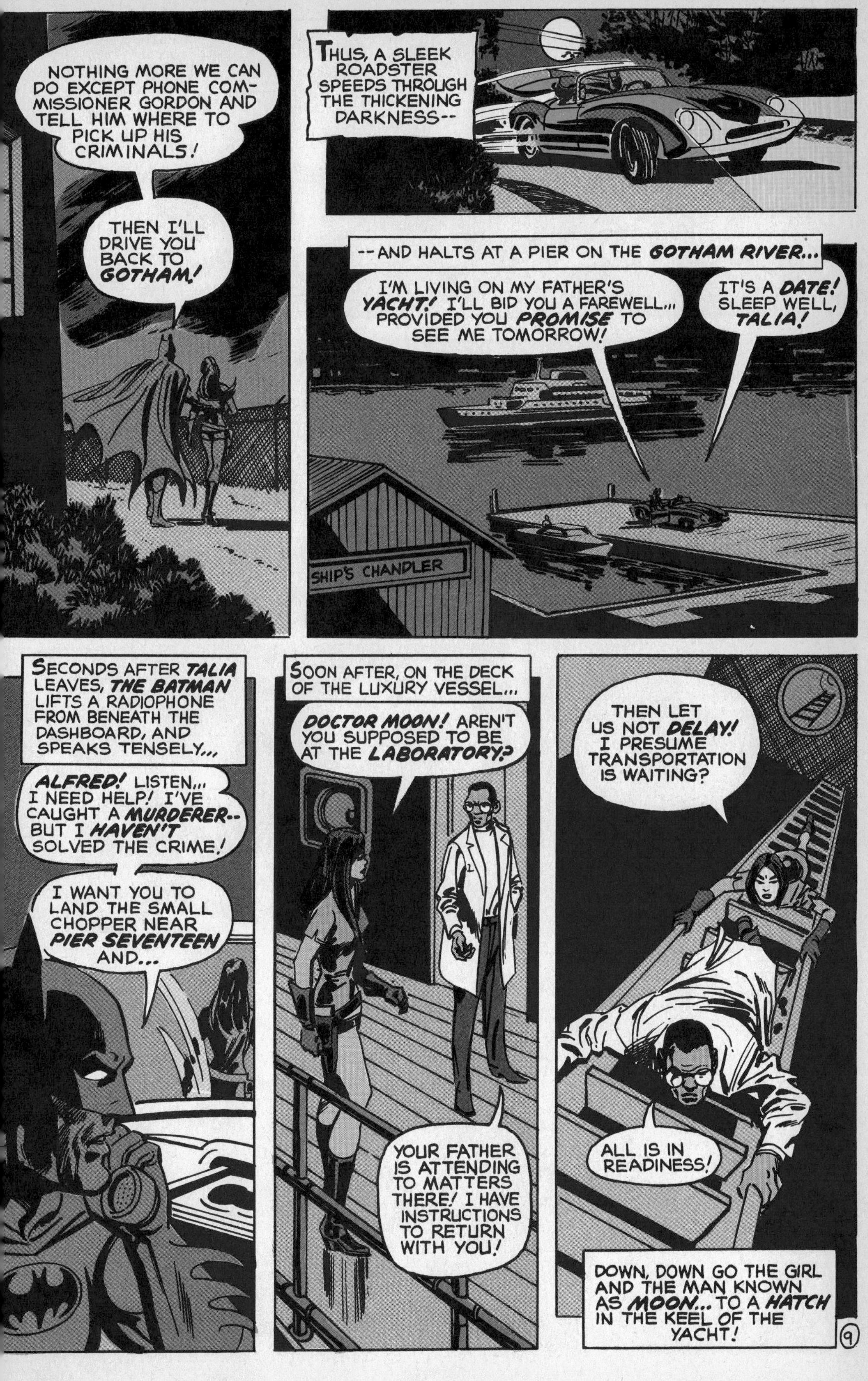
NOTHING MORE WE CAN DO EXCEPT PHONE COMMISSIONER GORDON AND TELL HIM WHERE TO PICK UP HIS CRIMINALS!
THEN I'LL DRIVE YOU BACK TO GOTHAM!
THUS, A SLEEK ROADSTER SPEEDS THROUGH THE THICKENING DARKNESS--
--AND HALTS AT A PIER ON THE GOTHAM RIVER...
I'M LIVING ON MY FATHER'S YACHT! I'LL BID YOU A FAREWELL... PROVIDED YOU PROMISE TO SEE ME TOMORROW!
IT'S A DATE! SLEEP WELL, TALIA!
SHIP'S CHANDLER
SECONDS AFTER TALIA LEAVES, THE BATMAN LIFTS A RADIOPHONE FROM BENEATH THE DASHBOARD, AND SPEAKS TENSELY...
ALFRED! LISTEN... I NEED HELP! I'VE CAUGHT A MURDERER-- BUT I HAVEN'T SOLVED THE CRIME!
I WANT YOU TO LAND THE SMALL CHOPPER NEAR PIER SEVENTEEN AND...
SOON AFTER, ON THE DECK OF THE LUXURY VESSEL...
DOCTOR MOON! AREN'T YOU SUPPOSED TO BE AT THE LABORATORY?
YOUR FATHER IS ATTENDING TO MATTERS THERE! I HAVE INSTRUCTIONS TO RETURN WITH YOU!
THEN LET US NOT DELAY! I PRESUME TRANSPORTATION IS WAITING?
ALL IS IN READINESS!
DOWN, DOWN GO THE GIRL AND THE MAN KNOWN AS MOON... TO A HATCH IN THE KEEL OF THE YACHT!
9

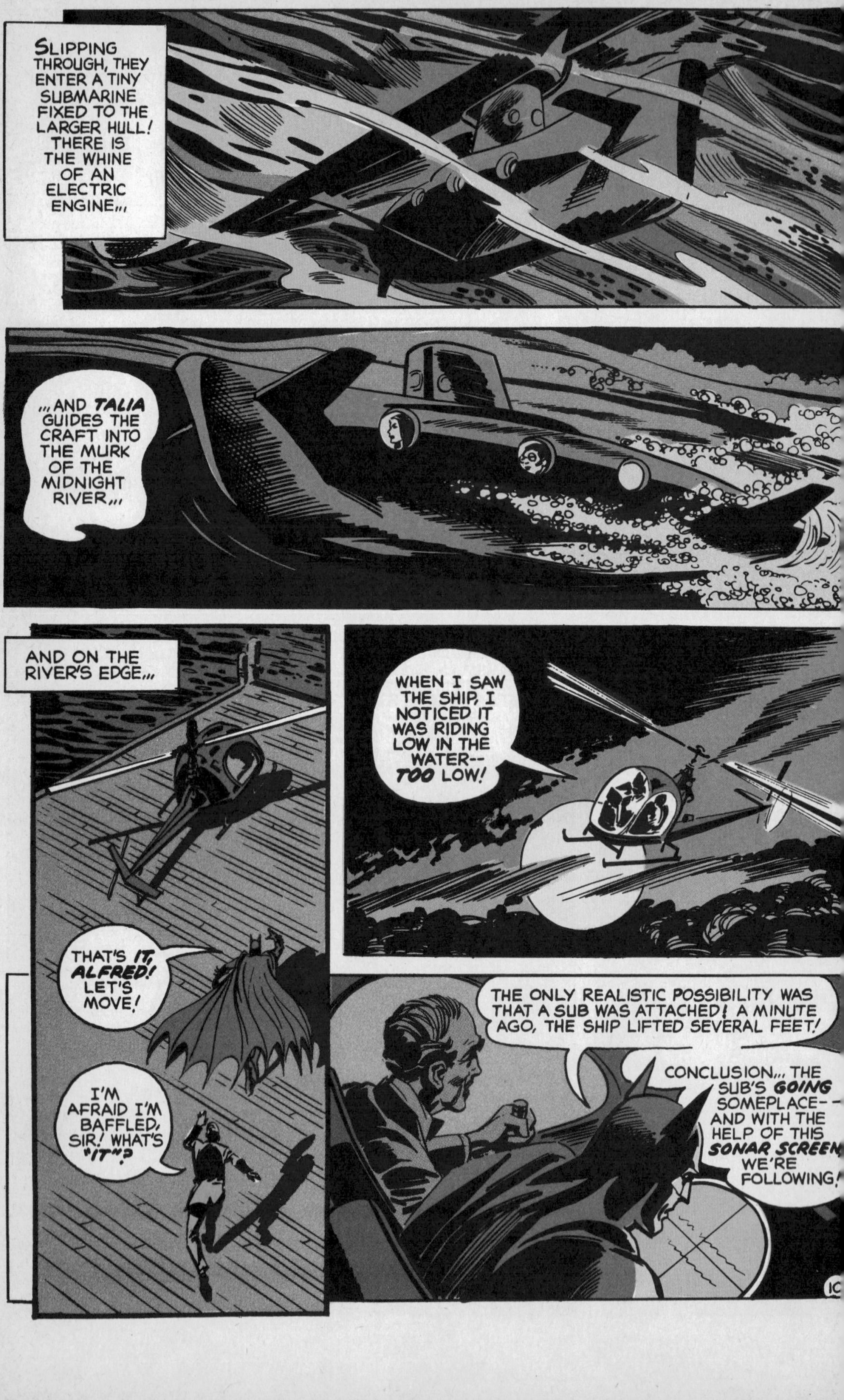
SLIPPING THROUGH, THEY ENTER A TINY SUBMARINE FIXED TO THE LARGER HULL! THERE IS THE WHINE OF AN ELECTRIC ENGINE...
...AND TALIA GUIDES THE CRAFT INTO THE MURK OF THE MIDNIGHT RIVER...
AND ON THE RIVER'S EDGE...
THAT'S IT, ALFRED! LET'S MOVE!
I'M AFRAID I'M BAFFLED, SIR! WHAT'S "IT"?
WHEN I SAW THE SHIP, I NOTICED IT WAS RIDING LOW IN THE WATER-- TOO LOW!
THE ONLY REALISTIC POSSIBILITY WAS THAT A SUB WAS ATTACHED! A MINUTE AGO, THE SHIP LIFTED SEVERAL FEET!
CONCLUSION... THE SUB'S GOING SOMEPLACE-- AND WITH THE HELP OF THIS SONAR SCREEN WE'RE FOLLOWING!

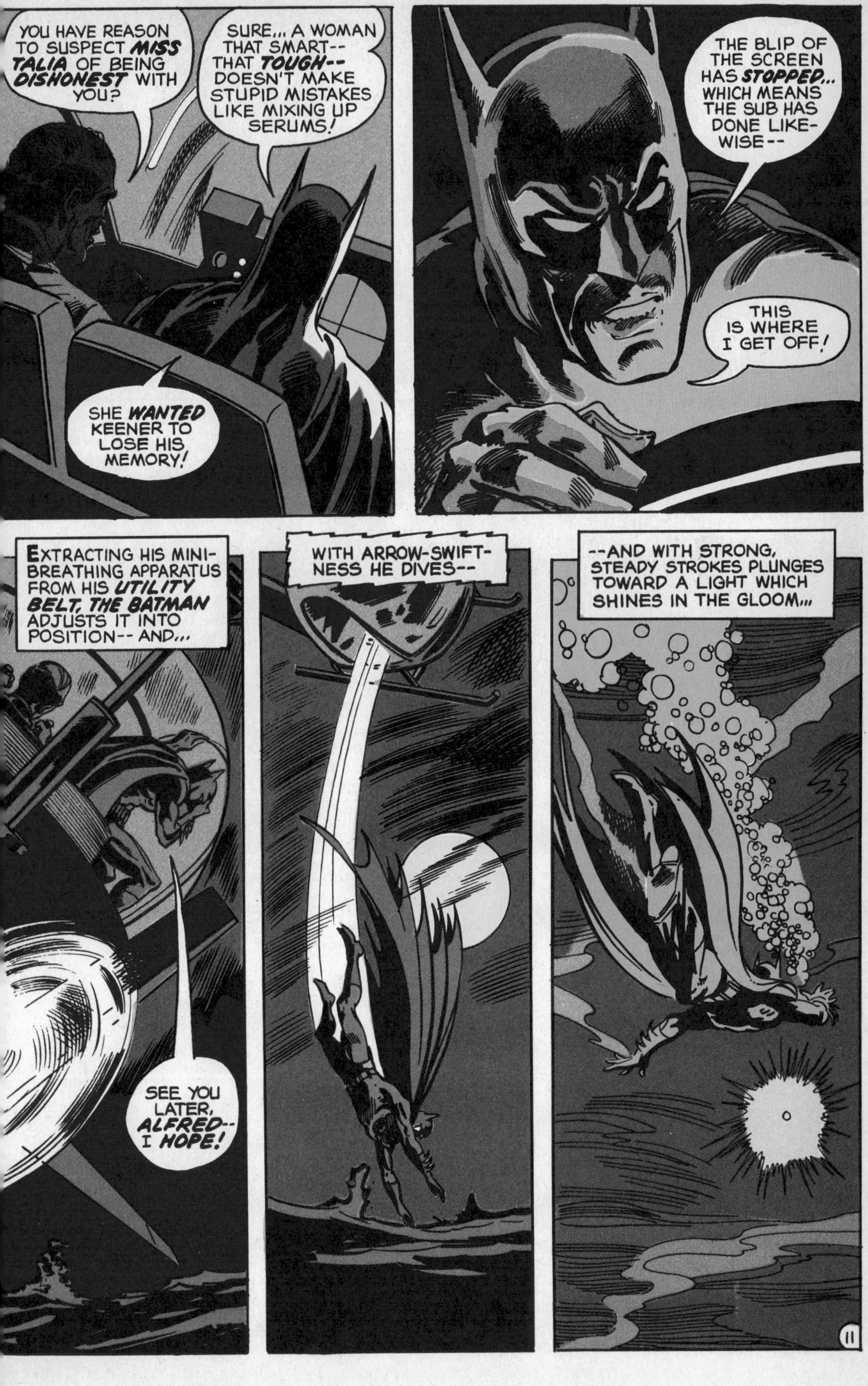
YOU HAVE REASON TO SUSPECT MISS TALIA OF BEING DISHONEST WITH YOU?
SURE... A WOMAN THAT SMART-- THAT TOUGH-- DOESN'T MAKE STUPID MISTAKES LIKE MIXING UP SERUMS!
SHE WANTED KEENER TO LOSE HIS MEMORY!
THE BLIP OF THE SCREEN HAS STOPPED... WHICH MEANS THE SUB HAS DONE LIKE-WISE--
THIS IS WHERE I GET OFF!
EXTRACTING HIS MINI-BREATHING APPARATUS FROM HIS UTILITY BELT, THE BATMAN ADJUSTS IT INTO POSITION-- AND...
SEE YOU LATER, ALFRED-- I HOPE!
WITH ARROW-SWIFT-NESS HE DIVES--
--AND WITH STRONG, STEADY STROKES PLUNGES TOWARD A LIGHT WHICH SHINES IN THE GLOOM...
11

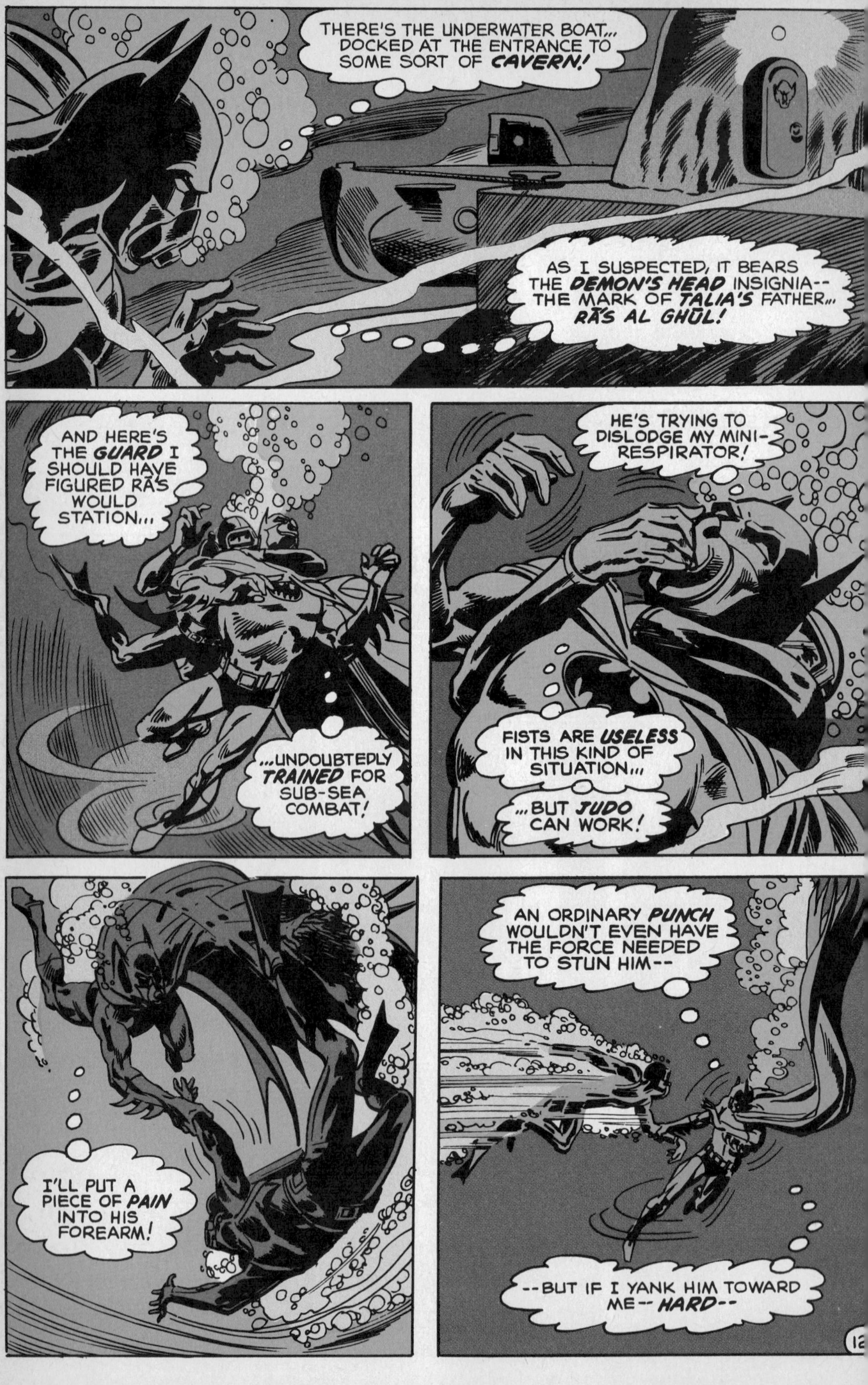
THERE'S THE UNDERWATER BOAT... DOCKED AT THE ENTRANCE TO SOME SORT OF CAVERN!
AS I SUSPECTED, IT BEARS THE DEMON'S HEAD INSIGNIA-- THE MARK OF TALIA'S FATHER... RĀ'S AL GHŪL!
AND HERE'S THE GUARD I SHOULD HAVE FIGURED RĀ'S WOULD STATION...
...UNDOUBTEDLY TRAINED FOR SUB-SEA COMBAT!
HE'S TRYING TO DISLODGE MY MINI-RESPIRATOR!
FISTS ARE USELESS IN THIS KIND OF SITUATION...
...BUT JUDO CAN WORK!
I'LL PUT A PIECE OF PAIN INTO HIS FOREARM!
AN ORDINARY PUNCH WOULDN'T EVEN HAVE THE FORCE NEEDED TO STUN HIM--
--BUT IF I YANK HIM TOWARD ME-- HARD--
12

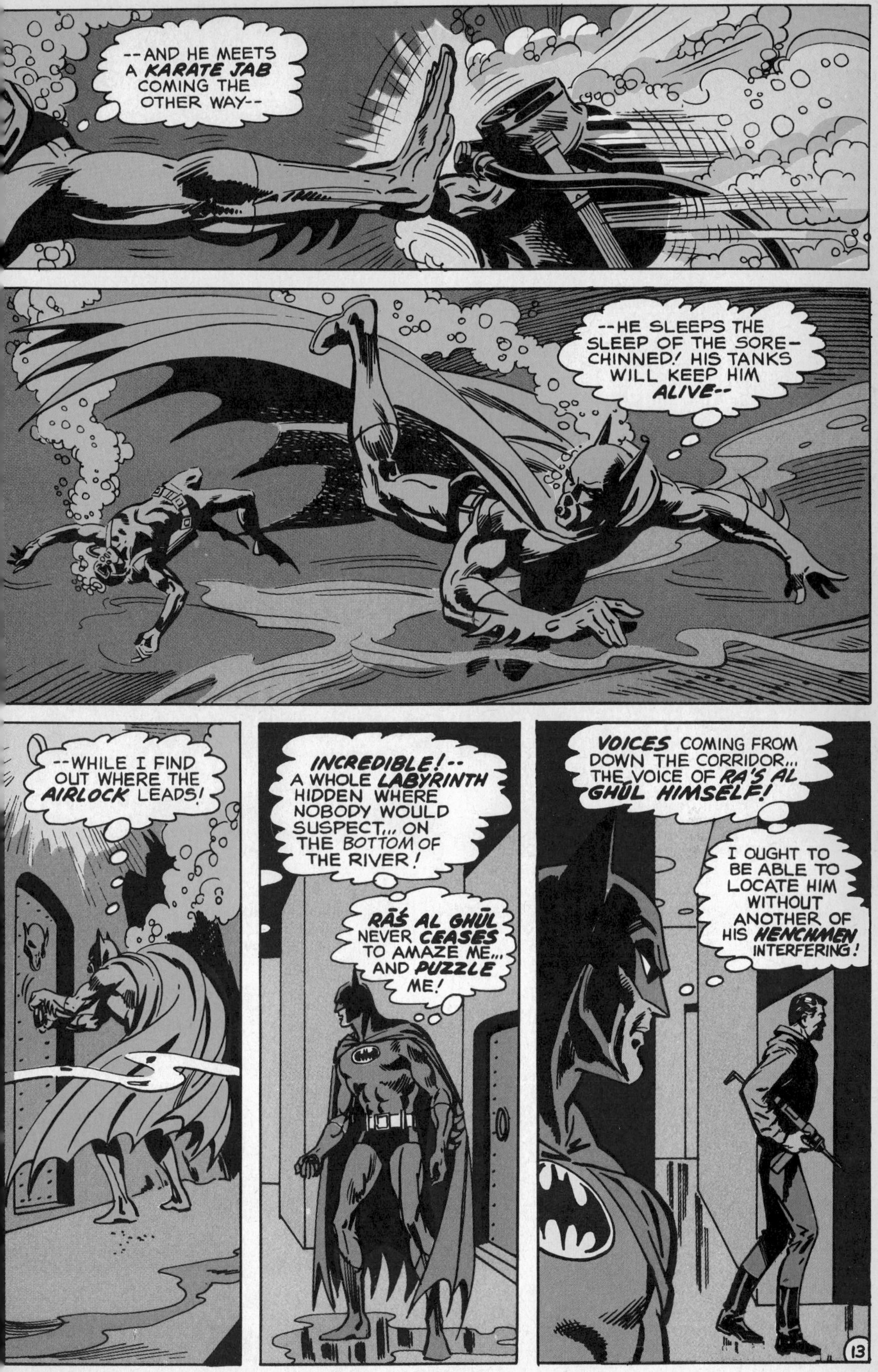
--AND HE MEETS A KARATE JAB COMING THE OTHER WAY--
--HE SLEEPS THE SLEEP OF THE SORE-CHINNED! HIS TANKS WILL KEEP HIM ALIVE--
--WHILE I FIND OUT WHERE THE AIRLOCK LEADS!
INCREDIBLE!-- A WHOLE LABYRINTH HIDDEN WHERE NOBODY WOULD SUSPECT... ON THE BOTTOM OF THE RIVER!
RA'S AL GHUL NEVER CEASES TO AMAZE ME... AND PUZZLE ME!
VOICES COMING FROM DOWN THE CORRIDOR... THE VOICE OF RA'S AL GHUL HIMSELF!
I OUGHT TO BE ABLE TO LOCATE HIM WITHOUT ANOTHER OF HIS HENCHMEN INTERFERING!
13

INDEED, IT *IS* AWESOME *RĀS AL GHŪL* THAT *THE BATMAN* HAS HEARD! FOR...

YOU ARE *PREPARED, DOCTOR MOON?*

YES, MASTER! TRUTH DRUGS HAVE BEEN ADDED TO THE SUBJECT'S *NUTRIENT* FLUIDS!

HE WILL ANSWER YOUR QUESTIONS!

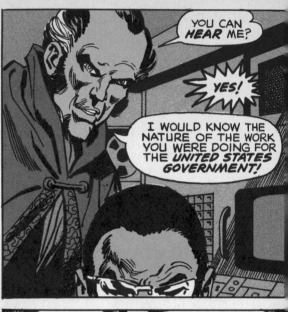

YOU CAN *HEAR* ME?

YES!

I WOULD KNOW THE NATURE OF THE WORK YOU WERE DOING FOR THE *UNITED STATES* GOVERNMENT!

WE PLANNED DIPLOMATIC MANEUVERS... FOR THE WAR IN *SOUTHEAST ASIA!*

AND THE EXACT *NATURE* OF THESE MANEUVERS?

DON'T ANSWER!

AH, OUR FRIEND THE MASTER *DETECTIVE!* ONCE MORE YOU DEMONSTRATE YOUR *PROWESS!* I HAD IMAGINED THIS FORTRESS *SECURE!*

SAVE THE *FLATTERY!* FROM *YOU,* IT'S *INSULTING*...UNLESS I'M *WRONG* ABOUT WHAT'S IN THAT TANK!

NO, I FEAR NOT! DETECTIVE, LOOK UPON ALL THAT REMAINS OF THE LATE *MISTER STERLING*... HIS *BRAIN!*

14

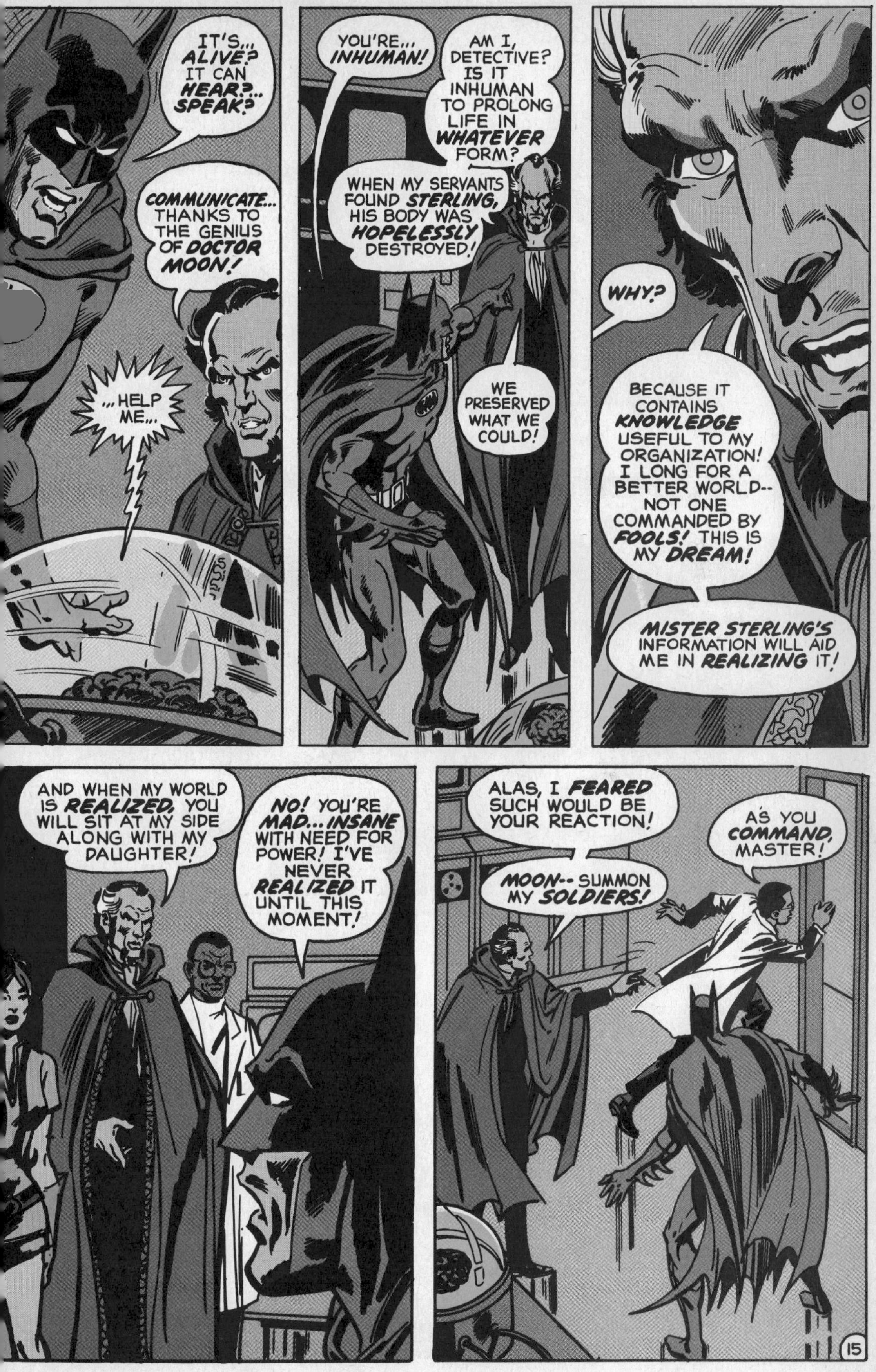
IT'S... ALIVE? IT CAN HEAR?... SPEAK?
COMMUNICATE... THANKS TO THE GENIUS OF DOCTOR MOON!
...HELP ME...
YOU'RE... INHUMAN!
AM I, DETECTIVE? IS IT INHUMAN TO PROLONG LIFE IN WHATEVER FORM?
WHEN MY SERVANTS FOUND STERLING, HIS BODY WAS HOPELESSLY DESTROYED!
WE PRESERVED WHAT WE COULD!
WHY?
BECAUSE IT CONTAINS KNOWLEDGE USEFUL TO MY ORGANIZATION! I LONG FOR A BETTER WORLD-- NOT ONE COMMANDED BY FOOLS! THIS IS MY DREAM!
MISTER STERLING'S INFORMATION WILL AID ME IN REALIZING IT!
AND WHEN MY WORLD IS REALIZED, YOU WILL SIT AT MY SIDE ALONG WITH MY DAUGHTER!
NO! YOU'RE MAD...INSANE WITH NEED FOR POWER! I'VE NEVER REALIZED IT UNTIL THIS MOMENT!
ALAS, I FEARED SUCH WOULD BE YOUR REACTION!
MOON-- SUMMON MY SOLDIERS!
AS YOU COMMAND, MASTER!
15

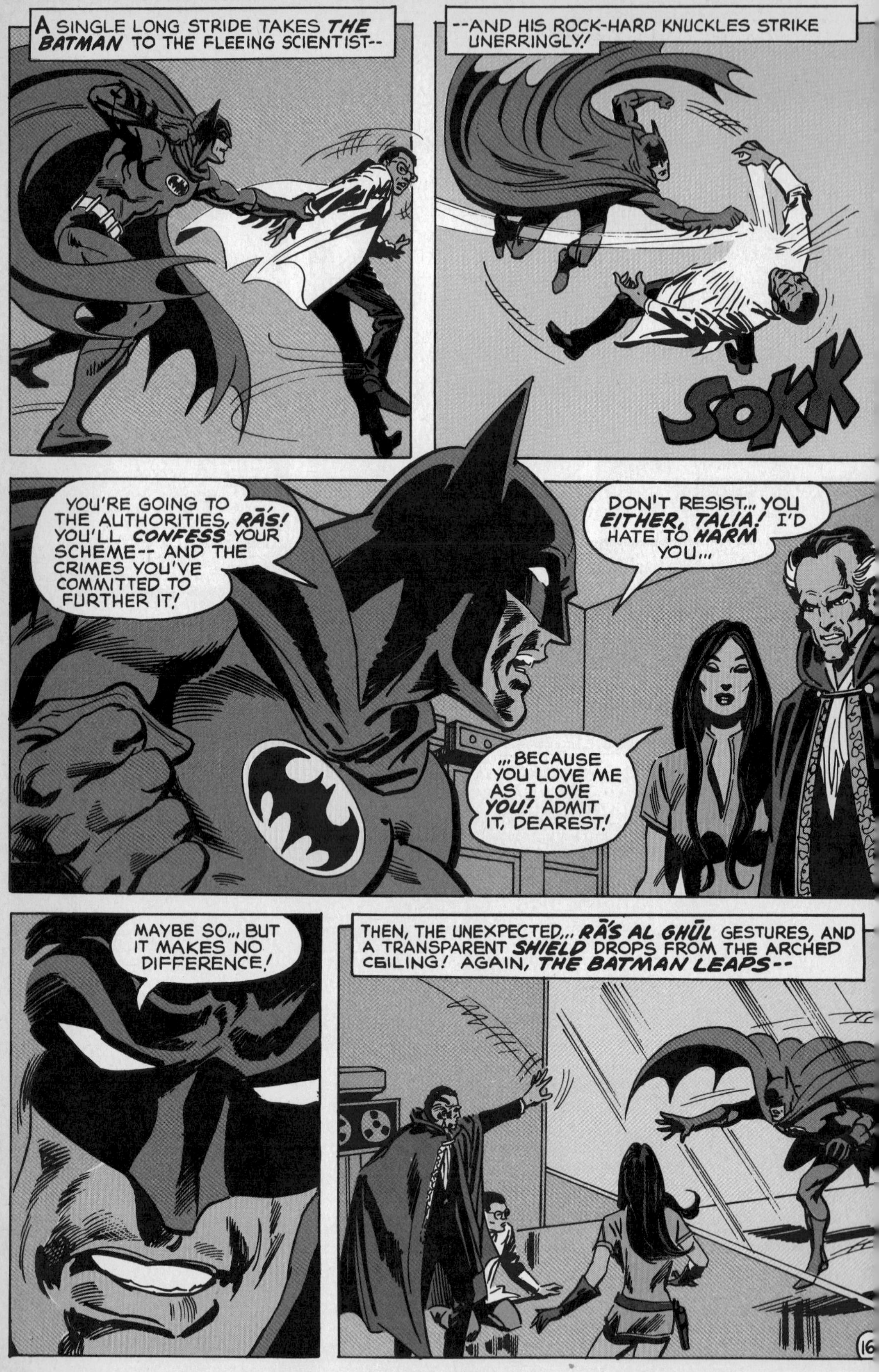
A SINGLE LONG STRIDE TAKES THE BATMAN TO THE FLEEING SCIENTIST--
--AND HIS ROCK-HARD KNUCKLES STRIKE UNERRINGLY!
SOKK
YOU'RE GOING TO THE AUTHORITIES, RĀ'S! YOU'LL CONFESS YOUR SCHEME-- AND THE CRIMES YOU'VE COMMITTED TO FURTHER IT!
DON'T RESIST... YOU EITHER, TALIA! I'D HATE TO HARM YOU...
...BECAUSE YOU LOVE ME AS I LOVE YOU! ADMIT IT, DEAREST!
MAYBE SO... BUT IT MAKES NO DIFFERENCE!
THEN, THE UNEXPECTED... RĀ'S AL GHŪL GESTURES, AND A TRANSPARENT SHIELD DROPS FROM THE ARCHED CEILING! AGAIN, THE BATMAN LEAPS--
16

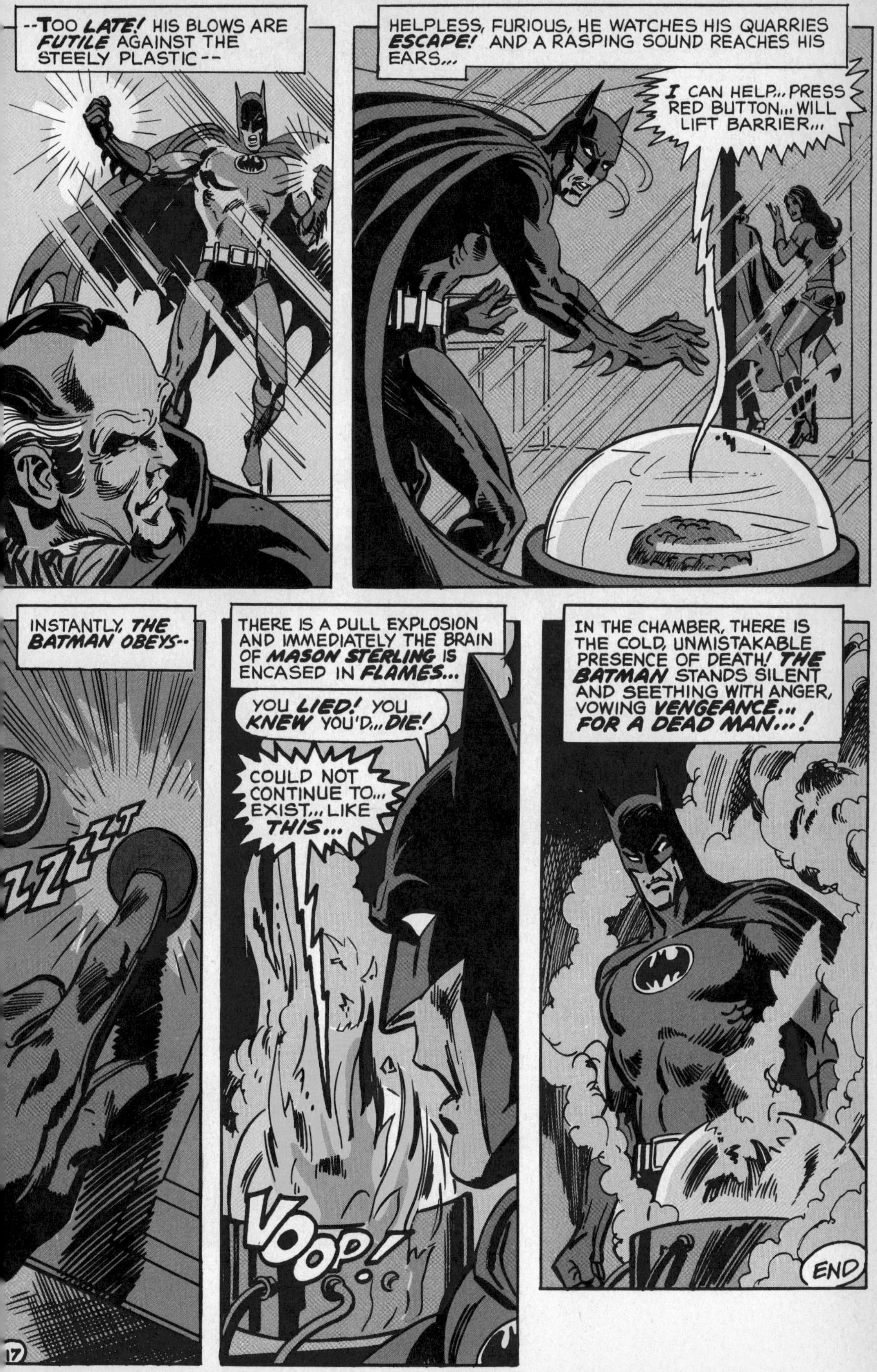
--TOO LATE! HIS BLOWS ARE FUTILE AGAINST THE STEELY PLASTIC--
HELPLESS, FURIOUS, HE WATCHES HIS QUARRIES ESCAPE! AND A RASPING SOUND REACHES HIS EARS...
I CAN HELP... PRESS RED BUTTON... WILL LIFT BARRIER...
INSTANTLY, THE BATMAN OBEYS--
ZZZZT
THERE IS A DULL EXPLOSION AND IMMEDIATELY THE BRAIN OF MASON STERLING IS ENCASED IN FLAMES...
YOU LIED! YOU KNEW YOU'D... DIE!
COULD NOT CONTINUE TO... EXIST... LIKE THIS...
VOOP!
IN THE CHAMBER, THERE IS THE COLD, UNMISTAKABLE PRESENCE OF DEATH! THE BATMAN STANDS SILENT AND SEETHING WITH ANGER, VOWING VENGEANCE... FOR A DEAD MAN...!
END
17

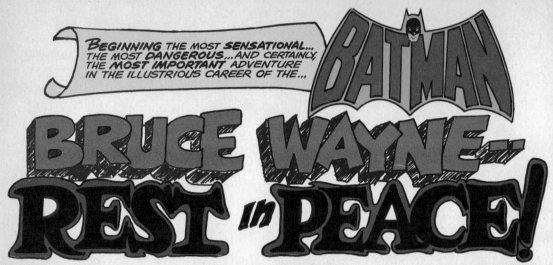

BEGINNING THE MOST SENSATIONAL... THE MOST DANGEROUS... AND CERTAINLY, THE MOST IMPORTANT ADVENTURE IN THE ILLUSTRIOUS CAREER OF THE...
BATMAN
BRUCE WAYNE-- REST in PEACE!
STORY: DENNY O'NEIL ART: IRV NOVICK & DICK GIORDANO EDITING: JULIUS SCHWARTZ
COLORS: TOM ZIUKO
AT THE OFFICE OF COMMISSIONER GORDON, OF THE GOTHAM CITY POLICE...
THE GOTHAM NEWS
15¢
BRUCE WAYNE VANISHES!
MILLIONAIRE BELIEVED DEAD IN JUNGLE PLANE CRASH!
IT'S TRAGIC, BATMAN... TRAGIC THAT WAYNE SHOULD DIE-- SO YOUNG... AND SO SENSELESSLY--!
HE WAS ONE MILLIONAIRE WHO USED HIS WEALTH-- INSTEAD OF LETTING IT USE HIM!
I WONDER WHY HE DARED FLY A SMALL PLANE OVER THAT JUNGLE-- ALONE?
WAYNE ALWAYS WAS A BIT HEADSTRONG!

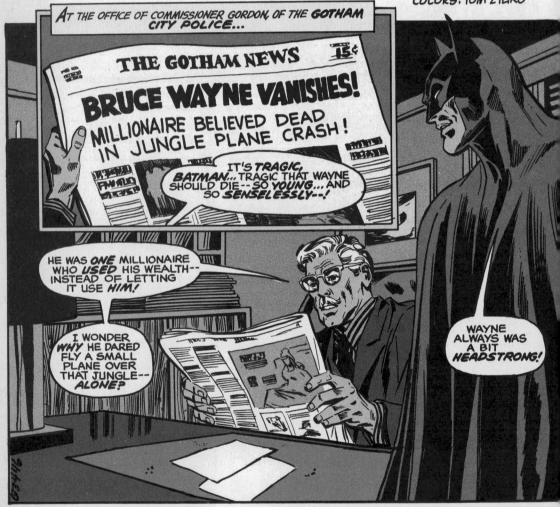

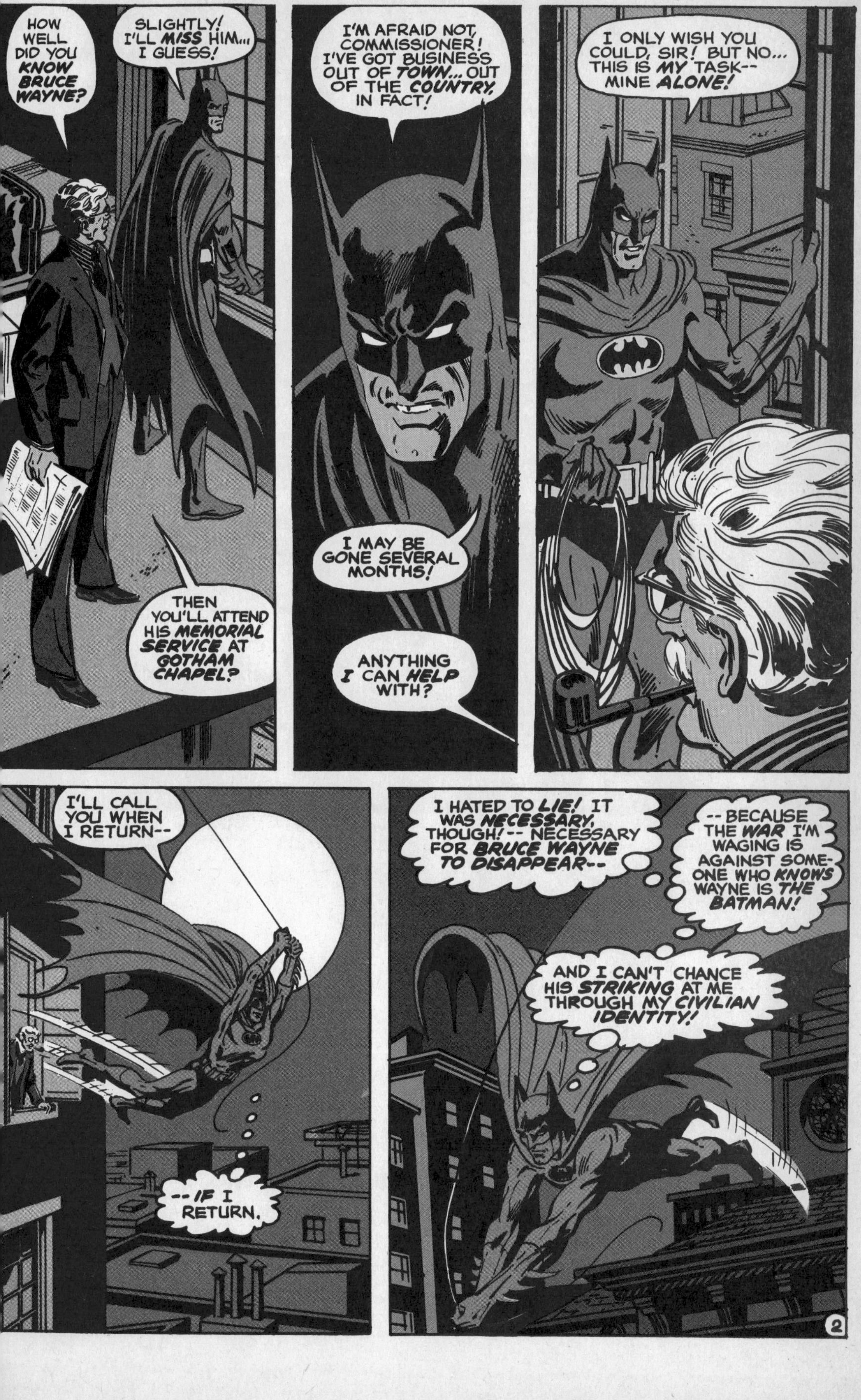
HOW WELL DID YOU KNOW BRUCE WAYNE?
SLIGHTLY! I'LL MISS HIM... I GUESS!
THEN YOU'LL ATTEND HIS MEMORIAL SERVICE AT GOTHAM CHAPEL?
I'M AFRAID NOT, COMMISSIONER! I'VE GOT BUSINESS OUT OF TOWN... OUT OF THE COUNTRY, IN FACT!
I MAY BE GONE SEVERAL MONTHS!
ANYTHING I CAN HELP WITH?
I ONLY WISH YOU COULD, SIR! BUT NO... THIS IS MY TASK-- MINE ALONE!
I'LL CALL YOU WHEN I RETURN--
--IF I RETURN.
I HATED TO LIE! IT WAS NECESSARY, THOUGH! -- NECESSARY FOR BRUCE WAYNE TO DISAPPEAR--
-- BECAUSE THE WAR I'M WAGING IS AGAINST SOMEONE WHO KNOWS WAYNE IS THE BATMAN!
AND I CAN'T CHANCE HIS STRIKING AT ME THROUGH MY CIVILIAN IDENTITY!
2

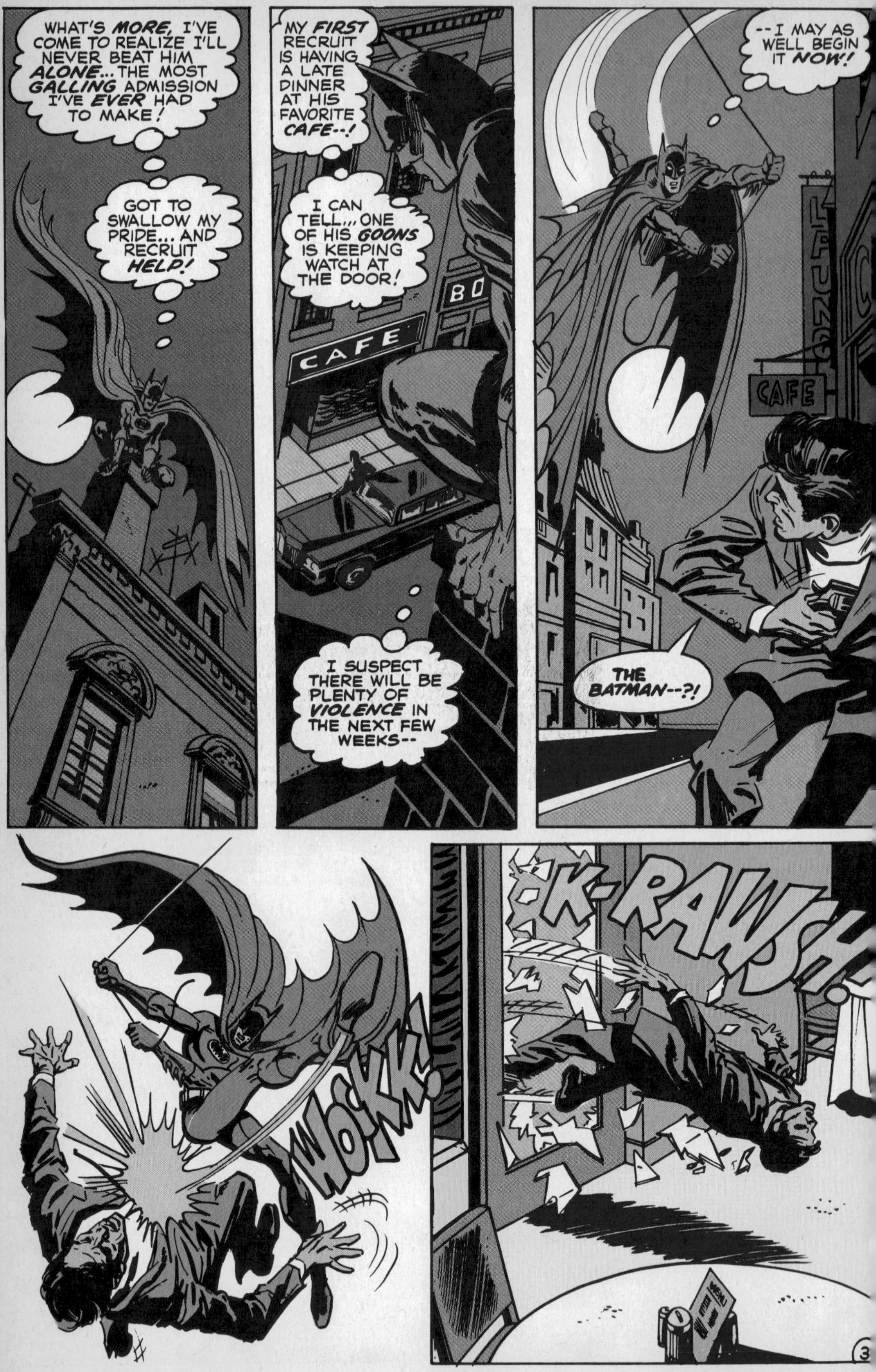
WHAT'S MORE, I'VE COME TO REALIZE I'LL NEVER BEAT HIM ALONE... THE MOST GALLING ADMISSION I'VE EVER HAD TO MAKE!
GOT TO SWALLOW MY PRIDE... AND RECRUIT HELP!
MY FIRST RECRUIT IS HAVING A LATE DINNER AT HIS FAVORITE CAFE--!
I CAN TELL... ONE OF HIS GOONS IS KEEPING WATCH AT THE DOOR!
CAFE
I SUSPECT THERE WILL BE PLENTY OF VIOLENCE IN THE NEXT FEW WEEKS--
--I MAY AS WELL BEGIN IT NOW!
CAFE
THE BATMAN--?!
WOKK!
K-RAWSH!
3

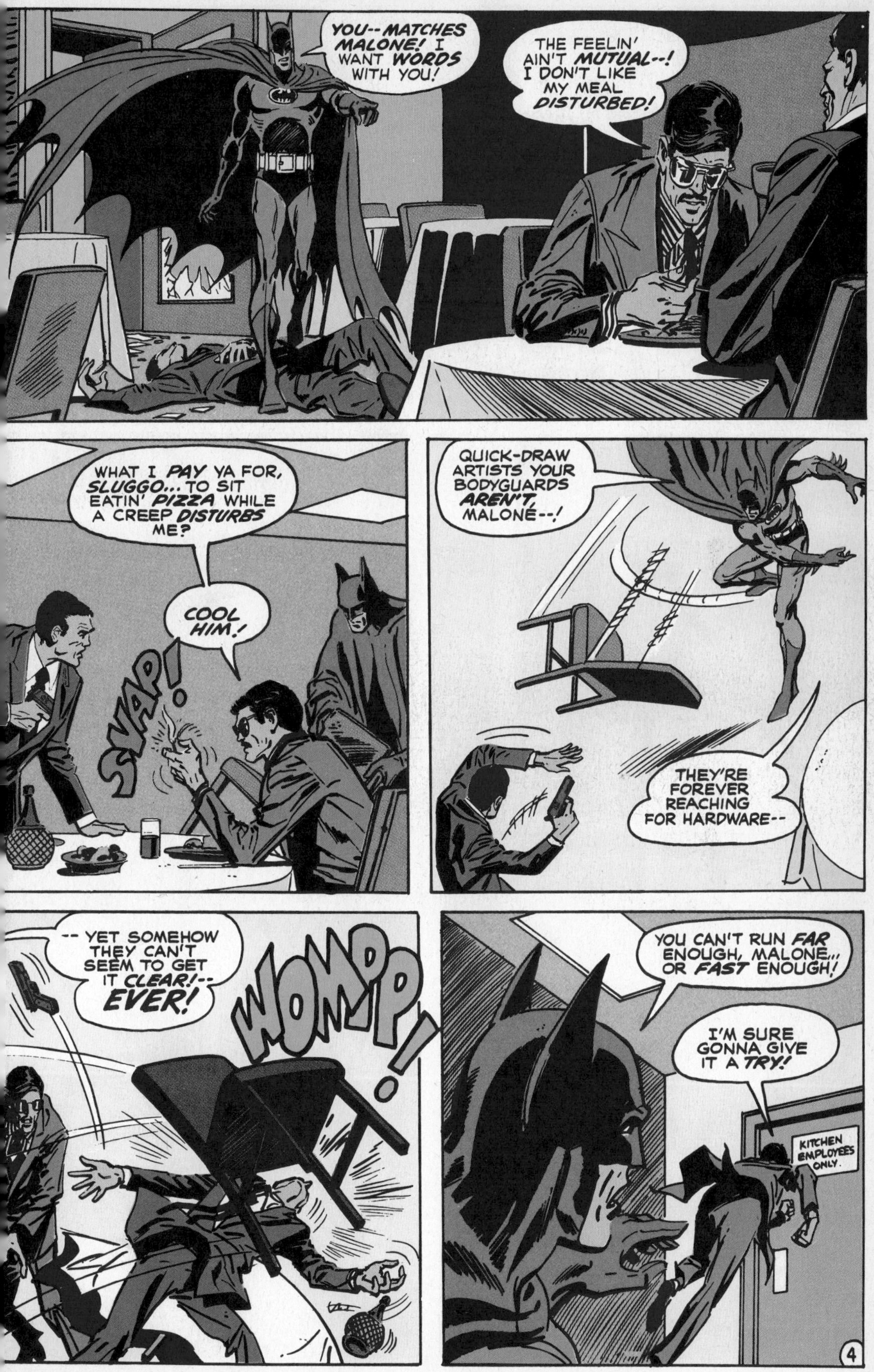
YOU--MATCHES MALONE! I WANT WORDS WITH YOU!
THE FEELIN' AIN'T MUTUAL--! I DON'T LIKE MY MEAL DISTURBED!
WHAT I PAY YA FOR, SLUGGO... TO SIT EATIN' PIZZA WHILE A CREEP DISTURBS ME?
COOL HIM!
SNAP!
QUICK-DRAW ARTISTS YOUR BODYGUARDS AREN'T, MALONE--!
THEY'RE FOREVER REACHING FOR HARDWARE--
-- YET SOMEHOW THEY CAN'T SEEM TO GET IT CLEAR!-- EVER!
WOMP!
YOU CAN'T RUN FAR ENOUGH, MALONE... OR FAST ENOUGH!
I'M SURE GONNA GIVE IT A TRY!
KITCHEN EMPLOYEES ONLY.
4

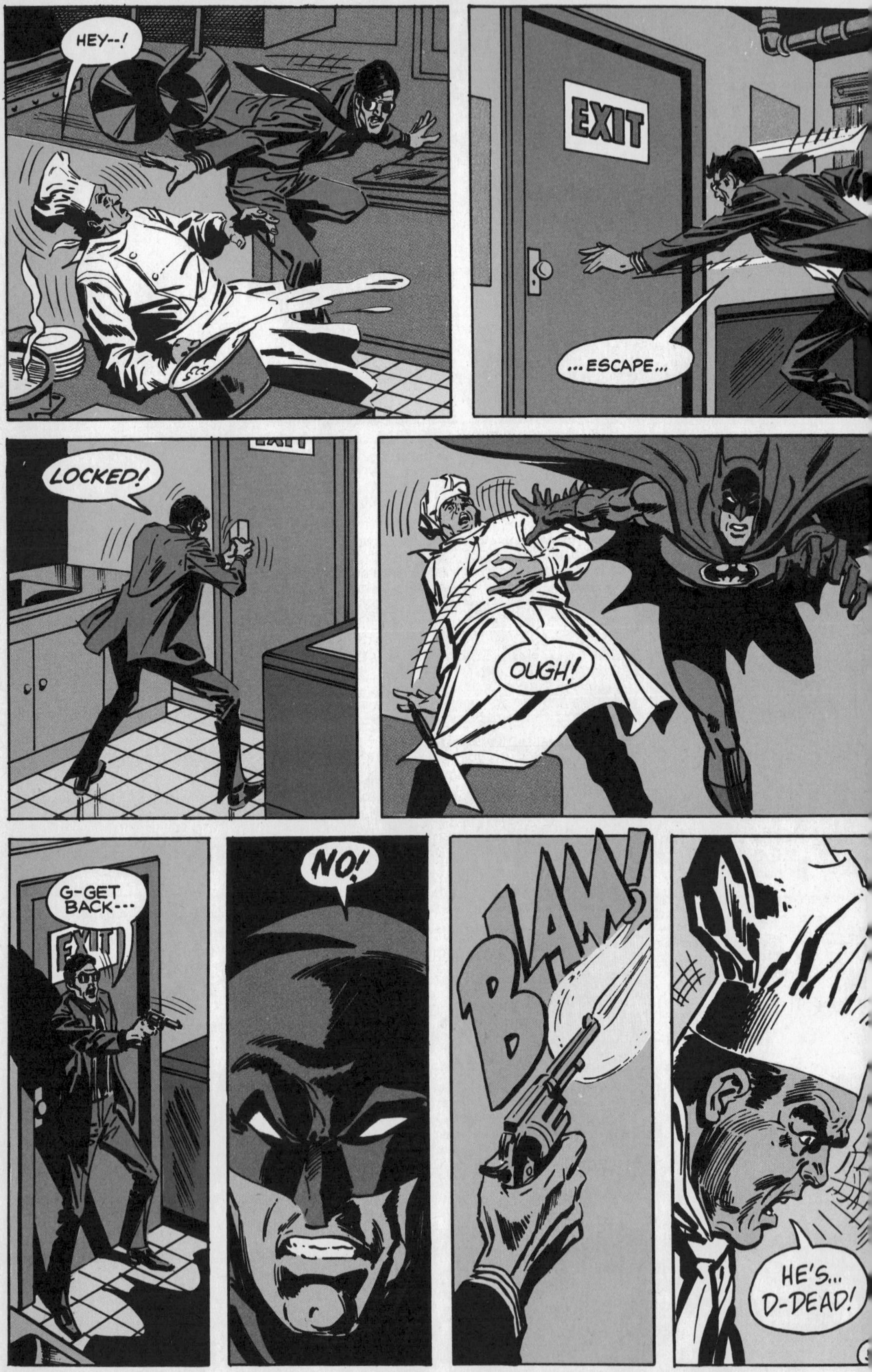
HEY--!
EXIT
...ESCAPE...
LOCKED!
OUGH!
G-GET BACK---
NO!
BLAM!
HE'S... D-DEAD!

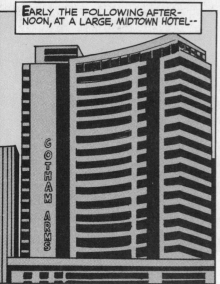

EARLY THE FOLLOWING AFTER-NOON, AT A LARGE, MIDTOWN HOTEL--

--A SINISTER FIGURE SCANS A CROWD...

MY *PIGEON* SHOULD BE PASSING THIS WAY! HE'S THE MAIN SPEAKER AT THE *BIOPHYSICS CONVENTION*--

--AND THOSE GUYS ARE THE *CONVENTIONEERS!*

SNAP

THERE HE IS-- *DOCTOR HARRIS BLAINE!* I'D BETTER WAIT TILL HE'S *ALONE* BEFORE I PUT MY *PROPOSITION* TO HIM!

HE'S HEADING FOR THE *ELEVATOR...* PROBABLY GOING TO HIS *ROOM!* AND SOMEBODY'S STICKING TO HIM LIKE *GLUE*--

--MAYBE SOMEBODY WITH THE SAME IDEA *I* HAVE!

I'LL JUST DRIFT IN *WITH* THEM...

A FEW MOMENTS LATER, ON THE TWENTY-EIGHTH FLOOR...

PARDON *ME*, DOCTOR BLAINE! MAY I *SPEAK* WITH YOU?

WHAT IS IT?

6

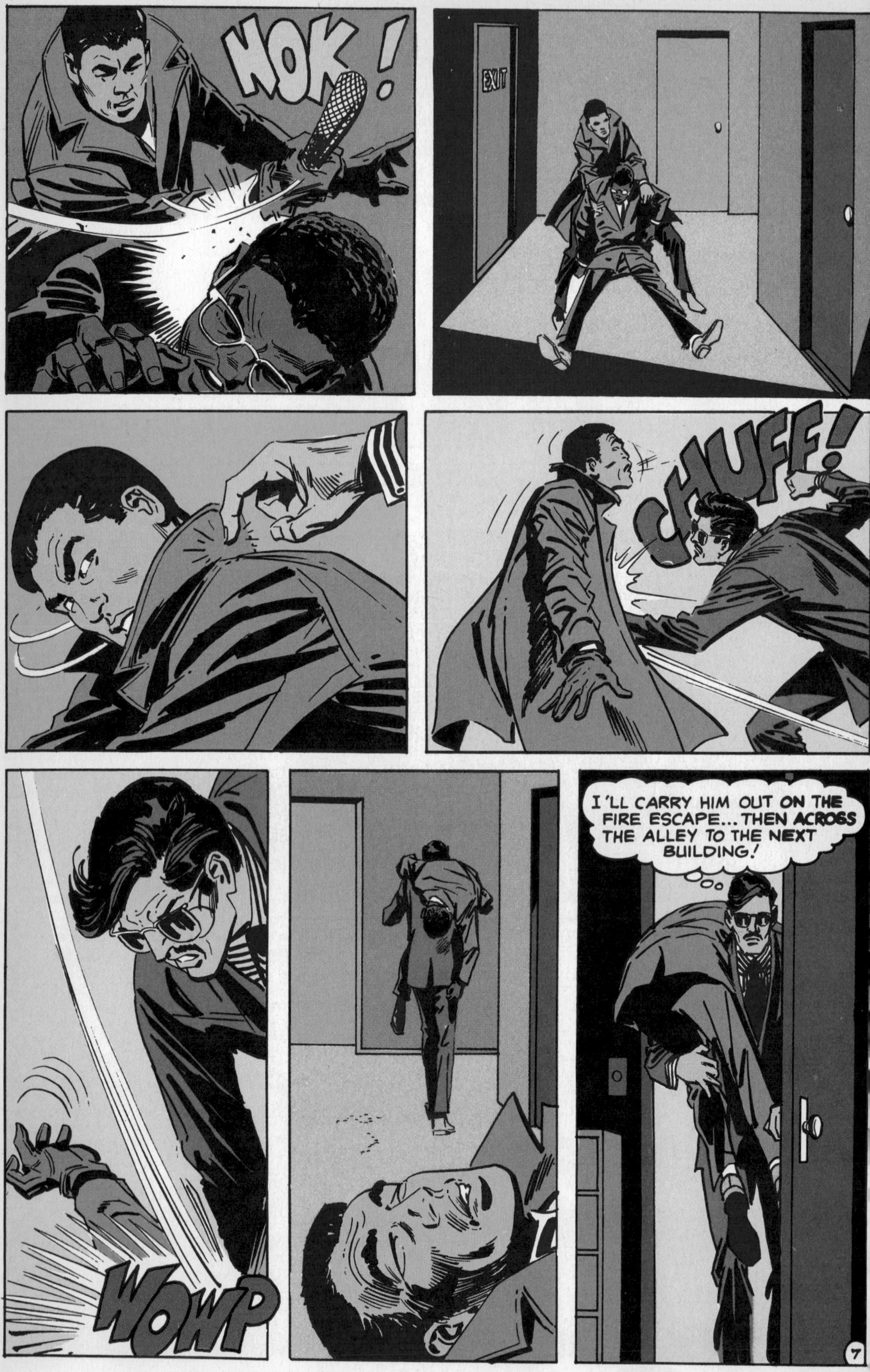
HOK!
EXIT
CHUFF!
WOWP
I'LL CARRY HIM OUT ON THE FIRE ESCAPE...THEN ACROSS THE ALLEY TO THE NEXT BUILDING!
7

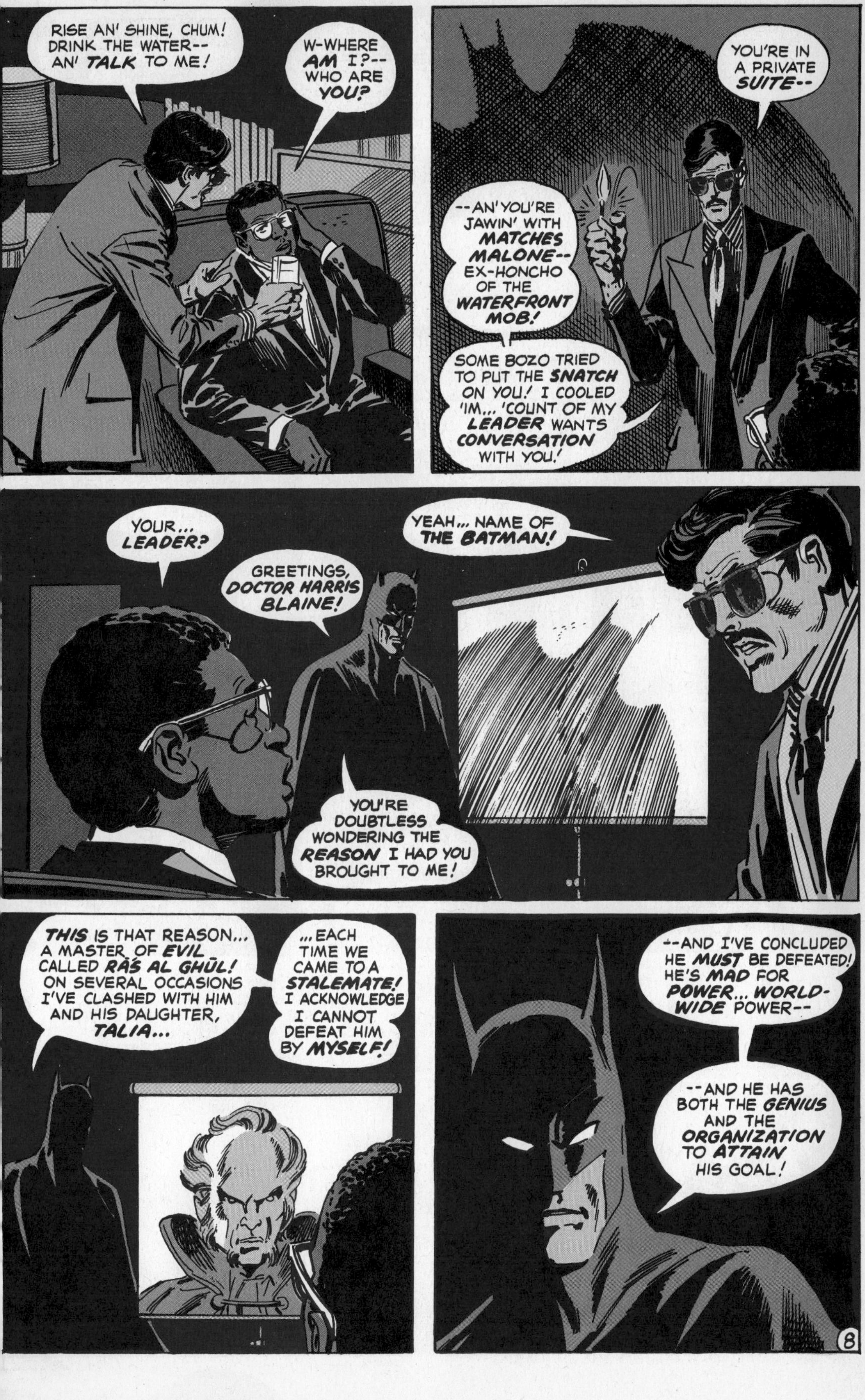
RISE AN' SHINE, CHUM! DRINK THE WATER-- AN' TALK TO ME!
W-WHERE AM I?-- WHO ARE YOU?
YOU'RE IN A PRIVATE SUITE--
--AN' YOU'RE JAWIN' WITH MATCHES MALONE-- EX-HONCHO OF THE WATERFRONT MOB!
SOME BOZO TRIED TO PUT THE SNATCH ON YOU! I COOLED 'IM... 'COUNT OF MY LEADER WANTS CONVERSATION WITH YOU!
YOUR... LEADER?
YEAH... NAME OF THE BATMAN!
GREETINGS, DOCTOR HARRIS BLAINE!
YOU'RE DOUBTLESS WONDERING THE REASON I HAD YOU BROUGHT TO ME!
THIS IS THAT REASON... A MASTER OF EVIL CALLED RĀS AL GHŪL! ON SEVERAL OCCASIONS I'VE CLASHED WITH HIM AND HIS DAUGHTER, TALIA...
...EACH TIME WE CAME TO A STALEMATE! I ACKNOWLEDGE I CANNOT DEFEAT HIM BY MYSELF!
--AND I'VE CONCLUDED HE MUST BE DEFEATED! HE'S MAD FOR POWER... WORLD-WIDE POWER--
--AND HE HAS BOTH THE GENIUS AND THE ORGANIZATION TO ATTAIN HIS GOAL!
8

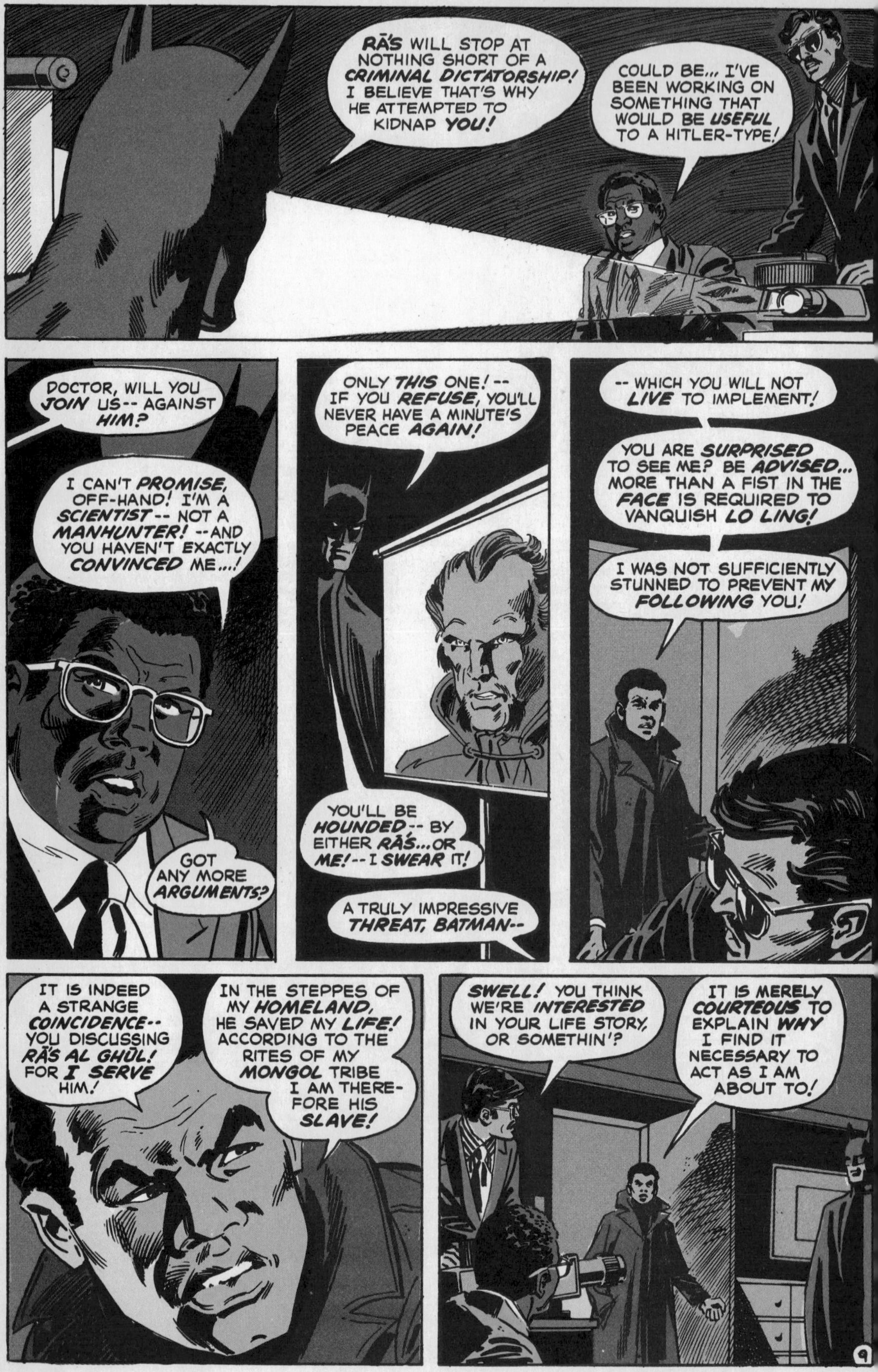
RĀ'S WILL STOP AT NOTHING SHORT OF A CRIMINAL DICTATORSHIP! I BELIEVE THAT'S WHY HE ATTEMPTED TO KIDNAP YOU!
COULD BE... I'VE BEEN WORKING ON SOMETHING THAT WOULD BE USEFUL TO A HITLER-TYPE!
DOCTOR, WILL YOU JOIN US-- AGAINST HIM?
I CAN'T PROMISE, OFF-HAND! I'M A SCIENTIST-- NOT A MANHUNTER! --AND YOU HAVEN'T EXACTLY CONVINCED ME...!
GOT ANY MORE ARGUMENTS?
ONLY THIS ONE! -- IF YOU REFUSE, YOU'LL NEVER HAVE A MINUTE'S PEACE AGAIN!
YOU'LL BE HOUNDED-- BY EITHER RĀ'S...OR ME!--I SWEAR IT!
A TRULY IMPRESSIVE THREAT, BATMAN--
-- WHICH YOU WILL NOT LIVE TO IMPLEMENT!
YOU ARE SURPRISED TO SEE ME? BE ADVISED... MORE THAN A FIST IN THE FACE IS REQUIRED TO VANQUISH LO LING!
I WAS NOT SUFFICIENTLY STUNNED TO PREVENT MY FOLLOWING YOU!
IT IS INDEED A STRANGE COINCIDENCE-- YOU DISCUSSING RĀ'S AL GHŪL! FOR I SERVE HIM!
IN THE STEPPES OF MY HOMELAND, HE SAVED MY LIFE! ACCORDING TO THE RITES OF MY MONGOL TRIBE I AM THEREFORE HIS SLAVE!
SWELL! YOU THINK WE'RE INTERESTED IN YOUR LIFE STORY, OR SOMETHIN'?
IT IS MERELY COURTEOUS TO EXPLAIN WHY I FIND IT NECESSARY TO ACT AS I AM ABOUT TO!
9

MASTER *RĂS AL GHŨL* CHARGED ME TO CAPTURE *DOCTOR BLAINE*-- UNLESS I HAPPENED TO MEET *THE BATMAN!*

IN SUCH AN INSTANCE, MY *GREATEST* PRIORITY IS TO *ELIMINATE THE BATMAN*-- A COMMAND THE MASTER'S *DAUGHTER* DISAGREES WITH, BY THE WAY!

HOWEVER, I AM NOT *TALIA'S* CREATURE-- BUT HER *FATHER'S!* THUS--

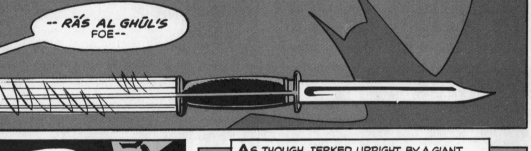

-- RĂS AL GHŨL'S FOE--

--DIES!

SHU**NK!**

AS THOUGH JERKED UPRIGHT BY A GIANT HAND, MALONE *STANDS*, AND SHOUTS--

YA DIRTY... MURDERIN'... SWINE! I'LL PUT YA ON A SLAB *PERSONALLY!*

10

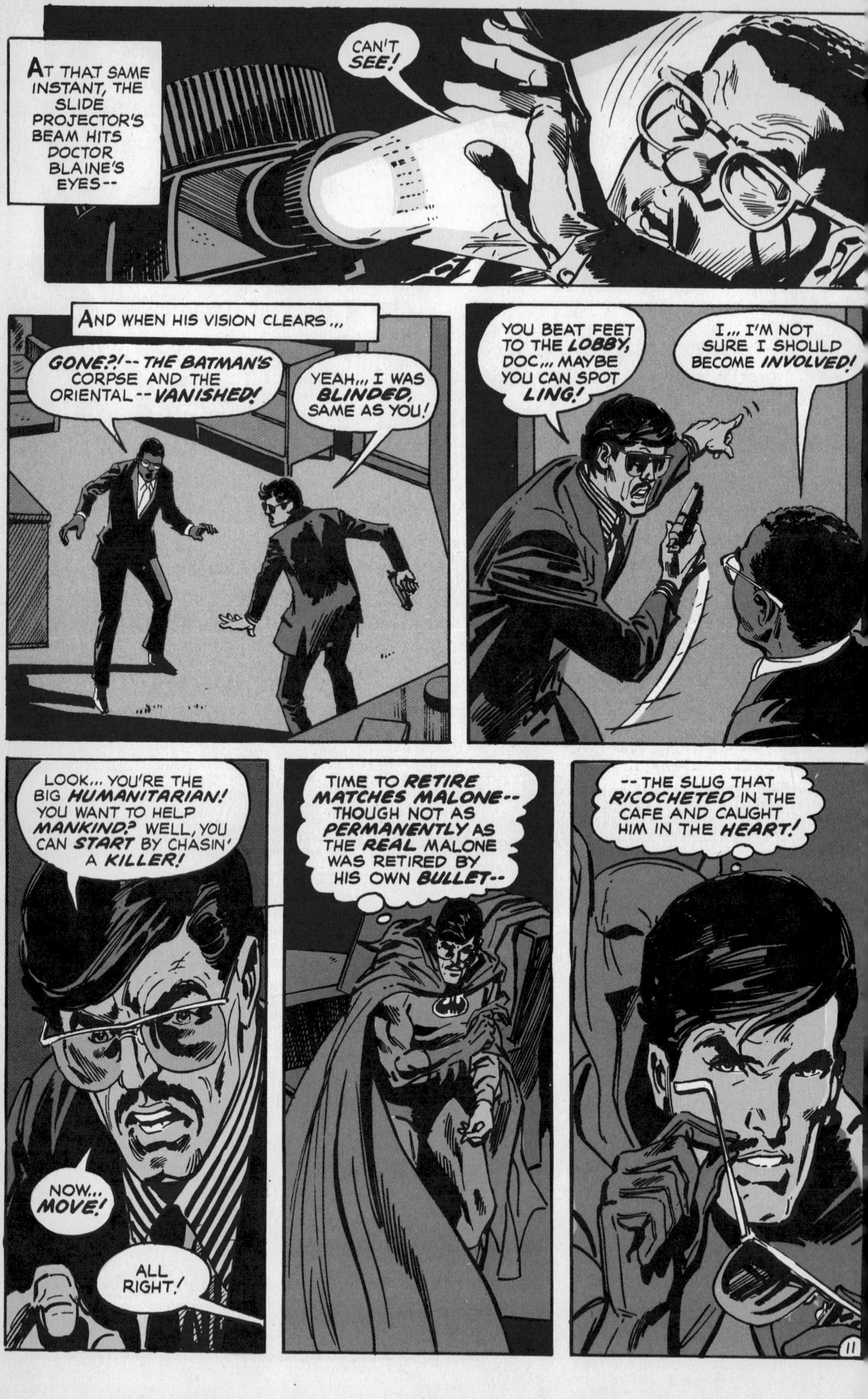
AT THAT SAME INSTANT, THE SLIDE PROJECTOR'S BEAM HITS DOCTOR BLAINE'S EYES--
CAN'T SEE!
AND WHEN HIS VISION CLEARS...
GONE?!--THE BATMAN'S CORPSE AND THE ORIENTAL--VANISHED!
YEAH... I WAS BLINDED, SAME AS YOU!
YOU BEAT FEET TO THE LOBBY, DOC... MAYBE YOU CAN SPOT LING!
I... I'M NOT SURE I SHOULD BECOME INVOLVED!
LOOK... YOU'RE THE BIG HUMANITARIAN! YOU WANT TO HELP MANKIND? WELL, YOU CAN START BY CHASIN' A KILLER!
NOW... MOVE!
ALL RIGHT!
TIME TO RETIRE MATCHES MALONE-- THOUGH NOT AS PERMANENTLY AS THE REAL MALONE WAS RETIRED BY HIS OWN BULLET--
--THE SLUG THAT RICOCHETED IN THE CAFE AND CAUGHT HIM IN THE HEART!
11

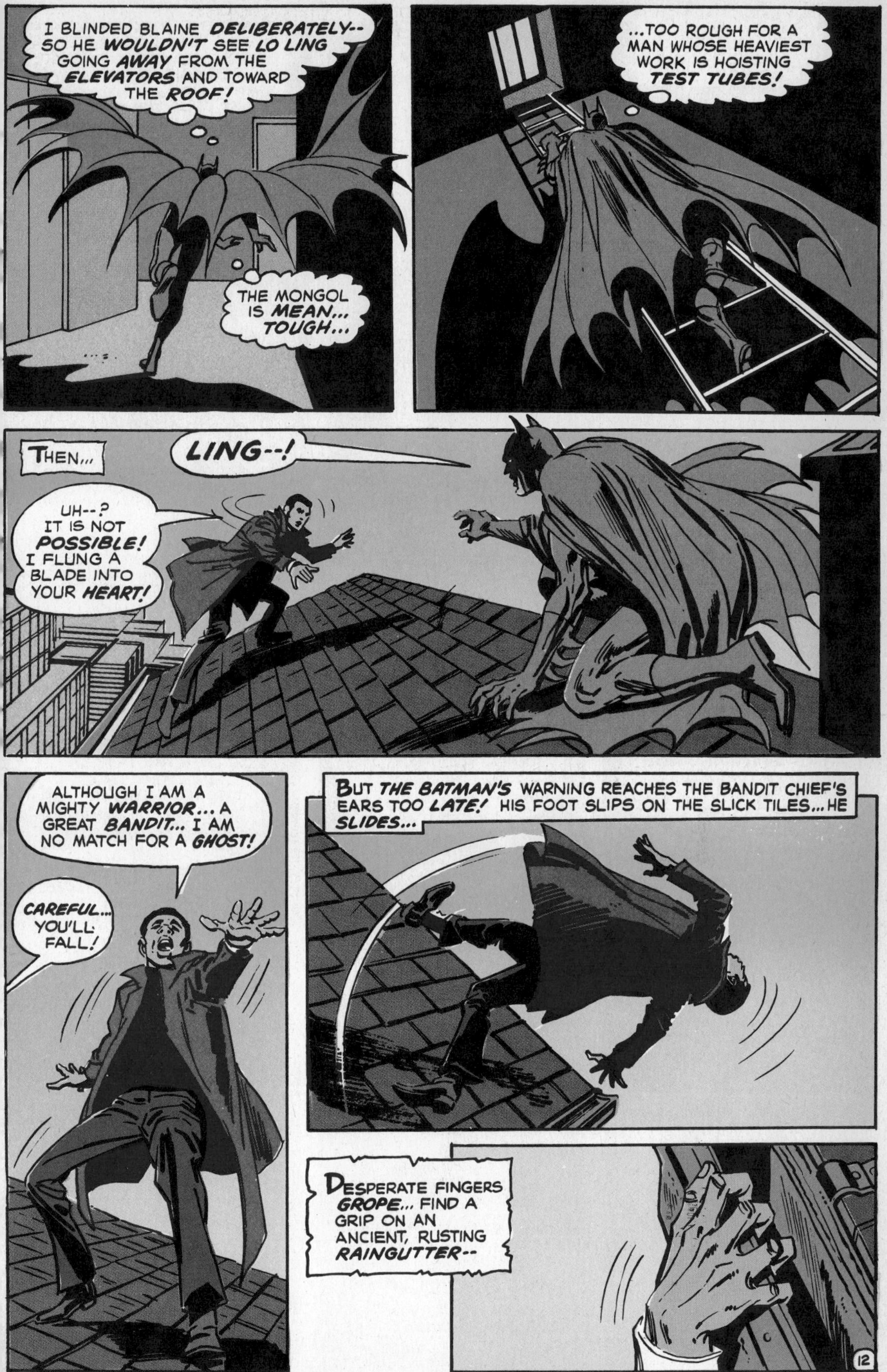
I BLINDED BLAINE DELIBERATELY-- SO HE WOULDN'T SEE LO LING GOING AWAY FROM THE ELEVATORS AND TOWARD THE ROOF!
THE MONGOL IS MEAN... TOUGH...
...TOO ROUGH FOR A MAN WHOSE HEAVIEST WORK IS HOISTING TEST TUBES!
THEN,,,
LING--!
UH--? IT IS NOT POSSIBLE! I FLUNG A BLADE INTO YOUR HEART!
ALTHOUGH I AM A MIGHTY WARRIOR... A GREAT BANDIT... I AM NO MATCH FOR A GHOST!
CAREFUL... YOU'LL FALL!
BUT THE BATMAN'S WARNING REACHES THE BANDIT CHIEF'S EARS TOO LATE! HIS FOOT SLIPS ON THE SLICK TILES... HE SLIDES...
DESPERATE FINGERS GROPE... FIND A GRIP ON AN ANCIENT, RUSTING RAINGUTTER--
12

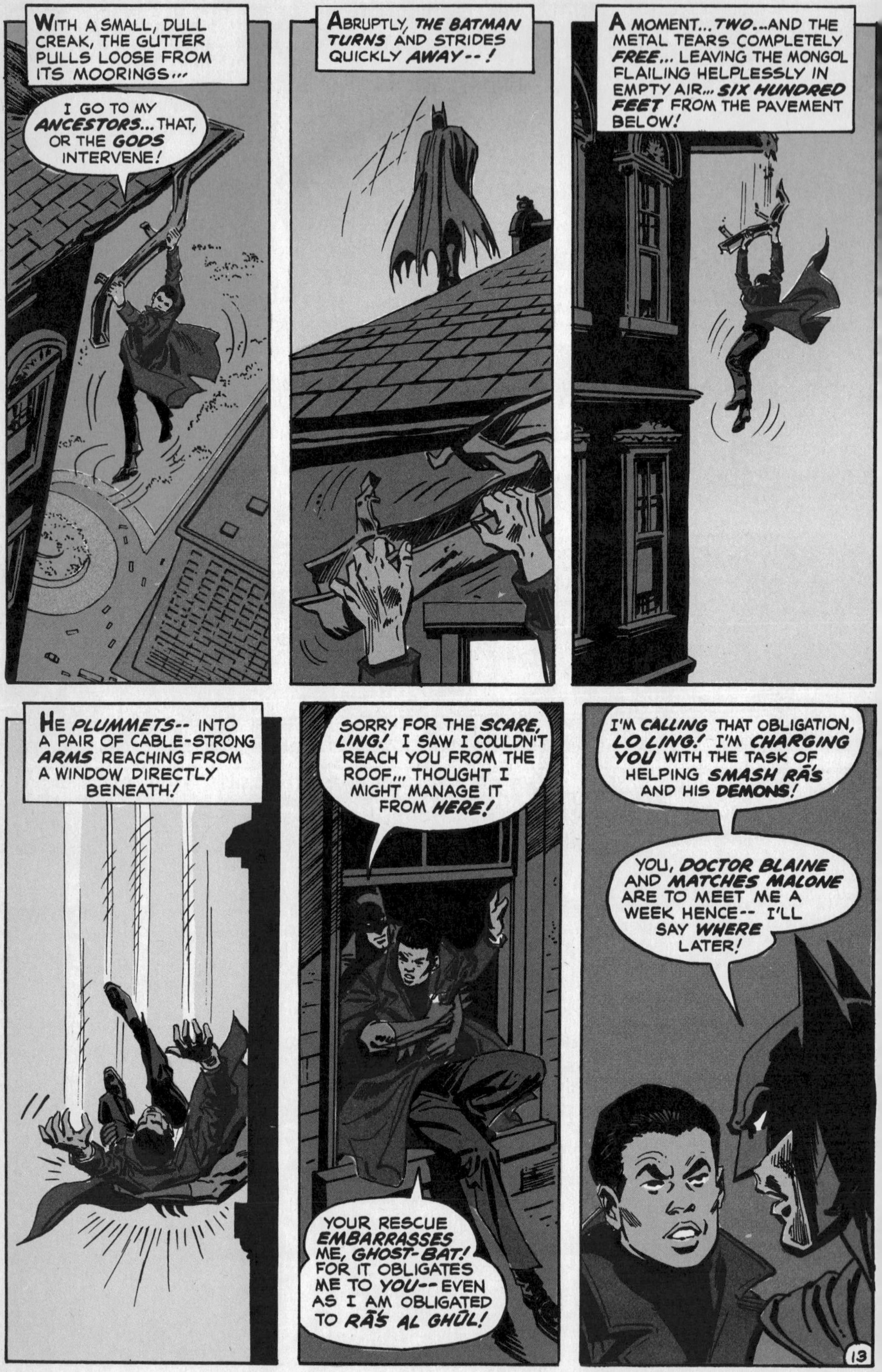
WITH A SMALL, DULL CREAK, THE GUTTER PULLS LOOSE FROM ITS MOORINGS...
I GO TO MY ANCESTORS... THAT, OR THE GODS INTERVENE!
ABRUPTLY, THE BATMAN TURNS AND STRIDES QUICKLY AWAY--!
A MOMENT... TWO... AND THE METAL TEARS COMPLETELY FREE... LEAVING THE MONGOL FLAILING HELPLESSLY IN EMPTY AIR... SIX HUNDRED FEET FROM THE PAVEMENT BELOW!
HE PLUMMETS-- INTO A PAIR OF CABLE-STRONG ARMS REACHING FROM A WINDOW DIRECTLY BENEATH!
SORRY FOR THE SCARE, LING! I SAW I COULDN'T REACH YOU FROM THE ROOF... THOUGHT I MIGHT MANAGE IT FROM HERE!
YOUR RESCUE EMBARRASSES ME, GHOST-BAT! FOR IT OBLIGATES ME TO YOU-- EVEN AS I AM OBLIGATED TO RĀ'S AL GHŪL!
I'M CALLING THAT OBLIGATION, LO LING! I'M CHARGING YOU WITH THE TASK OF HELPING SMASH RĀ'S AND HIS DEMONS!
YOU, DOCTOR BLAINE AND MATCHES MALONE ARE TO MEET ME A WEEK HENCE-- I'LL SAY WHERE LATER!
13

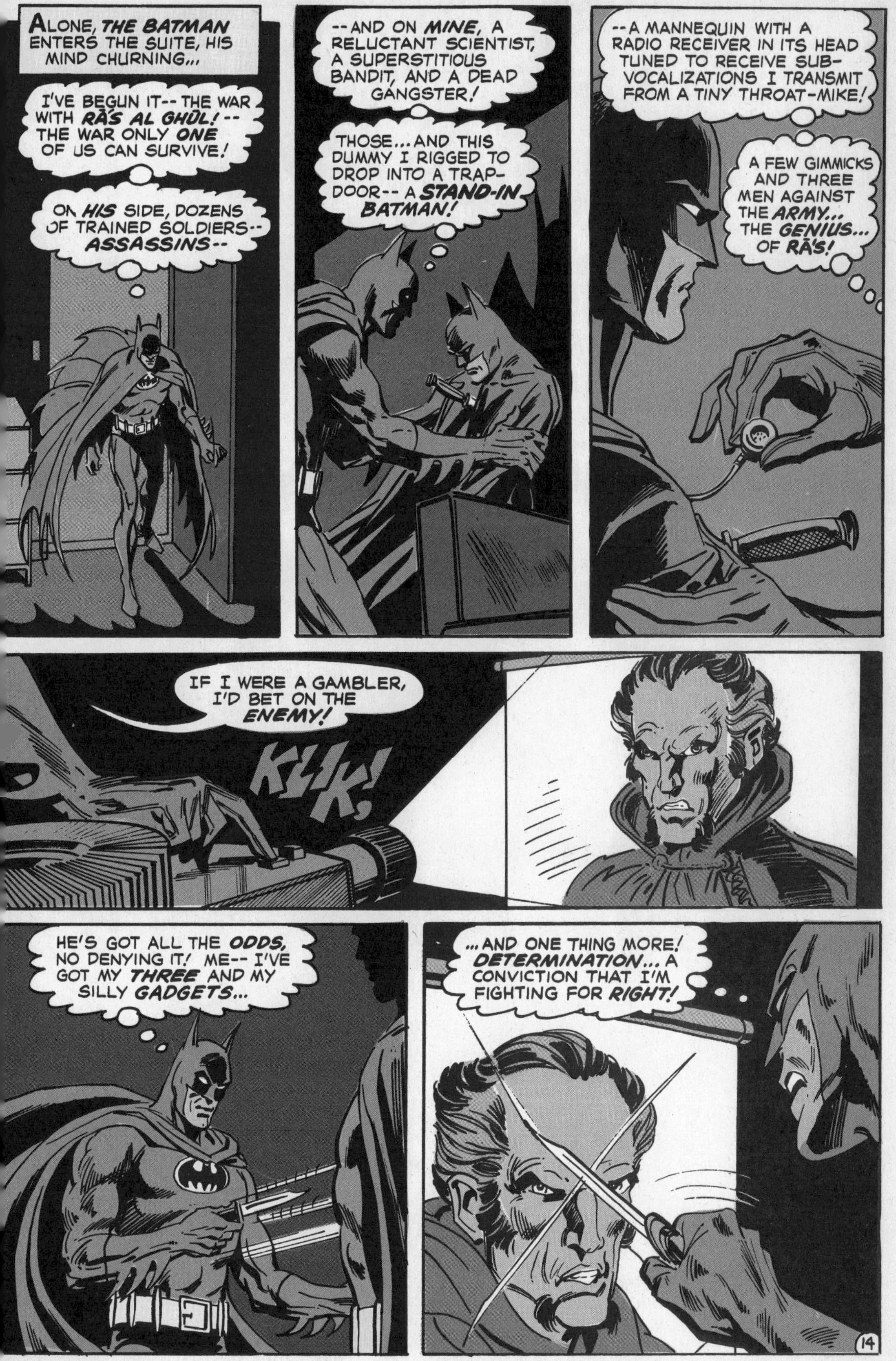
ALONE, THE BATMAN ENTERS THE SUITE, HIS MIND CHURNING...
I'VE BEGUN IT-- THE WAR WITH RĀ'S AL GHŪL! -- THE WAR ONLY ONE OF US CAN SURVIVE!
ON HIS SIDE, DOZENS OF TRAINED SOLDIERS-- ASSASSINS--
--AND ON MINE, A RELUCTANT SCIENTIST, A SUPERSTITIOUS BANDIT, AND A DEAD GANGSTER!
THOSE... AND THIS DUMMY I RIGGED TO DROP INTO A TRAP-DOOR-- A STAND-IN BATMAN!
--A MANNEQUIN WITH A RADIO RECEIVER IN ITS HEAD TUNED TO RECEIVE SUB-VOCALIZATIONS I TRANSMIT FROM A TINY THROAT-MIKE!
A FEW GIMMICKS AND THREE MEN AGAINST THE ARMY... THE GENIUS... OF RĀ'S!
IF I WERE A GAMBLER, I'D BET ON THE ENEMY!
KLIK!
HE'S GOT ALL THE ODDS, NO DENYING IT! ME-- I'VE GOT MY THREE AND MY SILLY GADGETS...
...AND ONE THING MORE! DETERMINATION... A CONVICTION THAT I'M FIGHTING FOR RIGHT!
14

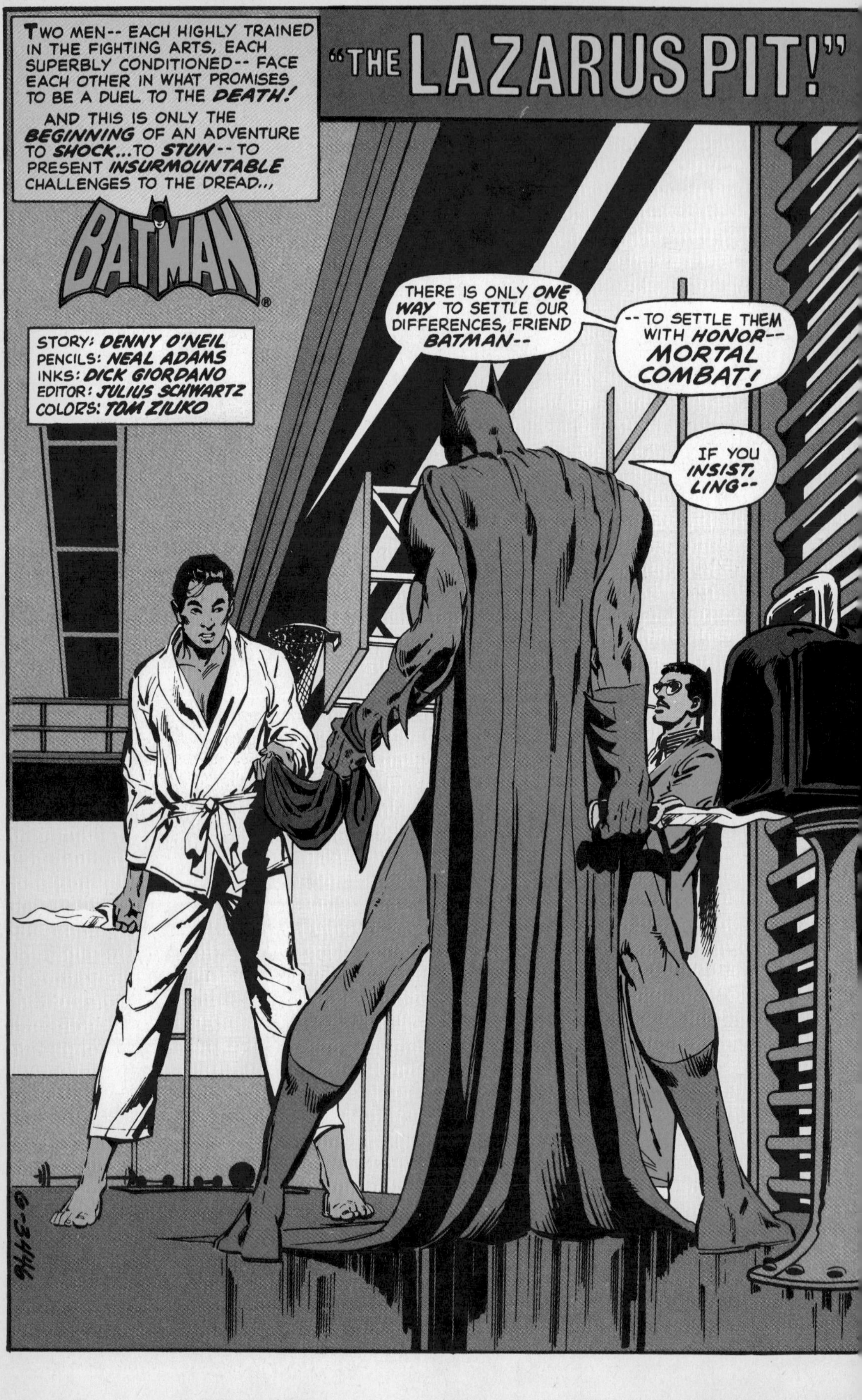
TWO MEN-- EACH HIGHLY TRAINED IN THE FIGHTING ARTS, EACH SUPERBLY CONDITIONED-- FACE EACH OTHER IN WHAT PROMISES TO BE A DUEL TO THE DEATH!
AND THIS IS ONLY THE BEGINNING OF AN ADVENTURE TO SHOCK...TO STUN-- TO PRESENT INSURMOUNTABLE CHALLENGES TO THE DREAD...,
BATMAN
"THE LAZARUS PIT!"
STORY: DENNY O'NEIL
PENCILS: NEAL ADAMS
INKS: DICK GIORDANO
EDITOR: JULIUS SCHWARTZ
COLORS: TOM ZIUKO
THERE IS ONLY ONE WAY TO SETTLE OUR DIFFERENCES, FRIEND BATMAN--
-- TO SETTLE THEM WITH HONOR-- MORTAL COMBAT!
IF YOU INSIST, LING--
G-3446

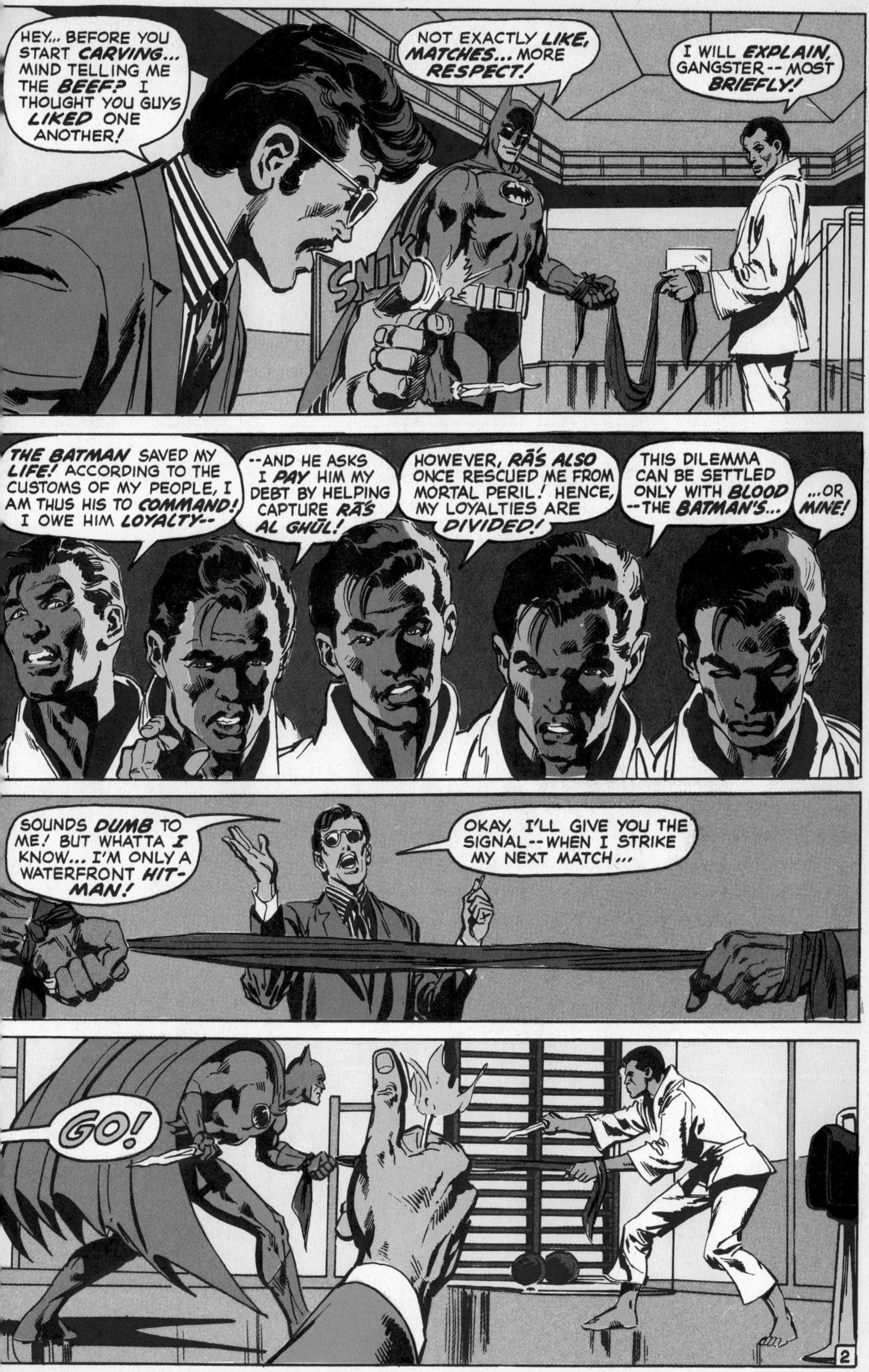
HEY... BEFORE YOU START CARVING... MIND TELLING ME THE BEEF? I THOUGHT YOU GUYS LIKED ONE ANOTHER!
NOT EXACTLY LIKE, MATCHES... MORE RESPECT!
I WILL EXPLAIN, GANGSTER -- MOST BRIEFLY!
SNIK
THE BATMAN SAVED MY LIFE! ACCORDING TO THE CUSTOMS OF MY PEOPLE, I AM THUS HIS TO COMMAND! I OWE HIM LOYALTY--
--AND HE ASKS I PAY HIM MY DEBT BY HELPING CAPTURE RĀ'S AL GHŪL!
HOWEVER, RĀ'S ALSO ONCE RESCUED ME FROM MORTAL PERIL! HENCE, MY LOYALTIES ARE DIVIDED!
THIS DILEMMA CAN BE SETTLED ONLY WITH BLOOD --THE BATMAN'S...
...OR MINE!
SOUNDS DUMB TO ME! BUT WHATTA I KNOW... I'M ONLY A WATERFRONT HIT-MAN!
OKAY, I'LL GIVE YOU THE SIGNAL--WHEN I STRIKE MY NEXT MATCH...
GO!
2

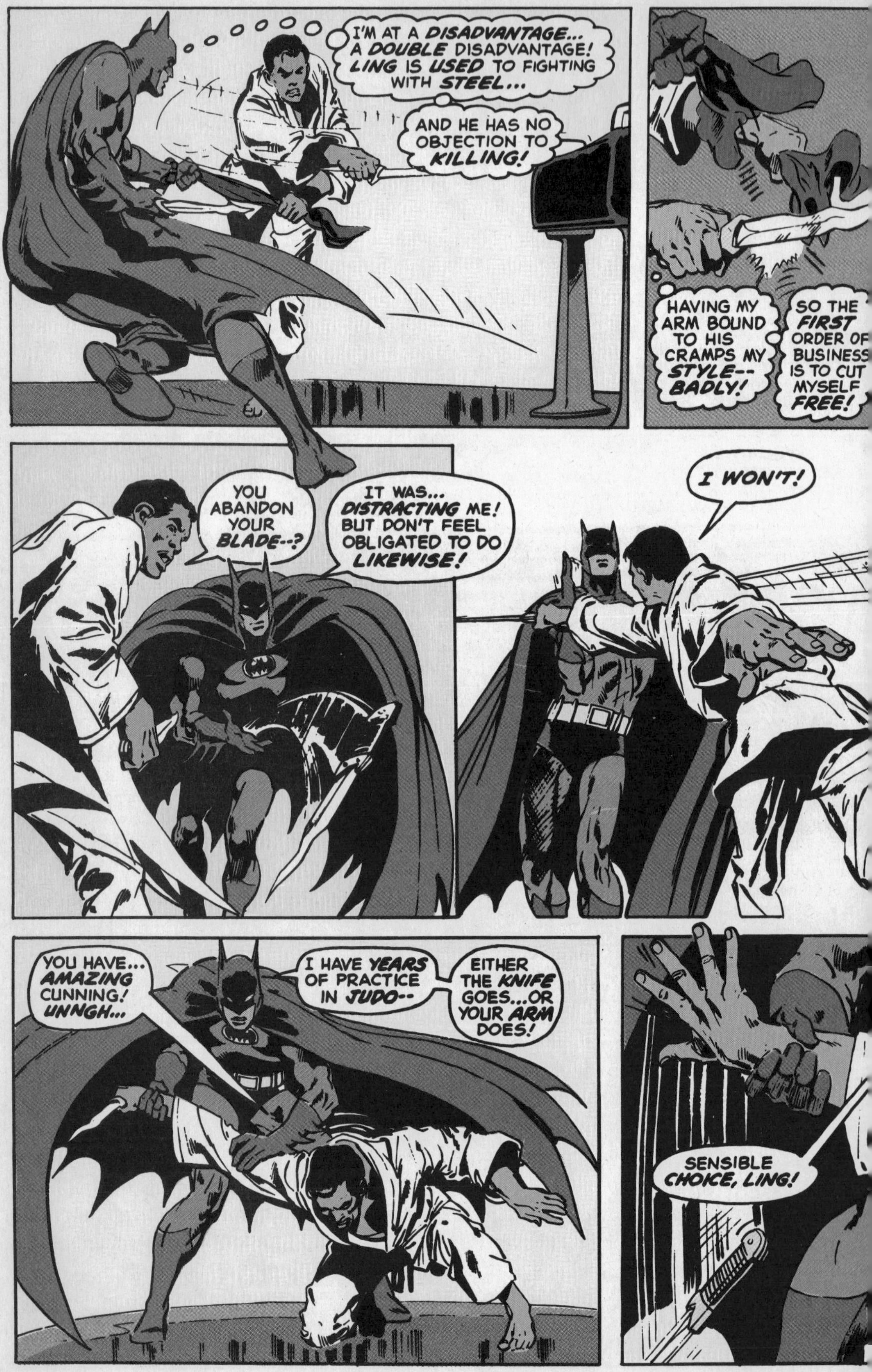
I'M AT A DISADVANTAGE... A DOUBLE DISADVANTAGE! LING IS USED TO FIGHTING WITH STEEL...
AND HE HAS NO OBJECTION TO KILLING!
HAVING MY ARM BOUND TO HIS CRAMPS MY STYLE-- BADLY!
SO THE FIRST ORDER OF BUSINESS IS TO CUT MYSELF FREE!
YOU ABANDON YOUR BLADE--?
IT WAS... DISTRACTING ME! BUT DON'T FEEL OBLIGATED TO DO LIKEWISE!
I WON'T!
YOU HAVE... AMAZING CUNNING! UNNGH...
I HAVE YEARS OF PRACTICE IN JUDO--
EITHER THE KNIFE GOES...OR YOUR ARM DOES!
SENSIBLE CHOICE, LING!

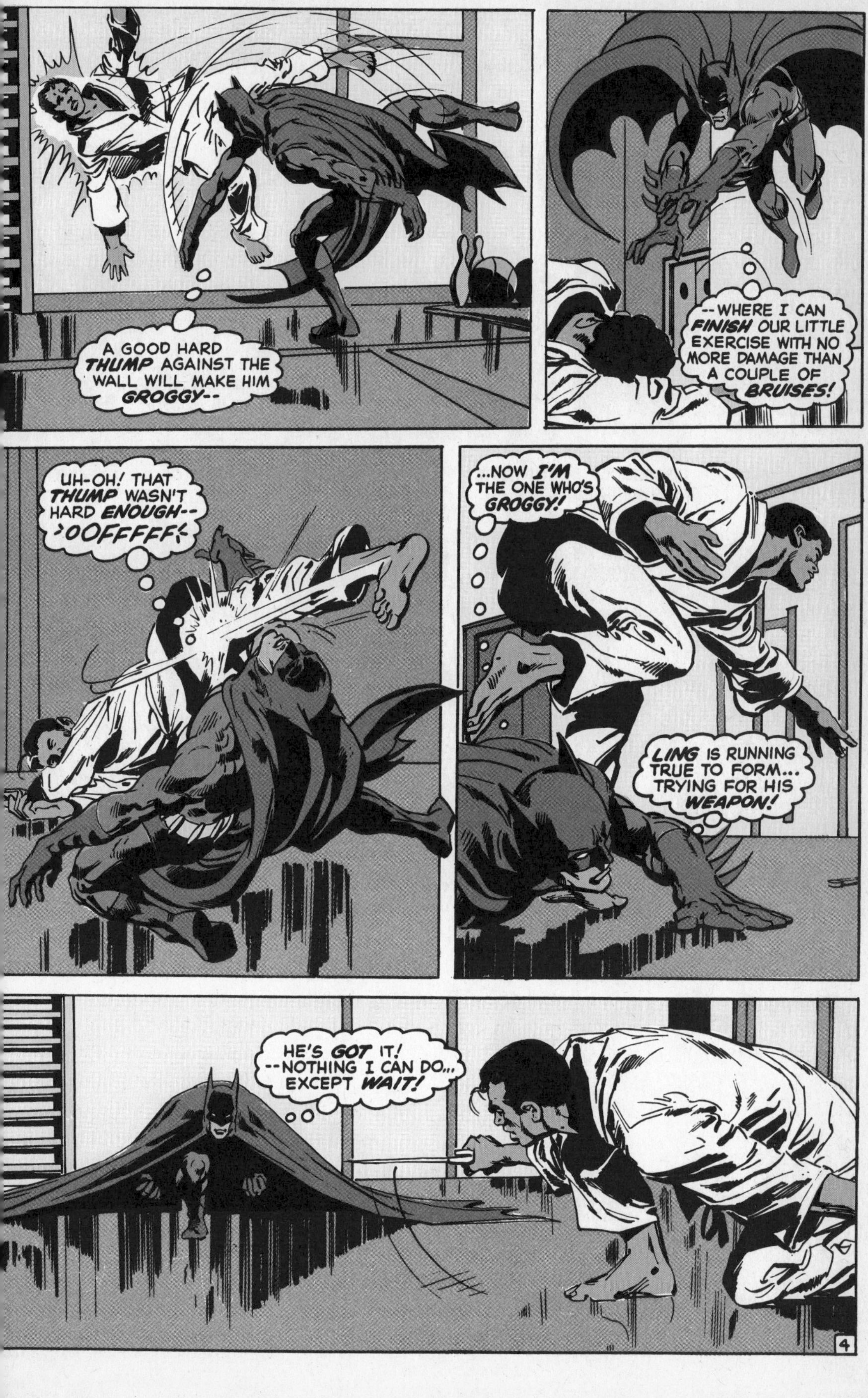
A GOOD HARD THUMP AGAINST THE WALL WILL MAKE HIM GROGGY--
--WHERE I CAN FINISH OUR LITTLE EXERCISE WITH NO MORE DAMAGE THAN A COUPLE OF BRUISES!
UH-OH! THAT THUMP WASN'T HARD ENOUGH-- >OOFFFFF<
...NOW I'M THE ONE WHO'S GROGGY!
LING IS RUNNING TRUE TO FORM... TRYING FOR HIS WEAPON!
HE'S GOT IT! --NOTHING I CAN DO... EXCEPT WAIT!
4

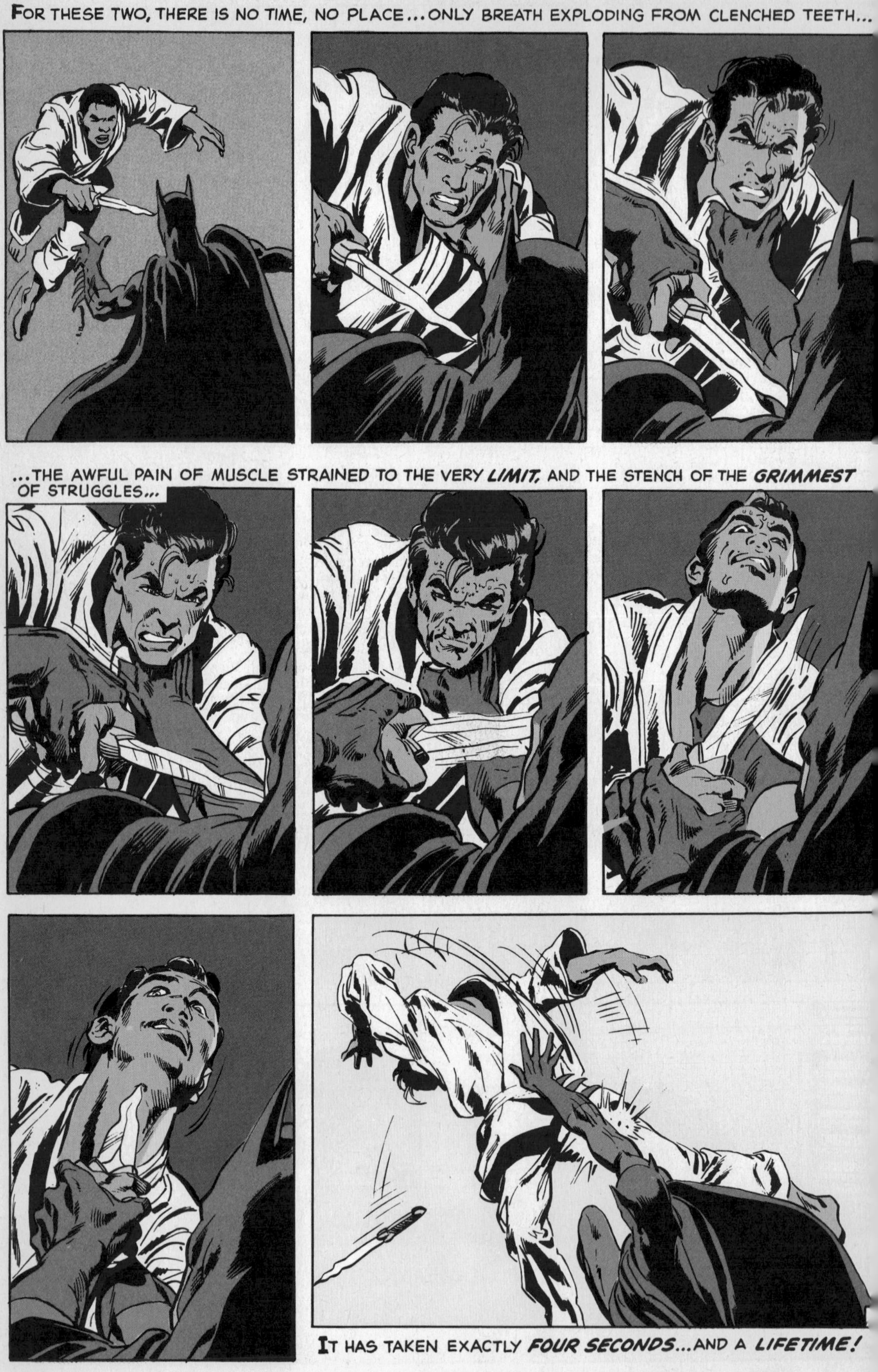
FOR THESE TWO, THERE IS NO TIME, NO PLACE... ONLY BREATH EXPLODING FROM CLENCHED TEETH...
...THE AWFUL PAIN OF MUSCLE STRAINED TO THE VERY LIMIT, AND THE STENCH OF THE GRIMMEST OF STRUGGLES...
IT HAS TAKEN EXACTLY FOUR SECONDS... AND A LIFETIME!

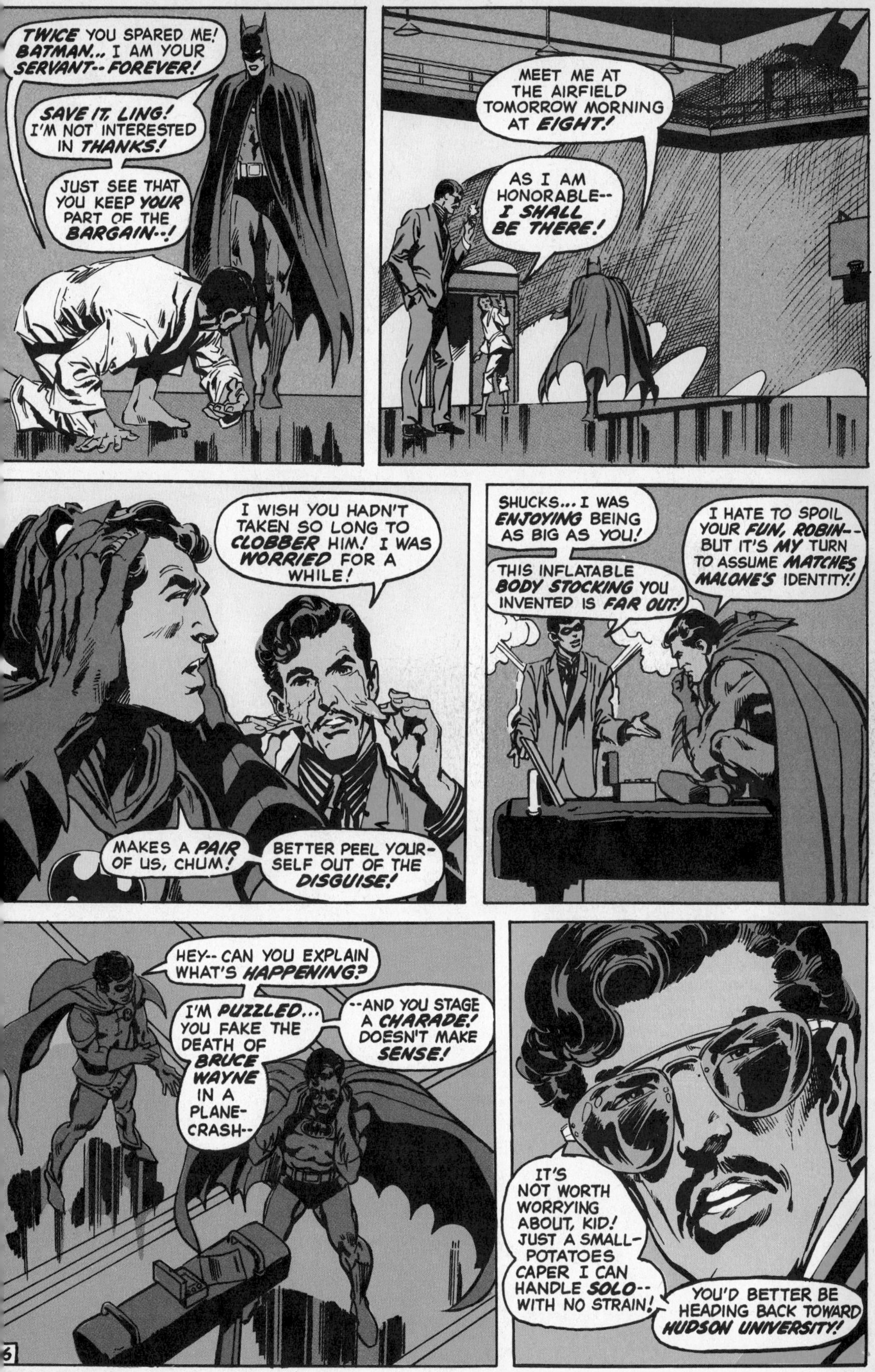
TWICE YOU SPARED ME! BATMAN... I AM YOUR SERVANT--FOREVER!
SAVE IT, LING! I'M NOT INTERESTED IN THANKS!
JUST SEE THAT YOU KEEP YOUR PART OF THE BARGAIN--!
MEET ME AT THE AIRFIELD TOMORROW MORNING AT EIGHT!
AS I AM HONORABLE-- I SHALL BE THERE!
I WISH YOU HADN'T TAKEN SO LONG TO CLOBBER HIM! I WAS WORRIED FOR A WHILE!
MAKES A PAIR OF US, CHUM!
BETTER PEEL YOURSELF OUT OF THE DISGUISE!
SHUCKS... I WAS ENJOYING BEING AS BIG AS YOU!
THIS INFLATABLE BODY STOCKING YOU INVENTED IS FAR OUT!
I HATE TO SPOIL YOUR FUN, ROBIN-- BUT IT'S MY TURN TO ASSUME MATCHES MALONE'S IDENTITY!
HEY-- CAN YOU EXPLAIN WHAT'S HAPPENING?
I'M PUZZLED... YOU FAKE THE DEATH OF BRUCE WAYNE IN A PLANE-CRASH--
--AND YOU STAGE A CHARADE! DOESN'T MAKE SENSE!
6
IT'S NOT WORTH WORRYING ABOUT, KID! JUST A SMALL-POTATOES CAPER I CAN HANDLE SOLO-- WITH NO STRAIN!
YOU'D BETTER BE HEADING BACK TOWARD HUDSON UNIVERSITY!

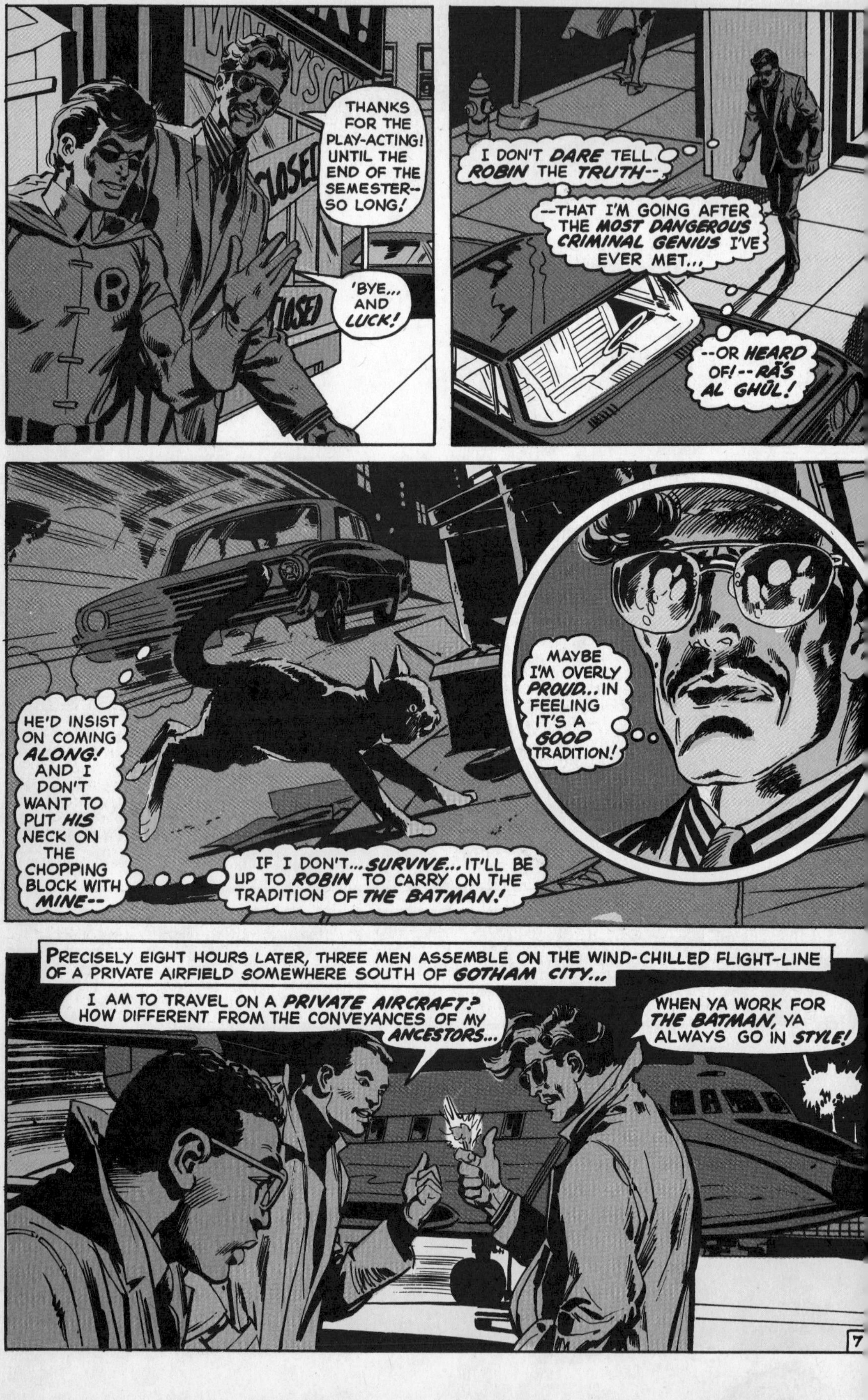
THANKS FOR THE PLAY-ACTING! UNTIL THE END OF THE SEMESTER-- SO LONG!
CLOSED
CLOSED
'BYE... AND LUCK!
I DON'T DARE TELL ROBIN THE TRUTH--
--THAT I'M GOING AFTER THE MOST DANGEROUS CRIMINAL GENIUS I'VE EVER MET...
--OR HEARD OF!--RĀ'S AL GHŪL!
HE'D INSIST ON COMING ALONG! AND I DON'T WANT TO PUT HIS NECK ON THE CHOPPING BLOCK WITH MINE--
IF I DON'T... SURVIVE... IT'LL BE UP TO ROBIN TO CARRY ON THE TRADITION OF THE BATMAN!
MAYBE I'M OVERLY PROUD... IN FEELING IT'S A GOOD TRADITION!
PRECISELY EIGHT HOURS LATER, THREE MEN ASSEMBLE ON THE WIND-CHILLED FLIGHT-LINE OF A PRIVATE AIRFIELD SOMEWHERE SOUTH OF GOTHAM CITY...
I AM TO TRAVEL ON A PRIVATE AIRCRAFT? HOW DIFFERENT FROM THE CONVEYANCES OF MY ANCESTORS...
WHEN YA WORK FOR THE BATMAN, YA ALWAYS GO IN STYLE!
7

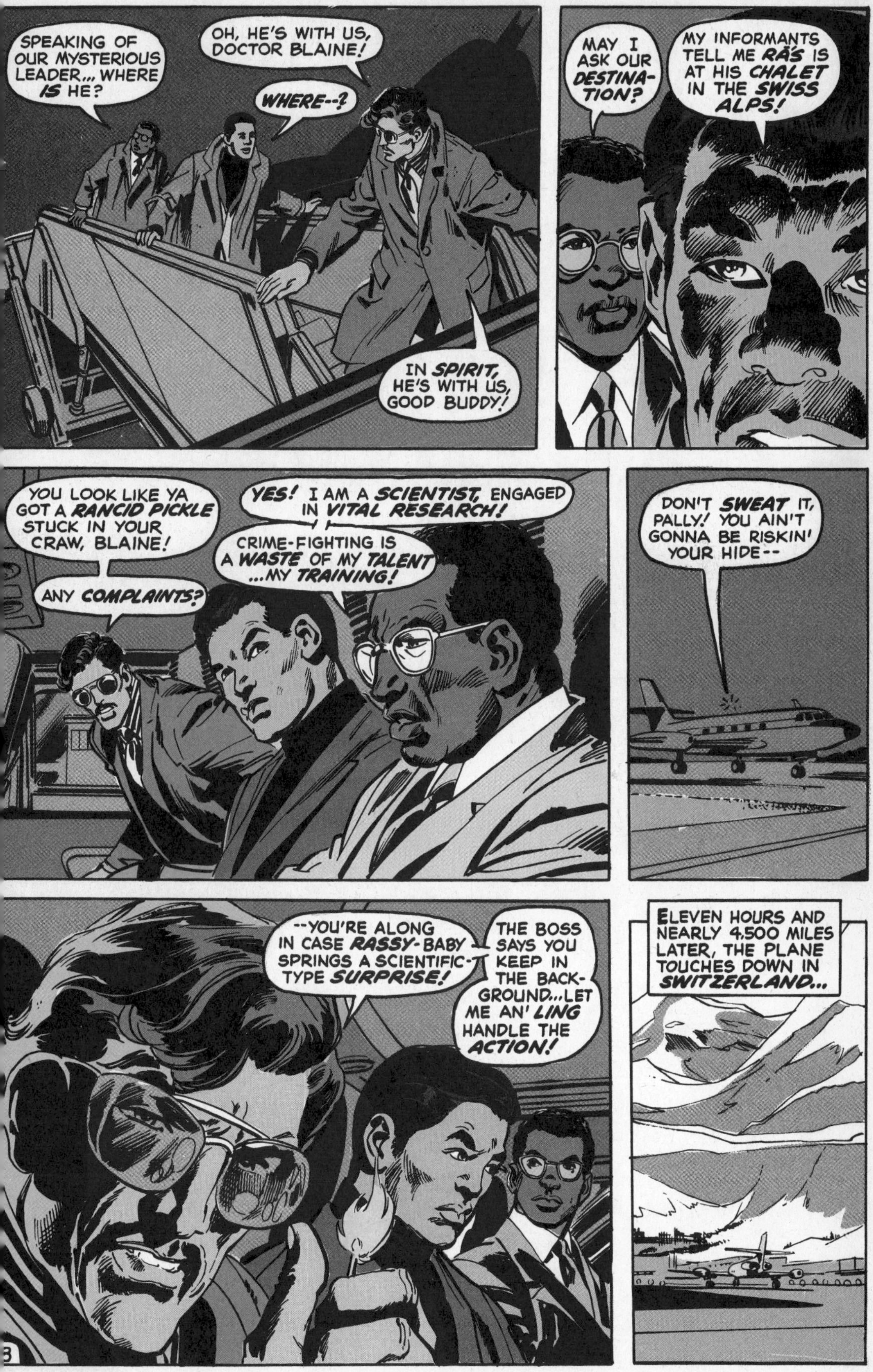
SPEAKING OF OUR MYSTERIOUS LEADER... WHERE IS HE?
OH, HE'S WITH US, DOCTOR BLAINE!
WHERE--?
IN SPIRIT, HE'S WITH US, GOOD BUDDY!
MAY I ASK OUR DESTINATION?
MY INFORMANTS TELL ME RĀS IS AT HIS CHALET IN THE SWISS ALPS!
YOU LOOK LIKE YA GOT A RANCID PICKLE STUCK IN YOUR CRAW, BLAINE!
ANY COMPLAINTS?
YES! I AM A SCIENTIST, ENGAGED IN VITAL RESEARCH!
CRIME-FIGHTING IS A WASTE OF MY TALENT ...MY TRAINING!
DON'T SWEAT IT, PALLY! YOU AIN'T GONNA BE RISKIN' YOUR HIDE--
--YOU'RE ALONG IN CASE RASSY-BABY SPRINGS A SCIENTIFIC-TYPE SURPRISE!
THE BOSS SAYS YOU KEEP IN THE BACKGROUND...LET ME AN' LING HANDLE THE ACTION!
ELEVEN HOURS AND NEARLY 4,500 MILES LATER, THE PLANE TOUCHES DOWN IN SWITZERLAND...
3

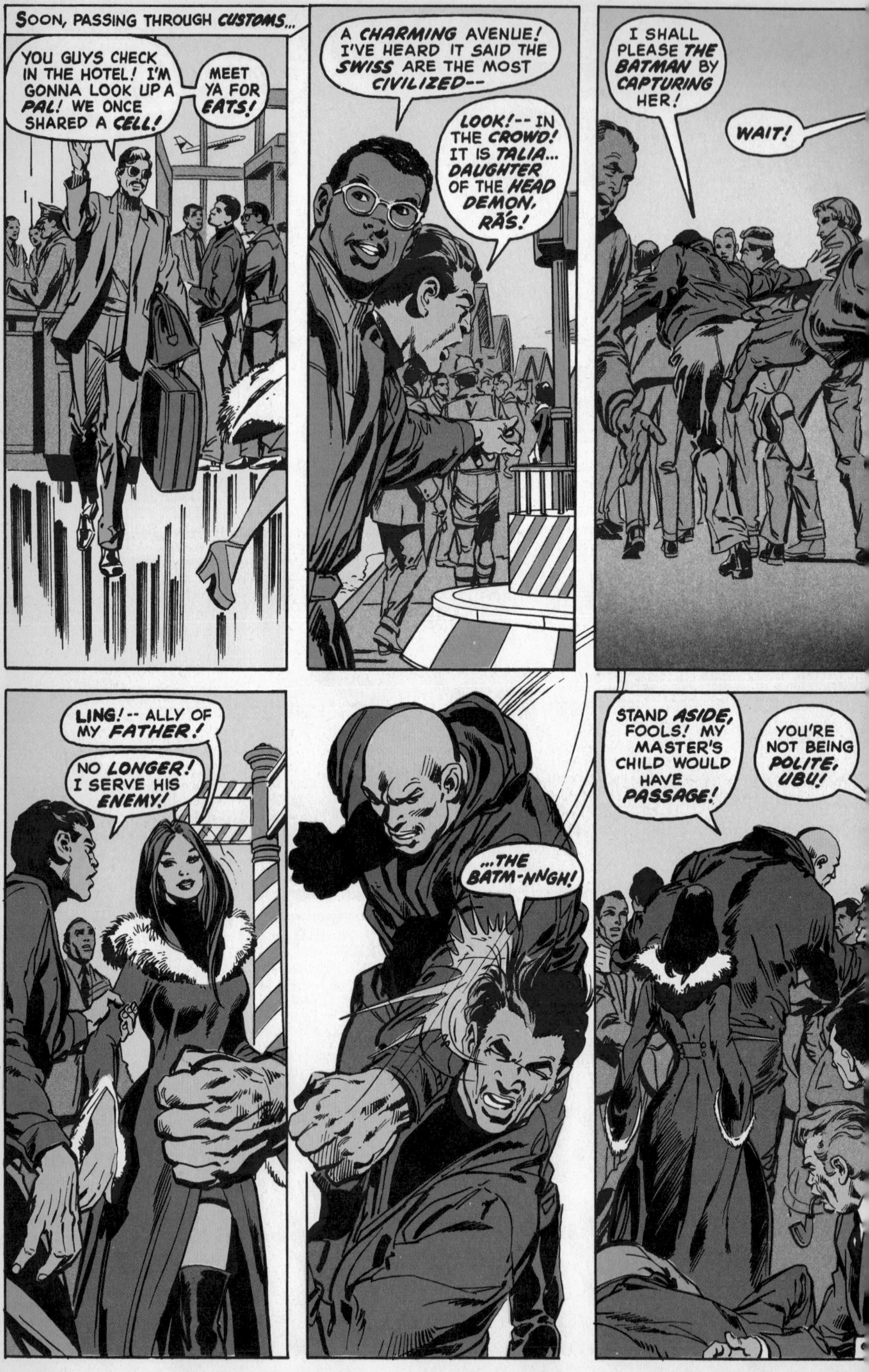
SOON, PASSING THROUGH CUSTOMS...
YOU GUYS CHECK IN THE HOTEL! I'M GONNA LOOK UP A PAL! WE ONCE SHARED A CELL!
MEET YA FOR EATS!
A CHARMING AVENUE! I'VE HEARD IT SAID THE SWISS ARE THE MOST CIVILIZED--
LOOK!-- IN THE CROWD! IT IS TALIA... DAUGHTER OF THE HEAD DEMON, RĀ'S!
I SHALL PLEASE THE BATMAN BY CAPTURING HER!
WAIT!
LING! -- ALLY OF MY FATHER!
NO LONGER! I SERVE HIS ENEMY!
...THE BATM-NNGH!
STAND ASIDE, FOOLS! MY MASTER'S CHILD WOULD HAVE PASSAGE!
YOU'RE NOT BEING POLITE, UBU!

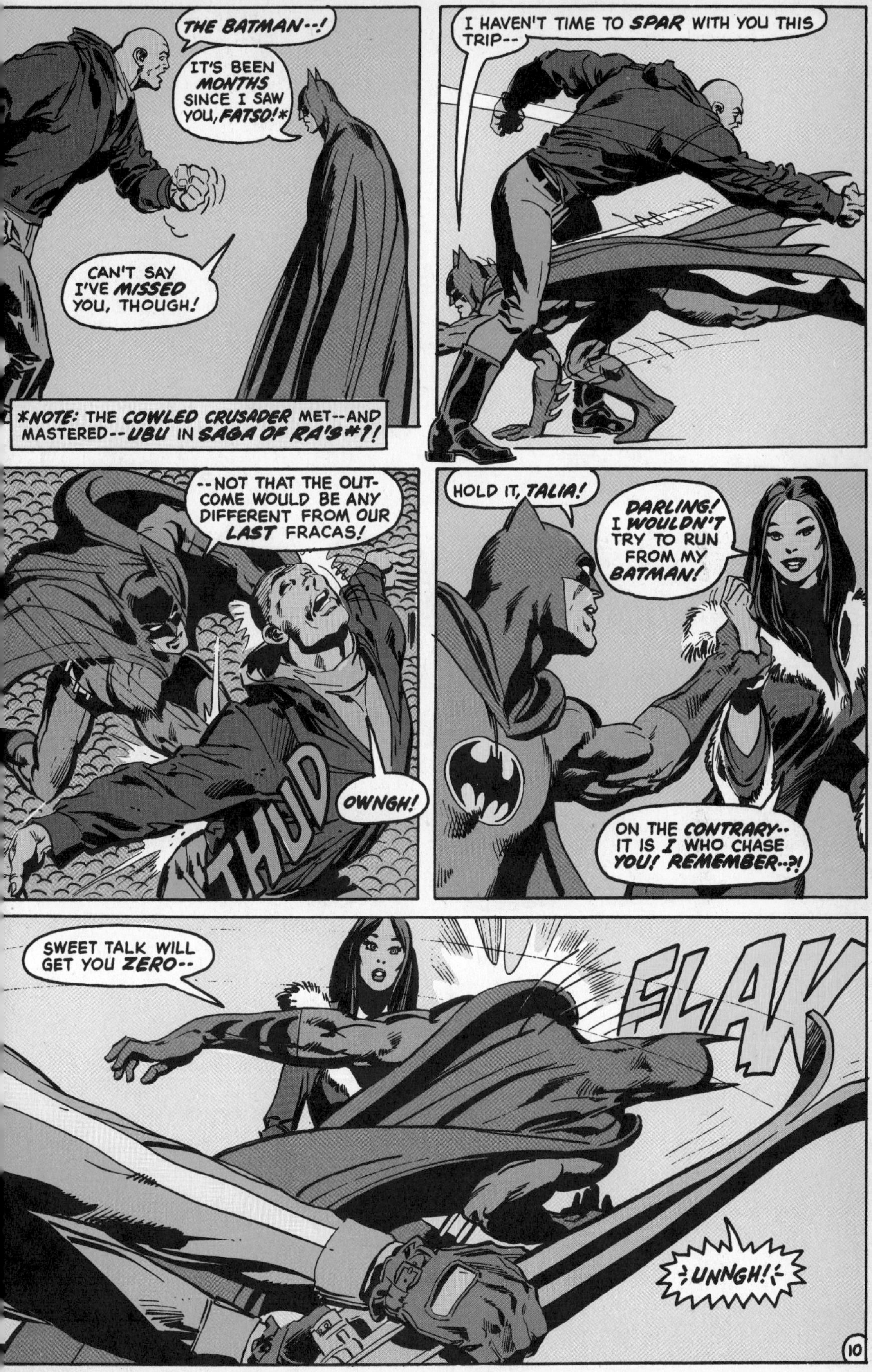
THE BATMAN--!
IT'S BEEN MONTHS SINCE I SAW YOU, FATSO!*
CAN'T SAY I'VE MISSED YOU, THOUGH!
*NOTE: THE COWLED CRUSADER MET--AND MASTERED--UBU IN SAGA OF RA'S #1!
I HAVEN'T TIME TO SPAR WITH YOU THIS TRIP--
--NOT THAT THE OUT-COME WOULD BE ANY DIFFERENT FROM OUR LAST FRACAS!
OWNGH!
THUD
HOLD IT, TALIA!
DARLING! I WOULDN'T TRY TO RUN FROM MY BATMAN!
ON THE CONTRARY-- IT IS I WHO CHASE YOU! REMEMBER--?!
SWEET TALK WILL GET YOU ZERO--
FLAK
UNNGH!
10

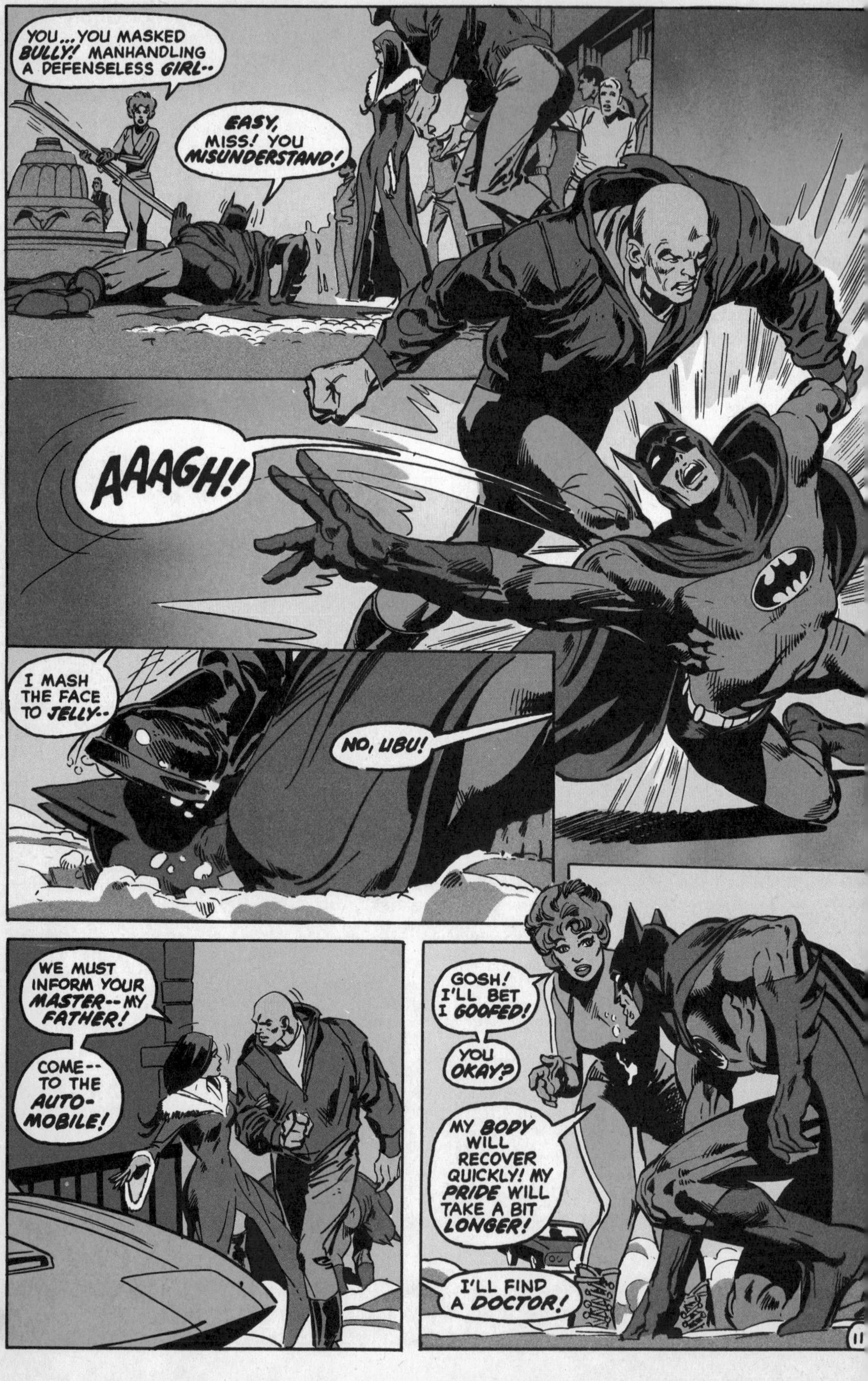
YOU...YOU MASKED BULLY! MANHANDLING A DEFENSELESS GIRL--
EASY, MISS! YOU MISUNDERSTAND!
AAAGH!
I MASH THE FACE TO JELLY--
NO, UBU!
WE MUST INFORM YOUR MASTER--MY FATHER!
COME-- TO THE AUTO-MOBILE!
GOSH! I'LL BET I GOOFED!
YOU OKAY?
MY BODY WILL RECOVER QUICKLY! MY PRIDE WILL TAKE A BIT LONGER!
I'LL FIND A DOCTOR!
11

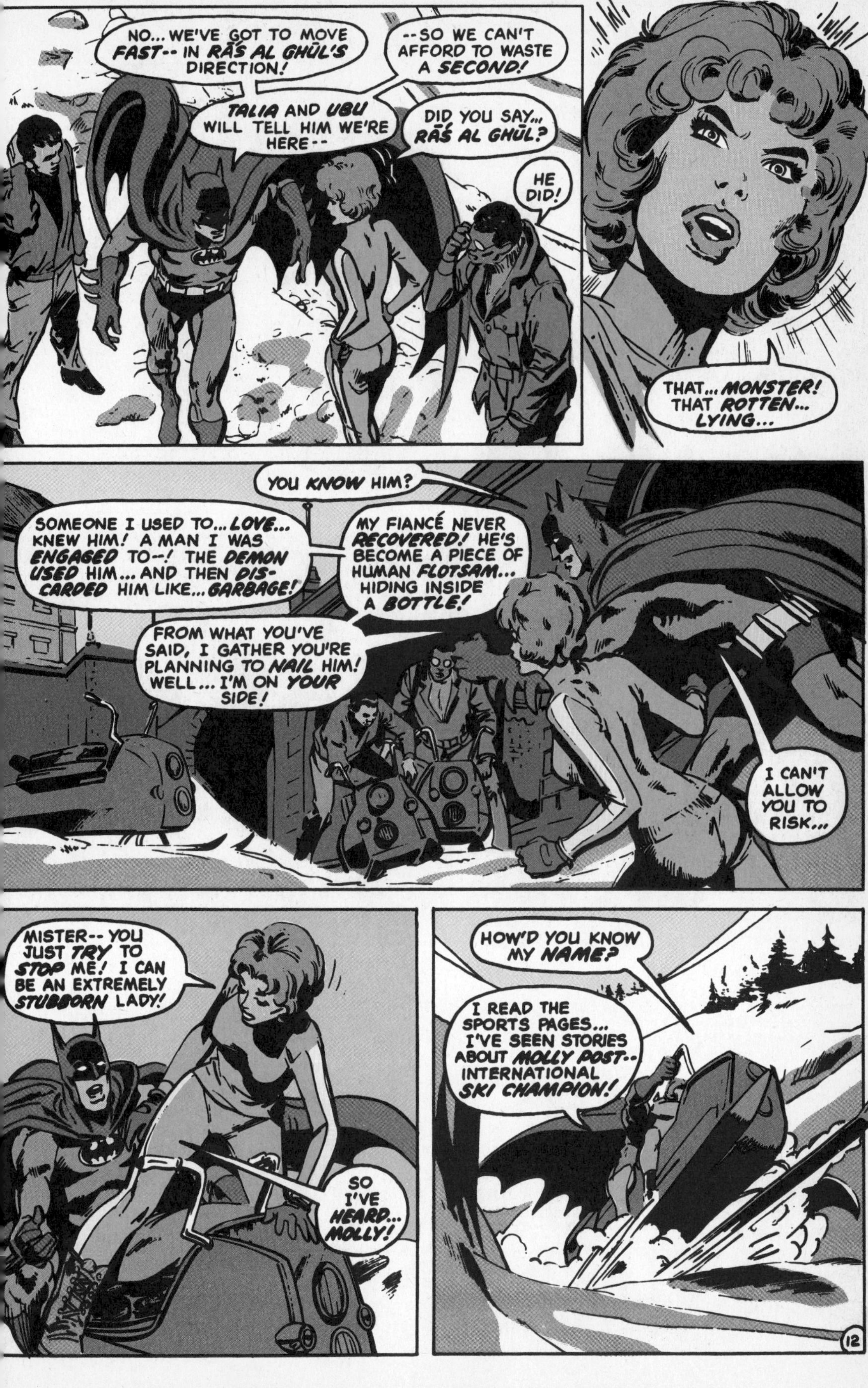
NO... WE'VE GOT TO MOVE FAST-- IN RĀS AL GHŪL'S DIRECTION!
--SO WE CAN'T AFFORD TO WASTE A SECOND!
TALIA AND UBU WILL TELL HIM WE'RE HERE--
DID YOU SAY... RĀS AL GHŪL?
HE DID!
THAT... MONSTER! THAT ROTTEN... LYING...
YOU KNOW HIM?
SOMEONE I USED TO... LOVE... KNEW HIM! A MAN I WAS ENGAGED TO--! THE DEMON USED HIM... AND THEN DISCARDED HIM LIKE... GARBAGE!
MY FIANCÉ NEVER RECOVERED! HE'S BECOME A PIECE OF HUMAN FLOTSAM... HIDING INSIDE A BOTTLE!
FROM WHAT YOU'VE SAID, I GATHER YOU'RE PLANNING TO NAIL HIM! WELL... I'M ON YOUR SIDE!
I CAN'T ALLOW YOU TO RISK...
MISTER-- YOU JUST TRY TO STOP ME! I CAN BE AN EXTREMELY STUBBORN LADY!
SO I'VE HEARD... MOLLY!
HOW'D YOU KNOW MY NAME?
I READ THE SPORTS PAGES... I'VE SEEN STORIES ABOUT MOLLY POST-- INTERNATIONAL SKI CHAMPION!
12

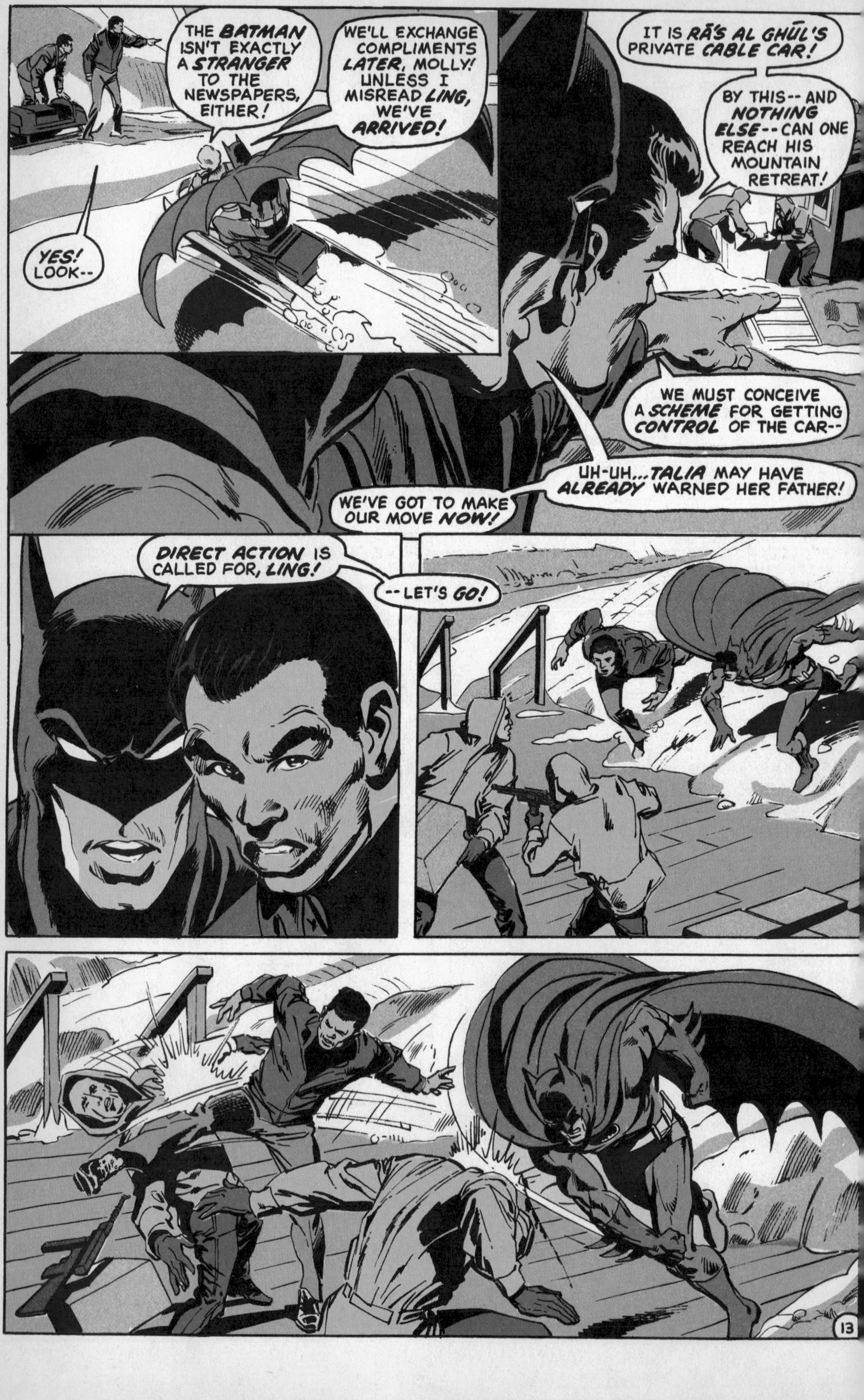
THE BATMAN ISN'T EXACTLY A STRANGER TO THE NEWSPAPERS, EITHER!
WE'LL EXCHANGE COMPLIMENTS LATER, MOLLY! UNLESS I MISREAD LING, WE'VE ARRIVED!
YES! LOOK--
IT IS RĀ'S AL GHŪL'S PRIVATE CABLE CAR!
BY THIS-- AND NOTHING ELSE-- CAN ONE REACH HIS MOUNTAIN RETREAT!
WE MUST CONCEIVE A SCHEME FOR GETTING CONTROL OF THE CAR--
UH-UH...TALIA MAY HAVE ALREADY WARNED HER FATHER!
WE'VE GOT TO MAKE OUR MOVE NOW!
DIRECT ACTION IS CALLED FOR, LING!
--LET'S GO!
13

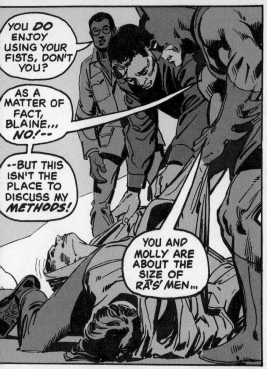

YOU *DO* ENJOY USING YOUR FISTS, DON'T YOU?

AS A MATTER OF FACT, BLAINE... *NO!*--

--BUT THIS ISN'T THE PLACE TO DISCUSS MY *METHODS!*

YOU AND MOLLY ARE ABOUT THE SIZE OF *RĀS'* MEN...

"...PUT THESE ON! KEEP YOUR FACES HIDDEN AND WE JUST *MIGHT* FOOL RĀS' LOOKOUTS!

AND *YOU* GUYS?

WE'LL BE WITH YOU-- *BELIEVE* IT!

THUS, WITHIN *MINUTES*...

THE *CABLE CAR* APPROACHES!

THE MASTER CAUTIONS THERE MAY BE *TREACHERY!*

OUR ORDERS ARE TO EXAMINE IT *CAREFULLY*--!

I OBSERVE NOTHING OUT OF THE *ORDINARY!*

THE CONVEYANCE CONTAINS NAUGHT SAVE THE *SUPPLIES*--

--AND THE MASTER'S *SLAVES!* WE HAVE NO CAUSE FOR *ALARM!*

14

WE ARE *DECEIVED!* THESE ARE NOT OUR *MATES--!*

BRATA-TAT

THEY ARE *IMPOSTORS...* AGGH!

WE MOVE AS *ONE BEING,* BATMAN! SURELY NO FINER FIGHTERS *EXIST!*

DON'T LET'S CONGRAT- ULATE OURSELVES *YET,* LING! THAT GUARD GOT OFF A COUPLE OF *SHOTS--*

..UNDOUBT- EDLY ALERTING *RÄS* AND COMPANY!

BATMAN! --*DUCK!*

BRA TA TA TAK

SPVG SPANG SPANG SPANG

BEEOW TZING SPANG VIIP VIIP

I HAPPENED TO GLANCE AROUND--AND SAW THE SUN GLINTING ON A *MACHINE GUN --*

--*ABOVE* US,..ON TOP OF THE *SLOPE!*

15

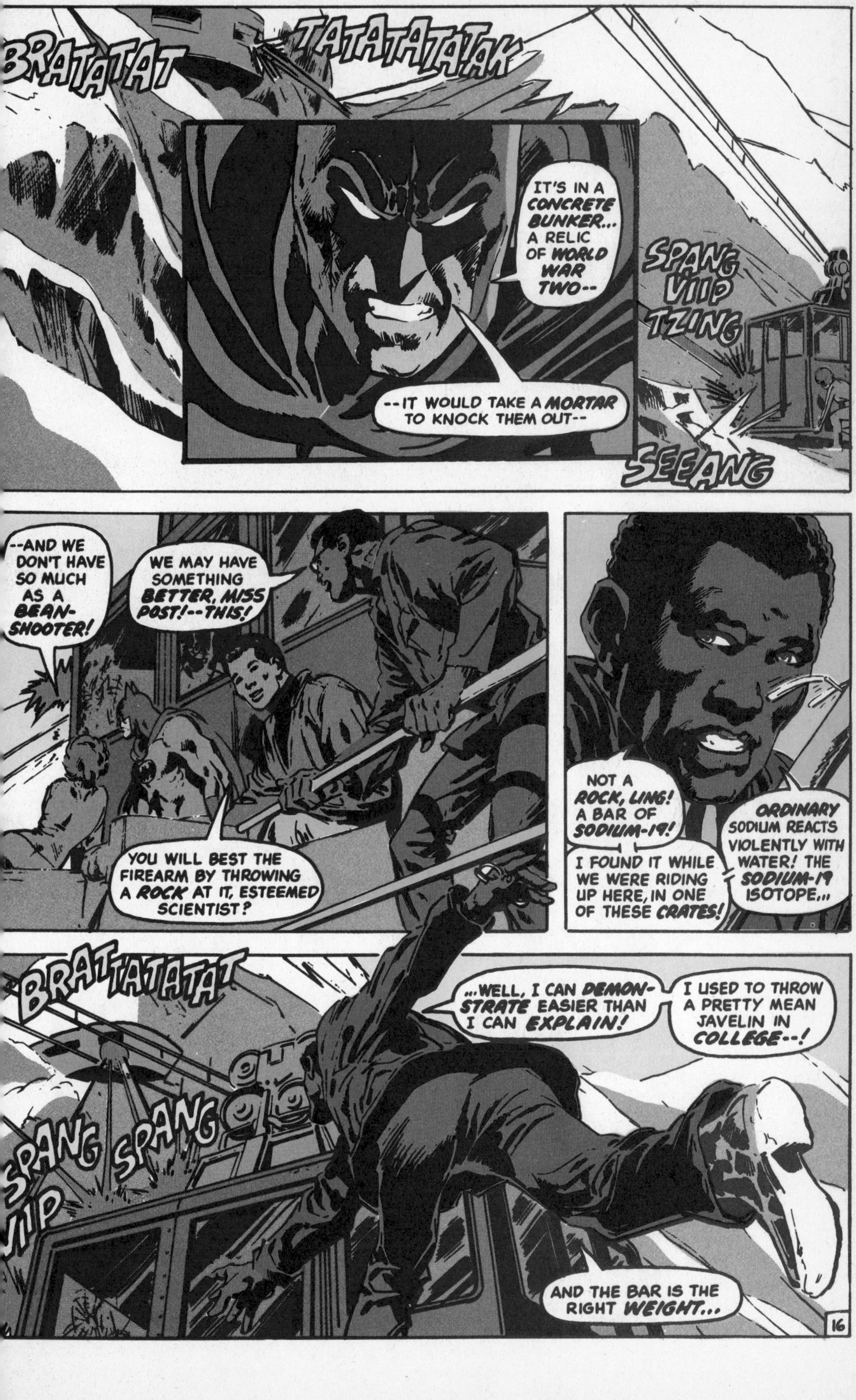
BRATATAT
TATATATATAK
IT'S IN A CONCRETE BUNKER... A RELIC OF WORLD WAR TWO--
--IT WOULD TAKE A MORTAR TO KNOCK THEM OUT--
SPANG VIIP TZING
SEEANG
--AND WE DON'T HAVE SO MUCH AS A BEAN-SHOOTER!
WE MAY HAVE SOMETHING BETTER, MISS POST!--THIS!
YOU WILL BEST THE FIREARM BY THROWING A ROCK AT IT, ESTEEMED SCIENTIST?
NOT A ROCK, LING! A BAR OF SODIUM-19!
I FOUND IT WHILE WE WERE RIDING UP HERE, IN ONE OF THESE CRATES!
ORDINARY SODIUM REACTS VIOLENTLY WITH WATER! THE SODIUM-19 ISOTOPE...
BRATTATATAT
...WELL, I CAN DEMON-STRATE EASIER THAN I CAN EXPLAIN!
I USED TO THROW A PRETTY MEAN JAVELIN IN COLLEGE--!
SPANG SPANG
VIIP
AND THE BAR IS THE RIGHT WEIGHT...
16

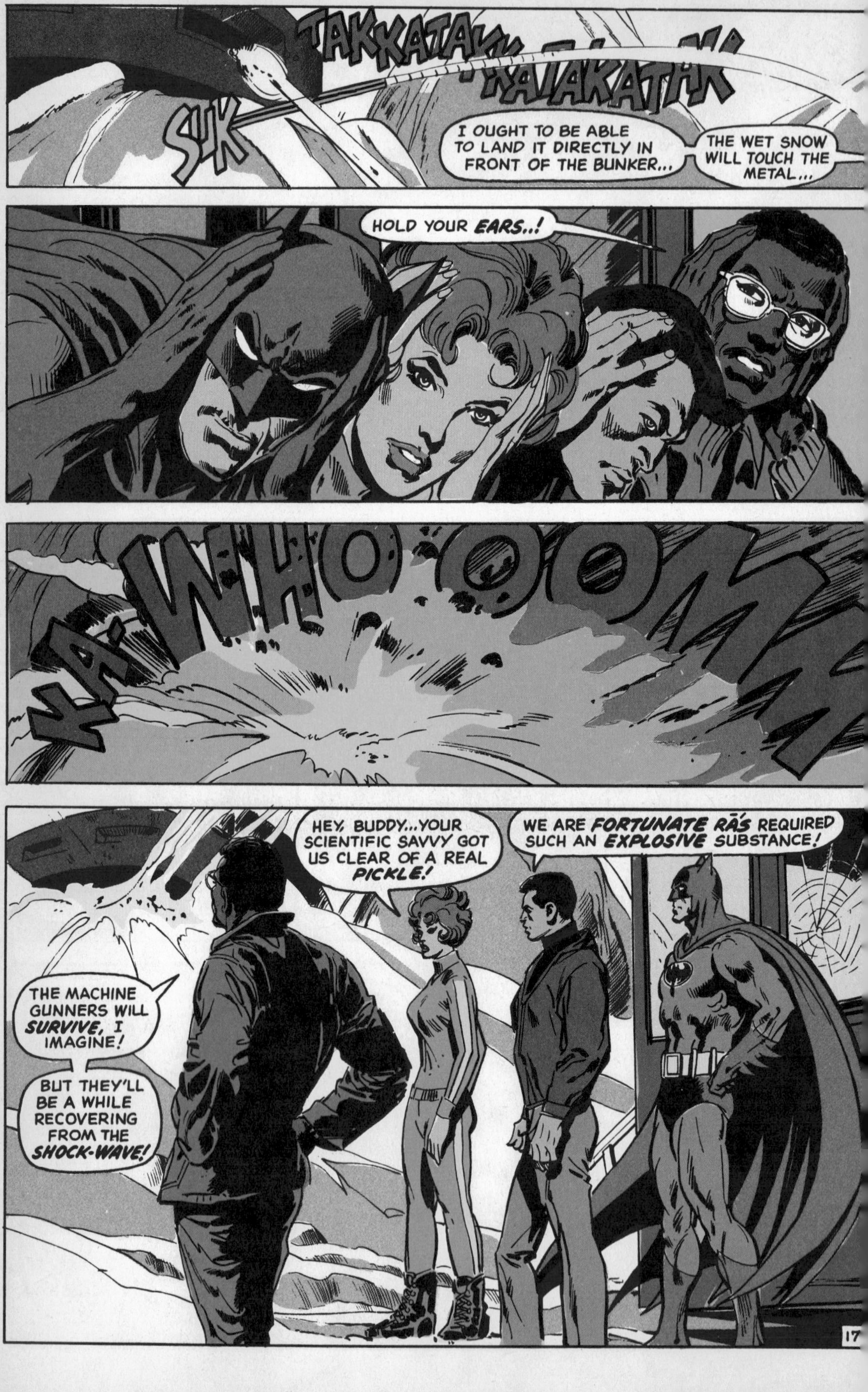
TAKKATAKK
TAKATAKATHK
SUK
I OUGHT TO BE ABLE TO LAND IT DIRECTLY IN FRONT OF THE BUNKER...
THE WET SNOW WILL TOUCH THE METAL...
HOLD YOUR EARS..!
KA-WHOOOOM
HEY, BUDDY...YOUR SCIENTIFIC SAVVY GOT US CLEAR OF A REAL PICKLE!
WE ARE FORTUNATE RĀ'S REQUIRED SUCH AN EXPLOSIVE SUBSTANCE!
THE MACHINE GUNNERS WILL SURVIVE, I IMAGINE!
BUT THEY'LL BE A WHILE RECOVERING FROM THE SHOCK-WAVE!
17

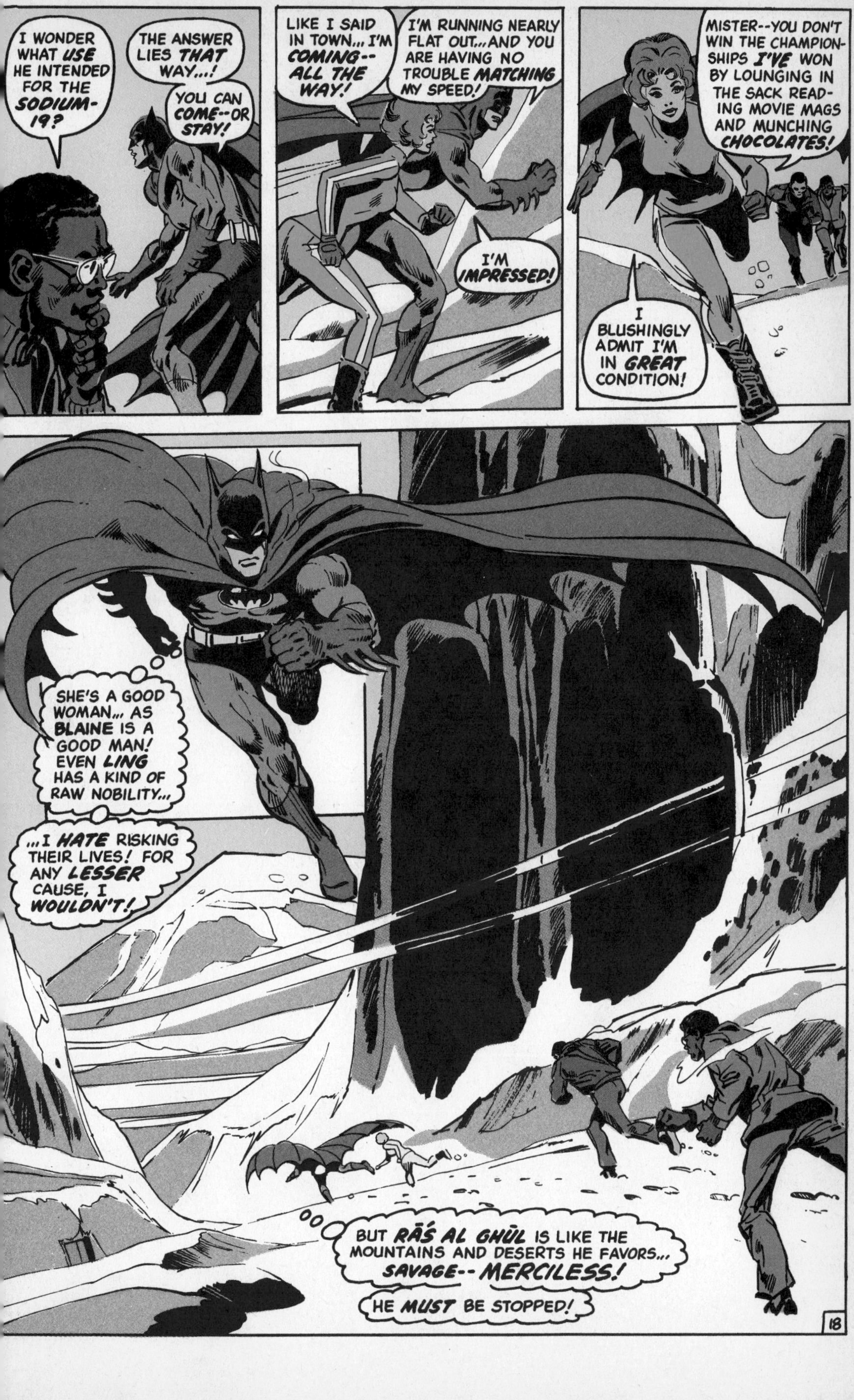
I WONDER WHAT USE HE INTENDED FOR THE SODIUM-19?
THE ANSWER LIES THAT WAY...!
YOU CAN COME--OR STAY!
LIKE I SAID IN TOWN... I'M COMING--ALL THE WAY!
I'M RUNNING NEARLY FLAT OUT...AND YOU ARE HAVING NO TROUBLE MATCHING MY SPEED!
I'M IMPRESSED!
MISTER--YOU DON'T WIN THE CHAMPIONSHIPS I'VE WON BY LOUNGING IN THE SACK READING MOVIE MAGS AND MUNCHING CHOCOLATES!
I BLUSHINGLY ADMIT I'M IN GREAT CONDITION!
SHE'S A GOOD WOMAN... AS BLAINE IS A GOOD MAN! EVEN LING HAS A KIND OF RAW NOBILITY...
...I HATE RISKING THEIR LIVES! FOR ANY LESSER CAUSE, I WOULDN'T!
BUT RĀS AL GHŪL IS LIKE THE MOUNTAINS AND DESERTS HE FAVORS... SAVAGE--MERCILESS!
HE MUST BE STOPPED!
18

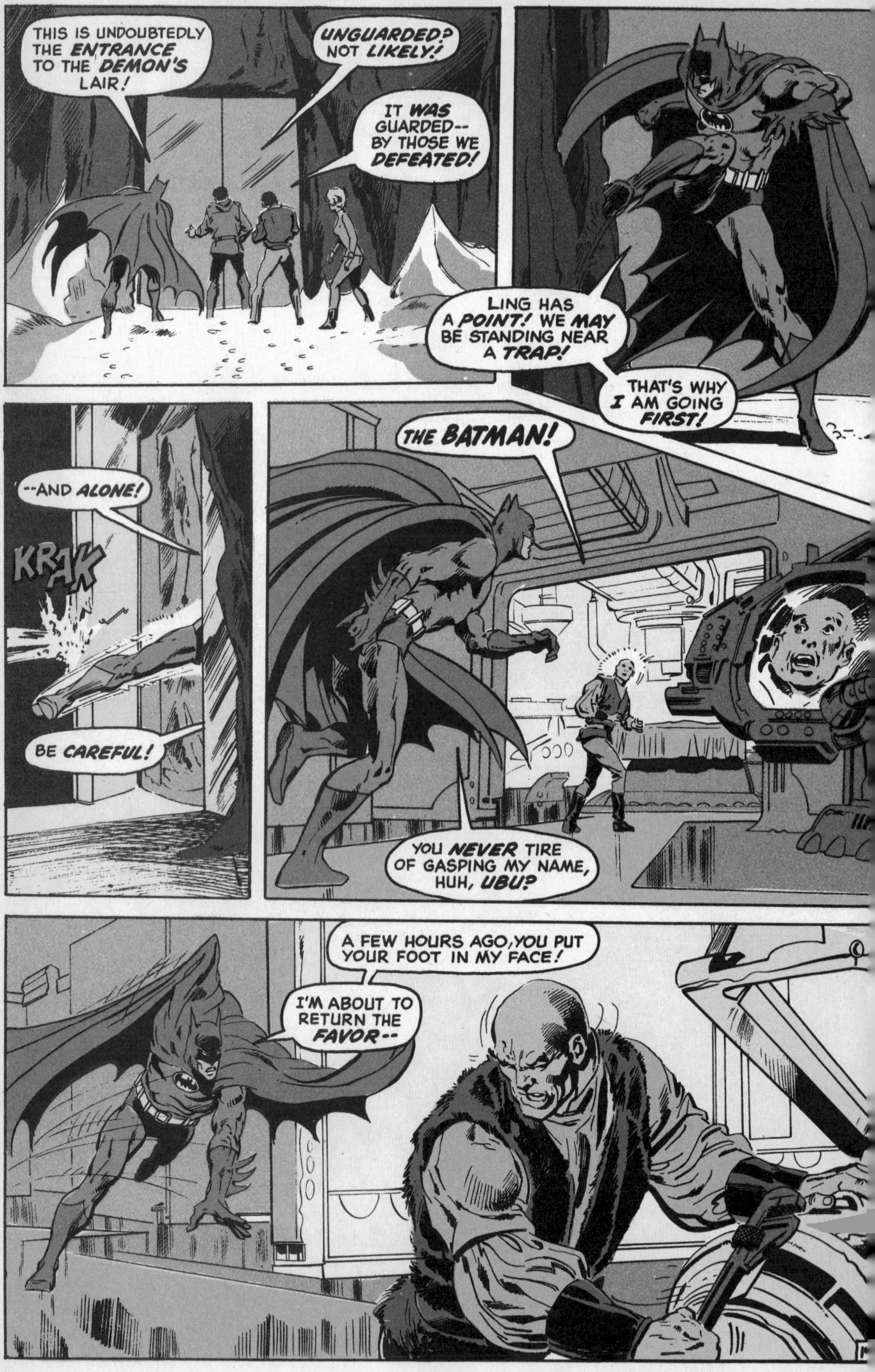
THIS IS UNDOUBTEDLY THE ENTRANCE TO THE DEMON'S LAIR!
UNGUARDED? NOT LIKELY!
IT WAS GUARDED-- BY THOSE WE DEFEATED!
LING HAS A POINT! WE MAY BE STANDING NEAR A TRAP!
THAT'S WHY I AM GOING FIRST!
--AND ALONE!
KRAK
BE CAREFUL!
THE BATMAN!
YOU NEVER TIRE OF GASPING MY NAME, HUH, UBU?
A FEW HOURS AGO, YOU PUT YOUR FOOT IN MY FACE!
I'M ABOUT TO RETURN THE FAVOR--

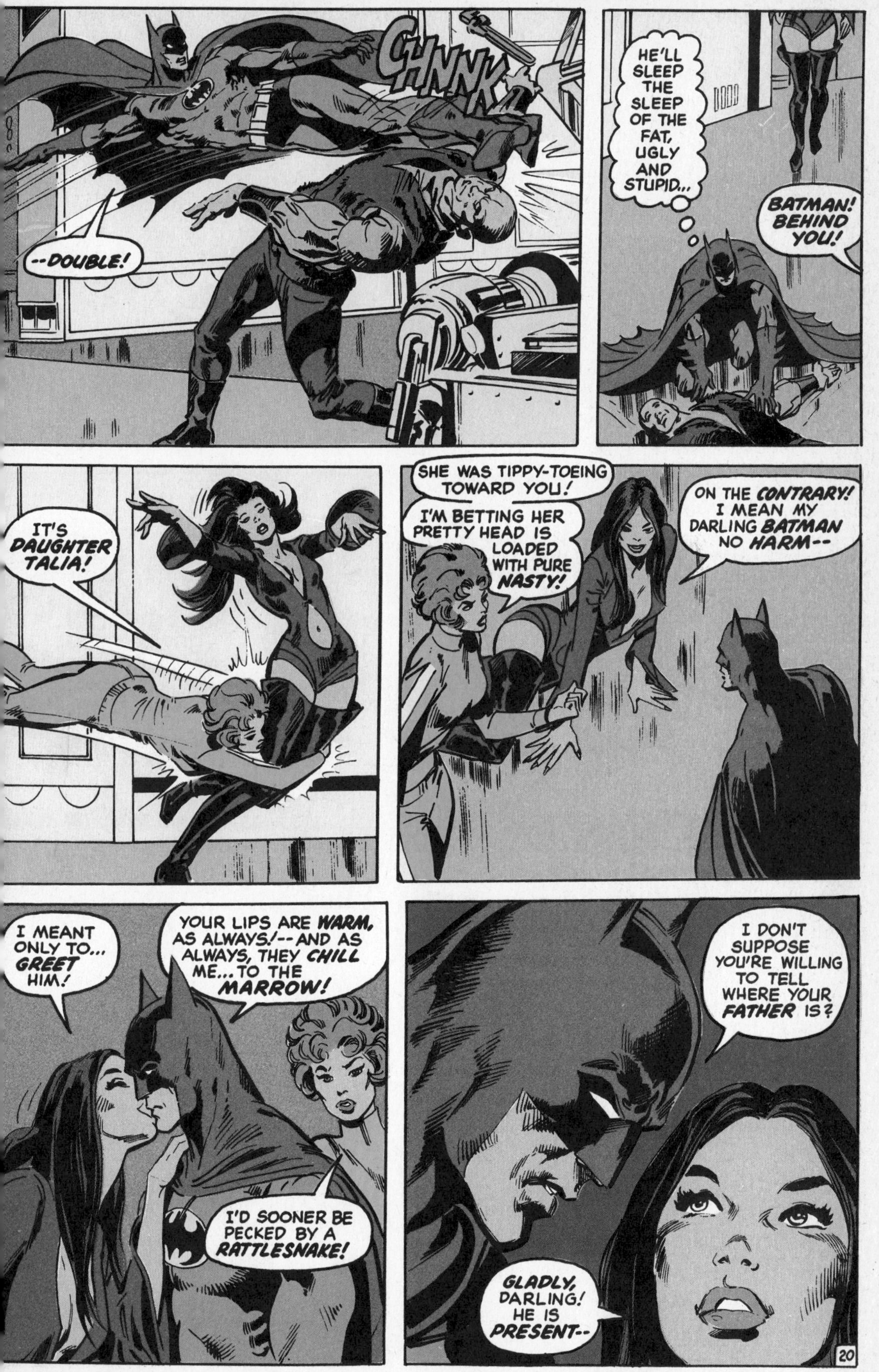
CHNNK
--DOUBLE!
HE'LL SLEEP THE SLEEP OF THE FAT, UGLY AND STUPID...
BATMAN! BEHIND YOU!
IT'S DAUGHTER TALIA!
SHE WAS TIPPY-TOEING TOWARD YOU!
I'M BETTING HER PRETTY HEAD IS LOADED WITH PURE NASTY!
ON THE CONTRARY! I MEAN MY DARLING BATMAN NO HARM--
I MEANT ONLY TO... GREET HIM!
YOUR LIPS ARE WARM, AS ALWAYS!--AND AS ALWAYS, THEY CHILL ME...TO THE MARROW!
I'D SOONER BE PECKED BY A RATTLESNAKE!
I DON'T SUPPOSE YOU'RE WILLING TO TELL WHERE YOUR FATHER IS?
GLADLY, DARLING! HE IS PRESENT--
20

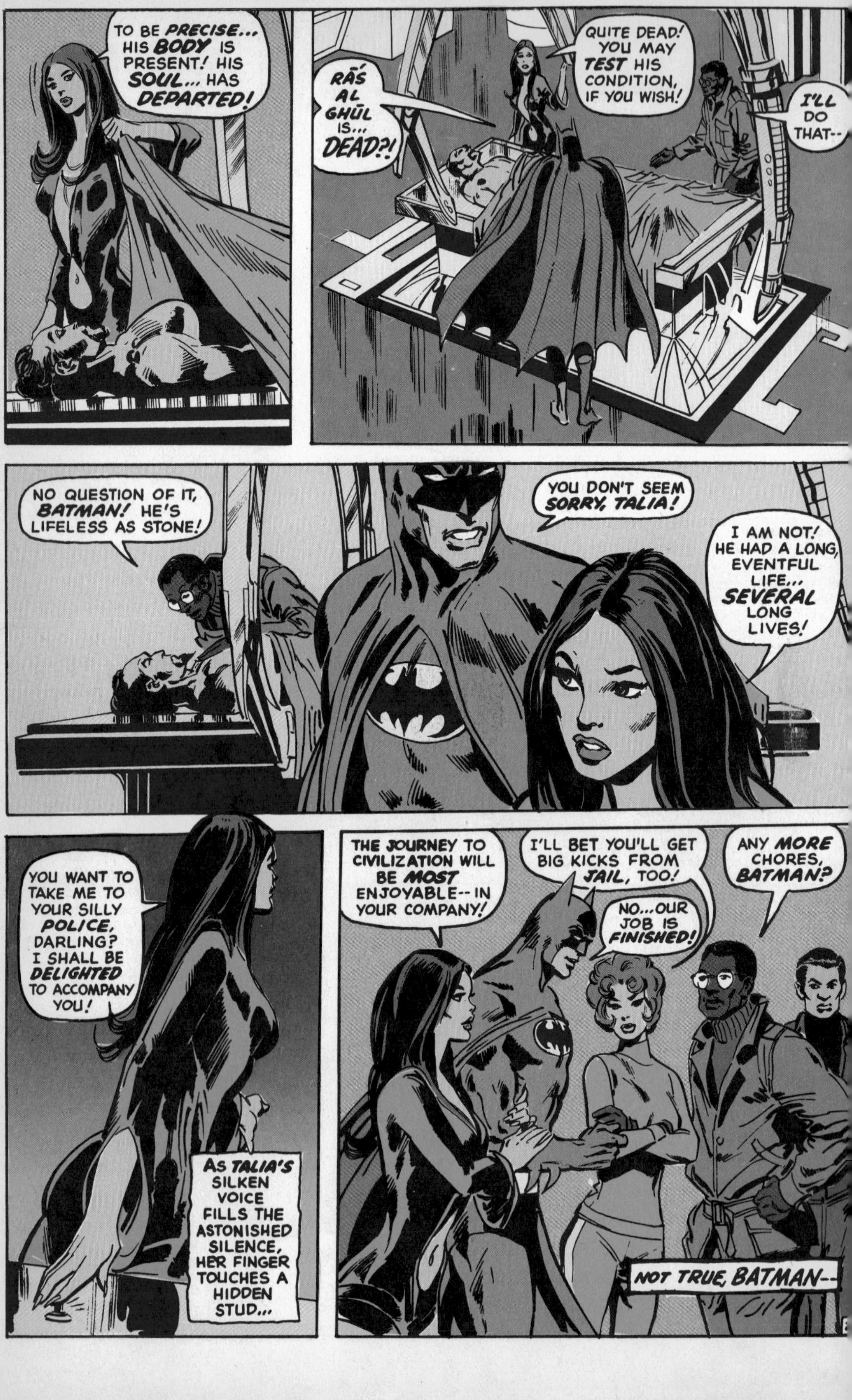
TO BE PRECISE... HIS BODY IS PRESENT! HIS SOUL... HAS DEPARTED!
RĀS AL GHŪL IS... DEAD?!
QUITE DEAD! YOU MAY TEST HIS CONDITION, IF YOU WISH!
I'LL DO THAT--
NO QUESTION OF IT, BATMAN! HE'S LIFELESS AS STONE!
YOU DON'T SEEM SORRY, TALIA!
I AM NOT! HE HAD A LONG, EVENTFUL LIFE... SEVERAL LONG LIVES!
YOU WANT TO TAKE ME TO YOUR SILLY POLICE, DARLING? I SHALL BE DELIGHTED TO ACCOMPANY YOU!
AS TALIA'S SILKEN VOICE FILLS THE ASTONISHED SILENCE, HER FINGER TOUCHES A HIDDEN STUD...
THE JOURNEY TO CIVILIZATION WILL BE MOST ENJOYABLE-- IN YOUR COMPANY!
I'LL BET YOU'LL GET BIG KICKS FROM JAIL, TOO!
NO...OUR JOB IS FINISHED!
ANY MORE CHORES, BATMAN?
NOT TRUE, BATMAN--

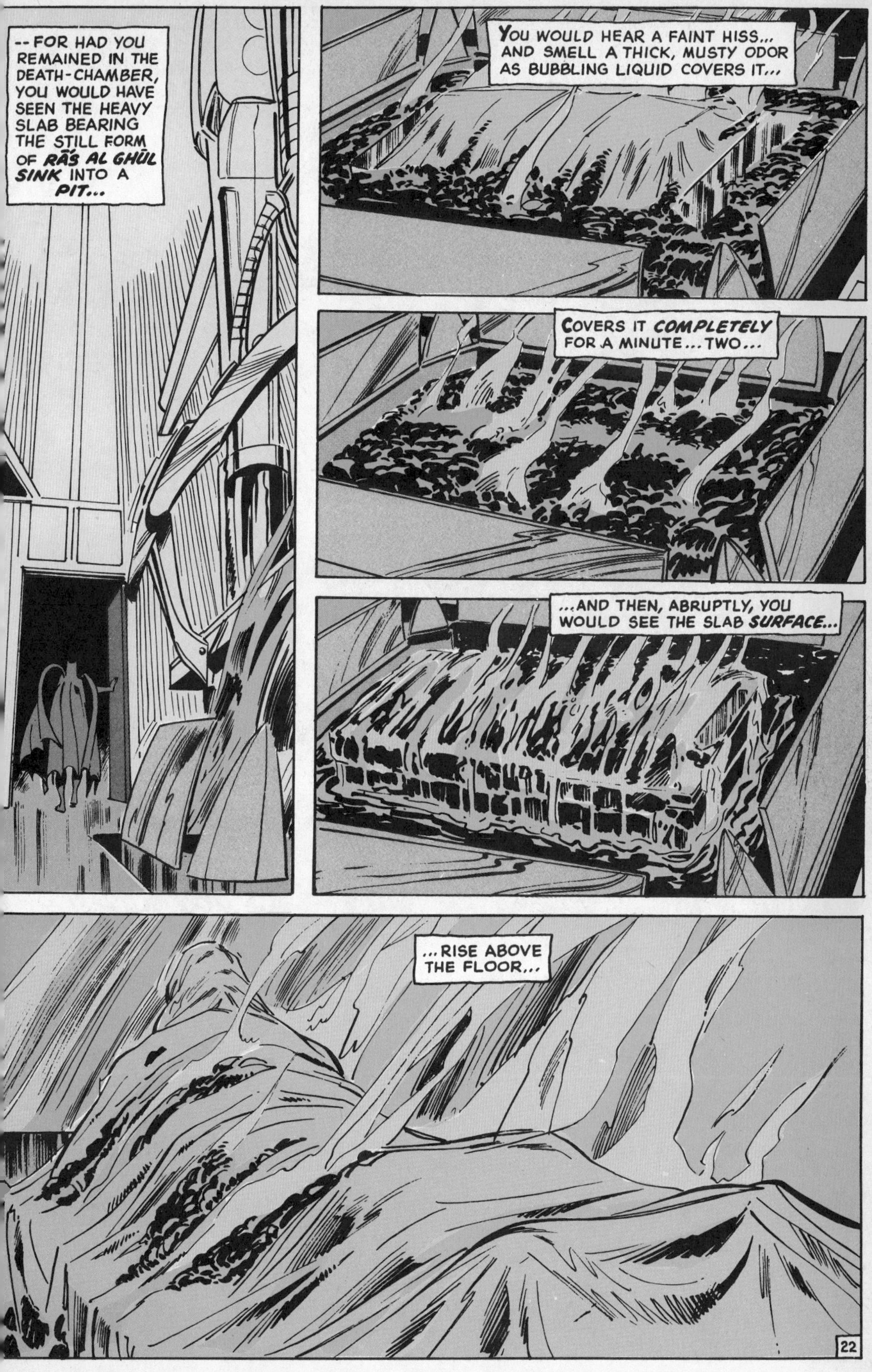
--FOR HAD YOU REMAINED IN THE DEATH-CHAMBER, YOU WOULD HAVE SEEN THE HEAVY SLAB BEARING THE STILL FORM OF *RĀS AL GHŪL* *SINK* INTO A *PIT...*
YOU WOULD HEAR A FAINT HISS... AND SMELL A THICK, MUSTY ODOR AS BUBBLING LIQUID COVERS IT...
COVERS IT *COMPLETELY* FOR A MINUTE... TWO...
...AND THEN, ABRUPTLY, YOU WOULD SEE THE SLAB *SURFACE...*
...RISE ABOVE THE FLOOR...
22

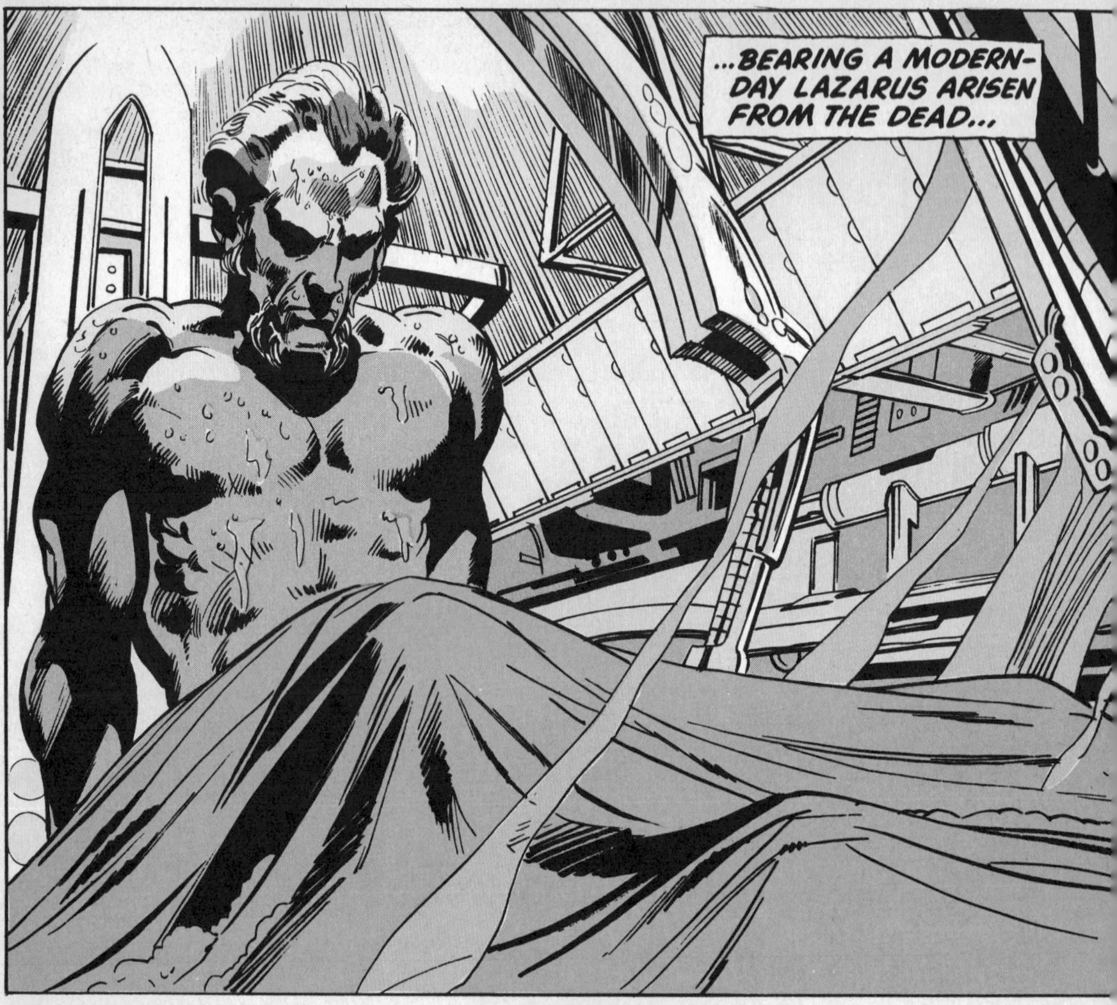
...BEARING A MODERN-DAY LAZARUS ARISEN FROM THE DEAD...

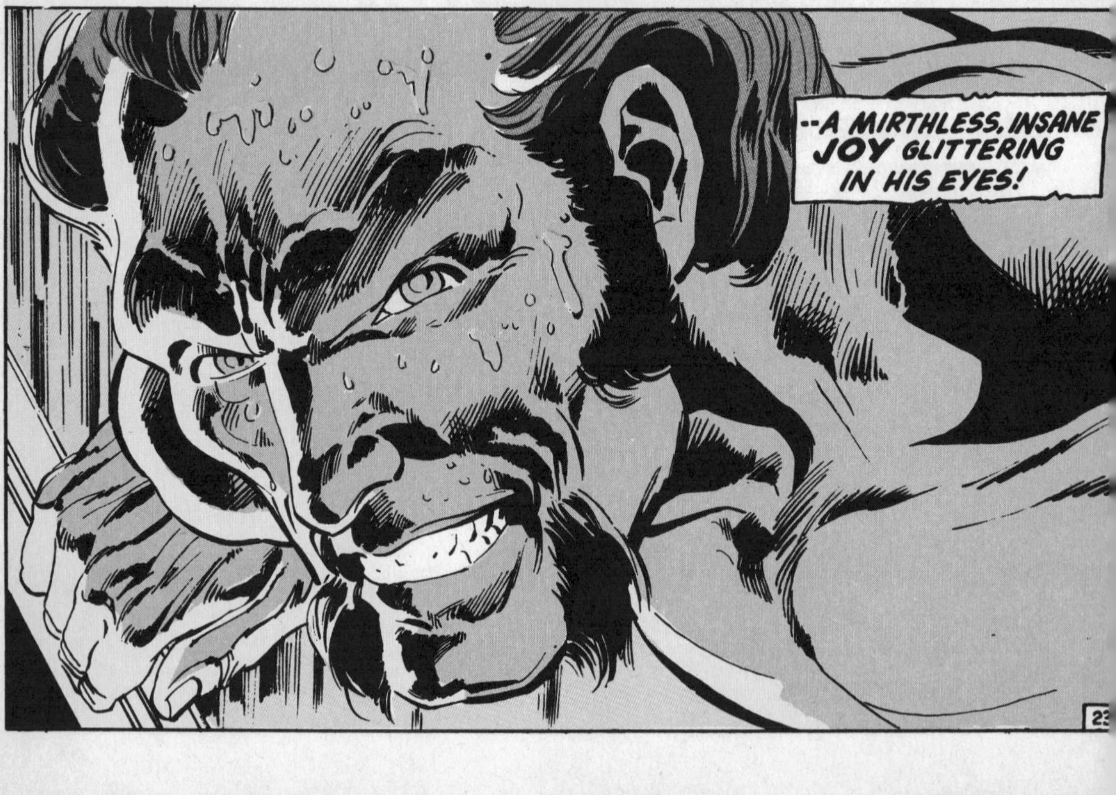
--A MIRTHLESS, INSANE JOY GLITTERING IN HIS EYES!

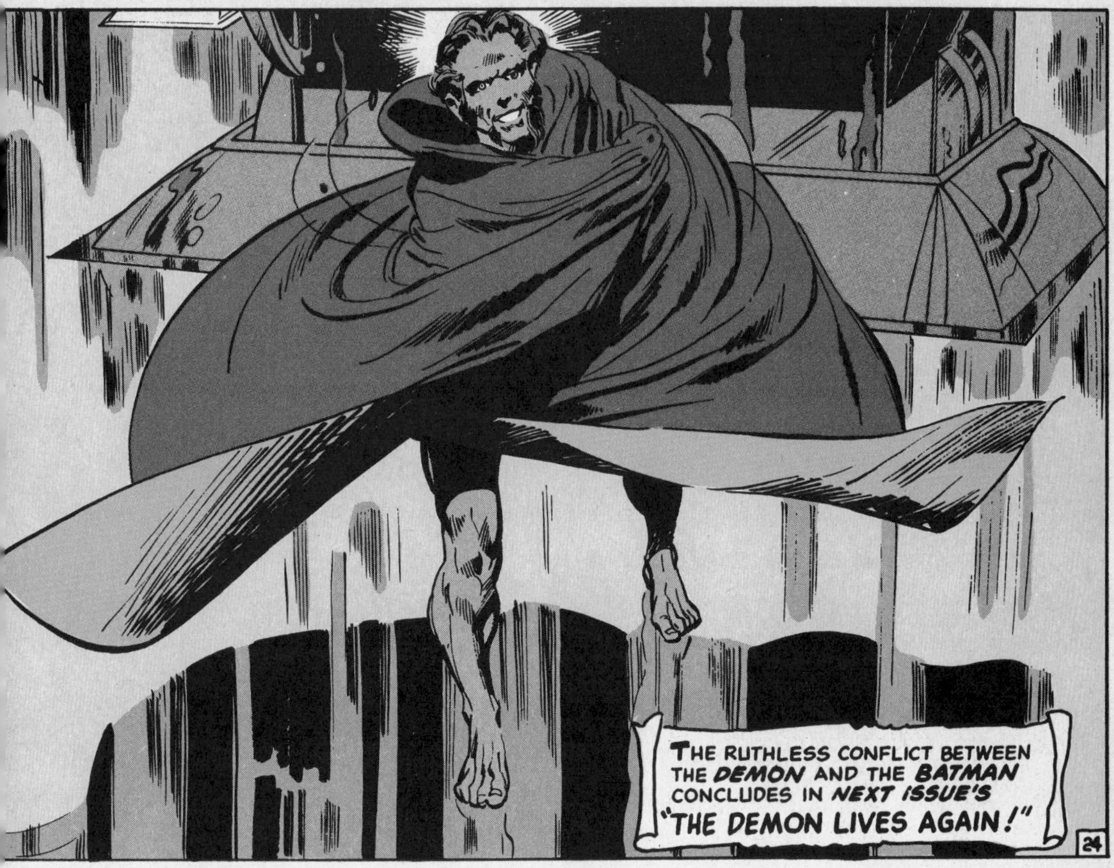
THE RUTHLESS CONFLICT BETWEEN
THE DEMON AND THE BATMAN
CONCLUDES IN NEXT ISSUE'S
"THE DEMON LIVES AGAIN!"
24

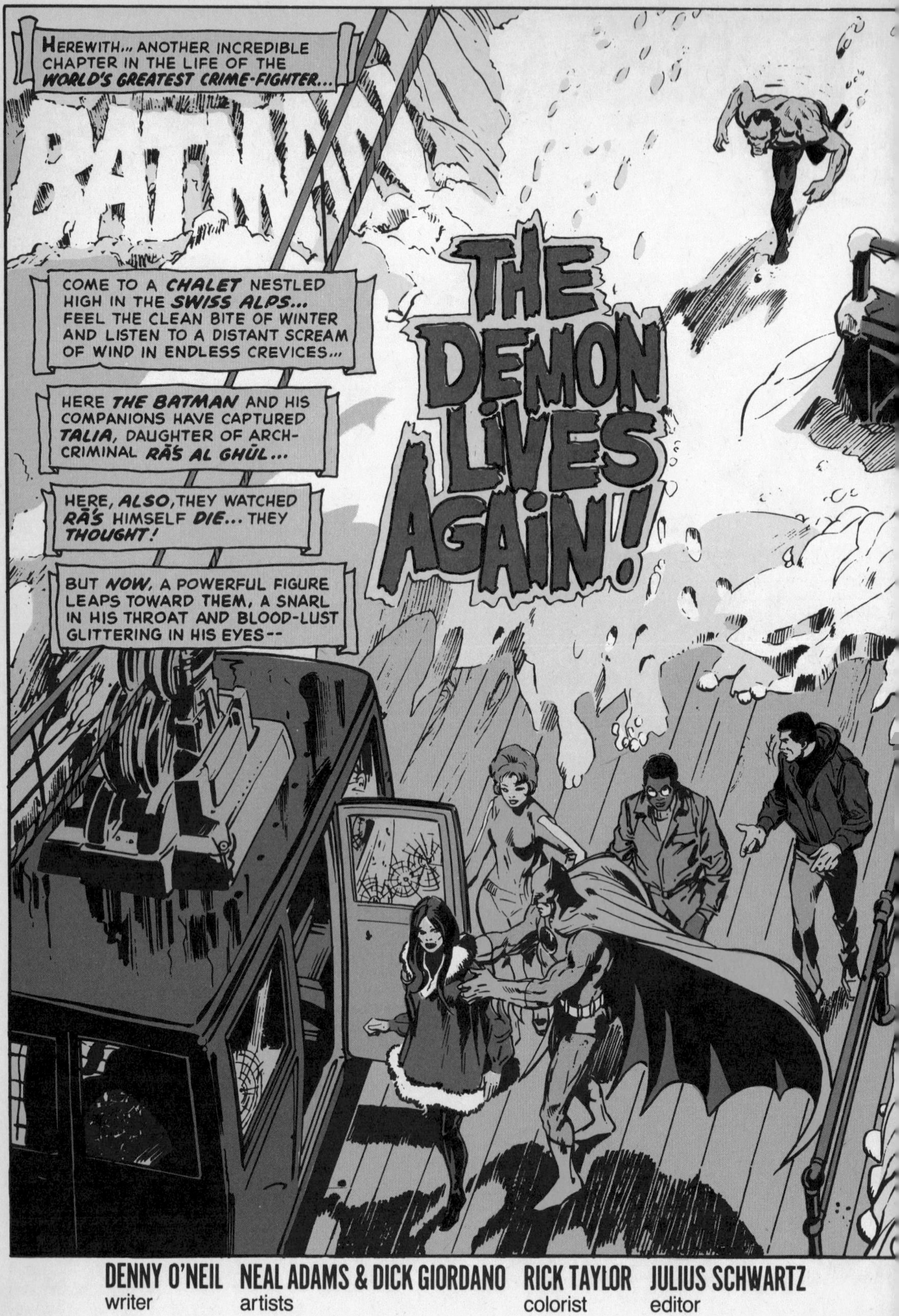
HEREWITH... ANOTHER INCREDIBLE CHAPTER IN THE LIFE OF THE WORLD'S GREATEST CRIME-FIGHTER...
BATMAN
THE DEMON LIVES AGAIN!
COME TO A CHALET NESTLED HIGH IN THE SWISS ALPS... FEEL THE CLEAN BITE OF WINTER AND LISTEN TO A DISTANT SCREAM OF WIND IN ENDLESS CREVICES...
HERE THE BATMAN AND HIS COMPANIONS HAVE CAPTURED TALIA, DAUGHTER OF ARCH-CRIMINAL RĀ'S AL GHŪL...
HERE, ALSO, THEY WATCHED RĀ'S HIMSELF DIE... THEY THOUGHT!
BUT NOW, A POWERFUL FIGURE LEAPS TOWARD THEM, A SNARL IN HIS THROAT AND BLOOD-LUST GLITTERING IN HIS EYES--

DENNY O'NEIL writer **NEAL ADAMS & DICK GIORDANO** artists **RICK TAYLOR** colorist **JULIUS SCHWARTZ** editor

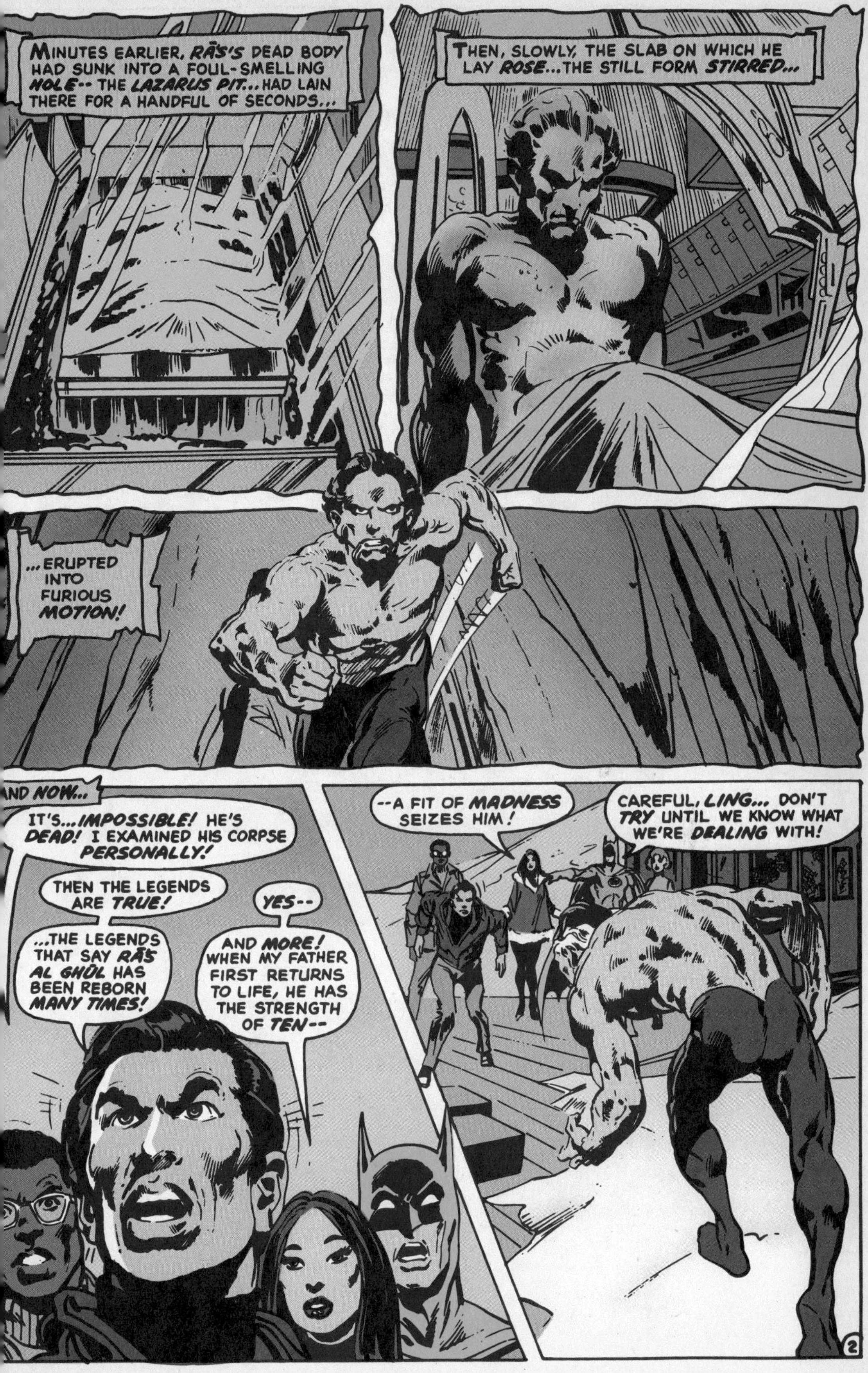
MINUTES EARLIER, RĀ'S'S DEAD BODY HAD SUNK INTO A FOUL-SMELLING HOLE-- THE LAZARUS PIT... HAD LAIN THERE FOR A HANDFUL OF SECONDS...
THEN, SLOWLY, THE SLAB ON WHICH HE LAY ROSE...THE STILL FORM STIRRED...
...ERUPTED INTO FURIOUS MOTION!
AND NOW...
IT'S...IMPOSSIBLE! HE'S DEAD! I EXAMINED HIS CORPSE PERSONALLY!
THEN THE LEGENDS ARE TRUE!
...THE LEGENDS THAT SAY RĀ'S AL GHŪL HAS BEEN REBORN MANY TIMES!
YES--
AND MORE! WHEN MY FATHER FIRST RETURNS TO LIFE, HE HAS THE STRENGTH OF TEN--
--A FIT OF MADNESS SEIZES HIM!
CAREFUL, LING... DON'T TRY UNTIL WE KNOW WHAT WE'RE DEALING WITH!
2

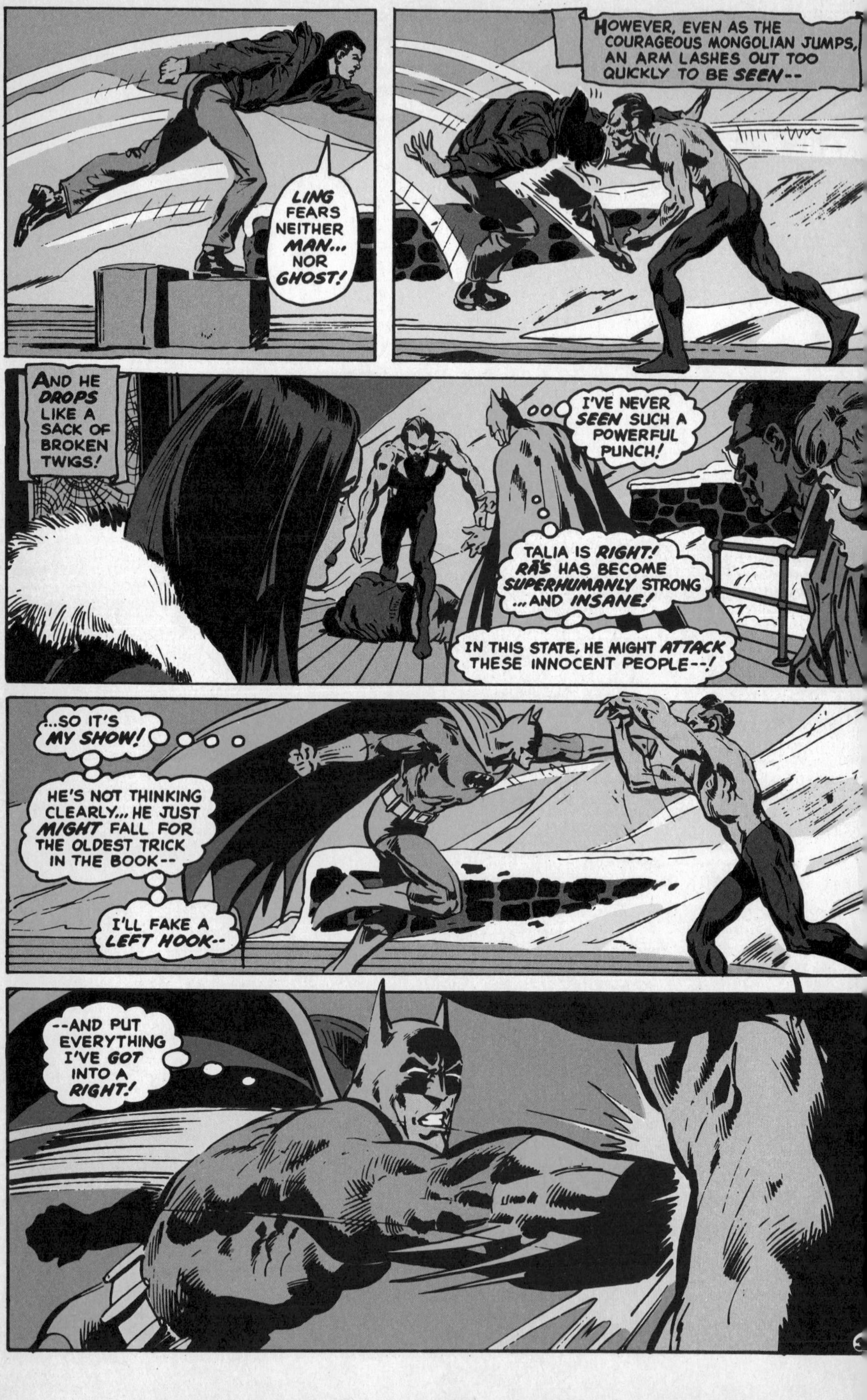
LING FEARS NEITHER MAN... NOR GHOST!
HOWEVER, EVEN AS THE COURAGEOUS MONGOLIAN JUMPS, AN ARM LASHES OUT TOO QUICKLY TO BE SEEN--
AND HE DROPS LIKE A SACK OF BROKEN TWIGS!
I'VE NEVER SEEN SUCH A POWERFUL PUNCH!
TALIA IS RIGHT! RĀ'S HAS BECOME SUPERHUMANLY STRONG ...AND INSANE!
IN THIS STATE, HE MIGHT ATTACK THESE INNOCENT PEOPLE--!
...SO IT'S MY SHOW!
HE'S NOT THINKING CLEARLY... HE JUST MIGHT FALL FOR THE OLDEST TRICK IN THE BOOK--
I'LL FAKE A LEFT HOOK--
--AND PUT EVERYTHING I'VE GOT INTO A RIGHT!

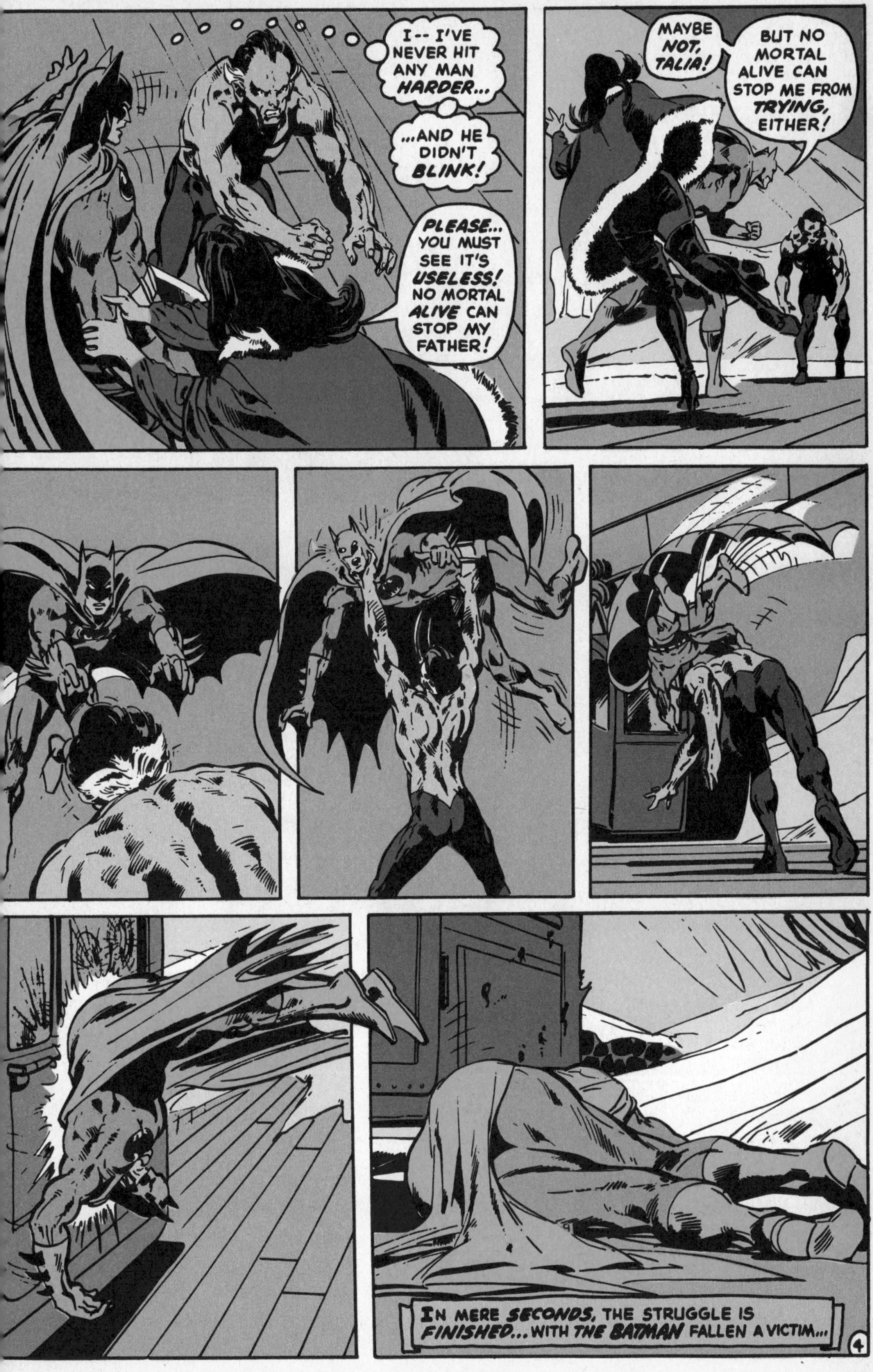
I-- I'VE NEVER HIT ANY MAN HARDER...
...AND HE DIDN'T BLINK!
PLEASE... YOU MUST SEE IT'S USELESS! NO MORTAL ALIVE CAN STOP MY FATHER!
MAYBE NOT, TALIA!
BUT NO MORTAL ALIVE CAN STOP ME FROM TRYING, EITHER!
IN MERE SECONDS, THE STRUGGLE IS FINISHED... WITH THE BATMAN FALLEN A VICTIM...
4

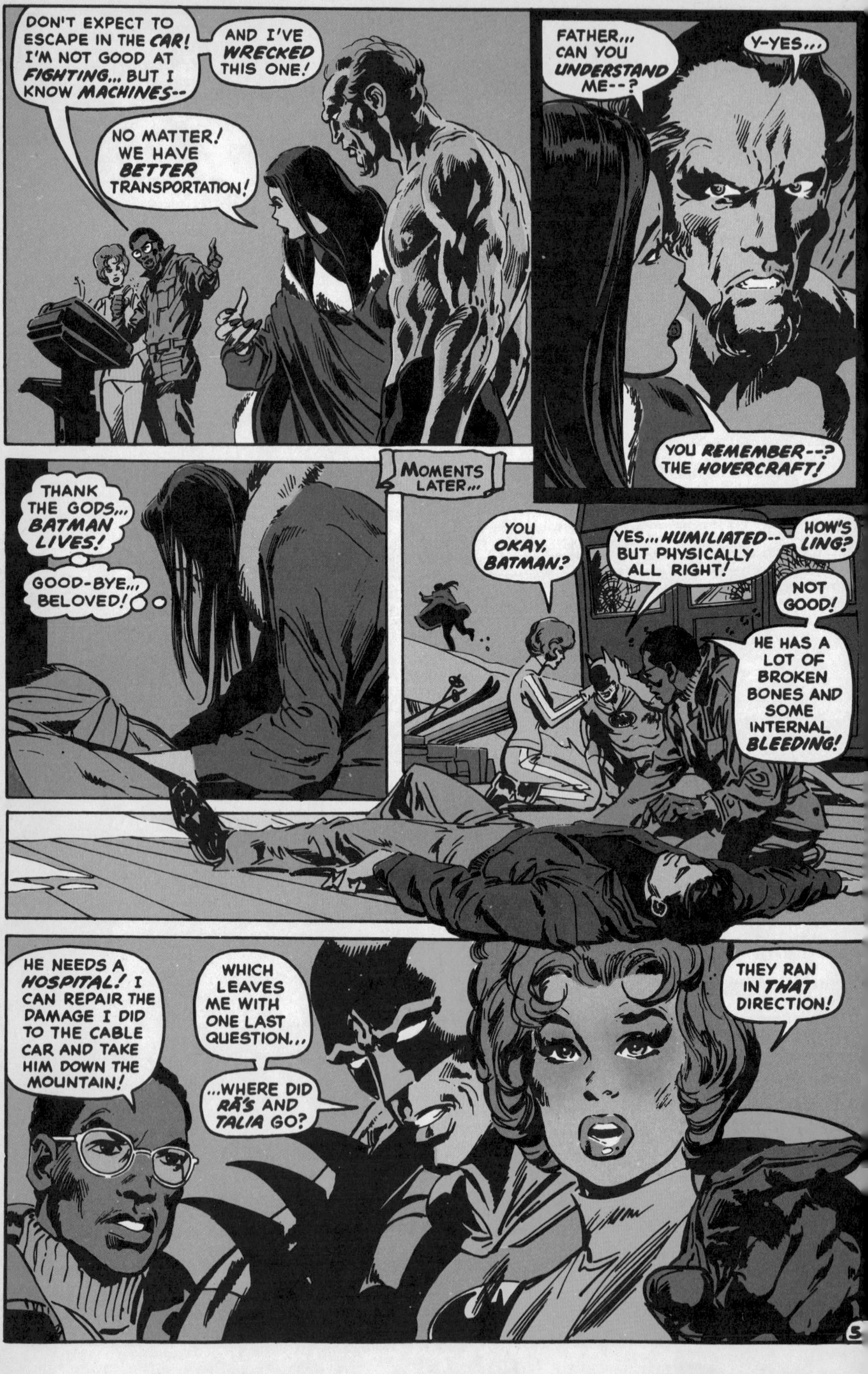
DON'T EXPECT TO ESCAPE IN THE CAR! I'M NOT GOOD AT FIGHTING... BUT I KNOW MACHINES--
AND I'VE WRECKED THIS ONE!
NO MATTER! WE HAVE BETTER TRANSPORTATION!
FATHER... CAN YOU UNDERSTAND ME--?
Y-YES...
YOU REMEMBER--? THE HOVERCRAFT!
MOMENTS LATER...
THANK THE GODS... BATMAN LIVES!
GOOD-BYE... BELOVED!
YOU OKAY, BATMAN?
YES... HUMILIATED-- BUT PHYSICALLY ALL RIGHT!
HOW'S LING?
NOT GOOD!
HE HAS A LOT OF BROKEN BONES AND SOME INTERNAL BLEEDING!
HE NEEDS A HOSPITAL! I CAN REPAIR THE DAMAGE I DID TO THE CABLE CAR AND TAKE HIM DOWN THE MOUNTAIN!
WHICH LEAVES ME WITH ONE LAST QUESTION...
...WHERE DID RA'S AND TALIA GO?
THEY RAN IN THAT DIRECTION!
5

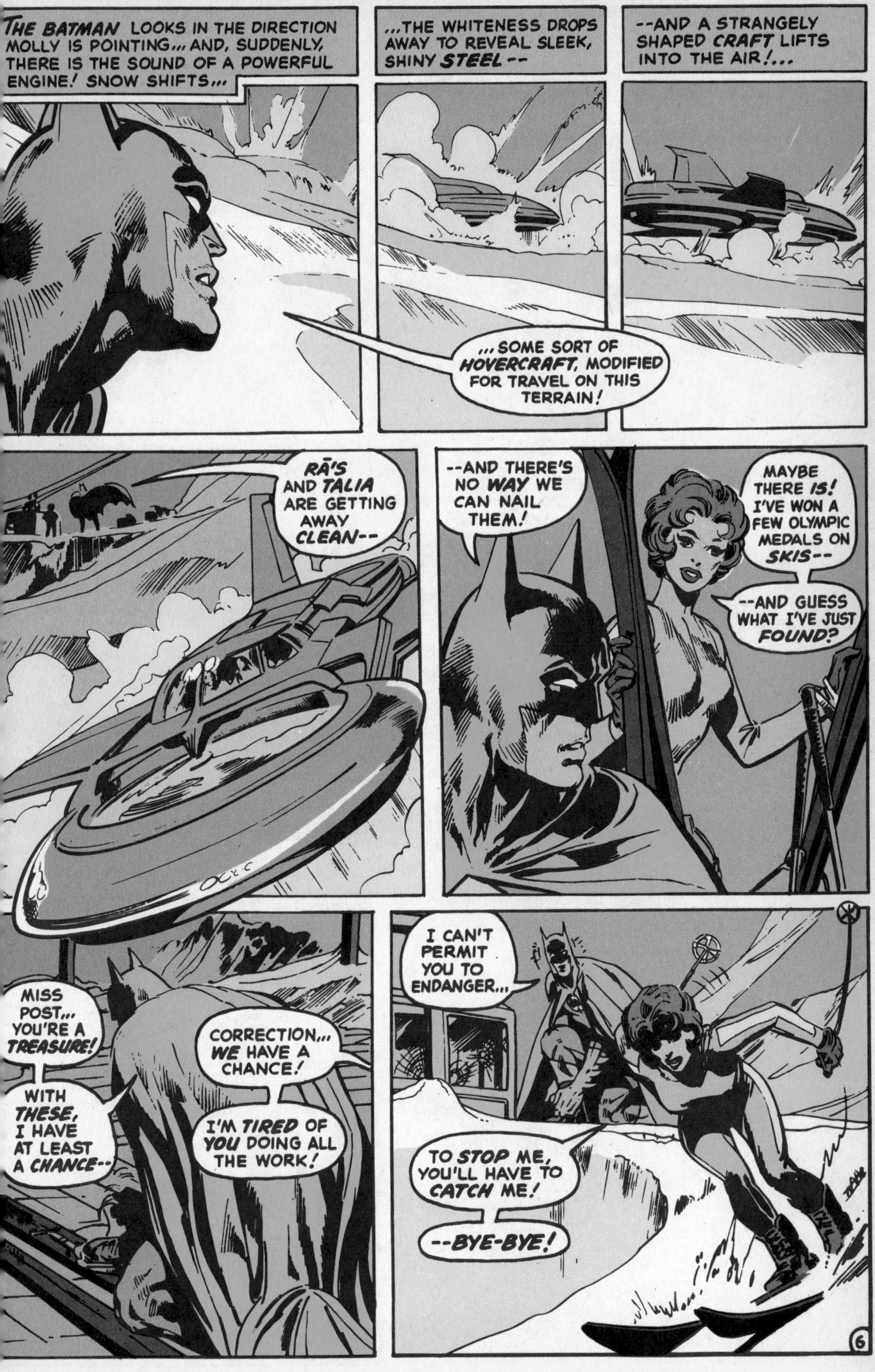
THE BATMAN LOOKS IN THE DIRECTION MOLLY IS POINTING... AND, SUDDENLY, THERE IS THE SOUND OF A POWERFUL ENGINE! SNOW SHIFTS...
...THE WHITENESS DROPS AWAY TO REVEAL SLEEK, SHINY STEEL--
--AND A STRANGELY SHAPED CRAFT LIFTS INTO THE AIR!...
...SOME SORT OF HOVERCRAFT, MODIFIED FOR TRAVEL ON THIS TERRAIN!
RĀ'S AND TALIA ARE GETTING AWAY CLEAN--
--AND THERE'S NO WAY WE CAN NAIL THEM!
MAYBE THERE IS! I'VE WON A FEW OLYMPIC MEDALS ON SKIS--
--AND GUESS WHAT I'VE JUST FOUND?
MISS POST... YOU'RE A TREASURE!
WITH THESE, I HAVE AT LEAST A CHANCE--
CORRECTION... WE HAVE A CHANCE!
I'M TIRED OF YOU DOING ALL THE WORK!
I CAN'T PERMIT YOU TO ENDANGER...
TO STOP ME, YOU'LL HAVE TO CATCH ME!
--BYE-BYE!
6

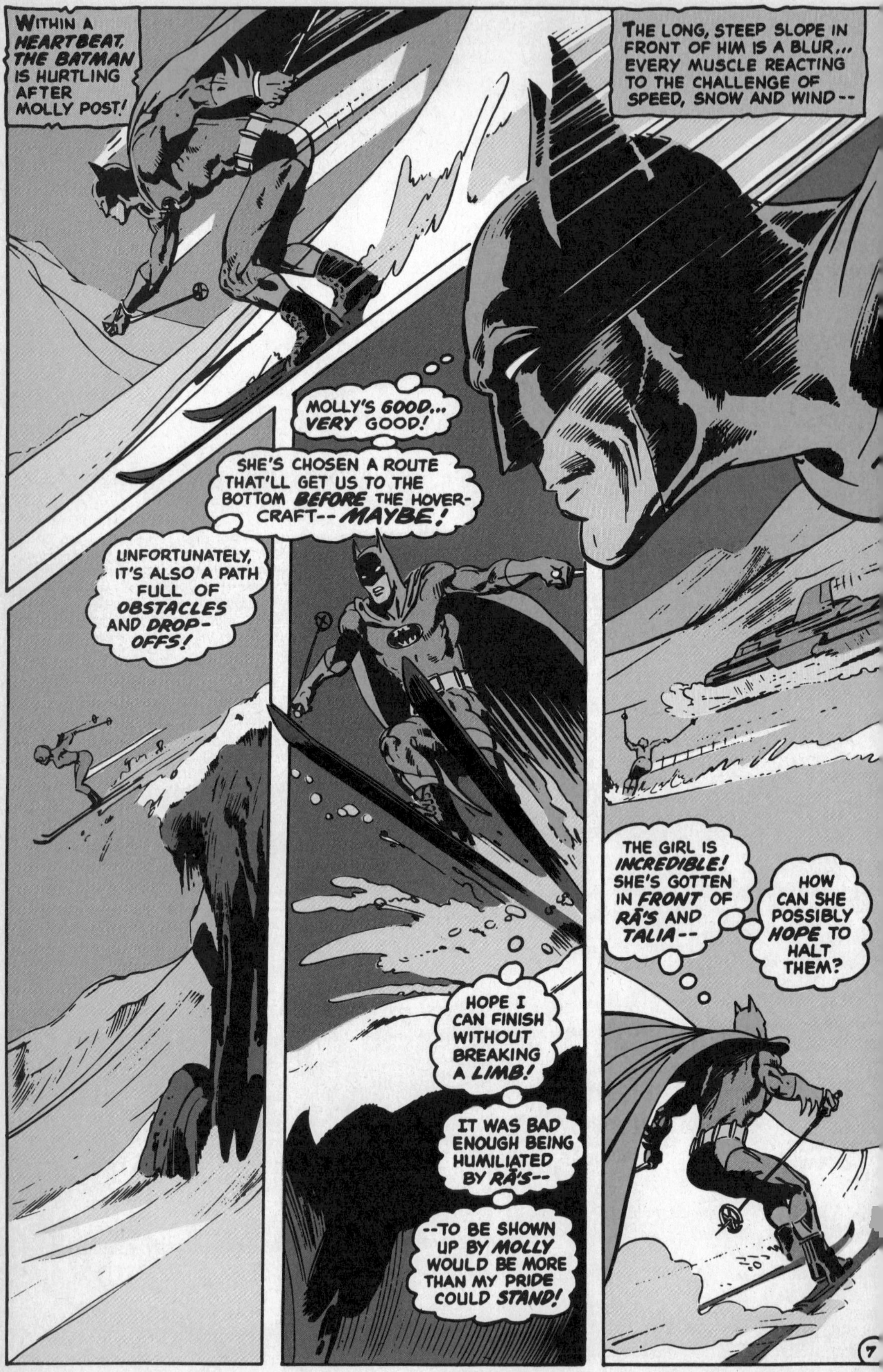
WITHIN A HEARTBEAT, THE BATMAN IS HURTLING AFTER MOLLY POST!
THE LONG, STEEP SLOPE IN FRONT OF HIM IS A BLUR... EVERY MUSCLE REACTING TO THE CHALLENGE OF SPEED, SNOW AND WIND--
MOLLY'S GOOD... VERY GOOD!
SHE'S CHOSEN A ROUTE THAT'LL GET US TO THE BOTTOM BEFORE THE HOVER-CRAFT-- MAYBE!
UNFORTUNATELY, IT'S ALSO A PATH FULL OF OBSTACLES AND DROP-OFFS!
HOPE I CAN FINISH WITHOUT BREAKING A LIMB!
IT WAS BAD ENOUGH BEING HUMILIATED BY RĀ'S--
--TO BE SHOWN UP BY MOLLY WOULD BE MORE THAN MY PRIDE COULD STAND!
THE GIRL IS INCREDIBLE! SHE'S GOTTEN IN FRONT OF RĀ'S AND TALIA--
HOW CAN SHE POSSIBLY HOPE TO HALT THEM?
7

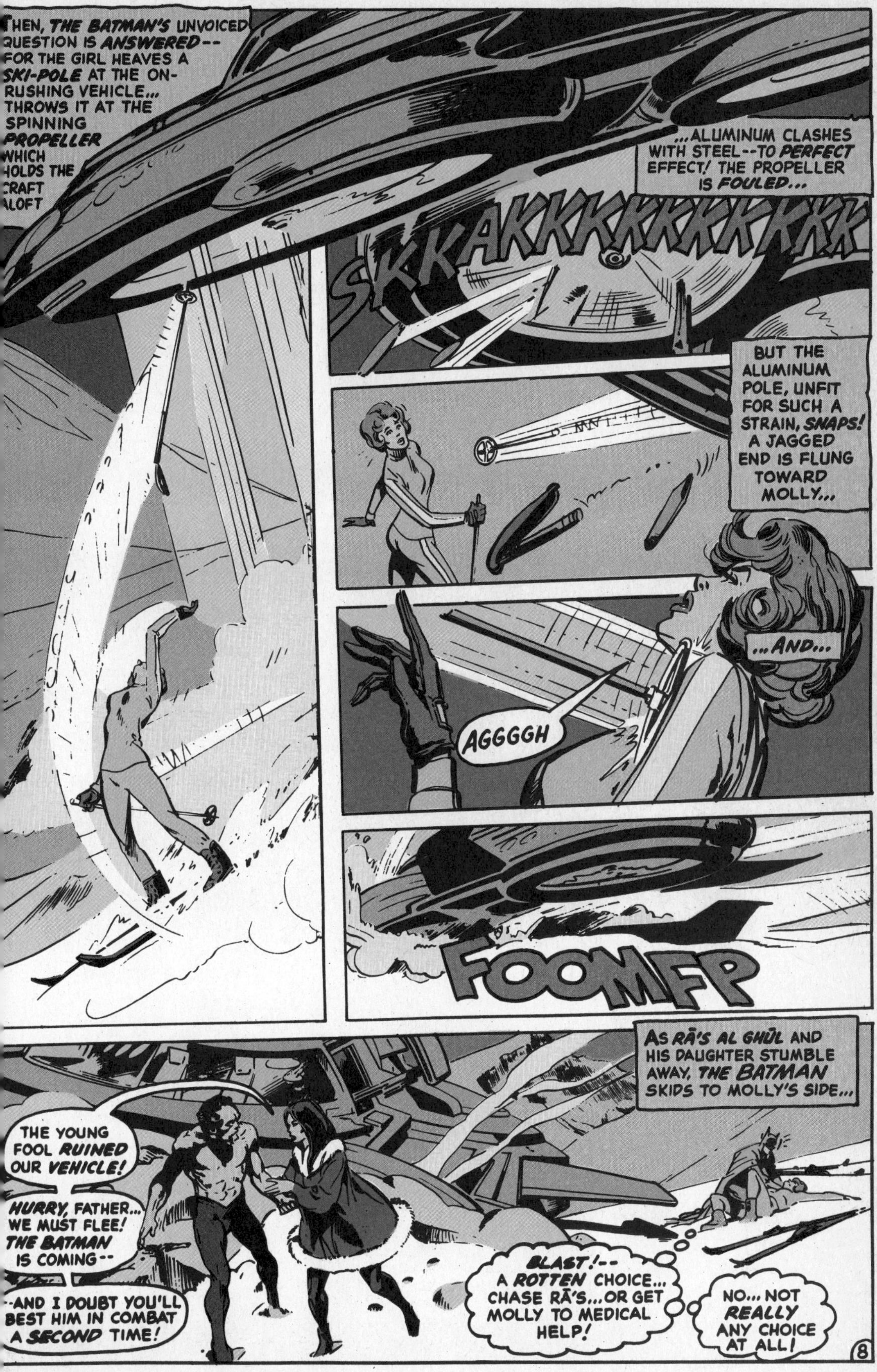
THEN, THE BATMAN'S UNVOICED QUESTION IS ANSWERED-- FOR THE GIRL HEAVES A SKI-POLE AT THE ON-RUSHING VEHICLE... THROWS IT AT THE SPINNING PROPELLER WHICH HOLDS THE CRAFT ALOFT
...ALUMINUM CLASHES WITH STEEL--TO PERFECT EFFECT! THE PROPELLER IS FOULED...
SKKAKKKKKKKKKK
BUT THE ALUMINUM POLE, UNFIT FOR SUCH A STRAIN, SNAPS! A JAGGED END IS FLUNG TOWARD MOLLY...
...AND...
AGGGGH
FOOMFP
AS RĀ'S AL GHŪL AND HIS DAUGHTER STUMBLE AWAY, THE BATMAN SKIDS TO MOLLY'S SIDE...
THE YOUNG FOOL RUINED OUR VEHICLE!
HURRY, FATHER... WE MUST FLEE! THE BATMAN IS COMING--
--AND I DOUBT YOU'LL BEST HIM IN COMBAT A SECOND TIME!
BLAST!-- A ROTTEN CHOICE... CHASE RĀ'S...OR GET MOLLY TO MEDICAL HELP!
NO... NOT REALLY ANY CHOICE AT ALL!
8

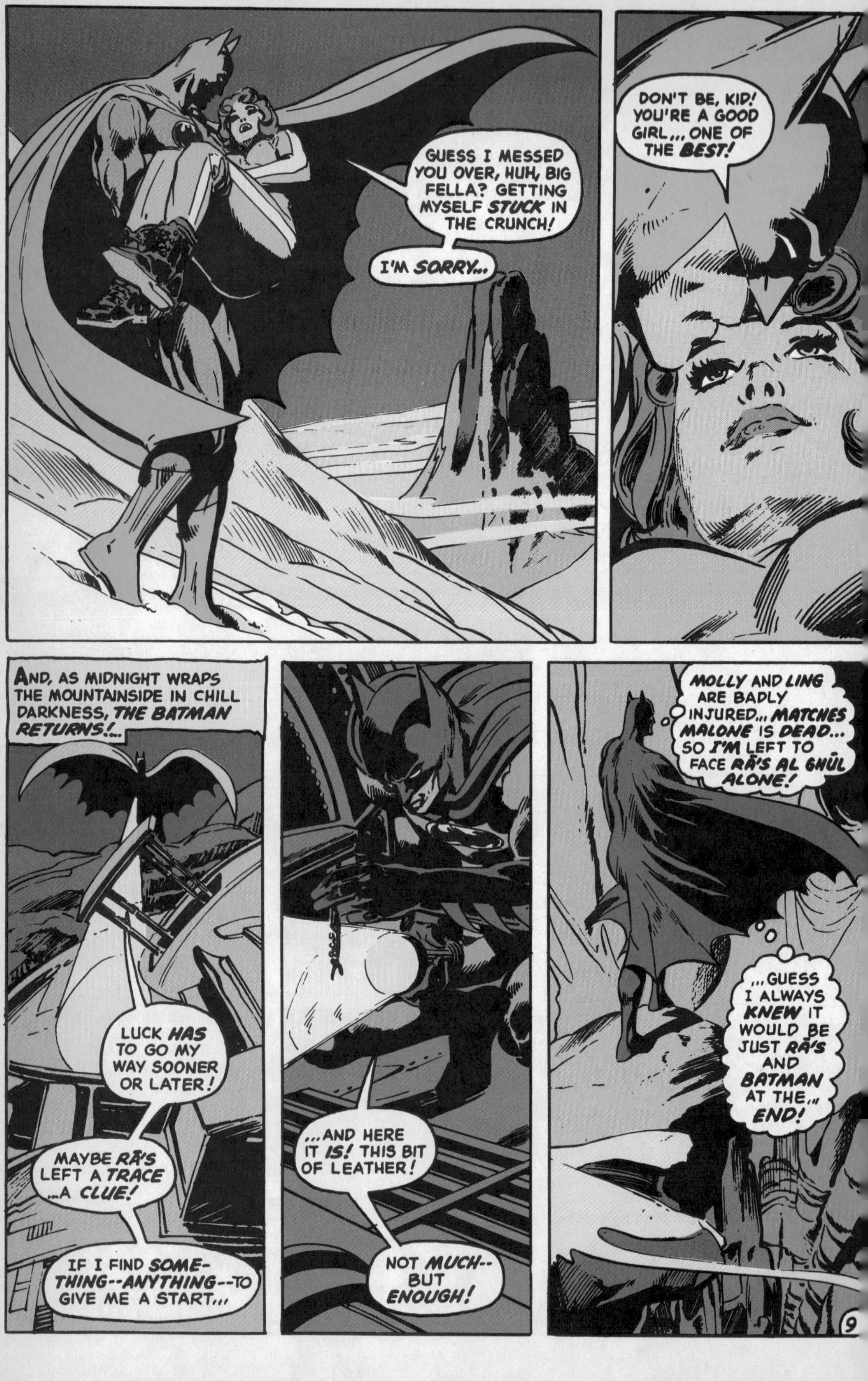
GUESS I MESSED YOU OVER, HUH, BIG FELLA? GETTING MYSELF STUCK IN THE CRUNCH!
I'M SORRY...
DON'T BE, KID! YOU'RE A GOOD GIRL... ONE OF THE BEST!
AND, AS MIDNIGHT WRAPS THE MOUNTAINSIDE IN CHILL DARKNESS, THE BATMAN RETURNS!...
LUCK HAS TO GO MY WAY SOONER OR LATER!
MAYBE RĀ'S LEFT A TRACE ...A CLUE!
IF I FIND SOME-THING--ANYTHING--TO GIVE ME A START...
...AND HERE IT IS! THIS BIT OF LEATHER!
NOT MUCH--BUT ENOUGH!
MOLLY AND LING ARE BADLY INJURED... MATCHES MALONE IS DEAD... SO I'M LEFT TO FACE RĀ'S AL GHŪL ALONE!
...GUESS I ALWAYS KNEW IT WOULD BE JUST RĀ'S AND BATMAN AT THE... END!
9

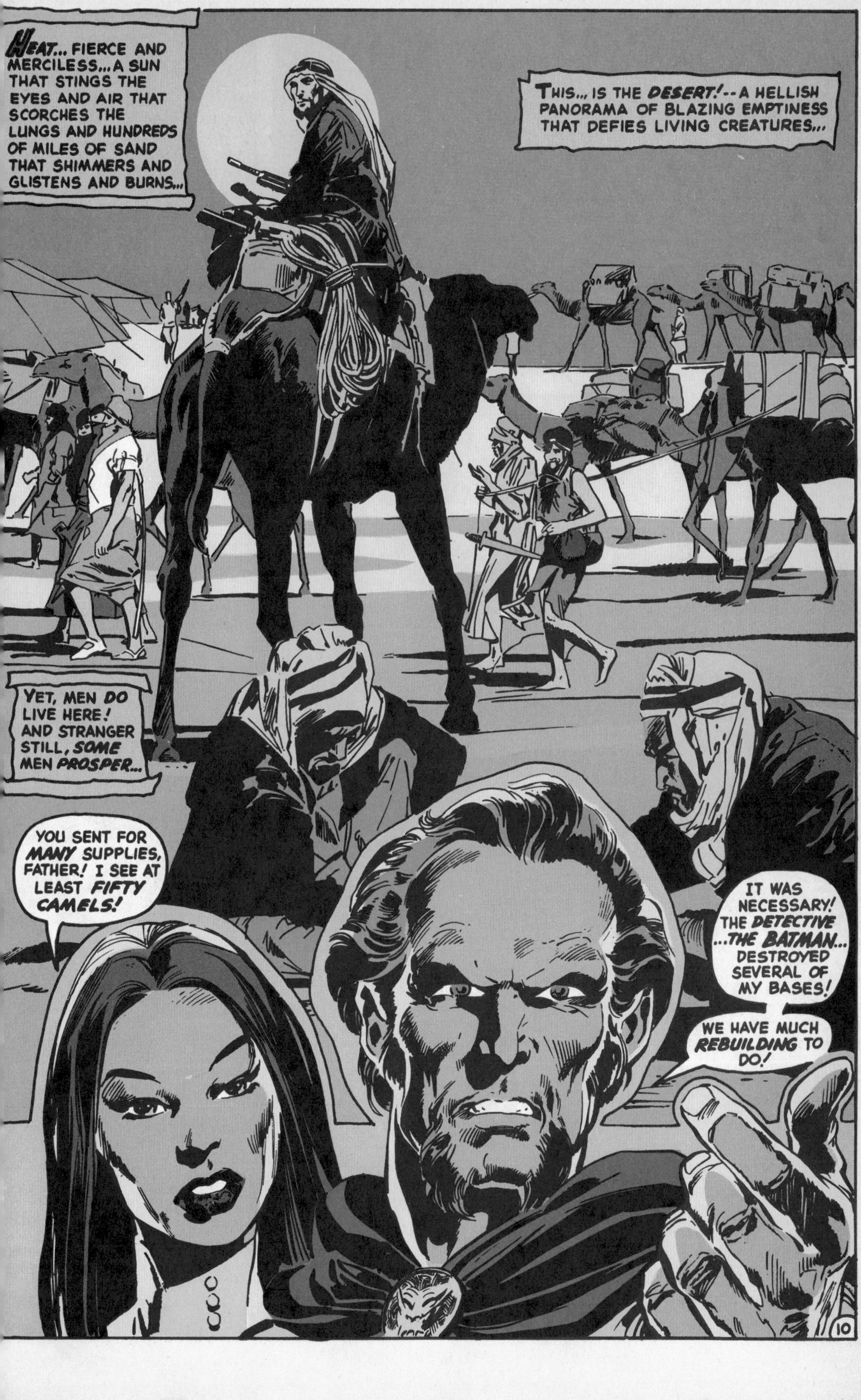
HEAT... FIERCE AND MERCILESS... A SUN THAT STINGS THE EYES AND AIR THAT SCORCHES THE LUNGS AND HUNDREDS OF MILES OF SAND THAT SHIMMERS AND GLISTENS AND BURNS...
THIS... IS THE DESERT!--A HELLISH PANORAMA OF BLAZING EMPTINESS THAT DEFIES LIVING CREATURES...
YET, MEN DO LIVE HERE! AND STRANGER STILL, SOME MEN PROSPER...
YOU SENT FOR MANY SUPPLIES, FATHER! I SEE AT LEAST FIFTY CAMELS!
IT WAS NECESSARY! THE DETECTIVE ...THE BATMAN... DESTROYED SEVERAL OF MY BASES!
WE HAVE MUCH REBUILDING TO DO!
10

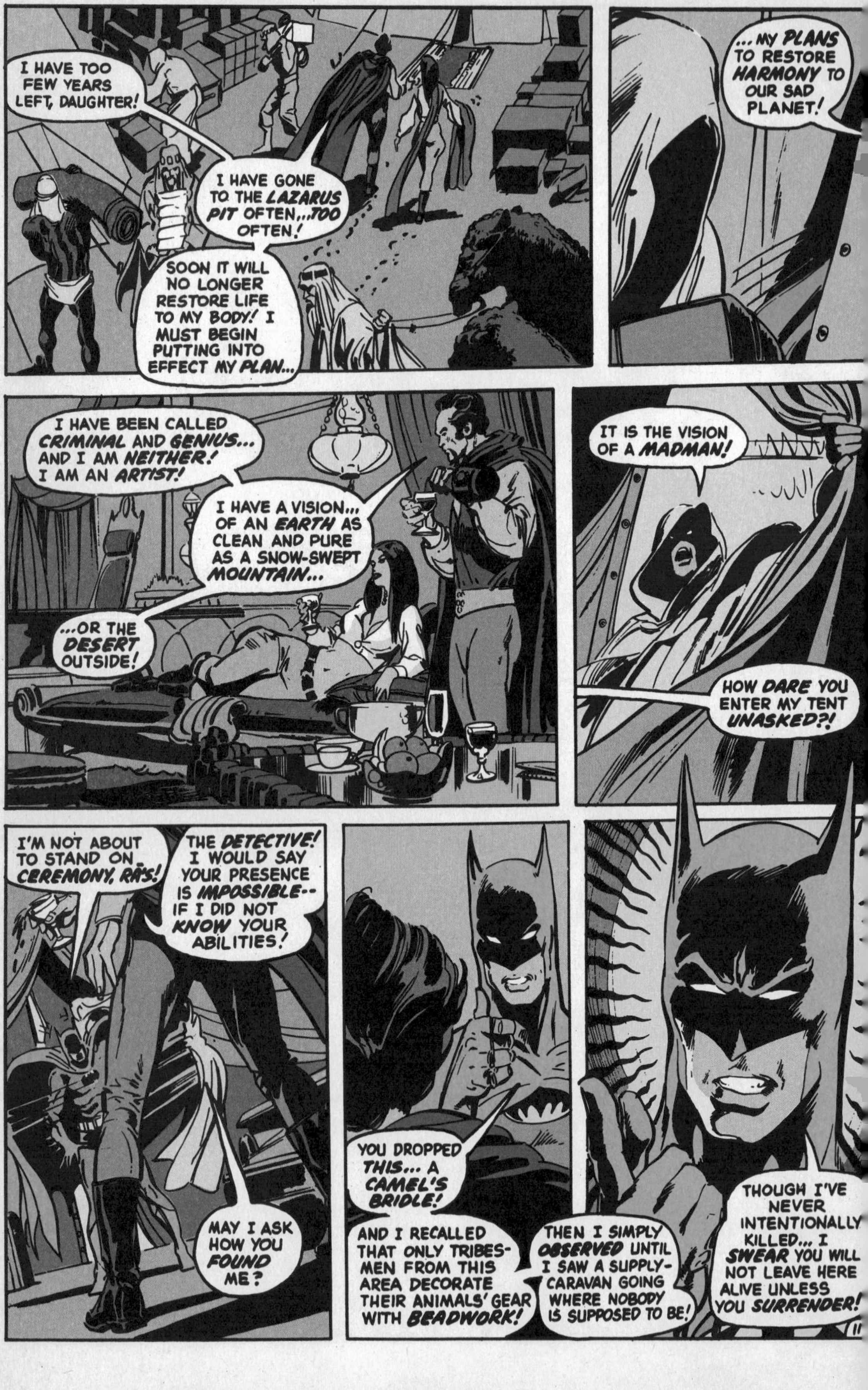
I HAVE TOO FEW YEARS LEFT, DAUGHTER!
I HAVE GONE TO THE LAZARUS PIT OFTEN,...TOO OFTEN!
SOON IT WILL NO LONGER RESTORE LIFE TO MY BODY! I MUST BEGIN PUTTING INTO EFFECT MY PLAN...
...MY PLANS TO RESTORE HARMONY TO OUR SAD PLANET!
I HAVE BEEN CALLED CRIMINAL AND GENIUS... AND I AM NEITHER! I AM AN ARTIST!
I HAVE A VISION... OF AN EARTH AS CLEAN AND PURE AS A SNOW-SWEPT MOUNTAIN...
...OR THE DESERT OUTSIDE!
IT IS THE VISION OF A MADMAN!
HOW DARE YOU ENTER MY TENT UNASKED?!
I'M NOT ABOUT TO STAND ON CEREMONY, RĀ'S!
THE DETECTIVE! I WOULD SAY YOUR PRESENCE IS IMPOSSIBLE-- IF I DID NOT KNOW YOUR ABILITIES!
MAY I ASK HOW YOU FOUND ME?
YOU DROPPED THIS... A CAMEL'S BRIDLE!
AND I RECALLED THAT ONLY TRIBES-MEN FROM THIS AREA DECORATE THEIR ANIMALS' GEAR WITH BEADWORK!
THEN I SIMPLY OBSERVED UNTIL I SAW A SUPPLY-CARAVAN GOING WHERE NOBODY IS SUPPOSED TO BE!
THOUGH I'VE NEVER INTENTIONALLY KILLED... I SWEAR YOU WILL NOT LEAVE HERE ALIVE UNLESS YOU SURRENDER!
11

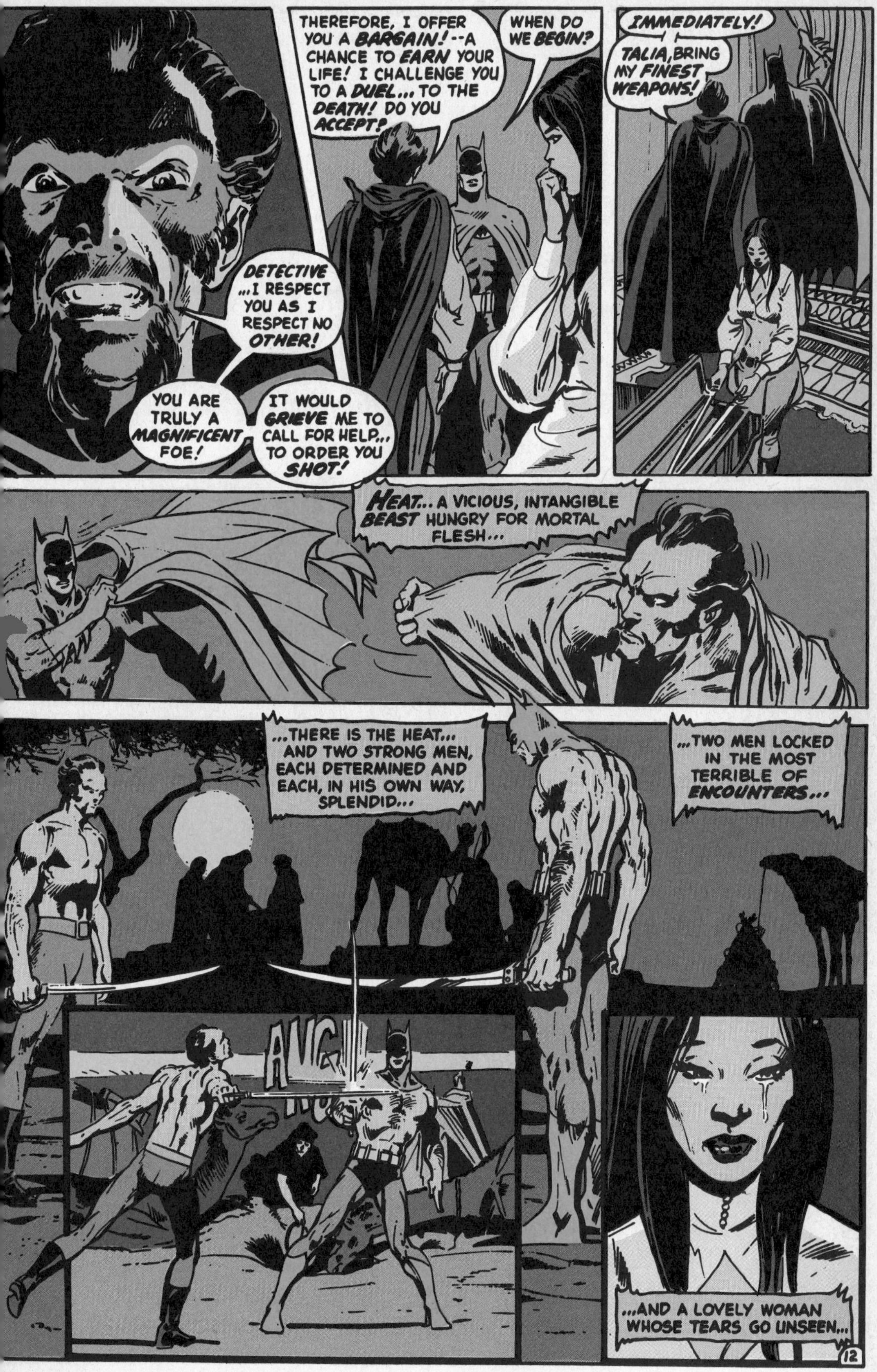
DETECTIVE ...I RESPECT YOU AS I RESPECT NO OTHER!
YOU ARE TRULY A MAGNIFICENT FOE!
IT WOULD GRIEVE ME TO CALL FOR HELP... TO ORDER YOU SHOT!
THEREFORE, I OFFER YOU A BARGAIN! --A CHANCE TO EARN YOUR LIFE! I CHALLENGE YOU TO A DUEL... TO THE DEATH! DO YOU ACCEPT?
WHEN DO WE BEGIN?
IMMEDIATELY!
TALIA, BRING MY FINEST WEAPONS!
HEAT... A VICIOUS, INTANGIBLE BEAST HUNGRY FOR MORTAL FLESH...
...THERE IS THE HEAT... AND TWO STRONG MEN, EACH DETERMINED AND EACH, IN HIS OWN WAY, SPLENDID...
...TWO MEN LOCKED IN THE MOST TERRIBLE OF ENCOUNTERS...
ANG
...AND A LOVELY WOMAN WHOSE TEARS GO UNSEEN...
12

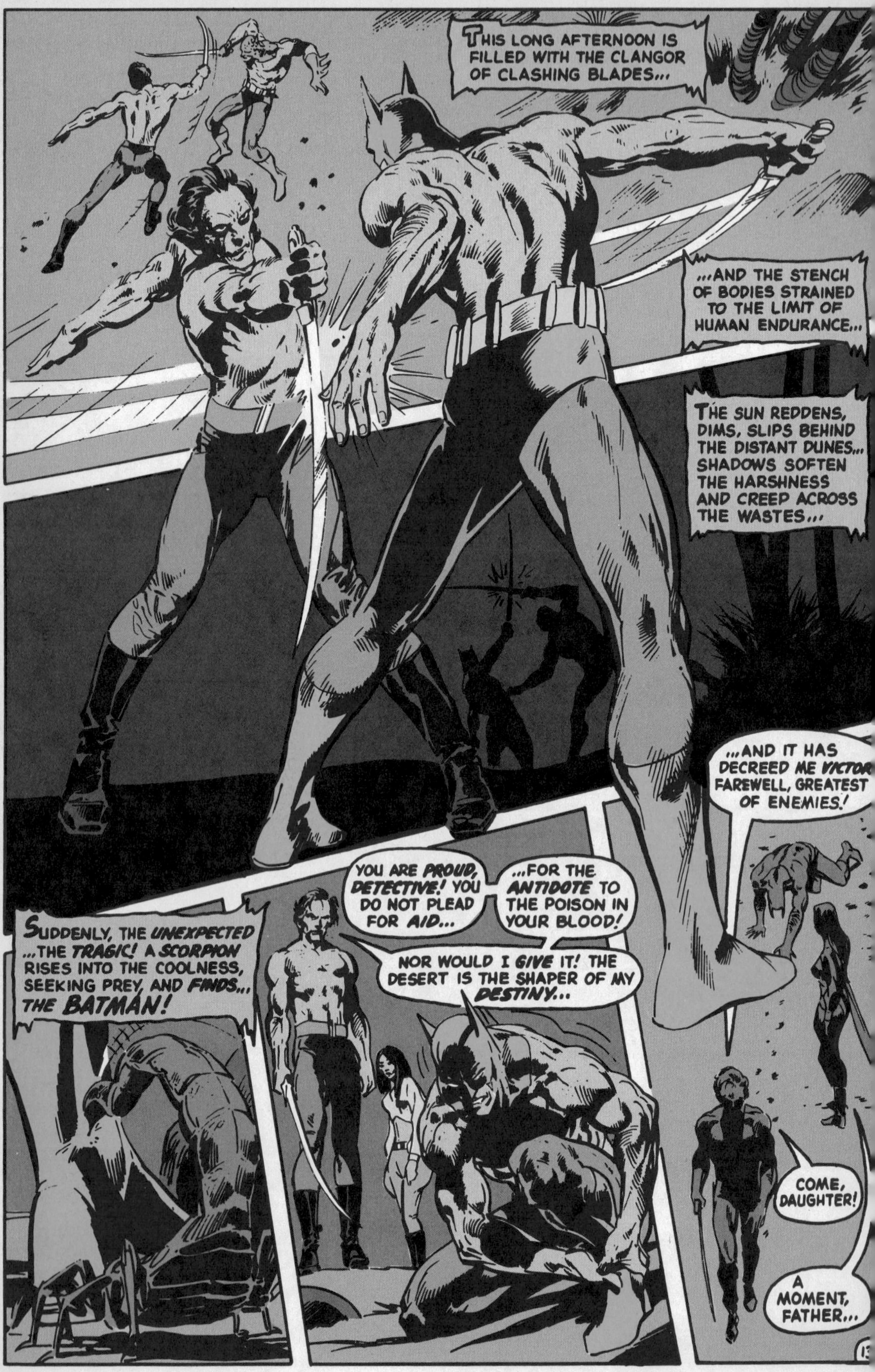
THIS LONG AFTERNOON IS FILLED WITH THE CLANGOR OF CLASHING BLADES...
...AND THE STENCH OF BODIES STRAINED TO THE LIMIT OF HUMAN ENDURANCE...
THE SUN REDDENS, DIMS, SLIPS BEHIND THE DISTANT DUNES... SHADOWS SOFTEN THE HARSHNESS AND CREEP ACROSS THE WASTES...
SUDDENLY, THE UNEXPECTED ...THE TRAGIC! A SCORPION RISES INTO THE COOLNESS, SEEKING PREY, AND FINDS... THE BATMAN!
YOU ARE PROUD, DETECTIVE! YOU DO NOT PLEAD FOR AID...
...FOR THE ANTIDOTE TO THE POISON IN YOUR BLOOD!
NOR WOULD I GIVE IT! THE DESERT IS THE SHAPER OF MY DESTINY...
...AND IT HAS DECREED ME VICTOR FAREWELL, GREATEST OF ENEMIES!
COME, DAUGHTER!
A MOMENT, FATHER...

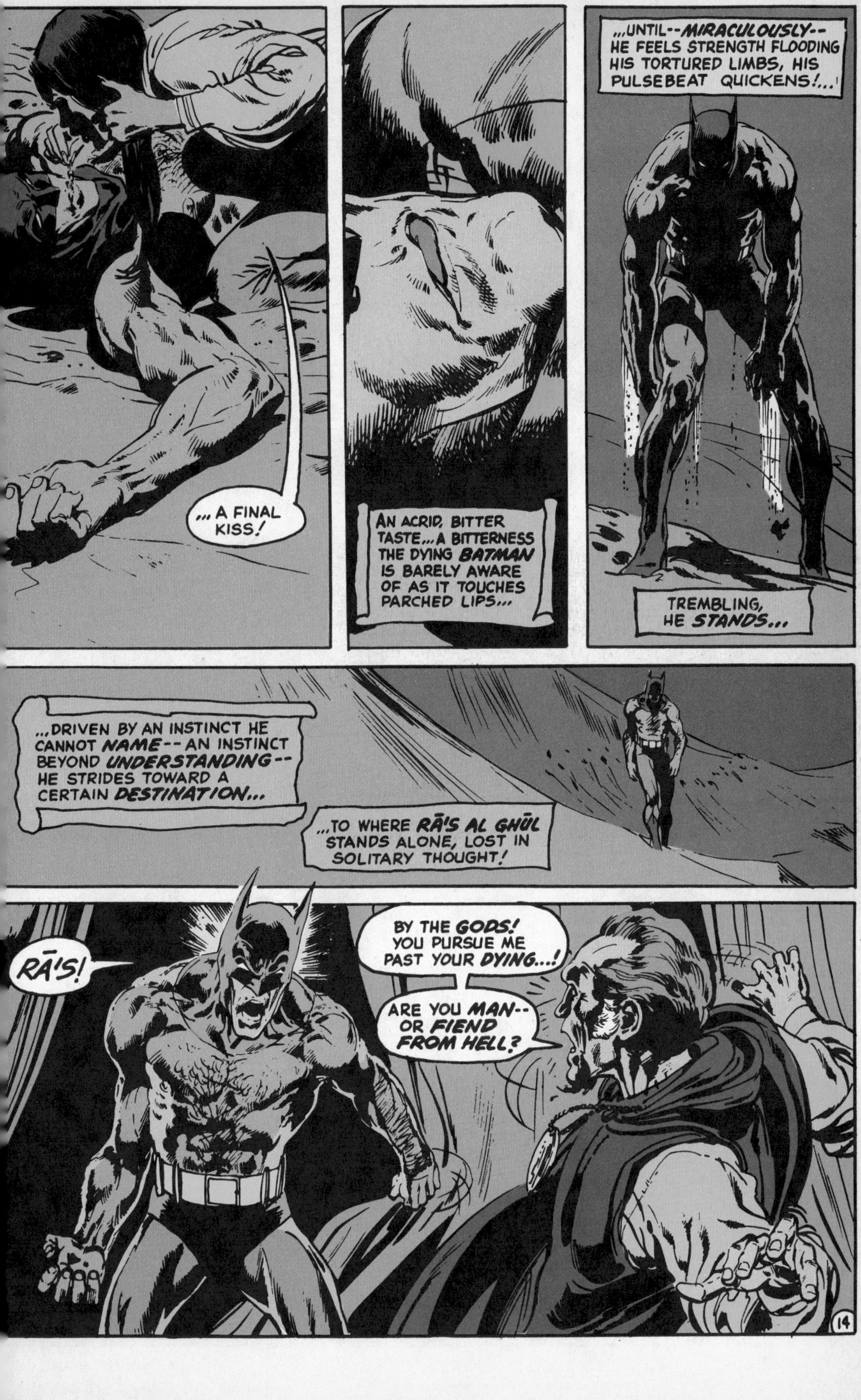
...A FINAL KISS!
AN ACRID, BITTER TASTE... A BITTERNESS THE DYING BATMAN IS BARELY AWARE OF AS IT TOUCHES PARCHED LIPS...
...UNTIL--MIRACULOUSLY--HE FEELS STRENGTH FLOODING HIS TORTURED LIMBS, HIS PULSEBEAT QUICKENS!...
TREMBLING, HE STANDS...
...DRIVEN BY AN INSTINCT HE CANNOT NAME-- AN INSTINCT BEYOND UNDERSTANDING-- HE STRIDES TOWARD A CERTAIN DESTINATION...
...TO WHERE RĀ'S AL GHŪL STANDS ALONE, LOST IN SOLITARY THOUGHT!
RĀ'S!
BY THE GODS! YOU PURSUE ME PAST YOUR DYING...!
ARE YOU MAN--OR FIEND FROM HELL?
14

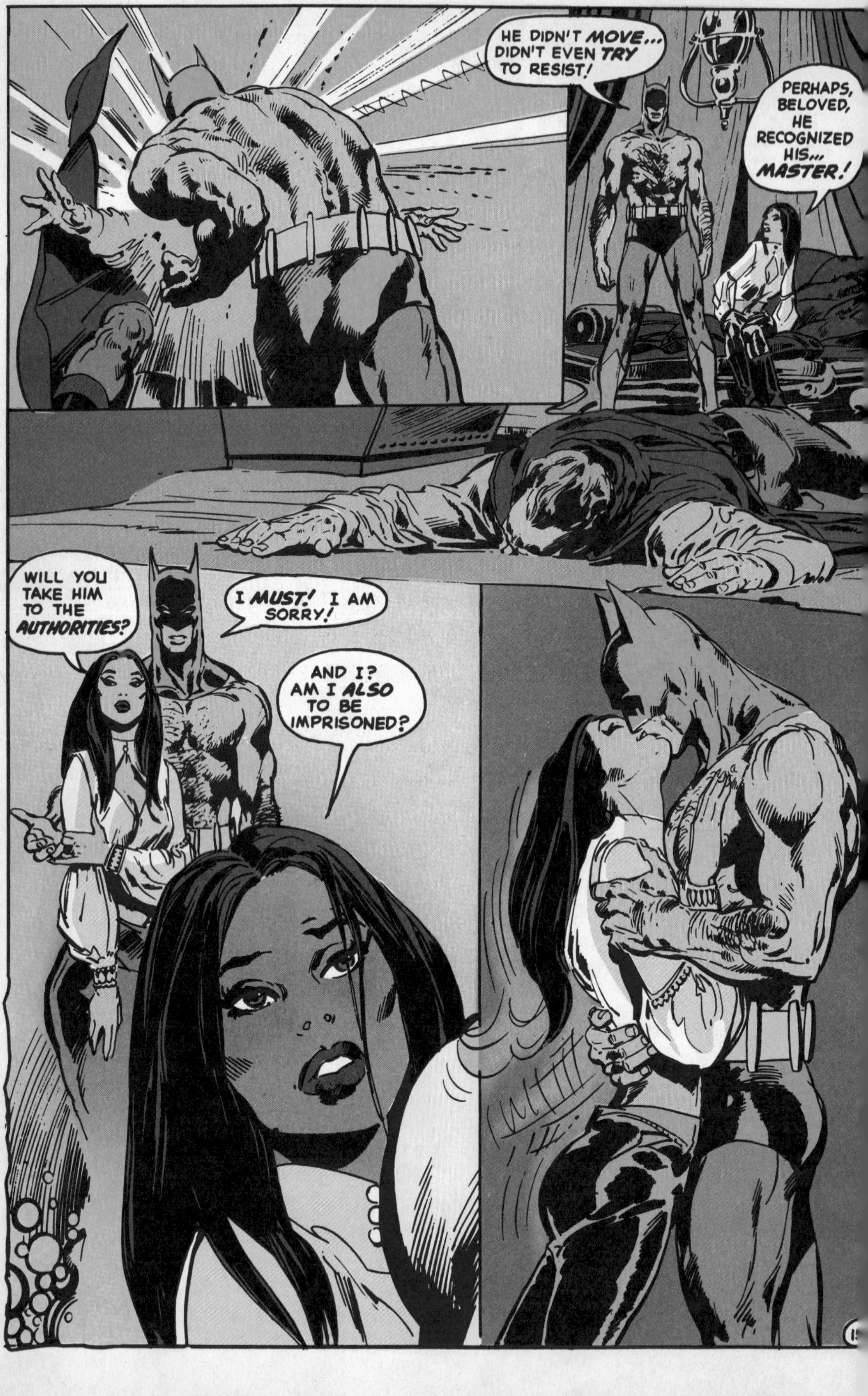
HE DIDN'T MOVE... DIDN'T EVEN TRY TO RESIST!
PERHAPS, BELOVED, HE RECOGNIZED HIS... MASTER!
WILL YOU TAKE HIM TO THE AUTHORITIES?
I MUST! I AM SORRY!
AND I? AM I ALSO TO BE IMPRISONED?

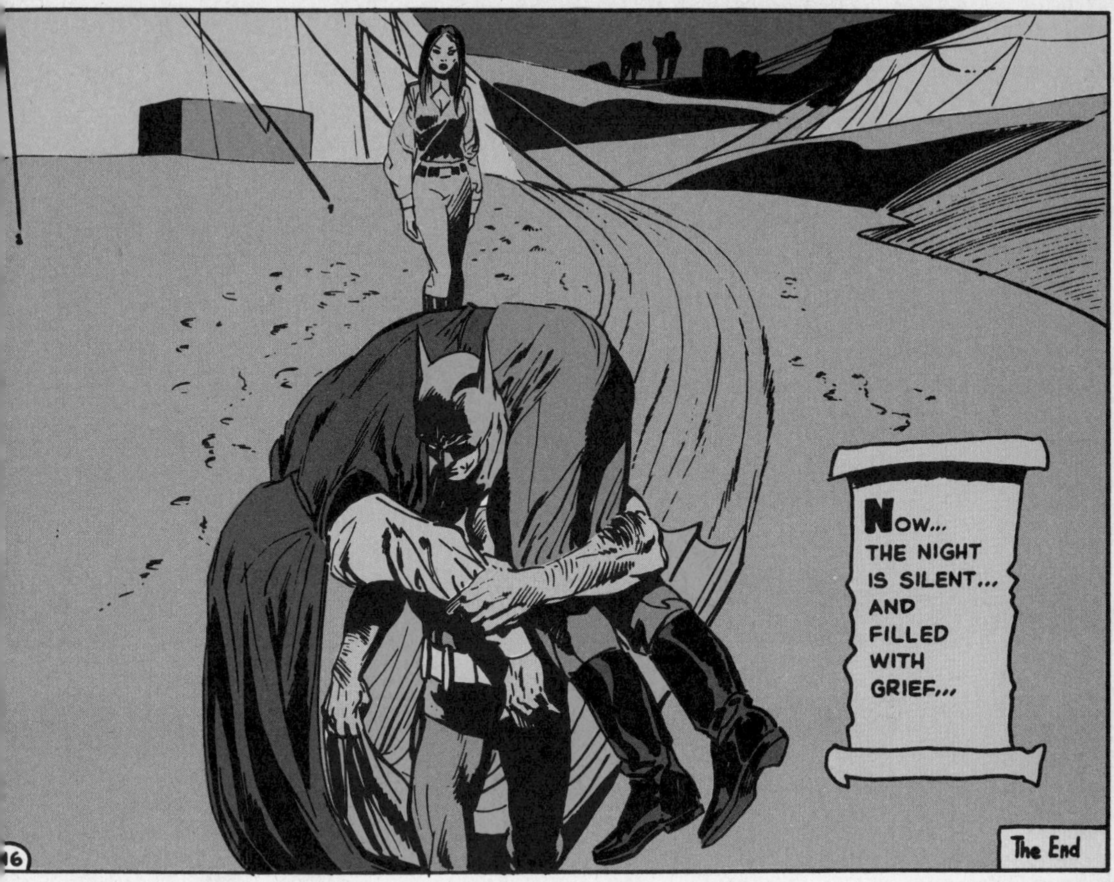
16
NOW...
THE NIGHT
IS SILENT...
AND
FILLED
WITH
GRIEF...
The End

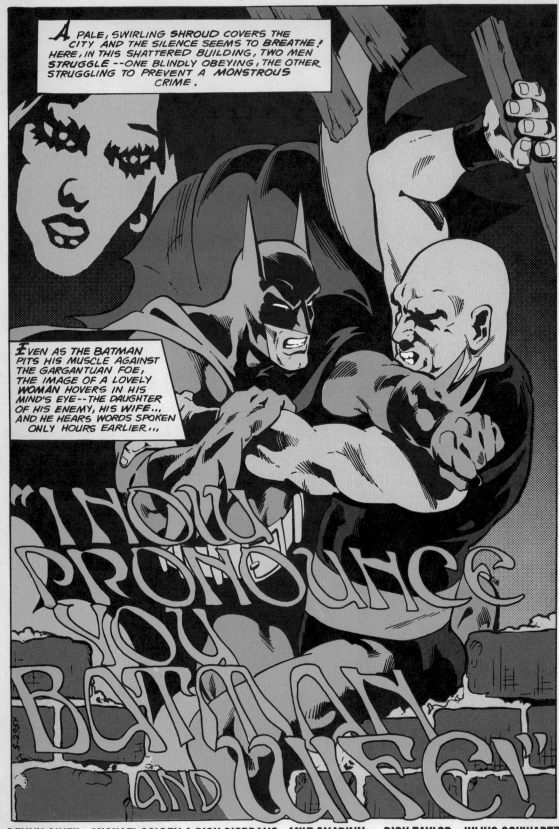

A PALE, SWIRLING SHROUD COVERS THE CITY AND THE SILENCE SEEMS TO BREATHE! HERE, IN THIS SHATTERED BUILDING, TWO MEN STRUGGLE --ONE BLINDLY OBEYING, THE OTHER STRUGGLING TO PREVENT A MONSTROUS CRIME.

EVEN AS THE BATMAN PITS HIS MUSCLE AGAINST THE GARGANTUAN FOE, THE IMAGE OF A LOVELY WOMAN HOVERS IN HIS MIND'S EYE--THE DAUGHTER OF HIS ENEMY, HIS WIFE... AND HE HEARS WORDS SPOKEN ONLY HOURS EARLIER...

"I NOW PRONOUNCE YOU BATMAN AND WIFE!"

DENNY O'NEIL writer **MICHAEL GOLDEN & DICK GIORDANO** artists **MILT SNAPINN** letterer **RICK TAYLOR** colorist **JULIUS SCHWARTZ** editor

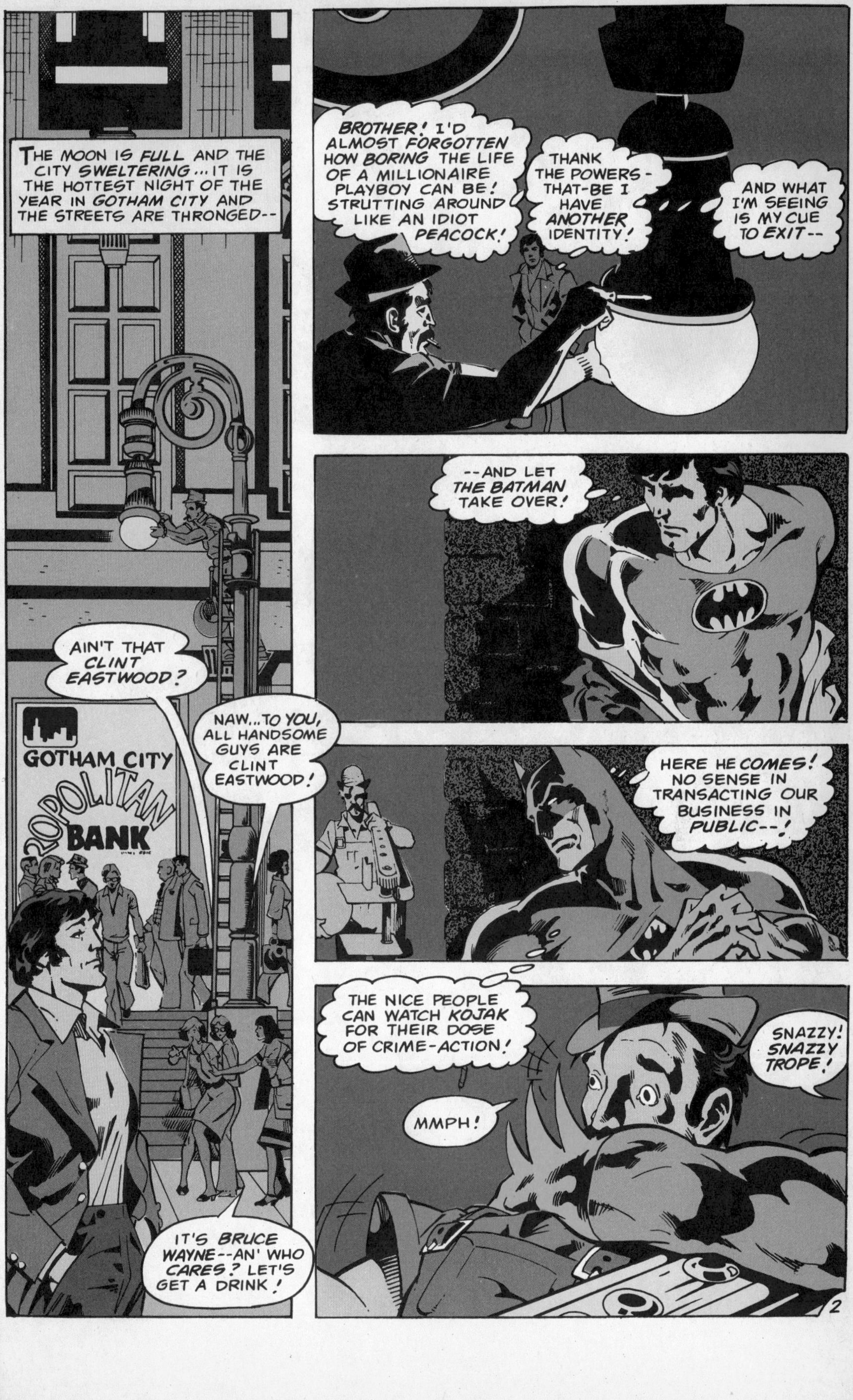
THE MOON IS FULL AND THE CITY SWELTERING... IT IS THE HOTTEST NIGHT OF THE YEAR IN GOTHAM CITY AND THE STREETS ARE THRONGED--
AIN'T THAT CLINT EASTWOOD?
NAW... TO YOU, ALL HANDSOME GUYS ARE CLINT EASTWOOD!
GOTHAM CITY
ROPOLITAN
BANK
IT'S BRUCE WAYNE--AN' WHO CARES? LET'S GET A DRINK!
BROTHER! I'D ALMOST FORGOTTEN HOW BORING THE LIFE OF A MILLIONAIRE PLAYBOY CAN BE! STRUTTING AROUND LIKE AN IDIOT PEACOCK!
THANK THE POWERS-THAT-BE I HAVE ANOTHER IDENTITY!
AND WHAT I'M SEEING IS MY CUE TO EXIT--
--AND LET THE BATMAN TAKE OVER!
HERE HE COMES! NO SENSE IN TRANSACTING OUR BUSINESS IN PUBLIC--!
THE NICE PEOPLE CAN WATCH KOJAK FOR THEIR DOSE OF CRIME-ACTION!
MMPH!
SNAZZY! SNAZZY TROPE!
2

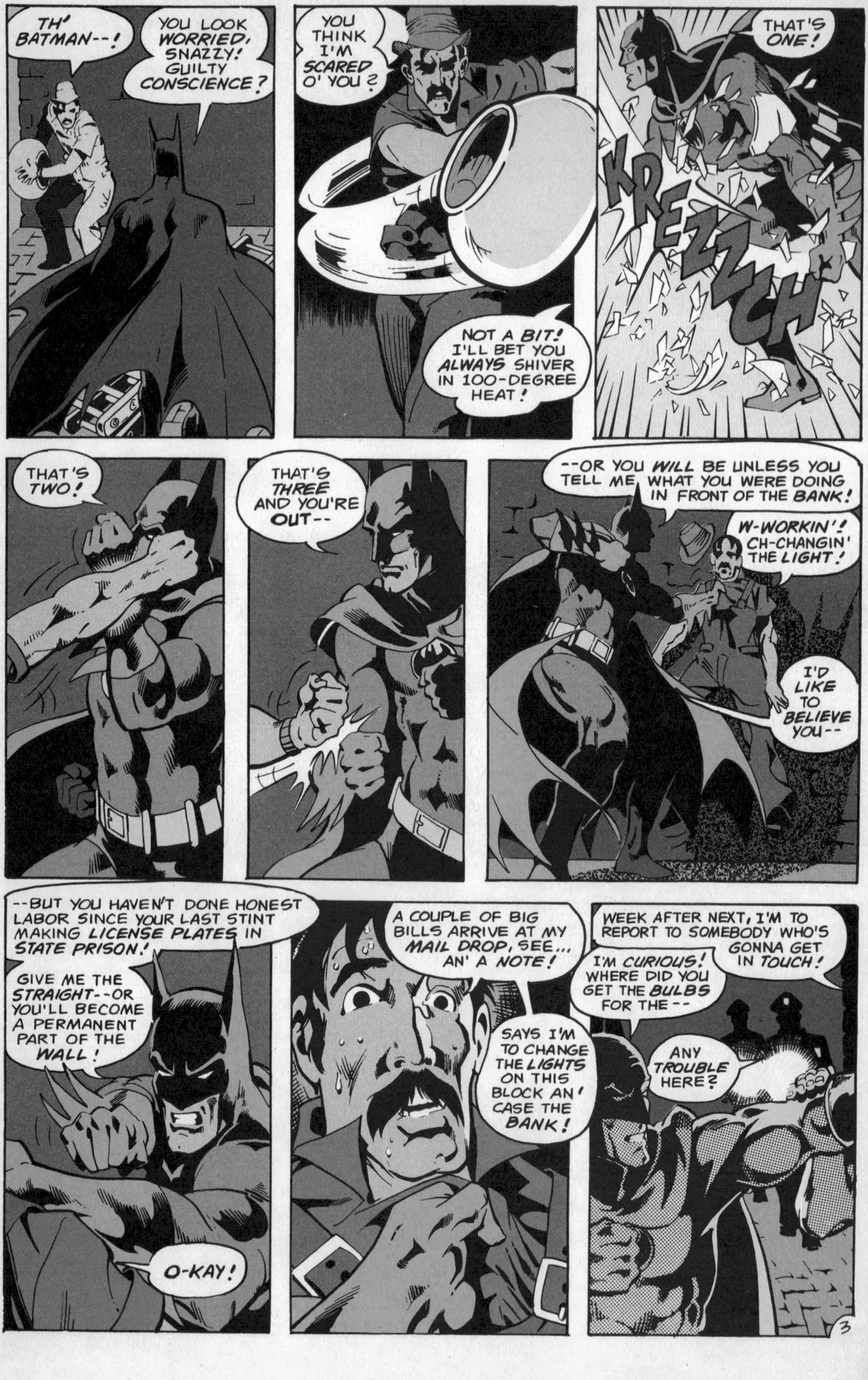
TH' BATMAN--!
YOU LOOK WORRIED, SNAZZY! GUILTY CONSCIENCE?
YOU THINK I'M SCARED O' YOU?
NOT A BIT! I'LL BET YOU ALWAYS SHIVER IN 100-DEGREE HEAT!
THAT'S ONE!
KREZZZCH
THAT'S TWO!
THAT'S THREE AND YOU'RE OUT--
--OR YOU WILL BE UNLESS YOU TELL ME WHAT YOU WERE DOING IN FRONT OF THE BANK!
W-WORKIN'! CH-CHANGIN' THE LIGHT!
I'D LIKE TO BELIEVE YOU--
--BUT YOU HAVEN'T DONE HONEST LABOR SINCE YOUR LAST STINT MAKING LICENSE PLATES IN STATE PRISON!
GIVE ME THE STRAIGHT--OR YOU'LL BECOME A PERMANENT PART OF THE WALL!
O-KAY!
A COUPLE OF BIG BILLS ARRIVE AT MY MAIL DROP, SEE... AN' A NOTE!
SAYS I'M TO CHANGE THE LIGHTS ON THIS BLOCK AN' CASE THE BANK!
WEEK AFTER NEXT, I'M TO REPORT TO SOMEBODY WHO'S GONNA GET IN TOUCH!
I'M CURIOUS! WHERE DID YOU GET THE BULBS FOR THE--
ANY TROUBLE HERE?
3

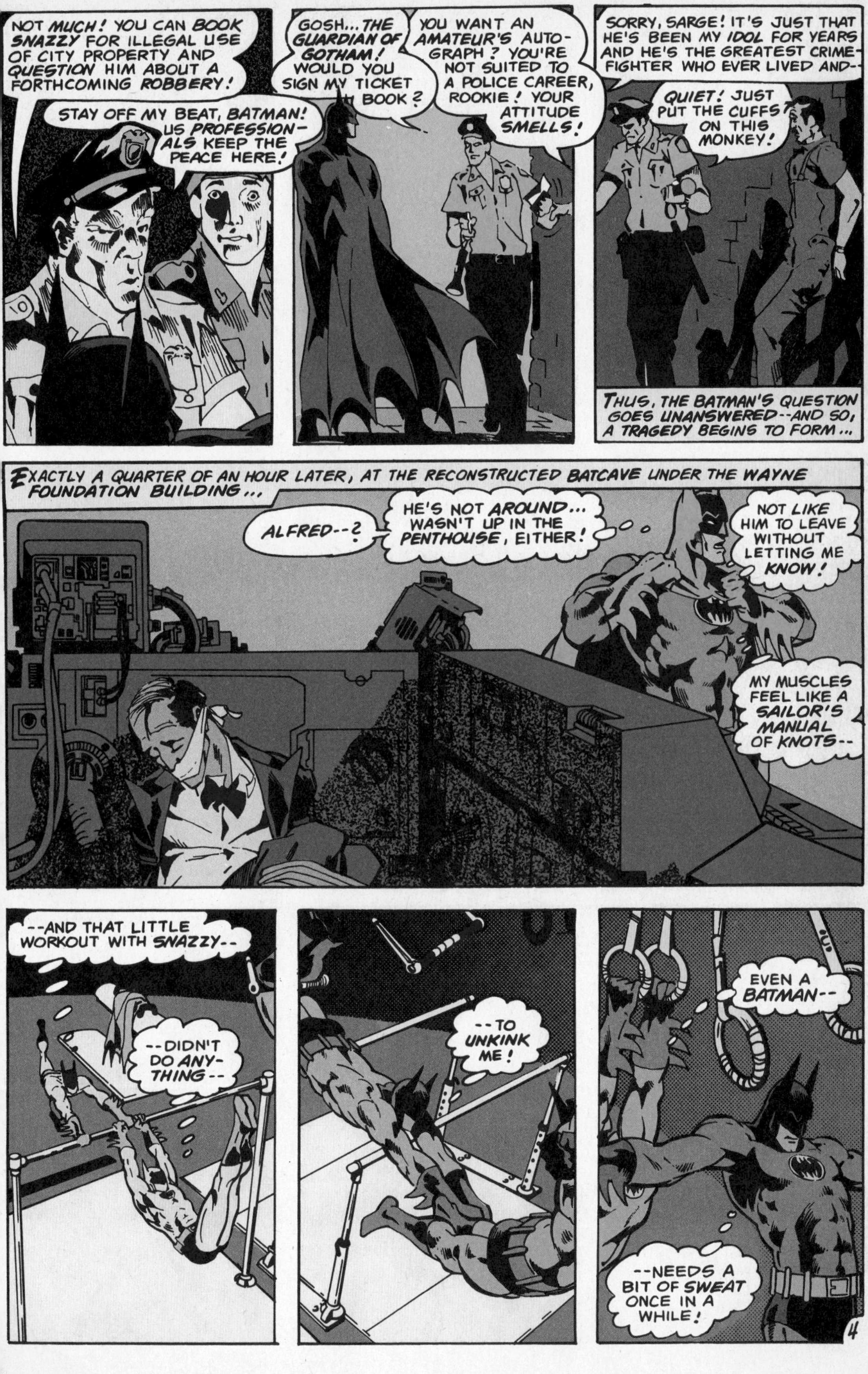
NOT MUCH! YOU CAN BOOK SNAZZY FOR ILLEGAL USE OF CITY PROPERTY AND QUESTION HIM ABOUT A FORTHCOMING ROBBERY!
STAY OFF MY BEAT, BATMAN! US PROFESSION-ALS KEEP THE PEACE HERE!
GOSH... THE GUARDIAN OF GOTHAM! WOULD YOU SIGN MY TICKET BOOK?
YOU WANT AN AMATEUR'S AUTO-GRAPH? YOU'RE NOT SUITED TO A POLICE CAREER, ROOKIE! YOUR ATTITUDE SMELLS!
SORRY, SARGE! IT'S JUST THAT HE'S BEEN MY IDOL FOR YEARS AND HE'S THE GREATEST CRIME-FIGHTER WHO EVER LIVED AND--
QUIET! JUST PUT THE CUFFS ON THIS MONKEY!
THUS, THE BATMAN'S QUESTION GOES UNANSWERED--AND SO, A TRAGEDY BEGINS TO FORM...
EXACTLY A QUARTER OF AN HOUR LATER, AT THE RECONSTRUCTED BATCAVE UNDER THE WAYNE FOUNDATION BUILDING...
ALFRED--?
HE'S NOT AROUND... WASN'T UP IN THE PENTHOUSE, EITHER!
NOT LIKE HIM TO LEAVE WITHOUT LETTING ME KNOW!
MY MUSCLES FEEL LIKE A SAILOR'S MANUAL OF KNOTS--
--AND THAT LITTLE WORKOUT WITH SNAZZY--
--DIDN'T DO ANY-THING--
--TO UNKINK ME!
EVEN A BATMAN--
--NEEDS A BIT OF SWEAT ONCE IN A WHILE!
4

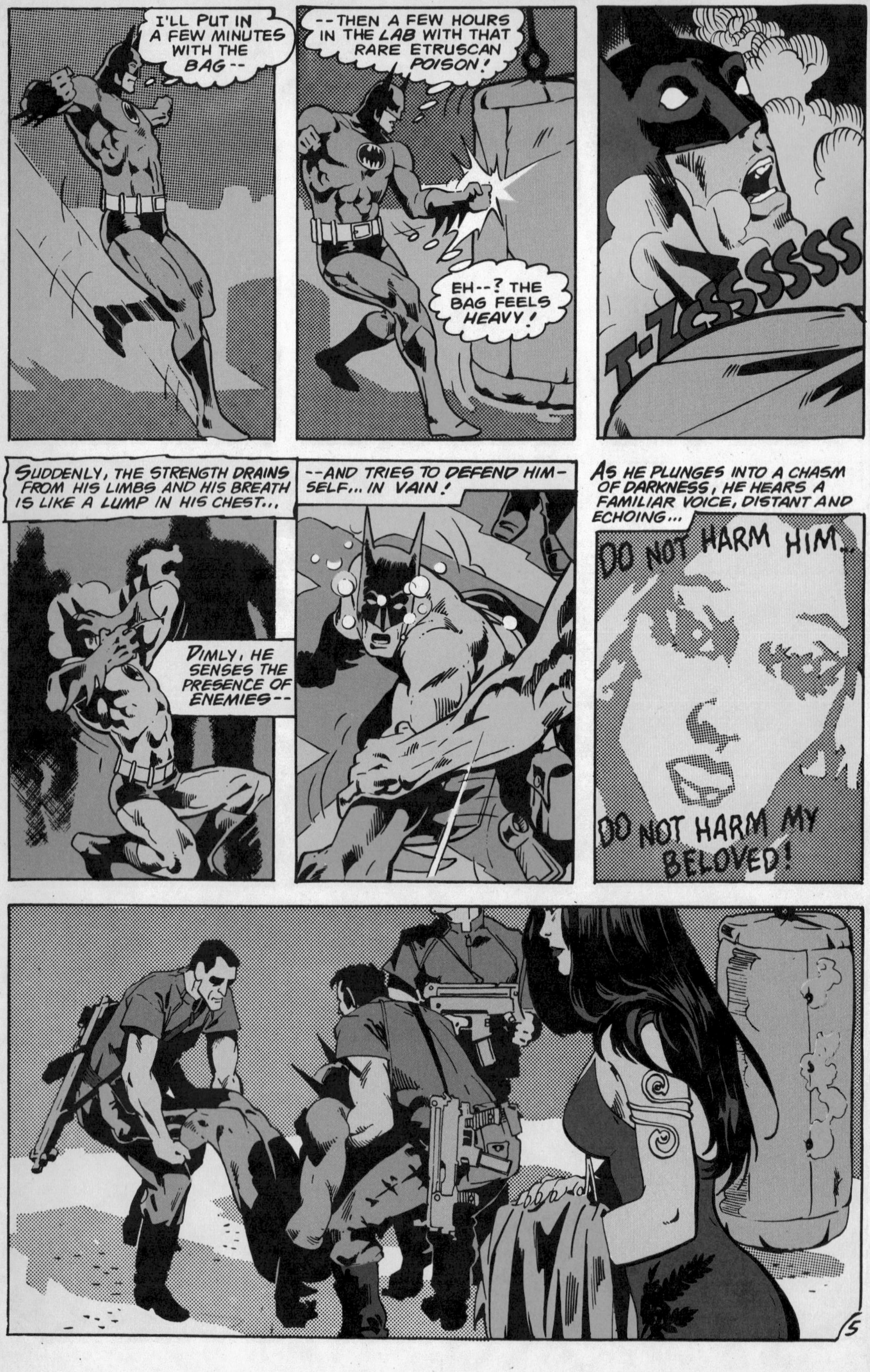
I'LL PUT IN A FEW MINUTES WITH THE BAG--
--THEN A FEW HOURS IN THE LAB WITH THAT RARE ETRUSCAN POISON!
EH--? THE BAG FEELS HEAVY!
T-ZCSSSSSSS
SUDDENLY, THE STRENGTH DRAINS FROM HIS LIMBS AND HIS BREATH IS LIKE A LUMP IN HIS CHEST...
DIMLY, HE SENSES THE PRESENCE OF ENEMIES--
--AND TRIES TO DEFEND HIMSELF... IN VAIN!
AS HE PLUNGES INTO A CHASM OF DARKNESS, HE HEARS A FAMILIAR VOICE, DISTANT AND ECHOING...
DO NOT HARM HIM...
DO NOT HARM MY BELOVED!
5

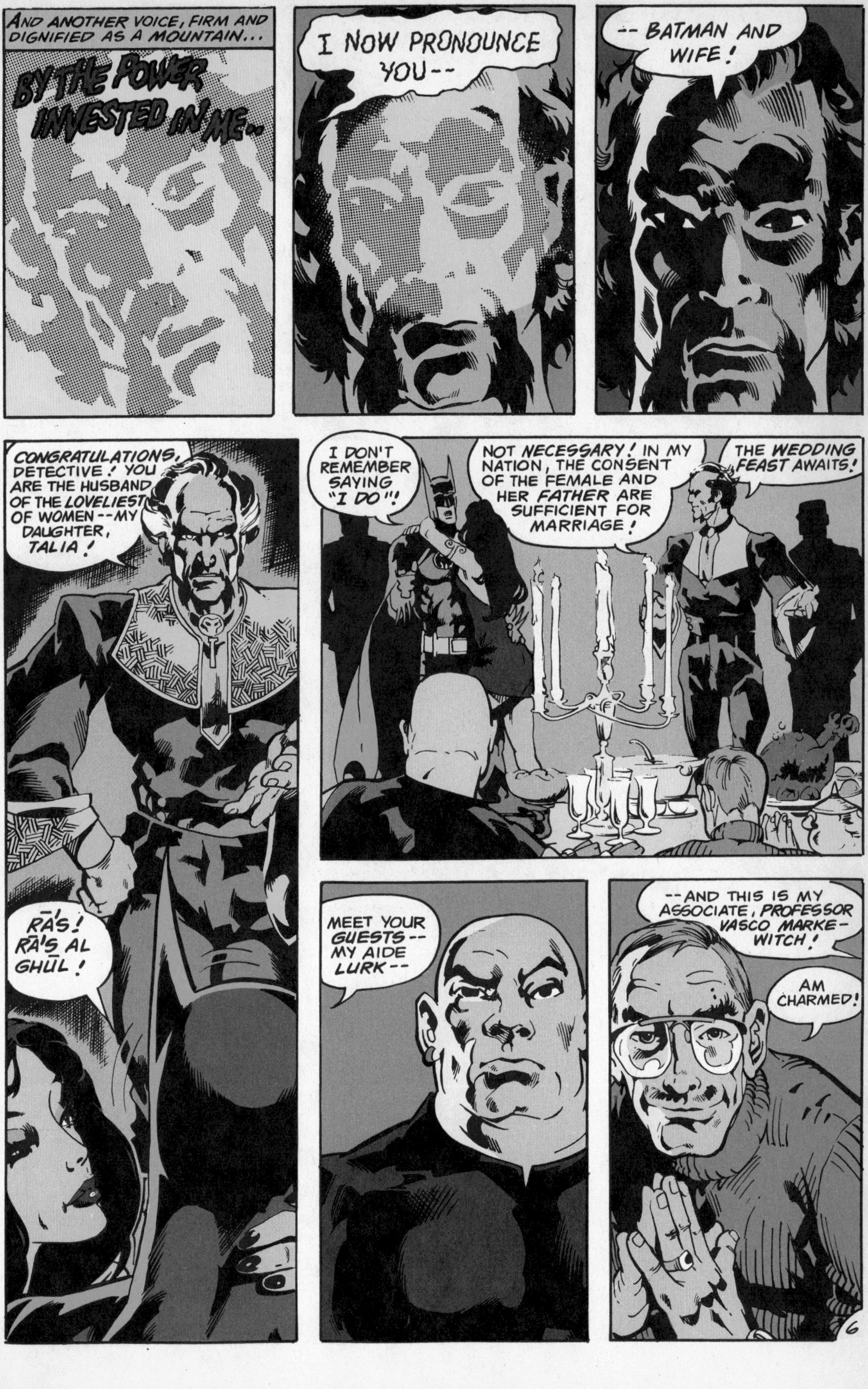
AND ANOTHER VOICE, FIRM AND DIGNIFIED AS A MOUNTAIN...
BY THE POWER INVESTED IN ME..
I NOW PRONOUNCE YOU--
--BATMAN AND WIFE!
CONGRATULATIONS, DETECTIVE! YOU ARE THE HUSBAND OF THE LOVELIEST OF WOMEN--MY DAUGHTER, TALIA!
--! RA'S! RA'S AL GHUL!
I DON'T REMEMBER SAYING "I DO"!
NOT NECESSARY! IN MY NATION, THE CONSENT OF THE FEMALE AND HER FATHER ARE SUFFICIENT FOR MARRIAGE!
THE WEDDING FEAST AWAITS!
MEET YOUR GUESTS-- MY AIDE LURK--
--AND THIS IS MY ASSOCIATE, PROFESSOR VASCO MARKE-WITCH!
AM CHARMED!
6

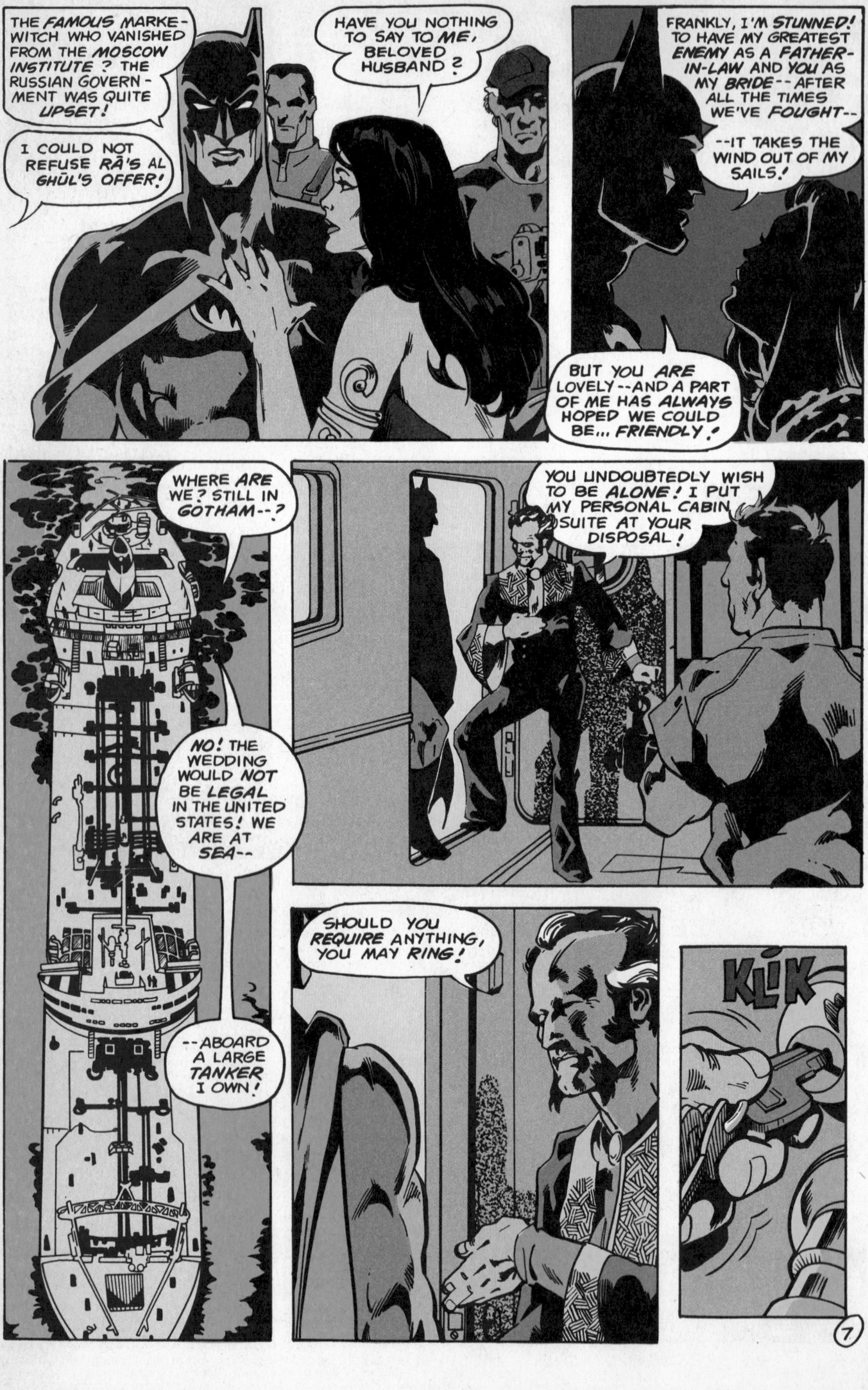
THE FAMOUS MARKE-WITCH WHO VANISHED FROM THE MOSCOW INSTITUTE? THE RUSSIAN GOVERN-MENT WAS QUITE UPSET!
I COULD NOT REFUSE RĀ'S AL GHŪL'S OFFER!
HAVE YOU NOTHING TO SAY TO ME, BELOVED HUSBAND?
FRANKLY, I'M STUNNED! TO HAVE MY GREATEST ENEMY AS A FATHER-IN-LAW AND YOU AS MY BRIDE--AFTER ALL THE TIMES WE'VE FOUGHT--
--IT TAKES THE WIND OUT OF MY SAILS!
BUT YOU ARE LOVELY--AND A PART OF ME HAS ALWAYS HOPED WE COULD BE... FRIENDLY!
WHERE ARE WE? STILL IN GOTHAM--?
NO! THE WEDDING WOULD NOT BE LEGAL IN THE UNITED STATES! WE ARE AT SEA--
--ABOARD A LARGE TANKER I OWN!
YOU UNDOUBTEDLY WISH TO BE ALONE! I PUT MY PERSONAL CABIN SUITE AT YOUR DISPOSAL!
SHOULD YOU REQUIRE ANYTHING, YOU MAY RING!
KLIK
7

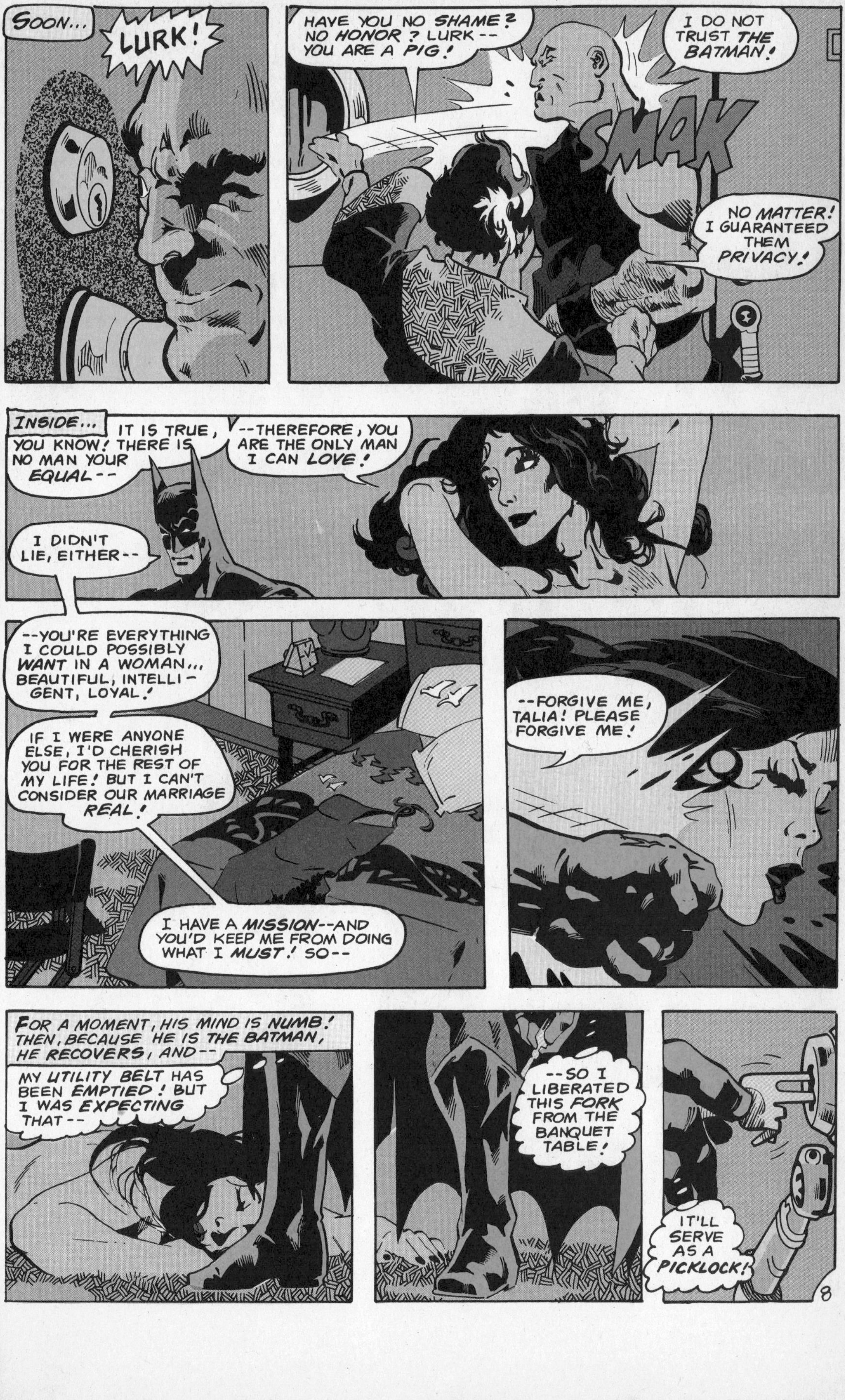

SOON...
LURK!
HAVE YOU NO SHAME? NO HONOR? LURK-- YOU ARE A PIG!
I DO NOT TRUST THE BATMAN!
SMAK
NO MATTER! I GUARANTEED THEM PRIVACY!
INSIDE...
IT IS TRUE, YOU KNOW! THERE IS NO MAN YOUR EQUAL--
--THEREFORE, YOU ARE THE ONLY MAN I CAN LOVE!
I DIDN'T LIE, EITHER--
--YOU'RE EVERYTHING I COULD POSSIBLY WANT IN A WOMAN... BEAUTIFUL, INTELLI-GENT, LOYAL!
IF I WERE ANYONE ELSE, I'D CHERISH YOU FOR THE REST OF MY LIFE! BUT I CAN'T CONSIDER OUR MARRIAGE REAL!
I HAVE A MISSION--AND YOU'D KEEP ME FROM DOING WHAT I MUST! SO--
--FORGIVE ME, TALIA! PLEASE FORGIVE ME!
FOR A MOMENT, HIS MIND IS NUMB! THEN, BECAUSE HE IS THE BATMAN, HE RECOVERS, AND--
MY UTILITY BELT HAS BEEN EMPTIED! BUT I WAS EXPECTING THAT--
--SO I LIBERATED THIS FORK FROM THE BANQUET TABLE!
IT'LL SERVE AS A PICKLOCK!
8

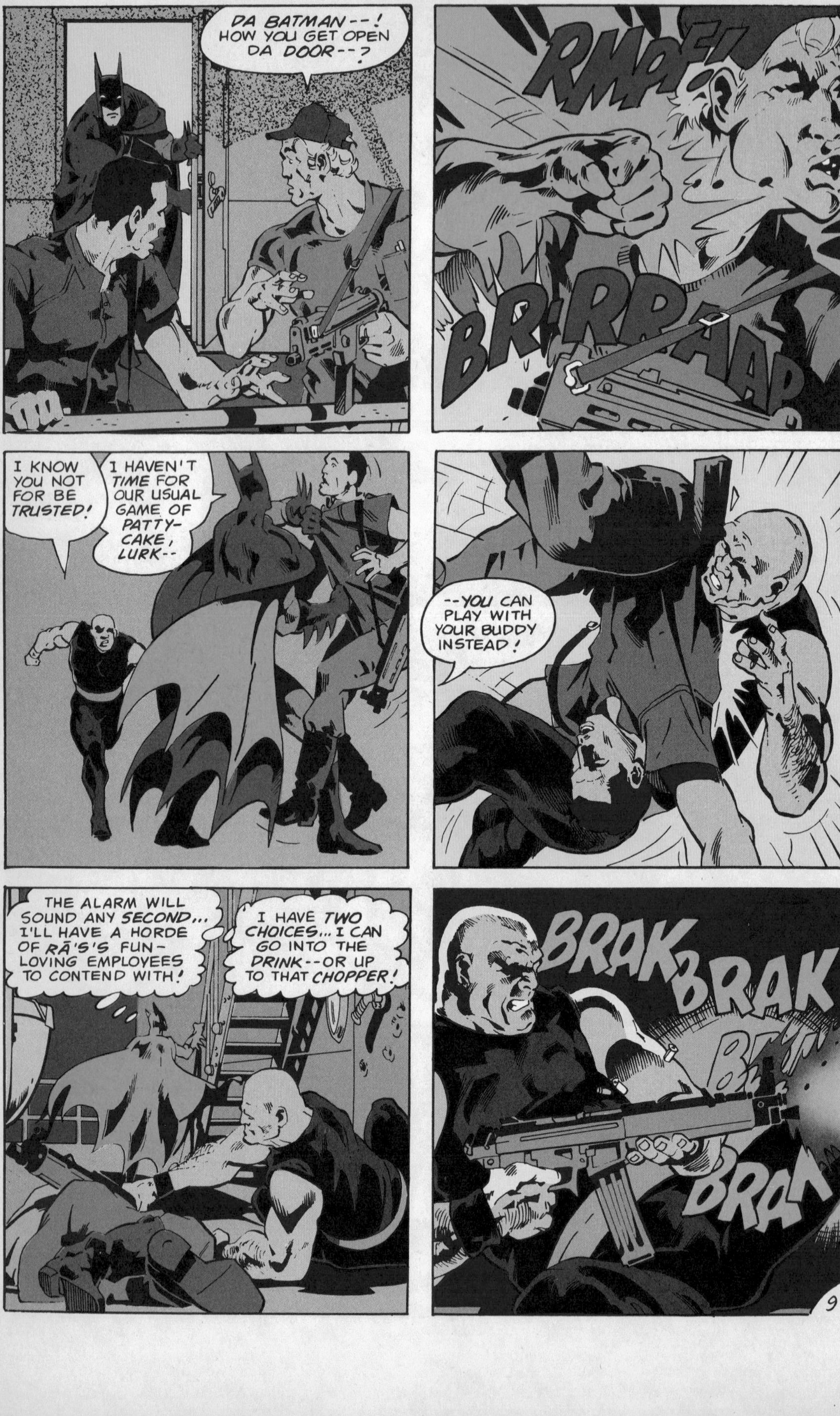
DA BATMAN--! HOW YOU GET OPEN DA DOOR--?
RMPF!!
BR-RRAAAP
I KNOW YOU NOT FOR BE TRUSTED!
I HAVEN'T TIME FOR OUR USUAL GAME OF PATTY-CAKE, LURK--
--YOU CAN PLAY WITH YOUR BUDDY INSTEAD!
THE ALARM WILL SOUND ANY SECOND... I'LL HAVE A HORDE OF RĀ'S'S FUN-LOVING EMPLOYEES TO CONTEND WITH!
I HAVE TWO CHOICES... I CAN GO INTO THE DRINK--OR UP TO THAT CHOPPER!
BRAK BRAK
BRAK
9

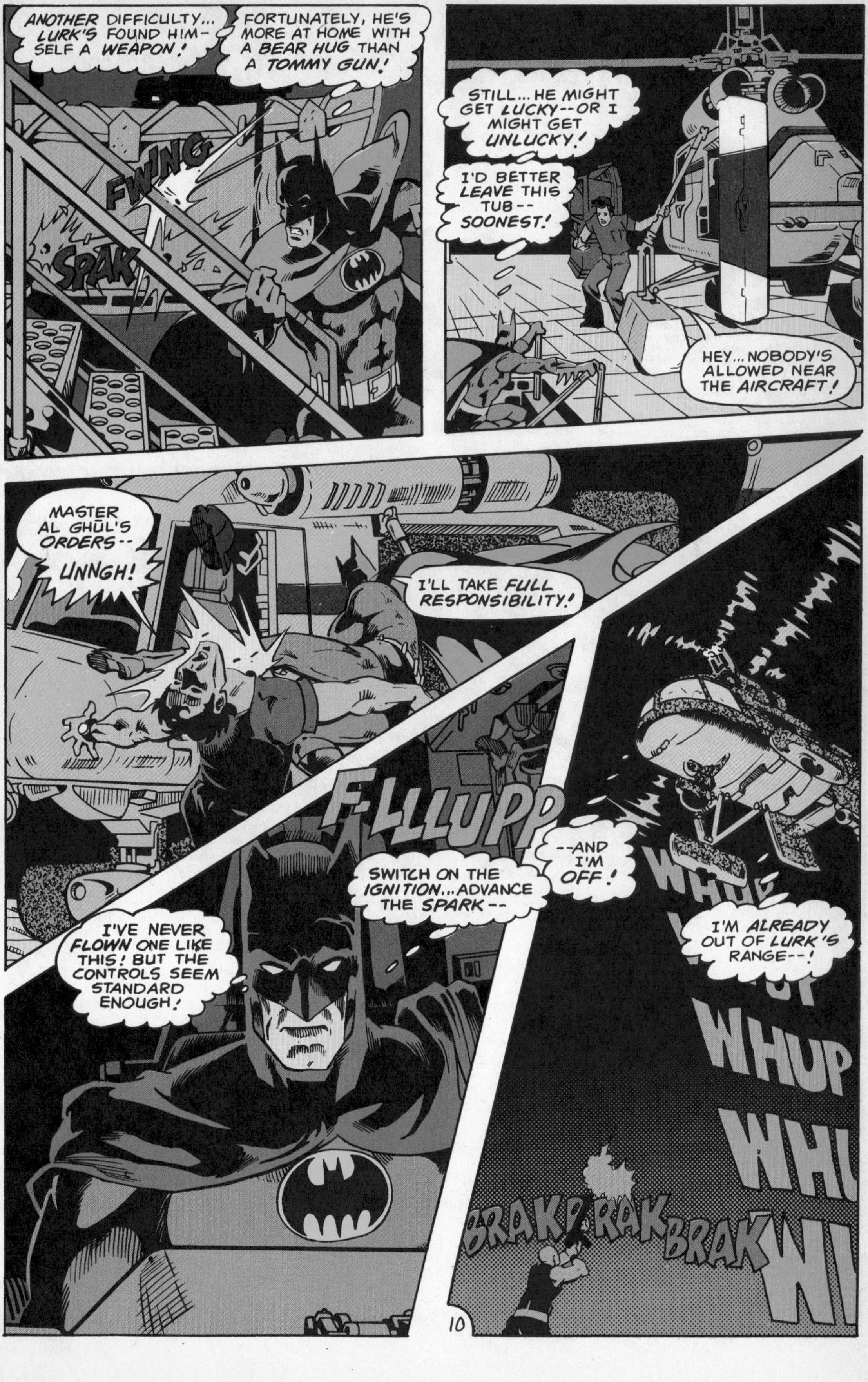
ANOTHER DIFFICULTY... LURK'S FOUND HIMSELF A WEAPON!
FORTUNATELY, HE'S MORE AT HOME WITH A BEAR HUG THAN A TOMMY GUN!
FWING
SPAK
STILL... HE MIGHT GET LUCKY--OR I MIGHT GET UNLUCKY!
I'D BETTER LEAVE THIS TUB--SOONEST!
HEY... NOBODY'S ALLOWED NEAR THE AIRCRAFT!
MASTER AL GHŪL'S ORDERS--
UNNGH!
I'LL TAKE FULL RESPONSIBILITY!
F-LLLUPP
SWITCH ON THE IGNITION... ADVANCE THE SPARK--
--AND I'M OFF!
I'VE NEVER FLOWN ONE LIKE THIS! BUT THE CONTROLS SEEM STANDARD ENOUGH!
I'M ALREADY OUT OF LURK'S RANGE--!
WHUP
WHU
BRAKD RAK BRAK
10

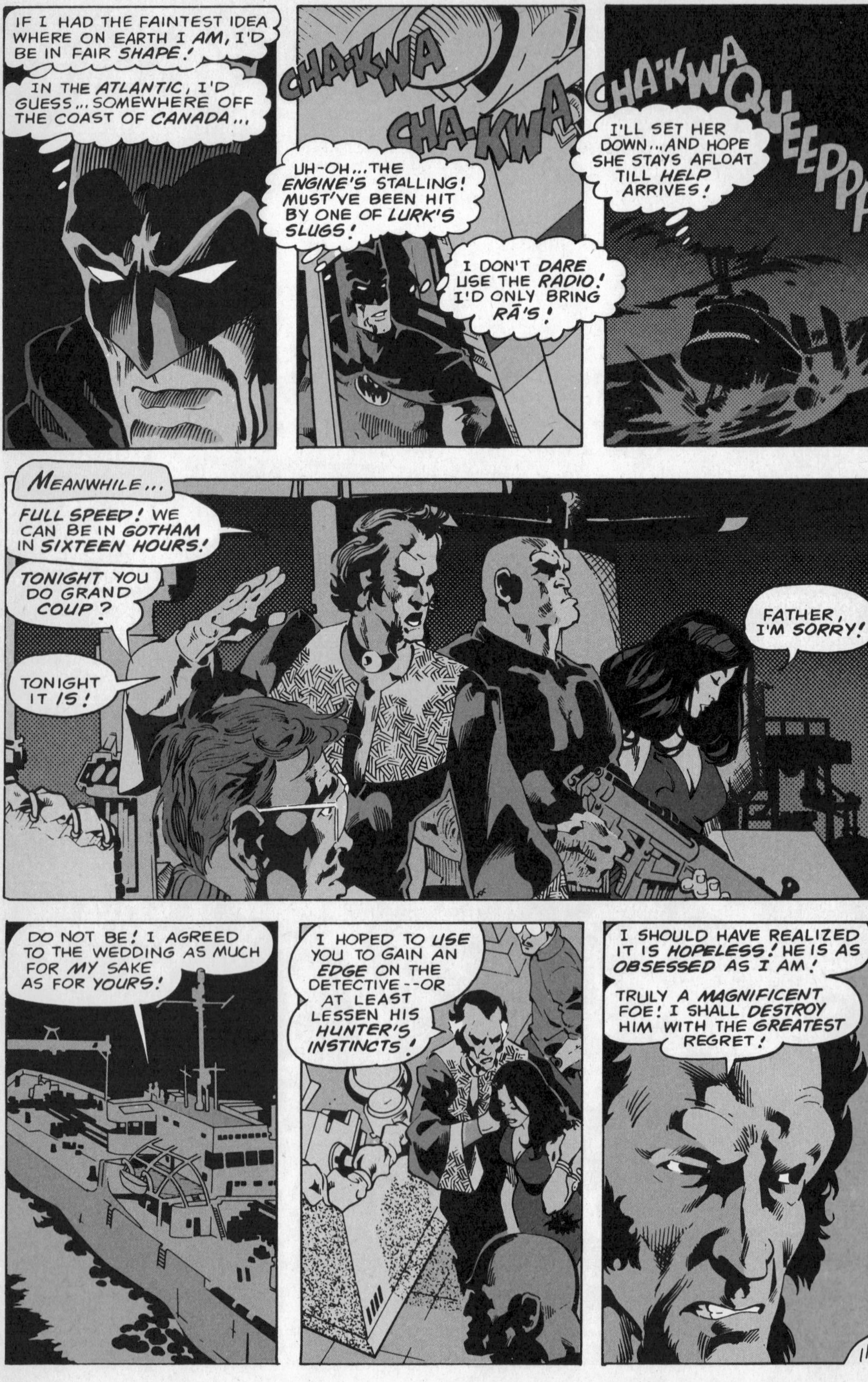
IF I HAD THE FAINTEST IDEA WHERE ON EARTH I AM, I'D BE IN FAIR SHAPE!
IN THE ATLANTIC, I'D GUESS... SOMEWHERE OFF THE COAST OF CANADA...
CHA-KWA
CHA-KWA
UH-OH... THE ENGINE'S STALLING! MUST'VE BEEN HIT BY ONE OF LURK'S SLUGS!
I DON'T DARE USE THE RADIO! I'D ONLY BRING RĀ'S!
CHA'KWA CHA'KWA
QUEEEPPPP
I'LL SET HER DOWN... AND HOPE SHE STAYS AFLOAT TILL HELP ARRIVES!
MEANWHILE...
FULL SPEED! WE CAN BE IN GOTHAM IN SIXTEEN HOURS!
TONIGHT YOU DO GRAND COUP?
TONIGHT IT IS!
FATHER, I'M SORRY!
DO NOT BE! I AGREED TO THE WEDDING AS MUCH FOR MY SAKE AS FOR YOURS!
I HOPED TO USE YOU TO GAIN AN EDGE ON THE DETECTIVE--OR AT LEAST LESSEN HIS HUNTER'S INSTINCTS!
I SHOULD HAVE REALIZED IT IS HOPELESS! HE IS AS OBSESSED AS I AM!
TRULY A MAGNIFICENT FOE! I SHALL DESTROY HIM WITH THE GREATEST REGRET!
11

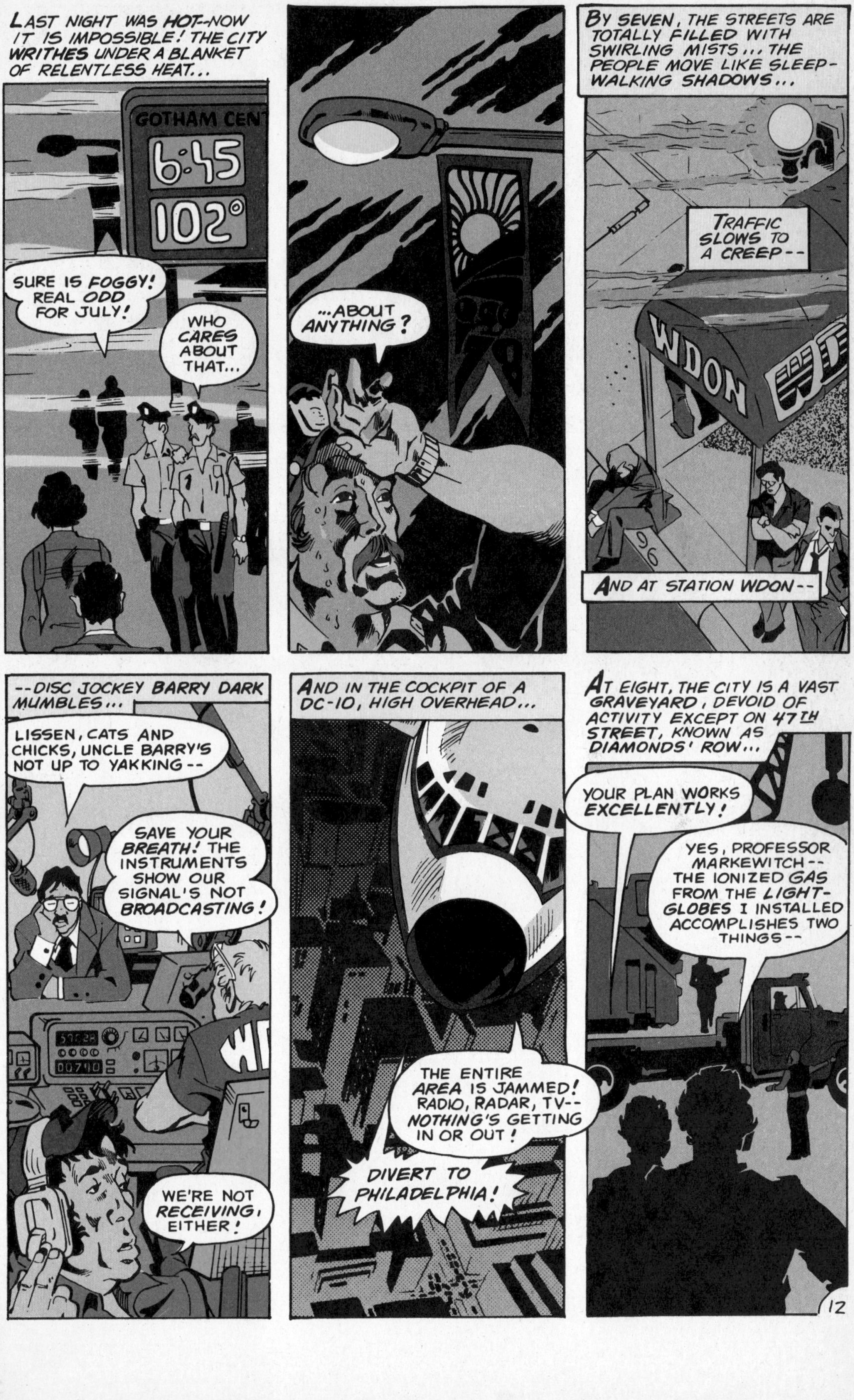
LAST NIGHT WAS HOT--NOW IT IS IMPOSSIBLE! THE CITY WRITHES UNDER A BLANKET OF RELENTLESS HEAT...
GOTHAM CEN
6:45
102°
SURE IS FOGGY! REAL ODD FOR JULY!
WHO CARES ABOUT THAT...
...ABOUT ANYTHING?
BY SEVEN, THE STREETS ARE TOTALLY FILLED WITH SWIRLING MISTS... THE PEOPLE MOVE LIKE SLEEP-WALKING SHADOWS...
TRAFFIC SLOWS TO A CREEP--
WDON
AND AT STATION WDON--
--DISC JOCKEY BARRY DARK MUMBLES...
LISSEN, CATS AND CHICKS, UNCLE BARRY'S NOT UP TO YAKKING--
SAVE YOUR BREATH! THE INSTRUMENTS SHOW OUR SIGNAL'S NOT BROADCASTING!
WE'RE NOT RECEIVING, EITHER!
AND IN THE COCKPIT OF A DC-10, HIGH OVERHEAD...
THE ENTIRE AREA IS JAMMED! RADIO, RADAR, TV--NOTHING'S GETTING IN OR OUT!
DIVERT TO PHILADELPHIA!
AT EIGHT, THE CITY IS A VAST GRAVEYARD, DEVOID OF ACTIVITY EXCEPT ON 47TH STREET, KNOWN AS DIAMONDS' ROW...
YOUR PLAN WORKS EXCELLENTLY!
YES, PROFESSOR MARKEWITCH--THE IONIZED GAS FROM THE LIGHT-GLOBES I INSTALLED ACCOMPLISHES TWO THINGS--
12

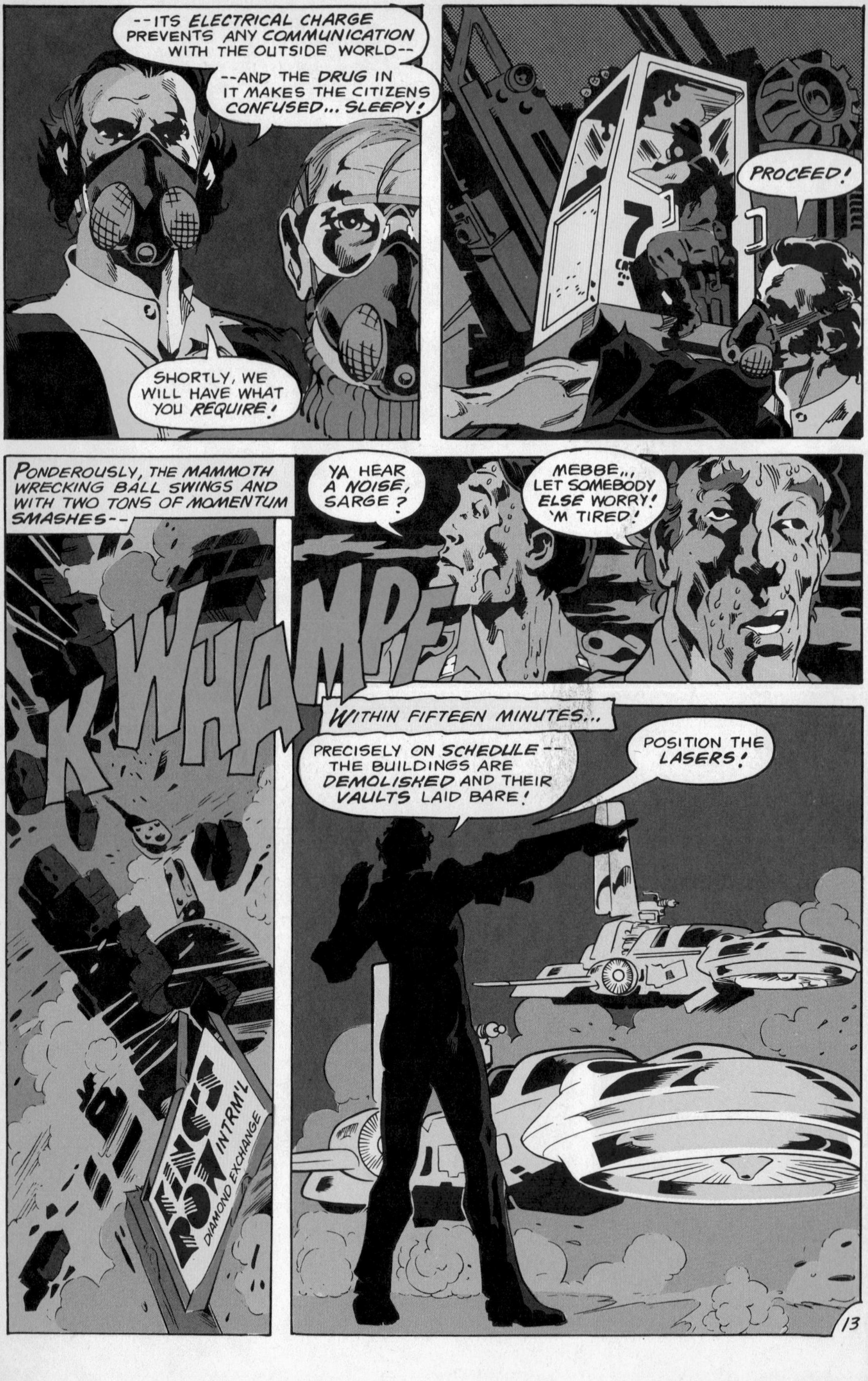
--ITS ELECTRICAL CHARGE PREVENTS ANY COMMUNICATION WITH THE OUTSIDE WORLD--
--AND THE DRUG IN IT MAKES THE CITIZENS CONFUSED... SLEEPY!
SHORTLY, WE WILL HAVE WHAT YOU REQUIRE!
PROCEED!
PONDEROUSLY, THE MAMMOTH WRECKING BALL SWINGS AND WITH TWO TONS OF MOMENTUM SMASHES--
KWHAMPF
INTRM'L
DIAMOND EXCHANGE
YA HEAR A NOISE, SARGE?
MEBBE... LET SOMEBODY ELSE WORRY! 'M TIRED!
WITHIN FIFTEEN MINUTES...
PRECISELY ON SCHEDULE-- THE BUILDINGS ARE DEMOLISHED AND THEIR VAULTS LAID BARE!
POSITION THE LASERS!
13

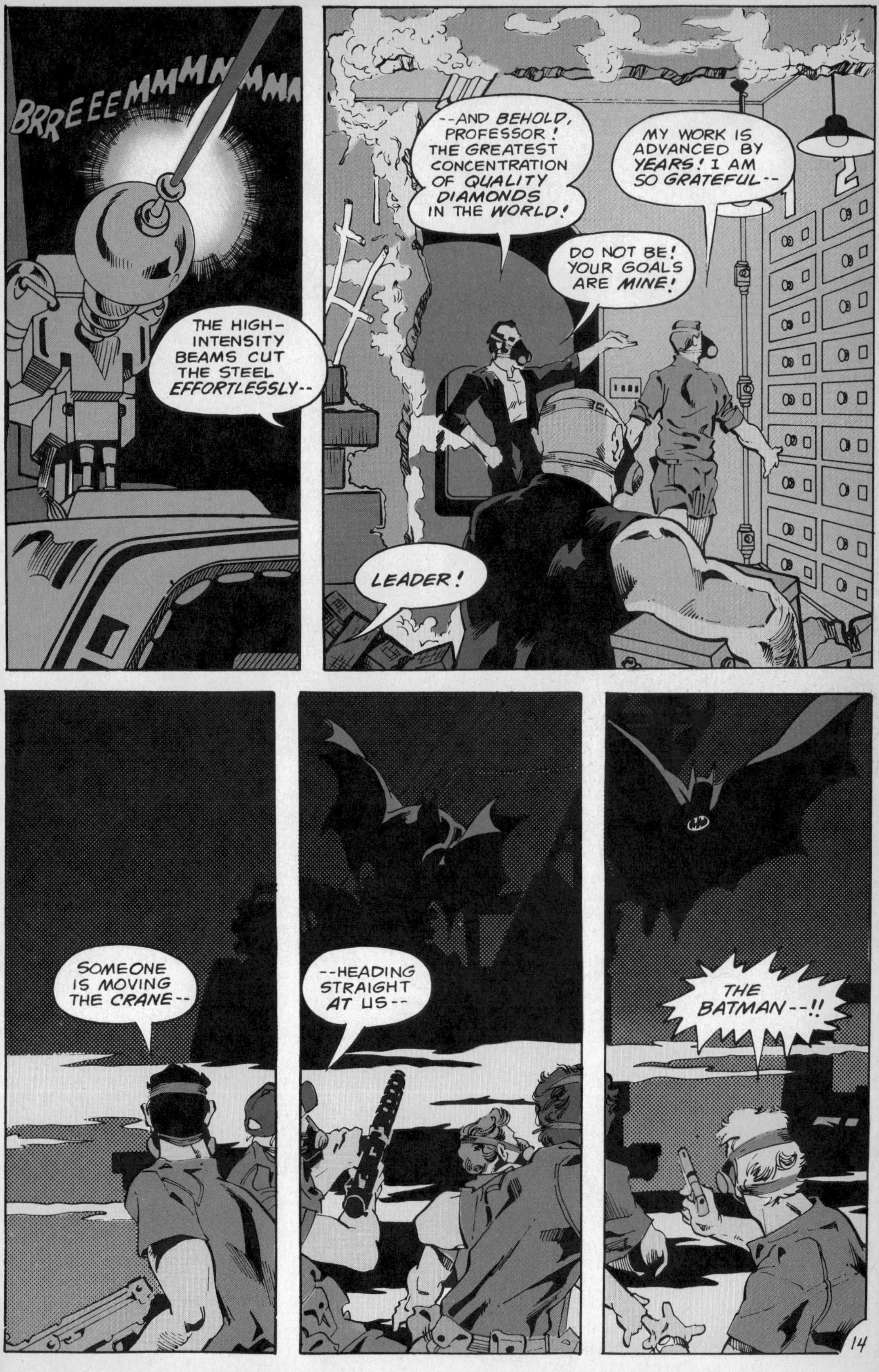
BRREEEMMMMMMMM
THE HIGH-INTENSITY BEAMS CUT THE STEEL EFFORTLESSLY--
--AND BEHOLD, PROFESSOR! THE GREATEST CONCENTRATION OF QUALITY DIAMONDS IN THE WORLD!
MY WORK IS ADVANCED BY YEARS! I AM SO GRATEFUL--
DO NOT BE! YOUR GOALS ARE MINE!
LEADER!
SOMEONE IS MOVING THE CRANE--
--HEADING STRAIGHT AT US--
THE BATMAN--!!

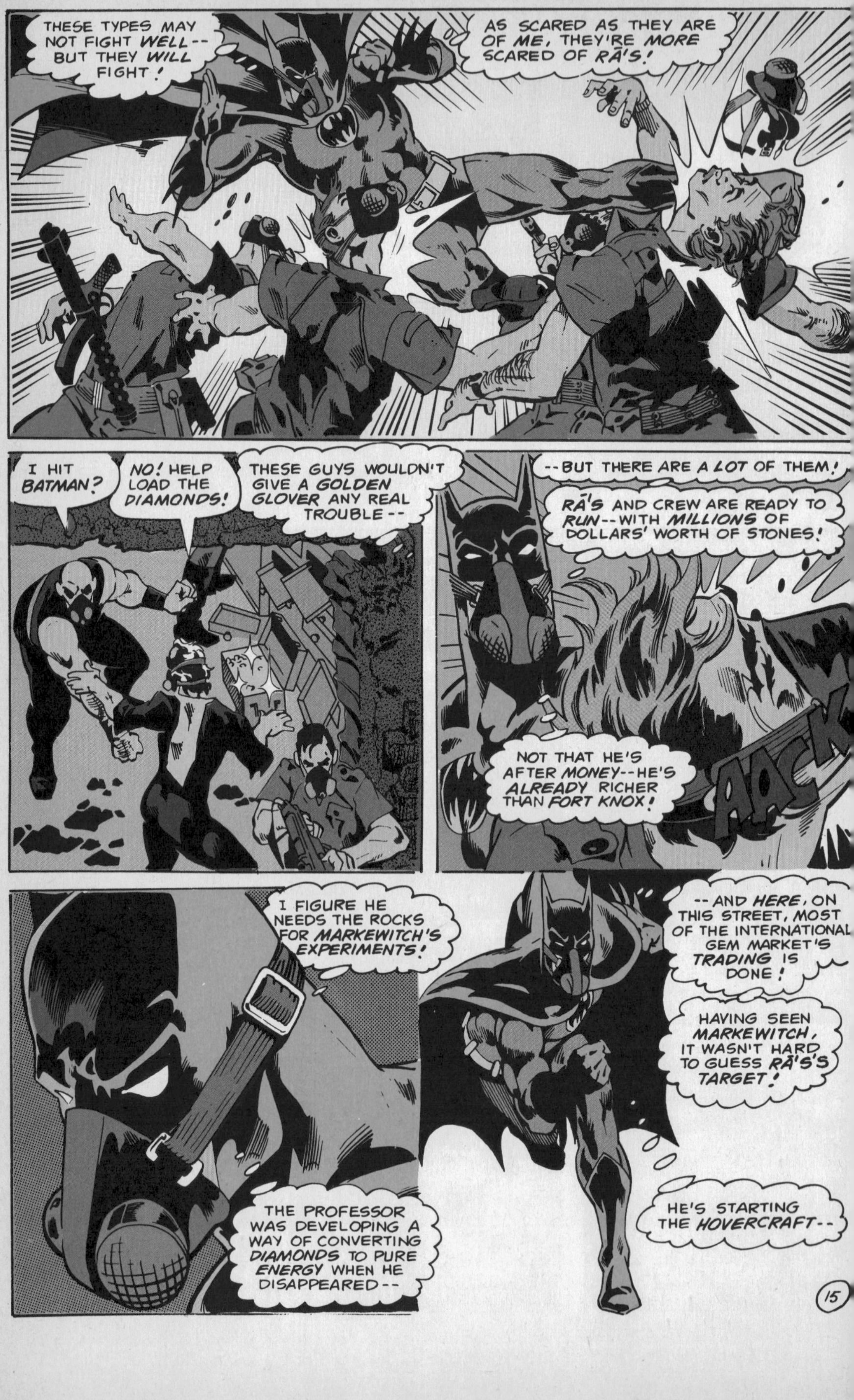
THESE TYPES MAY NOT FIGHT WELL-- BUT THEY WILL FIGHT!
AS SCARED AS THEY ARE OF ME, THEY'RE MORE SCARED OF RĀ'S!
I HIT BATMAN?
NO! HELP LOAD THE DIAMONDS!
THESE GUYS WOULDN'T GIVE A GOLDEN GLOVER ANY REAL TROUBLE--
--BUT THERE ARE A LOT OF THEM!
RĀ'S AND CREW ARE READY TO RUN--WITH MILLIONS OF DOLLARS' WORTH OF STONES!
NOT THAT HE'S AFTER MONEY--HE'S ALREADY RICHER THAN FORT KNOX!
AACK
I FIGURE HE NEEDS THE ROCKS FOR MARKEWITCH'S EXPERIMENTS!
THE PROFESSOR WAS DEVELOPING A WAY OF CONVERTING DIAMONDS TO PURE ENERGY WHEN HE DISAPPEARED--
--AND HERE, ON THIS STREET, MOST OF THE INTERNATIONAL GEM MARKET'S TRADING IS DONE!
HAVING SEEN MARKEWITCH, IT WASN'T HARD TO GUESS RĀ'S'S TARGET!
HE'S STARTING THE HOVERCRAFT--
15

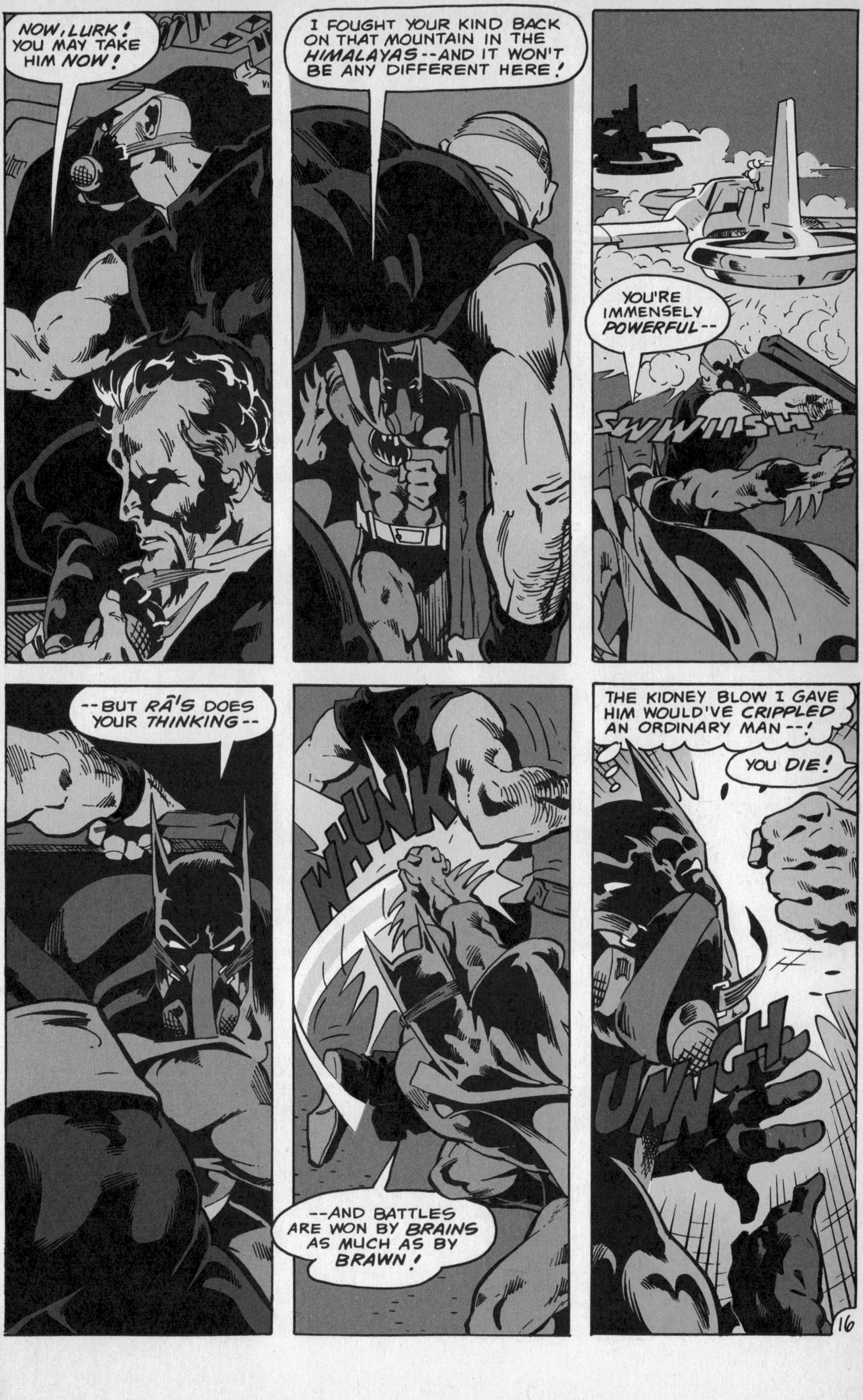
NOW, LURK! YOU MAY TAKE HIM NOW!
I FOUGHT YOUR KIND BACK ON THAT MOUNTAIN IN THE HIMALAYAS--AND IT WON'T BE ANY DIFFERENT HERE!
YOU'RE IMMENSELY POWERFUL--
SWWISH
--BUT RĀ'S DOES YOUR THINKING--
WHUNK
--AND BATTLES ARE WON BY BRAINS AS MUCH AS BY BRAWN!
THE KIDNEY BLOW I GAVE HIM WOULD'VE CRIPPLED AN ORDINARY MAN--!
YOU DIE!
UNNGH
16

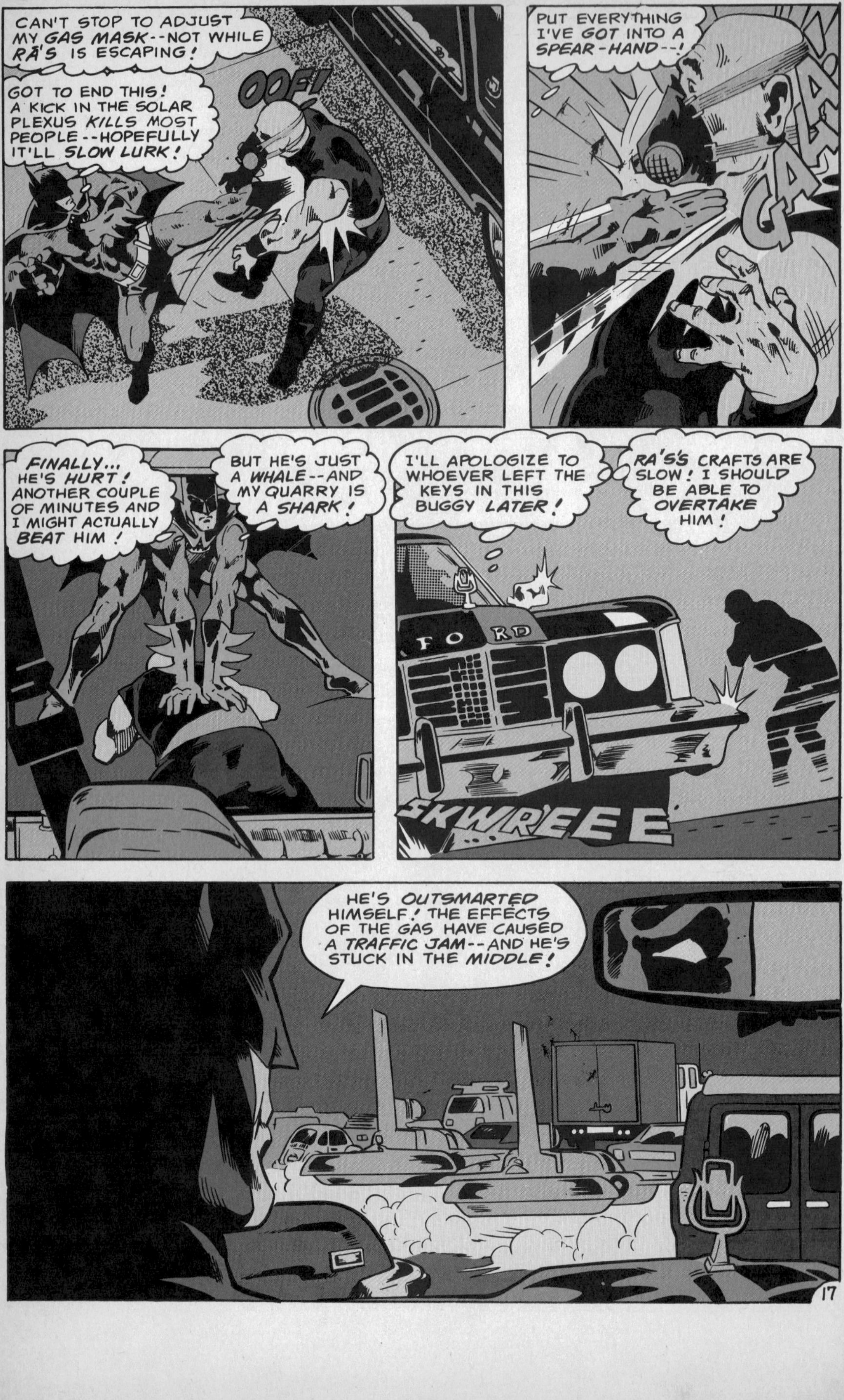
CAN'T STOP TO ADJUST MY GAS MASK--NOT WHILE RA'S IS ESCAPING!
GOT TO END THIS! A KICK IN THE SOLAR PLEXUS KILLS MOST PEOPLE--HOPEFULLY IT'LL SLOW LURK!
OOF!
PUT EVERYTHING I'VE GOT INTO A SPEAR-HAND--!
GAA
FINALLY... HE'S HURT! ANOTHER COUPLE OF MINUTES AND I MIGHT ACTUALLY BEAT HIM!
BUT HE'S JUST A WHALE--AND MY QUARRY IS A SHARK!
I'LL APOLOGIZE TO WHOEVER LEFT THE KEYS IN THIS BUGGY LATER!
RA'S'S CRAFTS ARE SLOW! I SHOULD BE ABLE TO OVERTAKE HIM!
FORD
SKWREEEE
HE'S OUTSMARTED HIMSELF! THE EFFECTS OF THE GAS HAVE CAUSED A TRAFFIC JAM--AND HE'S STUCK IN THE MIDDLE!
17

NO...I'M OUTSMARTED! THE TRAFFIC JAM WAS *PART* OF HIS PLAN--!

THE HOVERCRAFTS ARE GOING *ABOVE* IT...RIDING ON AN *AIR CUSHION!*

BY ELEVEN, A STRONG BREEZE SWEEPS FROM THE OCEAN, DISSIPATING THE FUMES, AND THE MOON REAPPEARS IN THE INKY SKY...

AT A PIER SOUTH OF GOTHAM--

HURRY!

SOON, THE POLICE WILL *RECOVER!* WE MUST HAVE THE SUBMARINE LOADED AND BE UNDER WAY BEFORE THEY *ORGANIZE!*

WE CAN BE AT THE TANKER BY SUNRISE...

YOU'LL BE NOWHERE--

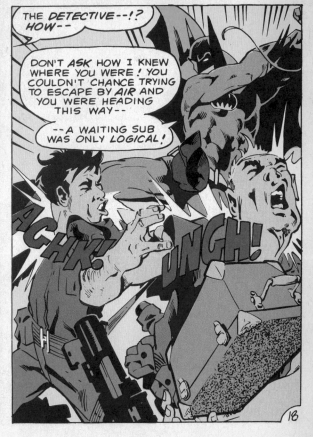

THE *DETECTIVE--!?* HOW--

DON'T *ASK* HOW I KNEW WHERE YOU WERE! YOU COULDN'T CHANCE TRYING TO ESCAPE BY *AIR* AND YOU WERE HEADING THIS WAY--

--A WAITING SUB WAS ONLY *LOGICAL!*

AGHK!

UNGH!

18

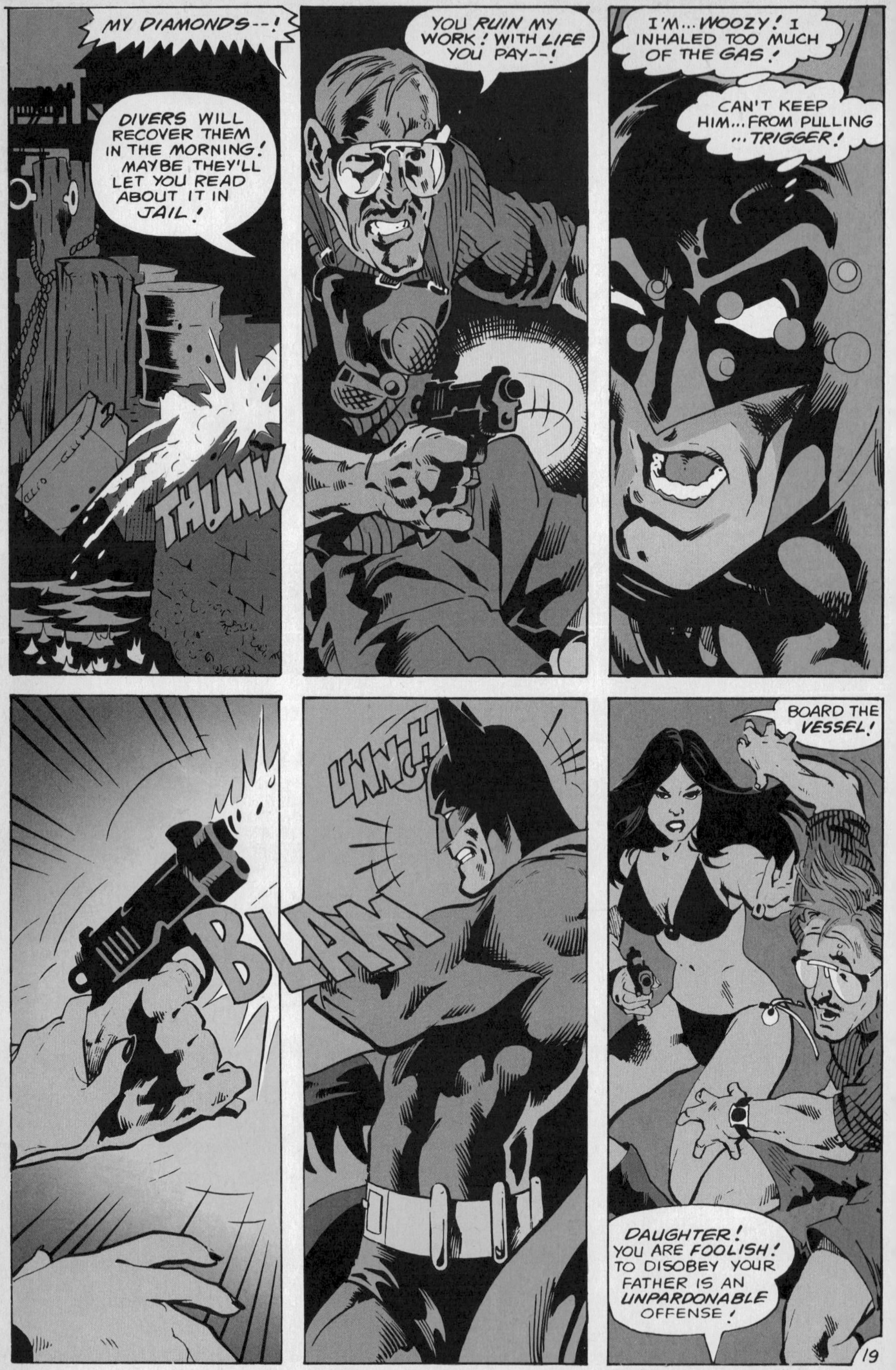
MY DIAMONDS--!
DIVERS WILL RECOVER THEM IN THE MORNING! MAYBE THEY'LL LET YOU READ ABOUT IT IN JAIL!
THUNK
YOU RUIN MY WORK! WITH LIFE YOU PAY--!
I'M...WOOZY! I INHALED TOO MUCH OF THE GAS!
CAN'T KEEP HIM...FROM PULLING ...TRIGGER!
BLAM
UNNCH
BOARD THE VESSEL!
DAUGHTER! YOU ARE FOOLISH! TO DISOBEY YOUR FATHER IS AN UNPARDONABLE OFFENSE!
19

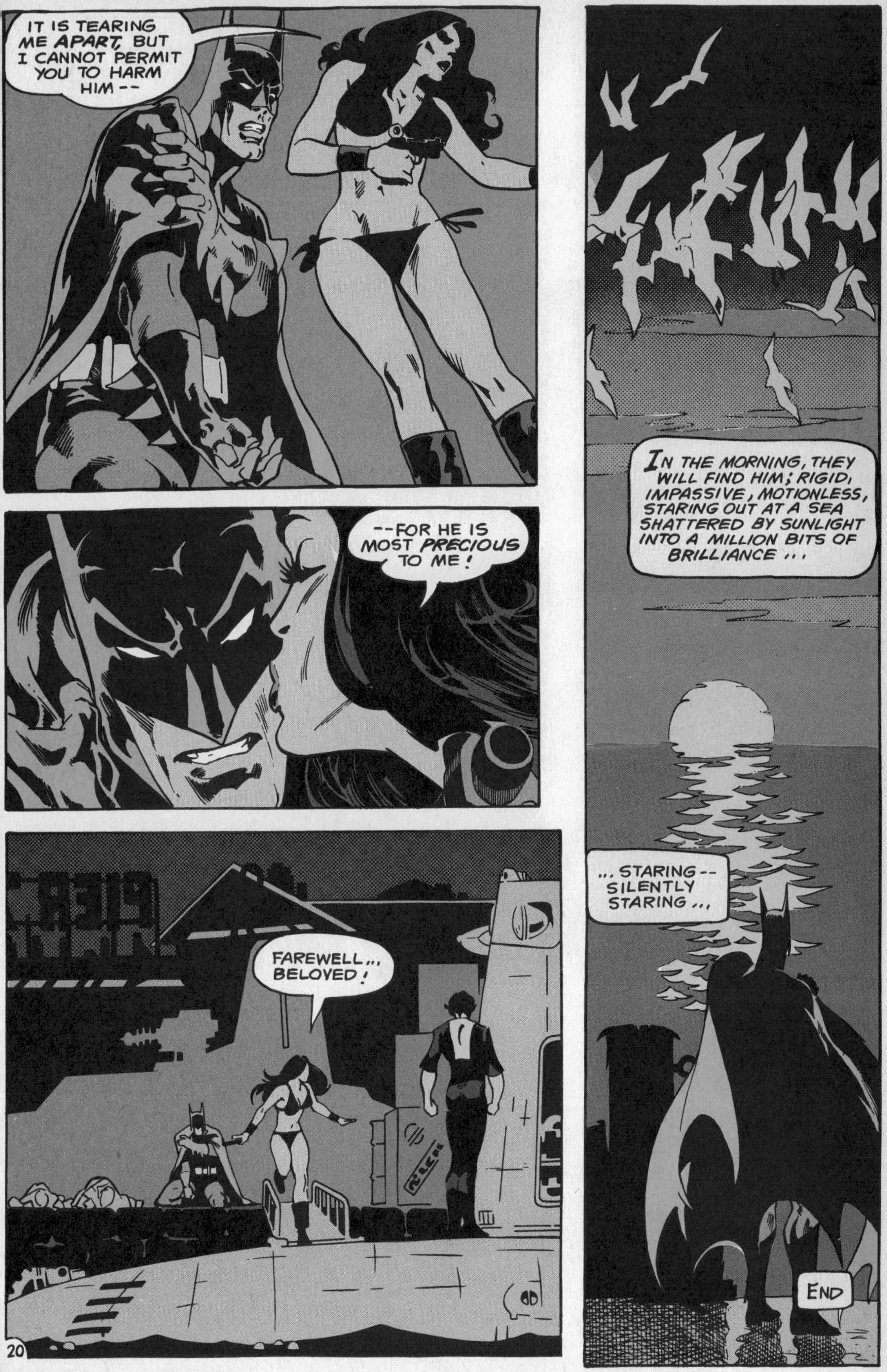
IT IS TEARING ME APART, BUT I CANNOT PERMIT YOU TO HARM HIM --
--FOR HE IS MOST PRECIOUS TO ME!
FAREWELL... BELOVED!
20
IN THE MORNING, THEY WILL FIND HIM; RIGID, IMPASSIVE, MOTIONLESS, STARING OUT AT A SEA SHATTERED BY SUNLIGHT INTO A MILLION BITS OF BRILLIANCE ...
... STARING -- SILENTLY STARING ...
END

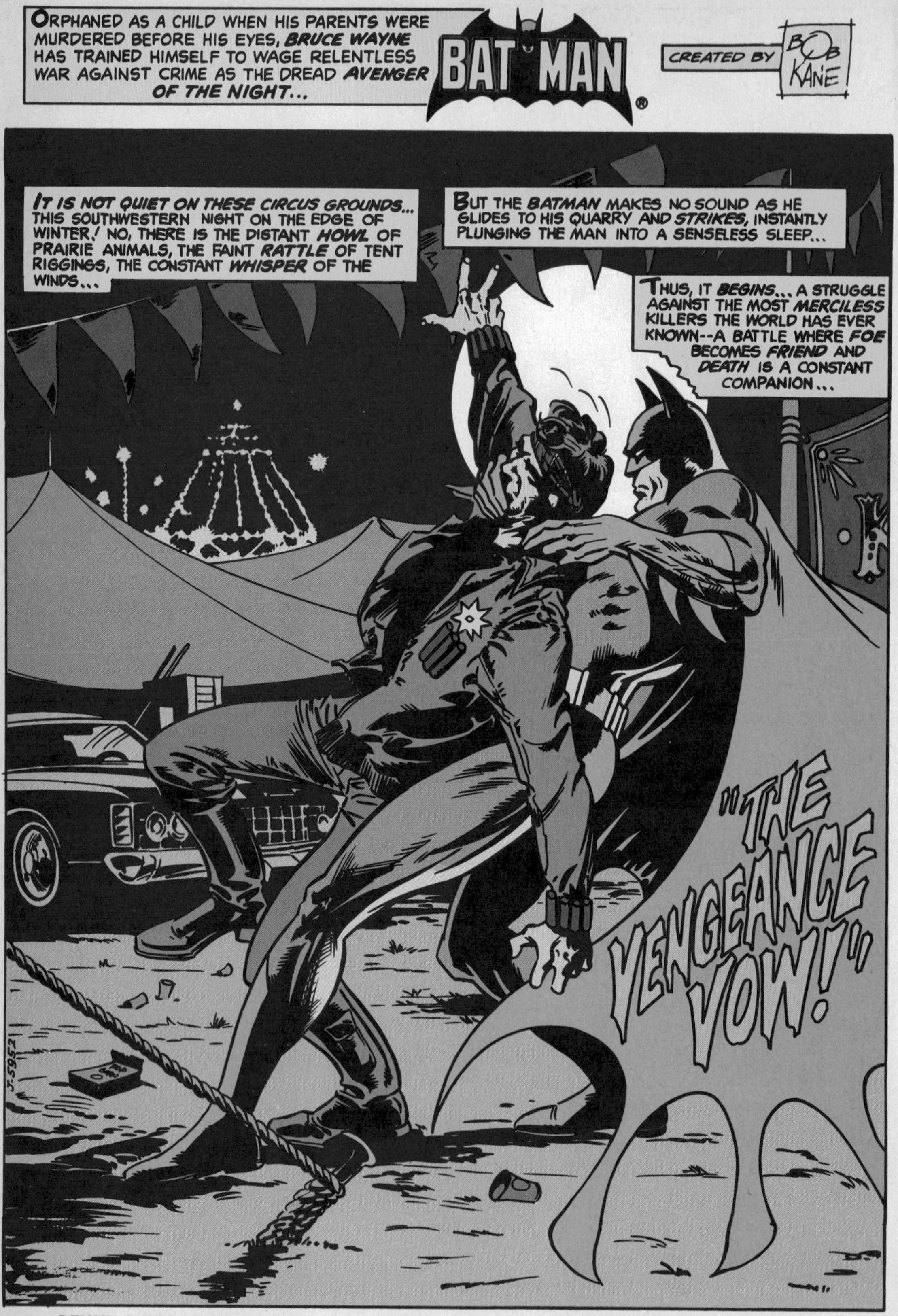
ORPHANED AS A CHILD WHEN HIS PARENTS WERE MURDERED BEFORE HIS EYES, BRUCE WAYNE HAS TRAINED HIMSELF TO WAGE RELENTLESS WAR AGAINST CRIME AS THE DREAD AVENGER OF THE NIGHT...
BATMAN
CREATED BY BOB KANE
IT IS NOT QUIET ON THESE CIRCUS GROUNDS... THIS SOUTHWESTERN NIGHT ON THE EDGE OF WINTER! NO, THERE IS THE DISTANT HOWL OF PRAIRIE ANIMALS, THE FAINT RATTLE OF TENT RIGGINGS, THE CONSTANT WHISPER OF THE WINDS...
BUT THE BATMAN MAKES NO SOUND AS HE GLIDES TO HIS QUARRY AND STRIKES, INSTANTLY PLUNGING THE MAN INTO A SENSELESS SLEEP...
THUS, IT BEGINS... A STRUGGLE AGAINST THE MOST MERCILESS KILLERS THE WORLD HAS EVER KNOWN--A BATTLE WHERE FOE BECOMES FRIEND AND DEATH IS A CONSTANT COMPANION...
"THE VENGEANCE VOW!"

DENNY O'NEIL writer **DON NEWTON & DAN ADKINS** artists **BEN ODA** letterer **GLENN WHITMORE** colorist **PAUL LEVITZ** editor

Special thanks to sensei RICHARD HILL for martial arts advice.

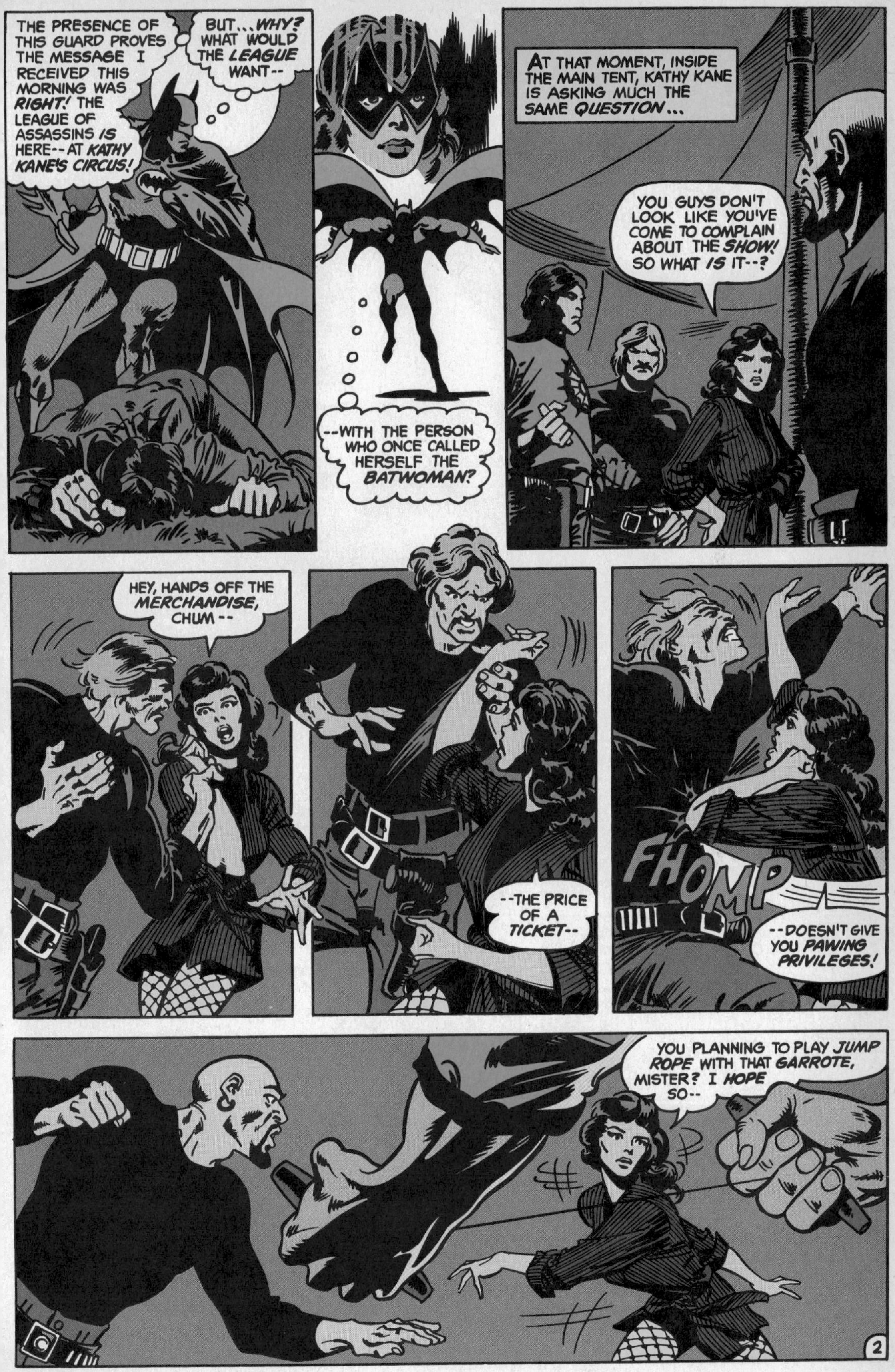
THE PRESENCE OF THIS GUARD PROVES THE MESSAGE I RECEIVED THIS MORNING WAS RIGHT! THE LEAGUE OF ASSASSINS IS HERE--AT KATHY KANE'S CIRCUS!
BUT...WHY? WHAT WOULD THE LEAGUE WANT--
--WITH THE PERSON WHO ONCE CALLED HERSELF THE BATWOMAN?
AT THAT MOMENT, INSIDE THE MAIN TENT, KATHY KANE IS ASKING MUCH THE SAME QUESTION...
YOU GUYS DON'T LOOK LIKE YOU'VE COME TO COMPLAIN ABOUT THE SHOW! SO WHAT IS IT--?
HEY, HANDS OFF THE MERCHANDISE, CHUM--
--THE PRICE OF A TICKET--
FHOMP
--DOESN'T GIVE YOU PAWING PRIVILEGES!
YOU PLANNING TO PLAY JUMP ROPE WITH THAT GARROTE, MISTER? I HOPE SO--
2

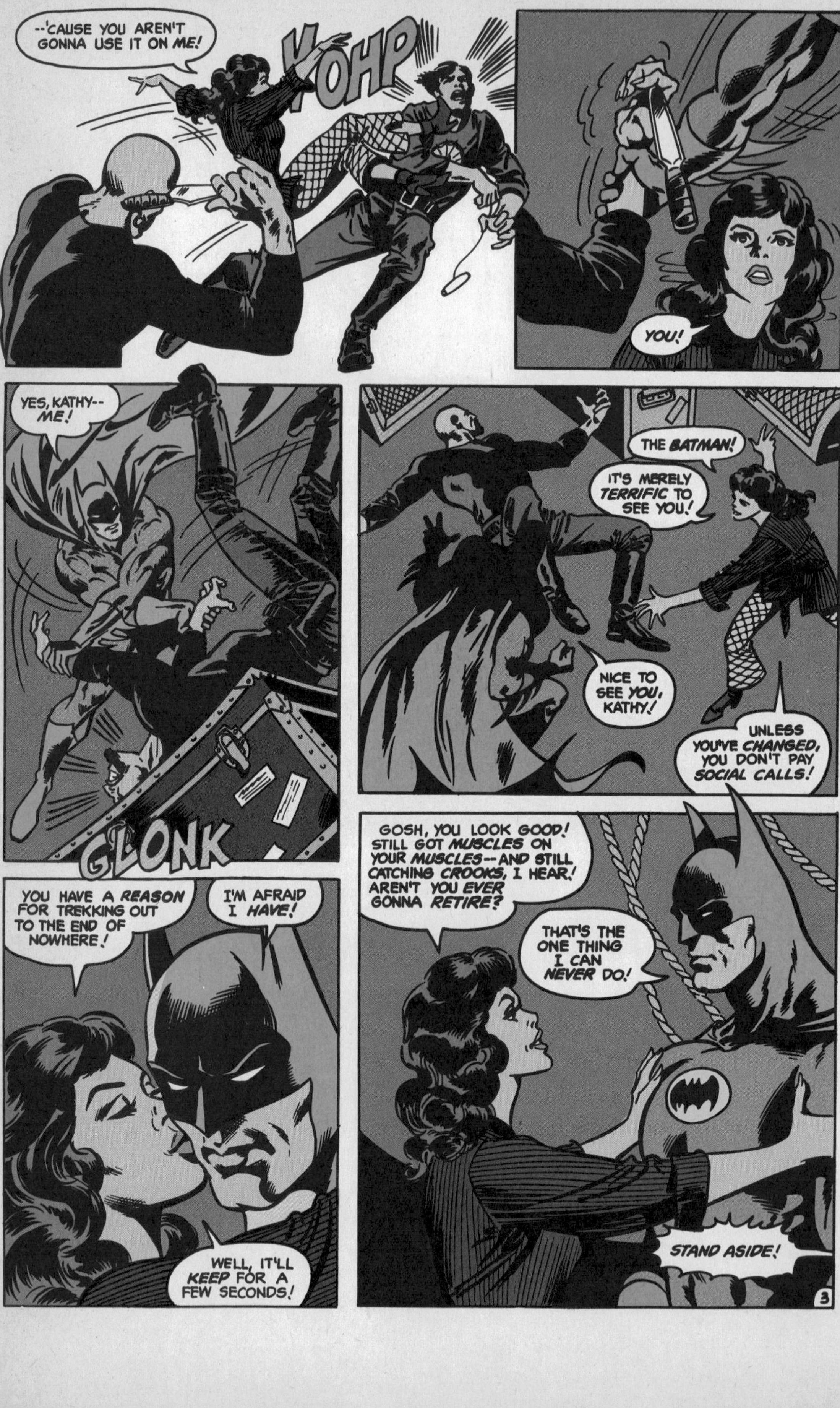
--'CAUSE YOU AREN'T GONNA USE IT ON ME!
YOHP
YOU!
YES, KATHY-- ME!
GLONK
THE BATMAN!
IT'S MERELY TERRIFIC TO SEE YOU!
NICE TO SEE YOU, KATHY!
UNLESS YOU'VE CHANGED, YOU DON'T PAY SOCIAL CALLS!
YOU HAVE A REASON FOR TREKKING OUT TO THE END OF NOWHERE!
I'M AFRAID I HAVE!
WELL, IT'LL KEEP FOR A FEW SECONDS!
GOSH, YOU LOOK GOOD! STILL GOT MUSCLES ON YOUR MUSCLES--AND STILL CATCHING CROOKS, I HEAR! AREN'T YOU EVER GONNA RETIRE?
THAT'S THE ONE THING I CAN NEVER DO!
STAND ASIDE!
3

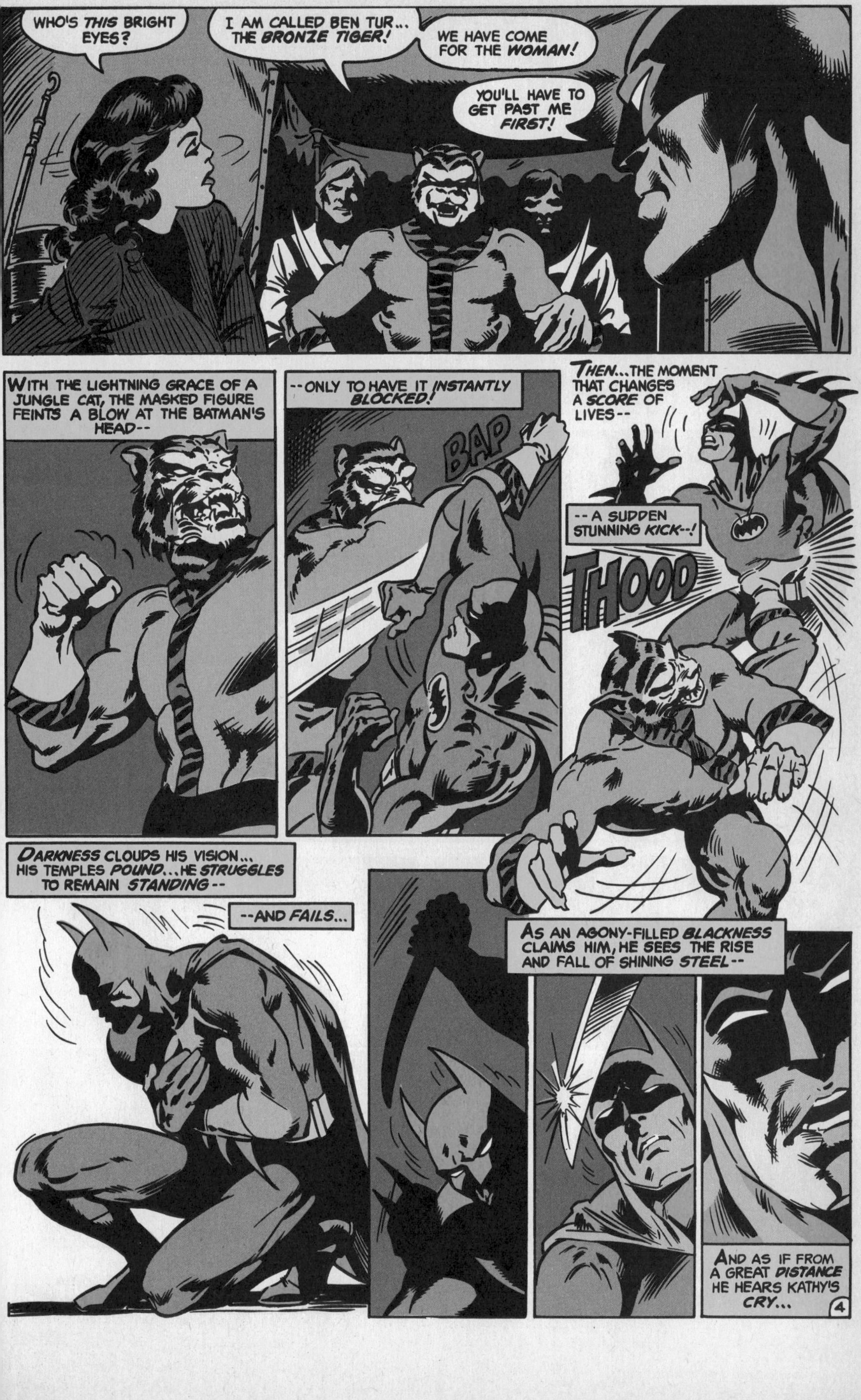
WHO'S THIS BRIGHT EYES?
I AM CALLED BEN TUR... THE BRONZE TIGER!
WE HAVE COME FOR THE WOMAN!
YOU'LL HAVE TO GET PAST ME FIRST!
WITH THE LIGHTNING GRACE OF A JUNGLE CAT, THE MASKED FIGURE FEINTS A BLOW AT THE BATMAN'S HEAD--
--ONLY TO HAVE IT INSTANTLY BLOCKED!
BAP
THEN...THE MOMENT THAT CHANGES A SCORE OF LIVES--
--A SUDDEN STUNNING KICK--!
THOOD
DARKNESS CLOUDS HIS VISION... HIS TEMPLES POUND...HE STRUGGLES TO REMAIN STANDING--
--AND FAILS...
AS AN AGONY-FILLED BLACKNESS CLAIMS HIM, HE SEES THE RISE AND FALL OF SHINING STEEL--
AND AS IF FROM A GREAT DISTANCE HE HEARS KATHY'S CRY...
4

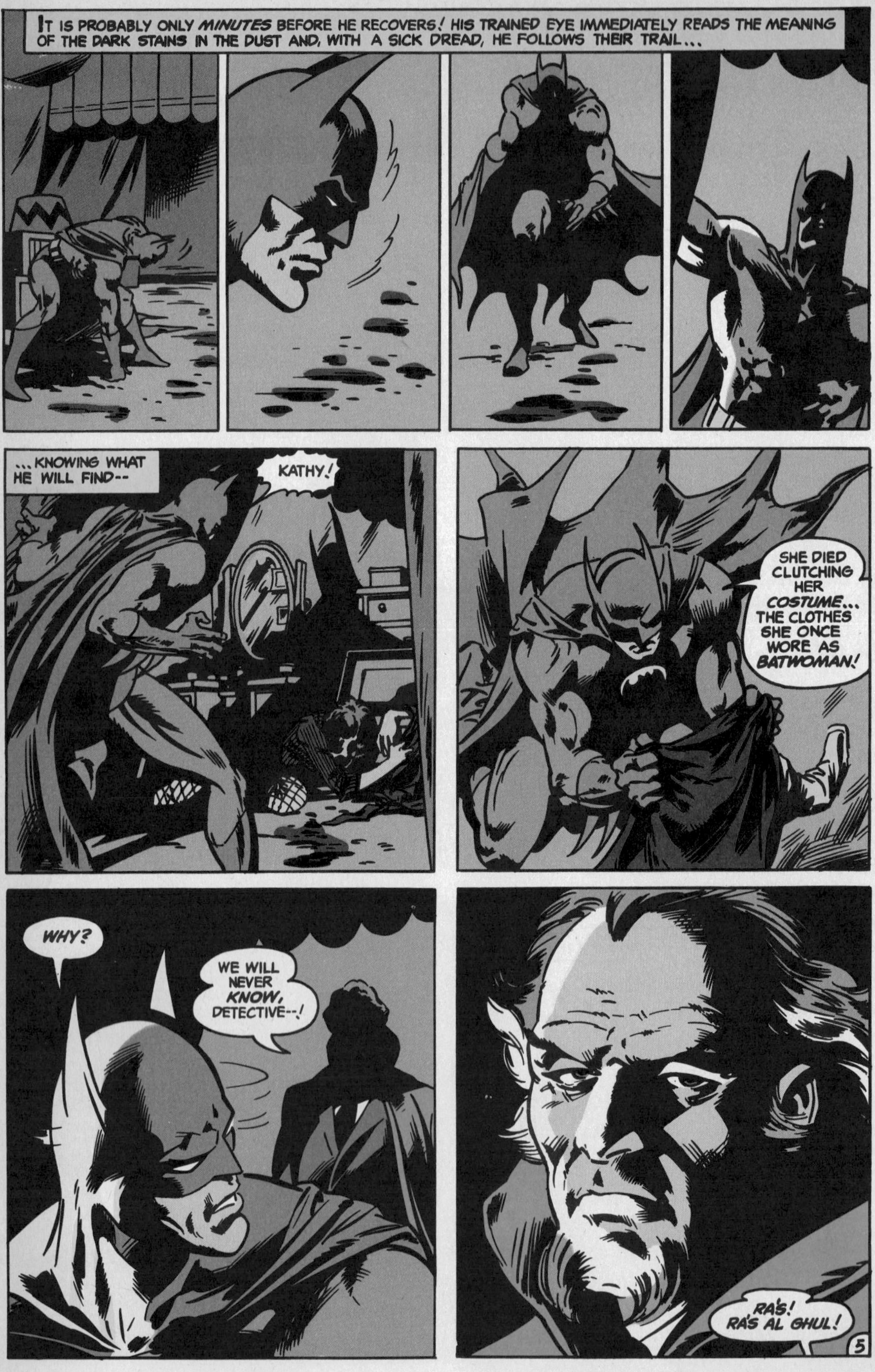
IT IS PROBABLY ONLY MINUTES BEFORE HE RECOVERS! HIS TRAINED EYE IMMEDIATELY READS THE MEANING OF THE DARK STAINS IN THE DUST AND, WITH A SICK DREAD, HE FOLLOWS THEIR TRAIL...
...KNOWING WHAT HE WILL FIND--
KATHY!
SHE DIED CLUTCHING HER COSTUME... THE CLOTHES SHE ONCE WORE AS BATWOMAN!
WHY?
WE WILL NEVER KNOW, DETECTIVE--!
RA'S! RA'S AL GHUL!
5

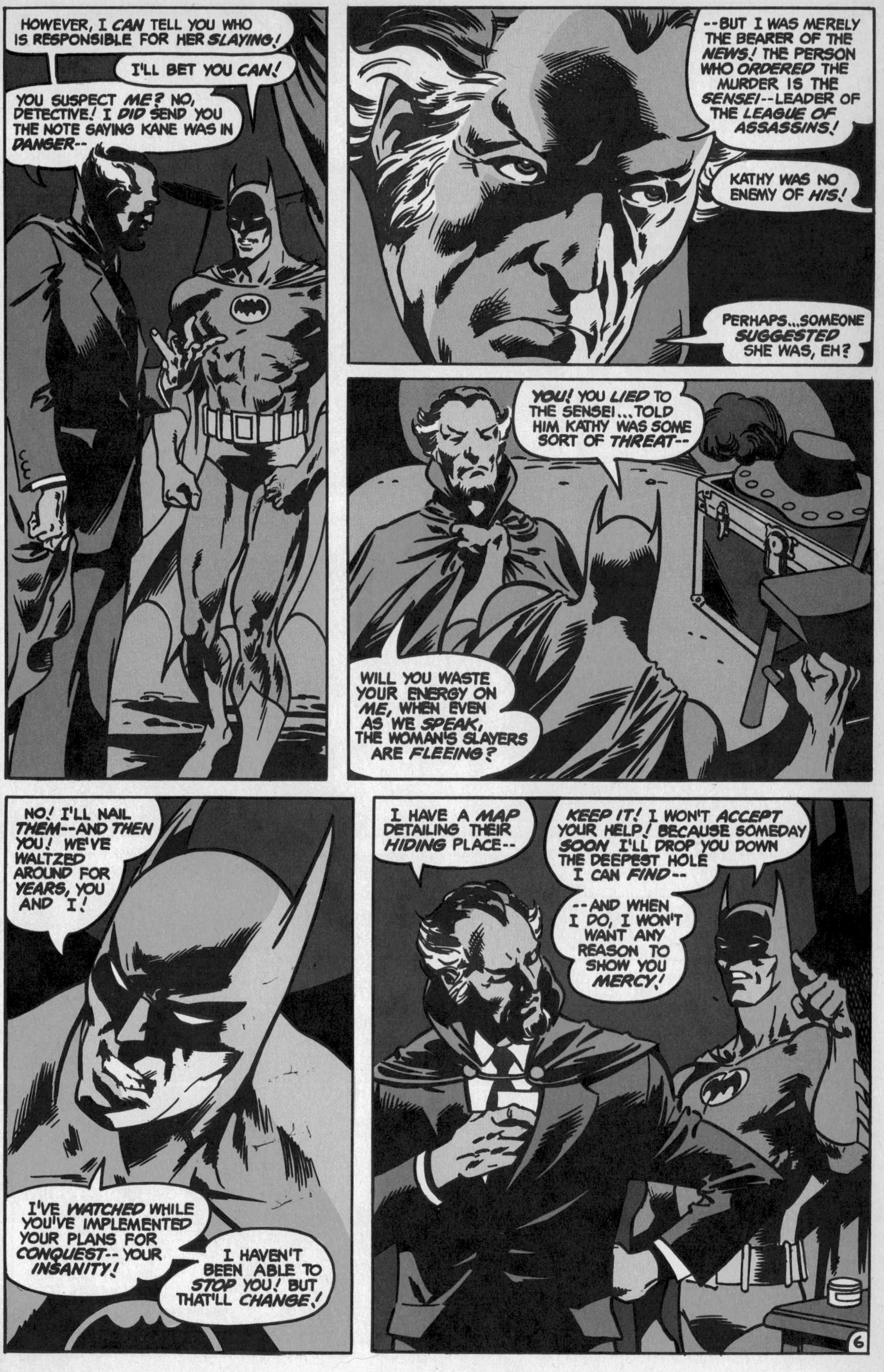
HOWEVER, I CAN TELL YOU WHO IS RESPONSIBLE FOR HER SLAYING!
I'LL BET YOU CAN!
YOU SUSPECT ME? NO, DETECTIVE! I DID SEND YOU THE NOTE SAYING KANE WAS IN DANGER--
--BUT I WAS MERELY THE BEARER OF THE NEWS! THE PERSON WHO ORDERED THE MURDER IS THE SENSEI--LEADER OF THE LEAGUE OF ASSASSINS!
KATHY WAS NO ENEMY OF HIS!
PERHAPS...SOMEONE SUGGESTED SHE WAS, EH?
YOU! YOU LIED TO THE SENSEI...TOLD HIM KATHY WAS SOME SORT OF THREAT--
WILL YOU WASTE YOUR ENERGY ON ME, WHEN EVEN AS WE SPEAK, THE WOMAN'S SLAYERS ARE FLEEING?
NO! I'LL NAIL THEM--AND THEN YOU! WE'VE WALTZED AROUND FOR YEARS, YOU AND I!
I'VE WATCHED WHILE YOU'VE IMPLEMENTED YOUR PLANS FOR CONQUEST-- YOUR INSANITY!
I HAVEN'T BEEN ABLE TO STOP YOU! BUT THAT'LL CHANGE!
I HAVE A MAP DETAILING THEIR HIDING PLACE--
KEEP IT! I WON'T ACCEPT YOUR HELP! BECAUSE SOMEDAY SOON I'LL DROP YOU DOWN THE DEEPEST HOLE I CAN FIND--
--AND WHEN I DO, I WON'T WANT ANY REASON TO SHOW YOU MERCY!
6

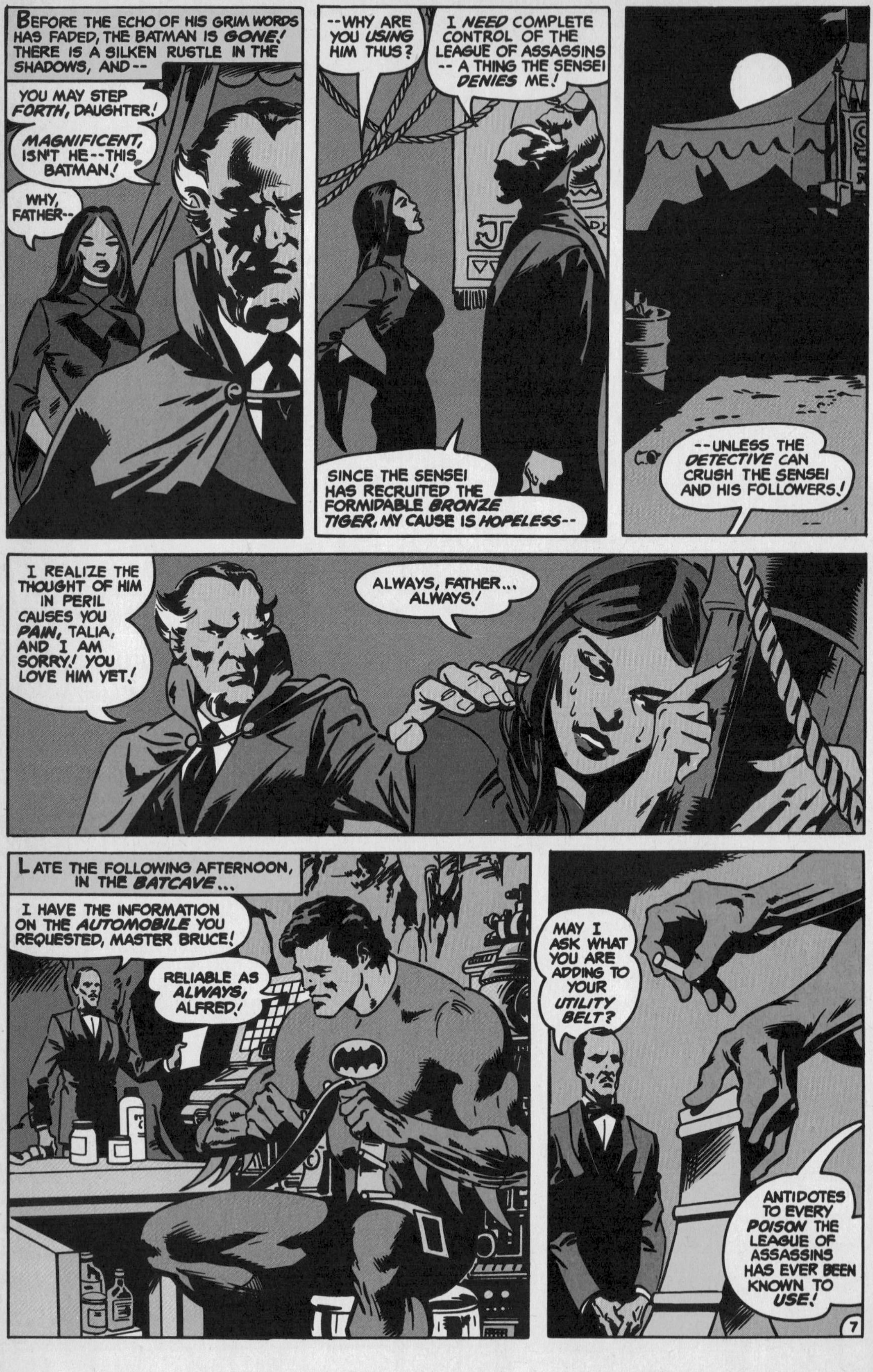
BEFORE THE ECHO OF HIS GRIM WORDS HAS FADED, THE BATMAN IS GONE! THERE IS A SILKEN RUSTLE IN THE SHADOWS, AND--
YOU MAY STEP FORTH, DAUGHTER!
MAGNIFICENT, ISN'T HE--THIS BATMAN!
WHY, FATHER--
--WHY ARE YOU USING HIM THUS?
I NEED COMPLETE CONTROL OF THE LEAGUE OF ASSASSINS -- A THING THE SENSEI DENIES ME!
SINCE THE SENSEI HAS RECRUITED THE FORMIDABLE BRONZE TIGER, MY CAUSE IS HOPELESS--
--UNLESS THE DETECTIVE CAN CRUSH THE SENSEI AND HIS FOLLOWERS!
I REALIZE THE THOUGHT OF HIM IN PERIL CAUSES YOU PAIN, TALIA, AND I AM SORRY! YOU LOVE HIM YET!
ALWAYS, FATHER... ALWAYS!
LATE THE FOLLOWING AFTERNOON, IN THE BATCAVE...
I HAVE THE INFORMATION ON THE AUTOMOBILE YOU REQUESTED, MASTER BRUCE!
RELIABLE AS ALWAYS, ALFRED!
MAY I ASK WHAT YOU ARE ADDING TO YOUR UTILITY BELT?
ANTIDOTES TO EVERY POISON THE LEAGUE OF ASSASSINS HAS EVER BEEN KNOWN TO USE!
7

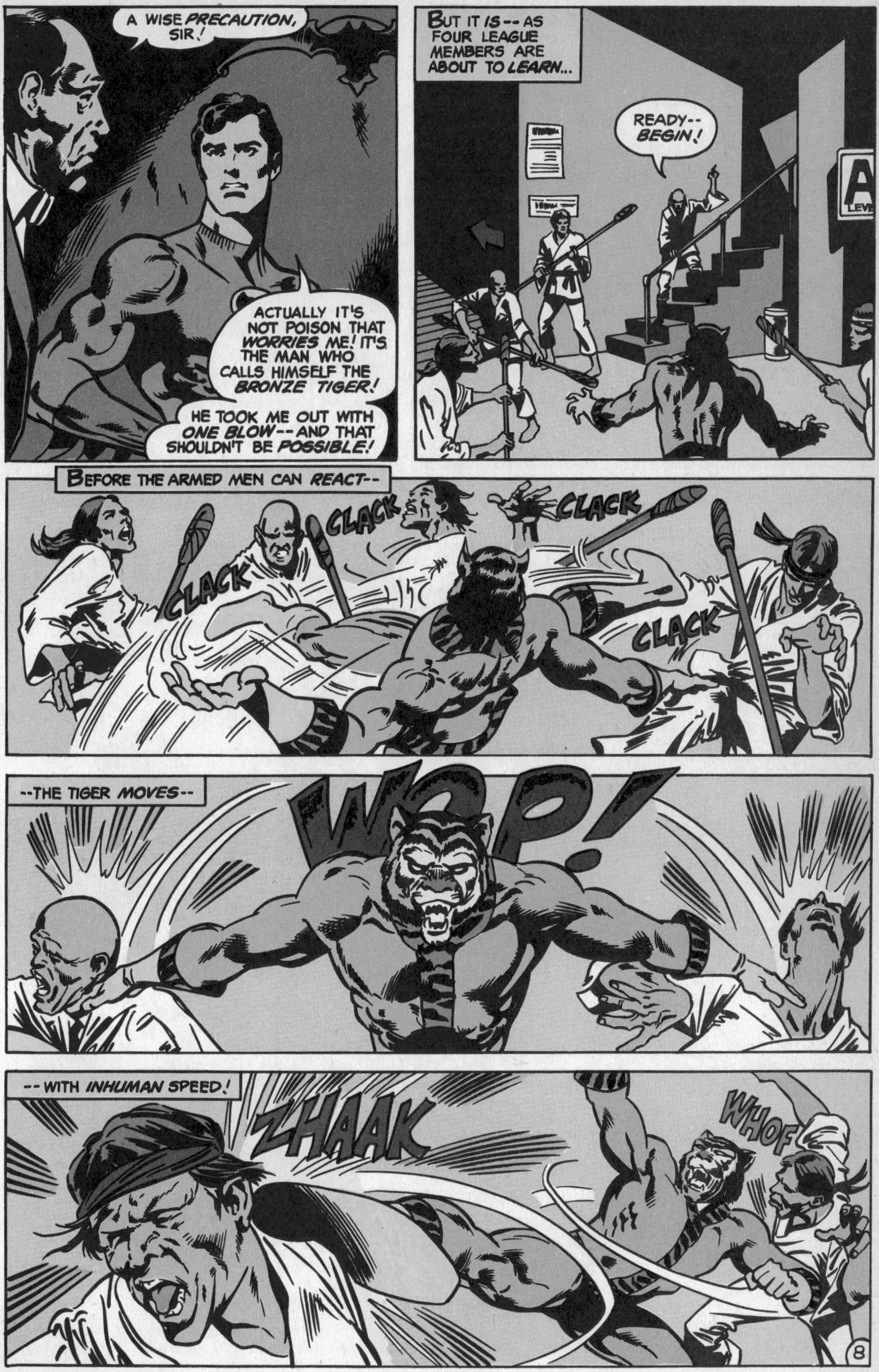
A WISE PRECAUTION, SIR!
ACTUALLY IT'S NOT POISON THAT WORRIES ME! IT'S THE MAN WHO CALLS HIMSELF THE BRONZE TIGER!
HE TOOK ME OUT WITH ONE BLOW--AND THAT SHOULDN'T BE POSSIBLE!
BUT IT IS--AS FOUR LEAGUE MEMBERS ARE ABOUT TO LEARN...
READY-- BEGIN!
BEFORE THE ARMED MEN CAN REACT--
CLACK
CLACK
CLACK
CLACK
--THE TIGER MOVES--
WOP!
--WITH INHUMAN SPEED!
ZHAAK
WHOF
8

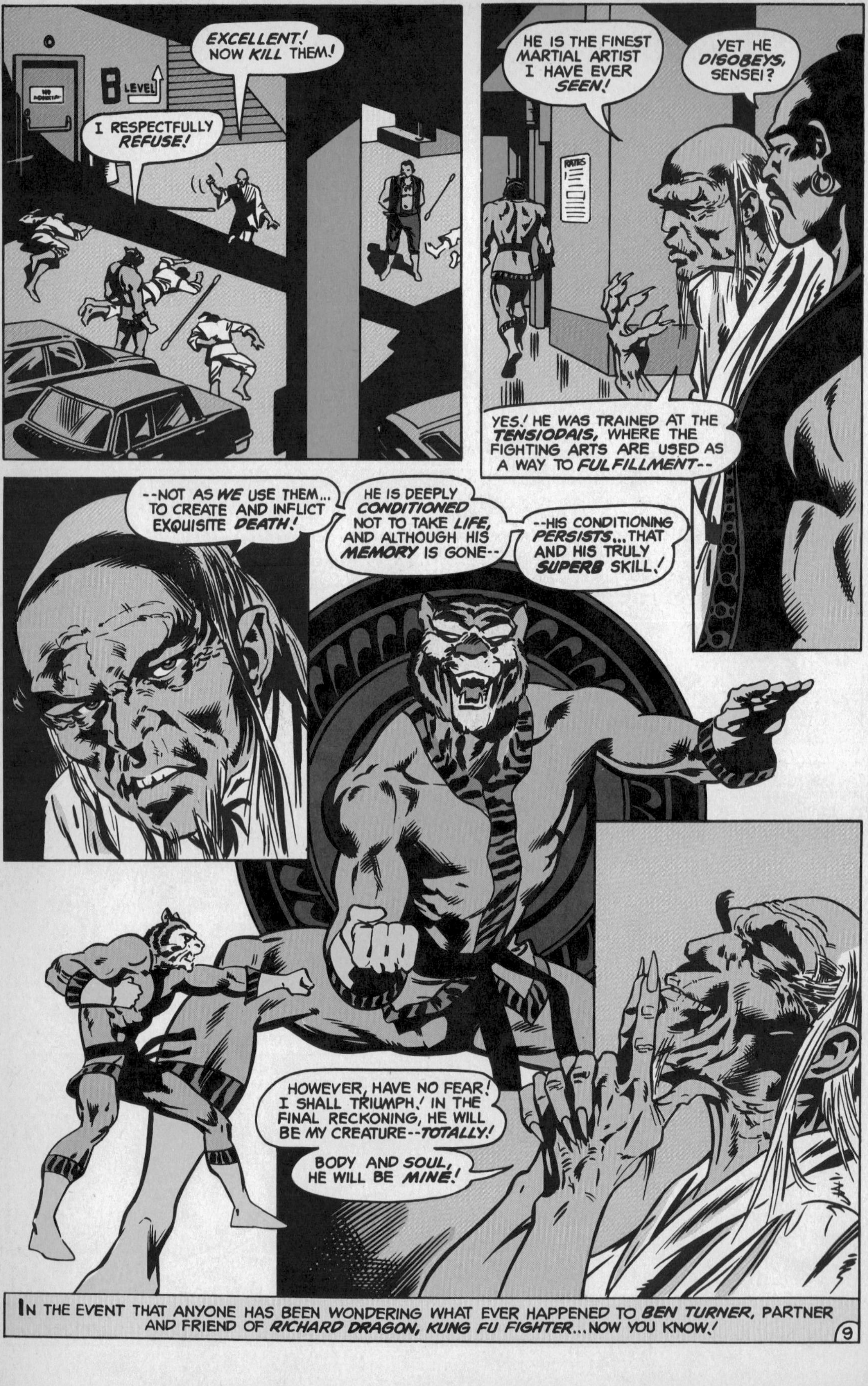
EXCELLENT! NOW KILL THEM!
I RESPECTFULLY REFUSE!
B LEVEL
HE IS THE FINEST MARTIAL ARTIST I HAVE EVER SEEN!
YET HE DISOBEYS, SENSEI?
RATES
YES! HE WAS TRAINED AT THE TENSIODAIS, WHERE THE FIGHTING ARTS ARE USED AS A WAY TO FULFILLMENT--
--NOT AS WE USE THEM... TO CREATE AND INFLICT EXQUISITE DEATH!
HE IS DEEPLY CONDITIONED NOT TO TAKE LIFE, AND ALTHOUGH HIS MEMORY IS GONE--
--HIS CONDITIONING PERSISTS...THAT AND HIS TRULY SUPERB SKILL!
HOWEVER, HAVE NO FEAR! I SHALL TRIUMPH! IN THE FINAL RECKONING, HE WILL BE MY CREATURE--TOTALLY!
BODY AND SOUL, HE WILL BE MINE!
IN THE EVENT THAT ANYONE HAS BEEN WONDERING WHAT EVER HAPPENED TO BEN TURNER, PARTNER AND FRIEND OF RICHARD DRAGON, KUNG FU FIGHTER...NOW YOU KNOW!
9

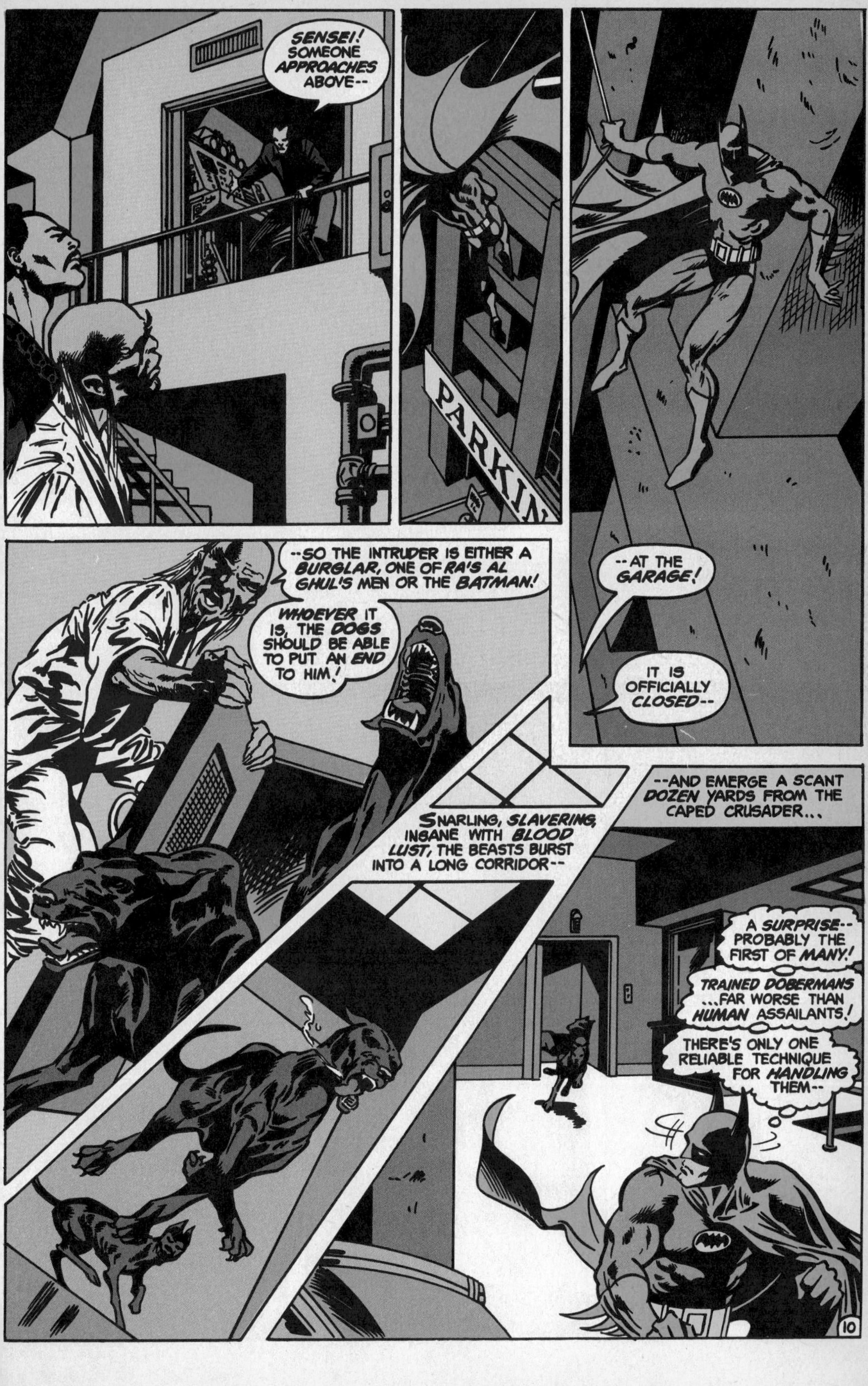
SENSEI! SOMEONE APPROACHES ABOVE--
PARKIN
--AT THE GARAGE!
IT IS OFFICIALLY CLOSED--
--SO THE INTRUDER IS EITHER A BURGLAR, ONE OF RA'S AL GHUL'S MEN OR THE BATMAN!
WHOEVER IT IS, THE DOGS SHOULD BE ABLE TO PUT AN END TO HIM!
SNARLING, SLAVERING, INSANE WITH BLOOD LUST, THE BEASTS BURST INTO A LONG CORRIDOR--
--AND EMERGE A SCANT DOZEN YARDS FROM THE CAPED CRUSADER...
A SURPRISE-- PROBABLY THE FIRST OF MANY!
TRAINED DOBERMANS ...FAR WORSE THAN HUMAN ASSAILANTS!
THERE'S ONLY ONE RELIABLE TECHNIQUE FOR HANDLING THEM--
10

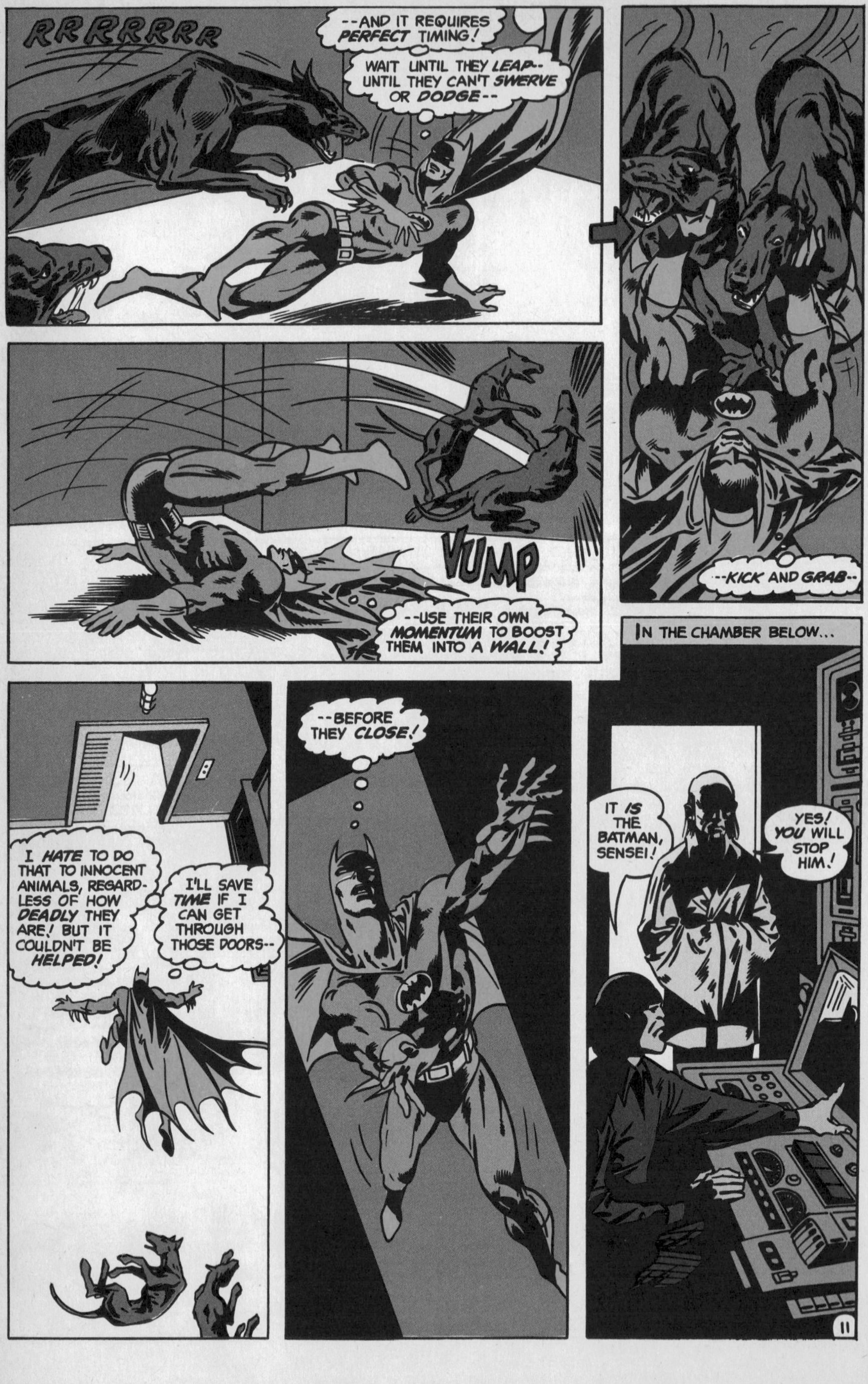
RRRRRRRR
--AND IT REQUIRES PERFECT TIMING!
WAIT UNTIL THEY LEAP--UNTIL THEY CAN'T SWERVE OR DODGE--
--KICK AND GRAB--
VUMP
--USE THEIR OWN MOMENTUM TO BOOST THEM INTO A WALL!
IN THE CHAMBER BELOW...
I HATE TO DO THAT TO INNOCENT ANIMALS, REGARDLESS OF HOW DEADLY THEY ARE! BUT IT COULDN'T BE HELPED!
I'LL SAVE TIME IF I CAN GET THROUGH THOSE DOORS--
--BEFORE THEY CLOSE!
IT IS THE BATMAN, SENSEI!
YES! YOU WILL STOP HIM!
11

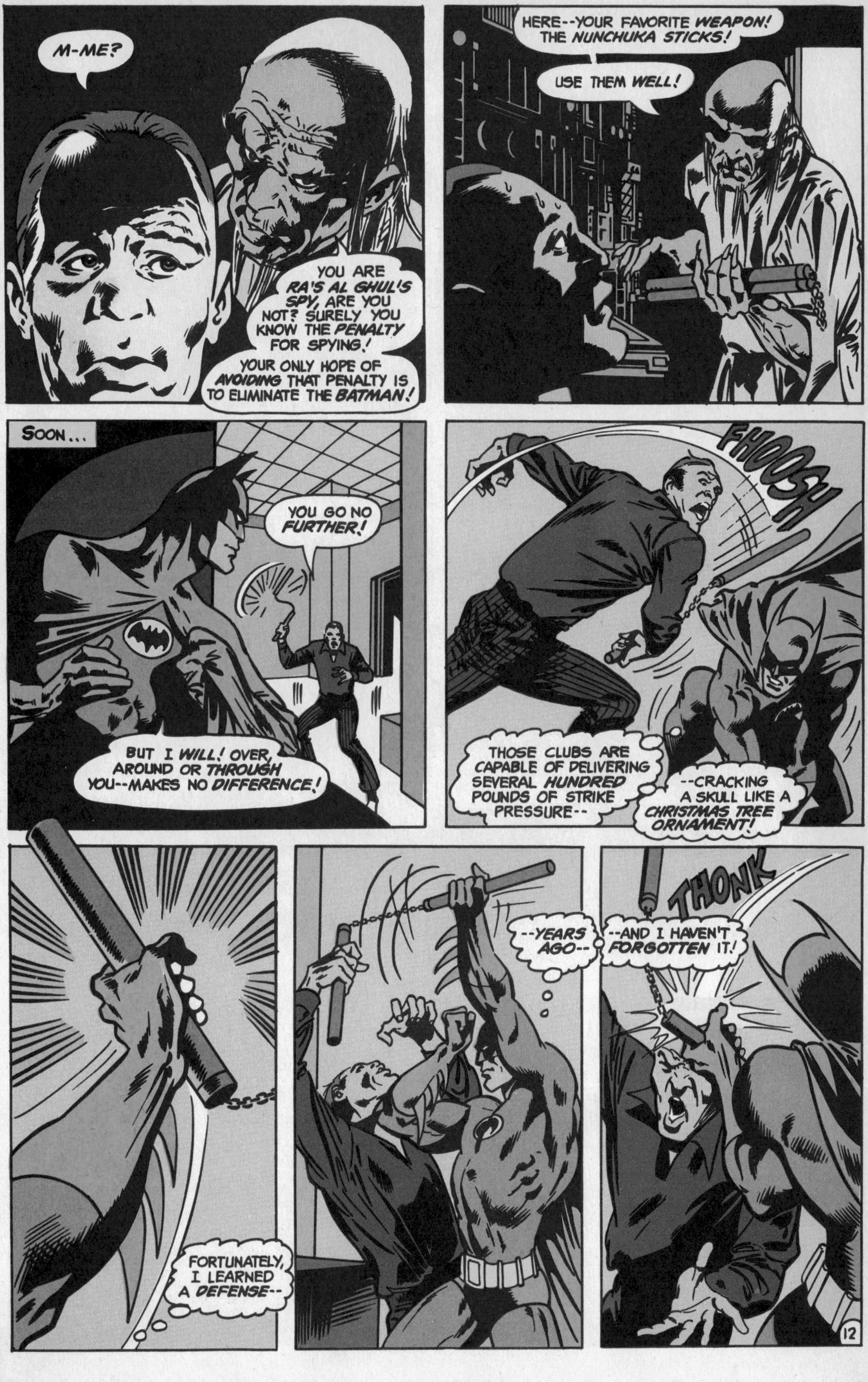
M-ME?
YOU ARE RA'S AL GHUL'S SPY, ARE YOU NOT? SURELY YOU KNOW THE PENALTY FOR SPYING!
YOUR ONLY HOPE OF AVOIDING THAT PENALTY IS TO ELIMINATE THE BATMAN!
HERE--YOUR FAVORITE WEAPON! THE NUNCHUKA STICKS!
USE THEM WELL!
SOON...
YOU GO NO FURTHER!
BUT I WILL! OVER, AROUND OR THROUGH YOU--MAKES NO DIFFERENCE!
FHOOSH
THOSE CLUBS ARE CAPABLE OF DELIVERING SEVERAL HUNDRED POUNDS OF STRIKE PRESSURE--
--CRACKING A SKULL LIKE A CHRISTMAS TREE ORNAMENT!
FORTUNATELY, I LEARNED A DEFENSE--
--YEARS AGO--
--AND I HAVEN'T FORGOTTEN IT!
THONK
12

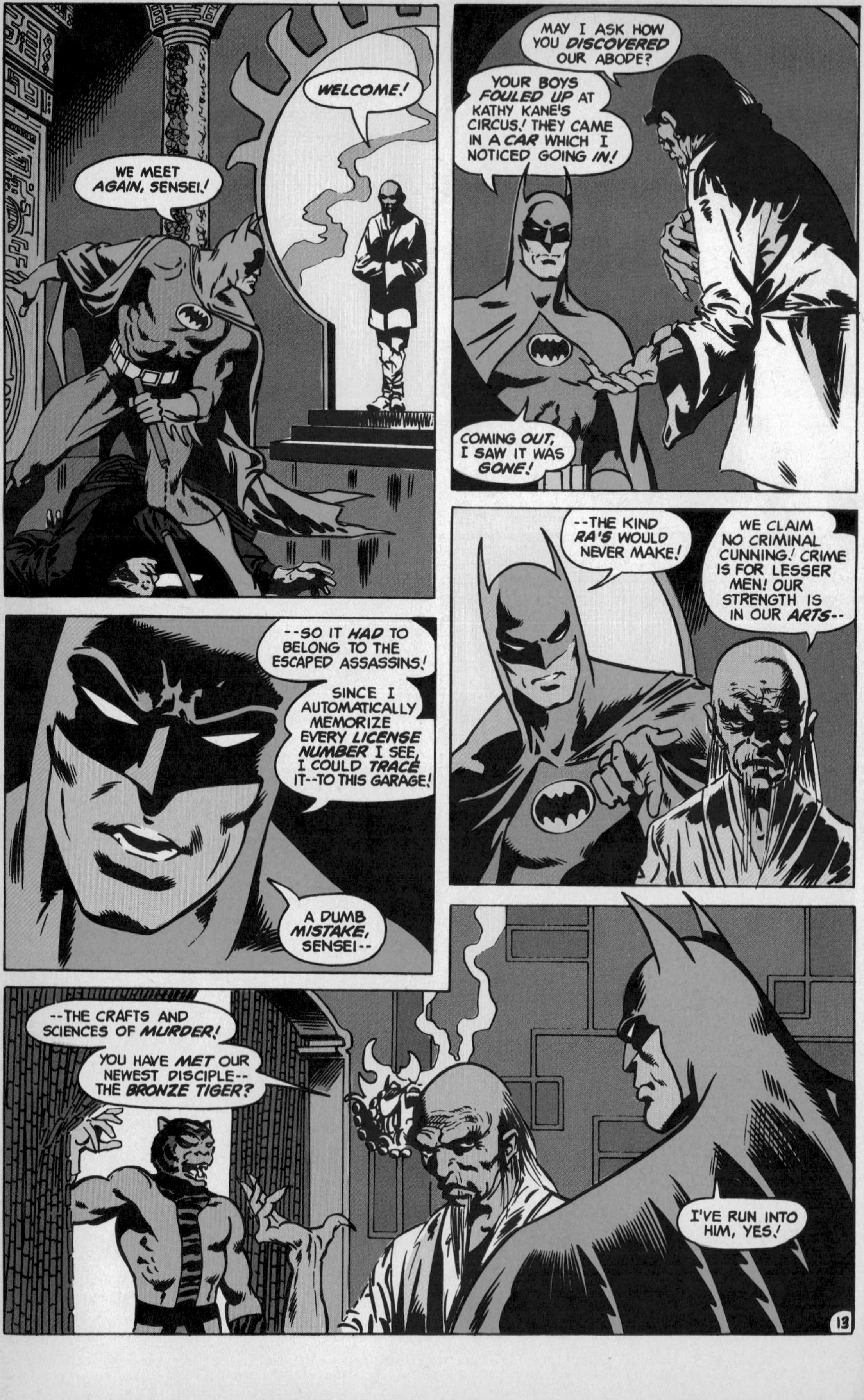
WELCOME!
WE MEET AGAIN, SENSEI!
MAY I ASK HOW YOU DISCOVERED OUR ABODE?
YOUR BOYS FOULED UP AT KATHY KANE'S CIRCUS! THEY CAME IN A CAR WHICH I NOTICED GOING IN!
COMING OUT, I SAW IT WAS GONE!
--SO IT HAD TO BELONG TO THE ESCAPED ASSASSINS!
SINCE I AUTOMATICALLY MEMORIZE EVERY LICENSE NUMBER I SEE, I COULD TRACE IT--TO THIS GARAGE!
A DUMB MISTAKE, SENSEI--
--THE KIND RA'S WOULD NEVER MAKE!
WE CLAIM NO CRIMINAL CUNNING! CRIME IS FOR LESSER MEN! OUR STRENGTH IS IN OUR ARTS--
--THE CRAFTS AND SCIENCES OF MURDER!
YOU HAVE MET OUR NEWEST DISCIPLE-- THE BRONZE TIGER?
I'VE RUN INTO HIM, YES!
13

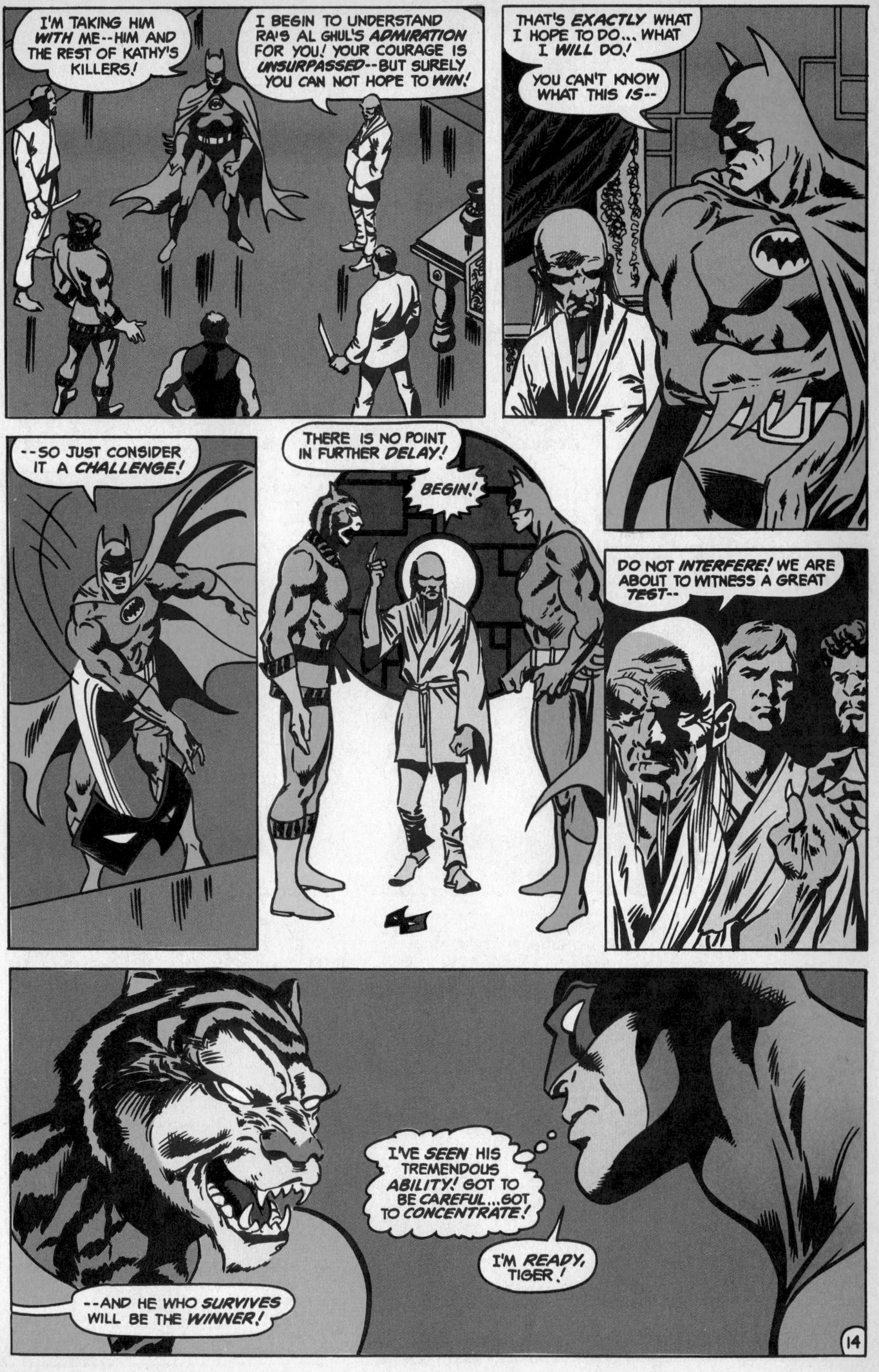
I'M TAKING HIM WITH ME--HIM AND THE REST OF KATHY'S KILLERS!
I BEGIN TO UNDERSTAND RA'S AL GHUL'S ADMIRATION FOR YOU! YOUR COURAGE IS UNSURPASSED--BUT SURELY YOU CAN NOT HOPE TO WIN!
THAT'S EXACTLY WHAT I HOPE TO DO... WHAT I WILL DO!
YOU CAN'T KNOW WHAT THIS IS--
--SO JUST CONSIDER IT A CHALLENGE!
THERE IS NO POINT IN FURTHER DELAY!
BEGIN!
DO NOT INTERFERE! WE ARE ABOUT TO WITNESS A GREAT TEST--
I'VE SEEN HIS TREMENDOUS ABILITY! GOT TO BE CAREFUL...GOT TO CONCENTRATE!
I'M READY, TIGER!
--AND HE WHO SURVIVES WILL BE THE WINNER!
14

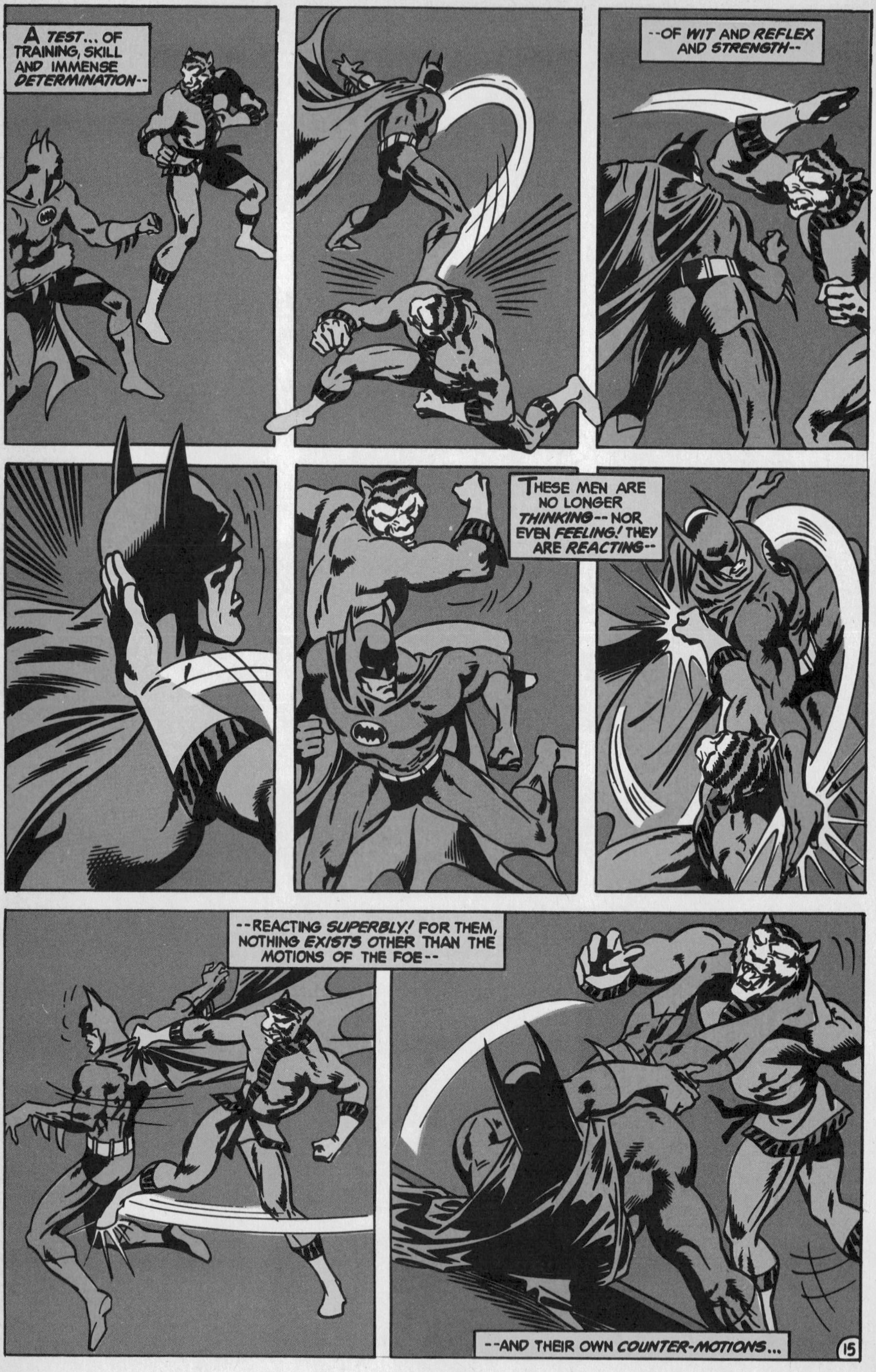
A TEST... OF TRAINING, SKILL AND IMMENSE DETERMINATION--
--OF WIT AND REFLEX AND STRENGTH--
THESE MEN ARE NO LONGER THINKING-- NOR EVEN FEELING! THEY ARE REACTING--
--REACTING SUPERBLY! FOR THEM, NOTHING EXISTS OTHER THAN THE MOTIONS OF THE FOE--
--AND THEIR OWN COUNTER-MOTIONS...
15

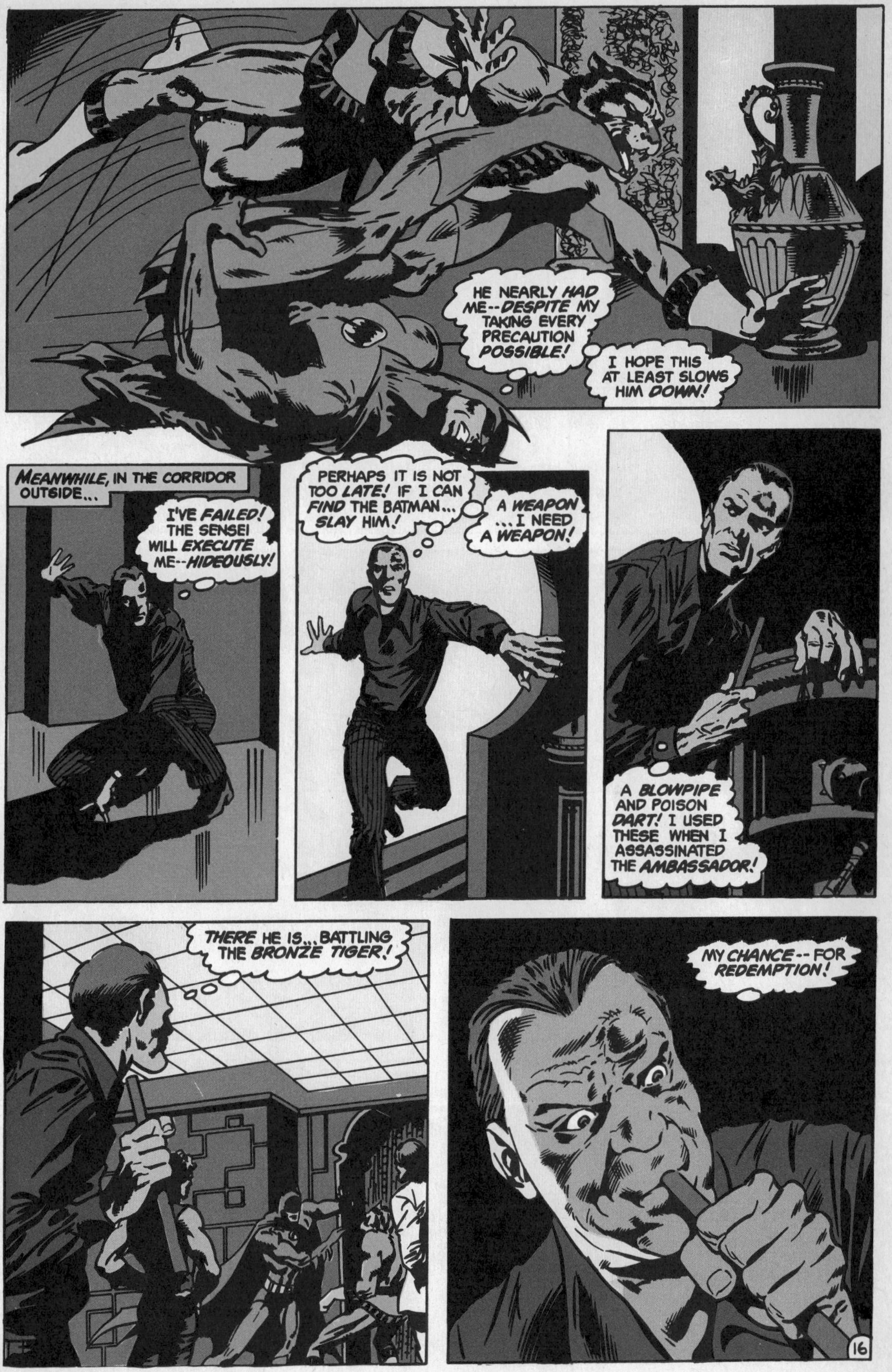
HE NEARLY HAD ME--DESPITE MY TAKING EVERY PRECAUTION POSSIBLE!
I HOPE THIS AT LEAST SLOWS HIM DOWN!
MEANWHILE, IN THE CORRIDOR OUTSIDE...
I'VE FAILED! THE SENSEI WILL EXECUTE ME--HIDEOUSLY!
PERHAPS IT IS NOT TOO LATE! IF I CAN FIND THE BATMAN... SLAY HIM!
A WEAPON ...I NEED A WEAPON!
A BLOWPIPE AND POISON DART! I USED THESE WHEN I ASSASSINATED THE AMBASSADOR!
THERE HE IS...BATTLING THE BRONZE TIGER!
MY CHANCE--FOR REDEMPTION!
16

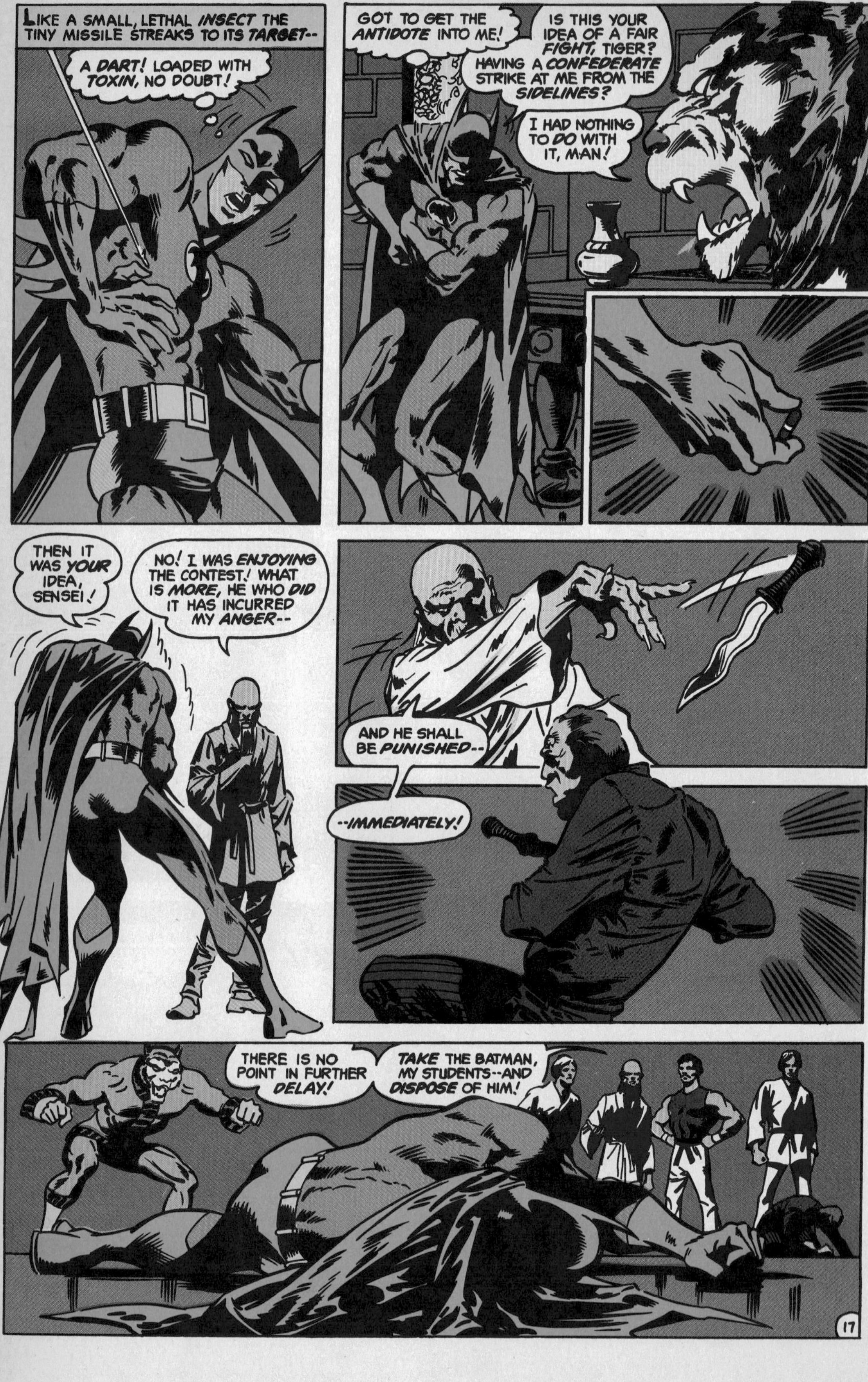
LIKE A SMALL, LETHAL INSECT THE TINY MISSILE STREAKS TO ITS TARGET--
A DART! LOADED WITH TOXIN, NO DOUBT!
GOT TO GET THE ANTIDOTE INTO ME!
IS THIS YOUR IDEA OF A FAIR FIGHT, TIGER? HAVING A CONFEDERATE STRIKE AT ME FROM THE SIDELINES?
I HAD NOTHING TO DO WITH IT, MAN!
THEN IT WAS YOUR IDEA, SENSEI!
NO! I WAS ENJOYING THE CONTEST! WHAT IS MORE, HE WHO DID IT HAS INCURRED MY ANGER--
AND HE SHALL BE PUNISHED--
--IMMEDIATELY!
THERE IS NO POINT IN FURTHER DELAY!
TAKE THE BATMAN, MY STUDENTS--AND DISPOSE OF HIM!
17

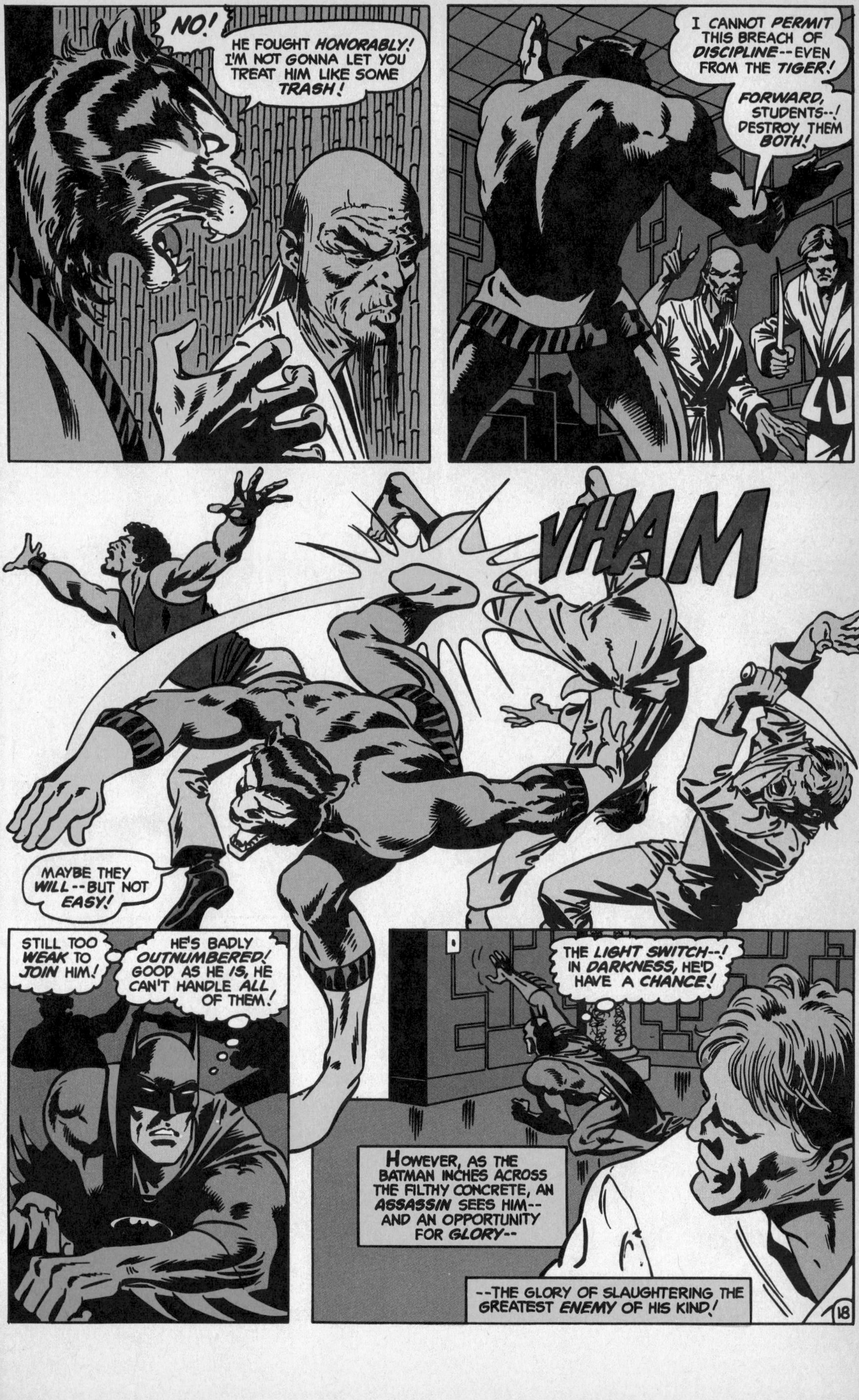
NO!
HE FOUGHT HONORABLY! I'M NOT GONNA LET YOU TREAT HIM LIKE SOME TRASH!
I CANNOT PERMIT THIS BREACH OF DISCIPLINE--EVEN FROM THE TIGER!
FORWARD, STUDENTS--! DESTROY THEM BOTH!
VHAM
MAYBE THEY WILL--BUT NOT EASY!
STILL TOO WEAK TO JOIN HIM!
HE'S BADLY OUTNUMBERED! GOOD AS HE IS, HE CAN'T HANDLE ALL OF THEM!
THE LIGHT SWITCH--! IN DARKNESS, HE'D HAVE A CHANCE!
HOWEVER, AS THE BATMAN INCHES ACROSS THE FILTHY CONCRETE, AN ASSASSIN SEES HIM--AND AN OPPORTUNITY FOR GLORY--
--THE GLORY OF SLAUGHTERING THE GREATEST ENEMY OF HIS KIND!
18

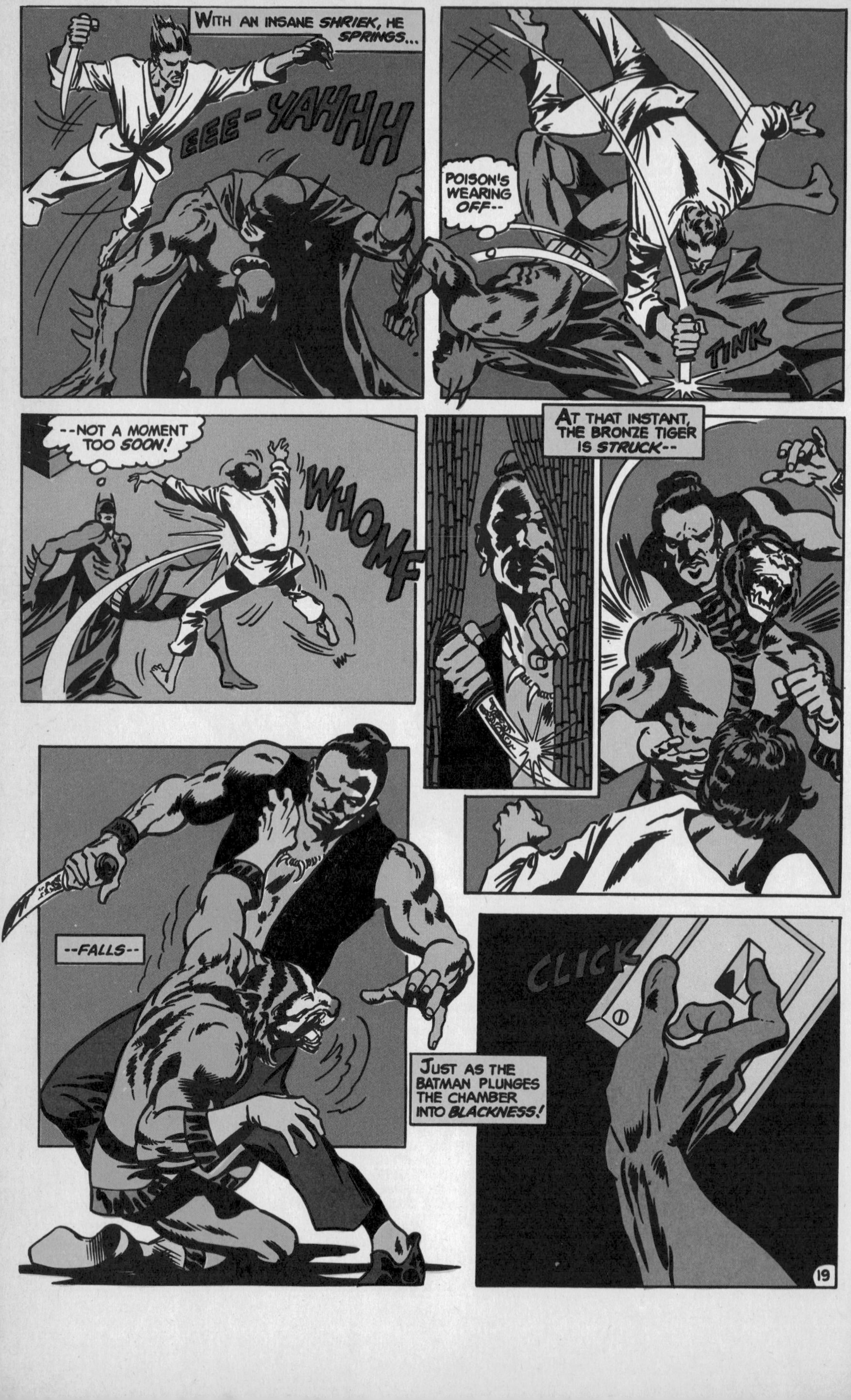
WITH AN INSANE SHRIEK, HE SPRINGS...
EEE-YAHHH
POISON'S WEARING OFF--
TINK
--NOT A MOMENT TOO SOON!
WHOMF
AT THAT INSTANT, THE BRONZE TIGER IS STRUCK--
--FALLS--
JUST AS THE BATMAN PLUNGES THE CHAMBER INTO BLACKNESS!
CLICK
19

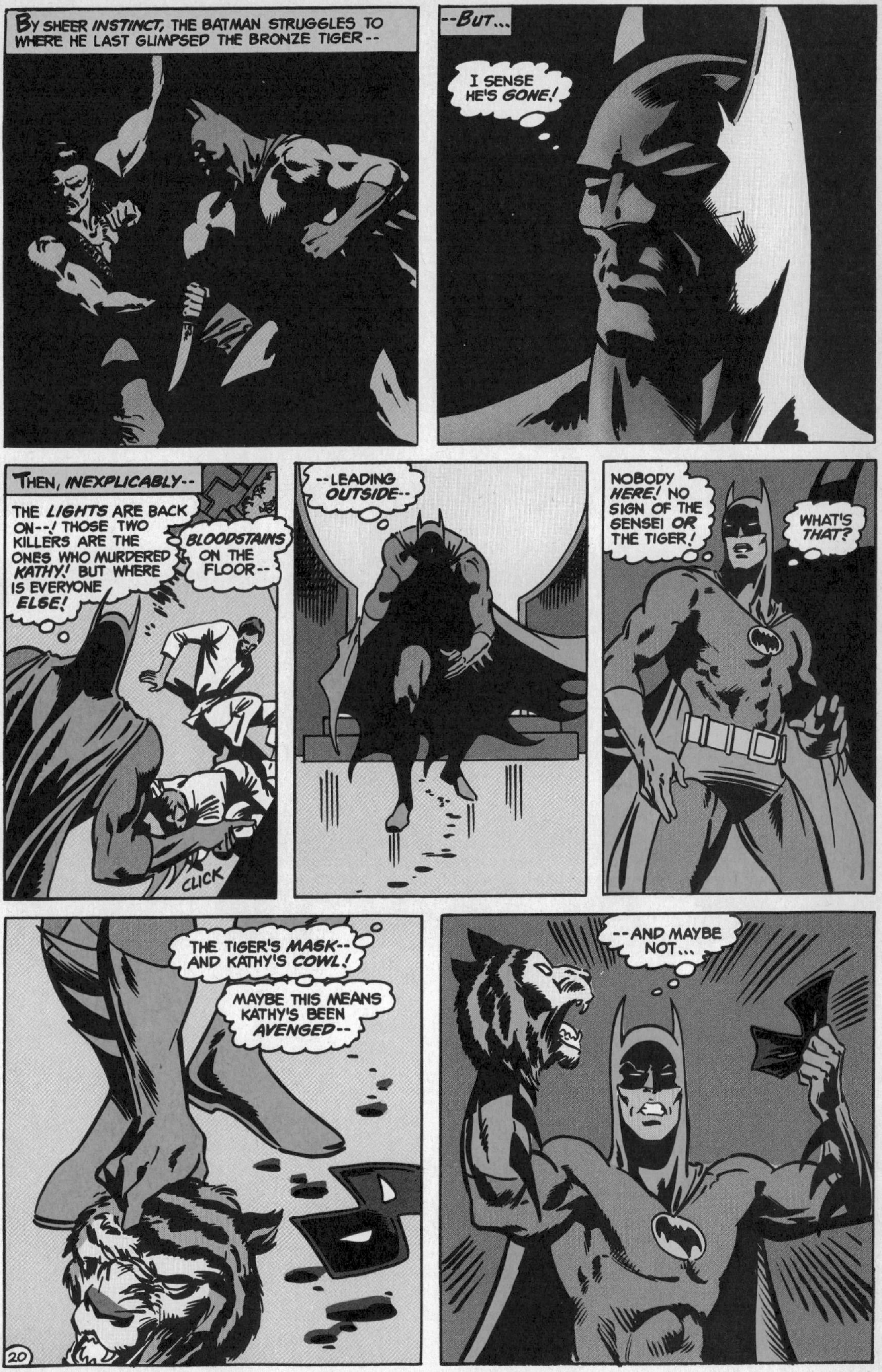
BY SHEER INSTINCT, THE BATMAN STRUGGLES TO WHERE HE LAST GLIMPSED THE BRONZE TIGER--
--BUT...
I SENSE HE'S GONE!
THEN, INEXPLICABLY--
THE LIGHTS ARE BACK ON--! THOSE TWO KILLERS ARE THE ONES WHO MURDERED KATHY! BUT WHERE IS EVERYONE ELSE!
BLOODSTAINS ON THE FLOOR--
CLICK
--LEADING OUTSIDE--
NOBODY HERE! NO SIGN OF THE SENSEI OR THE TIGER!
WHAT'S THAT?
THE TIGER'S MASK-- AND KATHY'S COWL!
MAYBE THIS MEANS KATHY'S BEEN AVENGED--
20
--AND MAYBE NOT...

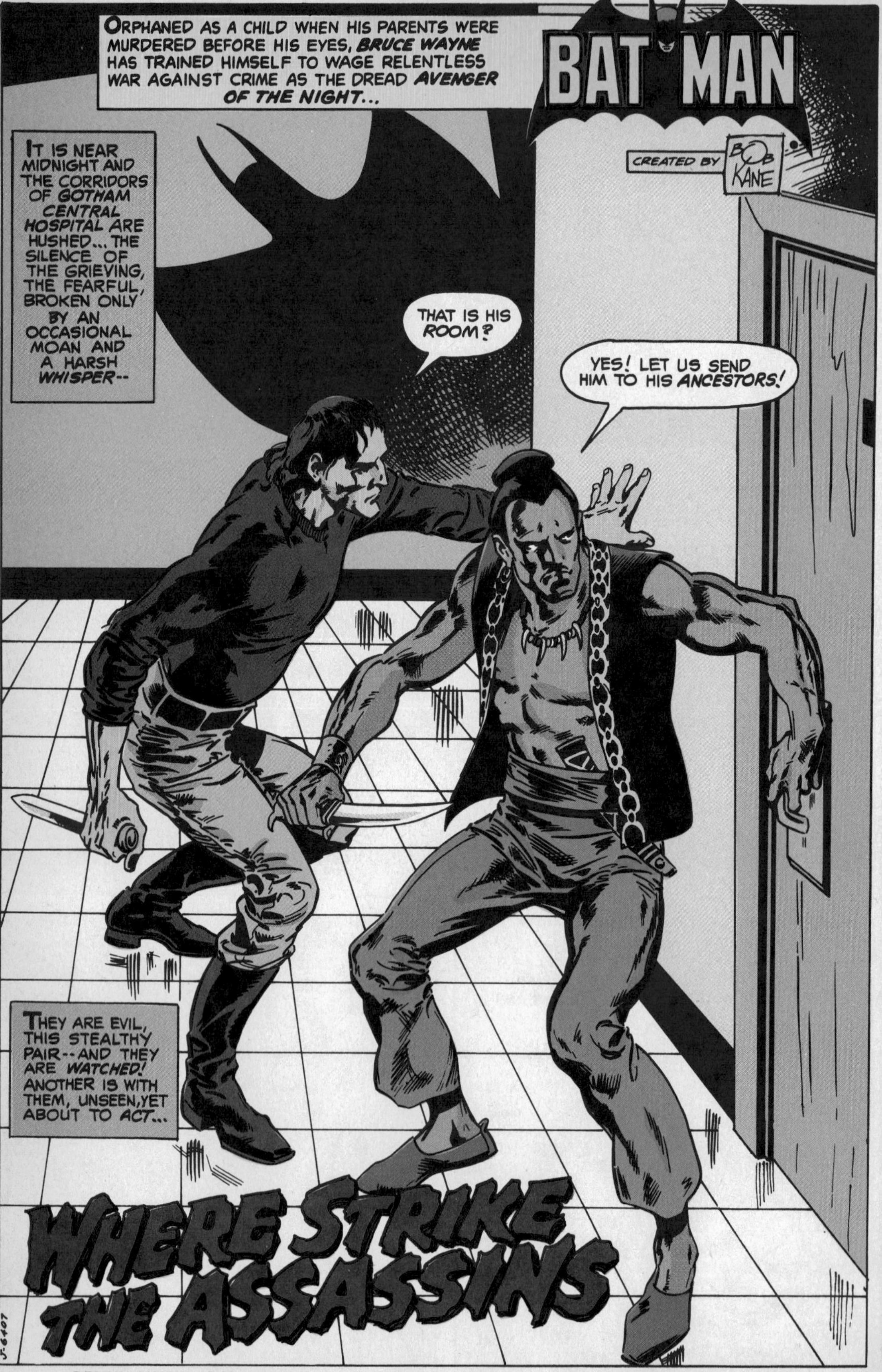

ORPHANED AS A CHILD WHEN HIS PARENTS WERE MURDERED BEFORE HIS EYES, BRUCE WAYNE HAS TRAINED HIMSELF TO WAGE RELENTLESS WAR AGAINST CRIME AS THE DREAD AVENGER OF THE NIGHT...
BATMAN
CREATED BY BOB KANE
IT IS NEAR MIDNIGHT AND THE CORRIDORS OF GOTHAM CENTRAL HOSPITAL ARE HUSHED... THE SILENCE OF THE GRIEVING, THE FEARFUL, BROKEN ONLY BY AN OCCASIONAL MOAN AND A HARSH WHISPER--
THAT IS HIS ROOM?
YES! LET US SEND HIM TO HIS ANCESTORS!
THEY ARE EVIL, THIS STEALTHY PAIR--AND THEY ARE WATCHED! ANOTHER IS WITH THEM, UNSEEN, YET ABOUT TO ACT...
WHERE STRIKE THE ASSASSINS
J-6407

DENNY O'NEIL writer | DON NEWTON & DAN ADKINS artists | BEN ODA letterer | TOM McCRAW colorist | PAUL LEVITZ editor

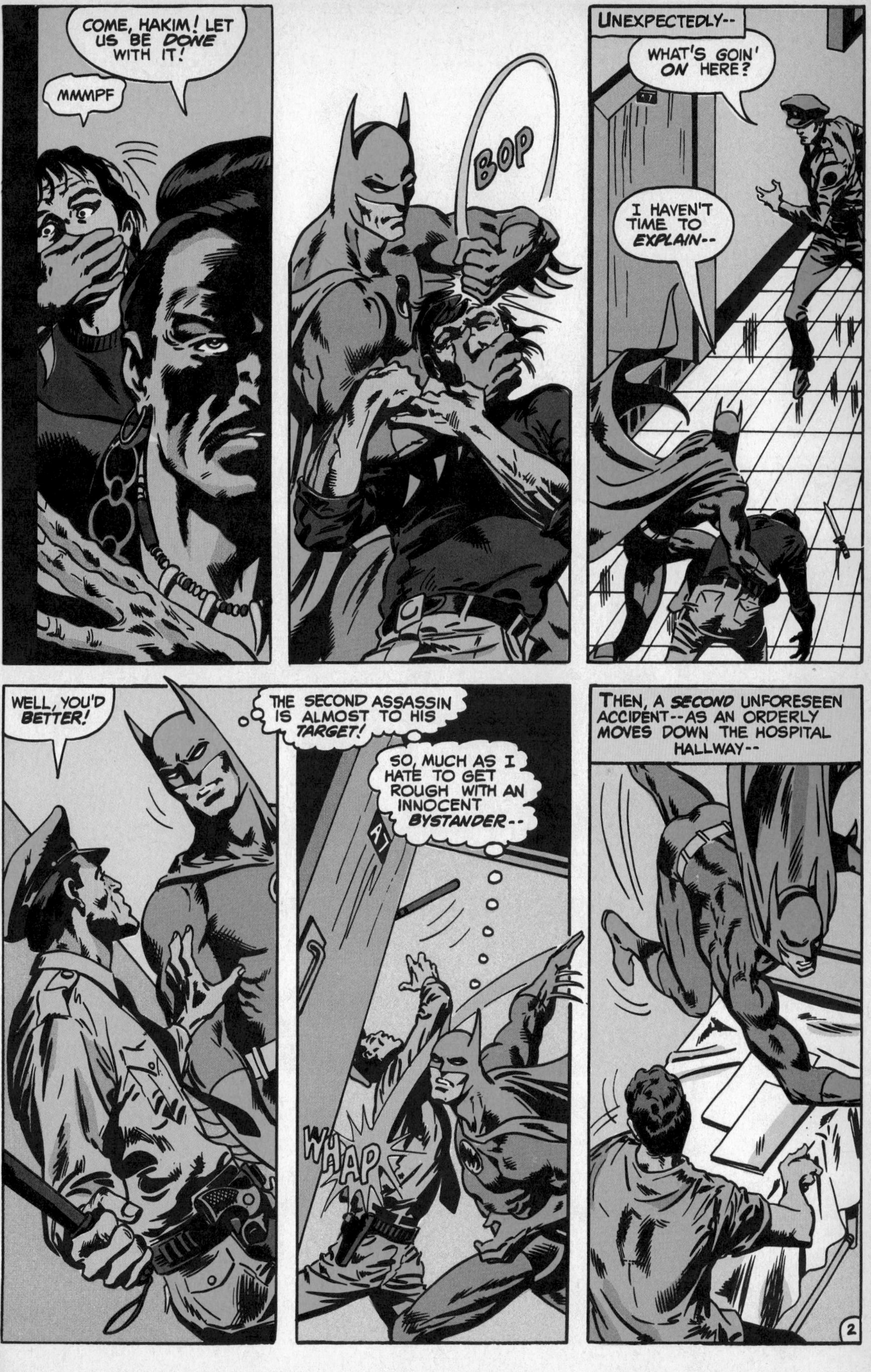
COME, HAKIM! LET US BE DONE WITH IT!
MMMPF
BOP
UNEXPECTEDLY--
WHAT'S GOIN' ON HERE?
I HAVEN'T TIME TO EXPLAIN--
WELL, YOU'D BETTER!
THE SECOND ASSASSIN IS ALMOST TO HIS TARGET!
SO, MUCH AS I HATE TO GET ROUGH WITH AN INNOCENT BYSTANDER--
WHAP
THEN, A SECOND UNFORESEEN ACCIDENT--AS AN ORDERLY MOVES DOWN THE HOSPITAL HALLWAY--
2

WHILE THE *BATMAN* COLLIDES WITH THE GURNEY, INSIDE THE ROOM--

FOR THE HONOR OF THE *LEAGUE OF ASSASSINS*-- AND THE *SENSEI!*...

IF THAT'S YOUR *PRODUCT*--

--I AIN'T *BUYIN'!*

LOOKS LIKE YOU DON'T NEED *ME*, FRIEND--

THUD

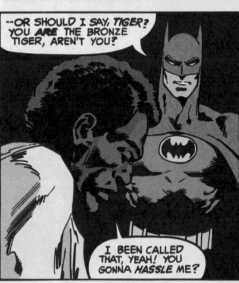

--OR SHOULD I SAY, *TIGER?* YOU *ARE* THE BRONZE TIGER, AREN'T YOU?

I BEEN CALLED THAT, YEAH! YOU GONNA *HASSLE* ME?

NOT AFTER THE HAND YOU GAVE ME AT THE SENSEI'S *HEADQUARTERS!* NO, I'M ASKING FOR YOUR *HELP!*

YOU MUST REALIZE YOU WERE *WRONG* TO PUT IN WITH THE LEAGUE!

I DON'T KNOW *WHAT* I REALIZE! I STILL CAN'T REMEMBER WHO I AM!

I ONLY KNOW THE SENSEI TURNED *AGAINST* ME... DID A NUMBER THAT PUT ME *HERE!*

CAN YOU RECALL ANYTHING *ELSE?*

3

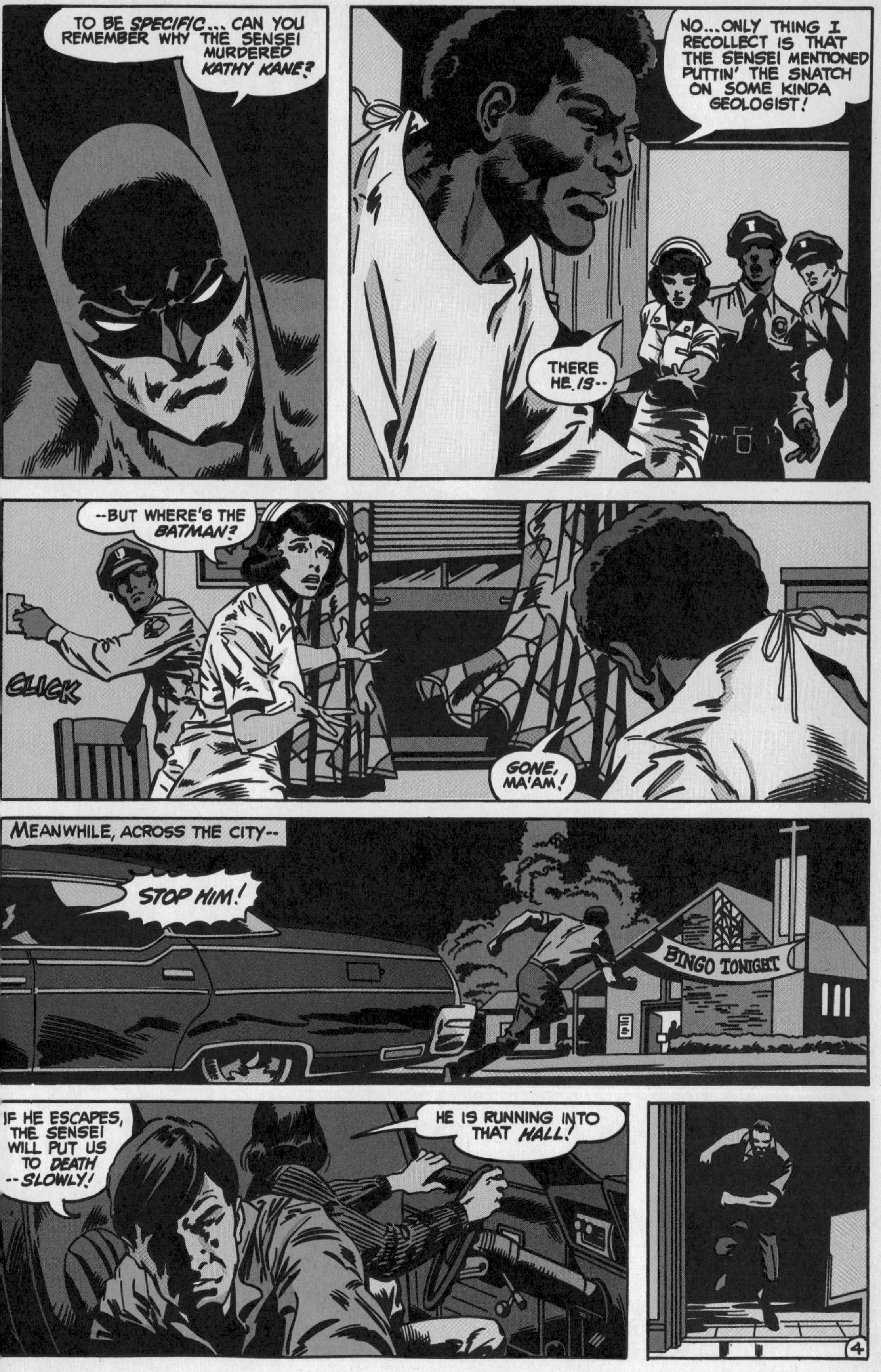
TO BE SPECIFIC... CAN YOU REMEMBER WHY THE SENSEI MURDERED KATHY KANE?
NO...ONLY THING I RECOLLECT IS THAT THE SENSEI MENTIONED PUTTIN' THE SNATCH ON SOME KINDA GEOLOGIST!
THERE HE IS--
--BUT WHERE'S THE BATMAN?
CLICK
GONE, MA'AM!
MEANWHILE, ACROSS THE CITY--
STOP HIM!
BINGO TONIGHT
IF HE ESCAPES, THE SENSEI WILL PUT US TO DEATH --SLOWLY!
HE IS RUNNING INTO THAT HALL!
4

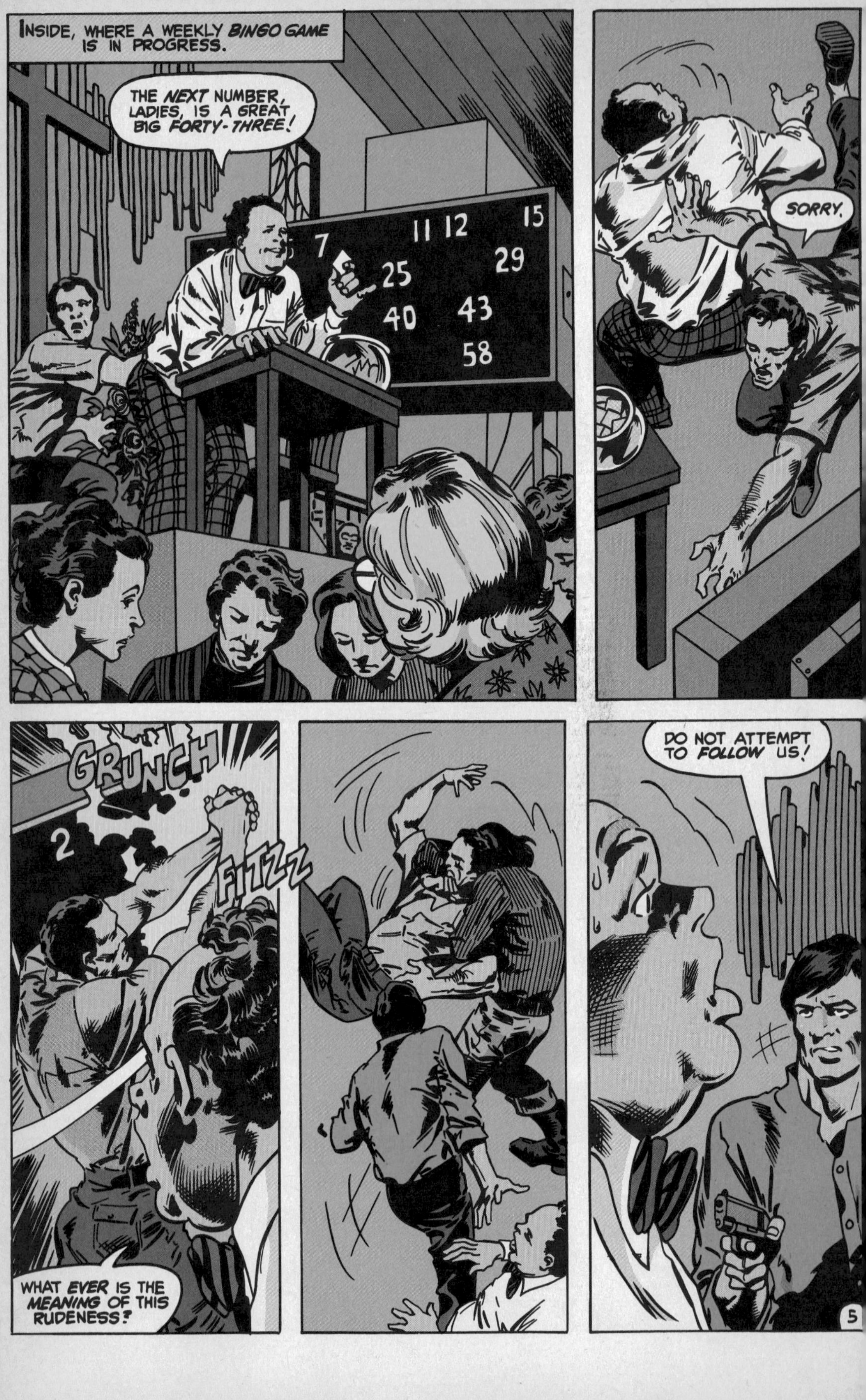
INSIDE, WHERE A WEEKLY BINGO GAME IS IN PROGRESS.
THE NEXT NUMBER, LADIES, IS A GREAT BIG FORTY-THREE!
7 11 12 15 25 29 40 43 58
SORRY.
GRUNCH
2
FITZZ
WHAT EVER IS THE MEANING OF THIS RUDENESS?
DO NOT ATTEMPT TO FOLLOW US!
5

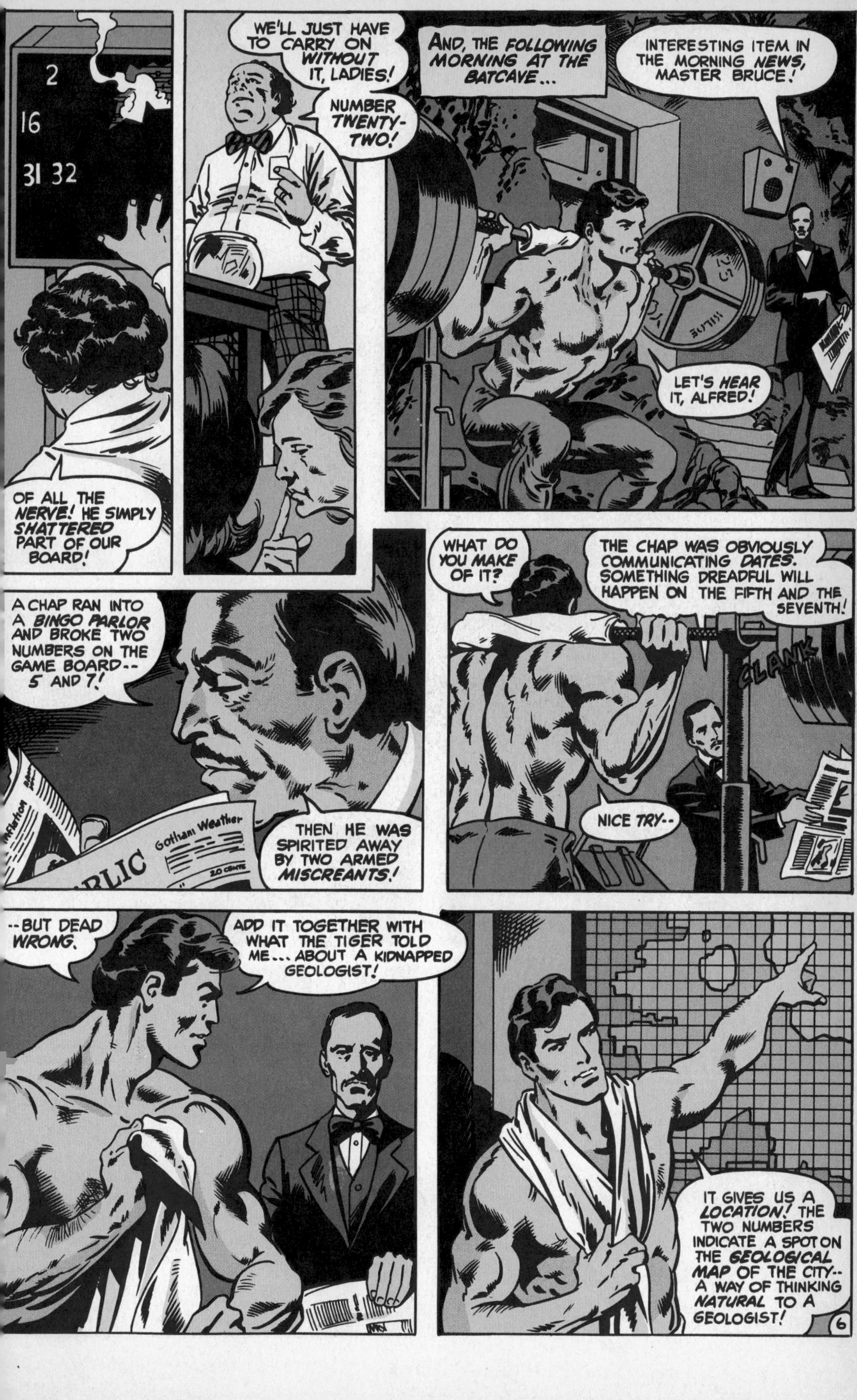
2
16
31 32
OF ALL THE NERVE! HE SIMPLY SHATTERED PART OF OUR BOARD!
WE'LL JUST HAVE TO CARRY ON WITHOUT IT, LADIES!
NUMBER TWENTY-TWO!
AND, THE FOLLOWING MORNING AT THE BATCAVE...
INTERESTING ITEM IN THE MORNING NEWS, MASTER BRUCE!
LET'S HEAR IT, ALFRED!
A CHAP RAN INTO A BINGO PARLOR AND BROKE TWO NUMBERS ON THE GAME BOARD-- 5 AND 7!
THEN HE WAS SPIRITED AWAY BY TWO ARMED MISCREANTS!
Gotham Weather
WHAT DO YOU MAKE OF IT?
THE CHAP WAS OBVIOUSLY COMMUNICATING DATES. SOMETHING DREADFUL WILL HAPPEN ON THE FIFTH AND THE SEVENTH!
CLANK
NICE TRY--
--BUT DEAD WRONG.
ADD IT TOGETHER WITH WHAT THE TIGER TOLD ME... ABOUT A KIDNAPPED GEOLOGIST!
IT GIVES US A LOCATION! THE TWO NUMBERS INDICATE A SPOT ON THE GEOLOGICAL MAP OF THE CITY-- A WAY OF THINKING NATURAL TO A GEOLOGIST!
6

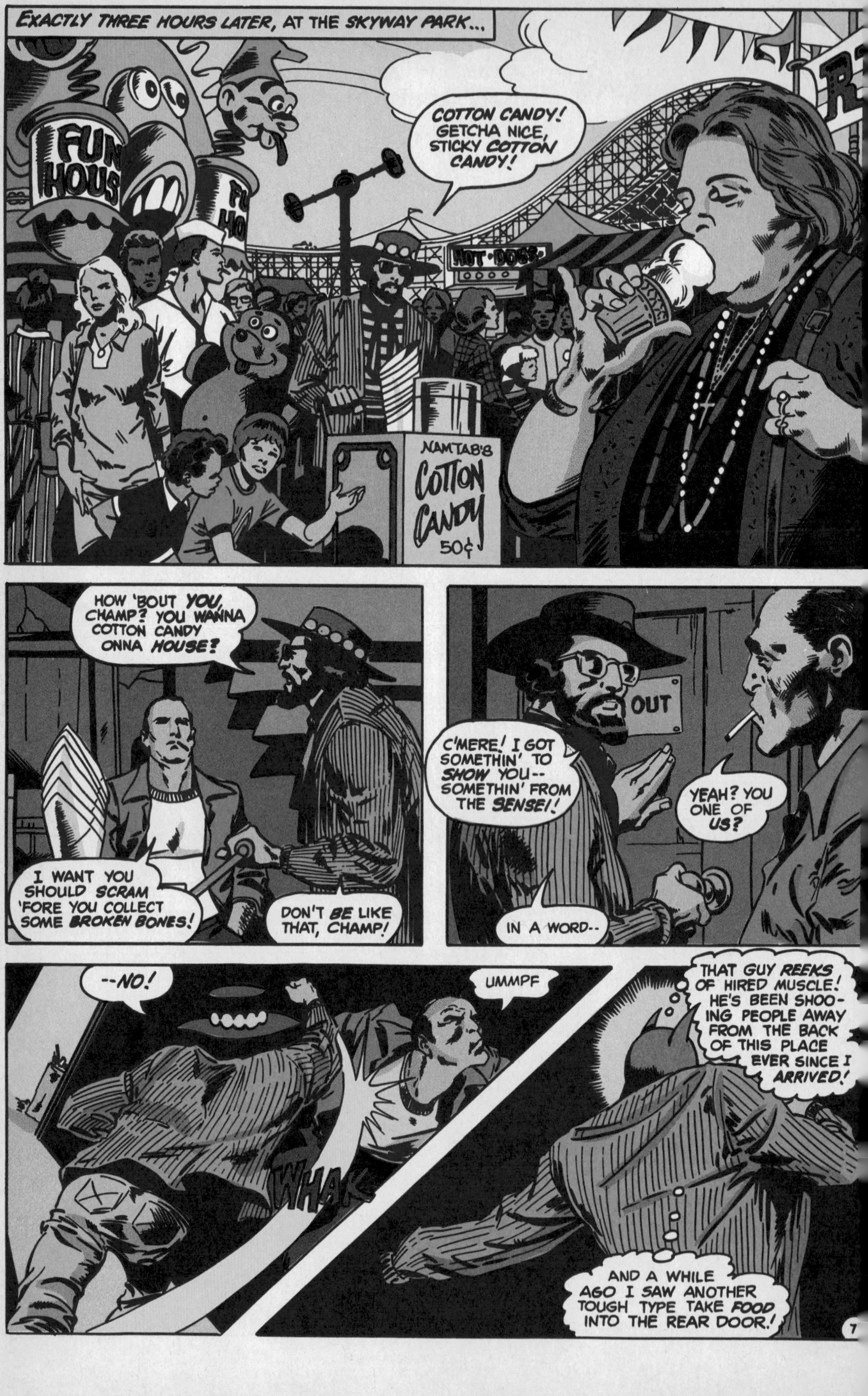
EXACTLY THREE HOURS LATER, AT THE SKYWAY PARK...
FUN HOUS
HOT DOGS
COTTON CANDY! GETCHA NICE, STICKY COTTON CANDY!
NAMTAB'S COTTON CANDY 50¢
HOW 'BOUT YOU, CHAMP? YOU WANNA COTTON CANDY ONNA HOUSE?
I WANT YOU SHOULD SCRAM 'FORE YOU COLLECT SOME BROKEN BONES!
DON'T BE LIKE THAT, CHAMP!
OUT
C'MERE! I GOT SOMETHIN' TO SHOW YOU-- SOMETHIN' FROM THE SENSE!
YEAH? YOU ONE OF US?
IN A WORD--
--NO!
UMMPF
WHAK
THAT GUY REEKS OF HIRED MUSCLE! HE'S BEEN SHOOING PEOPLE AWAY FROM THE BACK OF THIS PLACE EVER SINCE I ARRIVED!
AND A WHILE AGO I SAW ANOTHER TOUGH TYPE TAKE FOOD INTO THE REAR DOOR!
7

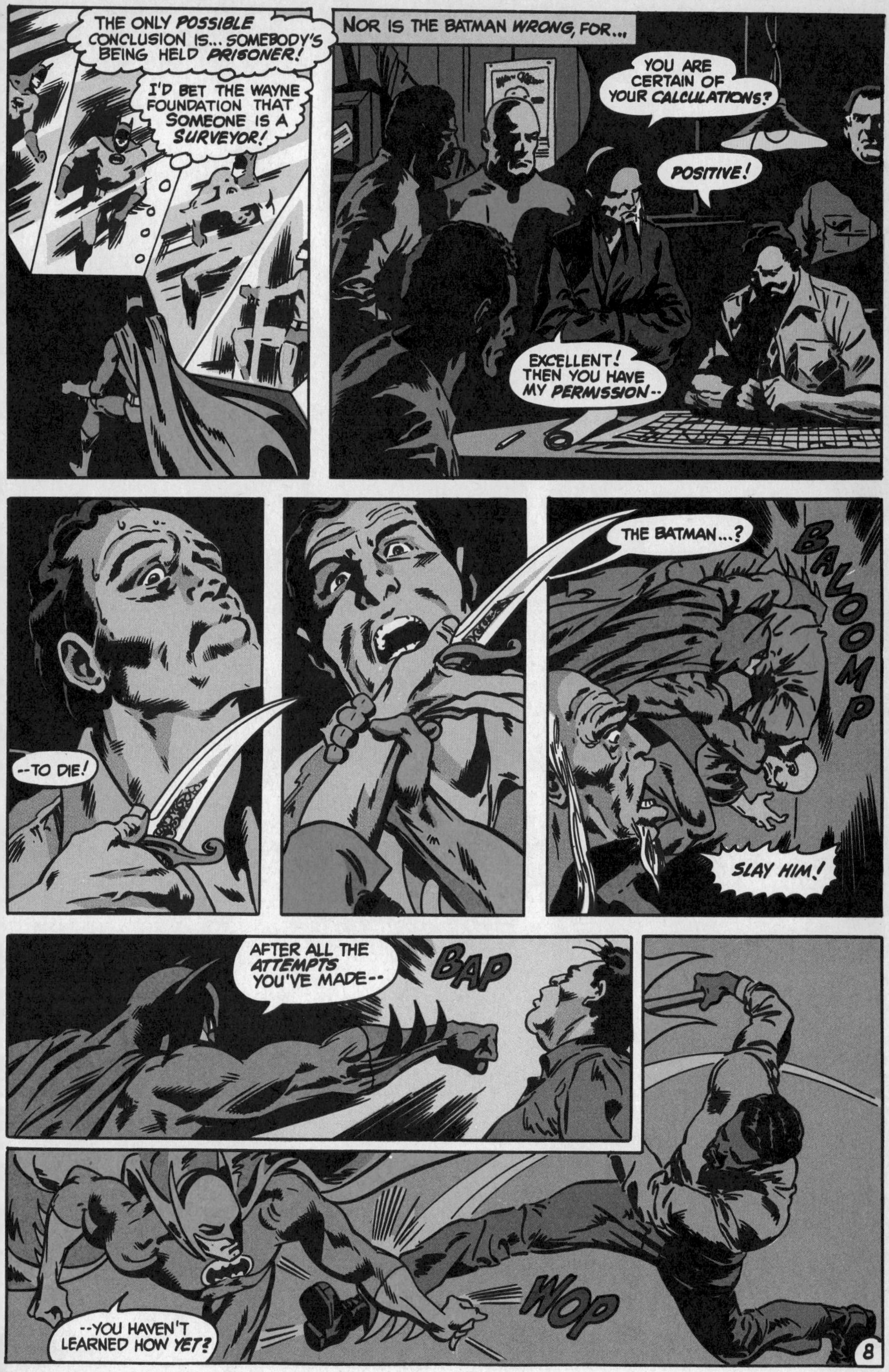
THE ONLY POSSIBLE CONCLUSION IS... SOMEBODY'S BEING HELD PRISONER!
I'D BET THE WAYNE FOUNDATION THAT SOMEONE IS A SURVEYOR!
NOR IS THE BATMAN WRONG, FOR...
YOU ARE CERTAIN OF YOUR CALCULATIONS?
POSITIVE!
EXCELLENT! THEN YOU HAVE MY PERMISSION--
--TO DIE!
THE BATMAN...?
BALOOMP
SLAY HIM!
AFTER ALL THE ATTEMPTS YOU'VE MADE--
BAP
--YOU HAVEN'T LEARNED HOW YET?
WOP
8

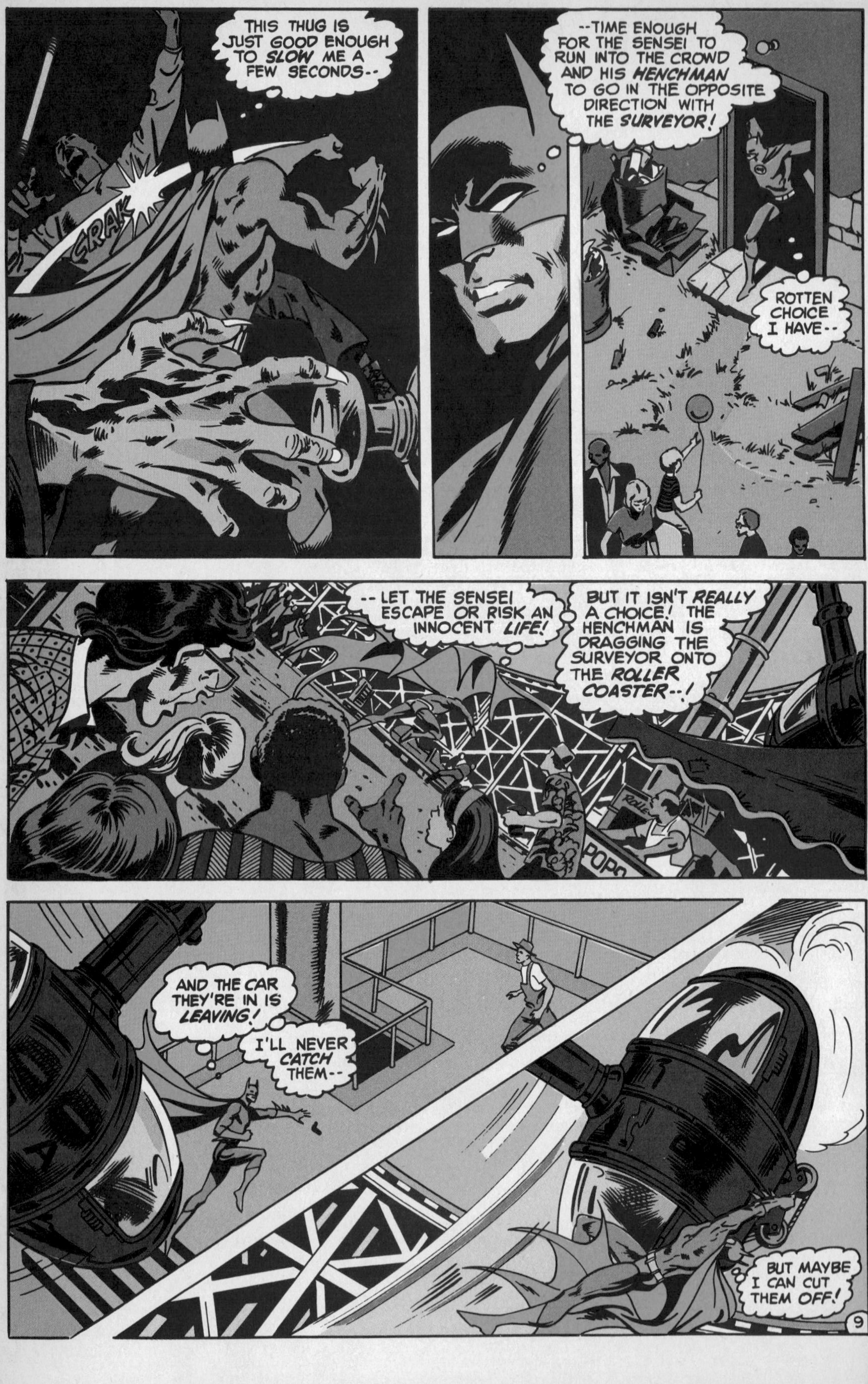
THIS THUG IS JUST GOOD ENOUGH TO SLOW ME A FEW SECONDS--
CRAK
--TIME ENOUGH FOR THE SENSEI TO RUN INTO THE CROWD AND HIS HENCHMAN TO GO IN THE OPPOSITE DIRECTION WITH THE SURVEYOR!
ROTTEN CHOICE I HAVE--
--LET THE SENSEI ESCAPE OR RISK AN INNOCENT LIFE!
BUT IT ISN'T REALLY A CHOICE! THE HENCHMAN IS DRAGGING THE SURVEYOR ONTO THE ROLLER COASTER--!
AND THE CAR THEY'RE IN IS LEAVING!
I'LL NEVER CATCH THEM--
BUT MAYBE I CAN CUT THEM OFF!
9

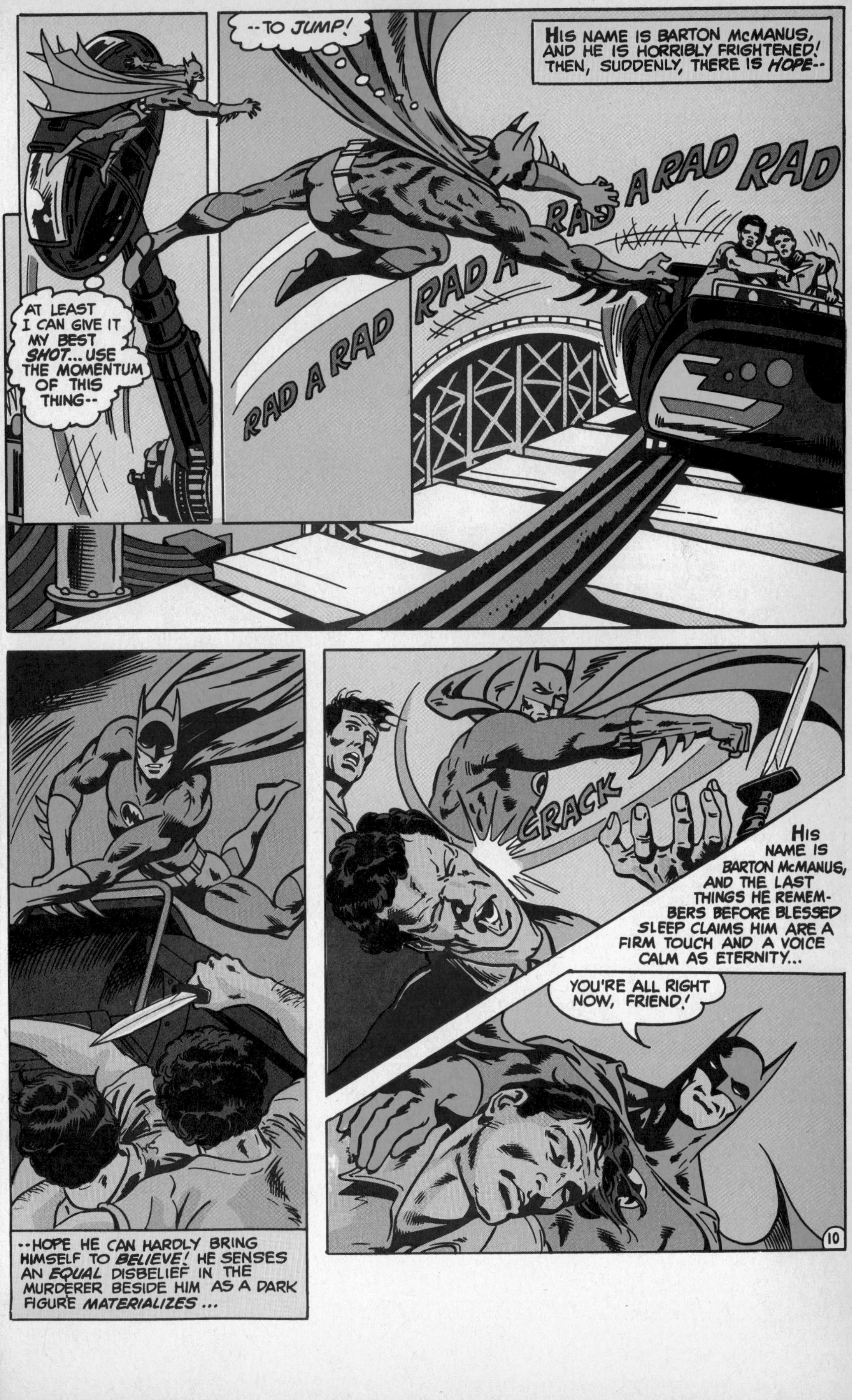
--TO JUMP!
HIS NAME IS BARTON McMANUS, AND HE IS HORRIBLY FRIGHTENED! THEN, SUDDENLY, THERE IS HOPE--
AT LEAST I CAN GIVE IT MY BEST SHOT... USE THE MOMENTUM OF THIS THING--
RAD A RAD RAD A RAD A RAD RAD
--HOPE HE CAN HARDLY BRING HIMSELF TO BELIEVE! HE SENSES AN EQUAL DISBELIEF IN THE MURDERER BESIDE HIM AS A DARK FIGURE MATERIALIZES...
CRACK
HIS NAME IS BARTON McMANUS, AND THE LAST THINGS HE REMEMBERS BEFORE BLESSED SLEEP CLAIMS HIM ARE A FIRM TOUCH AND A VOICE CALM AS ETERNITY...
YOU'RE ALL RIGHT NOW, FRIEND!
10

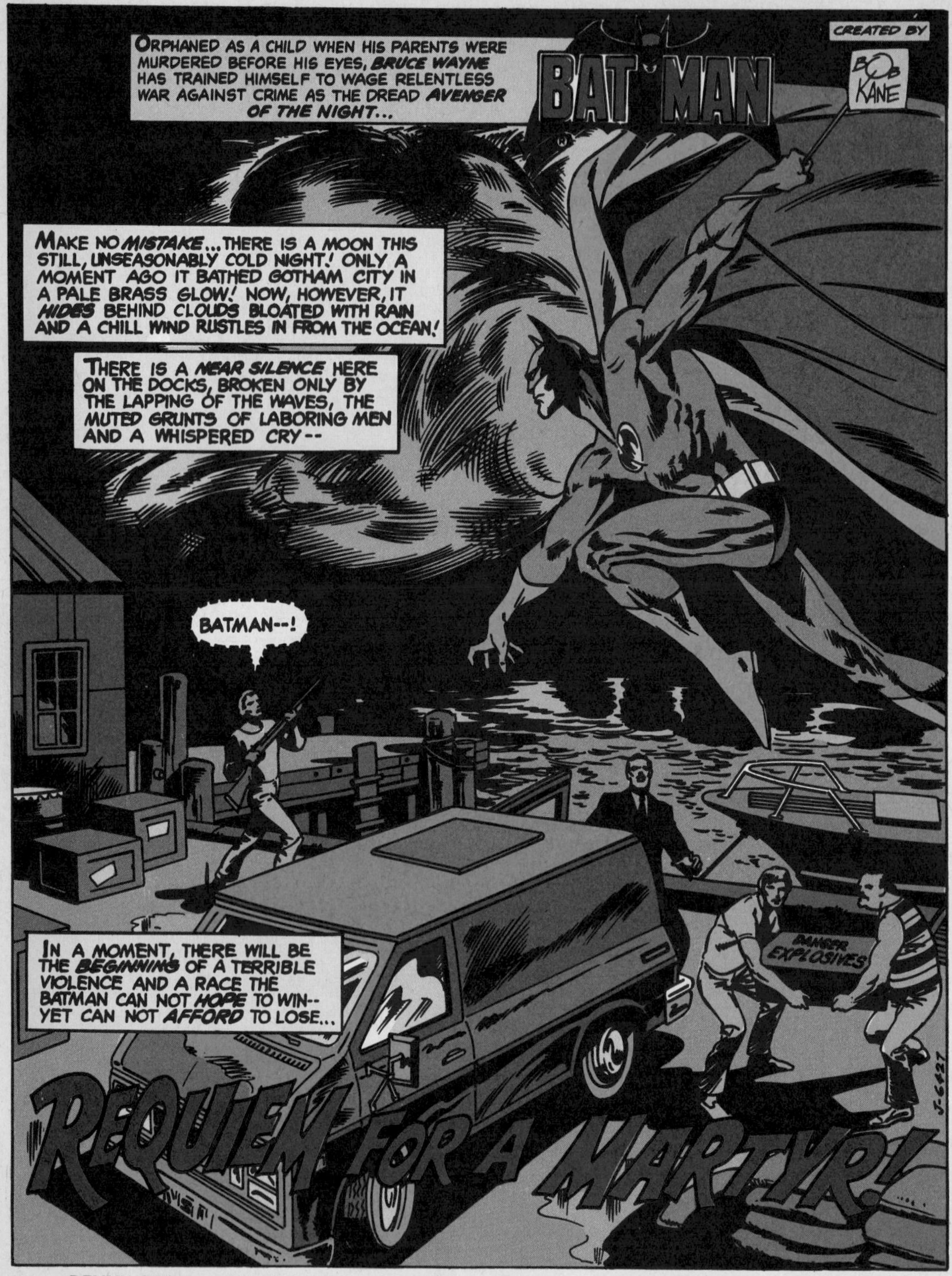
ORPHANED AS A CHILD WHEN HIS PARENTS WERE MURDERED BEFORE HIS EYES, BRUCE WAYNE HAS TRAINED HIMSELF TO WAGE RELENTLESS WAR AGAINST CRIME AS THE DREAD AVENGER OF THE NIGHT...
BATMAN
CREATED BY
BOB KANE
MAKE NO MISTAKE...THERE IS A MOON THIS STILL, UNSEASONABLY COLD NIGHT! ONLY A MOMENT AGO IT BATHED GOTHAM CITY IN A PALE BRASS GLOW! NOW, HOWEVER, IT HIDES BEHIND CLOUDS BLOATED WITH RAIN AND A CHILL WIND RUSTLES IN FROM THE OCEAN!
THERE IS A NEAR SILENCE HERE ON THE DOCKS, BROKEN ONLY BY THE LAPPING OF THE WAVES, THE MUTED GRUNTS OF LABORING MEN AND A WHISPERED CRY--
BATMAN--!
DANGER EXPLOSIVES
IN A MOMENT, THERE WILL BE THE BEGINNING OF A TERRIBLE VIOLENCE AND A RACE THE BATMAN CAN NOT HOPE TO WIN-- YET CAN NOT AFFORD TO LOSE...
REQUIEM FOR A MARTYR!

DENNY O'NEIL writer | **DON NEWTON & DAN ADKINS** artists | **BEN ODA** letterer | **JULIA LACQUEMENT** colorist | **PAUL LEVITZ** editor

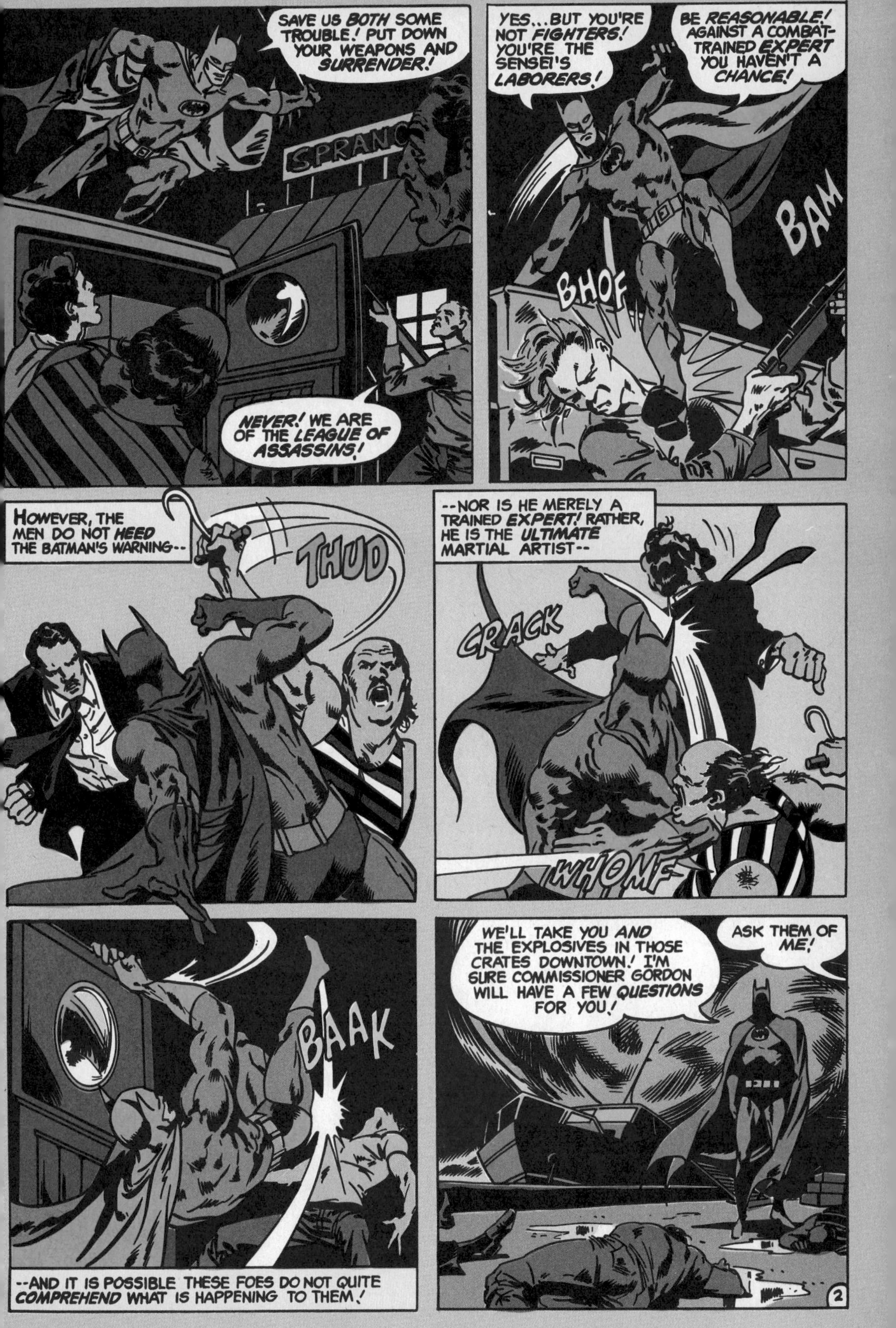
SAVE US BOTH SOME TROUBLE! PUT DOWN YOUR WEAPONS AND SURRENDER!
SPRANG
NEVER! WE ARE OF THE LEAGUE OF ASSASSINS!
YES...BUT YOU'RE NOT FIGHTERS! YOU'RE THE SENSEI'S LABORERS!
BE REASONABLE! AGAINST A COMBAT-TRAINED EXPERT YOU HAVEN'T A CHANCE!
BAM
BHOF
HOWEVER, THE MEN DO NOT HEED THE BATMAN'S WARNING--
THUD
--NOR IS HE MERELY A TRAINED EXPERT! RATHER, HE IS THE ULTIMATE MARTIAL ARTIST--
CRACK
WHOMF
BAAK
--AND IT IS POSSIBLE THESE FOES DO NOT QUITE COMPREHEND WHAT IS HAPPENING TO THEM!
WE'LL TAKE YOU AND THE EXPLOSIVES IN THOSE CRATES DOWNTOWN! I'M SURE COMMISSIONER GORDON WILL HAVE A FEW QUESTIONS FOR YOU!
ASK THEM OF ME!
2

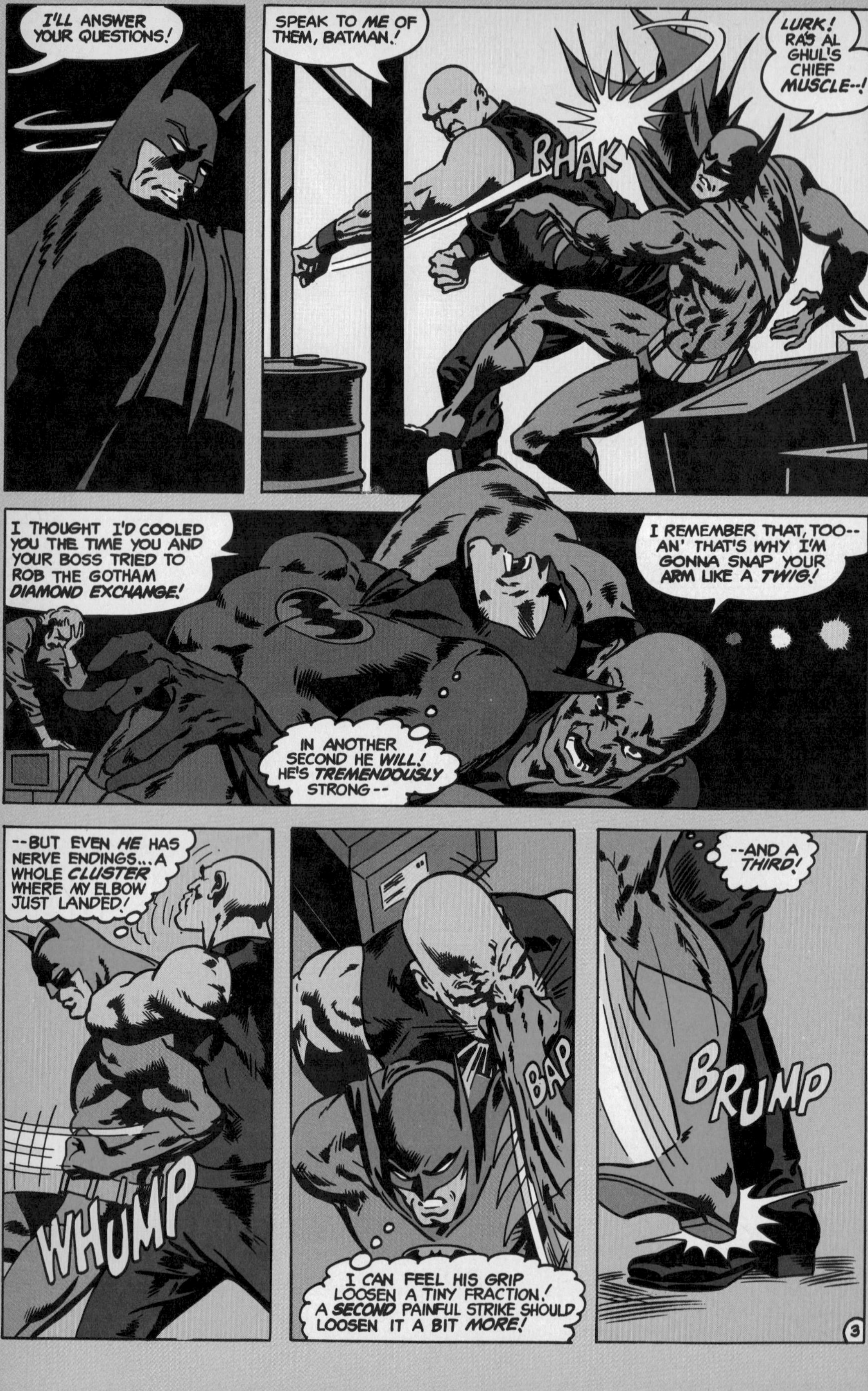
I'LL ANSWER YOUR QUESTIONS!
SPEAK TO ME OF THEM, BATMAN.!
RHAK
LURK! RA'S AL GHUL'S CHIEF MUSCLE--!
I THOUGHT I'D COOLED YOU THE TIME YOU AND YOUR BOSS TRIED TO ROB THE GOTHAM DIAMOND EXCHANGE!
I REMEMBER THAT, TOO--AN' THAT'S WHY I'M GONNA SNAP YOUR ARM LIKE A TWIG!
IN ANOTHER SECOND HE WILL! HE'S TREMENDOUSLY STRONG--
--BUT EVEN HE HAS NERVE ENDINGS...A WHOLE CLUSTER WHERE MY ELBOW JUST LANDED!
WHUMP
BAP
I CAN FEEL HIS GRIP LOOSEN A TINY FRACTION! A SECOND PAINFUL STRIKE SHOULD LOOSEN IT A BIT MORE!
--AND A THIRD!
BRUMP
3

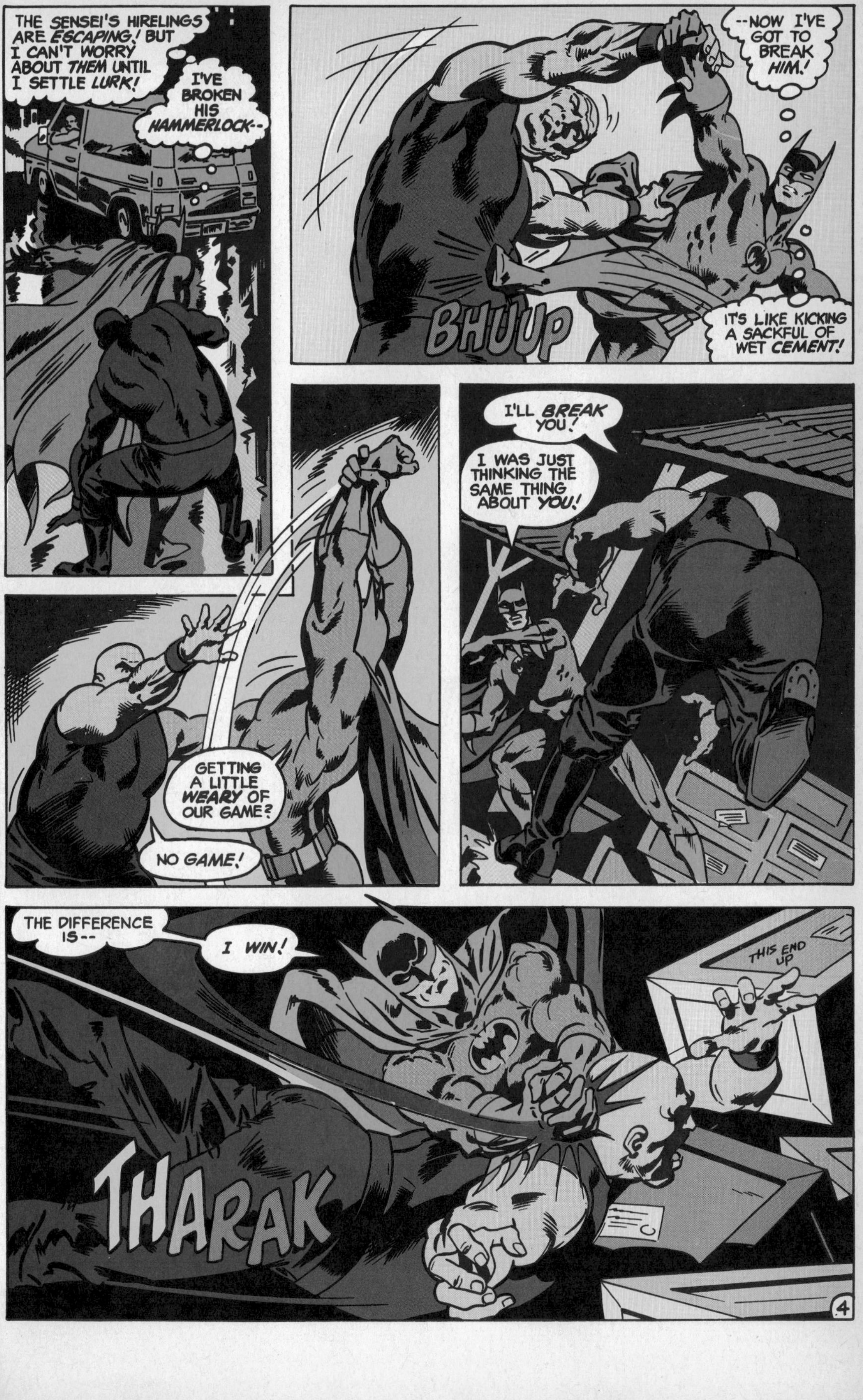
THE SENSEI'S HIRELINGS ARE ESCAPING! BUT I CAN'T WORRY ABOUT THEM UNTIL I SETTLE LURK!
I'VE BROKEN HIS HAMMERLOCK--
--NOW I'VE GOT TO BREAK HIM!
BHUUP
IT'S LIKE KICKING A SACKFUL OF WET CEMENT!
GETTING A LITTLE WEARY OF OUR GAME?
NO GAME!
I'LL BREAK YOU!
I WAS JUST THINKING THE SAME THING ABOUT YOU!
THE DIFFERENCE IS--
I WIN!
THIS END UP
THARAK
4

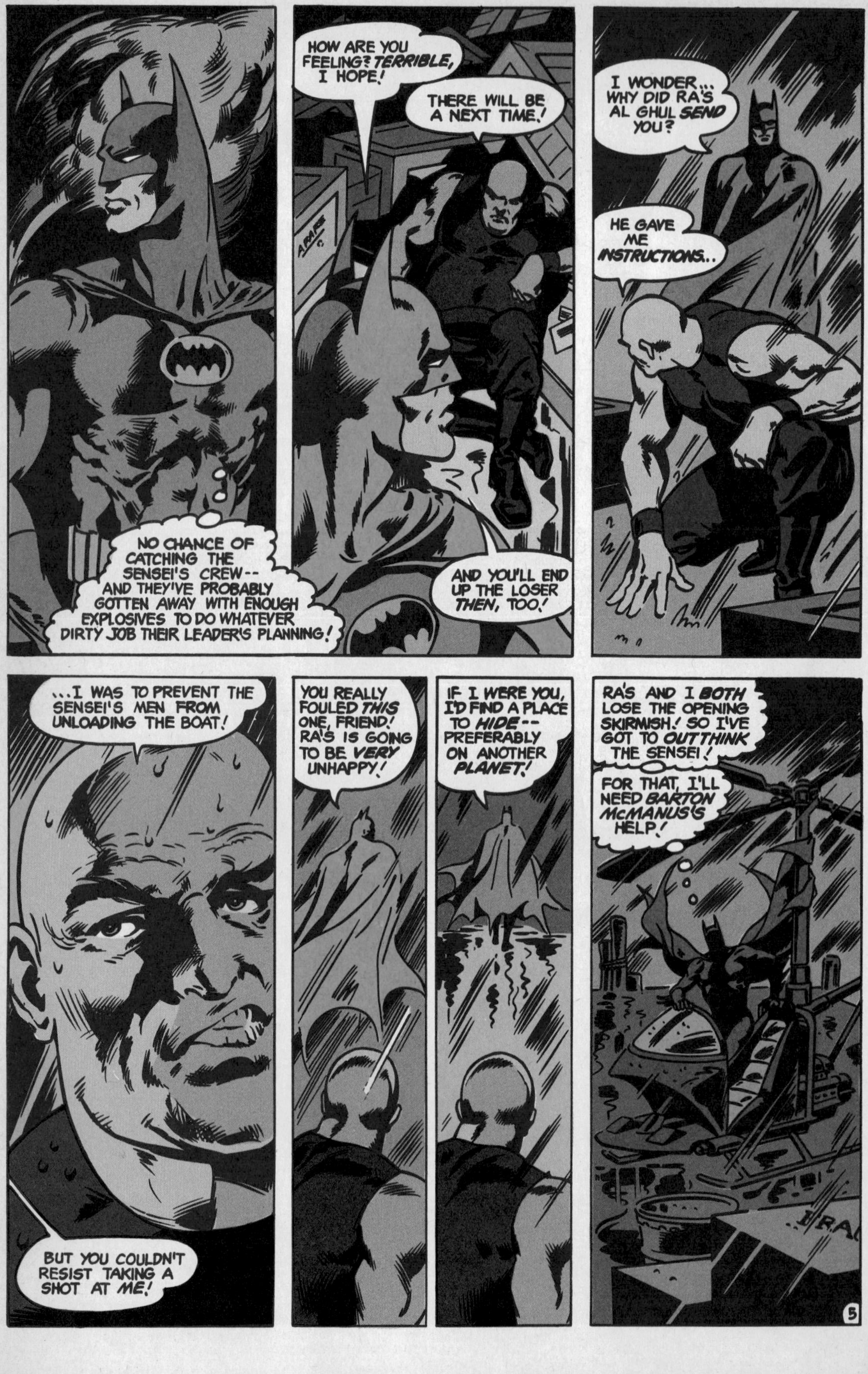
NO CHANCE OF CATCHING THE SENSEI'S CREW-- AND THEY'VE PROBABLY GOTTEN AWAY WITH ENOUGH EXPLOSIVES TO DO WHATEVER DIRTY JOB THEIR LEADER'S PLANNING!
HOW ARE YOU FEELING? TERRIBLE, I HOPE!
THERE WILL BE A NEXT TIME!
AND YOU'LL END UP THE LOSER THEN, TOO!
I WONDER... WHY DID RA'S AL GHUL SEND YOU?
HE GAVE ME INSTRUCTIONS..
...I WAS TO PREVENT THE SENSEI'S MEN FROM UNLOADING THE BOAT!
BUT YOU COULDN'T RESIST TAKING A SHOT AT ME!
YOU REALLY FOULED THIS ONE, FRIEND! RA'S IS GOING TO BE VERY UNHAPPY!
IF I WERE YOU, I'D FIND A PLACE TO HIDE-- PREFERABLY ON ANOTHER PLANET!
RA'S AND I BOTH LOSE THE OPENING SKIRMISH! SO I'VE GOT TO OUTTHINK THE SENSEI!
FOR THAT, I'LL NEED BARTON McMANUS'S HELP!
5

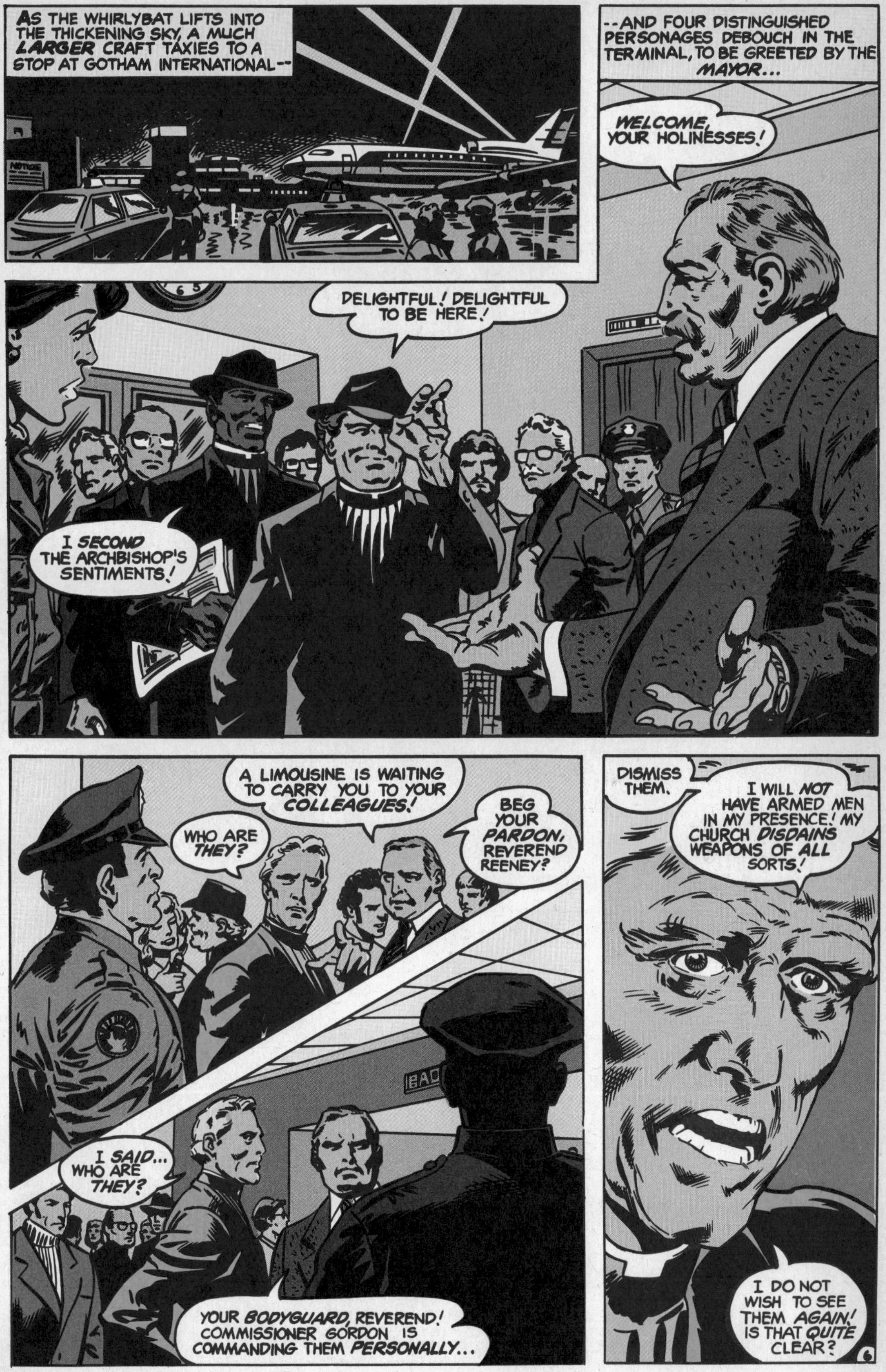
AS THE WHIRLYBAT LIFTS INTO THE THICKENING SKY, A MUCH LARGER CRAFT TAXIES TO A STOP AT GOTHAM INTERNATIONAL--
--AND FOUR DISTINGUISHED PERSONAGES DEBOUCH IN THE TERMINAL, TO BE GREETED BY THE MAYOR...
WELCOME, YOUR HOLINESSES!
DELIGHTFUL! DELIGHTFUL TO BE HERE!
I SECOND THE ARCHBISHOP'S SENTIMENTS!
A LIMOUSINE IS WAITING TO CARRY YOU TO YOUR COLLEAGUES!
WHO ARE THEY?
BEG YOUR PARDON, REVEREND REENEY?
I SAID... WHO ARE THEY?
YOUR BODYGUARD, REVEREND! COMMISSIONER GORDON IS COMMANDING THEM PERSONALLY...
DISMISS THEM.
I WILL NOT HAVE ARMED MEN IN MY PRESENCE! MY CHURCH DISDAINS WEAPONS OF ALL SORTS!
I DO NOT WISH TO SEE THEM AGAIN! IS THAT QUITE CLEAR?
6

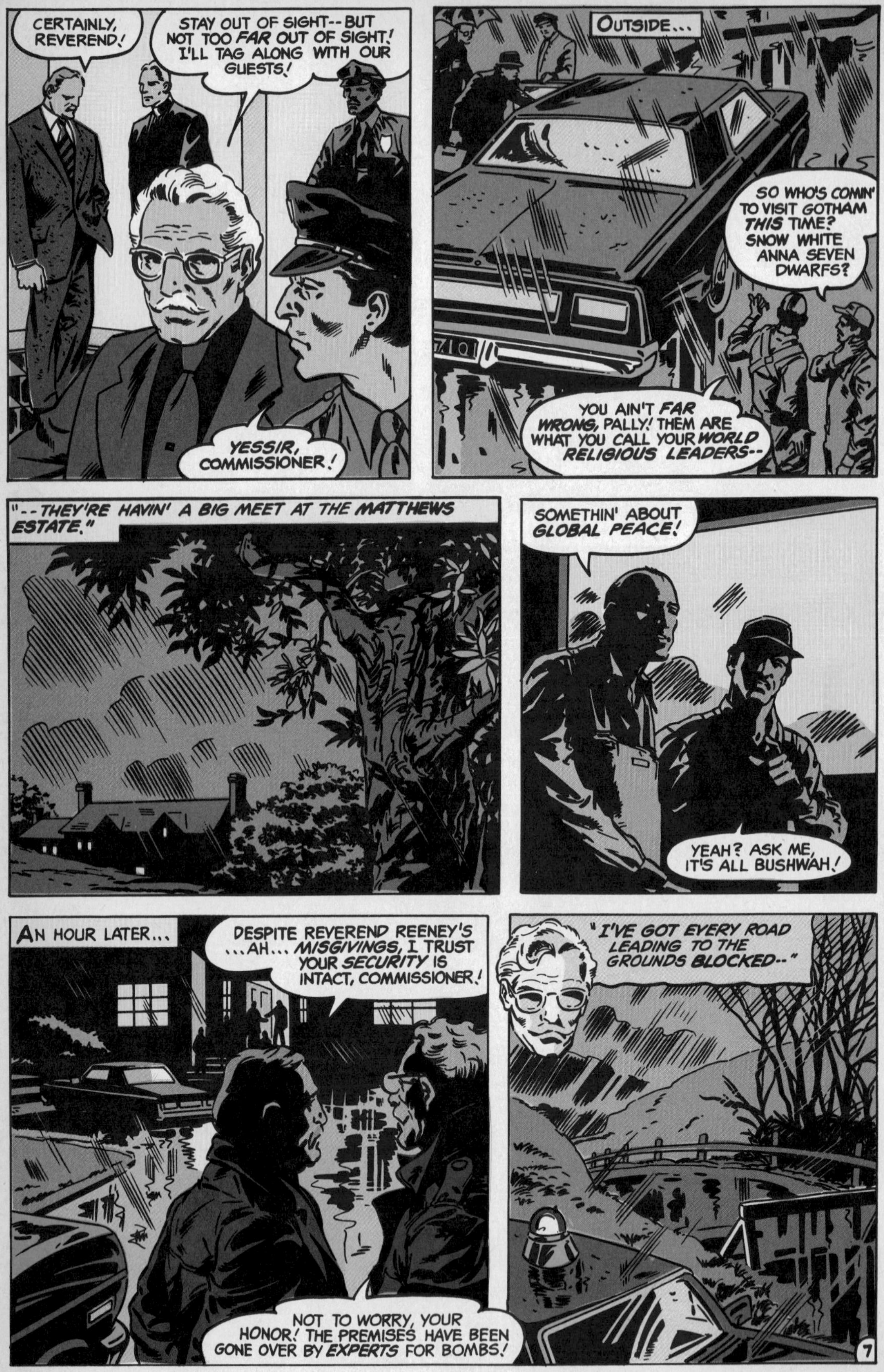
CERTAINLY, REVEREND!
STAY OUT OF SIGHT--BUT NOT TOO FAR OUT OF SIGHT! I'LL TAG ALONG WITH OUR GUESTS!
YESSIR, COMMISSIONER!
OUTSIDE...
SO WHO'S COMIN' TO VISIT GOTHAM THIS TIME? SNOW WHITE ANNA SEVEN DWARFS?
YOU AIN'T FAR WRONG, PALLY! THEM ARE WHAT YOU CALL YOUR WORLD RELIGIOUS LEADERS--
"--THEY'RE HAVIN' A BIG MEET AT THE MATTHEWS ESTATE."
SOMETHIN' ABOUT GLOBAL PEACE!
YEAH? ASK ME, IT'S ALL BUSHWAH!
AN HOUR LATER...
DESPITE REVEREND REENEY'S ...AH... MISGIVINGS, I TRUST YOUR SECURITY IS INTACT, COMMISSIONER!
NOT TO WORRY, YOUR HONOR! THE PREMISES HAVE BEEN GONE OVER BY EXPERTS FOR BOMBS!
"I'VE GOT EVERY ROAD LEADING TO THE GROUNDS BLOCKED--"
7

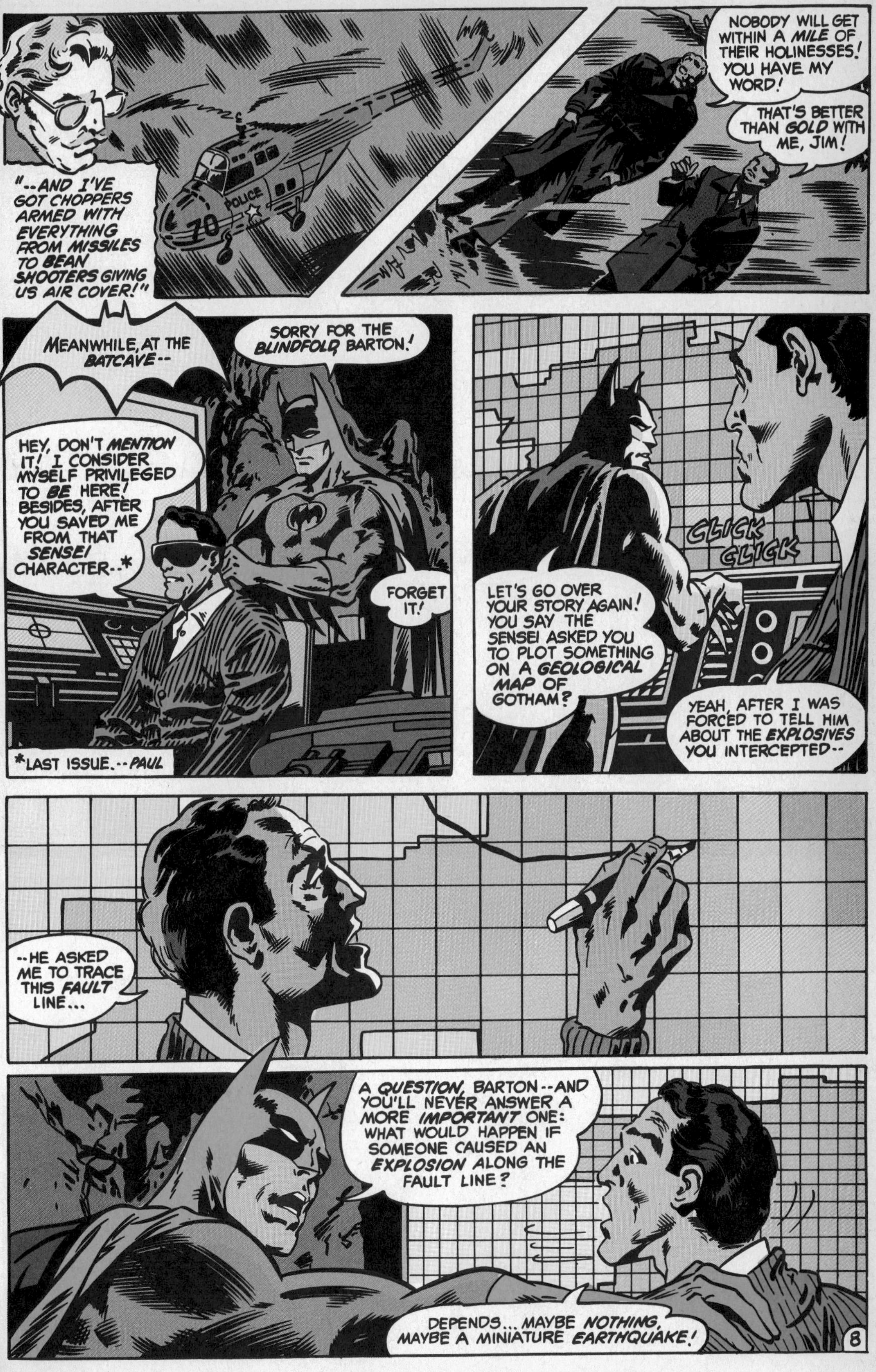
"--AND I'VE GOT CHOPPERS ARMED WITH EVERYTHING FROM MISSILES TO BEAN SHOOTERS GIVING US AIR COVER!"
POLICE
70
NOBODY WILL GET WITHIN A MILE OF THEIR HOLINESSES! YOU HAVE MY WORD!
THAT'S BETTER THAN GOLD WITH ME, JIM!
MEANWHILE, AT THE BATCAVE--
SORRY FOR THE BLINDFOLD, BARTON!
HEY, DON'T MENTION IT! I CONSIDER MYSELF PRIVILEGED TO BE HERE! BESIDES, AFTER YOU SAVED ME FROM THAT SENSEI CHARACTER--*
FORGET IT!
*LAST ISSUE.--PAUL
CLICK
CLICK
LET'S GO OVER YOUR STORY AGAIN! YOU SAY THE SENSEI ASKED YOU TO PLOT SOMETHING ON A GEOLOGICAL MAP OF GOTHAM?
YEAH, AFTER I WAS FORCED TO TELL HIM ABOUT THE EXPLOSIVES YOU INTERCEPTED--
--HE ASKED ME TO TRACE THIS FAULT LINE...
A QUESTION, BARTON--AND YOU'LL NEVER ANSWER A MORE IMPORTANT ONE: WHAT WOULD HAPPEN IF SOMEONE CAUSED AN EXPLOSION ALONG THE FAULT LINE?
DEPENDS... MAYBE NOTHING, MAYBE A MINIATURE EARTHQUAKE!
8

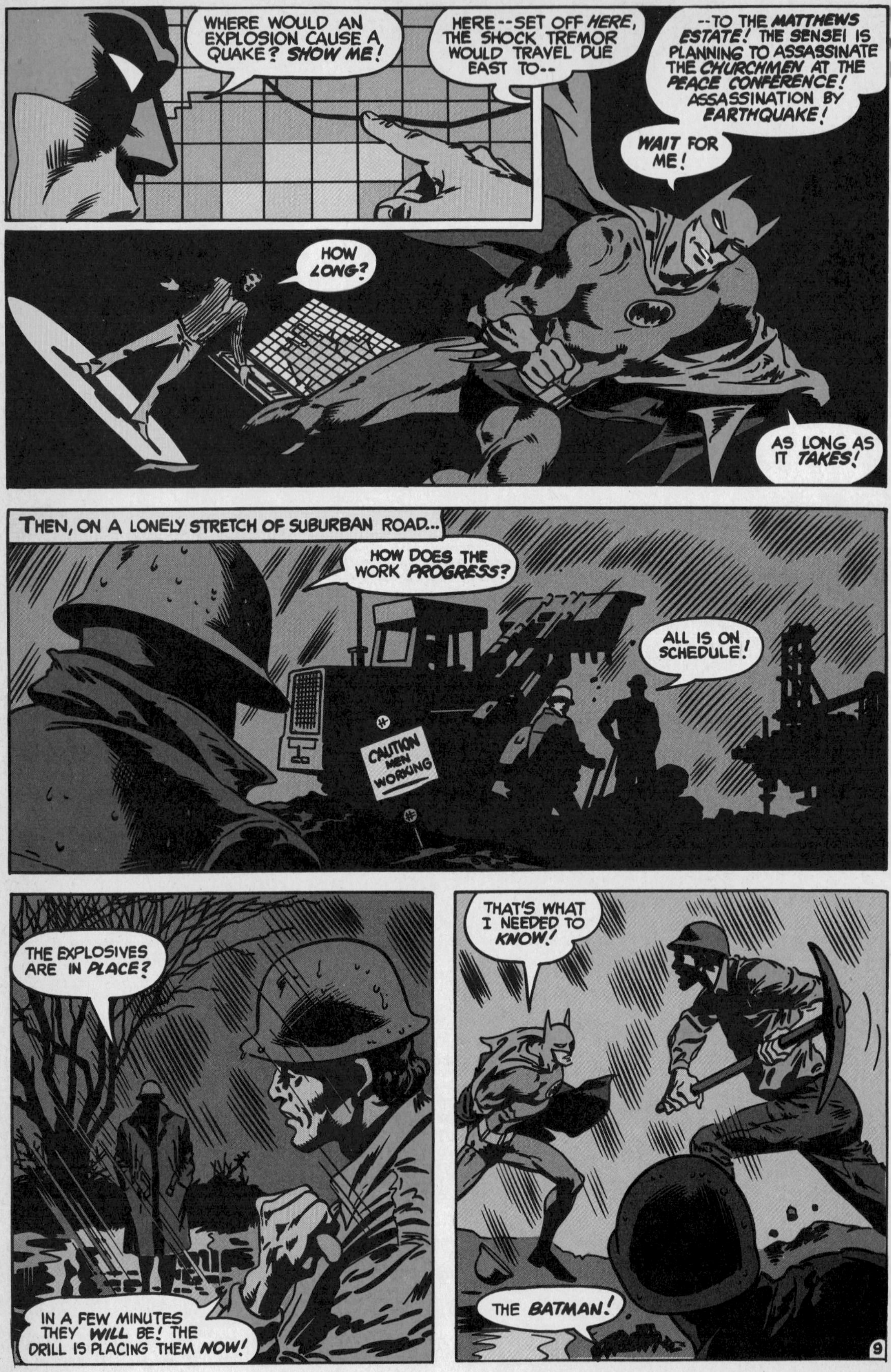
WHERE WOULD AN EXPLOSION CAUSE A QUAKE? SHOW ME!
HERE--SET OFF HERE, THE SHOCK TREMOR WOULD TRAVEL DUE EAST TO--
--TO THE MATTHEWS ESTATE! THE SENSEI IS PLANNING TO ASSASSINATE THE CHURCHMEN AT THE PEACE CONFERENCE! ASSASSINATION BY EARTHQUAKE!
WAIT FOR ME!
HOW LONG?
AS LONG AS IT TAKES!
THEN, ON A LONELY STRETCH OF SUBURBAN ROAD...
HOW DOES THE WORK PROGRESS?
ALL IS ON SCHEDULE!
CAUTION MEN WORKING
THE EXPLOSIVES ARE IN PLACE?
IN A FEW MINUTES THEY WILL BE! THE DRILL IS PLACING THEM NOW!
THAT'S WHAT I NEEDED TO KNOW!
THE BATMAN!
9

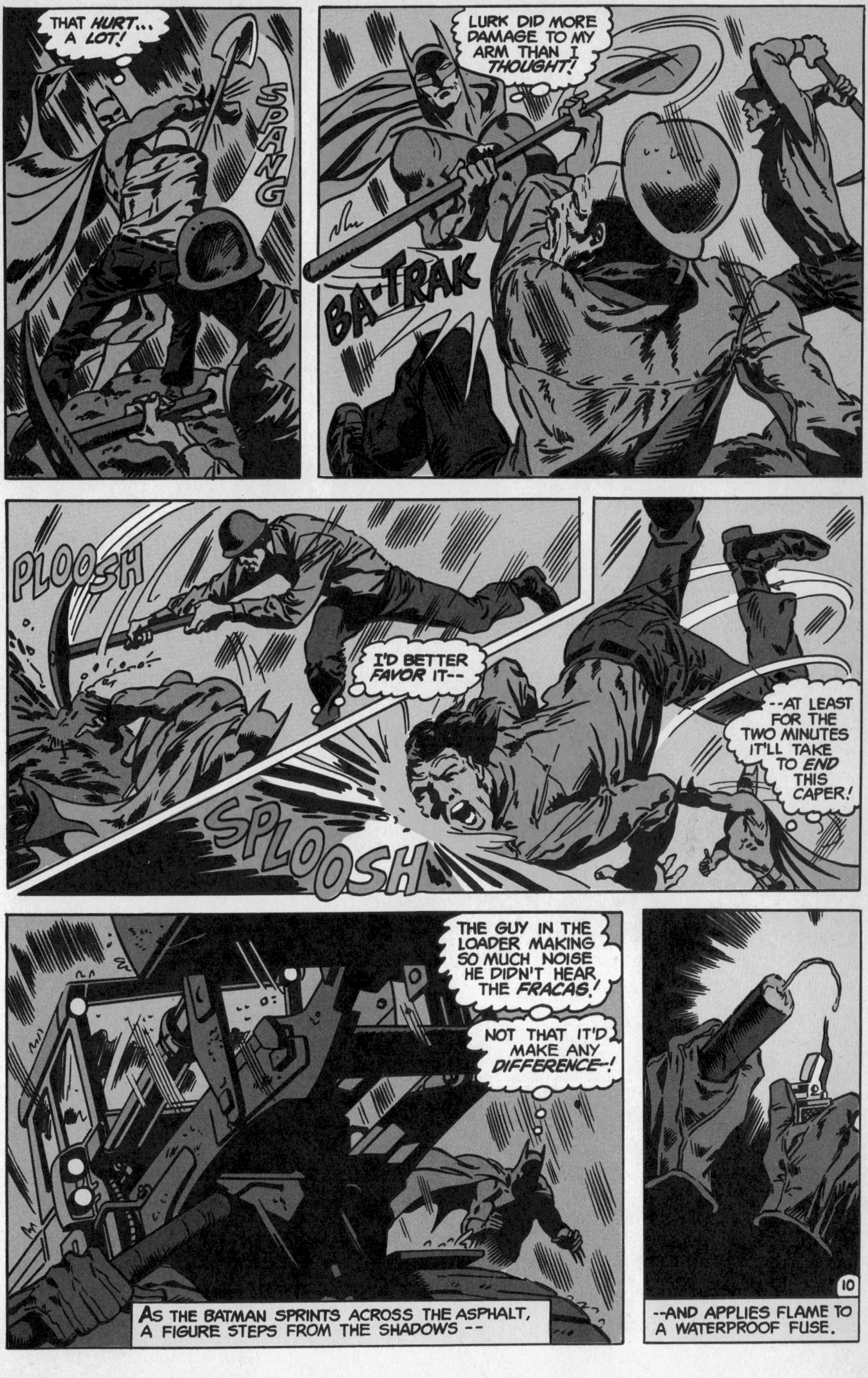
THAT HURT... A LOT!
SPANG
LURK DID MORE DAMAGE TO MY ARM THAN I THOUGHT!
BA-TRAK
PLOOSH
I'D BETTER FAVOR IT--
--AT LEAST FOR THE TWO MINUTES IT'LL TAKE TO END THIS CAPER!
SPLOOSH
THE GUY IN THE LOADER MAKING SO MUCH NOISE HE DIDN'T HEAR THE FRACAS!
NOT THAT IT'D MAKE ANY DIFFERENCE--!
AS THE BATMAN SPRINTS ACROSS THE ASPHALT, A FIGURE STEPS FROM THE SHADOWS --
10
--AND APPLIES FLAME TO A WATERPROOF FUSE.

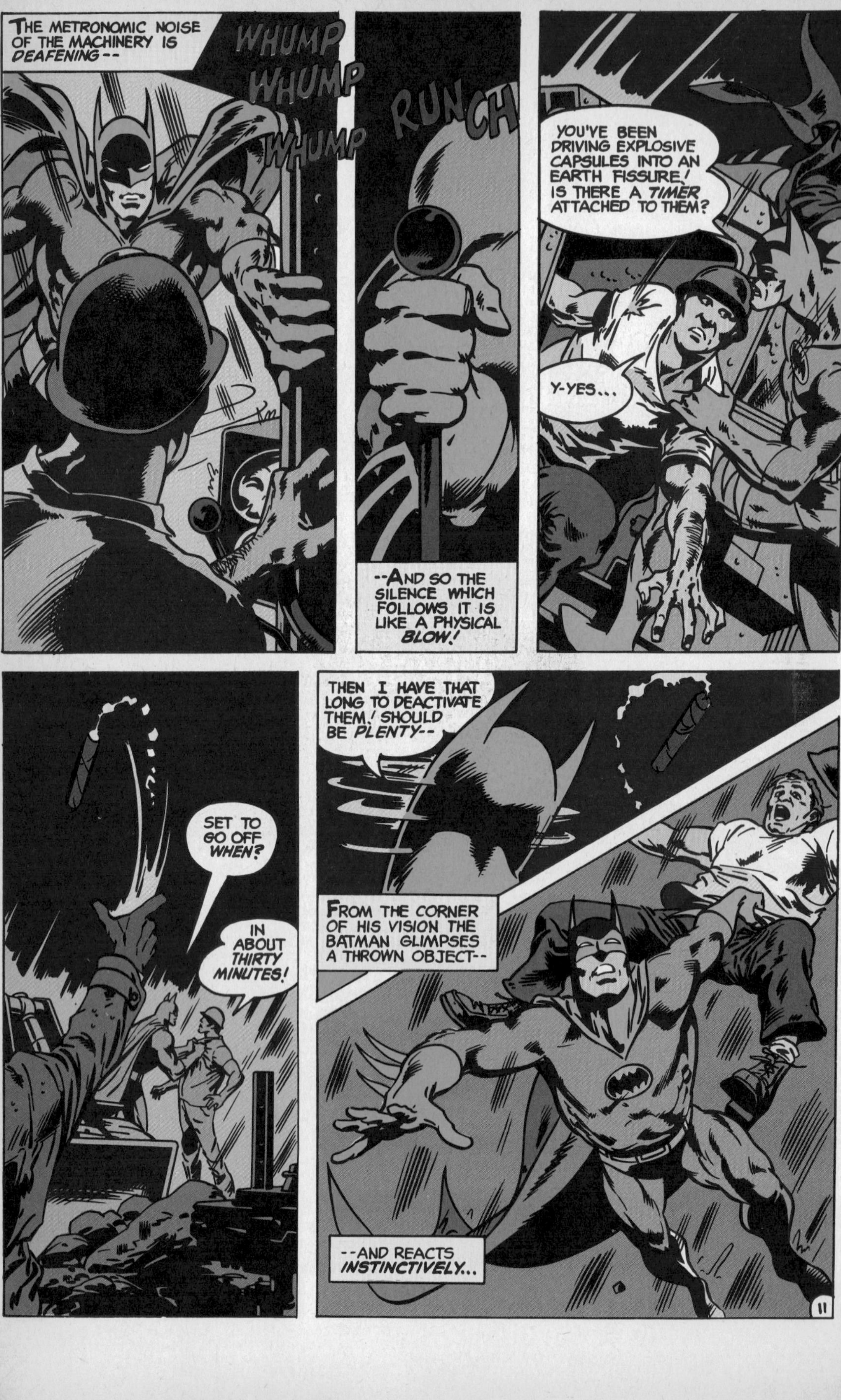
THE METRONOMIC NOISE OF THE MACHINERY IS DEAFENING--
WHUMP WHUMP WHUMP
RUNCH
--AND SO THE SILENCE WHICH FOLLOWS IT IS LIKE A PHYSICAL BLOW!
YOU'VE BEEN DRIVING EXPLOSIVE CAPSULES INTO AN EARTH FISSURE! IS THERE A TIMER ATTACHED TO THEM?
Y-YES...
SET TO GO OFF WHEN?
IN ABOUT THIRTY MINUTES!
THEN I HAVE THAT LONG TO DEACTIVATE THEM! SHOULD BE PLENTY--
FROM THE CORNER OF HIS VISION THE BATMAN GLIMPSES A THROWN OBJECT--
--AND REACTS INSTINCTIVELY...
11

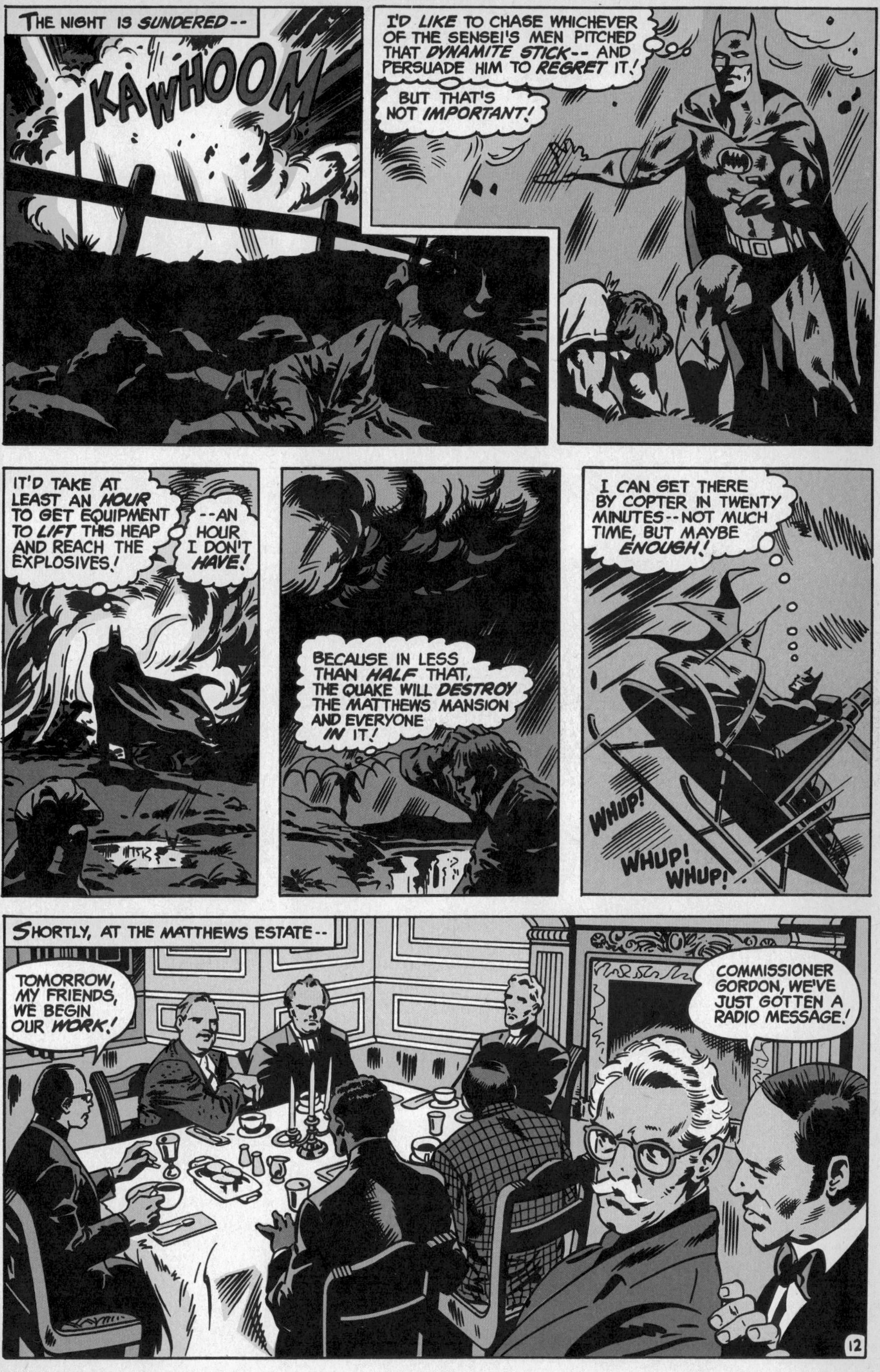
THE NIGHT IS SUNDERED--
KAWHOOM
I'D LIKE TO CHASE WHICHEVER OF THE SENSEI'S MEN PITCHED THAT DYNAMITE STICK-- AND PERSUADE HIM TO REGRET IT!
BUT THAT'S NOT IMPORTANT!
IT'D TAKE AT LEAST AN HOUR TO GET EQUIPMENT TO LIFT THIS HEAP AND REACH THE EXPLOSIVES!
--AN HOUR I DON'T HAVE!
BECAUSE IN LESS THAN HALF THAT, THE QUAKE WILL DESTROY THE MATTHEWS MANSION AND EVERYONE IN IT!
I CAN GET THERE BY COPTER IN TWENTY MINUTES--NOT MUCH TIME, BUT MAYBE ENOUGH!
WHUP!
WHUP!
WHUP!
SHORTLY, AT THE MATTHEWS ESTATE--
TOMORROW, MY FRIENDS, WE BEGIN OUR WORK!
COMMISSIONER GORDON, WE'VE JUST GOTTEN A RADIO MESSAGE!
12

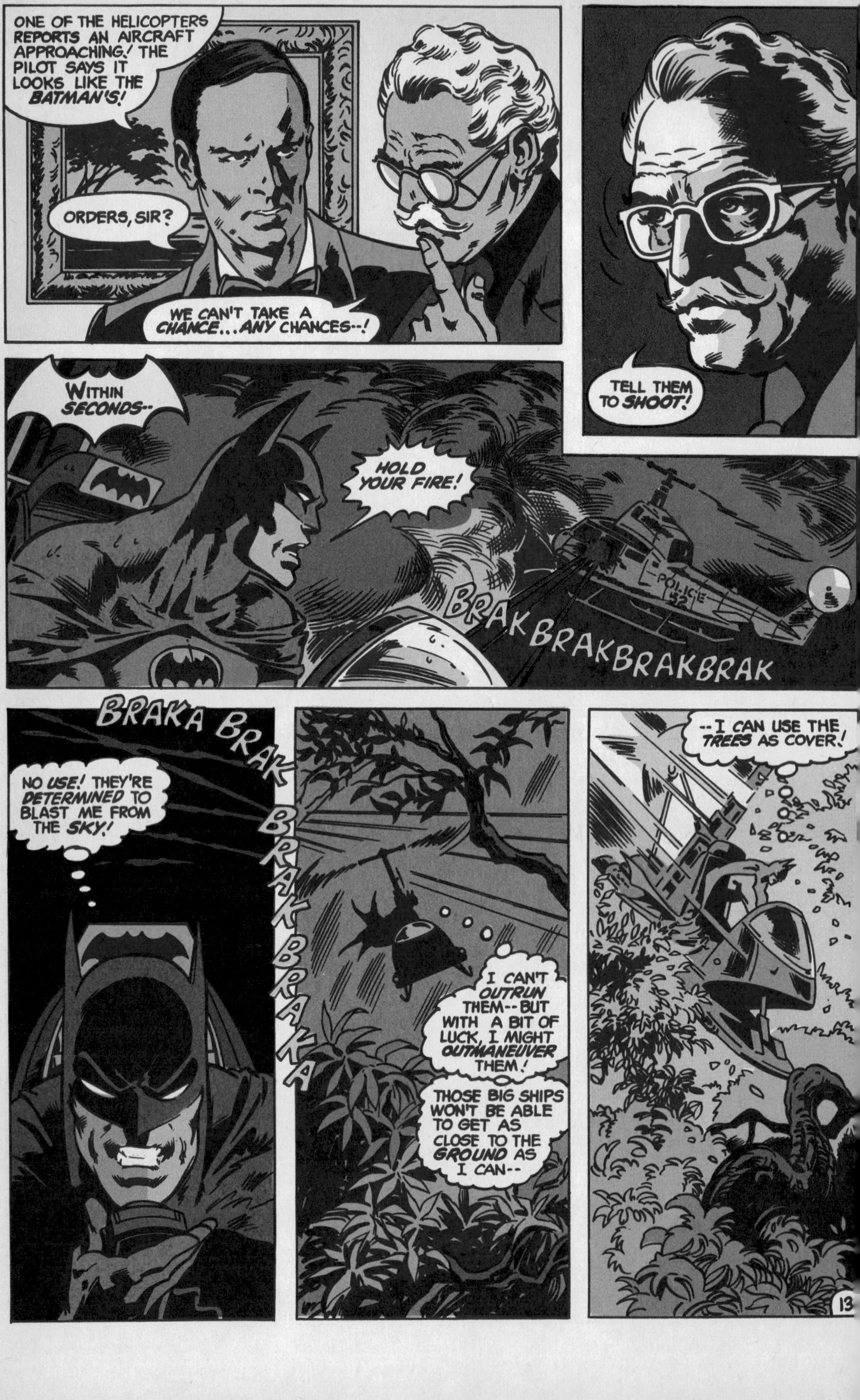
ONE OF THE HELICOPTERS REPORTS AN AIRCRAFT APPROACHING! THE PILOT SAYS IT LOOKS LIKE THE BATMAN'S!
ORDERS, SIR?
WE CAN'T TAKE A CHANCE...ANY CHANCES--!
TELL THEM TO SHOOT!
WITHIN SECONDS--
HOLD YOUR FIRE!
POLICE 32
BRAKBRAKBRAKBRAKBRAK
BRAKA BRAK
NO USE! THEY'RE DETERMINED TO BLAST ME FROM THE SKY!
BRAKBRAKA
I CAN'T OUTRUN THEM--BUT WITH A BIT OF LUCK, I MIGHT OUTMANEUVER THEM!
THOSE BIG SHIPS WON'T BE ABLE TO GET AS CLOSE TO THE GROUND AS I CAN--
--I CAN USE THE TREES AS COVER!
13

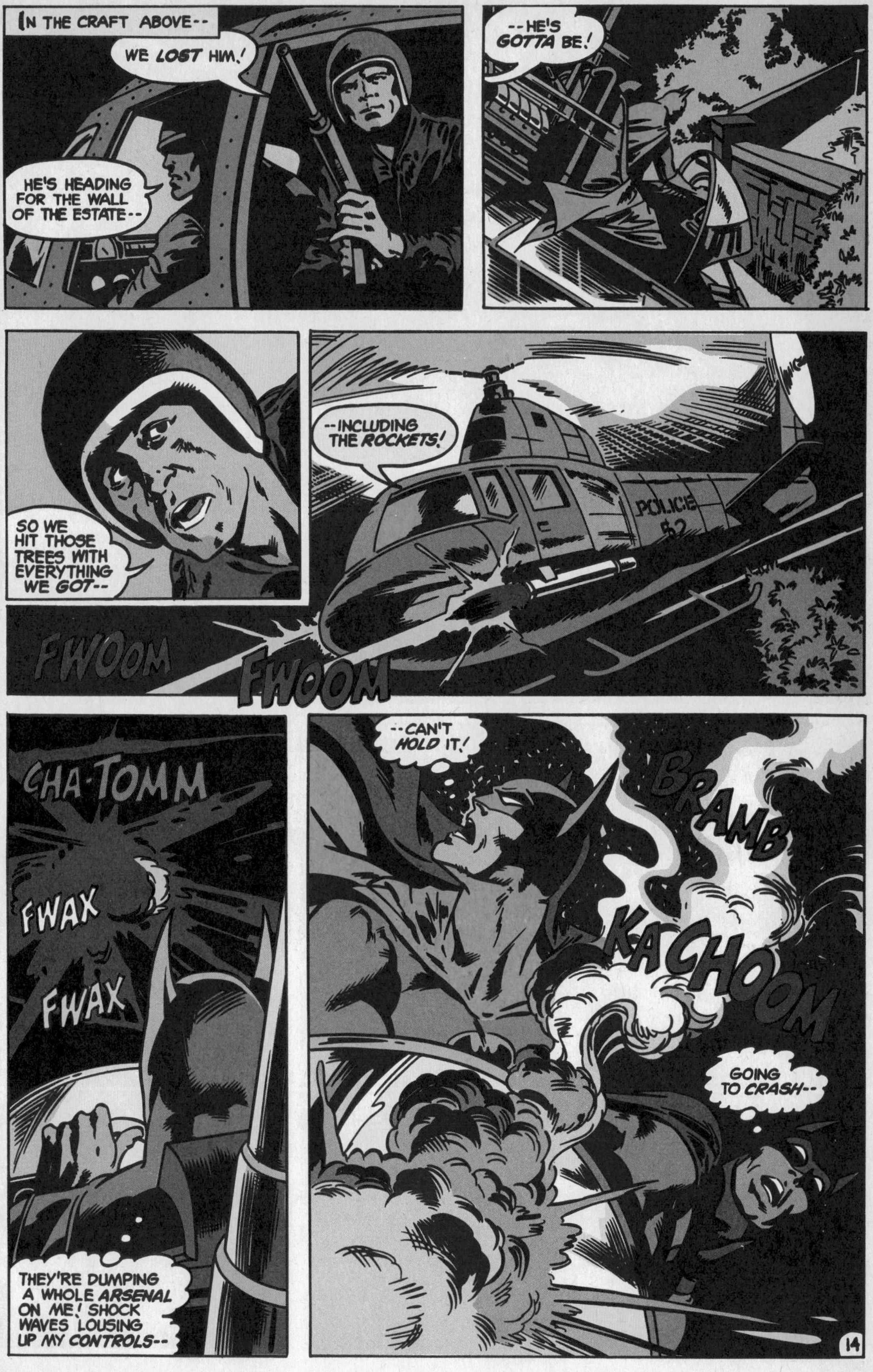
IN THE CRAFT ABOVE--
WE LOST HIM!
HE'S HEADING FOR THE WALL OF THE ESTATE--
--HE'S GOTTA BE!
SO WE HIT THOSE TREES WITH EVERYTHING WE GOT--
--INCLUDING THE ROCKETS!
POLICE
52
FWOOM
FWOOM
CHA-TOMM
FWAX
FWAX
THEY'RE DUMPING A WHOLE ARSENAL ON ME! SHOCK WAVES LOUSING UP MY CONTROLS--
--CAN'T HOLD IT!
BRAMB
KACHOOM
GOING TO CRASH--
14

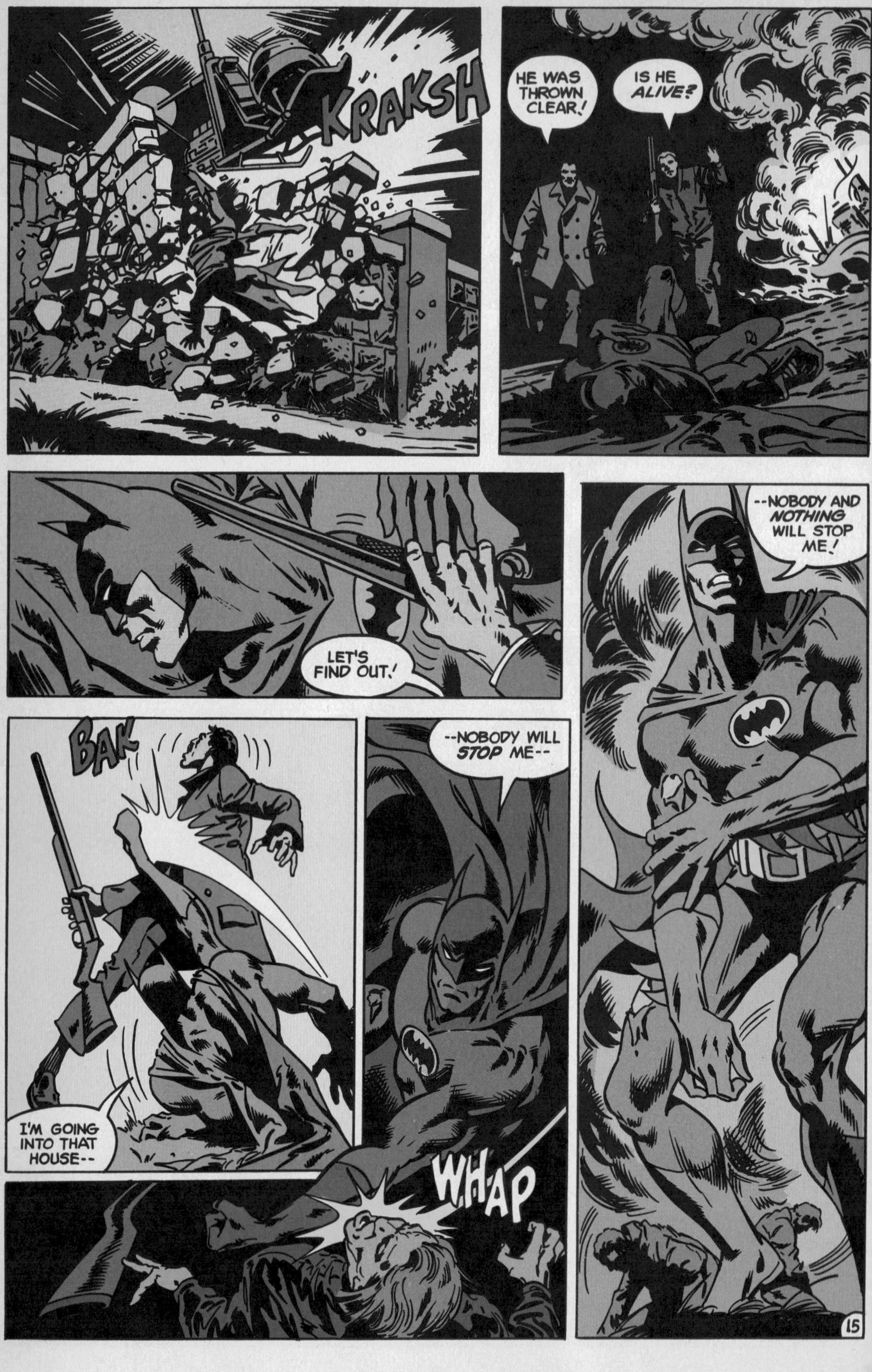
KRAKSH
HE WAS THROWN CLEAR!
IS HE ALIVE?
LET'S FIND OUT!
BAK
I'M GOING INTO THAT HOUSE--
--NOBODY WILL STOP ME--
WHAP
--NOBODY AND NOTHING WILL STOP ME!
15

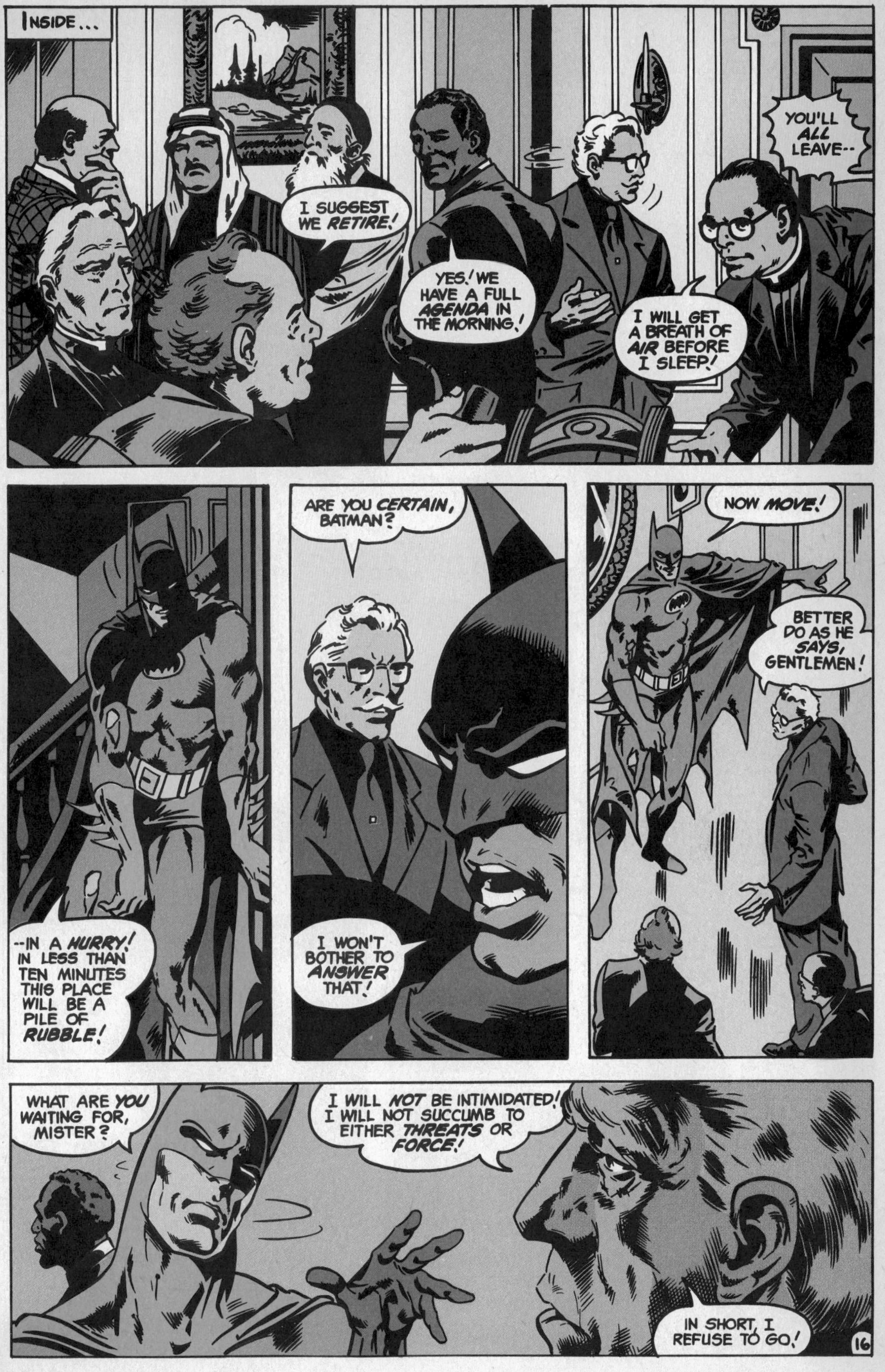
INSIDE...
YOU'LL ALL LEAVE--
I SUGGEST WE RETIRE!
YES! WE HAVE A FULL AGENDA IN THE MORNING!
I WILL GET A BREATH OF AIR BEFORE I SLEEP!
--IN A HURRY! IN LESS THAN TEN MINUTES THIS PLACE WILL BE A PILE OF RUBBLE!
ARE YOU CERTAIN, BATMAN?
I WON'T BOTHER TO ANSWER THAT!
NOW MOVE!
BETTER DO AS HE SAYS, GENTLEMEN!
WHAT ARE YOU WAITING FOR, MISTER?
I WILL NOT BE INTIMIDATED! I WILL NOT SUCCUMB TO EITHER THREATS OR FORCE!
IN SHORT, I REFUSE TO GO!
16

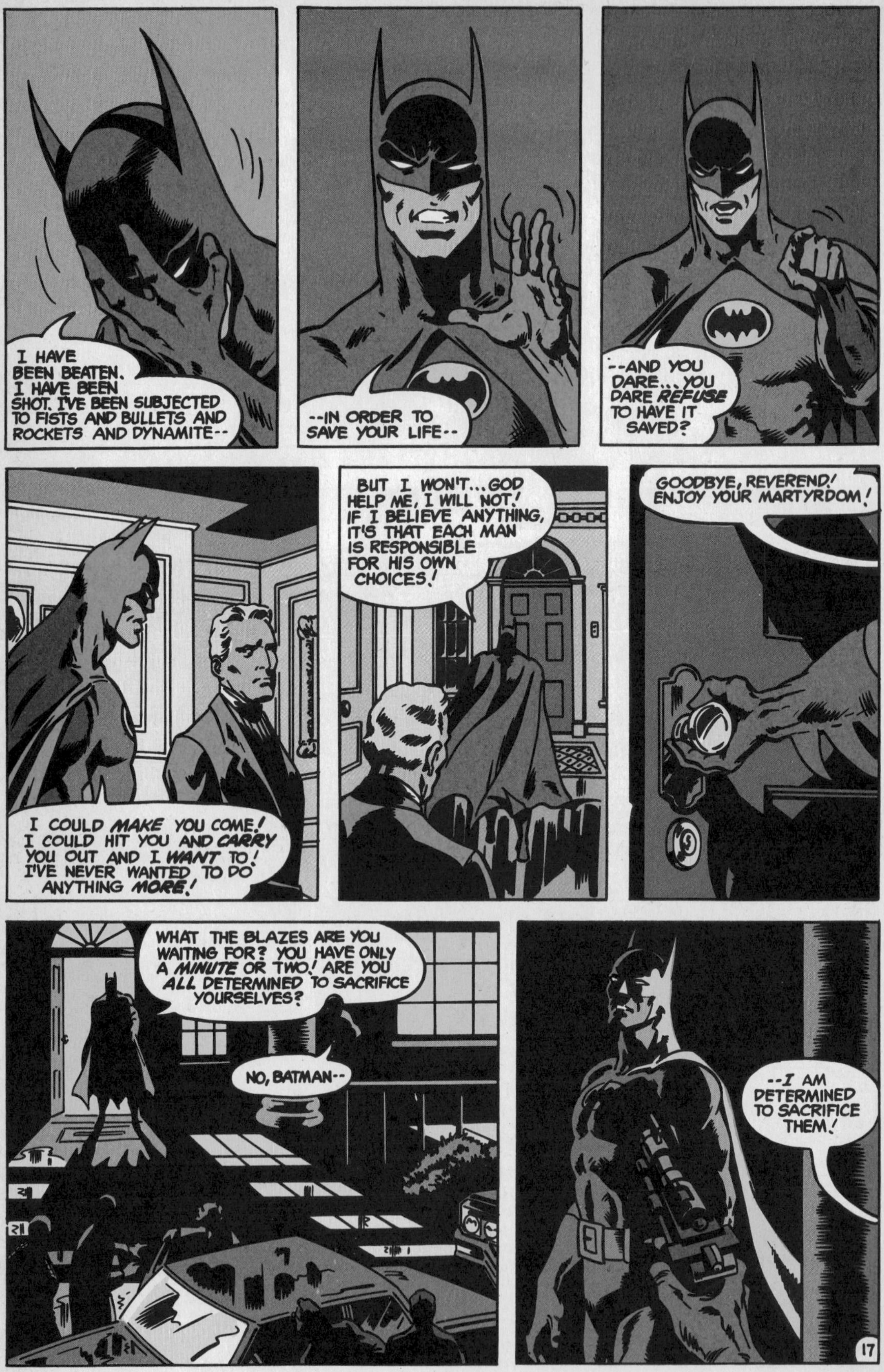
I HAVE BEEN BEATEN. I HAVE BEEN SHOT. I'VE BEEN SUBJECTED TO FISTS AND BULLETS AND ROCKETS AND DYNAMITE--
--IN ORDER TO SAVE YOUR LIFE--
--AND YOU DARE... YOU DARE REFUSE TO HAVE IT SAVED?
I COULD MAKE YOU COME! I COULD HIT YOU AND CARRY YOU OUT AND I WANT TO! I'VE NEVER WANTED TO DO ANYTHING MORE!
BUT I WON'T...GOD HELP ME, I WILL NOT! IF I BELIEVE ANYTHING, IT'S THAT EACH MAN IS RESPONSIBLE FOR HIS OWN CHOICES!
GOODBYE, REVEREND! ENJOY YOUR MARTYRDOM!
WHAT THE BLAZES ARE YOU WAITING FOR? YOU HAVE ONLY A MINUTE OR TWO! ARE YOU ALL DETERMINED TO SACRIFICE YOURSELVES?
NO, BATMAN--
--I AM DETERMINED TO SACRIFICE THEM!
17

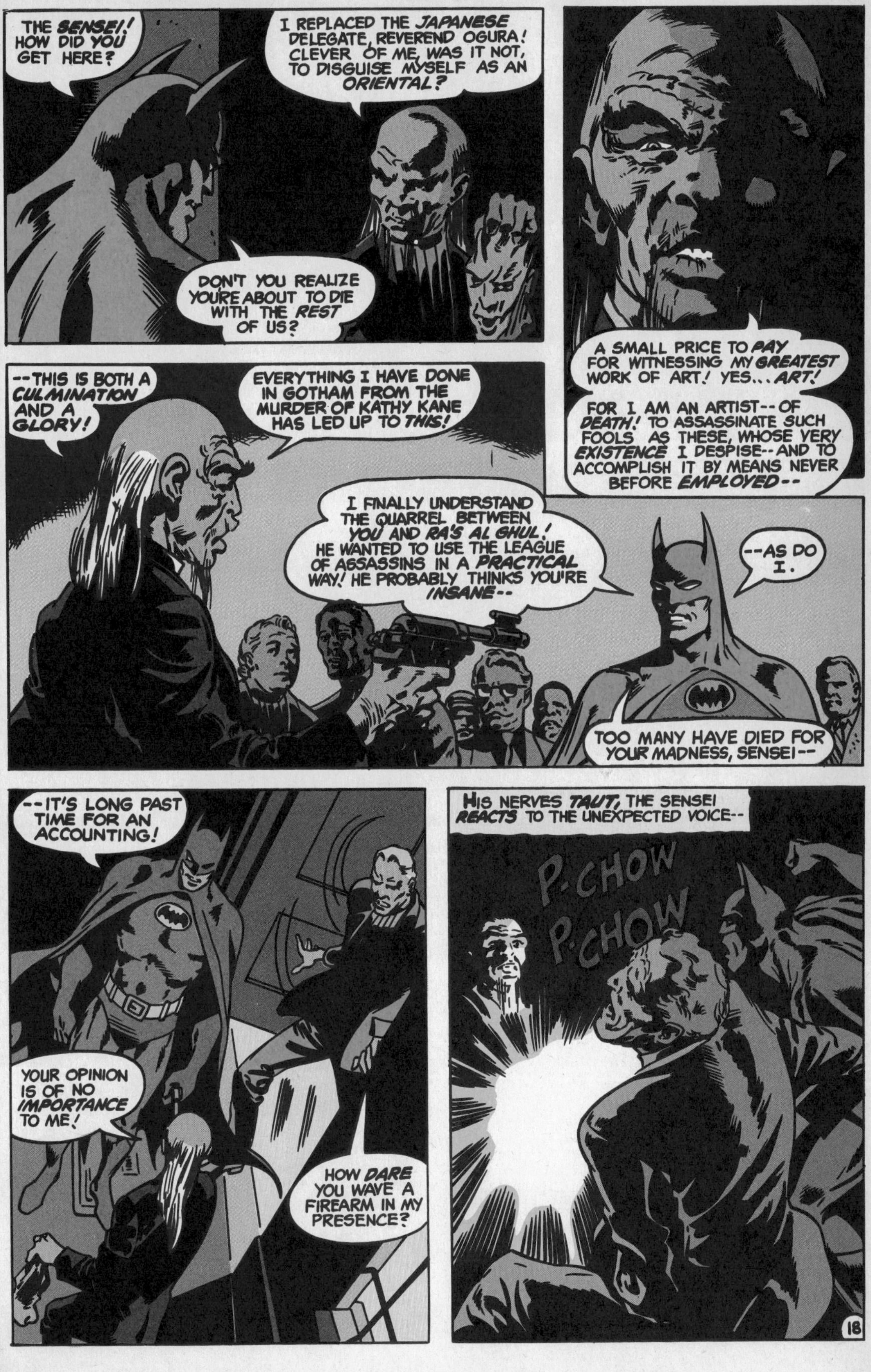
THE SENSEI! HOW DID YOU GET HERE?
I REPLACED THE JAPANESE DELEGATE, REVEREND OGURA! CLEVER OF ME, WAS IT NOT, TO DISGUISE MYSELF AS AN ORIENTAL?
DON'T YOU REALIZE YOU'RE ABOUT TO DIE WITH THE REST OF US?
A SMALL PRICE TO PAY FOR WITNESSING MY GREATEST WORK OF ART! YES... ART!
FOR I AM AN ARTIST-- OF DEATH! TO ASSASSINATE SUCH FOOLS AS THESE, WHOSE VERY EXISTENCE I DESPISE-- AND TO ACCOMPLISH IT BY MEANS NEVER BEFORE EMPLOYED--
--THIS IS BOTH A CULMINATION AND A GLORY!
EVERYTHING I HAVE DONE IN GOTHAM FROM THE MURDER OF KATHY KANE HAS LED UP TO THIS!
I FINALLY UNDERSTAND THE QUARREL BETWEEN YOU AND RA'S AL GHUL! HE WANTED TO USE THE LEAGUE OF ASSASSINS IN A PRACTICAL WAY! HE PROBABLY THINKS YOU'RE INSANE--
--AS DO I.
TOO MANY HAVE DIED FOR YOUR MADNESS, SENSEI--
--IT'S LONG PAST TIME FOR AN ACCOUNTING!
YOUR OPINION IS OF NO IMPORTANCE TO ME!
HOW DARE YOU WAVE A FIREARM IN MY PRESENCE?
HIS NERVES TAUT, THE SENSEI REACTS TO THE UNEXPECTED VOICE--
P-CHOW
P-CHOW
18

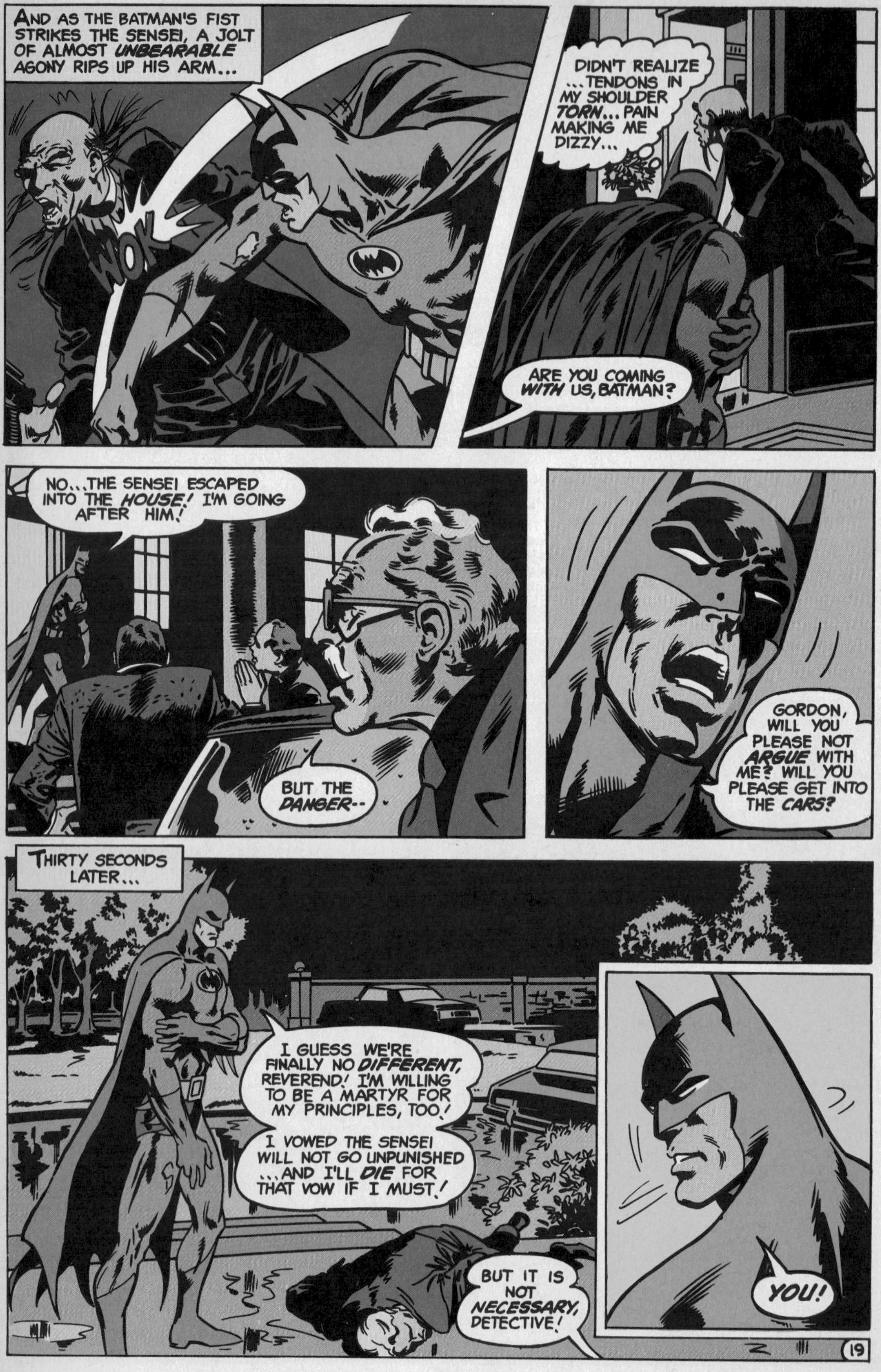
AND AS THE BATMAN'S FIST STRIKES THE SENSEI, A JOLT OF ALMOST UNBEARABLE AGONY RIPS UP HIS ARM...
WOK
DIDN'T REALIZE ...TENDONS IN MY SHOULDER TORN... PAIN MAKING ME DIZZY...
ARE YOU COMING WITH US, BATMAN?
NO...THE SENSEI ESCAPED INTO THE HOUSE! I'M GOING AFTER HIM!
BUT THE DANGER--
GORDON, WILL YOU PLEASE NOT ARGUE WITH ME? WILL YOU PLEASE GET INTO THE CARS?
THIRTY SECONDS LATER...
I GUESS WE'RE FINALLY NO DIFFERENT, REVEREND! I'M WILLING TO BE A MARTYR FOR MY PRINCIPLES, TOO!
I VOWED THE SENSEI WILL NOT GO UNPUNISHED ...AND I'LL DIE FOR THAT VOW IF I MUST!
BUT IT IS NOT NECESSARY, DETECTIVE!
YOU!
19

RA'S AL GHUL... I SUPPOSE I SHOULD HAVE *EXPECTED* YOU!

INDEED. HAVE I NOT *OPPOSED* THE SENSEI STEP BY STEP IN THIS MATTER... EVEN TO ENSURING YOUR *PRESENCE*...?

BUT *TOO LATE* TO HELP KATHY-- AND I'M STILL *NOT CONVINCED* THAT IT WASN'T *YOU* WHO ENDANGERED HER IN THE FIRST PLACE!

BE THAT AS IT MAY, BATMAN...

NOW, HOWEVER, YOU SHOULD *DEPART!* I WILL ASSUME THE TASK OF DEALING WITH THE SENSEI-- FOR HE IS A *GREATER* ENEMY OF *MINE* THAN YOURS!

THERE IS A *SWIFT* VEHICLE IN THE GARAGE!

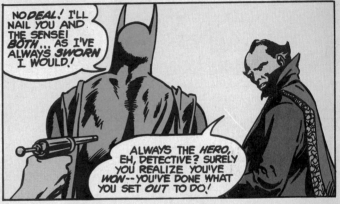

NO *DEAL!* I'LL *NAIL* YOU AND THE SENSEI *BOTH*... AS I'VE ALWAYS *SWORN* I WOULD!

ALWAYS THE *HERO*, EH, DETECTIVE? SURELY YOU REALIZE YOU'VE *WON*-- YOU'VE DONE WHAT YOU SET OUT TO DO!

PFSST

POISON DART...

...FROM BEHIND... NOT LIKE YOU...

TAKE HIM, DAUGHTER! HE DESERVES TO SURVIVE!

AND *YOU*, FATHER?

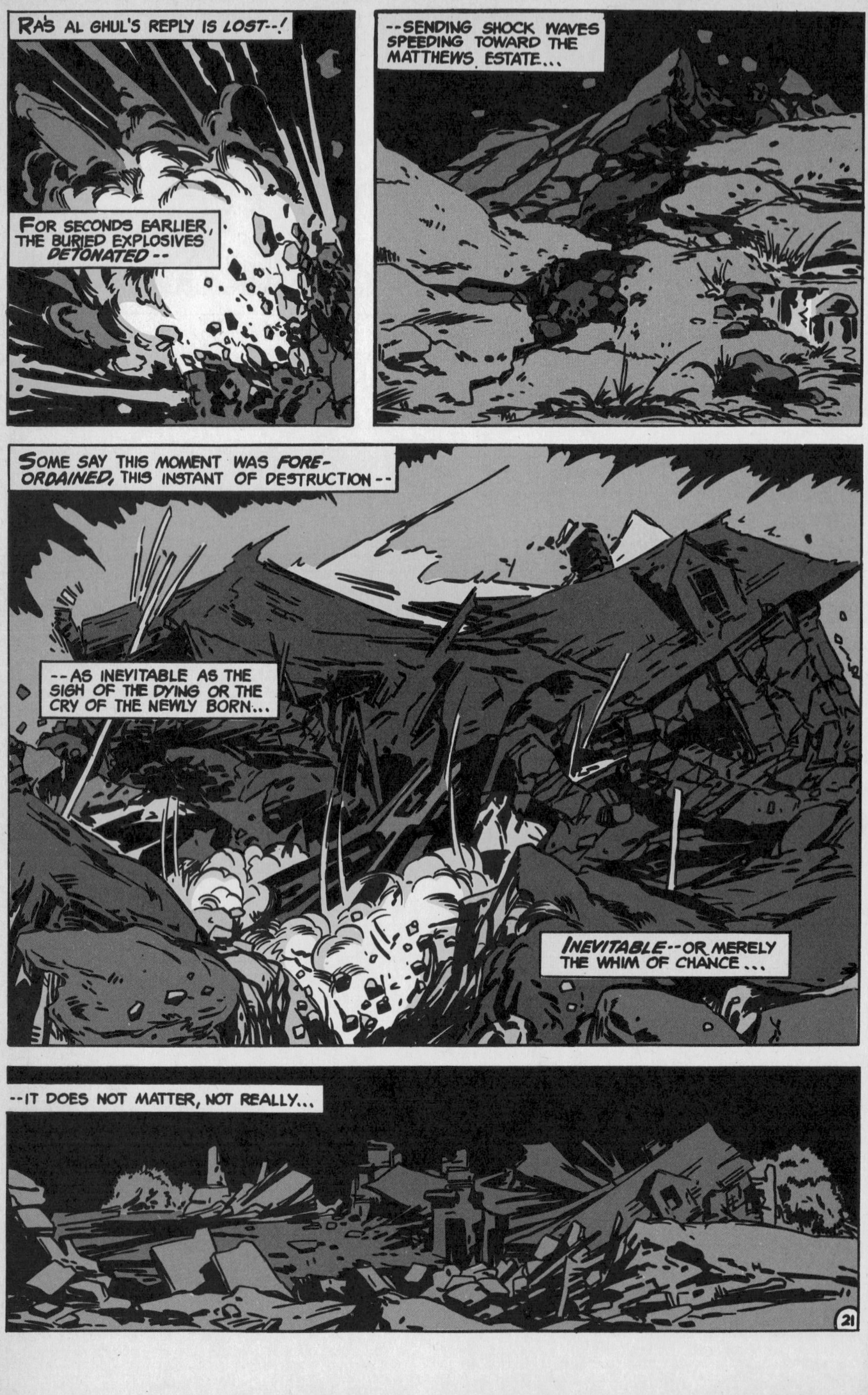
RA'S AL GHUL'S REPLY IS LOST--!
FOR SECONDS EARLIER, THE BURIED EXPLOSIVES DETONATED--
--SENDING SHOCK WAVES SPEEDING TOWARD THE MATTHEWS ESTATE...
SOME SAY THIS MOMENT WAS FORE-ORDAINED, THIS INSTANT OF DESTRUCTION--
--AS INEVITABLE AS THE SIGH OF THE DYING OR THE CRY OF THE NEWLY BORN...
INEVITABLE--OR MERELY THE WHIM OF CHANCE...
--IT DOES NOT MATTER, NOT REALLY...
21

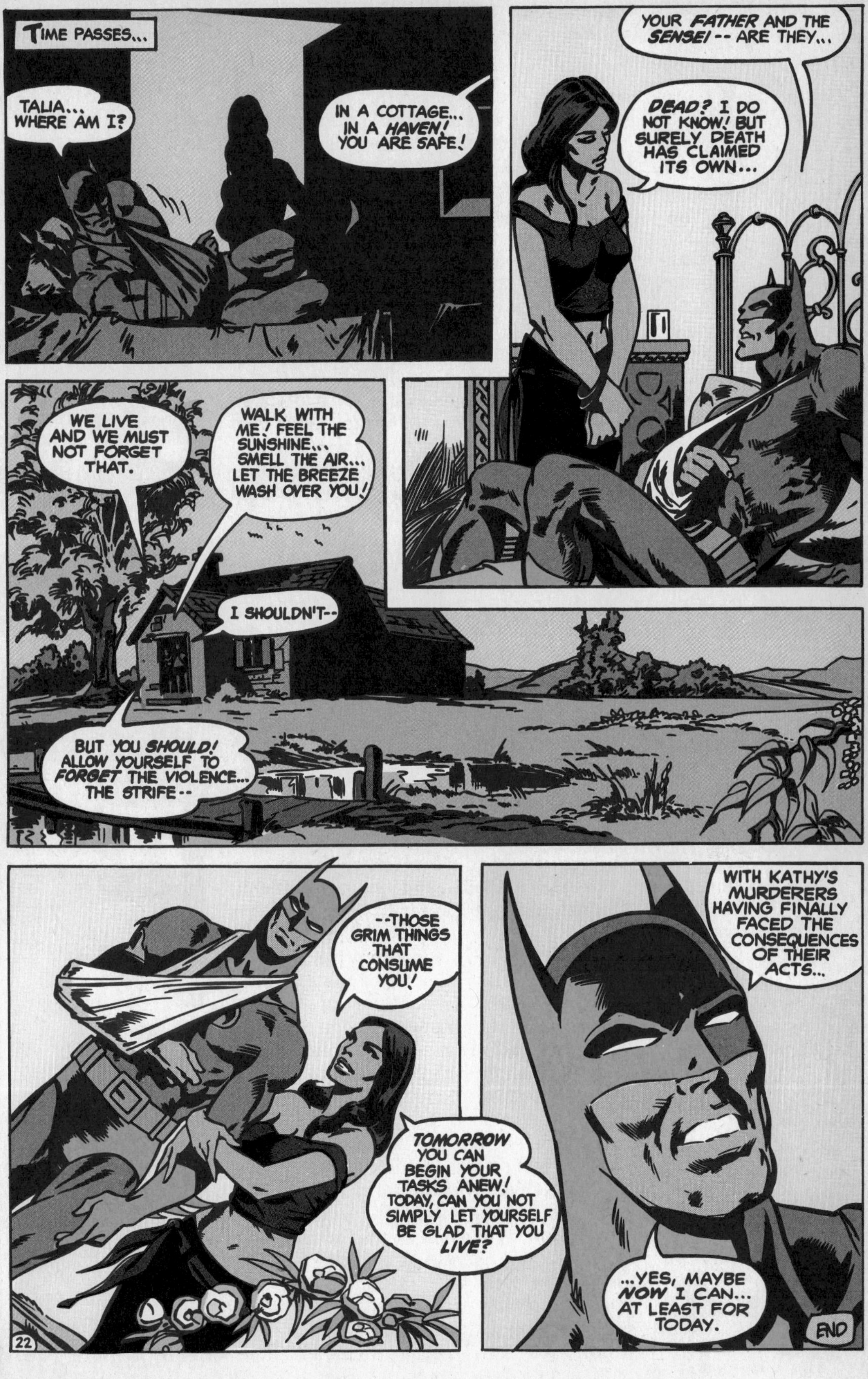
TIME PASSES...
TALIA... WHERE AM I?
IN A COTTAGE... IN A HAVEN! YOU ARE SAFE!
YOUR FATHER AND THE SENSEI -- ARE THEY...
DEAD? I DO NOT KNOW! BUT SURELY DEATH HAS CLAIMED ITS OWN...
WE LIVE AND WE MUST NOT FORGET THAT.
WALK WITH ME! FEEL THE SUNSHINE... SMELL THE AIR... LET THE BREEZE WASH OVER YOU!
I SHOULDN'T--
BUT YOU SHOULD! ALLOW YOURSELF TO FORGET THE VIOLENCE... THE STRIFE--
--THOSE GRIM THINGS THAT CONSUME YOU!
TOMORROW YOU CAN BEGIN YOUR TASKS ANEW! TODAY, CAN YOU NOT SIMPLY LET YOURSELF BE GLAD THAT YOU LIVE?
22
WITH KATHY'S MURDERERS HAVING FINALLY FACED THE CONSEQUENCES OF THEIR ACTS...
...YES, MAYBE NOW I CAN... AT LEAST FOR TODAY.
END

If you're reading these words after you've finished the stories collected in this volume, you may have noticed some things. For example, you may have observed that although the hero is often driven and desperate, he isn't quite as *grim* as today's Batman. He banters with the bad guys, he essays the occasional mild wisecrack, he is more openly compassionate. Nor is he quite so super-humanly *competent;* would the present Batman ever be flattened by Molly Post and her lousy *skis*? Not likely. You may wonder about some of the captions — the alliteration, the chatty little asides. ("Did you catch the key to the mystery, as did the Batman?" a typical one asks.) But then, you surely remind yourself, these tales first appeared almost two decades ago, at a point in Batman's 50-year history when a lot of the elements of his persona were still being defined, as he was evolving from the cheery, sun-drenched do-gooder of the fifties and mid-sixties to the present Dark Knight. As for those captions … like Batman himself, comic book conventions and technique were changing; in particular, many young comics professionals were influenced by Marvel Comics' Stan Lee, whose writing teems with friendly comments to the reader. And almost nobody working in the medium would admit, under torture, to taking the work seriously. *In a cutesy mood?*, a writer might ask himself. *Then knock out a cutesy caption. It's only a comic book…*

Okay, granting all that, you still have a question. You've given the stories titled "The Vengeance Vow" and "Where Strike The Assassins" your close attention and you want to know how the Batman found the Bronze Tiger in the hospital after the fight with the sensei's thugs. Well, try this: it was simple detective work. He knew, from the amount of blood on the ground, that the Tiger was badly wounded and so would probably seek help at the nearest medical facility. The hospital was it.

Not satisfied? No problem. There are other possible answers. (He spotted the killers and tailed them, hoping they'd lead him to the Tiger? He was able to follow the trail of the blood itself? He questioned someone who saw where the Tiger went?) You might be able to think of something better than any of these. Me — I don't know if I *had* an explanation and forgot to include it, or if some months passed between the writing of the two stories and I didn't remember that the Batman's fortuitous arrival at the Tiger's bedside hadn't already been explained, or what. Maybe I would have fretted if I'd noticed the omission after the story was published — maybe I even *did.* I don't know. We weren't taking notes back then. We were just dashing from assignment to assignment, producing monthly entertainments and, frequently, having a pretty good time doing it. What we *weren't* doing was expecting that those entertainments would ever be collected in a single, rather portly book with an introduction by Sam Hamm, a cover by Brian

AFTERWORD

P.S.

Stelfreeze, and a postscript by the undersigned.

But, having just reread the stuff, some of it for the first time since the original publication, I'm mildly amazed at how cohesive it all is. It really does form a single, unified narrative — what today would be called

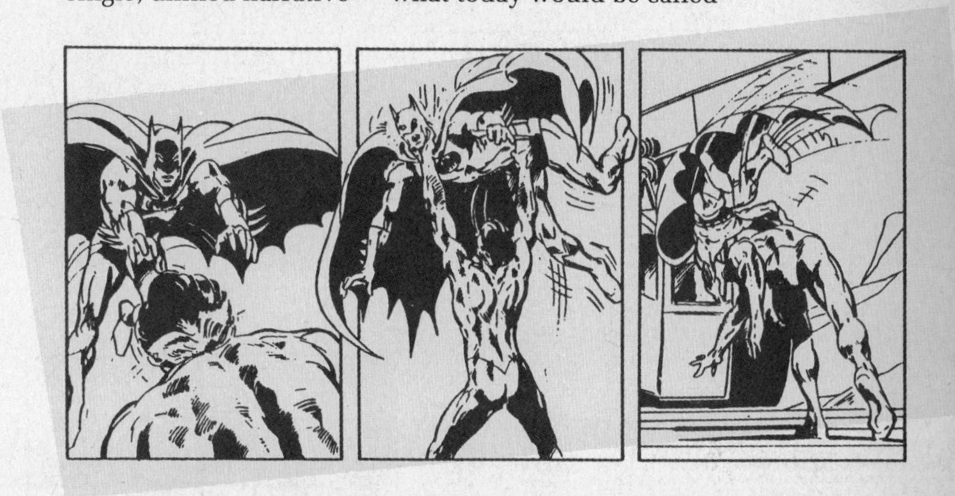

a graphic novel. Does that mean that when we introduced Talia we knew that eventually her father would be presumed dead, and she and Batman would finally enjoy a walk into the sunset? No, certainly not. Rather, I'm sure, we understood the characters well enough to keep them from doing anything alien to them and, with that as a constant, the narrative grew organically, each incident suggesting others. The overall design was never imposed on the material; rather, it emerged gradually as

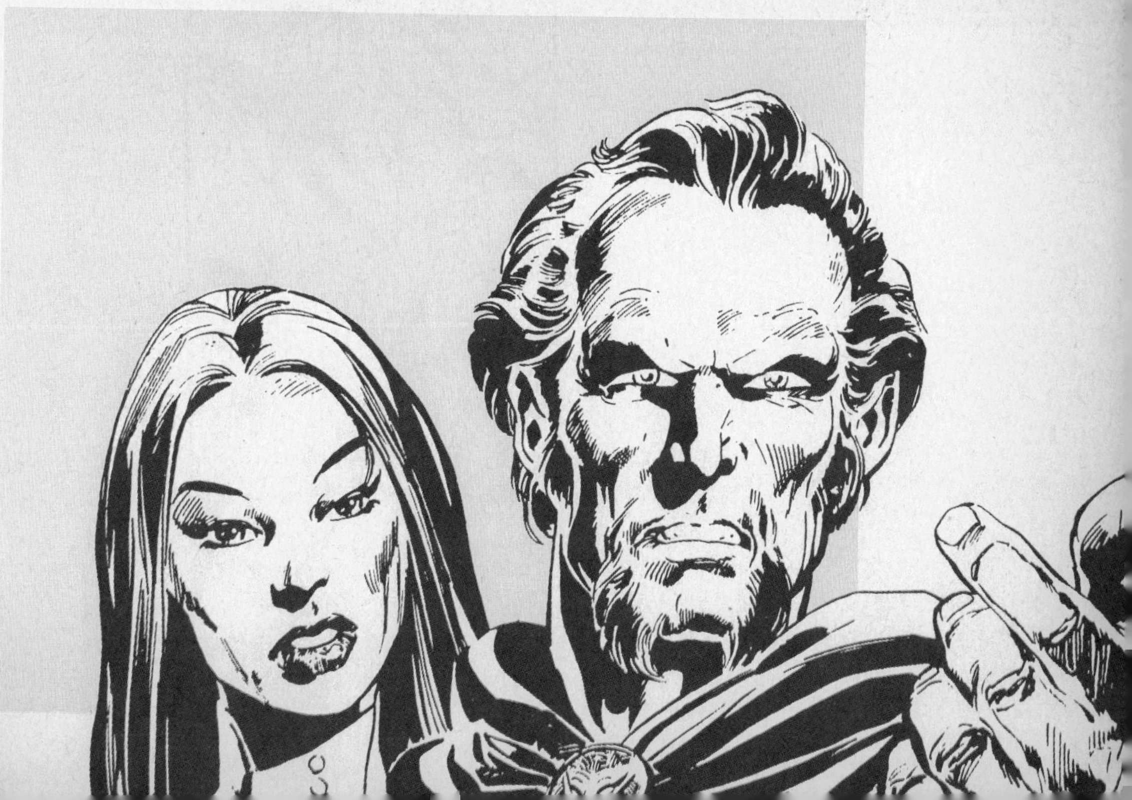

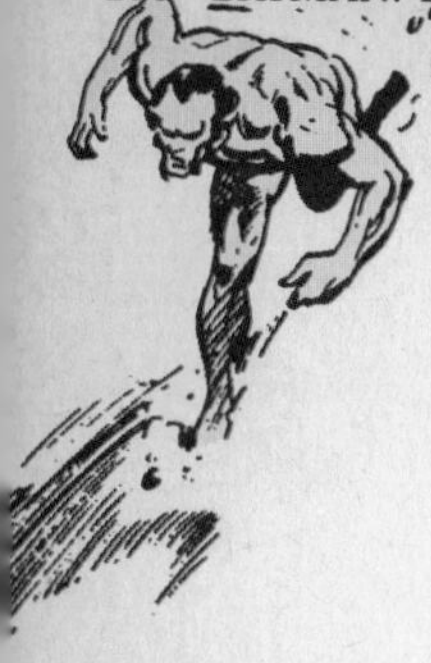

we produced the individual episodes. We were guys sticking tiles up on a wall, just interested in covering the space, and after a while, *Look at that! Darn if we didn't make a mosaic!* This kind of process is denied to storytellers who create conventional plays, movies, novels — forms that demand structure with clearly defined beginnings, middles and ends. It lets the writers and artists share, at least to some extent, in the audience's pleasure of anticipation, of being surprised by what happens next. It can be an absolute joy.

Of course, it does cause the occasional glitch, such as Batman arriving at a hospital without anyone, maybe including the writer (maybe *especially* the writer), knowing exactly how he got there.

Dennis O'Neil
January, 1991

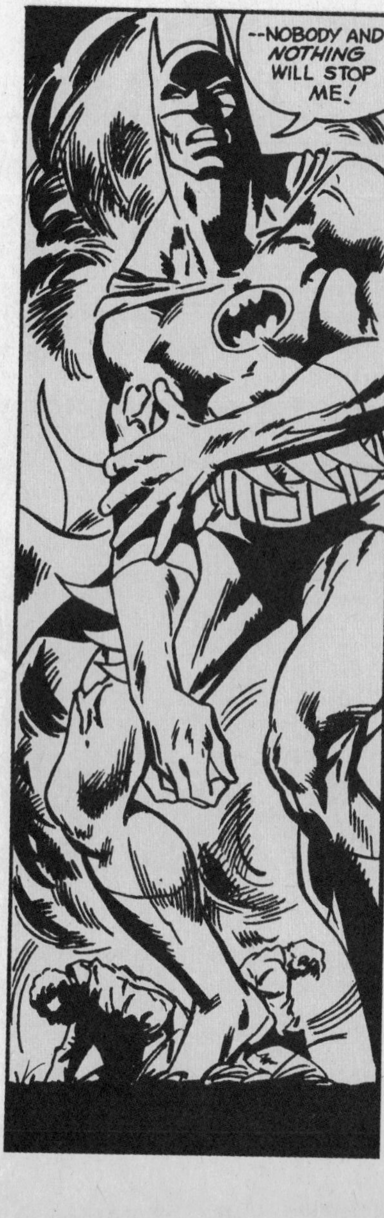
--NOBODY AND NOTHING WILL STOP ME!

Also From DC Comics:
Available at Specialty Retailers Everywhere

Trade Paperbacks

The Art of Walter Simonson

Batman: Arkham Asylum
Grant Morrison / Dave McKean

Batman: The Dark Knight Returns
Frank Miller / Klaus Janson / Lynn Varley

Batman: Year One
Frank Miller / David Mazzucchelli / Richmond Lewis

Batman: Year Two
Mike W. Barr / Alan Davis / Todd McFarlane / Paul Neary
Alfredo Alcala / Steve Oliff

Camelot 3000
Mike W. Barr / Brian Bolland

The Greatest Batman Stories Ever Told

The Greatest Joker Stories Ever Told

The Greatest Superman Stories Ever Told

The Greatest Team-Up Stories Ever Told

Green Arrow: The Longbow Hunters
Mike Grell / Lurene Haines / Julia Lacquement

Hawkman
Gardner Fox / Joe Kubert

Justice League: A New Beginning
Keith Giffen / J.M. DeMatteis / Kevin Maguire

Legion of Super-Heroes:
The Great Darkness Saga
Paul Levitz / Keith Giffen / Larry Mahlstedt

The New Teen Titans: The Judas Contract
Marv Wolfman / George Pérez

The Prisoner: Shattered Visage
Dean Motter / Mark Askwith
David Hornung / Richmond Lewis

Ronin
Frank Miller

Saga of the Swamp Thing
Alan Moore / Stephen Bissette / John Totleben

The Sandman: The Doll's House
Neil Gaiman / Mike Dringenberg / Malcolm Jones III

The Shadow: Blood and Judgment
Howard Chaykin

Superman: The Man of Steel
John Byrne / Dick Giordano

Swamp Thing: Love and Death
Alan Moore / Stephen Bissette
John Totleben / Shawn McManus

V for Vendetta
Alan Moore / David Lloyd

Watchmen
Alan Moore / Dave Gibbons

Hardcover Books

Batman Archives Volume 1
Bob Kane / Bill Finger / Gardner Fox
Jerry Robinson / George Roussos

Batman: Digital Justice
Pepe Moreno

Superman Archives Volume 1
Jerry Siegel & Joe Shuster

Superman Archives Volume 2
Jerry Siegel & Joe Shuster

Graphic Novels

Batman: Son of the Demon
Mike W. Barr / Jerry Bingham

Batman 3-D
John Byrne / Ray Zone

The Dragonlance Saga #4
Roy Thomas / Tony DeZuniga

Prestige Format Books

Batman Movie Adaptation
Dennis O'Neil / Jerry Ordway / Steve Oliff

Batman: Gotham by Gaslight
Brian Augustyn / Michael Mignola
P. Craig Russell / David Hornung

Batman: The Killing Joke
Alan Moore / Brian Bolland / John Higgins

Lex Luthor: The Unauthorized Biography
James D. Hudnall / Eduardo Barreto / Adam Kubert

Superman: The Earth Stealers
John Byrne / Curt Swan / Jerry Ordway / Bill Wray

Standard Format Books

Batman: A Death in the Family
Jim Starlin / Jim Aparo / Mike DeCarlo

Batman: A Lonely Place of Dying
Marv Wolfman / George Pérez / Jim Aparo
Tom Grummett / Mike DeCarlo / Bob McLeod

Secret Origins